A CERTAIN MS. BALL

by

Walter J. Kastner

CCB Publishing
British Columbia, Canada

A Certain Ms. Ball

Copyright ©2006, 2011, 2015 by Walter J. Kastner
ISBN-13   978-1-77143-211-5
Third Edition

Library and Archives Canada Cataloguing in Publication
Kastner, Walter J., 1932-, author
A certain Ms. Ball / by Walter Kastner. -- Third edition.
Issued in print and electronic formats.
ISBN 978-1-77143-211-5 (pbk.).--ISBN 978-1-77143-212-2 (pdf)
Additional cataloguing data available from Library and Archives Canada

Artwork credit: Benjamin Franklin and son William flying kite
© wynnter | iStockPhoto.com

Publisher: CCB Publishing
             British Columbia, Canada
             www.ccbpublishing.com

Acknowledgments

The following writers, and their areas of expertise, are listed below. We are deeply indebted to them, for without their assistance, this book would never have been published.

Nanncy J. Steward: much of Act I; Act II, half of Chapter 18, and Love Letter (chapter 20)
Carole Ann McCord: Act I, Chapter 3
Patricia Hammond: Act II, The Tale of the Silken Scarf (chapter 13)
Thomas K. Perry: Act II, Melchior's Tale (chapter 14); Act III, first part of chapter 33
Karen Bernardo: Act II, chapter 15; Act III, chapters 22 through 27; Act IV, The Case of the Ravished Inamorata (chapter 39)
Jules Verne: Act III, chapter 32
Sunshine Brewer: Act III, chapters 28, 29, 31; Act IV, chapter 38
Julie Sullivan: Act IV, chapters 40 and 41

Also, A.R.C. Science Simulation Software for the date of the astronomical event preceding the birth of Crystal

CONTENTS

LIST OF ILLUSTRATIONS

ACT I

Omén of Arabia

ACT II

Westward Ho!
(Riyadh to the Royal Society)

ACT III

The Captain of the Caucasus

ACT IV

Crystal and Her Mate

The story you are about to read
just might be true....

PROLOGUE

Dear Auggie,

My friends all say there is no real Crystal Ball, that a crystal ball cannot really allow you to see things yet unseen; that it is all in your imagination. My Mom says if there truly is a real Crystal Ball, then I should be able to see her at your place.

Please, Sir, do you have a real Crystal Ball?

Virginia (age 12)

Dear Virginia,

Your friends are mistaken. True, there have been crystal balls made in the past purporting to see the future, but these have been poor imitations, indeed. As is true even today, men thought that bigger is better, and had artisans make "bigger and better" crystal balls in the vain hope of better to see things yet unseen. Foolish, prideful creatures – "What fools we mortals be!" Can man improve upon what God has established as the true and never-changing order of things?

Yes, Virginia, there *is* a Crystal Ball. Born immortal at the junction of earth, air, fire and water, she lives today and lives forever. Men can laugh and taunt, and crush her under their feet, but she will return again and again, as long as there is a child on Earth and a God in Heaven. Not believe in Crystal Ball? Better that fairies do not play in the dell, or that gnomes do not work in the Black Forest. Better that Shahrazad did not live to tell all the wondrous Tales that Crystal showed to her. Better that Anton Leeuwenhoek never met her and let her show him all the "amazing little beasties" in a drop of water. Even today there are grown men and women who will laugh when you try to tell them all the things you see with your Crystal Ball. Poor, proud, foolish, blind people!

Yes, Virginia, there *is* a Crystal Ball, and you *can* see her at our place.

Warmest regards,
Auggie

The World of Microscopic Photographs

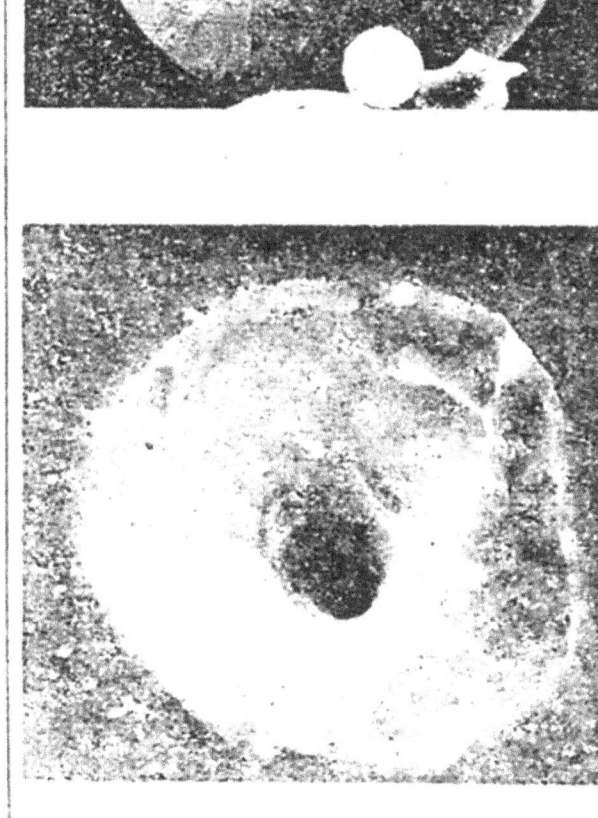

What looks like the entrance to a bottomless pit (left) is actually a photograph of a laser-drilled hole in a silicon wafer made with the benefit of a scanning electron microscope. The picture is the work of microscopist Bob Woods of the Engineering Research Center at Princeton, N.J. The image was magnified 2,400 times. What appears to be an unusual organism being hatched from an egg (right) is a photograph of a group of glass beads.

xvii

ASTER NEW ERA

LANCASTER, PA., TUESDAY EVENING, DECEMBER 8, 1981   Price 25¢ — Daily Home Delivered $1.20 A Week

Local Weather

Windy, colder tonight, Wednesday, chance of snow flurries. Lows tonight 25 to 30, highs Wednesday mid 30s.

(Details on Page 3)

'Explosion' Heard Six Miles Away

Thunderbolt Knocks Out 300 Runway Lights at Airport

An intense bolt of lightning struck in the middle of Lancaster Airport around 8:30 a.m. today, blowing out the airport's extensive network of runway and taxi lights and causing an "explosion-like" roar of thunder that was felt and heard for miles around.

Shoppers and shop workers in downtown Lancaster, six miles away, were talking about the "explosion."

A resident in Lancaster Township reported her cats fled at the noise. She knew it was thunder, she noted, "that's the only thing that frightens them."

An indignant Manheim Township resident, however, called the airport office later in the morning to file a protest with the manager. A resident of nearby Weatherburn development, he was calling, he explained, about "that large transport plane that flew so low over my house at 8:30 this morning. It rattled my roof and things in my house. It must have been large: it was very noisy."

Norman Lamar, the airport manager, was enroute downtown when it happened. He heard shoppers talking about the "explosion."

He said that there was no mistaking it for a sonic boom, a different type of sound caused when a high-flying jet breaks the sound barrier.

"This was more like an explosion," Lamar said. There could be no mistaking the roll of thunder for what it was."

Back at the airport, workers in the terminal reported that the windows and doors rattled.

"Where physically it struck we're not really sure," said a worker at the airport tower. "We saw the light flash near the terminal area, but we don't know exactly where."

A airport authority repairman said that it appeared the bolt had hit somewhere on the field, sending its millions of volts of electricity skittering across the ground surface and blowing all the runway lamps.

The bulbs, encased in plastic-topped metal housings, all stand about 3 to 16 inches off the ground.

Two maintenance workers at the field were a little too close for comfort. They were out on the field when the bolt hit, about 100 yards from them.

"What did we say? It would be unprintable," said David Eberly. He and Tim Brennan said they knew it was lightning. They were unhurt, but shaken.

Lamar said the bolt blew all the

—See THUNDERBOLT —Page 2

ACT I

Omén of Arabia

1
Genesis

Thunder and Lightning – thunder and lightning. All night it had gone on: Zeus's bolts from heaven onto the dry sandy beach on the shore of the Arabian Sea. The shepherds were silent. They watched and listened in awe, transfixed as the leaders hurried down to meet the wispy stringers from the ground just an instant before the mighty arm-thick bolts were thrown.

Bedouins were they, five in number; four of them born in the nearby village of Muscat, the fifth a restless wanderer from far away Kuwait, or so he said.

Near daybreak the storm moved away over the water and they came out of the tent to watch the display. Suddenly a thunderbolt, mightier even than any of the others, hissed and crackled and exploded not twenty feet in front of them! They fell back from the force and were blinded. Inshallah! All was silent.

When dawn came with her rosy hue, the Bedouins stirred, then cried out, "Praise be to Allah – we see! We must gather the flock and be out of here to the next watering hole before high noon, else we perish." The wanderer went about his tasks, then went to the place the gods had sanctified to offer up prayers of thanksgiving.

What was this? The sand for yards around was glazed, and at the center was a thick crust of shiny water. Then the sun arose and streamed upon the scene. A dazzling rainbow as from a dewdrop on the spider web struck the wanderer's eye. He looked closely. Near the edge of the thickened crust was a tiny ball, smaller than a baby's tear, but of a perfect roundness and clarity, much more than of any pearl of great price. He looked even closer and saw a tiny sand grain behind the sphere, but to his eye it seemed a boulder. "Praise be to Allah – I will keep this ball of crystal!" He carefully lifted the palm-sized crust and placed it into a small sheepskin pouch.

"Come, Omén from Oman," the others teased him, "A dreamer you are and a dreamer you will always be, Sultan Omén." And they bowed in derision; yet they looked when he showed them his treasure.

Fairer than Venus who sprang fully clothed from Jupiter's brow;
More perfect than the full Moon;
Alive with knowledge and wisdom of things past and things yet to come;
Stay with me always, my Crystal Ball.
Allah be praised!

2
Exodus

Omén sat in the sunlight on the hillside overlooking the flock of sheep entrusted to him. Although he kept a watchful eye on them, his mind kept returning to his dream of a better life in Kuwait. Ever since he was a young boy he had dreamed of a better life. His dreams were filled with visions of great deeds: saving an exalted Sultan from a terrible fate, and in his gratitude the Sultan would take Omén into his service – Omén saw himself climbing to positions of power with the Sultan's help. Or he would rescue a princess from her captors and marry her. The dreams went on and on ... played out daily in his mind.

He knew they were only dreams, but they helped pass the time. He had discovered the life of a shepherd was lonely – very lonely indeed. He had not realized a shepherd spent so much time alone, so much time walking about checking the area for dangers while the sheep grazed on the sparse grass. There were so many hours with nothing to occupy his mind but the dreams of the future. He often found himself mesmerized by the crystal ball he kept in his sheepskin pouch, safely protected in the soft wool. Somehow he could feel a kind of strength emitting from the tiny sphere. He marveled at the spell it had begun to weave upon him.

Sometimes he thought of his home. It had been almost six months since he left. He wondered if they really missed him. He didn't want to remember his life there. Nevertheless his mind would drift back to the days that led up to his decision to leave. He thought of his mother's dancing eyes when she looked at him. She worked so hard caring for his brothers and baby sister; she was always so tired. But she always faithfully cared for his father's needs.

His father worked hard and expected the same from his family. Omén knew his father expected more from him since he was the eldest son, yet he never seemed to be able to do anything that pleased his father. He always drove Omén to his limit and criticized him for wanting more out of life than his small village of Sur had to offer. His father could never understand that Omén wanted more out of life than to marry, raise children and barely exist off the land. Somehow Omén knew he was destined to be something more in his life.

Tears stung his cheeks as he remembered the angry words his father had shouted that last night at home. "Omén, you will never be more than what you were born into. You are a fool and a dreamer if you believe those day-dreams that uselessly occupy your mind. If you applied your energy more to your responsibilities than the foolish nonsense in your head, you would like your life better. Dreams are for young girls who have nothing better to do. Ah, Omén, what am I to do with you?" Omén had held back the tears then, but the words pierced his very soul.

Omén was jarred from his thoughts when he saw a movement out of the corner of his eye. As he looked closer he could see one of the older shepherds headed his way. Rather than be taunted for the tears streaming down his cheeks, he quickly wiped them away and leaned against the rock behind him pretending to be asleep.

The shepherd quietly strode up to Omén. He gently shook the boy's shoulder to wake him. "Ah, Omén, why must you dream so much?" he teased.

Omén jumped and looked around as if unsure of where he was. He rubbed his eyes like he was struggling to focus on the man before him. "I only…" He looked to the flock. "Praise to Allah, the sheep have not been harmed." Omén was visibly embarrassed that he had almost been caught with tears in his eyes, like a girl.

"Praise be to Allah, indeed. Omén, you must pay more attention to your duties. The sheep are fine…this time. Be glad it was I who caught you napping."

Omén smiled to himself as the shepherd turned to go back to the encampment. He knew Abdul was his only true friend among the shepherds he had joined. He didn't mind Abdul's teasing as much as the others'. He felt they gave him more than his fair share of grief.

"It won't happen again," Omén called to his friend.

"See that it doesn't, my young dreamer. You best see that none have strayed." He waved his walking stick and continued down the hill.

Omén stared after Abdul for a moment, then decided he should check the outlying area for danger. He stooped to pick up his staff, pausing to survey the grazing flock before setting out to look for strays. "A dreamer indeed!" he mumbled to himself. "I'll show all of you someday. I am not just another fool with idle dreams. By Allah, I will be a man of means before I grow old."

In the months that followed, Omén began to realize that his future dreams lay in his knowledge of sheep herding. He promised himself he would learn everything he could from his friend Abdul and the other shepherds. And when they would meet other shepherds in their travels, Omén would talk to them into the night learning all he could.

"Ho, Omén," said one of the young sheepherders gruffly one morning as they broke camp, "it looks like you will never get the hang of it. Abdul thinks it is time for me to take over my old job." He took the tent poles from Omén, finished bundling up the tent, and heaved it onto the back of an old ram, kept for that purpose until it could no longer carry, whereupon they would celebrate with a feast of mutton.

Out of the corner of his eye, Omén saw the young man smile as the ram sagged with the weight. "Perhaps we will have some real meat soon," he thought. "For all the time I have spent with these men, I have never seen Bahlul smile until now."

Now the shepherds he traveled with were beginning to treat Omén with more respect. They were as eager to teach him as he was to learn. They still teased him but it was not as hurtful as it had been. The other shepherds commented that he was no longer the dreamy-eyed youngster that had joined them in Muscat. When he asked questions they answered him with an enthusiasm they had not felt for years. Sheep herding was gaining a new purpose for them as well. They had a young man among them who was willing to learn and often do the unpleasant tasks that went along with their profession. They too had begun to think that Omén might be a man of importance some day.

At night around the campfire when Omén would pull the palm-sized stone from his pouch, they would all gather 'round to look at the tiny marvel perched thereon. Omén would hold Crystal up in front of the fire, letting her soak up the warmth before returning her to the pouch so she would not be cold through the night. The shepherds teased him about the way he cared for the tiny gem.

"Omén, someday you will take that stone and bathe it in a stream before you bathe yourself." Omén laughed along with them but he knew that he might very well do just that. He wondered why he had not thought of that himself. The shepherds teased him some more before they turned in for the night. But Omén had learned to take their taunts in stride. He had discovered they did not mean to hurt him as his father had. Rather, it was their way of showing him that they cared.

Omén developed an air of confidence about him that was ever growing. He was learning to hold his head high and proud no matter what anyone said to him. He had a purpose in life, he wanted everyone to notice the changes taking place inside him. He had begun to direct all his energies towards this new feeling of belonging. He now understood that he was a person too and maybe, just maybe, he could forget his life with his father. He would never again be made to feel that his worth was less than that of a mongrel dog. He had a place in this life…he had yet to discover how great his fate would be. He found he didn't even mind having to stay with the whole herd while the others went into a village for occasional supplies and to seek their pleasures. He was content for the time being to remain in this simple life of a shepherd, learning all it had to offer him.

Although he still dreamed while he tended his flock, he no longer dreamed idle dreams about saving sultans or lost princesses. Now his thoughts turned to the day he would reach Kuwait as a knowledgeable herdsman, the wealth he would obtain from his sheep, the fine-boned horses he would own, the possibilities of having a wife and family someday.

Each morning he would awaken before the others and watch for the Sun to rise in the East, bathing the land in crimson and orange. He would remove Crystal from his pouch, turning her over and over, wondering what secrets were hidden inside the precious gem. As he walked with the sheep he pondered the mysterious power the crystal seemed to hold over him. He examined the new direction his life was taking since she came into his possession. At times he wondered if it wasn't the other way around…maybe it was he who came into *her* possession.

In the lazy afternoons as the Sun beat mercilessly on the desert land, Omén sat near the sheep watching the flock with a wary eye. He would take Crystal out for a quick peek and find himself hours later still sitting on the ground looking at the sparkling gem.

Looking *at*, or looking *through*? Staring at his treasure, he would drift into a trance, the sunlight reflecting off of the tiny orb numbing his optic nerve until he no longer saw it. With unfocused eyes, images began to dance around in his mind's eye. Later, the setting sun behind him would reflect inside the frozen drop and re-emerge back to his eyes – the light dispersed, as with a prism, into a rainbow of colors. Omén would be startled, remember his first encounter with Crystal, and awaken from his trance.

He often had the impression that Crystal was somehow trying to communicate with him. But that was nonsense…wasn't it? How could a tiny gem like this talk to him? Deep inside something told him to be patient, someday he would learn the mysteries of the wondrous prize. Slowly he began to believe that when the time was right he would have the knowledge to unfold the secrets locked away within the crystal.

As he dreamed of one day talking with Crystal, it never once occurred to him that she was already guiding him towards his dreams and his destiny.

The loneliness he had felt when he first left home was beginning to ebb. That was due, in part, to the fact that he had befriended a stray wolfhound outside the last village near where they had camped. No one in the village had wanted the poor beast since its master had died. Omén couldn't bear to see the magnificent animal turned out into the desert, so he coaxed the dog to follow when they broke camp.

"Ah, Omén, you are soft in the heart, as well as a dreamer," teased his fellow shepherds as the dog ran after Omén.

"It's true, I may be," he grinned, "but at least I'll have somebody to keep me company during these cold and lonely nights."

With the dog running ahead, Omén set his pace for the day, herding the sheep north. He grinned to himself as the shepherds called taunts to him. Deep down he knew they envied him for taking in the dog. He knew they wished they had a faithful companion who could offer them loyalty and protection from the hazards of the desert. The days were dull at best, tending the sheep, but the endless nights were worse. Besides, now he had somebody to share his hopes and dreams without the fear of being laughed at, and the dog could help him with the sheep as well.

So Omén spent hours each day dreaming with the stone in his hand, bathing Crystal with the warm rays of the Sun. The wolfhound occasionally nudged his arm for affection, and placing his head in Omén's lap would sniff at Crystal and the stone, and wag his tail. Omén would scratch him behind the ears and tell him that he was a dreamer too!

3
Delirium and Mirages

Abdul had given him a few sheep for his wages, and they parted – the shepherds returning south, Omén continuing north toward Kuwait. Several years pass, and he has a fight with some bandits who leave him for dead, which is not far from the truth. He has been rationing his water severely.

Omén was weary. He had traveled all day in the heat until his feet ached from plodding in the shifting sands. "What I need is a horse," he thought grimly, as he sat down to have a sip of water from his dwindling supply. Then he froze, bottle lifted to his lips – a scream had shattered the dry air like glass. It was high and desperate and unmistakably human.

He started to his feet as the scream came again; this time the cry was longer and mixed with the frantic neighing of a horse. Without hesitation Omén ran up a sandy ridge in the direction of the noise, drawing his short sword as he went. He topped the hill and made out darting shadows from behind a huge rock outcropping. He loped down the hill to the near side of the rock and stopped to flatten himself against the stone. When he edged around the sandstone corner, however, he was quite unprepared for what he saw – a young, slightly-built woman on a milk-white mare was struggling with three swarthy men who clearly had evil intentions. Two of the men were holding the struggling mare's bridle while the other was trying to extricate the fighting woman from the saddle.

Omén burst from the shadows with a great cry that made everyone, including the panicked mare, stop and stare with looks of utter terror in their eyes. "I must look awesome," he thought grimly to himself as he advanced upon the lady's attackers. Suddenly he felt rather than saw the shadow coming up from behind him, and heard the thunder of hooves and the rush of a plunging body.

A black stallion with fiery red eyes swooped down upon one of the men still clutching the little mare's bridle, and grabbed him by the neck, his horse teeth crunching through flesh and bone. The mare reared free and the woman delivered a savage blow to her assailant with her small dagger. Omén, recovering from his surprise, rushed to tackle the third man, who had thrown down his sword and was retreating into the rock formation. The stallion left his dying victim crumpled on the sand and went after the remaining man, who stared transfixed in terror as the black fury reared above him and came down with a sickening crunch. The stallion turned towards Omén, blood in his eyes, and then stopped as though bewitched. The woman, still astride the mare, was murmuring to it and holding out a glistening stone. Omén gasped; could it be? The crystal on the stone flickered in the sunlight as if beckoning him. Was it – could it be – *his* crystal, the one stolen on that dark night months ago? Omén strode towards the woman, not even heeding the angry snorts and stamps from the stallion.

"Stay!" the lady commanded, holding the stone before her.

The crystal had no numbing effect on Omén, although it obviously did on the stallion. Omén smiled to himself; surely this must be his crystal.

"I threaten you not," he told the woman on the prancing mare. "I had come to offer aid when he (nodding toward the stallion) came before me."

"That crystal," Omén continued slowly, "where did you get it?"

"That is no concern of yours," the lady snapped. "I'll ask the questions now. You say you came to rescue me – from where and to where, traveler?"

Briefly, Omén described his latest travels and troubles, including the theft of his crystal, "that could be the sister of yours, my lady," he ended respectfully, hoping she could relax enough to tell him about her crystal.

She sat on her prancing mare considering his words. At last she turned her eyes to the west. "The sun moves lower," she said. "We must retire to my stronghold to find out more about each other. Come." She wheeled her mare westward toward the sinking sun.

"Wait!" cried Omén, visualizing his running across blazing sands to keep up with the fleet-footed pair. "Can your mare ride both of us?"

"Never!" She looked shocked at the suggestion. "I had forgotten you were afoot. Ride the Black."

"The stallion?" Omén reeled — put himself at the mercy of that killer?

The lady smiled at his discomfiture, and waved vaguely at the snorting stallion, that walked up to Omén and stood calmly waiting. With one more look at the lady, Omén gingerly swung himself aboard the gleaming Black, and rode after the lady and her mare.

They rode at an easy canter, and before long came to an oasis that had seemingly sprung up out of nowhere. A golden tent was set up under the trees, and a small herd of about fifteen mares and colts stood in the shade behind the tent. Like the white mare and the black stallion, they were the most magnificent horses Omén had ever seen. His eyes were wrenched away from the horses, however, by the emergence of two exquisite women, who were raven-haired and dark like the lady on the mare. Clearly, these were sisters.

"Your father must be a great lord to have this wealth in horses," Omén said as he slid down from the Black.

"Our father has been dead these fifteen years," said the lady, unsaddling the mare. "Allow us to introduce ourselves. This is Mari," indicating the taller of the two women, "and this is Sian. I am Neva. We will welcome you to our hospitality tonight and discuss this matter of crystals."

The inside of the tent was as luxurious as the three sisters were beautiful, and after a sumptuous dinner liberally accompanied by a white wine that to Omén had a strange but heavenly taste, they all sat upon thick silk pillows and stared at the crystal between them. Omén was sure it was his, until Mari produced an identical one, and then Sian produced hers. He could not believe it. "Are there others?" he finally asked, not taking his eyes off the glittering gems. Neva smiled and reached into her pockets – this crystal was like the others, but it had a golden glow when put in front of Omén. Omén gasped and reached for the crystal, but Neva stilled his hand.

"I believe you to be an honorable man," she said, looking him straight in the eye with a gaze that was disquieting, "and honest. If we return your treasure, which we believe to be yours, will you promise to tell no one of us or our crystals or to ever seek us again?" She stopped and smiled. "We owe you a debt for helping to save me from that scum this afternoon. There is a black colt of the stallion you rode today. Upon your vow of secrecy the crystal is yours again as is the colt." Omén stared at her lovely face and lovelier figure, and thought it would be a crime not only to never see her or her exquisite sisters again but also to never mention their beauty – but then he seemed to be in over his head altogether this time.

"I will take my crystal and do as you say, lady," he said. His beloved crystal was placed in his hand and he was given more wine to savor while Mari played a golden harp. Omén's eyes grew heavy......

The next morning Omén woke with a fearful headache and a sore back that felt as if he had slept on the sand instead of silk pillows. As he came fully awake, he realized he *was* on the sand. The pillows, the tent, the horses and oasis were gone! He grasped his belt – yes, Crystal was still there…it hadn't been a dream. Or had it? He shrugged as he rubbed his aching head. "Well," he told himself, "at least I have *you* back," – he held her to the light – "but I do wish I could have kept the colt." He sighed.

4

Rest and Relaxation

Omén sat on the sun-bleached shore along the Arabian Sea watching the sea-weary ships anchor and depart from the village of Dhahran. It had been four years since he had begun his journey to Kuwait. He had been resting in the friendly village for several months now. Badly in need of help, he and the wolfhound had somehow managed to stagger to the outskirts of the village, where a kindly merchant and his daughter had found them.

Time passed slowly here, even more slowly than it had on the journey. But Omén was thankful for the quiet life and the safety Dhahran offered. He said a daily prayer to Allah for granting him a second chance to fulfill his dream. He was ashamed of his rash actions that had almost destroyed him and his animals in the desert. Yet he was grateful for the wisdom he had gained through the ordeal. He was grateful also for the strengthened bond that now lay between Crystal and himself. Had it not been for her words of encouragement, he doubted he would have had the will to guide the flock towards help.

Each day he and the wolfhound would stroll down to the shoreline watching the grey-green waves ripple onto the burning beach. For hours on end they would sit watching the ships depart on the silvery waves until they were but tiny black specks on the horizon. Often Omén would sit with the stone cupped within his large hands letting Crystal enjoy the salt mist that blew off the sea. He sensed that she enjoyed watching the sea vessels almost as much as he. He thought that someday he would like to sail on one of those fine ships and maybe even own one…some day. He had heard that many of these ships were dhows made in Kuwait; perhaps that was why they held his interest. Maybe he could sail to Kuwait. But when he asked his God about this, he got no answer, and Crystal would want him to remain a shepherd for a time yet. For now he was content to accept the hospitality offered by the merchant until he could gather his strength for the rest of the journey.

The last few months Omén had employed two local shepherd boys to watch over his flock, promising them a better life in Kuwait if they would make the journey with him. He could see so much of himself in them. It made him smile when he thought of how green he had been when he joined Abdul and the other shepherds. He only hoped he could pass some wisdom on to them before they impulsively rushed into a birdbrain idea as he had. He doubted he would ever get over his folly in the desert.

In spite of his doubts, there were many in the village who admired his courage. There were few young men who would have set out alone in the desert to try to make their dreams come true. As he walked the dirty streets of Dhahran the shop keepers and the fellaheen alike would bid him welcome and invite him to share their humble meals. Omén always eagerly accepted; he was hungry for company after the months alone in the desert. But after a few pleasant hours he would excuse himself, saying only that he had many preparations to make for the journey north. The truth was that he could sense the conversation beginning to tread dangerously near the subject of his ordeal in the desert; he had no intention of telling them – he could not bear to hear their scorn of his folly.

Walking through the market place, Omén could see the young girls of the village staring at him, whispering to each other and giggling. He was so consumed with shame that it never occurred to him the women of the village found him handsome. Many a wife met the angry tongues of their husbands when they commented on Omén's appearance. He had grown from a gangly youth of sixteen into a man. He had grown tall with sturdy shoulders and walked with the grace of a dancer. His dark brown eyes danced when he spoke and they twinkled with a spark of mischief. He had long unruly locks he bound with a leather thong. Any girl in Dhahran would have been proud to receive Omén's attention.

He had grown mentally as well. He no longer spent his time dreaming about the glorious future in Kuwait but prepared himself for the day when he would finally reach his destination. Before taking his "short cut" into the desert he worked in the villages he passed through whenever possible, earning a little money to buy supplies or more sheep. Occasionally he would work for other shepherds along the way, accepting a lamb or two for his pay. He was developing a business head, as was evidenced by the way he haggled with the merchants in the market place for a higher price for the sheep he sold to buy supplies to continue his journey.

Rarely did he let his mind wander back to his home life – it was all still painful. He sometimes wondered how his mother was, and tried not to think about his father. He laughed to himself when he thought of the endless dreams that had filled his mind; the dreams of Sultans, of Princesses and of great riches seemed a life time ago. But they had helped pass the time when life became too much of a burden.

When Omén returned to the merchant's home one evening he found the village elders seated around the main room of the dwelling. All were eager to speak with Omén. Over the months he spent tending to his wounds, he had not been questioned about the desert and the only explanation he offered was that he had been attacked by bandits on his way to Kuwait to seek his fortune. He could sense the time had come…he owed it to them for their kindness. As the chill of the evening settled over the land Omén began his tale….

It had been almost four years since he had parted company with the band of shepherds. They had followed the ancient trade route from Muscat as far as Fahal before Abdul and the other shepherds decided to head back to Muscat. Omén was paid for his hard work in the knowledge he had gained of sheep herding. Plus Abdul gave him a small flock of sheep – what they owed him in wages, they said. But he knew it was a gift, showing their faith in his dream.

As Omén and the wolfhound and the sheep started out on their own, the dream burned stronger than ever. The shepherds called goodbye, watching their young friend disappear into the desert heat. He had promised to get word back to them when he reached Kuwait. They advised him to stay on the well-traveled routes with his flock and to stay near villages for protection. Omén waved goodbye to his friends as tears trickled down his sun-baked cheeks. He was not ashamed of these tears; they were tears of love and admiration for the men.

At first Omén did as the shepherds advised and stayed near villages and well-worn routes. Yet his anxiety about traveling so slowly was getting the best of him. He began asking questions about other routes north. Each time he was told there were indeed other routes but they were dangerous, especially for a young man traveling alone. Besides the fact there was little water in the vast desert, marauding bandits roamed looking for victims. Omén scoffed at their warnings, only seeing a way to cut the travel time. Many nights he sat before the campfire trying to decide what to do. He would hold the stone in his hand, gently brushing Crystal with the splayed end of a knotted cord, caressing her smooth body, wishing she could tell him what to do. Finally one night around midnight he made his decision to go into the desert. Following the coast line to Kuwait would take too long…he felt he would be an old man by the time he got there, were he not to go into the desert. As he settled down into his blanket he sent the dog out to check the sheep.

For several months the journey went smoothly. They had encountered few people in the desert. He grew lonely for the sight of civilization but felt he was doing the right thing. Once he encountered a caravan heading south. He eagerly sought their company for news and companionship. They offered the same advice: head east to the coast before you run into trouble. The caravan leader told him the watering hole north of them had dried up for the season and the bandits were getting bolder. Still Omén had scoffed at their advice. But now Omén was beginning to wonder if he had made the right decision after all. To try to find answers he sat by the campfire holding Crystal in a dreamlike trance, starting up suddenly hours later feeling as though he had been dreaming. Wearily he would place Crystal back into her warm woolen bed in the pouch and drift off to sleep.

The realization of his mistake hit Omén full force the day they reached the watering hole and found it dried up, as the caravan leader had told him. He knew he had to get back to the main route before they all perished in the heat. He had already lost two weak lambs to the burning sun and feared the others were getting weaker as well. Even the wolfhound was beginning to grow listless, often searching out the shade of a boulder or scrub brush rather than watching the sheep. Omén prayed the night would soon fall over the land, offering a bit of comfort as he headed the thirsty flock to the east.

"If only Allah will grace us for a while longer," he said out loud. "Just another day or two…please…" His words trailed off as he thought of how he had almost destroyed everything. Not only his dreams, but the lives of the innocent sheep and his faithful wolfhound. And Crystal, what would become of her? His head hurt, his tongue was thick, his heart beat slowly and painfully, but the shame he felt for his folly made everything else seem unimportant. "I am such a fool!" he screamed into the darkness.

Sensing his master's distress the wolfhound went out to check on the flock. Trying to seek some comfort, Omén sought out Crystal, hoping to lose himself in the visions she spun before his eyes. Suddenly his mind was jerked back to the present by a noise in the distance. The wolfhound was barking, warning his master of the coming disaster.

Thundering hooves shattered the silence of the velvet night. Instinctively, Omén knew it was the bandits. Hurriedly, he placed the stone back into the pouch, dug a small hole, placed the pouch into it and covered it up. He would not let the bandits get his most prized possession. A sheep bleated in the distance as the thundering hooves drew nearer. He whistled into the darkness for the dog. With scimitar drawn, the leader of the bandits rode his horse to within inches of Omén. He laughed as he edged the horse forward, knocking Omén to the ground.

"Please, sir, I am just a poor shepherd," Omén pleaded. "I have nothing …" The bandit merely grinned as his men dismounted, grabbing Omén roughly as they ripped through his bed roll and tore at his clothes. A bandit with a wicked-looking scar was about to strike him when the wolfhound sprang out of the shadows and grabbed the bandit's shoulder with his powerful jaws. Without warning, something struck the back of Omén's head. As the darkness closed in on his senses, the last thing he heard was a yelp of pain from the dog.

As the sun began to rise overhead, Omén awoke, his head pounding fiercely.

Looking about, trying to focus, he heard the familiar thump, thump of the wolfhound's wagging tail. Somehow, in spite of his wounds, the dog had gathered the sheep and they were all waiting patiently by his side for their master to wake up. Omén smiled at the dog, tears running down his face. He did not deserve such devotion. He rose dizzily from where he lay and went to dig up the pouch containing his beloved Crystal. He began walking east with the weary sheep, the wounded dog following behind. He had to get them to safety … somehow.

Omén looked up from his tale, glancing at the men around him, expecting to see scorn on their faces. Instead he saw concern and awe at the ordeal he had survived. They did not laugh, but urged him on. When he realized they admired him for his courage, he pulled Crystal from her snug bed. He told them how she had coaxed him on with a soothing but demanding voice when his will had failed. The men looked at Omén in even more awe than before and gathered around to get a better look at the wondrous crystal ball. They marveled at the young man who dared to follow his destiny.

5

She Speaks!

The sun baked the landscape from overhead, the heat rising and falling in waves along the sun-parched trail as a small band of travelers headed north to Kuwait.

Omén had finally gained back his strength and courage to continue the journey in search of his dream. As he left Dhahran the dream blazed even stronger in his soul, like a flame that could not be put out.

He held his head high as they walked down the dirty streets. Villagers called their good-byes and well wishes. He still did not understand why the villagers thought him a hero. He was angry with himself for endangering so many lives because of his impatience. But these people thought him courageous for his daring. Maybe he was, but he knew it would take a long time, perhaps years, before he saw the misadventure in that light.

For now he had more important things to occupy his mind. He had a sizeable herd to watch out for along with two green shepherd boys. Then there was the faithful wolfhound to care for as well as the wondrous crystal ball. She had become more of a puzzle to him since the ordeal in the desert. How could she have spoken to him? Stones do not speak. Yet, he knew by the life that flowed through his veins she had guided him on to safety. What were the hazy visions she rolled before his eyes as he sat before the campfire at night? Why did he feel such a bond to this sparkling gem? Crystal was even more puzzling than the first day he found her. A puzzle he intended to unravel as soon as possible.

The wolfhound playfully nipped at his heels, bringing his attention back to the present. He called out several commands to the two shepherds and turned to wave a final goodbye to the villagers. His eyes misted over as he spotted the merchant's daughter standing away from the crowd. He smiled and waved just to her. He had become very fond of her over the months. But deep down he knew that what he felt for her was gratitude for nursing him back to health. Although he and the merchant had discussed the possibility of marriage and Omén sending for her when he got to Kuwait, he knew it would never come to pass. He was a man with a grand destiny to follow and he knew he could not settle down until he had fulfilled his dreams.

That evening as the shepherds bedded down the flock and the velvety darkness enclosed the tiny encampment, Omén sat before the campfire with the stone cupped between his hands. He turned it over and over inspecting Crystal's smooth surface. "What a wonder you are," he mumbled. He wearily put her into the pouch and settled down into his blanket. He was too tired to contemplate her magic; the day, though uneventful, had taken its toll on him after so many months of inactivity. But it felt good to be back on the road to Kuwait. He drifted into slumber, thoughts of the glorious city filling his brain.

Soon Omén fell into the familiar pattern of tending the sheep and stopping in the nearby villages for supplies. Now that he had two shepherd boys to look after the sheep he could occasionally afford himself the luxury of relaxing in a village. Even the wolfhound found a new sense of adventure, following him wherever he went. Omén guessed the dog did not feel the need to remain with the flock all the time now that the shepherds were there. Omén enjoyed the dog's company on these outings. Often he would buy something for the two of them to eat as they rested in the common area of the village before returning to camp.

He found his mind ever more preoccupied with thoughts of the crystal ball as they walked. He couldn't understand how she could have possibly talked to him, urging him on through the relentless heat, yet someone or something had. He decided he must have been half mad from the lack of water and only thought he heard that soothing voice. "Enough of this foolishness," he said out loud. He was eager to get back on the road and quickened his pace. So many things were troubling him, especially the walking dream he had in the desert heat. The road would offer him the time to sort out his thoughts. Tonight, after the boys had gone to tend to their duties with the sheep, Omén intended to try to get some answers from Crystal.

As the darkness fell across the encampment and the silence of night crept over the desert, Omén took Crystal from her warm woolen bed. He held her before the fire, watching the reflection of the flame dance about her sparkling surface.

He shook his head from side to side as he spoke. "Sometimes, my lovely gem, I think I must be mad! I talk to you, tell you my dreams and problems as if you can help me." He glanced about the shadows, then turned back to the fire, satisfied no one was listening.

"That night the bandits came I placed your safety above my own because I could not bear the thought of being separated from you. I do not understand this bond between us. By the Gods, I do not understand." He sat in silence for a time watching the flames wander to and fro, caressing each other, then fleeing away.

"Ah, Crystal, I know you speak. I heard you urge me on when my strength failed. I do not want to believe that the voice I heard was just another walking dream, as were the beautiful horse and the sisters who returned you to me. Please tell me you spoke to me, Crystal Ball."

His mind wandered to the hallucination. He could still feel the black stallion's powerful muscles rippling beneath him as they rode through the desert. He knew it had been a dream, but it all seemed so real. Especially the beautiful raven-haired sisters who had returned his stolen crystal to him, with the promise that he never tell anyone about them. Yet the dream persisted to plague his thoughts. He wondered if it was brought on because of his fear of losing his most prized possession; or was it a premonition of what was to come?

"Why won't you speak to me, my beauty?" Omén whispered. "Must we be in danger before you will speak again?"

The silence was deafening to Omén. He wanted to cry, to curse, to rage at the world all at the same time. In defeat he decided to put Crystal away for the night. He was tired and it was obvious she would not speak to him.

Suddenly a small voice shattered the silence. "No, my friend, we do not have to be in danger again before I'll speak." Startled, Omén almost dropped Crystal to the ground. He sat staring at her for several minutes. Tears of joy began to roll down his cheeks – she *did* speak!

As if reading his thoughts she began again. "Yes, Omén, I can speak. But you were not ready to listen until the desert ordeal. And since then I have been more concerned with your regaining your strength…" She paused, seeing the tears well up in his eyes again.

After a few moments Omén wiped the tears away. He still could not believe his ears. "But how is it you can talk?"

"That need not concern you for now, love," she cooed. "We have a whole lifetime before us to learn of my secrets."

Omén sat staring into the flames for a time. "Just tell me one thing…the walking dream…"

"Do not worry yourself," she broke in. She knew it was troubling him.

"It was nothing more than a delirium brought on by the many days you had gone without water in the burning sun." She studied his finely chiseled features for a moment before continuing. "Now perhaps, my friend, you should get some rest. You have had enough of a shock for one night. We will talk more later; besides, we have a long day ahead of us tomorrow."

He smiled. "As you say, little one, it is a long day tomorrow." He held her up to the light, then placed her in the sheepskin pouch. For the first time since the desert folly he felt more at ease with himself. He settled down into the blanket and fell into a peaceful sleep with his arm around the wolfhound.

Omén woke early the next morning. His heart skipped a beat as he thought of the conversation with Crystal. Had she really spoken to him or did he just dream it? Was the desire for her to speak so overpowering that he dreamed their conversation? Surely she had spoken…he couldn't be going mad…not with Kuwait this close. Had the desert affected his mind so much he was hallucinating again? No! He would not believe such a thing. She *had* to have spoken.

He busied himself with rekindling the campfire. After putting some tea on to heat, he sat back and took Crystal from the pouch. As the sun peeked over the horizon he was greeted by a cheery voice.

14

"Good morning, Omén."

With trembling hands he tightened his grasp on the stone. "Praise be to Allah, you do speak!"

"Do you doubt your own ears?" she asked.

"I … I thought … I was afraid that perhaps I had dreamed you spoke to me last night," he stammered.

"No, dearest, you did not dream it," she said. "I do speak."

As if dumbfounded Omén sat, alternately watching Crystal and the luminous sunrise. He was in awe of both the wonders before him. The wolfhound nudged Omén's arm, then sat down beside him to get a better look at the crystal and hear what she was saying.

"Ah, Wolf, she speaks," he murmured, patting the dog absentmindedly on the head. The steady thump, thump, thump of the wolfhound's wagging tail was his answer. The two boys came in from their night's vigil for breakfast.

Hours later as the sun finished its golden ascent high into the heavens, the small motley band of travelers resumed their trek to the north. The two young shepherds took positions on either side of the flock and Omén took up the rear. The wolfhound bounded to the head of the flock, then raced back to Omén. It seemed as though his new found happiness was infectious to the dog as well.

Crystal's words were music to his ears as they made their way along the trail. "We have a whole lifetime before us to learn of my secrets." The sky clouded up and a warm, gentle rain began to fall.

My secrets you may learn,
As others will in turn.
The sand will make clear stone,
To see what can't be known
Up close and yet out far,
Beyond the farthest star.
Quartz crystals time their watch,
Transmitter and all such;
Make fiber optics too,
To talk across the blue.

My silicon is neat,
For chips that can't be beat
In computation tests —
To beat you all at chess
Designing many things
For paupers and for kings.
Yet too much more I fear
So let us meet your dear.

Crystal Ball

6
Omén Meets Shahrazad

Omén stumbled down the dark and dirty streets of Kuwait on his way back to camp. He had spent a pleasant evening with friends, drinking and swapping stories.

It was hard to believe that he had been here for three months. This was the city he had only seen in his dreams since childhood. It had taken him a little over six years to get here, but in spite of all the obstacles he had made it. His heart raced even now as he thought of the day he approached the city gates. He wanted to scream out his joy to everyone he met. What a spectacle he must have made of himself when he fell

15

to his knees and kissed the ground before him. He felt so foolish when he looked up into the faces of passers-by. Omén laughed at his foolishness.

He staggered on into the darkness towards the encampment. As he neared the welcoming campfire he called out a hearty greeting to the boys tending the flock. He almost called out a cheery greeting to his faithful dog as well, but caught himself in time. Painfully he blinked back the burning tears welling up in his eyes. Sitting down by the fire, he mumbled an order to the shepherds and they scampered off to check the sheep. Omén poured himself a cup of tea hoping to steady his swimming head.

This had been a night for remembering. Memories filled his mind even now. Once again he let his mind drift back to the fateful day the wolfhound died. It had been more than a year since the dog had dropped in the noon-day heat; he suspected the animal's heart had finally given out. Tears rolled freely down his face now as he wished he had gotten around to giving the dog a more proper name. But Wolf had never seemed to mind and had served him well for five years. Five years….

"That's a fine looking dog you have there, Ma'am." "Tis just a cur, part wolf-hound. The bitch died giving the litter and this one is still here. The master has departed and we will no longer keep it. Would you care to take the dog?" "I...oh ... what's its name?" "We call it 'Dog'. It comes and goes. It was nursed by a black sheep, as the litter came in the Spring – it seems to like sheep."

The dog eyed its 'mistress' warily from its resting place on the ground. "Here, Wolf" The dog's eyes brightened. It rose, and the tail began to wag. It walked up to Omén and stood quietly by his side, the tail still wagging. "It looks like he is yours, young man. Good luck to both of you. Kuwait, you say? That is a far piece. The dog will never make it. He is already four years old."

"Ah, enough of this," he thought. "I only hope Wolf is happy now." He reached for the pouch at his side, removing Crystal from her bed of wool. He gently caressed her smooth surface as he stared into the fire, watching the flames dance for a time before his eyelids grew heavy. Sighing, he returned Crystal to the sheepskin, then settled down into his blankets. He awoke in the morning with a grand sized headache. He wondered if he would ever get used to the effects of the wine he shared with his friends. He often wondered why he tried to keep up with them, especially the giant of a man called Zeus. The man could surely drink an ocean without harm. Omén laughed in spite of the pain in his head when he thought of the day they met….

… In his haste to get away from the quizzical faces that had witnessed his strange behavior at the gates the day he arrived, Omén had carelessly rounded a corner, not bothering to watch where he was going. Abruptly he found himself sprawled in the dirt on his butt. In a daze, Omén looked up and saw a blur of gold and amber towering above him. He scrambled to get up but before he could turn a large hand gently lifted him to his feet. Omén stared in disbelief at the sight before him – he had never seen anyone so tall or so powerfully built. In front of him stood a giant of a man, dark skinned, chocolate brown, with light brown (almost amber) eyes and hair, contrasting strongly with his dark skin. Below each eye was a wide streak of gold dust. Dangling from his right ear lobe was a large round gold earring. On his neck was a curiously shaped collar of gold. His deerskin vest was the color of his hair. A gold-stranded braided rope held up his baggy purple pantaloons. His sandal straps were gilded. The giant smiled, his pure white teeth gleaming against his dark skin. "Welcome to Kuwait, Sahib," the giant said, still smiling down on the dusty, disheveled creature in his grasp. Omén warily returned the smile. "Please let me down, Sir," he finally said in a strained voice — the giant had him lifted by the back of his shirt, and it was cutting into his neck.

Omén soon found himself warming up to the giant's bravado. And would soon discover the man had a heart of gold buried in his massive chest. Zeus had taken an immediate liking to the young shepherd. He showed Omén about Kuwait, introducing him to merchants and villagers, treating him like a long lost brother. Omén marveled at the attention this stranger bestowed upon him. Zeus and Omén became frequent companions at the local inn, passing the time away on lonely nights…"And passing away even more time recuperating from the effects of the wine," Omén lamented. He lay back on his blanket, closed his eyes and prayed that the swelling wave of nausea would quickly pass. From outside his lean-to a deep laugh boomed through the early morning solitude. Omén opened his eyes to find Zeus watching him. He knew from the amused look on his face that Zeus found his condition comical. "Come, friend shepherd, the market place awaits your wares." Omén raised on one elbow, shading his eyes from the rising sun. "It's not funny, Zeus. My head feels as though a thousand camels have raced through it." The giant threw back his head and let out a deep throaty laugh. "Besides, I did not think you would remember your offer to help me this morning." "Omén, you underestimate your friend Zeus!" he scolded, pretending to be hurt. "Zeus' word is as good as gold. Now hurry; the morning is wasting."

Omén hesitated a moment, then rose to a spinning world. Unsteadily he made his way to the stream; surely the cool water would clear his fuzzy head. He heard a chuckle rise from within Zeus' throat. The man never ceased to amaze him…last night he had promised to help take some sheep to the market and here he was bright and early. Omén groaned as he submerged his head in the cold soothing water and his senses began to awaken.

Less than an hour later they were headed for the market with the sheep. Omén hung back, amused at the way the towering giant coddled the sheep along. The man was a source of constant wonder; one minute he was a raging bull full of drink, the next an overgrown child coaxing a wayward lamb. He had to turn away quickly, pretending to look at the scenery, to hide his smile from Zeus.

As they neared the city gates Zeus stopped abruptly. He nervously fingered the golden collar about his neck as he watched a small group of slaves being herded towards the market. Omén watched his friend silently. He knew the giant wore the golden collar to remind him of his past in his native land. He had heard that Zeus had made a vow to avenge the wrong done him some day. Suddenly Zeus found a thousand things he had to do, leaving Omén standing in the middle of the road with his mouth open.

Hours later as the noise of the market died down Omén leaned against a stone wall, congratulating himself on the fine deal he had made selling the sheep. Not only did he have enough money to buy supplies but also to pay the two shepherds for their help. He knew he did not always need their help, he could manage well enough without them, but he cherished the companionship they had given him. They had helped to ease his loneliness this last year. But he supposed they would be leaving one day soon to seek their own fortunes.

With the money left over, he bought two fine ewes he had seen headed to market the day before. He knew the ewes would make a grand addition to his flock and improve his stock. He had heeded the words of wisdom from Abdul over the years to always be on the lookout for a prize ewe or ram to improve the quality of his breeding stock. Now that he was settled in Kuwait and had plenty of water and pasture to graze the sheep, he intended to do just that. Almost regretfully he headed the ewes out of the city. He had hoped Zeus would seek him out when the market place began to clear. He guessed the memory of having once been a slave was too painful for him to be anywhere near the market place today. Omén shrugged his shoulders; he'd more than likely see Zeus tonight.

Nearing the campsite, Omén spotted three riders crossing the lush pasture. He watched the graceful horses canter, wishing that one day he too would own such a beautiful horse and race the desert sands. After a few moments he urged the ewes on to their new home. He had better things to do than daydream. As the riders drew nearer he could see the splendid clothing they wore, dyed in the richest of colors. He decided they must be headed for the palace. He saw the brightly colored tassels dangling from the horses' bridles and heard the tiny bells on the horses' breast collars jangle at each step. He watched the powerful stride of the horses, their coats glistening in the sunlight. He noted that the rider in the middle was smaller than the others.

The closer they came, the surer he was that the one in the center was not a man, but a woman. But he could not fathom a woman riding so well, in complete control. In all his days he had never seen a woman sit a horse so well. When they were but a hundred paces from him, he noticed the Sultan's emblem, but his attention was drawn to the woman. Although she was dressed in a tunic and her head was covered with a long veil gliding to her feet (leaving only her eyes exposed), she also wore men's breeches for riding. Despite all the clothing he could see she was small and fine boned; dainty hands with slim fingers held the reins tightly. As they passed by at thirty paces she boldly looked at him, their eyes locking for the briefest of moments before she bowed her head and looked away. Omén watched them disappear into the heat waves of the landscape. He felt a thrill of excitement, a haunting glimmer that he had seen her somewhere before – he could never forget those enchanting brown eyes peering over the veil.

As the days passed he found his thoughts were ever filled with visions of the woman. He could not seem to get her out of his mind. His dreams were filled with those enchanting eyes. Her graceful movements upon the fiery horse glided across his sleeping eyes. Each morning he arose wondering how this woman could possess his thoughts so. He had known women before but none affected him as this one. He often consulted Crystal, but her words of wisdom did not appease him. Logic told him to forget this woman he would probably never see again. Zeus said he was acting like a love-sick calf, and he had to agree.

Early one afternoon he heard hooves thundering across the earth, but for once he did not run to see who it was. He knew he could not drop what he was doing every time he heard a horse. A few moments passed as Omén continued to work. He had the odd sensation that someone was watching him. He slowly turned to see if anyone was there. As he turned, his pulse began to race. His gaze traveled over the vision before him and then locked onto those beautiful eyes. His sight dimmed and he thought he was going to pass out.

The woman quickly jumped down from her mount and tethered the horse; then she boldly stepped close. "Hello, shepherd boy," she said, smiling beneath her veil. Omén felt he was dreaming and the dream would vanish if he dared move. He could do nothing but stare at her. He was surprised. And delighted. She was as tall as he. The guards, and the horses, must be huge indeed. She smiled again and removed the heavy veil from her face, revealing a sheer veil beneath. "Do not worry," she said, observing the look of apprehension on his face. "Today I have managed to get away from the palace unnoticed."

"I think…I think I must be dreaming," Omén finally managed to get out. "I am Omén."

"And I am Shahrazad," she said as she headed towards the stream. Omén followed, still feeling as though he were dreaming. For a long time they sat in silence watching the ripples in the stream. Both seemed content just to share each other's company. At last Omén broke the silence. "I hope you do not think me too bold when I say that you have been in my thoughts ever since I first saw you."

"No, Omén, you are not too bold…you have been in my thoughts as well," she smiled; then looked coyly away. "I have seen you many times when I rode out with the guards."

For a time longer they sat in silence watching each other. Omén moved slowly towards her. She looked away, then rose as if to leave. Their eyes met and searched deeply into each others' souls. They touched finger tips. Omén felt mesmerized in the depths of those enchanting eyes. "Shahrazad…."

Shahrazad began her inquiry. "You are not from around here, are you? Your speech is of the southern regions."

Omén replied in turn, "You are correct. I am from far to the South, in Oman, born in the village of Sur."

"Did you then journey with a caravan this past year, or are you perhaps the young caravan leader?"

"My lady, I am but an humble shepherd, come with my flock these past six years."

"Indeed! This is hard to believe. You are very young; you are hardly a man. You must have been but a youth when you began your journey. What possessed you to come to Kuwait?"

"My lady, I was but sixteen when I left my family and friends. Allah told me that I would find my destiny in Kuwait – and if it be his will, I have."

"Is Allah then your father, and would he allow such a young man to leave him?"

"Allah is my God, and I speak to him often. He speaks to me in the sound of the windstorm in the desert. My father would not let me leave, but I escaped and became a shepherd for livelihood on my journey."

"Your God Allah is a new name to my ears. Your tribal god?"

"Yes, my lady."

"I have a younger sister about your age, but no brothers…"

"I am the oldest in my family. I have two brothers…and a baby sister I was glad to be rid of."

"I should not be speaking to you as an equal. I should not dishonor my father, the Wezir, the court advisor to the Sultan. Are you married, Omén?"

"No, my lady, but I have found the one I have been seeking."

"That is good. You have been in town long enough now to know about the Sultan, and the dearth of available maidens. You should marry your love promptly, before the Sultan finds her and she dies. My father mentioned the problem directly to me not six weeks ago, and I have vowed to become the Sultan's bride and perhaps end the horror of this age. You look sad; why am I telling you all this? It is too depressing. My father has raised us and has kept the two of us from the company of men since our youth, so that we would be an honor to him when we marry. We read books and play together, and attend school – I am presently managing the kitchen help at the Palace. Whenever we can, we race each other around the Palace grounds to let off tensions. Also I love to ride horses, but my sister does not care for the sport. I can run like the wind. My father says I am too old for that – I am twenty four. Dunyzad, my sister, is twenty two. How old are you, Omén?"

"Twenty two years, my lady."

"I like you. Will you be my brother? The marriage to the Sultan will be soon enough, and I feel my youth slipping away. Do you run? Do you think you can keep up with me? Come, let us race to yonder hill and back."

After the race, they sat down beside each other, arms braced behind them, legs spread apart. Unexpectedly, Shahrazad leaned over and put her arms around Omén's neck and pushed him to the ground. She kissed him on the neck until their breath became more regular. "I have never been with a man before," she said. "Show me what I must do to keep the Sultan happy, Brother Omén."

Shahrazad – I have never known woman like you.

Shahrazad – Your dear lips are like morning's sweet dew.

Shahrazad – My whole head's filled with thoughts kind and true.

Shahrazad – Without *you* my whole being is blue.

Omén – Your name brings a promise to be.

Omén – I love you when first you I see.

Omén – If only we both may be free,

Omén – Then I would take you, and you me.

7

The Arabian Nights

Omén huddled beneath his blankets next to the fire as the windstorm raged against his small hut. He would give almost anything for a little companionship to sit out this nagging wind and pelting sand. His two young helpers were with the sheep, and besides, they were finding their own friends. He sighed, he would have to make do on his own; he certainly would not try to walk into Kuwait on a night such as this. At least he still had half a flask of wine that Zeus had brought the other day. He felt beneath the blankets for his pouch and pulled out the stone with tiny Crystal. He turned her over and over in the fire light, marveling at her sleek, unblemished surface.

"Ah, sweet Crystal, at times like this you are my only salvation." He smiled as she began to purr in his hand. For a long time he sat mesmerized by the calm that filled the air while Crystal hummed an ancient melody to him.

At last he settled back into his bed roll, contemplating the good turn his life had taken here in Kuwait. He had believed since he was a boy that if he could only get to Kuwait he would become a man of means. Suddenly a dark thought clouded his mind as he thought of his father. He hadn't really thought of him in years; had he changed any? He found he still harbored bitter feelings toward his father, but that was in the past and best forgotten. A warm feeling began to creep through his body as he thought of his mother. How did she fare now? He would never forget her kindness. His thoughts drifted to his brothers and his little sister; where were they now? How they must have grown since he left home. Home. He didn't think of Sur as home any more…no, home was now Kuwait. Kuwait, the city of dreams! The future he envisioned was no longer a dream but the reality he lived each day. He had learned to be a good businessman when dealing with his sheep; he sometimes marveled at his ability to haggle in the marketplace for the best price. Thanks to Shahrazad he now provided quality sheep to the Sultan of Kuwait for a tidy profit. She often told him the Sultan praised the mutton highly.

Omén had prospered in friendship as well. He was the favorite sight to many of the old merchants in the city. He always had time to stop and chat no matter how busy he was. In the evenings he passed many a night with his companions at the tavern. He enjoyed swapping tales with Zeus; each story became more outrageous than the last, giving them up to great fits of laughter. The gentle giant proved more and more to be his most trusted friend. He shared Omén's secrets and watched out for any dangers that might befall him. But the most precious and wondrous thing to happen to Omén came in the form of the lovely Shahrazad.

"Shahrazad." The name fairly flowed from his lips. She was everything he had ever dreamed of…so lovely, such creamy skin, those dark brown eyes that danced as she spoke, and so very intelligent. He was awed by the knowledge she possessed, awed by her ability to read and write; but most of all he was amazed that she could care for him…a mere shepherd. It never seemed to bother her, though, that he was ignorant and of low birth, while she was of the nobility – a beautiful, intelligent woman promised to a Sultan….

Night after night he cursed himself for being so stupid to have fallen in love with Shahrazad. There were other pretty young maids in the city; why was it only Shahrazad could set his heart aflame? The mere thought of her set his pulse racing. Over and over he vowed never to see her again but each time they met his resolve melted. He decided that he might as well accept the fact he was totally besotted, something

21

Zeus never tired teasing him about. What good did it do to curse himself for loving such a beautiful woman? It was not something he could turn on and off at will. At times like this even clever conversation with Crystal did not ease his emotional turmoil. He found it best to let sleep come and wash away his musings as the storm outside was washing the desert clean.

Early the next morning Zeus appeared in Omén's doorway with two loaves of bread and honey for breakfast. "Ho, young friend, how fare you from the storm?" Zeus boomed.

"As well as can be expected," Omén replied. "What brings you out so early in the day?"

Laughter erupted from deep within Zeus' throat. He had a reputation for sleeping late in the day due to his nightly carousing. "You wound me to think I cannot rise early to check on a friend! But you are right – I have another reason for coming."

"Don't keep me in suspense, Zeus. Tell me."

Again the giant smiled. He took a deep drink of honey-thickened wine and broke off a hunk of bread.

"Zeus!"

"Oh, very well." Zeus tried to look contrite. "I have a message from Shahrazad. She will meet you at the usual place this afternoon." He studied the young shepherd's face as it went from exasperation with his friend to elation at the prospect of seeing Shahrazad. "Shahrazad seemed a bit troubled when I spoke with her, though she did not go into detail." He watched a dark shadow pass over Omén's face at this. "You be careful, my brother. The desert has a thousand eyes. I cannot be everywhere to see to your safety."

A few hours later Omén was getting ready to leave to meet Shahrazad when he heard hoofbeats pound across the pasture. He went to watch the riders' approach…from the colors they wore they were the Sultan's guard. What could they be doing here he wondered. Unless…No! That was impossible…no one could have found out about his meetings with Shahrazad. No, he had been too careful. No one knew about the affair except Zeus, and he would tell no one.

The riders came to a halt before him. "Greetings, shepherd," the head guard called out.

"Good day to you," Omén said, looking nervously about the guard.

"A fine day, is it not?" the guard mused.

"Yes, indeed it is," Omén cautiously replied, wondering what doom was about to befall him.

"The Sultan sends his regards and requests you bring three sheep to the Palace no later than tomorrow morning. A page will pay you as usual."

"Oh…yes…yes, I will deliver them later this afternoon," Omén stammered, relief washing over him. He managed a smile and the guard pivoted his mount (who reared and snorted not three feet from Omén's face, frightening him thoroughly yet again) and ordered his men on to their next assignment.

Omén watched the guard until it was out of sight, until his heart stopped pounding, before he started to his rendezvous with Shahrazad. As he walked he thought over Zeus' words – 'The desert has a thousand eyes.' – They had to be careful...nothing had been amiss today, but he was visibly shaken by the sudden appearance of the guard. A short time later he approached the grassy knoll. He took a quick look around to see if anyone was watching. Satisfied there was no danger, he sat down to wait.

Morning dragged into high noon, and as the sun began its descent from the zenith, Omén headed forlornly back. Shahrazad had not come. Something must be very wrong. He thought of the rumors circulating through the countryside about the Sultan. Even Zeus had told him the Sultan was very disturbed. He had been cuckolded and he was taking out his wrath on young virgins in the realm. Zeus knew of parents who feared for the life of their daughters because the Sultan had put many maidens to death. But this could not be what was disturbing Shahrazad, could it? He would get some answers after he delivered the sheep to the Palace. If anyone would know what was going on, it would be Zeus.

He hurried the sheep through the entrance of the palace to a small paddock by the stables. He waited patiently for the page to return with the payment. A noise within the stable caught his attention and he moved closer to get a glimpse of one of the Sultan's beautiful horses. He cautiously entered the stable, letting his eyes adjust to the darkness, when a stone grazed his shoulder. He stopped, about to turn and investigate, when a voice came from the shadows.

"Do not turn around," a frightened woman's voice whispered. "Meet me in two days at the knoll." Before he could speak, a side door slammed shut and he was alone, staring into the shadows.

Never had he imagined time could pass so slowly as the last two days. He tried to keep himself busy with the sheep to pass the hours but found even the most menial tasks dragged on forever. He could not sleep more than a few hours without waking to spend the rest of the night staring into the black abyss of the cloudy moonless night sky. Zeus had tried to make him eat but he had no appetite and picked at his food. Even Crystal had no luck. She tried endlessly to ease his worries by telling him stories and singing to him, to no avail. At last she gave up, leaving Omén to his private thoughts. Nothing mattered to him except the fate of his lovely Shahrazad.

"Omén. Omén, I say, get your mind on other things. Have you not wondered about the golden collar about my neck?" said Zeus on the morning of the second day.

"What? What? I'm sorry, Zeus. You were saying something about a golden collar? Oh! Yes. I've wondered about that. What is the story behind it?" said Omén absentmindedly.

The Tale of the Golden Collar

Know, O Brother Omén, that I am an Indian of the Hindu religion. My mother was of the highest caste and betrothed to the King. She was of an independent spirit and would on occasion walk the markets incognito, in disguise.

But my mother one day was accosted by a madman of the lowest caste. He pulled her into his stall where he was butchering a pig, and had his way with her. At his trial, just before he was put to the sword, it came out that his wife had died not a week before, having been run over by the King's charioteers as they were returning to the city from one of their exercises; and as was the custom of his caste he could take no other to wife, but could become a eunuch for the palace, as they were always in short supply, the King not desiring slaves.

Naturally, my mother could no longer be the King's bride, and was ostracized. No man would have her, since she had been defiled. When I was born, her relatives begged that the infant be left in the fields to die or be devoured by wolves or jackals, as was the custom of the barbarian Romans. But my mother could not do this – I was the only child she would ever have, and she found me comely, and nursed me. She took all her possessions and sold them and had a golden collar made, one that could expand to fit a growing boy, and placed it around my neck and declared to all that could hear: "No harm shall come to my son. When he comes of age you will sell him to a caravan as a slave so that he may grow up in a distant land with the hope of manumission, unlike here where he would live and die, unwanted by high born and pariah alike."

When I became a man I was sold as a slave, still with my golden collar. I fetched a goodly price. My mother desired to travel with me and so we departed India. After many adventures we arrived here in Kuwait. The Sultan's Wezir, having lost his wife to a sickness, and having two small children, desired a cook and housekeeper and caretaker for the children. He saw my mother was highborn and intelligent and handsome, and approached her concerning this matter with his two daughters.

She replied, "Yes, on condition you buy the slave with the golden collar and free him." The Wezir was taken aback by her reply and asked her if I was her slave and if she was dissatisfied with my performance of duties. "The slave was sold to the caravan leader to pay for this trip. I was well satisfied with him and wish to see him free." And it was done. I work for the Wezir and others for wages as I see fit and am friend to high born and those of low estate alike. The collar I keep as a reminder of man's inhumanity to man.

*****

Know, also, Omén: While my mother was betrothed to the King, she became privy to much knowledge and stories not known to others. One of these stories concerned a certain water-clear sapphire chip, not a normal blue sapphire, nor yet one with a star blazing in its belly, but a chip as one of the points of a star – Sapphire Star was it called. To the ordinary mortal it appeared nothing. But the sages polished and mounted this chip, and by looking through it up into the deep blue sky (the sky so blue that the moon may be seen in full sunlight, or yet even the star Venus) they could discern worlds not visible to mortal, worlds even unto the foundations of the earth, and the substance from which all creation springs. My mother told me this tale many times when I was a child, and I have never forgotten it.

*****

Zeus' warning rang through his mind even now as he made his way to the knoll:

"I'm sorry, Omén, but rumor has it that Shahrazad's time with the Sultan is drawing near. Should she not please him I'm afraid she may perish like the others before her."

"NO!" he nearly shouted. "I'll not let harm come to her...even if I have to steal her away in the night."

Quickly yet cautiously Omén approached the knoll from the far side. Shahrazad's back was turned to him as she nervously watched for the approach of riders. Omén paused briefly to watch her. He felt as if he were memorizing her perfect form. Shahrazad sensed his presence and turned. Before he could move closer she was in his arms, hot tears flowing down her face.

"Sh-h-h, my love," he cooed. "Everything will be alright."

"Oh," she sobbed. "What am I to do? I fear so for the lives of us all."

"Shahrazad, certainly the Sultan would not be so cruel..."

"You do not know the full depths of it, my love." She looked out into the desert, fighting the tears burning behind her eyelids. "I must think of a way to give the Sultan peace of mind."

Omén stared out into the desert for a long time without saying a word. He felt so helpless. He loved her so much but was powerless to do anything. At last he guided her towards the stream, motioning for her to sit. When he joined her she leaned back into the security of his strong arms. Finally Omén broke the silence. "Shahrazad, come away with me. We'll go somewhere far away from here. Zeus can arrange passage..."

"No, my love," she broke in. "It is sweet of you to suggest, but you know he would send his guards for us, and find us wherever we went." She sighed forlornly.

"It is so unfair ..."

"Don't worry yourself, Omén," she half whispered. "I'll think of something." She buried her head deep into his chest, a small tear trickling down her satiny cheek. She clung to him a while, then fell into a fitful sleep.

Omén watched her, memorizing her features one by one. He didn't want to believe it, but this might be the last time he would ever hold her in his arms. He wanted to cherish each moment and file it away in his memory. How could a Sultan be so cruel as to punish an innocent for another's folly? There had to be some safe plan to steal her away. "Shahrazad," he whispered as he traced her lips with his shepherd-soft fingertips.

Several hours later Shahrazad stirred. She looked about, uncertain of her surroundings; she felt Omén's arms tighten about her shoulders, and she relaxed. For a minute she lay in silence before turning to look at the shepherd boy. The faintest hint of a smile played across her full lips as she spoke. "My love, I think I have come upon the solution to the problem ... Mayhaps I can tell the Sultan a story that he likes, and so live another day." After another minute she was wide awake; she frowned and became dejected. "I am well read, but my genius is small and the ideas few. I fear I die also like the others. How many stories, and how many days?"

Then the shepherd told Shahrazad of his discovery on the shores of the Arabian Sea and how this crystal could excite the genius in one, if he but gaze into its eye.

"Oh," said Shahrazad, "I will give thee great treasure if thou wilt give me thy crystal."

"Alas, ever since I was blinded by the lightning flash at her birth, and my sight fully restored by her at the first piercing ray of the morning sun, I have taken a vow upon my eyes never to part with my Crystal Ball."

"Thou hast vowed a mighty vow, and strong it is indeed. Since thou canst not break thy vow, come, show me how it works. Thou canst take the place of my sister to be at my side in the King's chambers, and when thou seest a convenient time, do thou say to me, 'O my sister, relate to me some strange story to beguile our waking hour:' – and I will (if it be the will of Allah, and with the help of thy magic crystal) relate to thee a story that shall be the means of deliverance."

Omén and Shahrazad parted in a mood of hope and faith. Shahrazad spent this last week at the Palace with fasting and prayer. The day arrived soon enough; the Sultan sent his summons.

Her father the Wezir, then took Shahrazad to the King, who, when he saw him, was rejoiced, and said, Hast thou brought me what I desired? He answered Yes. When the King, therefore, introduced himself to her, she wept; and he said to her, What aileth thee? She answered, O King, I have a young sister, and I wish to take leave of her. So the King sent to her; and she came to her sister, and embraced her, and sat near the foot of the bed; and after she had waited for a proper opportunity, she said, By Allah! O my sister, relate to us a story to beguile the waking hour of our night. Most willingly, answered Shahrazad, if this virtuous King permit me. And the King, hearing these words, and being restless, was pleased with the idea of listening to the story; and thus, on the first night of the thousand and one, Shahrazad commenced her recitations.

And during all of the thousand-and-one she told of Aladdin, and of Es-Sindibad of the Sea, and of Ali Baba, and of powerful Jinn, and of the City of Brass, and of much more. And after the first night, when she knew she would be spared, Shahrazad taught the shepherd to read and to write and to cipher. And Omén listened to the tales that the Crystal Ball told to Shahrazad, and remembered them, and when he had learned to write, he wrote them down, for he loved his Crystal Ball exceedingly, even as he truly loved Shahrazad as a brother loves his sister. And when the thousand and one nights had spent their course, he gave the book to Shahrazad to be saved until such time as men may want to hear these strange tales from his lovely little Crystal.

Now the Sultan, after the first night, learned of the shepherd, and of the magic crystal, and said in his heart, "Meat have I such as I have never tasted, from the shepherd, to fill my belly, and tales such as I have never heard, from the magic crystal, to fill my mind, and delights such as I have never known, from Shahrazad, to fill my senses. My soul longs for this to never end, yet must I still present a stern visage to keep all afrighted, lest they think I am grown soft, and I lose my meat and my tales and my Shahrazad."

And thus he kept them there, until such time as the shepherd grew weary of the stay and wished once again to take leave for distant lands. And the Sultan did not stay the shepherd but for one more week for the wedding feast.

Shahrazad relating a story to the Sultan

8
On to Riyadh

The sun blazed in the eastern sky as Omén left the city of his dreams. For so long had Kuwait been the object of his thoughts that it was hard for him to believe he was actually moving on. In one respect Kuwait represented all his dreams come true, yet in another it represented a shattered reality. He had indeed found a better life in this city. He had made his fortune and had made many new and trusted friends, especially Zeus. But his most precious dream was shattered when he could not find a way to free Shahrazad from her betrothal to the Sultan. More than anything else in his whole life he had wanted Shahrazad as his wife. "Ah, Shahrazad...."

What sweetness thoughts of her conjured. She was the warmth of the morning sun, in her eyes glowed the fire of life, the softness of her skin was finer than any silk from China...His love for her would never die, yet she belonged to another. She was married to the Sultan now. Never again would he hold her in his arms or kiss her lovely lips. She was gone.

Wearily Omén turned to look back at the gates of Kuwait. It saddened him to think of all that he was leaving behind ... friends he would probably never see again, his flock (although they were just sheep they were in a way his family), and ... Shahrazad, the woman of his dreams. It would be so hard to forget it all, but he could not stay. Having her so near but beyond his grasp would be more torture than he could bear. He had to leave.

The battle between his heart and mind raged as he watched the gates. His heart said, 'Stay, wait a while; maybe she will ride today and you can see her one more time,' while his mind argued, 'Go! It will do no good to prolong the pain.'

His mind won the battle and he urged the gentle beast beneath him onward to their new destination. He patted the neck of the sure-footed horse as she took him south towards Riyadh.

The horse had been a gift from Zeus. The giant handed him the reins as they left the tavern the night before. He had said he'd won the mare in a game of chance and had no use for her as she was too small for him to ride. Besides, he couldn't let Omén wander through the desert on foot and alone. The mare was a chestnut-brown roan with a blaze, and light brown mane and pasterns; Omén called her Kiyah. Zeus hugged Omén and told him to take the horse and go before he refused to let them leave. Before Omén could reply, the giant turned and walked away, hiding his emotions from Omén.

Omén was almost as sad about leaving Zeus as he was Shahrazad. He had heard that Zeus was returning to his native land to seek out those who had stigmatized him so long ago. He said a prayer for his friend's safety, hoping with all his might that Allah would keep him from danger.

As the sun beat down overhead, his mind wandered back to the last time he saw Shahrazad. He thought of the pain he saw spilling from her lovely eyes. He clenched his fist to his heart as though he had been stabbed...would the pain ever cease?

Late that afternoon Omén wearily made camp. He offered the mare some dried fodder he had brought along and some water from his wine skin. After tethering her nearby, he settled back against his bed roll. There was not much else to do; the two boys that shepherded his flock had grown into young men and had bought all when Omén left Kuwait. They would continue the proud and noble tradition. Omén thought of them often; he was happy to have helped them in their career, even as Abdul had helped him. Abdul…his mother…his baby sister…the merchant's daughter in Dhahran. He was tired but he dreaded the onslaught of sleep…sleep brought dreams, and the dreams were always of the Shahrazad he could not possess.

Several weeks later Omén met up with a caravan heading south. With the consent of the leader, he reined Kiyah in behind the last camel. It would be good for some company for a few days. The news the caravan leader would have would be most welcome to take his mind off of Kuwait.

He hoped eventually to run into a caravan heading north from Riyadh so he could learn of the types of work the big city offered. He knew he could always find work as a shepherd but it no longer appealed to him. Thanks to Shahrazad he could now read and write, and had shown a head for numbers. He had passed many hours marveling over the manuscripts the Sultan possessed from the Greek scholars. He was in awe of the men who had translated them into Arabic. Some day he hoped to own such writings. He would always be grateful to Shahrazad for opening up the world to him. Never in his wildest dreams as a lad had he imagined the wonders she had shown him.

As the caravan settled down for the night, Omén wandered restlessly about the camp, images of Shahrazad flowing through his mind. "Shahrazad…you are never far from my thoughts," he whispered into the darkness. "If only there had been a way to free you from the Sultan's …" He walked a distance into the night, holding back the tears. "Shahrazad, you are my heart ... I will never love anyone but you. No other woman could compare. …"

He looked to the stars twinkling above and slowly edged his hand into the sheepskin pouch hanging from his belt until he felt the smooth stone. "By the gods, I swear I will never love another … my love I give only to you, Crystal, until the day I die."

The stillness of the night engulfed him like a cloak. The stars twinkled, signaling to the heavens in affirmation of his vow. In the distance campfires glowed invitingly; Kiyah whinnied from afar as Omén headed back.

As the days passed, Omén began to feel the excitement of being on the road again surging through his veins. He focused his thoughts on the new life he sought in Riyadh. He could feel in his bones that something special was going to happen. Nightly he consoled himself in counsel with Crystal, but she had become evasive about his future. She had decided he needed excitement and the element of surprise in his life to help him forget Shahrazad. So she refused to tell him of the great things she saw in his future. She was so pleased with the grand future she saw for him but knew it was best to keep it to herself for now. All she would say was, "You'll see, my dear, life will be grand in Riyadh."

The time on the road passed more quickly than Omén had hoped. He kept himself busy working whenever he stopped in a village. It mattered little to him what he did as long as it kept his mind occupied and produced a few coins. He discovered he was becoming adept at all trades and enjoyed the work whatever it was. He knew that when he became tired of the manual labors he could fall back on the money hidden in his bed roll, the money from the sale of his sheep. But he hoped to save most of the money for Riyadh, until he had a suitable position. For now, the work took his mind off his beloved, but to his distress, she was never far from his thoughts.

The nights were still the worst; although he worked himself to exhaustion, at times they passed slowly, with endless dreams of the days outside Kuwait with Shahrazad, and the nights in the Sultan's bedchamber as Shahrazad reeled off story after story. She passed across his sleeping eyes with the grace of a swan, her lips smiling, ever inviting, silent words of love spoken through stolen glances and touches....

Waking suddenly from one of these dreams, Omén sat huddled next to his campfire staring into the night. The dream had been all too real – he could feel her gentle but strong arms about him, feel her breath upon his cheek as she whispered words of love....

As the desert chill crept over the land and the silver moon rose full and high into the sky, Omén walked into the desert to write in the sand proclaiming his love for Shahrazad for all the world to see (until the wind scattered the sand and the words floated through eternity):

"Shahrazad, you are in
my heart and soul.
Never shall my love for you die,
Though time and distance
Part our company...
You are my heart."

"Goodbye, my love." he whispered into the air.

The days turned to weeks, the weeks to months, the months to years. The time flew before Omén's eyes. He found the journey to Riyadh exciting, almost as exciting as the journey to Kuwait had been. And he found that he enjoyed exploring his country. This journey, though, had less responsibility…he had only himself and a small roan mare to care for. How wise Zeus had been giving him the horse. She provided the companionship he needed; and Crystal, his sweet Crystal Ball, offered him conversation and freely gave him the love he craved. For her part, Crystal enjoyed this time immensely – she had grown quite weary of coming up with stories for the thousand and one nights.

A nasty windstorm blew across the desert, pelting everything in sight with stinging grains of sand. Omén sought refuge in a small, almost deserted village. He was grateful to the gods for offering this small respite from the storm. After bedding Kiyah down in an empty stable, he went in search of a meal and a place to sleep.

The innkeeper greeted him warmly. The man was overjoyed to have a customer on a night like this. Omén settled before the fire to rest his weary bones and drink his wine. For the first time in months he felt at peace with himself and the world. His heart still ached but the pain had eased to a dull throb. It amazed him that only two years on the road could erase those painful memories enough so that he could actually see a new beginning waiting for him in Riyadh.

A short time later the innkeeper settled down beside Omén to share his news. Like Omén, he was just grateful to have the company of another human being during the monstrous storm that raged outside. They shared several cups of wine in silence before the innkeeper began questioning Omén about his travels. The man was amazed at all that Omén had done and seen in his young life. He told Omén he had been born in this village and supposed he would probably die here as well. He had little time to travel, taking care of the inn. He told Omén his eldest son lived in Riyadh and sent word as often as he could, raising a family and all being very hard, and letters written by the official scribes being very expensive, and Riyadh being so very far away, so that unless a caravan was going northward through Riyadh, he very seldom heard anything, and likewise he seldom sent word unless a caravan was traveling south through Riyadh, and would Omén care to take a letter to his son in Riyadh, even though he would not get it for many months, Riyadh being so very far away and all, and he would be more than happy to give Omén his son's name and last address so he could look him up when he got to the city, and they frequently get windstorms like this in the village, which is why many of the villagers had left to seek a better life in Riyadh, the weather seeming to have changed here noticeably these past ten years, and when the storm comes, one should cover his head and neck with a large, heavy cloth well wet down with water, even though water is precious and you are dying of thirst, else you will breathe in much fine dust and your lungs will turn to stone and you will die then and there, which is why there are no more sheep or goats hereabouts, and what would Omén like for his dinner?

Omén gladly accepted the man's help and advice. He was more than pleased when the innkeeper assured him that a smart young man like himself would have no trouble finding work in Riyadh. Several hours and many cups of wine later he and the innkeeper parted company and Omén settled back onto the pallet before the fire. The windstorm had departed long ago, and Omén had checked and found Kiyah none the worse for wear, the windstorm not being of the type that formed fine dust. Sleep came easily for the first time in months. He sank back into the blankets and drifted into a sea of pleasant dreams.

As dawn broke over the horizon, Omén silently made his way to the stable to saddle Kiyah. The storm had left the landscape looking clean and untouched. Omén smiled at the sleepy stable boy as he mounted the mare; he tossed the boy a coin, then headed Kiyah out of the village. After riding several hours he reined her in. Omén sat quietly atop the mare for a time viewing the landscape. The world looked so fresh and new to him; the air even smelled of hope. At last he knew he had done the right thing in leaving Kuwait and all that was dear to him. Yes, he definitely felt confident with his decision to go on to Riyadh. With a smile on his face and a song in his heart, he spurred Kiyah on towards their new home.

Back in Kuwait, a young woman sat forlornly at her window.

"Omén, Omén, I miss you so!"

Blue, blue your collar,
    Sad, sad my heart.

Though I do not go to you,
    Why don't you send word?

Blue, blue your beltstone,
    Sad, sad my thoughts.
Though I do not go to you,
    Why don't you come?

Restless, heedless,
    I walk the gate tower.
One day not seeing you
    Is three months long.

(The Columbia History of the World, Pg. 119,
Chinese Book of Odes,
Burton Watson Translation)

9
The Zero

Thunk-a-lug, thunk-a-lug, rattle, rattle, creak and groan. The sounds of the endless bustle of the city filled the air of Riyadh. Hawkers calling their wares followed oxen pulling their dilapidated carts at a snail's pace down the narrow, dusty streets. Women hurried to the market, inspecting goods at the gaily colored booths. Children scampered underfoot, bringing many an angry oath from merchants and shoppers alike.

"Thunk-a-lug, thunk-a-lug," sang the protesting wheels of the vendors' carts.

Omén leaned back against the cool stone wall of the tavern, sipping his cup of wine. He was enjoying a rare afternoon off from his work. The noises from outside slowly faded into the background as he mulled over his life in Riyadh. He had been the Sultan's chief scribe and accountant for almost two years now…he had accomplished so much in his thirty-five years. More than he had ever dreamed possible!

As Crystal had promised, life was indeed grand in this city. How different from what he'd known in Kuwait! Riyadh was non-stop from dawn to dusk and beyond – even the night-life lasted 'til the crowing of the cock. He learned quickly to be wary as he walked the streets: more than one set of sticky fingers was waiting to relieve him of his possessions. For that reason he now kept his beloved Crystal in a small pouch hung from a cord around his neck. "All the closer to my heart," he told her.

In spite of the many faults of the city he was intrigued, invigorated with its never-ceasing activity. Riyadh had been good to him. It was hard to believe he had once regretted the move. As he thought back now, he guessed it was a natural reaction to a strange place.

Life had not been all that easy when he first came. He had wandered aimlessly from job to job…nothing seemed to satisfy him. Many times he was on the verge of packing up and leaving. But soon soothing words from Crystal always contented him,

32

eased his apprehension. To his despair he found the money from the sale of the flock went far too quickly. He found himself taking any job just to make a few coins to feed himself and the small mare. Though he contemplated it several times, he could not bring himself to sell Kiyah. She was a gift from the biggest and gentlest man he had ever known. He would get by…somehow.

Just as he thought he could never sink lower and was sure there was no hope in sight, things began to brighten. A guardian angel in the form of the innkeeper's son appeared. They had met briefly soon after Omén arrived in Riyadh, but he had been too proud to ask for help then. The young man (about Omén 's age) was doing very well, thank you, and offered him a place to stay until he could get back on his feet; the young man also could provide free of charge a lush, green pasture for Kiyah. All he asked in return was a foal from the fine-boned mare. Omén readily accepted his offer, tears of joy flowing freely down his face. Within her bed of sheepskin Crystal breathed a sigh of relief. She knew the worst was over… nothing but great things were to happen to her love, now.

Omén gingerly tossed down the last of his wine and strode into the bright sunlight. He shaded his eyes until they adjusted to me glare, then engaged himself in the bustle. "Thunk-a-lug, thunk-a-lug," sang in his ears as he walked to the stable at the end of the street. He had found long ago that nothing could soothe his nerves or put memories in perspective better than a ride on his fiery black stallion.

As he approached the stable he could hear the stallion's angry hooves kicking impatiently at the confining stall. Entering the barn, he smiled at the young stable boys prudently stepping away from the stall. The horse sensed his presence and quieted down. He walked quickly to the horse, offering him a sweet treat. Then he bridled the black and easily swung up onto the sleek, muscled back, not having bothered with a saddle. He smiled to himself as the stable boys watched with mouths wide open. "Ah, Zeus, you do love to make these boys think you're a mean one!" He threw back his head and laughed as the horse twitched its ears in agreement. It stamped its hoof, impatient to be on the way. Omén had named the jet black colt soon after Kiyah died giving birth. He thought Zeus a fitting name, in honor of his dear friend…he knew Kiyah would approve, too.

He rode some miles beyond the city before he reined in Zeus. It was good to be free of the confines of the city for a change. At times like this he longed for the carefree life on the road when he was young, when he had been but a boy with so many dreams…and wide-eyed, not yet seasoned to the realities of life. Though he had prospered beyond belief, he longed to be a care-free lad…but only sometimes. Then he urged the horse on as his thoughts drifted to the days before Kuwait, and to his new life in Riyadh. Memories of Kuwait were carefully guarded…he would not let them surface consciously; only in the wee hours of the morning would these visions assail him.

Quite abruptly he laughed out loud as his mind touched on the day he blundered into the clerk's job. How he had ever gotten the position was beyond all comprehension. In his nervousness he had knocked over a pot of ink, blackening a column of figures the clerk had been working on before he arrived for the interview. In his haste to right the inkpot, he knocked over a stack of ledgers and succeeded in covering his best shirt with India ink. Yet the old clerk took it in stride; he laughed so hard Omén thought the man would burst his sides. At the age of twenty-eight, almost a year after he arrived in Riyadh, Omén found himself employed in the government. As was fitting, his first job had been to recopy the stained ledger and refile the scrolls.

Over a period of three years he found himself rising through the ranks of the clerks. He knew his promotions were due to the long hours of hard work he poured into his job. He was always the first to arrive in the morning and the last to leave; some of the others did not bother to come back after lunch, and by the middle of the afternoon, Omén closed the door to an empty office. His co-workers teased him about his dedication, but he suspected they were jealous of his rise within the ranks. Several of those men had been in the Sultan's service most of their lives, but had never risen above the job they started with.

He was often given special projects to work on, at the Sultan's request. It was unusual to have the Sultan request a particular clerk to do the tasks. Omén sensed the Sultan was impressed with his hard work and dedication; he also sensed the Sultan had taken a liking to him. When the Sultan asked him to help with the translation of many manuscripts into Arabic, he was overjoyed at the prospect.

It had taken him and an old Greek scholar, Nicoli, most of two years to complete the translations. Omén was in awe of the scholar; not only did he know Greek, Hebrew, Latin and Arabic fluently along with several other languages, but he was learning some of the strange bastardized tongues coming out of the Frankish territories. Omén marveled how the scholar could one minute read in another language and the next translate it to him to write down. How he longed to have a mind as sharp as the aging scholar. Late one afternoon he expressed to Nicoli an interest in learning another language. The old gentleman said if there would be a time set aside for several evenings a week, he would be more than happy to school Omén.

Omén grew very fond of his mentor in the time they worked together. Not only was Nicoli his co-worker but his teacher, and most importantly, his friend. Omén enjoyed the company of his friends and often passed the hours with them at the tavern, but had found himself shunning friends and tavern to spend time with the old scholar. He told Omén stories of what lay beyond Arabia and of the wondrous things he had seen in his life; Omén came to view the world through Nicoli's eyes. When he was wakened early one morning to the news that the old man had passed peacefully away in his sleep, Omén was deeply saddened. He grieved in silence at his loss, plunging into his work, as always.

After the translations were finished, Omén found himself back in his cubicle tied down with ledgers and accounts. It wasn't that he disliked the mathematics so much as the Arabic method of counting. It was so tedious! So hard to count into me large numbers he often found himself working with.

"There must be a better way," he said to himself one afternoon as he finished the day's accounts. Wearily he rubbed his tired eyes and throbbing head. He put away the ledgers and headed home to rest before the evening meal. As he walked a thought nagged at his brain: there has to be a simpler way to extract the figures each day. He tried to put the thought out of his head; it made his headache worse, and he wanted to enjoy himself that evening. But the thought would not go away.

The next few weeks Omén again plunged into his work. He was determined to find an answer to the problem. He knew that somewhere he had seen the solution he sought. Day and night it nagged at him. There was a better method of counting … he just knew it. But where? Surely this wasn't just something he dreamed up to perplex his mind.

That evening Omén consulted Crystal again about the matter. But as usual she answered his questions evasively. She knew Omén was much more appreciative if he accomplished things through his own intelligence. Exhausted, he settled down upon his bed and as sleep was about to claim him, the answer eased into his mind. He bolted upright in bed. The Manuscripts!

The next week Omén spent every free moment searching the manuscripts in the Sultan's library. He asked the scholars endless questions, but to no avail. He was beginning to think he was on a wild goose chase, that he was just lazy and had wanted to find an easier way to do his accounts, that he had in fact dreamed it all up. He never thought it would be this hard, and he knew he wasn't enough of a mathematician to work out something of this importance himself.

More weeks passed and Omén still had not found what he was looking for. He was about to resign himself to the present way of counting when he remembered something the old scholar had told him about the Hindu arithmetic. At once he began to search for the scrolls they had translated from India. Several hours later he emerged from the stacks with the scrolls he had been searching for. He read through each one until he found the translations from the Hindu mathematicians. It was late at night and he was very tired as he began to put symbols down on paper:

"I don't like all these straight lines, and the six could be an eight. I will make the six a curlicue like a pig's tail – **6**. The seven is a combination of the three and the Greek delta four, but it could also be a two and a four, so I will change it. Let's make the seven look like the two, and add a stroke on the two and the three:

ı Z Ʒ △ ♤ 6 7 8 ⬜ ⋂

The nine is a problem. I could leave it a square, but that is cumbersome to write. What do you think, Crystal?"

"Turn the curlicue upside down for **9** for nine," she said.

"The two, three, four, five and eight (two deltas) look too Greek or Egyptian – I can round them off:

ı 2 3 φ S 6 7 8 9 ⋂

The four, five, six and nine can be confused:

$$1 \quad 2 \quad 3 \quad 4 \quad 5 \quad 6 \quad 7 \quad 8 \quad 9 \quad \cap$$

That looks good."

Omén reflected further, "The other scientific cultures have tens and powers of tens (hundreds, thousands, and so forth) in their calculations, denoting each by a separate symbol. The various symbols become very confusing. Suppose I count up to ten on my fingers. The Romans use 'X', the Egyptians use '*n*', the Greeks use the tenth letter in their alphabet 'K', the Babylonians have a different symbol. The Hindus have a different name for each power of ten – 'one sata, three dasan, five' would be a hundred, three tens and a five. This is all very complicated. I could set up a system based on five (for one hand) and powers of five, but I would still need different symbols for the powers.

Crystal looked at him with a baleful eye – ⊛. "Oh, Omén, look at me!"

"Why, Crystal, you are so tiny, you are practically a dot, a SIFR [cipher], something not there, something empty, like an empty wineskin. The space between powers of tens, if there is no number, can be indicated by a dot, something as small as you. Some scholars have taken to drawing a triangle or square or hexagon around the dot so that it will not be lost or thought of as an ink spatter or flyspeck."

"Omén! Look closer. Look at me very, very close." As Omén did so, the point of light from the distant candle refracting through Crystal became larger, and larger. When his eye practically touched her, the point of light had become a large circle of light, practically filling up his whole eye. "What do you see, Omén?"

"I see a large circle of light. How can this be? How can you do this? You are filling my whole head with light!"

"And can the masterful Omén make a quick sketch of what he sees?" asked Crystal mockingly.

"Yes, yes!" Omén took a pen and drew a large circle on the piece of paper.

"Why do you make it so big?" teased Crystal.

"Why, it fills my whole mind. It is very important!"

"Make it a little smaller, about the same size as your other symbols you have been working out for the ten numbers."

Omén did so: $0 \quad 1 \quad 2 \quad 3 \quad 4 \quad 5 \quad 6 \quad 7 \quad 8 \quad 9 \quad \cap$

"Why do you use '*n*?' asked Crystal. "Why not 'X' or 'K'?"

"Well, what symbol would you use for ten?" petitioned Omén.

"Why don't you try '1' with me after it?" said Crystal matter-of-factly.

"I don't understand you."

"Has the masterful Omén then become suddenly dumb?" And Omén put down a '1' and then the '0' after it. "Now, was that so hard?" smiled the little lady, "What do you have?"

"I have a 'one' with a big 'sifr' after it," said Omén with a blank expression on his face, not understanding what Crystal was up to.

"Why don't you call that 'ten'?" said Crystal in the manner of an older sister talking down to her little brother.

"Well, why not," said Omén angrily. "And why don't I just put another 'sifr' after it to make '*100*' and call that a hundred, instead of 'C' as is the Roman custom? And another 'sifr' after that to make that '*1000*' and call it a thousand instead of the 'M' symbol of the Romans? That is stupid, using two, three and more figures instead of one. Do you take me for a dolt? Crystal? Crystal, don't cry." But it was Omén who found himself crying, as he realized what had just happened. Crystal had shown him how to number the universe with just ten symbols! EUREKA!

In the weeks to come, Omén found himself the center of attention. He had at once implemented the sifr into his accounts. The accounts became much easier to work and he found he used up less space on the ledgers. News of Omén's discovery soon reached the Sultan. Omén was called before his sovereign to be honored for such a discovery.

But when the Sultan began to praise him, Omén begged his King's pardon, but in all honesty he could not accept the praise for being the originator of the idea. He explained how he had found the answer in the scrolls he had helped Nicoli translate. The Sultan was greatly impressed by Omén's humility. Finding the method in the translations was not an easy task. He was proud to have such an intelligent young man in his employ. So proud in fact, that the next day in a royal decree Omén was given an increase in salary and was promoted to the position of chief scribe and accountant to the Sultan.

"What is the largest number you can write with your system?" asked the Sultan some weeks after. Some in his cabinet did not like Omén, especially since they felt this young know-nothing was beginning to usurp their power, and in their desire to take Omén down a peg or two had plotted together for weeks, finally coming to an agreement to put this bug in the Sultan's ear.

Omén then showed him. "Let's take nine (9) and add one (1) to make ten, and we show it as a one and a sifr – "*10*" is the symbol for ten. Ten tens would be a hundred, represented by "*100*," or one with two sifrs. Ten hundreds would be a thousand, represented by "*1000*.""

"Well, yes, but what is the largest number you can write with your system?" persisted the Sultan.

Omén began adding zeroes; line after line of zeroes. "I could keep this up for my whole lifetime and would not reach the largest number."

"But again I say, what is the largest number you can write with your system, and what is it called?" The bug was working.

Crystal whispered to Omén, "Put me beside myself and call it 'without end.'"

Omén drew the symbol on the paper. "Here is the symbol for the number, and 'no end' is its name," he said quietly.

"Fine," said the Sultan. "That is easy enough to remember. It even looks like its name." Omén looked again, and was surprised to find that, indeed, it did. "What is the Latin name, Omén?"

"Why, 'no ending' would be … 'infinity', I suppose."

"And do all the numbers below the 'infinity' have names, Omén?" Those cabinet members had done their work well.

Omén thought about this for a long time. Then finally he said, "No, after the thousand, each and everyone has no name, or really needs no name – the symbol itself shows its value."

"Would there be a Latin name for these smaller numbers, Omén?" The Sultan was down to his last question; the blackguards had Omén by the jugular, he would trouble them no more.

"Why, no, there would be no name," said Omén abjectly. The Sultan looked downcast also. Omén mulled the problem over. No name, no thing, no body, no one. "'Nemo,' in Latin," said Omén at last. Crystal smiled. NEMO!

"Good," said the Sultan, and he turned and left the room.

And Omén, in his position of importance to the Sultan, began corresponding with notables and scientists in other lands, using his new notation for counting. Those men of government and commerce had their own methods, and did not think much of this upstart's approach, especially since it had no practical value. But the Hindu astrologers picked it up, seeing how they could easily count the stars, and the citizens of their crowded country, and even the grains of sand on the beach or the drops of water in the ocean, using only ten symbols. In less than a hundred years, Crystal as a zero [sifr, or cipher] was being used widely in India, and from thence returned through commerce to the country of her origin.

Omén the dreamer was without great honor in his lifetime in this matter – some great ideas take a little time to sink into small minds. His associates quickly became jealous of his rise in government. The Sultan, finding no real use for this system other than to save a little space on paper and a little space in his mind, and wishing to keep peace, did not promote the idea any further.

Mathematicians regard the Hindu-Arabic system as one of the world's greatest inventions. Its greatness lies in the principle of place value and in the use of zero. These two ideas make it easy to represent numbers and to perform mathematical operations that would be difficult with any other kind of system. (World Book Encyclopedia)

"Can you see me?" said the sifr [cipher],
"I am small as I can be.
Are you sure that you can see me?
(Are you barking up a tree?)
For I came from out of nowhere
and my name is no body."

"You can pump me up like crazy,
Like a big hot air balloon.
And then I know you'll see me,
Even though I'm not the Moon."

"You can use me like a number
(Although number I am not)
For to space your other numbers
Just when one you have not got."

> "When you tack me on the ending
> I increase value by ten,
> Even though I am but nothing.
> Is this truth beyond your ken?"

> "Crystal knew me from her birth:
> We are shaped the same as Earth,
> Planets, Moon and Stars – all round;
> Mostly empty space we found.
> We're the perfect shape to be –
> Ball or sphere through 'ternity."

Nemo Frankenstone

10
The Queen

"Omén," said the Sultan one fine day, "my brother is coming to visit next year and is bringing his family and entourage – four wives and sixteen children – or is it eighteen (who can keep track?). Would you please start the preparations for a proper greeting?"

"Yes, of course, Sir. Your brother, as yourself, must be of great importance and in high position to afford four wives. I am sorry, but I have kept to my work and have not perhaps heeded the local gossip too well – I am not familiar with your brother."

"Oh, everyone in Riyadh knows about my brother, but no one discusses it, under my edict. You arrived here several years after the proclamation. My brother suffered mightily in love, and it affected his mind. He had taken to bedding a virgin in his city every night and having her killed the next morning, because he believed no woman would be faithful to him, until his Wezir's daughter came and told him tales every evening and soothed his troubled mind, faithful to him for almost three years, until he finally married her. My brother is the Sultan of Kuwait. Perhaps you have heard of him, or have even written to him."

Omén's heart skipped a beat, then began pounding furiously. Kuwait! The Sultan! Shahrazad! Coming here to Riyadh! Will she still be alive and be one of his wives? Will she have children and be dumpy and fat? He told his clerks and assistants to take the day off, as he was not feeling well. For a month, he could scarcely think of anything else. Shahrazad, the beautiful Queen! His whole office was abuzz about his mood swings, from elation to depression and back again.

"You are working too hard," the Sultan finally told him. "Set everything aside and take a vacation. Pick out a pretty maid in this grand city and go sailing or something. Be back in two months. 'Bye."

Omén must obey. He had his orders. His notice was written thoughtfully and was posted the next day on the message center near the Palace:

All those young maidens of the City between the ages of 14 and 24 who would desire to take a pleasant two month trip by camel to the East Ocean and back (with some sailing if the winds be favorable), please meet with your chaperone at Market Square on the morning following the first sighting of the new crescent Moon. Only one will be chosen; must be adventuresome.

By Order of the Sultan Halidah
XX Omén, chief scribe

Those who could read spread the word, and in two weeks, on the proper morning, a group of about thirty giggling young maidens and older dowagers were in the Square. It was not market day and, except for the females, everything was quiet. After an hour or so, when no one showed up to tell them about the trip, some of them left. Then a man from the Palace walked in to the Square with two bodyguards, and stopped in front of the group. When the chatter finally stopped, the man began in a halting, stammering manner.

"I am from the Palace, and I assume you, uh, are here in, uh, response to the notice I, uh, had posted. Uh, my name is Omén, scribe to the Sultan. I do not presently know, uh, all the details, and assume, uh, the Sultan may desire a, uh, a, uh, con-concubine, or even a, uh, Qu-Qu-Queen. Are there any questions?"

"What about our safety on the trip?" said one of the older women.

"These two bodyguards will travel with us to ward off bandits." was Omén's reply.

"How many will be in the caravan, and will the Sultan be taking his wives?" said another.

"There will only be six camels and six of us – the two bodyguards, you and your chaperone, the Sultan, and myself." Omén reddened in embarrassment. Several more women left, muttering about the tiny caravan and lack of planning.

"I like to rise early, before high noon, so I will have time for my servant to do my hair and makeup and nails," said one of the pretty young girls. "She will have to go along. She is small, so can she not sit with me on my camel?"

"The caravan will be traveling from crack of dawn until it is dark, with only short rest stops. There will be no time or need for prettying up, unless you want to do it yourself after the evening meal around the campfire, when it gets dark and the stars come out."

"Oh, my!" And two more turned away.

"Can we be sure of returning in exactly two months or less? My boyfriend will wait no longer than that."

"If you are not a, uh, a virgin, the Sultan is, uh, is, uh, not interested."

"Oh."

There were only four pairs remaining. One of the older women had been ogling Omén through her veil all the time he was addressing them. It made him very uncomfortable. Her young companion, he noted, would turn away each time he answered a question, only to be pulled back by the woman with the ogling eyes.

"Please follow me to the Palace, and I will complete the inquiry in my office." As they entered the Palace, they all began "ooh"-ing and "ah"-ing and craning their necks up and down and side to side. All, that is, except two – the one kept ogling Omén and her companion kept her head down and her eyes averted. "Please have a seat." Omén took up his notebook and began checking off questions. "I will need your names and addresses, and you must swear that the young maiden is truly a virgin." And Omén blushed.

"We really must go," said one matron, "I just remembered some pressing matters that must be attended to." Three pairs.

The Sultan poked his head into the room and said, "Ah, Omén, the business is about finished. Haven't you forgotten something?"

"Oh, yes. The trip by camel and on the ship can be very confining, and we may see each other naked at times. Is this a problem? No? Will you all please remove your veils so the Sultan can get a better look." Omén was now red as a beet.

With that, one of the girls spoke up. "I was trained to never remove my veil for a man until the wedding night. And those two left.

Only two pairs remained; two girls, two chaperones. Eight eyes peered over black veils. Slowly the veils were removed. Omén kept his gaze on the ogler. His heart skipped a beat as a shock of recognition swept over him. Shahrazad? No, but very much like her. Where had he seen this face before? Then he looked at her companion. Another shock of recognition – almost like Dunyzad, Shahrazad's younger sister. Were his eyes playing tricks on him? The other two were very pretty also. He lowered his eyes to his notebook and began writing furiously.

"Well, hello, love." said the Sultan to the ogler.

"Hello, yourself. Do you want the regular tonight or something special?" she bantered.

"Just a kiss will do," he said, and came through the doorway and up to her, kissed her fully on the mouth and patted her behind.

"No touching the merchandise until after the wedding," she smiled as she broke loose. Then she patted him on his behind. The Sultan broke out into a full, hearty laugh.

"And who do we have here," he said, reaching out to take the hand of the other woman.

"Well, I never!" said the matron. "Come, child. You can do better than this. He is nothing but a dirty old man."

As they left, everyone could hear the girl's wail, "But Auntie, he seems like a kindly old gentleman to me. He reminds me of my dear father."

"Hmpff!"

So now we were down to two ladies. The Sultan asked the two, "What is it that allows you to take this trip with us? Will your family not miss you?"

The woman, the ogler, looked pleadingly into the Sultan's eyes and said seriously, "My husband is gone these many years on a dangerous voyage, and I long to have him back in my arms."

"May you find the one you are seeking," said the Sultan softly. "By the way, Omén, I almost forgot to tell you. Sudden business has come up that I must attend to, and I am unable to take off for two months. Have a nice time. Come along, guards."

Omén looked up from his notebook and bade the Sultan farewell. Then he turned to the two in the room. "Young lady, you are very pretty, but you do not seem to fit our requirements. You must be at least fourteen."

The girl kept her head down. "I am fourteen, Sir."

"She has just turned fourteen. Today is her birthday. And perhaps this trip will be her birthday present?"

"Can you two leave tomorrow morning?"

"Yes." The woman ogled him shamelessly.

"Very well, I will show you to your quarters. Make yourself comfortable. Go home and get anything you may need, after you get settled. Provisions should be plentiful; we will have a spare camel. And are you sure you like adventure?"

"Yes, yes," they both said.

"And you two are mother and daughter?"

"Yes, yes."

"And you both will have an enjoyable time?"

"Yes, yes."

So Omén shook hands with them and showed them to their quarters for the day.

The evening meal was most interesting. The two new arrivals were invited to eat with the Sultan and his many wives; Omén was invited for the occasion also. The wives were quite nice to the two and to Omén. Really. If there was any jealousy it was not noticeable. They carried on small talk and did not pry. The six beribboned children, all girls, were introduced during dessert. Two were close to the age of the birthday girl and the three went off to play. The smaller girls sang a little song and put on a skit, amid much shouting and laughter. A very pleasant time. Omén was impressed. And quite taken aback at how the flirt could keep up her end of the conversation, even being familiar with some of me Sultan's business.

It was shortly after midnight when it happened. A cry went up from the guests' bedroom and the maid hurried in to see what was wrong. She quickly woke Omén and he, half asleep, heard the words, "Blood. All over. Place a mess." Omén immediately ordered her to summon the court physician and the chief of police; he pulled on his robe and slippers and hurried over. The girl was sobbing uncontrollably.

"What happened, what happened?" he asked the mother.

"Nothing, really," she said. "Please go back to bed."

"Did you see the intruder?" asked Omén of the girl. "Where are you hurt, child?"

"Please, it is nothing. My daughter is all right."

By this time the physician and chief of police came in with the maid. While the maid was cleaning up, the physician was checking the girl and the chief was looking for clues left by the villain. Everything was back in order when the physician straightened up and whispered in the mother's ear.

"No intruder," said the chief firmly.

"No injuries," said the physician firmly.

"See, I told you it was nothing," said the mother to Omén.

"It was nothing. I feel better now," said the girl cautiously.

"But what, then?" asked Omén.

The mother smiled broadly. "Today, on the first day of our trip, my child is a woman!"

The caravan trip to the coast was quite uneventful. Omén marveled at how fast the ships of the desert could travel, and he reflected upon how many months and years it had taken him to travel the same distance with his flock of sheep. But that was many years ago. Every evening at the campfire, Omén would tell a little story, and soon the girl was becoming proficient in using Crystal also (for some reason, Omén trusted her with the stone). At night, when everyone was bedded down, Omén would think about many things and watch the stars. He would start discussing astrology and star names and soon everyone was fast asleep. His dreams were strange, and they always were about his childhood in Sur, and his family, but especially about his baby sister, whom he could not abide, although she adored him – she was five when he left home. Whatever became of her? He dreamt on.

There were only two other minor events worth recounting on this trip, both taking place on the ship they sailed for a month – a pleasure cruise. The first event concerns the storm; the second, what Omén learned about the women that evening after the storm.

The ship was out a week, in sight of Persia, before the winds died. There is nothing more monotonous than the slapping of the wavelets against the hull (which soon died out) unless it is the sound of your own breathing in the utter calm. In the calm, everything becomes monotonous – the food, the friends, the stories, the wine. Omén had taken to filling empty wineskins with air and tying a rope end to them. Then he would have the young woman throw them into the water and see if they drifted by.

It was about the third day of the calm, a very lazy afternoon. No one was speaking to anyone – everyone was surly and keeping their thoughts to themselves. A lifetime friendship can be lost with one word in anger in a calm. Omén had drunk too much and had nodded off in his deck chair. The two ropes, that at one end were tied to inflated wineskins floating motionless twenty yards from the boat, were draped across the deck and attached at the other end to sturdy fittings. The skins began drifting ever so slowly and presently the ropes were close to Omén's feet.

"The wind! The wind!" cried the lookout. Everyone began running to the front of the boat to see where the lookout was pointing. A strong wind had sprung up on shore and several smaller craft had already capsized. The dark cast to the water showed that the blow was heading directly toward them. As Omén jumped up from his stupor, his feet tangled in the ropes, and he fell, hitting his head on the deck. The unconscious caravan chief slipped over the side and into the water with a splash.

"Man overboard!" shouted a crew member as he ran forward.

"Down the sails!" ordered the Captain, and at once the crewmen were busy. Omén 's entourage returned, only to see his chair empty and Omén floating face down in the water.

"Help, help!" cried the mother, "Save him!" The guards found a grappling hook, but lacked a handspan of reaching him.

"Do something," said the daughter, wide-eyed.

"We cannot swim," said the guards, and they began agitating as to what they should do.

The girl took off her outer garments and plunged into the salty water. Dog paddling, she reached the ropes and then paddled to Omén and tied the ropes around his limp body. "Pull him up," she ordered. No more than a minute had elapsed from the time when Omén hit the water to when he was on deck. The guards turned him face down over a coil of rope to clear out his lungs. About this time the storm hit. With the fury of a hurricane the winds and rain pelted the ship, heeling it over to a dangerous angle. If the sails had been up, the boat surely would have capsized. In fifteen seconds it was all over, the sun came out, and a cool dry breeze began blowing. The mother and the guards got Omén breathing, and then they all started shivering uncontrollably, from the near catastrophe, from the cold rain that had drenched them, and from the cool dry breeze.

Suddenly, the mother cried, "Dona! Dona! Get my Dona out of the water!" Everyone – crew and Captain and all – looked over the side to where Dona was happily splashing around in the warm Persian Gulf, pushing two wineskins.

"I am all right, Mother, really. Have them pull me up when you are all dried off…and they better not look!"

The second minor event took place that very evening, after dinner. After Omén had fully recovered from his drowning, he rapped on the cabin door of Dona and her mother. "May I come in? It is Omén. I must talk to the both of you." When they were presentable they let him in and asked how he was feeling. "I must get right to the point. You saved my life today, Dona. I must know all about you. I am forever in your debt."

"There is nothing to tell, really. I have lived with my mother all my life in Riyadh and hope to marry someday."

"But, yes, but...where did you learn to swim?"

Dona cast her eyes down. Her mother said, "Is it really necessary to know? Girls do many things today."

"Yes, I must know."

Then the young woman began crying softly. Presently she spoke. "Your Crystal called to me to dive in and retrieve her."

"But where did you learn how to swim?"

The floodgates opened; with tears in her eyes, the words poured forth. "My boyfriend pushed me into the fountain late one night and taught me. I am homesick already. I miss him so. We were planning to be secretly married when he finds a good job. He helps a local sheep herder, but wants to become a gardener – he likes to watch trees and flowering plants and grape vines spring out of the ground like magic wherever there is fresh water. Sari does not like him – she wants me to marry up, out of my position in life." Dona began crying again.

"And Sari, what is your story?"

It was Sari's turn to cry. Presently she said, "You have been good to us. I must tell someone. I have been longing to tell someone I can trust. Please do not tell anyone else, especially the Sultan. If he knew, my dream would be shattered, for he would laugh at the dreams of an old woman." And Sari began her tale.

"I was born in a small town on the East Shore far away. When I was five my oldest brother left to seek his fortune to the North. I worshipped my brother and was heartbroken to see him leave – I would never see him again. When I became a woman, my parents tried to marry me to a local lad. I would have none of it. After two years of prodding my father was getting firm – I must be out, and I must be married. A caravan came through town that year, heading north. I hopped on secretly after disguising myself and away we went. Perhaps I would see my brother yet! Several weeks later bandits held up the caravan and took all the gold and silver. Then they spotted me. They talked and argued among themselves until their leader said to the trail master, 'We have need of a young maid more than your piddling gold and silver.' 'Would that I could help you, but it is impossible – there are no young maidens in the caravan,' said the trail master. 'That one there, sitting behind you.' 'I will go with them,' I said, 'They will not harm me.' 'You do not know what you are saying,' said the trail master. I slid off the camel and approached the leader. 'You will not harm me,' I said, and I brushed his lips with mine. 'Take your gold and silver, and a good day to you,' said the bandit leader to the trail master, and I was off with my new companions."

"I became with child at that time, but do not know the father, whether the trail master or one of the bandits. I like adventure, but that is the last time I was with a man. I vowed to wait for a rich nobleman who loved me. The bandits took me to Riyadh, their home base, and there have I lived ever since."

"My dream is to be truly loved by the Sultan and to have a boy child for him – he has no heirs to the throne, as you know. In Riyadh I took work as a barmaid and presently own the tavern – I am training my daughter in my profession. The Sultan comes in often, as does half the population of Riyadh, it seems. My tavern is on the south end, in a pretty rough district. I have never seen you there. So now you know why the Sultan and I acted as old friends. We are – we have known each other for years. He has told me much about you, Omén, and I decided that while I could never have the Sultan as a true love, perhaps my daughter could, or could have the shy clerk. I am sorry, I want only the best for my daughter. Please forgive an old woman." And she wept tears of remorse.

"What town were you born in?" asked Omén.

"Why, Sur, on the East Coast."

"Where did your brother say he was going?"

"Why, to Kuwait."

Omén felt the pulse beating more strongly in his temples. "What was your brother's name?"

"That is the strange part. His name is (or was) Omén, the same as yours."

"It is a common name. I had a baby sister, and left her in similar circumstances. But her name was not Sari."

Sari looked at him wide-eyed and her pulse quickened. "I hated my given name and am Sari from my first day on the caravan."

Now Omén looked at her wide-eyed, intently. "I had a nickname for my baby sister, for she would bother me no end and was always jumping all over me and putting her arms around my neck and kissing me. I called her 'Monkey.'"

"Oh!" The cry was out of Sari's mouth before she could put her hands over it. Then she composed herself after a minute and said, "Many older brothers no doubt call their bothersome baby sisters by that name."

45

"No doubt," said Omén, smiling, for he was quite certain by now, "but do baby sisters call their big brothers by this nickname?" And he took her to the corner of the small cabin and whispered…then he nibbled her ear.

"Ouch! Ha, ha, Omén, ha ha ha ha, oh, ohh, it is you!" Laughing and crying hysterically, Sari flung her arms around Omén's neck and pushed him onto the bed, kissing him all over his face, while he and Dona looked at each other helplessly. When her hysteria had died down, Sari realized where she was and jumped up from the bed. "I'm sorry, I'm sorry. We really do not know each other. It has been many years. We are both adults. I'm sorry, please forgive me. It is out of my system. It will never happen again, Omén, I promise."

Now it was Omén's turn. "Come here, Monkey." He pulled her to him, picked her up in his arms, and sat down on a chair, cradling her while he half-whispered lullabies in her ear. Sari's eyes were closed, but tears of joy were streaming out and her mouth was open as if crying. Her body shook with sobs, and she put her arms around his neck and hung on for dear life.

The sobs ceased, the tears ceased. Sari carefully got up and kissed Omén on the forehead. "Thank you, big brother. I love you very much. Look, Dona, say hello to your Uncle Omén." Uncle and niece smiled at each other and nodded.

"We have a lot of catching up to do, don't we?" said Omén to Dona.

"Tomorrow, love," teased Dona, "I must get my beauty sleep for the Sultan. "

The three were almost inseparable for the rest of the cruise. Every evening Omén would stay late in their cabin, or they in his, and the guards smiled knowingly at each other. "The Sultan will be very pleased. Two at one crack."

The caravan returned to Riyadh without further incident, and to the Palace within the allotted time, before the new crescent Moon made her appearance. Omén told the two ladies to stay in their assigned quarters while he conversed privately with the Sultan. The Sultan beamed profusely when Omén entered his chambers. "Hello, hello. The guards tell me you have done famously. You look like a new man. Congratulations. When is the wedding day?"

Omén told him all that had transpired, and that the ladies were indeed his sister and his niece. The Sultan frowned. "Then what do you plan to do? Your family, working in the seediest part of town?"

"I wish to take them in. It can be noised about that I have taken Sari as my concubine, and I will lawfully make Dona my adopted daughter. Her boyfriend can also move in, as they wish to be married soon. He can start work as the gardener's assistant. Does any of this make any sense to you? Is it acceptable?"

The Sultan put his fingers together and brought them under his chin; he pursed his lips and thought for many moments. Sari as Omén's concubine in the Palace complex would be very handy – perhaps at last he would get to bed her – he found her very attractive and he had been after her for years to no avail, as had all the others. Omén would need larger quarters and an increase in salary. His wives liked Sari very much, for so they had commented frequently during the past two months. The local gossips would be stilled, as there would be nothing to talk about. Men take concubines every day, and Omén would be supporting her child as well. The Palace gardener needed more help, especially with the preparations for his brother's visit. Dona was turning into a very pretty woman, as he had noted when he patted her behind the last time he was in the tavern. It could be like one happy family.

Sultan Halidah began his reply with a frown on his face. "Sari could sell the tavern. That might provide sufficient funds to cover the increase in rent I would have to charge for your larger quarters…Oh, hang it all, Omén, you are due for a big increase in salary. Yes, I will approve of what you wish. Call in the women and we will go over the details. Tell Sari to get a manager for her tavern. I still like to get out occasionally."

Omén still had a worried look on his face. "There is one other detail which I must mention, even though Sari begged me to tell no one. Do not laugh at what I tell you. Sari loves you very much. She knows she will never be your concubine, much less a Queen, but her dream is for you to truly love her, and she wants to give you a male child, seeing as how there are no heirs to the throne."

"She told you all that? Hmmm. Well, don't stand there like a bump on a log. Go bring them in!"

So Sari and Dona and Dona's husband-to-be moved in. Omén and they (and the Sultan) were very happy. For Omén, the happiness lasted for all of six weeks. Then he became despondent again. The Sultan decided a week's relaxation in the desert with his horse and a pretty woman would fix Omén up, and mentioned it to him – about taking a week off in the desert, that is.

Omén replied dutifully, "I will be leaving this afternoon if there is nothing more expected of me, Sire."

The Sultan laughed. "No, Omén. Get out of my sight. Go to your much needed rest."

"I will see you at new moon then, my lord." Omén bowed and turned to go.

"There is one more thing, Omén." Sultan Halidah paused, studying Omén's face. "Take one of those pretty new dancing girls with you for company."

Omén grinned sheepishly. "As you wish, my lord."

"Sari, I will be taking a week off in the desert to clear my mind. Please have Dona saddle up Zeus while I pack my things. As he left the apartments he couldn't help but wonder if he was forgetting something. He had his bed roll, a few changes of clothing in his saddle bags, and of course Crystal was tucked cozily in the pouch hanging from his neck. She would fill his need for conversation, as always, on a long trip. He mentally searched through the saddle bags trying to figure out what was missing. Across the garden a lithe figure moved silently toward him. He watched as the slender young woman approached. He smiled at her. She was lovely.

"Omén?" she half whispered, looking about nervously.

"I am Omén," he answered, wondering why she had sought him out.

"I am Akasha, one of the Sultan's dancing girls." A smile flickered over his lips. He should have known the Sultan would not let him forget. "If it pleases you, I am to accompany you on your vacation in the desert."

Omén threw his head back, shouting with laughter. "Ah, now I know what I am forgetting!" She looked puzzled.

"Yes, Akasha, you please me very much. Let me get you a horse from the stables."

Sultan Halidah watched from the window in his bed chamber. He smiled warmly as Omén helped Akasha onto her horse. If he had not sent the girl to Omén he knew the lad would have conveniently forgotten. "Perhaps Omén will be luckier with this one. It is a good beginning."

Omén decided to take a room in town – the desert reminded him too much of Shahrazad, Akasha was new to horses and frightened of them, and he truly wished to make Akasha happy. Akasha was curious as to why they took a room in Riyadh, but he explained he wanted to rest a few days before they headed out, and he wanted to get to know her better first. She readily accepted his explanation. She was so sweet, so eager to please; and so lovely with her long silken hair and creamy skin. Were circumstances different and his heart free to love another, he knew he could find happiness.

"My mind reels with business. Let us walk the streets and hold hands and visit the taverns. Take me to the gift shops and places you frequent and let me buy you what your heart desires," Omén whispered in her ear.

Akasha, being new in town and eager to explore, willingly led the way, enjoying herself immensely. When evening came, Omén was thoroughly worn out. In the cool bed, with Akasha chattering away about what they had seen and what they had done, and with the scent of her perfume in his nostrils, and with her soft body nestled in his arms, Omén quickly fell asleep. And so the week transpired. And for that week, Omén was a new man; and for many weeks after. But it would not last.

One evening Sari called her big brother to her bed and asked him, "Why are you so sad, Omén? Is something wrong? Come here and tell your sister while I rub your back."

"You do not understand, Sari. I love a woman I cannot have, and she loves me."

Sari was silent for a time, soothing his back. "What perfume does she wear?" Omén told her to the best of his ability. Sari thought for awhile, then asked, "What does she look like?"

"She looks like ... she looks a lot like you," Omén finally blurted, "but she has a hold on me I cannot shake. It is my destiny."

The next day Sari went to market and bought several perfumes; she experimented until she found a mix that might be what Omén's love wore. That evening she put on a sheer nightgown and a generous amount of the new perfume at the proper places, and as evening wore on and she heard Omén tossing in his bed in the adjoining room, she called out, "Big brother, come in and hold me. Monkey is 'fraid." It was dark in her room. Omén came in and stumbled around. Sari was sitting up in bed.

"Come here and lie down, love, and lay your head on my bosom and quiet my fears." And Sari began quietly singing nursery rhymes from her childhood as she massaged his body and kissed the back of his neck. When his breathing became peaceful, she said quietly, "I love you and you love me, and we cannot have each other."

"That is different, Monkey," and he bit her tenderly on a nipple.

"Ouch!" Her hand formed into a fist and she hit him gently on the top of his head. Omén grunted and fell into a deep sleep.

Sari carefully placed him in her bed, then dressed and went outside to the Sultan's chambers, where she gave a pre-arranged signal. Yes, the Sultan was available tonight. He came out in fifteen minutes. "Before we dance the night away, love, I must ask you not to pester Omén with available women any more."

"Why is that? I noticed his mood was down, and gave him Akasha, one of my new dancing girls, and the prettiest."

"Because he is under the spell of a beautiful woman, and she is under his spell."

"Fine. What is the problem?" asked the Sultan, completely bewildered.

"They cannot have each other – I do not know why. I will comfort him as best I can. I am acquainted with his grief." Sari kissed Halidah on the cheek.

"To the Tavern," they sang out together, and they had a thoroughly enjoyable evening there until the cock crowed and the tavern closed. Sultan Halidah then took Sari to his bedchamber while it was still dark.

When they were in the Sultan's bed in preparation for their embrace, Sari decided to tell her lover a story. "Please do not think me forward, my sweet," she whispered in his ear, "but I had heard a story in my travels, and I must tell it now."

ABU NUWAS AND THE CALIPH'S QUEEN

Once Abu Nuwas asked Harun Al Rasheed for permission to take one donkey from every husband in the kingdom who proved to be afraid of his wife. Some time later the caliph was sitting in a palace window when he saw a cloud of dust on the horizon. Soon he made out Abu Nuwas driving a herd of donkeys toward the cattle market. "What is this, Abu Nuwas?" he asked.

"This is the sad state of your kingdom, sire," said Abu Nuwas. "Did you not give me leave to demand one donkey from every man who fears his wife? By the way, on my journey I saw a girl with cheeks like pomegranates and breasts like marble. I immediately thought of you…"

"Shhh!" whispered the caliph. "Queen Zubeida is sitting behind that screen – she will hear you!"

"Sire," said Abu Nuwas, "from the men of your land I have taken one donkey; for the king the fine is two donkeys – and make them white ones."[*]

Sultan Halidah broke out into a loud, long laugh. Sari then began to giggle. The giggling and laughing and caressing lasted until well past sunup.

*****

The caravan arrived this afternoon, as Omén knew it would. He had planned the whole thing to a "T" – the welcome, the reception, the accommodations, the fetes, the music, the dancing, the banquets, the recreation, the flowers and decorations, the food and drink, the nursery, the programs for the older children, the swimming, the archery, the falconry and horse racing for the men, the games of skill and of chance, the

---

* From ARAB FOLK TALES by Inea Bushnaq, copyright © 1986 by Inea Bushnaq. Used by permission of Pantheon Books, a division of Random House, Inc.)

relaxation periods, the quarters for the servants and attendants, the stables for the hordes of camels and horses, even stocked the livery with a complete replacement of bridles and tassels and bells and stirrups. Not to mention the gifts for presentations and awards. And Sari mentioned other needs of the attendants and servants that must be filled.

So when the day arrived, Omén stayed away. He was sick of the whole thing. If it went well, fine; if not, he would not be there to be embarrassed.

The next morning he was at his desk as usual when the door to the office burst open and the two brothers came in. Halidah was showing his brother around. They conversed, but their words were drowned by a shrill yet muffled noise in the distance. All stopped work to look, all except Omén, who kept plugging away. The brothers left by the opposite door, and then the guide came and the children started pouring in, followed by four regal matrons in veils. Omén heard the noise, and finally could concentrate no longer and looked up. An assistant came up to him and shouted through the noise to be heard, "Omén, what are we to do with the children?" At that, a loud cry came from one of the ladies and she fainted. The others slowly lowered her to the floor and began to pat her hands and fan her face. The din from the children ceased.

The brothers came back into the room. "We heard a strange quiet," said the Sultan of Kuwait. "What happened?"

"Mommy died again!" cried a little girl.

"Hush, child, your mother just fainted," said one of the matrons.

Omén came up to the woman on the floor, who was now stirring, and helped her to her feet. "Would Madame care for some smelling salts?" proffered Omén, who was well stocked with all sorts of emergency supplies in his pockets for just such an occasion.

"Yes, please." The voice seemed very familiar.

"Oh, it's Shahrazad," said the Sultan of Kuwait. "Is she with child?"

Yes, nodded the other veiled women. "That explains many things. She has not been herself this past year. I thought she had completed her change of life." The brothers left again.

Queen Shahrazad turned and whispered in Omén's ear, "Meet me somewhere, anywhere. We must talk." The crowd moved on. Omén closed the office for the week – with pay! The boss was sure a great guy!

Omén left the office and went to the gardens where the tour would end up. Shahrazad was with the other Queens. He went up to her and asked solicitously, though his heart was pounding, "Is Madame feeling better?"

Shahrazad nodded, then took his hand and led him out of earshot. "How did you come to be in Riyadh, and in such a high position? Are you married? Oh, here comes my husband. I will find you later."

"Ah, here is the young gentleman who planned this whole affair. Remarkable, wonderful, beautiful; I love it. Sorry that Sher caused such a commotion earlier."

"I want the child, but really, darling, I am too old for this."

"You look familiar, son. What name do you go by? Omén? I have seen you somewhere before."

"Pshaw, love," said Shahrazad, "he must be running all over the place to get things in order. You probably saw him a dozen times since we arrived."

"Yes, of course," said the husband, unconvinced.

Omén was beside himself. He could be close to his love and yet there was no opportunity to talk to her privately or to appear as other than the master of ceremonies for the events. At one of these close encounters on the third day, Shahrazad took his hand in hers and whispered, "Understand you have a wife and daughter. Congratulations. Please bring your wife when we find the opportunity to talk. She sounds like a gem. All the men I have met here praise her in the most glowing terms."

Omén returned home disconsolate that evening. Sari had conveniently been away, busy at the tavern, along with the teenage lovebirds. She did not want to be in the way, just in case.

Sari came in to pick up some supplies, and Omén cornered her. "Sari, please tell me what to do. I am beside myself. I have not had the chance to talk to Shahrazad in private. She hopes the opportunity will arise, and she wants you to be there also. She has heard we are man and wife."

"So your love is still alive. Is she still beautiful? As beautiful as your baby sister?" Sari batted her eyes at Omén.

"Yes, Omén, love, I want to meet her. Are her feelings for you as strong?"

"I do not know. It doesn't seem so. She seems more mature."

Sari laughed, "I would hope so."

That afternoon before the great banquet the next day, which would signal the eve of the departure, that afternoon was more or less open to allow everyone to rest up and prepare for the final festivities. Omén told Sari to stay with him as he walked the grounds to direct the cleanup. It would probably be his last chance to see Sher in private... There she was! Sitting on a bench, her veil and royal robes off, in a more revealing tea gown, with but one attendant, soaking up the sun.

"Hello," said Sari, "I understand you know my husband."

"Shahrazad, please meet Sari, my love," said Omén, by way of more formal introduction.

The two women bowed to each other, and Sari continued, "May we sit with you?"

"Yes, indeed," replied Shahrazad, and she shooed her young girl away with the words, "We would talk in private. I will be fine."

"Your perfume is most pleasing," said Sari, "What is it, may I ask?"

"Why, thank you. It is only sandalwood... and patchouli...from India...I use very little...and only on special occasions."

Then Shahrazad turned and looked closely at Sari for the first time and gasped.

"What is the matter, Sher?" asked Omén puzzled.

"Your wife, Omén, your wife! By the gods, hers is the face I see in my looking glass!"

Omén looked at Shahrazad in amazement, then looked at Sari. "Sher," he said at last, "you were told that Sari was my concubine, not my wife, were you not?" She nodded. "Sari is not my concubine. She is my baby sister."

"Omén, I do not understand any of this. The new life inside me has stilled my passion. Put your head on my lap to quiet the pain in my belly." Sher looked at Sari to catch any sign of jealousy – there was none – Sari leaned over and kissed Shahrazad on the cheek. "Now tell me your story."

While the three were talking, the attendant slipped out of sight and sat down about thirty paces away, near the rose bushes, watching carefully. After an hour or so the Sultan of Kuwait came by with his Queen Dunyzad and saw the girl. "Child, what are you doing here?"

"Hush, Papa. Auntie Sher wishes to speak privately with the couple," and she pointed.

The father bent down and kissed his ten-year-old favorite on her forehead, tousled her hair, and slowly walked away down the path, his hands clasped behind his back, in reverie, while Dunyzad stayed for awhile and stared steadily at the trio on the bench. The girl had ducked her head and blushed when the Sultan of Kuwait tousled her hair; then she switched position, now sitting facing her father as he walked away, her arms clasped around her knees drawn up tightly to her chest.

She sighed. "I love him, Mama."

"Yes, dear," said Dunyzad, turning to her daughter with a sigh. Immediately she uttered a startled cry – she realized her daughter was not talking about Omén, but about her husband the Sultan, who was walking away in the distance. Dunyzad ran down the path, quickly catching up to him before he was aware that she had not been with him the whole time.

Omén told his whole story. The late afternoon air was a little cooler when he finished. "And so you see that Sari is indeed my sister, and that my passion for you will not go away. It is my destiny. Your husband the Sultan of Kuwait does not seem to desire you. Would he not be willing to allow you to leave?"

"Dearest Omén, if we became husband and wife, your passion would no doubt disappear in the hum-drum of daily life. Then where would I be?"

"That would never happen."

"Omén, do you still keep your Crystal with you, as you vowed those many years ago?"

"Yes, of course. I have her here with me now."

"Well, as you have never broken your vow, so I have never broken mine.

I am more a nurse to my husband than a wife and lover. If I left him, he would soon be back drinking wine and eating mutton, and the lives of the maidens in Kuwait would again be in danger. The local mutton has something in it that affects him untowardly, which your mutton did not. I learned as much in the three years we were together evenings in his chambers. Did he tell you about our long tryst?" she asked Sari. Sari only smiled.

ILLUSTRATION

His people, He would have instructed them to eat only well-cooked pork rather than no pork at all. Clearly, it is argued, Jahweh had something else in mind—something more important than mere physical well-being.

In addition to this theological inconsistency, Maimonides' explanation suffers from medical and epidemiological contradictions. The pig is a vector for human disease, but so are other domestic animals freely consumed by Moslems and Jews. For example, undercooked beef is a source of parasites, notably tapeworms, which can grow to a length of sixteen to twenty feet within a man's intestines, induce severe anemia, and lower resistance to other infectious diseases. Cattle, goats, and sheep are also vectors for brucellosis, a common bacterial infection in underdeveloped countries that is accompanied by fever, chills, sweats, weakness, pain, and aches. The most dangerous form is *Brucellosis melitensis*, transmitted by goats and sheep. Its symptoms are lethargy, fatigue, nervousness, and mental depression often mistaken for psychoneurosis. Finally, there is anthrax, a disease transmitted by cattle, sheep, goats, horses, and mules, but not by pigs. Unlike trichinosis, which seldom has fatal consequences and which does not even produce symptoms in the majority of infected individuals, anthrax often runs a rapid course that begins with body boils and terminates in death through blood poisoning. The great epidemics of anthrax that formerly swept across Europe and Asia were not brought under control until the development of the anthrax vaccine by Louis Pasteur in 1881.

Jahweh's failure to interdict contact with the domesticated vectors of anthrax is especially damaging to Maimonides' explanation, since the relationship between this disease in

"What is Palace life like for you? Tell me about Dunyzad and your husband and children," said Omén.

And Shahrazad told all about her boring life in the Palace. "Omén," she said at last, with a far-away look in her eyes, "when the passion strikes and I long for your arms, I bother my husband no end until he submits; then while I am in his arms I think of you. Do you not have someone you can hold thusly? What about Akasha, the dancing girl? Do you not find her attractive?"

"Yes, but...."

"Omén, you are making me very jealous." She tickled him until he held her hands firmly. "Omén, we are both nearing fifty years. We are much too old for this. And yet we cannot help ourselves. Yes, it is Karma...You mentioned once long ago that your god Allah had told you that you would have me one day."

"Yes, but when I ask when, I am told to go to his messenger, Crystal. And when I ask her, the stone dissolves. I feel a shape, as a tunnel, and I see you at the end of the tunnel, but yet not as a tunnel, for the image fills my whole eye. And do not laugh: you are upside down!"

Sher and Sari both started to laugh but kept themselves in check. "And what am I doing while upside down?" said Shahrazad, a giggle starting in her throat.

"You are running to me, you are all bloody, I long to comfort you. The dream has come upon me many times and I do not understand it at all." Omén closed his eyes and held her hands even closer. His eyelids glistened at the corners.

"Omén, promise me something." He nodded. "Promise me that you take Akasha as your concubine and do as I do. If it be the will of Allah, we will be together in our next life. For the present we will be brother and sister when we are together, as you and Sari."

"May I write to you in the Palace?" asked Omén.

"My husband reads all the mail, incoming and outgoing. You will have to get his acceptance if our letters are to be delivered."

"Then I will ask him; and I promise to do as you wish."

The Sultan of Riyadh, Halidah by name, spoke to Shahrazad at the evening banquet prior to the departure on the morrow, "Dear Sister, I have heard rumors that you can tell tales with the help of the magic stone which Omén carries with him. Is this true and would you care to entertain us?"

"Dear brother-in-law, it has been many years since that was accomplished. If you will make ready on the stage with a bedchamber, and if your brother is willing, and if my Brother Omén will allow me once more to hold his magic Crystal, and if my sister Dunyzad will accompany me in the tableau, then I will attempt another story."

"Yes, yes," the assemblage shouted. "A story! A story! Let us have a Story!" So while the stage was being made ready, Shahrazad told Dunyzad what she must do and say at the proper times; then she took Omén's Crystal, and standing by him, shoulder to shoulder, she peered into its eye. To Omén, it was as if the years had been erased. Shahrazad was with him, close to him, touching him. He watched her face intently all the while; he felt her faint trembling.

All was ready but Shahrazad did not move her gaze from the stone. A hush fell upon the assemblage, and still Shahrazad did not quit her gaze as she said out loud to Omén, "I do not understand what your Crystal is telling me. I feel anxious and afraid. Please, this MUST be the last time I tell a story by your Crystal."

Then the Sultan of Kuwait went up and settled comfortably in the bed, Shahrazad went up and snuggled in his bosom, Dunyzad went up and sat at the foot of the bed. When the attendants bowed and left the stage, Dunyzad spoke, "By Allah, oh my sister, relate to us a story to beguile the waking hour of our night."

"Most willingly," answered Shahrazad, "if this virtuous King permit me." The Sultan her husband nodded his head, and Shahrazad began, in a sing-song voice, as if repeating a childhood tale everyone knew:

"There once was a young boy who lived far to the South. One day his God Allah spoke to him and said, 'My son, you must go North, and there you will find your destiny.' So the boy took leave of family and friends and became a shepherd to sustain himself while he traveled. Many years he went on, until finally he reached his goal and found that for which he was searching. But this one, for it was a young maiden, had vowed to be true to another for good and sufficient reason. The shepherd, also, had taken a vow; neither vow could they break. After three years he took leave and traveled far away to begin a new life. He became very rich and powerful and died in honor, never having broken his vow. But it is the will of his God Allah that they will be husband and wife in the next life."

She stopped speaking, and an uneasy silence pervaded the room. Omén was embarrassed. This was a generic love story – half of those listening no doubt could tell similar tales from their personal experience. Quiet whisperings ensued. The Sultan, upon whose bosom Shahrazad rested, even turned somewhat red and embarrassed. Then she began again, her voice now that of a gypsy fortune teller – her face was blank and her eyes were closed.

"I was born of a thunderbolt. I was plucked the next morning from the sandy beach by a young dreamer. I was buried alive with this dreamer when he died. Soon after I was taken and sold to a passing caravan and traveled West and North, through Mecca and Istanbul, to a city on the sea far away, and at last to a city on an island where tree worshippers dwelt. I find my mate and await my dreamer so that we can lead him to his destiny far to the South."

Again Shahrazad ceased. Then her trance deepened and her voice lowered and became staccato as an African medicine man – you can almost hear jungle drums in the distance. "My lover comes to me in the mountains far to the North. We become husband and wife. Life stirs in my belly. Oh!" A cry comes from Shahrazad's lips in her own voice and her hands clasp her stomach. "The wife dies. The distraught husband has heard of a Frankish stone whereby one can magnify his vision, and to keep his sanity, he begins his search. Years pass ... Many years ... Many, many years. He finds the stone, now altered beyond recognition, and they direct him to me, born again in a faraway land. We become one again, and live happily ever after ... Together ... Forever ...."

Shahrazad ceased speaking, and slowly wrapped her arms around her husband's neck, the hint of a smile playing on her lips. In the hush, the audience can hear her softly snoring.

The Sultan of Kuwait broke the silence. "My Shahrazad is with child. This shall be the last. She is become too old to have more. Please excuse her ramblings. She has been like this now for almost a year." The Sultan excused himself and carried his "bride" to her bedchamber.

The banquet broke up after a few more rounds of drinks and entertainment of jugglers and dancers. As the guests were departing, Omén overheard one say, "The Queen's story was very strange; I do not understand it – yet it haunts me." When the banquet hall had almost cleared out, Omén spied the Sultan of Kuwait, who had returned for the festivities, and went up to him and said, "Sir, it is unlikely that I will ever see your Shahrazad again. However, may I write to her as a brother?"

"Yes, yes, please do, Omén. She has been very moody of late, and letters from a brother and a friend will be most welcome. Yes, indeed." And they embraced. Then the Sultan whispered in his ear, "I do not believe in an afterlife. She will be faithful to me in my lifetime, and this is enough."

That night in bed, Omén tossed and turned, but sleep did not come. Finally he arose and went to his desk, took a piece of parchment and began writing what Shahrazad had told – it was etched in his mind like chiseled stone:

Praise be to Allah, Maker of all things. This is the last tale told by the Crystal to Shahrazad:

*****

When he finished all that he had heard and observed, he added: Scribed by Omén of Sur, who as a lad found the Crystal on the Eastern Shore, created by a mighty stroke of lightning three days after the new moon with the messenger approaching her horn, the Seven Sisters watching from above, and the Little She Camels nearby.

The very next day, after all the guests from Kuwait had finally left in the caravan, Omén took his precious stone (upon which Crystal sat), and the parchment, and went to the lapidary craftsmen, where they finished the bottom of the stone flat, leaving the hollow (like a clamshell). Then he went to the woodcrafters and had an ebony wood plate made to fit the bottom, so the stone could be used as a paperweight. Then he went to the glassmakers and warmed the stone and plate in a small annealing oven. Then he neatly folded the parchment into the hollow and with sealing wax sealed the plate onto the stone, hiding the parchment for posterity. When all was cool and firmly fixed, he put the stone back in his pouch and resumed his duties.

*****

It was several months after the visit by the Sultan of Kuwait. Omén was feeling chipper – he had just received the first letter from Shahrazad. He read it aloud to Sari (after editing out some personal items) and then looked closely at her and announced, "Sis, you look a little plump. Is the Palace food agreeing too well with you?"

"So I've put on a little weight. So what? You are not all skin and bone like you used to be, either." Omén laughed. Then Sari continued, "Omén, brother dear, there is something I must tell you. The Sultan's sister in Mecca is with child and is having a hard time. She is really too old for this foolishness. The Sultan has asked me if I would go stay with her until her time is fulfilled. Is this agreeable with you? You won't get blue, moping around about your love? Is Akasha keeping you happy?"

"Go, go, I'll be fine. I'll have another room, and have Dona all to myself," he grinned at her.

"Well, all right. I'll leave now. See you in a year." They embraced warmly.

While Sari was gone, Omén learned all about living with his growing-up teenage daughter and her boyfriend. They were constantly making and re-making plans for the wedding that would take place soon after Sari returned. The lad showed Omén around the gardens and even had him plant a tree or two. Under the watchful eye of the gardener, of course.

The year was up. Sari returned, radiant and thin, with a healthy baby boy. The Sultan and his wives, and Omén, were there to greet her as the caravan stopped at the Palace gates.

Sari approached the Sultan downcast and said, "Greetings to you, Sultan Halidah. I am so sorry for you. You have gotten the message I sent ahead about your sister's hard delivery? But the baby survived. It is a boy. Here, take your little nephew."

"That's all right, Sari. If you wish, you may keep him to raise as your own, if that will not discomfit you or Omén. Did my sister name the child before she died?"

"Oh, yes, thank you, thank you. He is a lovely boy. No, he has no name as yet. We wait for you to make the official announcement." And so the announcement was duly proclaimed of the possible heir to the throne.

Sari raised the child with love, for it was her own, her dream come true. Omén suspected, but questioned not. He became a true father to the child. The Sultan would come now and then and play with the boy before taking Sari out. The gossip started again, about how fickle concubines had become, going out with more than one man. Dona married and they moved out – the sound of crying interfered with their nights…they would soon have enough crying of their own.

Akasha kept Omén very happy, and he actually had pangs of jealousy when she went out with a younger man. When she finally married the lad, she settled down completely, except she still came when Omén wished to do the town of an evening, which was less and less frequently. Sari was still there and gave him companionship — the child was taken into the Palace proper when he was six. Zeus, the black stallion, was getting old, the Sultan was getting old. Time would not stand still.

Omén was still being congratulated on his luck – two beautiful concubines, not a worry in the world. Some people are just born lucky, they said.

> In a gilded prison, she;
> Yearning always to be free.
> Kept in rein by high duty,
> Can she to her lover flee,
> Lovely, lonely girl you see?
> Shahrazad, please come to me;

We will be in ecstasy.
Karma – 'tis our destiny.

Omén

11
The Sultan

Omén was awakened from a deep sleep by one of the Sultan's young pages. Groggily he searched for his clothes in the dimly lit sleeping chamber. The page shuffled from foot to foot, impatiently waiting for Omén to get his wits about him.

He waved the boy on, following closely behind. As they padded through the halls of the great Palace, his senses began to return. He had been dreaming of Shahrazad. As always she was so near, yet just beyond his grasp. A smile parted his lips but he quickly controlled himself. He knew something must be very wrong, being summoned to the Sultan's bedside in the dark hours before dawn exploded upon the Arab world.

Omén stopped just outside the Sultan's chamber to gather his courage. He said a brief prayer for the Sultan and silently slipped inside. Many people were already there. The doctor hovered nearby, straightening upon seeing Omén. He shook his head from side to side at Omén's questioning look. The Sultan was gravely ill, yet until now Omén had held a glimmer of hope he would get better. But as he looked down upon the old man, shrunken with age and illness, he knew the time had come. As Omén watched, the Sultan opened his eyes, bright with fever, and motioned his chief scribe to his side. Omén kneeled beside the bed and took the outstretched hand. The Sultan tried to smile. Omén found himself fighting back the burning tears. This man had come to mean so much to him over the years; he was like a father, a kind father such as Omén had never known in his childhood. Omén would gladly do anything asked of him, if only he could turn the time back, making the old man young again, just beginning his reign …

For several long minutes they watched each other, silently conveying how each felt about the other. At last with some difficulty the Sultan began to speak. "Omén, my friend," He began to cough, having trouble catching his breath. "Your Grace," Omén said unsteadily, "You must save your strength; rest now. …"

"No!" the Sultan whispered. "I am dying…we have so much to say… so little time. …"

"Don't say such things …" Omén began, truly alarmed.

"It is so … we both know it to be so. Now listen as I tell you what is to be." Omén took an offered chair and began listening dutifully to the old man's words…words he had yet to comprehend. In a halting voice, the Sultan told of his past encounters with Omén, how he had grown to like him as a person and as an employee, how he had come to depend on Omén and value his advice, how Omén's family had become as part of his family, how he thought of Omén as a son. …

When the Sultan finished, he looked into Omén's eyes. "Promise me, Omén …

promise me you will take my place. ..." He started to cough again.

Suddenly Omén understood what the Sultan was saying. "But Sire, you cannot mean that I am to be Sultan... Surely you. ..."

"Omén, listen to me," the Sultan broke in. "I wish to appoint you as the next Sultan. I have gathered everyone to hear my last wishes."

"But ... how can this be?" Omén sat wide-eyed, afraid to believe what he was hearing.

"My son, you have served me well, let me honor you so! After your rule is ended, the next in line in my family shall resume the reign. Is that not fair?" He began coughing anew, his breaths coming in ragged gasps. "Omén, promise me ..." he whispered.

"Yes ... yes, my lord, I would be proud to rule ..." Omén's voice broke, tears running freely down his swarthy cheeks. The old man smiled, feebly squeezed the new Sultan's hand (for the handshake was to be the signal for the passing of authority), and slipped into the peaceful sleep of eternity.

Within days of the old man's death, Sultan Omén had called the grieving family to his new quarters in the Palace to explain that the Sultanship would indeed be returned to the family at the end of his reign. Like the Sultan before him, he had no male heirs to leave it to. He felt that a restless nephew might challenge his right to rule, but the boy seemed content with Omén's reassurances for now. Still, he knew there were those who thought his claim to the throne unfair. They believed Sultan Halidah was not capable of making such a momentous decision when his mind had been clouded by fever. Omén also had wondered about this, until three of the old advisors had come to him shortly after the new rule and informed him that Halidah had voiced his desire weeks before the illness. The three pledged their loyalty to Omén, and as a reward were made his chief advisors.

Several weeks after Sultan Halidah's death, Omén sat behind his desk hoping to make sense of the correspondence piling up. Wearily he rubbed his tired eyes and leaned back against the chair. He sighed; the last weeks had been so taxing. He still was not used to his new role in life … it had happened all so suddenly. Never in his wildest dreams after his giddy boyhood days did he actually think he would ever become a … a Sultan! His first act as Sultan had been to choose several advisors he could trust to help make decisions that would benefit his people of Riyadh. Like the Sultan before him, he saw the importance of gaining a good rapport within his domain. He intended to implement many ideas he had proposed before but which had been brushed aside as foolish.

Slowly he rose from his chair; he was tired and the papers on the desk could wait. He wanted nothing more than to ride the fiery Zeus into the desert to think. But he was no longer afforded the privacy. If he rode anywhere, an armed escort must now accompany him. The fiery Zeus, he smiled wryly, the black stallion, now turned out to pasture. There were other horses, to be sure, but the excitement was gone.

"Did I make the right decision, becoming Sultan?" he wondered aloud. He edged his hand into the small pouch he wore hanging from his neck, wrapping his fingers around the stone's smooth cool surface. "You always said I would become someone of great importance, my love," he whispered. Wearily he made his way to his private chambers, seeking the solitude the night hours offered. He sank onto his bed, not even bothering to remove his clothing. He lay a long time listening to the noises of the night, his mind refusing to turn off. Around midnight he closed his eyes at last, willing the dreams of the past.

The weeks and months marched swiftly by, finding Omén immersed in his duties as Sultan. One of his first priorities was to view the whole city on foot with his advisors. Omén found he did not like what he saw in his city ... the filth, the starving beggars, the thieves, and the children clad in rags were more than he could handle. Though there seemed little he could do for the beggars and the ragged children, other than throwing them an occasional coin, he could pass stiffer laws concerning theft. He, too, had once been the victim of a clever thief while walking down the streets of Riyadh. He wished to hear no more stories of innocent victims being robbed within this city.

He also made note of the increasing garbage heaps outside the city's edge. He had long ago suggested that a piece of land should be set aside away from the city for the garbage, but Sultan Halidah had scoffed at such an idea – why waste donkeys and drivers to carry useless garbage a useless distance into the wastelands? Omén believed that much of the city's sickness came from the rotting garbage, and he hoped to prevent some of the aches and pains of the populace. He also hoped to rid the city of some of the rodent population by removing the garbage. He sent two of his advisors out to stake off the land.

Late one night it occurred to Omén that if he increased the protection in the city to discourage thieves, then why not do so with the trade caravans plagued with bandits? If he increased the guard, then surely the precious goods would reach their destination intact. The desert bandits would think twice before attacking armed men traveling with the caravans. But where would he get the men needed for such an endeavor? There were many out-of-work young men in the city, but how could he entice them to undertake such a dangerous profession? He mulled over his dilemma for a time, sipping his spicy wine. He was tired, but the idea would not go away. How? How?

"How?" he murmured at last out loud to Crystal. He was about to dismiss the whole thing, when something old Nicoli had said came to mind – something about the horse legions of the Romans and the young English King who had taken to battle on a fiery stallion. The more he thought about it, the more he knew that a horse cavalry was the solution. He could easily outfit a cavalry of three or four armed horsemen to travel with each trade caravan on their long journeys through the wilderness and desert. That number would not place an insurmountable burden on even a small caravan. Not only would he solve the outlaw problem, he would be effectively eliminating much of the thievery problem by offering desirable and prestigious work to the young men who had been driven to theft to survive. Not only would the caravans be able to travel in safety, they could increase their trade and thus increase the economy of Riyadh ... and of the whole of Arabia!

As the years passed Omén watched his idea grow and prosper. He watched profits of trade double, then triple. The merchants became fat and lazy with the increased availability and profits. The shoppers in turn no longer complained of the exorbitant prices the merchants charged: at the gentle persuasion of Omén, the merchants had grudgingly lowered their prices for the goods, but had soon seen the wisdom … with the availability of more goods they no longer had to overcharge to gain a profit. Eventually he set up trade stations at certain oases with armed guards to further the availability of goods.

Omén extended his trade routes to China and Africa. He found himself the owner of several new merchant vessels that would bring goods from Canton, Malacca, Java and Sumatra. He even sent a small group of merchants to set up a trade colony in Bombay, many centuries before the famous British East Indies Company. His seamen traded up and down the East Coast of Africa as far south as Madagascar. They brought tales of riches from the fabled Gold Coast to the west.

Sultan Omén was well pleased with his efforts to increase commerce and wealth for his people. He had silks, cotton goods, tapestries, drugs and alum from China, spices and aromatics from India, tropical woods and a strange food called the "Coconut" that delighted his palate, from Africa – and a seemingly endless supply of gold. But he longed to do business with Europe – Nicoli had whetted his curiosity for this part of the world with his tales. Trade with Europe was not to be, however. The Barbarians had overrun this part of the world, until the Franks united under Clovis and established a feudal system which was closed to outside trade. Omén did not really understand this type of government but respected it, knowing that beyond his lifetime Arabia would trade with all the countries of the world.

Through the years Omén viewed the gifted craftsmen of Arabia with awe. In time he exported the fine gold and silver crafts to the outside world. He encouraged their work, often offering a small stipend to tide them over until the goods were sold. Many scoffed at his actions. "Sultan, you foolishly throw away your money," warned his advisors. Omén simply smiled and took great pleasure when the silver and goldsmiths' wares turned a tidy profit. He encouraged all artisans to perfect their wares, and he set up guilds funded by the government enabling the artisans to produce the goods for a salary.

The Sultan found he enjoyed the arts as well. He encouraged new poets to come to the Palace and recite for him. Word spread that traveling musicians were welcomed guests. The Palace was soon filled with aspiring writers, musicians and artists, to many of whom Omén was patron. It was his belief that all creative endeavors must be given a chance.

Much to Omén's amazement the years passed all too quickly. His hair was greying and his waist was thickening, but he didn't seem to mind. Life had been good to him. He looked back on his life and realized that these last few decades had been most pleasant, most pleasant indeed. Almost as pleasant as…. He had achieved greatness beyond all dreams – he was Sultan of the great city of Riyadh!! His work was fulfilling, his leisure hours well spent in his stables, or with his sister and adopted daughter and family, or in quiet conversation with Crystal. Sweet Crystal had given him so much friendship, advisement, love…what more could he ask for? Only one thing…the beautiful dark haired woman locked away in his dreams. But on nights like this with the poetry and music rippling through the night air he could almost feel her lying beside him, enclosed in his arms. "My, sweet, sweet memories," he murmured, settling back into his cushions. He gently placed Crystal upon his chest so she could enjoy the evening's entertainment. She began to hum contentedly.

Life had been good … very good indeed!

Omén faithfully wrote to Shahrazad every new moon, and she faithfully wrote back, keeping him informed of the happenings at her Palace and the trials and tribulations of his "nephews and nieces." These treasures he kept in a box upon which at night rested the pouch containing his greatest treasure.

One day her letter came in the post. It looked different and it was. She was informing him that her husband, the Sultan of Kuwait, had died, and she was in disfavor with the new ruler; instead of being Queen Mother she had been relegated to being a nanny for all the young children – a very demanding and thankless job. And soon after that, within the year, his letter came back, unopened. On the envelope was written tersely, "Unclaimed. Recipient deceased."

Omén felt a knife being twisted into his stomach. Why live any longer? What was there to live for? Going to his desk, he wrote his last letter to Shahrazad, put it in an envelope, and wrote on the envelope these words: "To Shahrazad only." Then putting on his slippers, he plodded down the corridor to the Hall of Honor, and with a thumbtack affixed the letter to the back of the frame holding his portrait, where it could be easily reached.

Soon after he took to his bed, a man old in years and old in spirit. He asked for his family and friends to gather 'round. When they were all there, he gave instructions as to the proper way to resume the reign, gave away his belongings in a verbal codicil, and then added, "I pray thee, bury my treasure with me when I die."

And old in years, Omén the shepherd closed his eyes forever, and met his Maker. They buried him as he requested, Omén the shepherd, doctor at Crystal's birth, friend and companion all his life, Omén the dreamer. Within a fortnight, grave robbers had come and taken his treasure, throwing the body back into the grave, purposely backwards from Mecca, in spite for having found so little of value.

Thou hast thy reward with Allah, gentle Omén. And those who defiled thy grave and of their ilk, they shall have their reward also, from thy namesake.

Beauteous Crystal, constant friend in life, now are you freed in death to seek your true love. Ages can pass as a day, time is timeless, you were made immortal by the gods. Wait expectantly, for your whole life is before you; and great will be your adventures.

Despair not, dear reader. Omén lived a full life well into his eighties without having broken his vow. Shahrazad did likewise. The good Karma thus generated brings them together in their next life and eventually they live happily ever after.

But before the ever-aftering (Act IV), he must find Crystal (Act III), who must be with her Mate on the isle where tree worshippers dwelt.

How Crystal finds her way to her Mate will be the subject of Act II.

ACT II

Westward Ho!

12
Crystal Comes to Mohammed

Now in the City of Mecca there was a certain widow, Khadija by name. "Oh, I am bored with my life! I will put on my veil and go to market and see if I can buy something to while away my time." And on this market day it happened that the Caravan was in town. What noise, what commotion, what festivities. The ships of the desert must be watered, fed and groomed. The men must have their gambling and evening entertainment. Shop owners checked to see what they could barter with the caravan. Many things there were – spices and brocades, pearls, and jewels and gold, frankincense and myrrh, animal skins and strange fruits, toys and games and chess sets and scimitars – a happy time for children of all ages.

Khadija stood watching all morning while the shopkeepers bartered. Then she heard in the distance a different cry. "Pearls and precious stones – and Crystal Balls. Pearls and precious stones – and Crystal Balls." Her ears perked up, and she went up to the old man who dealt in pearls and precious stones.

"Greetings, noble Abu, what have we today?"

"Ah, dear Khadija, and how is life treating you today?"

"Oh, – I am melancholy. What new things have you from the caravan?" she said with a hint of interest.

Abu replied, "See these exquisite pearls from the East, these colored rubies and emeralds from the Orient."

Khadija shook her head and said inquisitively, "You sang a new song today. What are crystal balls?"

"Ah, dear Khadija, the caravan has brought these frozen pools of water from China, as big as guinea hen's eggs – come see!"

Following Abu to the back of the shop, Khadija came to the tiny display and looked at them for a while, frowning. "They have no color, they are perfectly round, they don't look like much, how would I wear them? You know my position, I cannot afford more than two pieces of silver."

The old man's face fell – he had hoped to get at least a gold coin out of his dear departed cousin's wife, even though the estate was presently tied up until creditors were paid. He thought for a time. Then his countenance brightened. "It is not that we look at them, we look into them, and thus divine the future."

"Hmmpf," she said. "Let me look into one … I see nothing."

The old man took the sphere from her hand and held it close to his face for a long time. Then he quietly said, "I see a young handsome shepherd lad in your future who will give you much pleasure."

"Hmmpf," said Khadija. "How much?"

"Only six silver coins, dear sister."

"I cannot afford it."

"Five?" said Abu, not willing to go any lower, as this was a new item, and if he sold too low, he could never bring the price back up to a respectable level.

"I cannot afford it," said Khadija, turning away as if to go, hoping Abu would lower the price.

"Oh, well, here is a tiny ball (and yet two more) held fast to a limpid pool of crystal. It has a long history behind it." Khadija came back to look. "For others, I would ask five silver pieces, but for you, my dear sister, I will sacrifice for only two silver coins."

Khadija looked at what Abu held in his hand. "Faah, it is not worth one."

"Let me tell you its story," said Abu, motioning for her to sit down on the chair he used when business was slow. And he told, as the caravan leader had told him, of the shepherd and the stone, and how the shepherd became a great ruler, and how he died and was buried with only the stone (plus some old letters), his greatest treasure, and how grave robbers took it and sold it to the caravan.

Khadija liked to hear stories (as Abu knew quite well) and liked to tell stories, and so gave him the two silver pieces, took the tiny crystal ball on its couch, and went home and placed it next to her dear departed husband's ring.

Now it had come to pass that there were shepherds abiding in the fields. And Mohammed said to his companions, "I am sorely tired of this life. I must go home to Mecca and find me a rich widow and settle down." So Mohammed set off. As he approached the city, he came upon a caravan. "Go ye to Mecca?" said Mohammed.

"Yea, come along and be our guest." And the caravan leader, Melchior by name, a Persian, told Mohammed the latest tales concerning all the gods and goddesses of all the tribes and nations, of Baal and Marduk, Zeus and Apollo, Venus and Aphrodite, and all the others. "Even the Jews have a god, who they say is above all the others. But they have two names for him. One is like unto the thunderclap of a nearby stroke of Zeus' lightning — TDJ (the first crack), HOOOOOOOO (the nearby thunder that shakes the ground), WAAAAAA (the distant roll). The other name is like unto the sound of storm winds through the treeless valleys of Canaan – YAAAAAAAAA – Wehhhhhhhhhhh. They are a very strange breed – they are afraid to say the name aloud, and only write the hard sounds in their sacred writings — YHVH. Perhaps this is because different thunders or different strengths of wind or different shapes of valleys will make different open sounds, and thus their god could otherwise have many names. But they are not responsible; they say they are descended from the union of a one hundred-year-old man and a ninety-year-old woman. Anybody from a union like that would have to be a little different. But it matters not. Since the Diaspora hundreds of years ago they have not had a country to call their own and will no doubt disappear from the face of the earth shortly. Too bad they didn't listen to their prophet Moses when first he led them out of Egypt. Then they would now be living in peace in the land promised by their god through Abraham the prophet I told you about before (he with the ninety-year-old woman with child) – their promised land being not far from here, near Jabal Razih. Such is life."

The caravan leader continued, "Their last prophet, Yeshua by name, proclaimed himself their Savior, and said that by eating what he ate and by drinking what he drank, that man could live happy, hale and hearty more moons than Methuselah. But the Jewish leaders believed him not, and put out a contract on his life, and he died a terrible death (yet no more so than the thousands strung up by the hand of Rome). And now their god has forgotten them. Perhaps if daily we ate some living bread (bread that is yet to be baked) and drank some living water (wine that is yet fermenting), we could all live to be a thousand?" He turned to Mohammed and smiled. "You are a Semite also, as the Jews; perhaps your ancestor was Abraham? Perhaps these poor people will finally turn away from their false religious leaders (who are a stiff-necked people, as Moses himself said) and go to the promised land, where your Semite brothers will welcome them, for so they told me when last I passed through." And half to himself Melchior said quietly, "Abraham was a neighbor of ours to the west, from the land between the rivers, from Mesopotamia, was he not?"

"Woman, thou still dost not call me husband, lord and master, and we have been married two years."

To which Khadija replied, "Dear Mohammed, I truly love you, but you know I married beneath my station, and to one fifteen years my junior, and my relations approve not – the words come hard."

To which Mohammed replied, "Yes, even harder, for you still think of your late husband daily – you look at his ring and pray to his shrine morning, noon and evening."

"Tis no shrine, but merely a crystal ball to while away my time."

In exasperation, Mohammed declared, "Is that where all your strange tales come from? You have a different story to tell me every evening and I have understood them not. Go to market and rid yourself of the ring and the shrine." And to himself he muttered, "Women. I will never understand them. I could write a book."

So she did…and he did.
An orphan near birth, out of Mecca I flee.
For long years I wandered in desert and lea.
And now I return for my dear wife Khadjee;
But Crystal has cast a deep spell over me.
I go to the cave for to write my story.
My brain's all a swirl with ideas so misty.
The horde of the gods spins my head. Don't you see
There can be but One to whom they bend the knee.
I know not the voices in Canaan's valley,
The fury of storm over desert art Thee!

ᴀᴀᴀᴀᴀᴀALALALAᴀᴀᴀᴀᴀ

it sounds so mighty!
And I your last prophet for all time shall be.

13
To Medina

Four years had gone by since Khadija the widow (now happily married and with two healthy children and another on the way) sold Crystal back to Abu for one silver coin. Abu's stock-in-trade was at a low ebb – gold and silver had he much, but his best gems were gone (his three crystal balls from China he sold the first year) and he was left with only pieces for which he could ask but little – enough to keep him busy in the shop, and that was of no little importance. He was very wealthy now, a member of the council, but he still liked to dabble in his trade. "The Caravan is coming! Within a month it will be here!" Rumor no longer, but irrefutable fact. Travelers to Mecca had passed it in the east and had samples of wares to show off proudly. Merchants began cleaning and repairing their stalls; they would have to work hard to be ready in time.

*****

Melchior approached him. "Dear friend Abu, I have restocked your supply of precious gems, but I have saved the best for last." And with that he held out to Abu a brilliant blue sapphire. "Notice the deep blue color, as of the cool ocean. Notice the star imbedded within. Notice the exquisite shape and polish. Only five gold pieces."

Abu could not keep his eyes off the sapphire gleaming in Melchior's palm. He had never seen a stone so blue, so transparent, and with a shimmering star within. The longer he looked, the more rested his eyes became, but the faster his heart raced. He must have this gem for himself! "Indeed, perhaps you jest, for I would never give more than two pieces of gold for a piece of glass like that."

Melchior arched his brows; his eyes widened; he sucked in his breath. "Glass, you say? Get out your test stones."

So Abu got out his emerald-green alexandrite test-stone from his left pocket and rubbed the sapphire. The mark was seen on his stone. Then he got out his crimson ruby test-stone from his right pocket and rubbed the sapphire. No mark was seen on either stone. Beads of sweat appeared on Abu's forehead. "Three gold coins and no more."

Now Melchior had seen Crystal (that dusty rock of fused sand on which was the miniature elongated shrine enclosing her two daughters and she by the entrance) when he first came into the shop. He had missed her for six long years and was anxious to have her again, for his repertoire of stories was threadbare. Also, he was on his way again to Istanbul, and on his last journey he had learned that the people there were of a scientific bent of mind, and would be most anxious to acquire something of this nature, even to the tune of two or three gold pieces.

"I will not haggle, Abu. Four gold pieces – and I will even take that old dusty piece of crystal you have been unable to get rid of," he said, pointing to the stone hiding in the corner.

"Done, and done!" said Abu, and the exchange was made. When the caravan leader left the shop, Abu's smile broadened wider and wider. He had outfoxed Melchior at last! No one around Mecca had ever seen a blue star sapphire before – and he now owned one. He was a Very Important Person.

But Melchior, now some distance away, began to whistle a merry tune. It had been like taking candy from a baby. And in this manner did the caravan prosper.

On the road to Medina. The caravan made fast for the evening and the talk began slowly around the campfire. While the others exchanged tales of prowess with Mecca's pretties, Melchior gazed intently at Crystal. When the second lull came in the babble, he began to speak thusly:

The Tale of the Silken Scarf

Ah, Mecca! It lures the faithful and the curious, adventurers and wayfarers. It is a city of marvels and revelations for those who have eyes to see. But the eyes to see Mecca behind her everyday veils are given to but few, and everyone who enters her sees a different city. Mecca is like a woman of complex moods, and there are quarters of the city wherein time and possibility lose their meanings.

There is an old quarter of Mecca that is entered only by accident or despair, when the wretched mind is off guard. Then, in the aimless, blind wandering of desolation, one may slip through a doorway or behind a wall and find himself in a Mecca of indistinct edges and peculiar light.

Thus did a young woman enter the whispering alleyways of this other Mecca one day, in the lull of the afternoon. The light was yellowish and thick, and the young woman walked with head down, heedless of the yellow dust and stones at her feet. A beggar, looking up from the gutter, might have glimpsed diamonds beneath her costly veils – or are they tears? Certainly her vision must have been cloudy, for she moved as one asleep, or perhaps deep in grief.

Suddenly she stopped and looked up, as if for the first time becoming aware that she knew not where she was. She turned around several times, seeking a familiar wall or shop, but saw nothing that she recognized.

"Alas," she murmured, "not only am I forsaken in spirit, but now I have lost my way. Surely I was just now looking at silks in Bahrudin's shop? How then have I been transported to this strange alleyway?" She shivered, though the yellow light was warm about her. Alarmed, she realized that before too many hours hence, night would fall, and she was separated from her escort. And if she *did* find her way home eventually, who would believe her story? Not her mother-in-law, who would certainly have her disgraced before the household.

"Young madam, perhaps I can be of help?" came a voice from her side.

The young woman jumped. There beside her was an old figure dressed all in green. The young woman, whose name was Samrah, hesitated, perplexed. Surely just the moment before there had been only an old yellow dog asleep in the gutter where the old one now stood? The figure was slight and stooped, as if by the weight of years, yet her voice was rich and full, and her clasped hands strong and steady. She spoke again:

"Young madam, you appear distressed. Please allow me to help you." As she spoke, it seemed to Sarnrah that a fresh breeze blew through the alley, washing away the yellow dust in a green cool light like that of the oases of palms.

Samrah found her voice at last, and replied hesitantly, "Why thank you, good woman. It seems I have lost my way. If you know the way to Bahrudin's shop, the silk merchant, I should be very grateful to you."

"Bahrudin, yes, his shop is familiar to me. But it is far from here. Will you not take refreshment with me before venturing back? Surely you are weary and dusty from your walk?"

Samrah found herself eager for the respite and accepted as if the words were being spoken for her: "Thank you, may Allah bless you, I am indeed weary."

And so the two women walked in silence through the filtered air like unto green palm shade until they came to a doorway framed in exotic wood carvings. The old woman pulled aside a green curtain and they entered. She seated Samrah upon brocade cushions worked with all manner of trees and plants in fine silk thread, and brought her tea and sweet cakes. Samrah relaxed in the cool green room.

After a suitable interval, the old woman spoke again. "My name is Mushtar," she said, "and some say Allah blesses me with the gift of sight. I perceived that you are distressed about something. Will you not confide in me? Perhaps fate has brought you here for a reason."

Samrah smiled but shook her head. "I am grateful for your sympathy, Mushtar, but nothing except a miracle can help me. My plight is like that of many young brides. You see, my husband's mother dislikes me, and is always finding fault and speaking ill of me to my husband. I have grown pale and my husband accuses me of being sullen and unresponsive. He looks at me now as if he would put me aside. We have been married for nearly two years and I have not yet produced a child for him. I fear that I may be barren. If he takes another wife my life will be in ruins. And today, somehow, I have become separated from my chaperones. My mother-in-law will accuse me of having a lover, and then I will be not only disgraced but probably put to death!" And she began weeping silently.

Mushtar clucked her tongue in sympathy. "Ah, my dear, in truth it is difficult to be a woman! My own sons were late in being conceived, and many the harsh words I myself endured before I became with child. But all is not lost, dear girl, because by the grace of Allah you have come to this quarter of the city where anything is possible."

"Are you a magician, then, or a seller of herbs, Mushtar?" Samrah was mystified. But through her desolation, she felt the quickness of breath that marks the stirrings of hope, as when a spring breaks through the dry ground and begins to wake the land to life again. Indeed, as Samrah dried her tears, it seemed that the room had turned watery, the shadows blue and the cushions cloud-like. Samrah found herself holding a blue porcelain bowl of clear water, and realized that she was thirsty. She drank, and felt refreshed.

Mushtar smiled. "Who knows how fate works in the lives of those who fear God? All I know is that you are here. I shall give you something to ease your heart." So saying, Mushtar disappeared behind a curtain of blue silk, a curtain so full and rich that it whispered at her passage like the sound of a sleeping baby's breath. Samrah idly wondered, hadn't the curtains been green before? And the cushions around her, now showing embroideries of lakes and rivers and blue skies.

"Have I indeed finally gone mad?" Samrah marveled.

In a moment Mushtar returned, bearing a small package wrapped in blue cloth. Samrah blinked. Mushtar was now wearing blue veils that shimmered in the dim light. How could she have had time to change? She handed the packet to Samrah, saying, "When you return home, wear this scarf around your waist every day, and soon you shall see the fulfillment of your heart's desire."

Samrah could not hide her disbelief. "A scarf? But Mushtar, what can a piece of silk do to get me a child? I thank you for kind thoughts, but how can this help me?"

Mushtar pressed the packet on her and said firmly, "I myself do not know why things happen the way they do in this old quarter of Mecca, only that Allah graces our lives somehow when we are desperate." She smiled encouragingly. "Surely wearing the scarf cannot do any harm?"

Samrah smiled back. "Of course, dear friend, I am sorry for my lack of faith. I will wear the scarf and remember your wisdom and friendship."

"There now," said Mushtar, rising and going to the doorway. "You must be on your way. I will walk with you to Bahrudin's."

The two women went out into the street, and Samrah thought it must be very late indeed. Shadows were lengthening and there was a rosy cast to the air as if the sun were sending its prettiest colors to grace the dusk. Samrah felt oddly content, and walked with abstract vision as she pondered the events of the day. They had not walked more than a score of steps when Samrah, a question on her lips, turned toward her new friend. How startled she was to see that no one was there! She turned rapidly in circles, but Mushtar was nowhere to be found. There was only a rusty-colored dog rooting among the bricks of the alleyway. Samrah thought to herself, "Did I dream this last meeting? And how shall I ever find my way back by myself?"

Then her eyes caught the flicker of a rose-colored curtain before her, in a mahogany doorway, overlaid with beautiful carvings. Samrah went toward it, hearing voices inside. How surprised when she entered to find herself in Bahrudin's shop, the shopkeeper himself deep in animated discussion with her chaperones over a pile of silks!

"How strange," she murmured. "Have I been here all along?"

The women turned to her, as if continuing a conversation begun only moments before. "Mistress, do you not think this red cloth will be suitable for the master's new robe? Yet the price is so high!"

Samrah rejoined the conversation, her mind in turmoil. When no one was looking, she felt in her pockets. Yes! The packet was still there! So she had not imagined it after all. She shook her head in puzzlement, but had no time to think. She found herself actually enjoying the bargaining with Bahrudin, laughing at his protestations of bankruptcy but giving in ever so slightly. The chaperones gathered up the purchases and hustled her out to the waiting litter. The sun shone full and hot and she was glad to ride in the dim protection of the litter's curtains. Home they went, the ladies outside chattering all the while and bantering with the young litter bearers. Samrah was glad for their chatter, for it gave her time to think. Well, she decided, she would wear the scarf as instructed, and perhaps something would come of it, and perhaps not. She would worry no more; the outcome would be the will of Allah.

At home finally, her mother-in-law scolded about the fabric, naturally, but grudgingly admitted that at least she had not been cheated on the price.

Who knows how Allah works in the lives of the faithful? Samrah found a new ease and delight in her life, that brought color to her cheeks and a softness to her body. Her mother-in law's scolding twittered about her ears like harmless sparrows, and Samrah just smiled and went about her duties. Even her husband noticed her serenity and beauty, and came to her with renewed affection.

In time, to her great joy, a son was born to Samrah, a child with golden complexion. Soon after, a daughter was born, and later another son. All of them were rosy, strong, happy children that grew like saplings in the sunbeams of Samrah's affection. She dressed them in yellow, green and blue, and delighted in them for all the long years of her life until she died at last, an old woman, one night in her bed.

The handmaiden who found her the next morning gossiped to the other servants about the strange length of tattered and threadbare silk knotted about her waist, a rag so old that it simply disintegrated when removed. "The peculiar talismans of old women!" sighed a maidservant, shaking her head at the others.

The campfire was about out when Melchior at last became silent. There was a soft murmur, "A good story ... what is that stone he holds ... crystal ball ... an old friend ... where did ... near Riyadh ... last caravan ... crystal ball... Crystal Ball... CRYSTAL BALL."

"May your lovely young bride sleep with a different lover every night that you are gone, if that wasn't the best story I've heard from you in a long time," laughed Gaspar the cook as he stirred the camel fuel into red coals, for he was in charge of the campfire on this leg of the journey.

And Crystal blushed scarlet all over.

Several days later they approached Medina. Several of the camel drivers complained, "Can anything good come out of Medina? For it is a small town and has no pretty women (as we discovered on our last journey), not even anything of importance as the world famous Black Stone in the Kaaba in Mecca, which came down from Heaven many years ago as a messenger and was seen by shepherds abiding in the fields that night, and which is venerated to this very day, as it has magical properties.

Can anything good come out of Medina?"

"Perhaps some day," said Melchior.

So they stopped to rest and trade as best they could in this little town that had scarcely as many people as the number of camels and drivers in the caravan. Then they departed for Jerusalem and Damascus.

> Melchior from Persia,
> Gaspar his best friend,
> Balthasar a new man,
> Hired at the bend.

All the other drivers,
Good at what they do,
Seeking fame and fortune,
Just like me and you.

Istanbul comes closer;
It seems almost nigh.
After all their troubles,
Camels almost fly.

"What can ever harm us?
Melchior is here.
He is ever steadfast;
We have naught to fear."

Crystal Ball

14
On the Way to Istanbul

"May your camel spit in your eye," said one young driver on the day the caravan picked up the new man Balthasar at the western bend in the trail to Istanbul. They were well into Turkish country and Melchior had decided an interpreter would give added assurance for the safety of the trip.

The co-worker to whom this remark was addressed did not take kindly to the good-natured banter. "May your camel's bridle rope be caught in the eye of the tent-maker's needle."

The first driver did not like the vision he saw of his camel's head and neck being whipsawed as the tentmaker busily repaired a seam. "May your camel step on your foot when you command it to kneel."

The second driver was not to be outdone. "May your camel loose its water upon you while you are kneeling to remove the stones from his feet."

"May your camel have the hiccups."

"May your mother be sitting upon your camel when he has the hiccups."

And with that the fight began in earnest. Noses were bloodied, eyes were blackened, clothes were torn. "Gentlemen, gentlemen. Please refrain from this unseemly conduct," said Melchior.

"May all the she-camels be in heat at the same time," they shouted in unison, and the fight continued. Finally they could fight no longer, and they resumed their duties.

Melchior took them aside and said, "If you do this one more time, be forewarned that you two will walk and carry, for of a certainty your camels will go suddenly lame."

And so they took heed and soon became friends, for they knew Melchior to be a man of his word.

> "What is a man if he doth not keep his word?
> For any donkey can bray in the wind."
>
> Zoroaster

That evening around the campfire, everyone was grumbling. No one had a good word. Melchior turned the stone over and over in his hands, and finally began:

Melchior's Story

We treat our world, and ourselves, as if we were the favored of our one and only God Ahura Mazda. But what I tell you now, my brothers, is of an earth before our own. Indeed, it became the seed of our earth. The story of this lost time comes to us etched upon a many-sided crystal, the process of writing unknown to me. The stone and its secrets have passed from generation to generation in my family. Placed in a bowl of water, each side is magnified enough to read the words of the ancient dialect. And the words tell of the last days of this ancient world.

Upon this ancient globe, a whole civilization warred itself into oblivion. Spared were three mighty warriors, two evil and one good; a handful of slaves for the evil ones, one learned servant for the good. Two there were who would breed slaves like cattle, and create unto themselves a world where the masses served their lords. One there was who stood against them, one who valued freedom and dignity above all else.

Crantar the Mighty battled Ismandel the Just. "My consort and I have no need to bind together to destroy you, weakling! That I can accomplish quickly while she herds our slaves to gather food." His voice boomed over the plain, empty but for men whose battle decides the course of all creation! Lances sped toward their target, but Ismandel dodged, waiting for one chance to use his deadly sling.

With each miss, Crantar grew more angry. "You prolong the inevitable, mouse! Submit, and you will have the honor of dying quickly." Black hair matted to his forehead, huge arms and legs covered with sweat; dark eyes burned with hatred, and as strongly with a need to hear 'god', 'master', 'savior' from the mouths of men. "Very well, you choose to run, so die as a dog whose fear makes him quick! Another lance missed its mark, shattering a stone near the foot of the quiet adversary. Sharp fragments littered the ground."

73

N THE THOUSAND YEARS before the birth of Christ, from the Mediterranean to the Ganges, charismatic leaders arose to challenge ancient ecclesiastical assumptions and practices and to found new religions and philosophies that condemned the role of priests as ritual killers of people or animals and denied the efficacy of food offerings as a means of winning favors from the gods. Instructed by one or another form of transcendental experience or deep meditation, the new leaders insisted that gods could not be swayed by material bribes. Instead, what the gods or their prophets demanded was a lifetime devoted to good deeds defined as love and kindness to people and all living things. In exchange for defending the poor and the weak and for restraining appetites and other egotistical tendencies, one could expect great rewards. But delivery would occur after death in the form of heavenly immortality or eternal peace rather than rewards delivered in life in the form of food and other material benefits.

Zoroastrianism, the religion of ancient Iran, is the oldest nonkilling faith of which any historical record exists. It was founded in either the eleventh or the seventh century B.C. by the prophet Zoroaster, after he received a vision about Ahura Mazda, "Lord of Enlightenment." Ahura Mazda stood for good thoughts, truth, good government, meekness, health, and immortality. But Ahura Mazda was not supreme. He was opposed by Ahriman, who stood for evil thoughts, lies, misgovernment, rebelliousness, sickness, and death. Ahura Mazda and Ahriman were locked in a great struggle. Humans are free to choose to join one side or the other. Those who chose Ahura Mazda must cease the consumption of intoxicants, give up the ritual slaughter of animals, and refrain from the shedding of blood in general. After death, the virtuous will be admitted to Ahura Mazda's heaven; the rest will fall into Ahriman's hell. Mazdaism, a modified form of the religion Zoroaster founded, became the dominant faith of the people of Iran during the reign of the Persian emperors Darius

"You become worried, my *lord*," the last word spat hatefully toward the other. Ismandel moved to grasp the shards at his feet, lithe form bathed in sweat as well, dark hair long and flowing. His eyes were set hard, not from hatred but from a sense of purpose, alert to spy the one break in Crantar's defense…There! Slow to bend and grasp the lance upon the ground! Whish, whish, whish – the sling spinning faster and faster, cluster of jagged rocks launched. "Die, you who would enslave all that lives!"

Crantar, too, moved quickly then, hurling the lance just before the shards buried deeply into his neck. The lance struck Ismandel a mortal blow just beneath his left shoulder. Two cries – one of death, the other of pain not far from death. "And I shall die as well," Ismandel spoke softly, gazing at the lifeless form of Crantar. "They have won, he and his mate. Our world shall know only slavery and misery all its days!"

She watched the combat from a point high above the plain; she whose beauty was matched by her brutality. Pleyendon saw Crantar fall and in a frenzy set upon the slaves, killing them with her sword. She descended the hill and approached the wounded Ismandel, filled no longer with hatred but with loneliness and defeat. The ice blue eyes filled with tears that trickled over the most beautiful face this world had ever known. She spoke quietly.

"No, Ismandel, my approach is not the sign of a second battle. My anger is gone, spent on those poor wretches on the hillside," she said, her slender arms raised toward where the dead slaves lay. "My vanity surpassed even that of my lover. I needed more than servile worship, more than words ordered out of the mouths of fearful men. Crantar's desire for me, for my beauty – that made me alive. And…" stepping close to stroke his face with her soft hands, her hair brushing his skin, "you once desired me as well."

"That was long ago, Pleyendon, before treachery and murder, before the death of a selfish civilization. Your beauty was another of your weapons. Do me the courtesy, lady, and use your sword once more. Hasten my death an hour, if you remember our love."

For the first time since touching him, she saw his blood on her hands. Swiftly she raised the sword, but not to fulfill his request. Grasping the hilt, point gently probing her stomach, Pleyendon fell forward, a few feet away from Ismandel.

"It is finished," the just warrior whispered, painfully raising himself to a sitting position against a rock. From nearby his servant moved to comfort his master, offering water and bread. "A little water, kind Mada, my friend." Ismandel coughed, and blood trickled from the corner of his mouth:

"Lose no time with me, but take the crystal from the saddlebag, the sacred relic from our temple. Given to us by the Holy One, let us prepare to return it to Him, etching upon each side the story of our self-imposed destruction. Perhaps our God shall see fit to place it in other hands, in other times, that our mistakes may not be repeated."

Mada buried the three warriors and the unfortunate slaves. He was old and would not long survive the coming winter. 'No matter,' he thought, as the writing instrument fired into life, forming the first symbol into the clear stone. He noticed with satisfaction that his hands were steady.

Melchior finished his story. "And this Crystal, dear brothers, which I hold now in my hands, is a daughter of this ancient mother, brought to earth another time by the hand of Ahura Mazda."

Melchior put down the stone, and there was silence. No one uttered a word. Everyone looked down at the ground – some were stirring the loose dirt with a stick. The silence stretched out interminably. Only the camels moved about, restless.

Finally Gaspar spoke. "For two days now we have been arguing among ourselves and saying things we ought not. Even the camels are uneasy. Whether it be bad water has poisoned us or whether it be stale provisions, I know not. But when Melchior himself speaks madness, we must lose no time to turn aside from our journey and replenish our food and drink and rest ourselves, else this caravan will soon disappear from the face of the earth."

And Melchior, coming out of his trance, said to Gaspar, "What is it I have said that bodes ill?" When Gaspar repeated the story, Melchior exclaimed, "Indeed, we must turn aside. We have no time to lose! To the right, toward yonder mountains of Ararat, without delay, 'til we reach a village with a spring and get help!"

Instantly the noise and commotion began – all the banshees of Hell broke loose. Although it was approaching midnight, the stars were out in full glory and there was enough light to see to pack up – the moon would be coming up soon. The camels balked and groaned as the drivers packed them and beat their legs to rise. By late morning the caravan was approaching the foothills of majestic Mount Ararat.

Melchior stopped the caravan for a much needed rest. "Balthasar, you are somewhat familiar with this land, speaking the language also. You had pointed out the crest of Ararat when you joined us and told us it was the source of sweet water for this territory. We are now at the foothills and the camels refuse to climb more. Is there an oasis or spring or village nearby, off this trail, for we have seen nothing as yet."

Balthasar replied contritely, "I may have misled you, Melchior. I am unfamiliar with this place. But surely there is something nearby. If you will have a sturdy camel unloaded, I will mount and go to the top of yon hillock and perhaps spy something in the distance."

It was done and in ten minutes Balthasar was sitting on the camel atop the hillock surveying the horizon. The sun was high, and he could view the complete circle. Nothing was seen for an hour. It was approaching noonday and Balthasar's stomach was beginning to tell him as much. Presently he smelled the faintest aroma of venison cooking on the open fire. He licked his forefinger and held it high in the air to see which way the breeze was blowing. Facing the general direction, he began to search intently for signs of smoke. After a few minutes his eyes and brain began working with his growling stomach, and he spotted it – the tiniest wisp of smoke to the northeast. But the camels would have to do a little work. Perhaps an hour away. Then he spotted another wisp of smoke to the south-east, more in the direction from which the breeze was coming, and lower in the foothills. He saw the hint of a trail near the smoke, but it was farther away – two hours? Balthasar signaled the caravan with his polished bronze mirror and rode back to consult with Melchior.

ILLUSTRATION

Nicea in A.D. 325 to adjudicate doctrinal disputes about whether Jesus the Son was one and the same God as the Father. Three hundred bishops attended, setting the precedent for Councils in the fourth, fifth, and sixth centuries that settled issues surrounding the Trinity and Person of Christ without developing permanent schisms fatal to the unity of the Church.

By the end of Constantine's reign, the bulk of the imperial establishment consisted of Christians. His successors continued to introduce severe penalties against any kind of pagan worship, public or private, destroyed most of the remaining temples, barred pagans from civil service, the army, the practice of law, and the teaching professions. Finally, in 529, Justinian ordered all who refused to become Christians to surrender their property and go into exile. The wrath of the new nonkilling imperial religion fell with equal harshness on Judaism and rival nonkilling religions.

Early in the fifth century, the Romans forbade Jews and Samaritans to build synagogues, serve in the government or army, or practice law. They also took similar measures to suppress the alarming spread of Manichaeism, a rival nonkilling religion founded by the third-century A.D. Persian visionary Mani, who regarded himself as the final prophet in the line of Adam, Enoch, Zoroaster, Gautama, and Christ. Alas for Mani, no armies rose to his defense and his splendid ecumenical dream of uniting the nonkilling religions of Europe and Asia has never been fulfilled.

From OUR KIND by Marvin Harris, copyright © 1989 by Marvin Harris. Used by permission of Harper Collins Publishers.

Melchior had everyone gathered together to listen to what Balthasar had to say when he returned, and no one particularly liked what he had to say. "Gentlemen," said Melchior, "what have you to say?"

"An hour is better than two,

"The camels will not climb for an hour," said another.

"Will there be water at either place, enough for the caravan?" said a third.

"Any spring or water source might be larger at the lower place," said a fourth.

"What is venison?" asked a fifth.

"They must be having a big celebration, to have started cooking so early in the morning," said a sixth.

"Two hunters could have taken a deer and are now enjoying it," said a seventh.

"One small campfire at that distance would not be noticed," said an eighth.

Melchior waited until everyone had his say. Then he said quietly, "Then you are in agreement, gentlemen, that we will join the village in their celebration?"

"Yes, yes," they all shouted, and the caravan moved out to the southeast.

It was mid-afternoon when the caravan finally approached the village. The villagers had finished their meal and were relaxing with wine and dance and games. One of the villagers had seen a cloud of dust in the distance, and after he perceived the strange creatures coming into view, he called out, so that when the caravan neared, the trail to the village was lined with almost the whole population, curious to see if yet another army was come to take tribute from their meager supply, and eager to get a glimpse of the strange beings from another world, this village being situated well away from the caravan routes.

Melchior called out, "Do you have water for the camels?" No one understood him. Then Balthasar called out in their native tongue, "Have you lakes of clear wine from the sky or have you fountains of clear milk from the rocks with which to fill the bellies of these outlandish creatures whom our God has seen fit to deliver into your hands?"

"Yes, indeed, a large lake of wine from the sky for your creatures," they pointed, and of a truth there was a sizeable lake of sweet water in sight. "And for you and your men, a fountain of clear milk from the rocks. Come down off your creatures, and if you all (and your creatures) mind your manners, we will take you there."

In no time at all, the caravan stocked up on fresh, sweet water. Balthasar then spoke to the village elders, "What feast do you celebrate, and may we partake somewhat?"

"We celebrate the birth of our prophet Mani, whom the whole world reveres. We have only scraps left, which we may burn on the altar or feed to the dogs. But you may help yourself."

At the mention of the name 'Mani', Melchior blanched, but said not a word. One of his friends in Persia was descended from this prophet who had lived several hundred years before, declaring himself the final revelator, of whom the Budda, Zoroaster and Jesus had been forerunners. The authorities had cracked down hard on Mani's followers, and these people were still being punished for the sin of having a heretic as a precursor – they must remain as laborers, not being allowed to be merchants or craftsmen or join the army even, much less becoming nobility or priests.

Now Gaspar the cook did not think much of eating scraps hardly fit for dogs, so he approached Balthasar and whispered in his ear, "Perhaps we can buy flour and dry meat and fodder from them and so be on our way."

Balthasar was about to relay this message to the village elders when a commotion was heard in the distance. Several of the villagers spoke the words, "Bu-Bu", then all became silent as heads craned in the direction of the facing hillside.

Down from the hillside lumbered the object of their foreboding. Not quite a man in age, Bu-Bu was more than any villager in size, in strength, in meanness. Very seldom is it given by the Creator to excel in everything, and this was no exception. Bu-Bu was big and powerful everywhere but in his brain. Bu-Bu was dimwitted. Yet no more so than the villagers who had laughed at him and caused his meanness. He could not increase his intelligence, try as he might, but the villagers could hold their tongues if they chose. Those who had laughed at Bu-Bu to his face were no longer of this world. The villagers had at last learned this much. So Bu-Bu stayed by himself.

This day, however, the smell of the roasting venison had finally become too much, and Bu-Bu came down to finish off the scraps. His head was down and he swung it from side to side, like a lumbering ox. When he approached the festive crowd, it parted to make way, and he was soon facing the village elders.

"Look, Bu-Bu, at the strange creatures these men ride." Bu-Bu looked up, saw some camels at the clearing that were being shown to the crowd, and stared at one for the longest time. The small children were playing tag under this one's legs. Finally a light dawned and a smile spread across his face. He went up to the camel (upon which event the children scattered), put his shoulders under its belly, stretched out his arms with his hands fore and aft under the camel, and grunted. Slowly the legs of the camel left the ground. The villagers cheered. The camel craned its neck around and bit Bu-Bu in the seat of his pants. Bu-Bu dropped his load and turned around to face the camel eye to eye. The camel spat in his face. Bu-Bu smiled again – the camel was his friend, he put his arms around its neck. The villagers cheered again.

Bu-Bu had done his morning workout and went up to the tables to eat. Balthasar talked to the elders, and after much haggling they came to an agreement. For their part, the villagers were in dire need of unguents for their dear departed brothers and sisters. It was not yet harvest time, and while there was much pasture and fodder for the camels, there was little food for the caravan drivers; but, true to the precepts of their prophet, the villagers would sell what they could spare. The goods were brought out of hiding, the coins were brought out, the exchanges were made. Bu-Bu took note of this as he ate.

Finally Bu-Bu finished eating and drinking. He had watched Melchior closely, because Melchior was different somehow. He did not haggle with his coin purse out, but kept it to himself, guarding it closely – it certainly looked like it held coins. Bu-Bu decided he wanted the pouch. He went up to Melchior and tried to put his hand on the pouch. Melchior signaled 'No'. Bu-Bu thought about this for some time, then decided he would buy it, as the others had done with their purchases. He held out an old dull copper coin to Melchior and put his hand on the pouch. Melchior stepped back and again signaled, 'No, not for sale'. Bu-Bu wasn't used to people saying 'No' to him. He became angry. He swung at Melchior and knocked him to the ground.

Then he stooped over and took the pouch.

Loosening the string, he tipped the pouch upside down at a table, expecting coins to fall out. Nothing came out. Bu-Bu felt the pouch and knew something was in there. He loosened the string further and put his finger in and gradually extracted the stone. Bu-Bu furrowed his brow. Why was this stone so important to the one sitting in the dust that he would risk life and limb? Bu-Bu turned the stone over and over in his big hands until he finally saw the gleam from Crystal's smooth body. He brought the stone closer and looked at Crystal eye to eye. His brow was still furrowed. Then he lifted the stone to the blue sky, facing the solitary cloud overhead, and held Crystal almost to his eye, his mouth wide open. One of the villagers nearby picked up a tiny bird feather from the ground and said, "Bu-Bu, let me dust the rock for you to clear out its eyes." Some children tittered.

The villager brought the feather up to Crystal as if to clean her. Bu-Bu cried out, dropped the stone, began shaking violently, then ran away, shouting. Melchior had lunged for the stone as it fell and caught it before it hit the ground.

The villagers were flabbergasted. This little stone had much power! Melchior asked Balthasar what Bu-Bu was shouting. Balthasar replied, "The stone holds a big bird captive – its wing covers the whole sky!"

Everyone wanted to see the stone. Melchior let everyone take a good look, then the elders were allowed to look at the feather through Crystal in the manner of Bu-Bu. The elders were quite astonished, almost as much as Bu-Bu had been. Melchior was now curious, and he took a look. Ahura Mazda! Every tiny barb, every hook of the tiny feather could be clearly discerned; and the tiny feather did indeed 'cover the whole sky.' Melchior was amazed. He had never noticed this property of Crystal before. Of a certainty she would fetch a goodly sum in Constantinople! Melchior could contain himself no longer, and he had Balthasar announce that he would tell the story of the stone, if everyone would gather 'round.

Story-time! Everyone there liked a good story. Speaking slowly, so that Balthasar could translate, Melchior told of the shepherd boy who had found the stone, and because of it had found his love, etc. At the conclusion he added, "And this stone will bring them together in a future life." 'Now why did I say that?' thought Melchior to himself. Then out loud, "I must take her to Constantinople, the center of the world, so that in this future life he may go there to find the stone, and thus find his love."

"Ah," said the village elders, "the stone whereby men may enlarge their vision, will bring the lovers together in an afterlife. This is indeed a day to remember. On the birthday of our prophet we have received many gifts from the Magi of Persia – gifts of gold and frankincense and myrrh. But also the greatest gift...the gift of love." Dusk had fallen.

"Please take your stone to Constantinople for the sake of the lovers." The villagers heard the halting voice from outside the circle; it was a different voice and they could not place whose it was. They turned to look. "Bu-Bu! Bu-Bu speaks! Bu-Bu has come back!" Some of the children went up to Bu-Bu and put their arms around him, the young man who had secretly returned and had listened to the whole story. And the village elders told Balthasar excitedly, "From the day his mother died when he was very young, until today, Abu has spoken not a word."

The caravan stayed near the little village for the night, then departed without fanfare early the next morning, even before any of the villagers were stirring. They continued westward without further incident to Constantinople, where Melchior sold Crystal for a good price to a wealthy Greek physician, who was told of its history, shown its powers, and admonished that it should remain in Constantinople to await the lovers. So Crystal at last arrived in Europe, in the western part of the city at the trade crossroads of the world, where she resided for many years, many centuries, first in the family of the physician, then into the hands of a rich merchant. And from the little village sprang the legend of "the stone whereby men may enlarge their vision." The legend gained in stature as it traveled into the mountainous regions to the north and to the east.

The trip home to Persia was quite uneventful. Relating of his adventures to his friends and family in Tehran, Melchior could not help but laugh when he told of the side trip to the foothills of Ararat near the country of Georgia of the Caucasus, with the large rock in the sky and the immense bird whose wings covered the whole sky. And thus was born the Persian legend, now part of the Arabian Nights, of the Roc, in the story of Es-Sindibad of the Sea.

(Looking, however, with a scrutinizing eye, there appeared to me on the island a white object, indistinctly seen in the distance, of enormous size; so I descended from the tree, and went towards it, and proceeded in that direction without stopping until I arrived at it; and lo, it was a huge white dome, of great height and large circumference. I drew near to it, and walked round it; but perceived no door to it; and I found that I had not strength nor activity to climb it, on account of its exceeding smoothness.

The close of the day, and the setting of the sun, had now drawn near; and behold, the sun was hidden, and the sky became dark, and the sun was veiled from me. I therefore imagined that a cloud come over it; but this was in the season of summer; so I wondered; and I raised my head, and, contemplating that object attentively, I saw that it was a bird, of enormous size, bulky body, and wide wings, flying in the air; and this it was that concealed the body of the sun, and veiled it from view upon the island. At this my wonder increased, and I remembered a story which travelers and voyagers had told me long before, that there is, in certain of the islands, a bird of enormous size, called the rukh, that feedeth its young ones with elephants. I was convinced, therefore, that the dome which I had seen was one of the eggs of the rukh.)

From The Thousand and One Nights,
The Harvard Classics

15

Five Adventures

In the twenty-fourth year of their travels, the three Polos, Maffeo, Nicolo, and Nicolo's son Marco, arrived at last in Constantinople, the last major stop of their journey home. The Venetians had amassed wealth beyond reckoning during their seven years in the service of the Kublai Khan; a bit of it had been lost to the treacherous Lord Comnenos in the city of Tabriz, but enough remained to make the fear of robbers an ever-present companion. To avoid the notice of burglars, the Polos dressed roughly, more like Tartars than proud Venetians, and they carried their most precious acquisitions – the jewels of the Khan – stitched securely in the linings of their coats.

But there were still treasures – carpets from Persia, golden idols from Cathay – that the merchants could not hide so easily. It occurred to Maffeo that many of these items could be profitably traded for more jewels, which could be more inconspicuously transported. He began to inquire discreetly where such fine gems could be purchased; and he was led at once to the home of an obscure Greek trader in the oldest quarter of the city.

Maffeo was surprised at the squalor of the district in which he found himself, but realized that the Greek practiced the same deception as he did. In a dark corner of the shop, almost completely veiled in shadows and smoke, sat a small swarthy man with a pipe. Maffeo drew near.

"You are the trader Stavros?" he inquired.

"Who asks?"

"Maffeo Polo of Venice – late of the court of Kublai Khan of Cathay in the East."

Maffeo heard, but did not see, the sharp intake of breath. "And you wish to buy....?"

"To trade. Large wares for small." The Greek did not reply for several minutes, and Maffeo grew impatient. "If you have not the goods I seek."

"Let me see what you have," the Greek said.

Maffeo snapped his fingers, and at once his servants began to crowd the shop with the treasures of the Orient. Intricate carpets, coffers of embroidered silk, statuary of purest gold, coffee, spices, tea – all were strewn about the dark shop before the eyes of the astonished Greek.

"What have you to equal the value of what you see here?" Maffeo asked.

Without a word, the Greek produced, from the folds of his own poor robes, a hefty leather purse. Onto the exquisite swath of silk at his feet he scattered a dozen, two dozen, three dozen cut jewels – emeralds, rubies, sapphires, diamonds, all flawlessly struck and polished, none smaller than a robin's egg.

"They are yours," he told the Venetian.

Maffeo examined the largest, trying to control the shaking of his hands. Before him lay a collection of jewels, the equal of the Great Khan's. He opened his mouth to speak, but the words that came out were not at all what he had intended.

"These are very good, Stavros. But have you nothing else?"

In the instant that followed, Maffeo would have cut out his own tongue had there been a knife close at hand. What impudence! Has the Savior Christ more to offer than salvation? But Stavros seemed to have been waiting for these words. Incredibly, the trader reached into his robes again, slowly, reluctantly, his own hand shaking this time. Then he spoke. "I have something worth more than jewels," and he brought out from his garments the stone with Crystal. He held it in his cupped hands.

"It appears of no value," said Maffeo.

"Let me tell you its history," said Stavros. "This story was told me by my grandfather when I was a boy. His grandfather had told him when he was a boy, and his grandfather likewise, and for many years before." And Stavros told the whole story, of the Arab boy who found the stone on the shore of the Arabian Sea – a gift of Zeus himself. And how the boy, now a young man, found his love, and how he became a great Sultan, and how the grave robbers came after he died, and how the stone came to be in Constantinople.

"Look closely and you will see the tiny Crystal ball perched upon the stone, the source of its great power. And look at the bottom of the stone, a well-fitted flat piece of ebony, polished with much patience. It looks like a paperweight, but is much too light – it must be hollow inside. Feel its weight, young man." And Stavros gave the stone to Marco, nephew of Maffeo, who had come along to help out and to relearn the trading practices of the Europeans after those many long years in the East; Marco, the only one in the shop who seemed to take a genuine interest in his story.

Marco inspected the stone very carefully. "Yes, indeed, it is of little weight. And the tiny crystal sphere is perfect. And there are two larger spheres in the tunnel atop the stone!"

The trader blinked; he had never noticed these.

Marco handed the stone back. "Yes, it is priceless, but we cannot take it."

"Take it you must," replied Stavros. "I have no children nor grandchildren to give her to (for my wife died young and I never remarried, being more interested in amassing great wealth), and for these past twenty years she has told me, 'I wish new adventure. Give me to the Western merchant who comes from the East.'"

"But I must give you something in return, something priceless," said Marco. "This ruby and this sapphire, each as large as a hen's egg, given me by the Great Kublai Khan himself."

"Marco Polo!" exclaimed his uncle.

But Marco had already ripped the seam of the pocket and took out the huge gems; the two men switched treasures.

When the Polos and their men departed, Stavros looked after them until they were out of sight. Tears were in his eyes. "You were my only friend for lo these many years, and I have only two more baubles to take your place. But now you are free to seek your destiny."

Stavros took the week off to grieve. Then he resumed his trade. He bought and sold as well as ever, but people noticed a difference: there was no longer a twinkle in his eye; he seemed to have suddenly grown old. He lived on for two more years, then a fever came upon him and he took to his bed. Business acquaintances came to help him, but he only said to them, "When the right person comes, tell him, 'I gave to the Venetian Marco Polo the sage's stone.'"

"But what of your great wealth? You have no relatives. To whom do you wish to give all your wealth?"

With his last dying breath, the old merchant repeated, "When the right person comes, tell him, 'I gave to the Venetian Marco Polo the philosopher's stone.'"

His wealth was taken soon after by the government of Constantinople. The government buried him in style, and on his stone marker, had the words engraved, in Greek, and in Latin, and in Turkish, and in Arabic: "When the right person comes, tell him, 'I gave to the Venetian Marco Polo the philosopher's stone.'"

When the three Polos, Marco, Maffeo and old Nicolo, arrived home in Venice after twenty-five years in the Orient, their relatives did not recognize them. They had adopted the mode of dress and many of the habits of the Tartars among whom they had lived, and were taken for rough barbarians instead of cultivated Europeans. When Maffeo's wife finally agreed to admit the "filthy beggars" into her house and dress them in decent clothing, she could still scarcely believe it was her family, back at last. As the days wore on, however, she became used to them again, and exulted in the change her husband's wealth had made in their household.

One thing she could not understand was her husband's obsessive attachment to the old coat he had worn among the Tartars. He could now hire the finest tailors in all Venice to clothe him, and clothe him they did, like a prince; but he still kept his tattered skin coat by his bedside and examined it lovingly every night.

"You love that coat more than you do me!" she accused him petulantly. "Deep down in your heart, you wish you were back with the Tartars!"

"Nothing of the kind, my sweet," he would console her. "I'll never leave your side again."

But one day, Maffeo's nephew Marco came to the house to bid his uncle goodbye. The life of a burgher was too tame for him, Marco explained; He'd been on the road with his father and uncle since he was fifteen years old, and the wanderlust was in his blood.

Maffeo's wife was overcome with panic at this news. What if Maffeo should decide to accompany his nephew? What if he should leave her again? Quickly she seized the old skin coat at her husband's bedside and handed it to one of the beggars that now camped beside her door.

Back in the dining room, Marco was taking his leave. "I do not know when I will return to you, dear Maffeo; the war with Genoa makes the seas unsafe for any Venetian, and yet I feel a bit of me dies each day I stay here."

Maffeo shook his head. "The times for traveling are never propitious; one fears the Karaunas and Assassins in one place, the Genoese in another. But in Constantinople you were handed the sacred stone, an amulet, by the trader Stavros, which was said to have special powers. I have had it with me for safekeeping until you matured. It is now time; she will see to your safety – I would feel more confident if you took her with you."

With that he went into his bedchamber to fetch his coat, in the linings of which were hidden the riches of the Orient; but he found the coat gone. And upon hearing the story of its disappearance, Maffeo the Venetian screamed and wept and tore out his hair in handfuls.

Like a crazed man, he burst out of the house, wearing a cape of the finest velvet over his nightshirt, and carrying the first thing he could lay his hand on, which happened to be a small spinning wheel. A gondolier ferried the weeping man to the Bridge of the Rialto at the center of the city, where Maffeo, still clutching his spinning wheel, disembarked, sat down upon the bridge, and began to go through the motions of spinning. And as he worked the wheel, he sobbed,

"He will come, God willing; God willing, he will come!"

News of Maffeo's mental collapse spread like wildfire through Venice. The once-esteemed world traveler sat on the bridge for days, and during that time every citizen of Venice passed by to see him, shaking their heads in pity and wonder. Though Maffeo seemed to be oblivious to everything, he was not.

Finally, toward the end of the third day, the beggar to whom Maffeo's wife had given his coat chanced by the Bridge of Rialto, ostensibly to cross the canal, but actually to see the madman who was the talk of Venice. Immediately Maffeo ceased his lamentations and offered the beggar his velvet cape for the tattered skin coat. The beggar, wishing to appease the afflicted man as well as better his wardrobe, agreed. And Maffeo returned to his own home, completely restored to sanity.

That very evening he gave the small, shining Crystal to his nephew Marco Polo, who promised to guard the treasure with his life on his voyage across the sea.

Marco Polo set sail on what was to be his second voyage in 1296, bound from Venice across the Adriatic Sea. The Venetian had in his possession, along with the merchandise he planned to trade, a small clear Crystal given him as a good luck charm by his Uncle Maffeo. Venice at that time was engaged in a long and bloody war with Genoa over trading rights, and Genoese ships thronged the seas, looking for rival merchant ships to capture, plunder, and sink. The danger was so great that Venetian ships sailed in convoys for mutual protection.

Late at night, on the deck of a narrow galley, Marco fingered the lining of his plain wool jacket. His Crystal was unobtrusively stitched inside the lining; there was a legend attached to this amulet he knew, but he had never really believed what the trader Stavros had said. He let his mind wander over the possibilities. Regardless of legend, however, there was something about the feel of the stone, even through the coarse-nubbed wool, that filled his heart with peace. And peace, not stories, was what he needed out here on a sea teeming with enemy vessels.

With a last squeeze of his Crystal, Marco made his way across the heaving deck to his bed.

He was awakened at the barest crack of dawn by a shout. His eyes, like those of every man on deck, snapped instantly to the lookout on the mainmast top. The sailor on the mast was gesturing wildly toward the greying east, where against the horizon an ominous grouping of ships converged. Within moments all the passengers on the Venetian convoys were awake and in battle stations. It was light enough now to see that the vessels were Genoese ships.

Marco's hand found its way to the secret pocket of his jacket. Aside from a strange warmth emanating from the Crystal, he felt nothing: no peace, no comfort, no message. "Now, if ever…" he murmured to himself; but the stone was silent.

The Genoese advanced. Despite the valiant effort of the Venetian crews, there was nothing the heavy-laden merchant galleys could do to get out of the path of the swifter warships. As the distance between them diminished, volleys of arrows filled the air, and many Venetians lay dying on the decks; it was clear there was no hope of victory or escape. By noon the battle was over and the remaining Venetians, including the renowned adventurer Marco Polo, were on their way to Genoa as prisoners of war.

The defeated passengers and crew were driven up the narrow stone steps from Genoa's harbor to its rocky pitched streets. There the passengers of rank were separated from the common sailors and freemen, and conducted to the red granite prison at the Palazzo del Capitano del Populo. There Marco was left, anxious and humiliated, but glad to be alive and still in possession of Crystal.

He found his prison to be a former palace; the noble prisoners were free to roam from room to room, consorting with each other and complaining about the cramped conditions and bad food. But rather than banding together as brothers in a bad situation, the inmates tended to form associations according to their cities of origin, befriending those who came from their home district and reviling those who did not.

Disturbed by this, Marco took pains to befriend a former author from Pisa named Rustichello. Noting that every day Marco was besieged by the other prisoners for tales of his Eastern adventures, Rustichello suggested that they pass the time by turning Marco's stories into a book.

Marco demurred. "Friend, I have forgotten more than I remember. And the recollections that do come to mind are as motes in the sunlight, isolated in time, forming no pattern."

"That is of no consequence," Rustichello told him. "What is important is not the details, but the breadth and variety of the world, and how you lived among the most diverse men as a brother."

Still Marco protested, until at last he agreed to write his father in Venice to ask for the log of their travels; and because of his great reputation, he obtained permission from his gaolers to do so. But when the notes arrived, Marco found them too spare to be of much use. He advised Rustichello to abandon all thought of the project.

But one night, in the meanderings of mind just before sleep, a voice like the ringing of thumb over long-stemmed wine glass filled Marco's thoughts.

"Take pen in hand," sang the voice, "and write my song. I shall sing it all night long; take pen in hand and write my song."

The refrain echoed over and over in Marco's ears until at last he got up, lit a lamp, and began to write. In the morning he showed the results to Rustichello, who was amazed at the tide of memories that had flowed over his friend in the night.

"There was no way to capture it all," Marco said in wonder. "There were too many ideas for my pen to contain; every time I tried to figure out where a memory fit in time, it would be gone."

"Don't worry about the order," advised Rustichello. "We can organize your memories afterwards. Just listen to your Muse, and write what you remember."

So night after night, moon cycling into moon, the voice recalled and Marco wrote. At last he could contain his curiosity no longer.

"You are of me, but not me," he addressed the voice. Who then, are you?

"I am the Crystal you hold over your heart," she told him, "the one given to you by your Uncle Maffeo; the one you purchased from the trader Stavros for a king's ransom. You prayed on me as a charm to keep you safe from the Genoese, but that was not the will of Him who sent me; for if you had never come to the Palazzo, you would never have met Rustichello, and you would never have written how you lived in the service of the Kublai Khan, with all the people of the East as brothers."

And Marco knew this to be true, but never did he confide it to his dear Rustichello, who organized so carefully the memories Crystal sang.

At last, after three years, a truce was declared between Genoa and Venice, and all Venetian prisoners were set free. Marco bid goodbye to his dear friend Rustichello. "Were it possible for me to buy your freedom from the Genoese," the Venetian said, "I would do so. But all my goods have been taken from me, and it is only by the generosity of my captors that I am able to return to my home."

"Think nothing of it," said his friend. "Your love, and the inspiration of your story, have been reward enough."

"But I do have something to give you," Marco continued. With the edge of his thumbnail he slit the lining of his jacket, and Crystal, unseen all these years, emerged. "This Crystal has been my true inspiration. Since you are a poet, and will undoubtedly live to weave many more romances, I think it only right that she should work for you. I now tell you her story."

So with deep love and sorrow, the stone passed again from friend to friend, and Rustichello placed it in a small pouch over his heart. Crystal stayed in his family for generations, her story told and retold at Christmastime and at important family gatherings.

Genoa in the spring of 1456 was alive with gossip; Piero Medici, heir to the fabulously wealthy first family of Florence, was in town for the express purpose of spending his father's money.

It seemed that Cosimo, Piero's father, was taking advantage of the fleeting peace between the two republics to add Genoese art and jewelry to his already extensive collection. Even the smallest child in the city knew that Piero was the guest of Umberto Capozzi, the most prominent merchant in Genoa and himself a discerning collector of art.

Piero was welcomed into the Capozzi home and shown at once into Umberto's private chambers.

"I have acquired many fine pieces from the East," the Genoese commented, "as well as artifacts dating from ancient times, and no small cache of rare jewels. And of course I have commissioned many works from artists under my patronage. See here." And Umberto indicated, with a wave of his hand, an exquisite tempera Venus on the wall.

"Lovely, truly," murmured Piero approvingly. "I don't suppose she is ... for sale?"

"All beautiful women have their price," smiled Umberto. An amount was named and agreed upon. The bargaining continued over an authentic Etruscan bust, a room-sized Persian carpet, a French tapestry, and a Chinese silk.

At last Piero held up his hands. "Enough, enough. You have been more than generous. Let us now put business aside, and tomorrow we shall devote the remainder of my time in Genoa to pleasure."

Accordingly, Umberto clapped his hands, and a servant, who had been lurking in the shadows, was instructed to show Piero to the guest chambers.

As soon as they were alone in the hall, however, the servant asked the Florentine for leave to speak.

"My master has many beautiful things," he told Piero, "but I myself, a poor man, possess something of value as well." From an ancient pouch on a thong around his neck, the man produced a palm-sized shiny stone upon which sat tiny Crystal, and he extended it in his hand.

Piero took it and examined it carefully. "An extraordinarily tiny, perfect, clear stone, to be sure…but perhaps there is some story behind it?"

"Ah, the story is the thing!" exclaimed the servant eagerly. "I am the descendent of one Rustichello, a poet once imprisoned here in Genoa with the great Marco Polo. Polo himself was said to have given this stone to my great great-grandfather in thanks for his aid in writing his book of travels. There is a legend attached to the stone itself. My father said the stone tells stories – though it's never told any to me. My father told me this story, told him by his father, and so back to the poet, who was told the story by Marco Polo himself. Would you care to listen?"

Piero held his hand to his mouth to stifle a yawn, indicated he was tired and wished to sit down, upon which the servant directed them to an alcove where the gentleman sat down with his eyes half closed. The storyteller then repeated the whole tale as he had heard it many times, including the word that had gotten back to Marco Polo of the inscription on the tomb of the trader Stavros.

The story was long, but the storyteller did not falter, and Piero did not fall asleep; his eyes were open as if in a trance when the story concluded. The silence stretched out.

"A true philosopher's stone," laughed Piero at last, and he stood up and clapped the servant on the back. "A gold piece for your story and your stone, my good man! At least this will be a fine bauble for the amusement of my children."

He dropped the gold piece into the servant's palm, tucked the soft leather pouch into his own clothing, and retired to his chambers for the night.

"Mama, when will Papa come? Where is he?" The five young Medicis clamored noisily at their mother's skirts. Since dawn, when the messenger arrived announcing Piero's safe return to the gates of the city, his children had been wild with excitement. Their mother prepared to explain for the twentieth time.

"Your father has been to Genoa on a diplomatic mission, so naturally he has to report to your grandfather first. But if he is indeed in the city, as the messenger has told us, he will be home very soon."

As if by divine command, the door opened and the children fell with delight into their father's arms. The second-youngest boy, Lorenzo, began patting his father's shirt, looking for the sweet or trinket he knew would be there.

"All right, Lorenzo! Yes, children! Yes, I have brought you all something, as you will soon see!"

As if by magic, he produced a long silk ribbon for Maria, the eldest, who squealed with delight. Bianca and Nannina received little poppets of cloth, and the baby Guiliano received a stick of barley-sugar. Only seven-year-old Lorenzo, Piero's favorite, was confronted with a stern face and empty hands.

"You tease too much, Lorenzo," his father admonished him. "I was no more in the door than you were searching me for gifts. You are too greedy, and therefore. ..."

Seeing the boy's stricken face, Piero melted. "I cannot tease you, it is too cruel. Here." And into the boy's eager hands went the Crystal.

"What is it?" asked the boy. "Is it candy?"

"It is a Legend," said Piero impressively. "It was brought to Genoa by Marco Polo himself!"

"And you give this to a child?" asked the children's mother. She took the Crystal from Lorenzo's palm and gazed at it. "Piero, this is no gift for a child. When the boy is older, perhaps ... but mark my words, this is a stone of power. To mix it in with a small boy's aggies and trinkets would be sacrilege."

Acquiescing to his wife, Piero appeased the boy with a stick of barley-sugar like his brother's, and the children ran out to play.

"Is Lorenzo well?" Piero asked his wife after the children had gone. "When I laid my hand on his head a moment ago, he seemed feverish."

"He's been so anxious for your return," replied the lady, secreting Crystal in her bosom. "It's just the excitement."

But it was not excitement that brought the flush and fever to the child's face. That very night he came down with a fever so violent and strange that the servants whispered suspicions of plague. None of the doctors of the Medici household knew what to do for him, and it was commonly expected the boy would die.

On the evening of the second day, however, a stranger appeared at the Medici villa. He was shown into Piero's presence, where he introduced himself.

"I am Paolo dal Pozzo Toscanelli, born here in Florence but lately of Alexandria. It was there that I learned my art ... and I think I can help your son."

The young doctor was at once ushered into the sickroom. After examining the child carefully, he set to work with a mortar and pestle, grinding genuine pearls and precious oils into a poultice which he applied to the child's chest. Then he called for a chair to be placed next to the boy's bedside, and he sat by the bed until dawn. During the night the boy's fever broke, and in the morning he opened his eyes and asked for something to eat.

The child's parents were beside themselves with joy. "How can we repay you?" they asked the young doctor. "Our home, our riches – anything you ask for is yours."

"I ask for nothing," the doctor replied. "God has seen fit to heal the child through my art. That is reward enough for me."

But the Medicis were not satisfied. All at once the boy's mother remembered the stone she had placed next to her heart. She removed it and pressed it into the good doctor's hands.

"Take this, please," she said, "as a token of our gratitude. I know not what power this Crystal has, but I know it has some, as well as a long and noble history; and if anyone can harness such power for the greatest good, I know it will be you."

"Can you stay a while and listen to the story of this stone?" asked Piero. "The story was told me by a servant whose ancestor knew Marco Polo the adventurer quite intimately, but the story commences in Arabia many, many years ago."

"I have been up all night," said the good doctor. "If you will allow me to lie down and rest for a while, why, yes, I would certainly enjoy hearing the story."

So everyone – Piero's wife, the five children and the doctor on the couch – listened to the tale for the first time. When Piero at last finished, little Lorenzo said, "Thank you, Papa, for the bestest gift of all."

They all smiled; Doctor Toscanelli got up refreshed, thanked them profusely for their generosity and hospitality, and took Crystal back to his own home.

16

The Moment of Truth

The young man lay on the beach, face up in the evening sunset. His blue shirt was tattered to shreds, with a hint of black, as from burning. His dark pants with wide bottoms indicated a sea-faring lad. His feet were bare and swollen and pointed sunward. Tied to his belt at his right side was a pouch – a money-bag perhaps. Nearby was a long oar. The tall, muscular man was somewhat up on the beach, having lain there some hours – the tide was now out. Shreds of burnt skin were here and there on his arms. His hair was reddish blond, his long face freckled, with a sunburn starting on his normally pale skin; his nose long, his countenance sad and tired – the appearance of a bloodhound comes to mind.

An old retired fisherman was taking his evening walk on the beach when he spotted the lad. The body did not stir. The old man spotted the pouch, but saw the body was breathing. He bent down and slapped the sunburned face from behind. No movement other than the chest slowly rising and falling. The fisherman kneeled and carefully began to open the pouch. A hand reached over and held the pouch tightly. The fisherman walked quickly into town to get assistance.

The fire and acrid smoke from the tar and wood of the burning ship was clearing out of the young man's nose and lungs.

The ship had sunk and he was one of the few survivors, using the long oar as a life-raft as he swam ashore the two leagues,. He was the only survivor on this beach. It was August. Faint traces of meadowland and of sweet-scented flower blossoms began to subconsciously assail the nostrils of the lad, the fragrance coming on the westerly wind across the water toward the setting sun. [Even today, highly sophisticated scientific equipment is no match for the subtleties of perfumes and of wines to a well-trained, well-rested nose; and dogs are used to sniff out hidden unlawful drugs.] As with any man suspended between life and death, scenes and images from his young life began to flash before his mind's eye.

"Momma, why is Poppa so sad all the time?" "Dear, your father is having a hard time making a living, as is true for many families nowadays. It was not always thus. Your father used to be care-free and fun-loving, and that is why I married him. But know that on May 29, not yet two years after you were born, the devil Turks captured Constantinople and the Straits, and Pera also. Your father's trade was cut off. He tries other things, but they are not too successful as yet. When you get bigger, you will understand how he feels. For now, you must help him at the inn."

"Poppa, I don't want to be a wool-weaver. I like the sea. Some day I will be a sailor and buy and sell for a profit." "Son, why do you always want to do things out of your class? Your grandfather came down here from the mountain valleys and became a wool-weaver. I was apprenticed to the trade, and became very important in town – I was appointed 'Keeper of the Gate'. Why do you not follow in my footsteps?"

"Poppa, there is no future in it for me, or for you, either!"

"Oh, do not talk to your father like that. And on the friars' property yet. They may have heard you. Confess your sins this Sabbath."

"Hello, lad, waiting for a ship to come in?"

"No, I am just watching the ships. I would like to sail some day."

"You look like a strapping lad. Perhaps we could use another crew member. How old are you?"

"Thirteen, sir. My father has goods he would like to trade."

"Well, well. You are large for your age. Have you had any schooling?"

"At the sacristy I learn reading, writing and spelling, and the seafaring arts."

"Well, well. Well, come along. We will go see the Captain. If he likes you, perhaps he will take you on now and then."

"This is indeed a large ship."

"Large enough. The Roxana is a three master and requires many hands."

"Is the name of any significance?"

"The ship is named in memory of a beautiful woman of your country of Liguria who was kidnapped by Turkish pirates. She became a slave but was freed by the love of a prince who later became Sultan and who married her. Her tomb is in Constantinople – some call it Istanbul now."

"Dear Poppa. I write you from Chios. I am here some months and am financially rather well off as a sailor/merchant. I am enjoying my adventures. I am enclosing a bank draft. Momma has written me concerning your fortunes."

"We head for Flanders and England, all five of the ships in convoy out through the Straits and into the Atlantic.

"The cannon and firearms are for the pirates who frequent the waters"...

"Throw the pots of fire at the French pirates – we will triumph over Captain Casenove yet"...

"The ships are too close! The fire is spreading to ours! We are engulfed in flames! Holy Mary, Mother of God, save us!" The soldiers in full armor are jumping overboard to their watery grave – the fire is intense – do you want to burn or drown, young man? Over you go. Oh, the water is cold!

"The oar, the oar, grab the oar and save yourself!"

"How do you know so much about the Roxana and all, Sir?"

"I am Paolo dal Pozzo Toscanelli, a physician of Florence. I have studied much and have acquired a treasure from Venice, brought by Marco Polo the adventurer from Constantinople. This treasure came from the shores of Arabia a millennium ago, and enlarges a man's vision so that he knows things otherwise unknown. For instance, did you know that Cathay and Cipango lie not many days' sailing west of the

Canary Islands?"

[They talked many hours during the voyage to Chios.]

"My son, I have learned all I can from this stone. Take it and preserve it with your life, even as all the others have done; and when it has done for you all it can do, give it to another for safekeeping ... Here are some maps I have drawn up. The earth is round, like an orange, you see. ..."

The young man half awoke out of his delirium. The sun had set. A hum was heard from the pouch. "The oar, the oar, grab the oar and save yourself!" she cried again.

"Crystal, you saved my life. I must protect yours." The hum continued:

> Silently you breathe the sea.
> Do you smell the scent of tea
> Coming on the West Wind free
> Drifting so enticingly?
>
> Can it be from Cathay? No,
> India nor Cipango;
> Trust me when I tell you so.
> Gold and silver, spices, – Oh!
>
> Comes aplenty from yon shore
> If you but sail westward for
> Less than forty days my love.
> First you gain your treasure trove
>
> From the Spanish Queen – that dove.
> She, like you, trusts God above
> And will give your quest a shove:
> She will find what you're made of.
>
> Now you must rest up anon,
> Gain a wife and have a son.
> Time to wait ere job is done,
> Time to grow and have some fun.

Crystal Ball

The fisherman returned with help and they took the young man to their village. Not many months later he set sail from Lisbon on a convoy bound for England and Iceland. On the return voyage they stopped for provisions at Ireland, which had many monasteries. It was time to give Crystal a safe, new home. The young man arrived at the monastery near the harbor, and in halting Latin discussed his proposal. The monks, whose Celtic ancestors had been converted in the distant past, were receptive to the idea.

Before they parted, Crystal spoke to the young man. "I give you some last words, friend. Your fortune will be found through Spain. Your name in Spanish – Cristóbal – is very much like mine. As you have seen that I have two daughters, so you will have two sons; and you will have much adventure."

"May God keep you safe, Crystal Ball."

"And may Allah protect you in your quest, Cristóbal Colon, Cristoforo Colombo."

The Irish Monks, after one hundred years to the day (1574 A.D.) in which Columbus gave Crystal to them, decided to give the stone to the Cambridge University in England, which University had been founded in the 1200's A.D. by fellow monks from Ely, a town close by Cambridge. They reasoned that they had learned all they could from her, and it seemed somewhat sacrilegious to be speaking to a non-human creature (although they talked with God, another non-human Being), and perhaps she had much to offer in the way of science and the arts.

Now William Shakespeare left his home in Stratford-on-Avon in 1585 and traveled to Cambridge, where, under an assumed name (because he was wanted back in Stratford for a run-in with the law), he enrolled at the University and picked up considerable knowledge and polish, both there and at the inn where he waited table to pay for his quarters and his lessons. Browsing the Museum on a day off, he came across Crystal, sitting in her box along with all the other fulgurites in their boxes. He signed her out (under the assumed name) and kept her in his room to tell him stories to while away the time. His wife (six years his senior, and quite well off) and his children remained back in Stratford. Shakespeare graduated finally and moved to London in 1591, after returning Crystal to the Museum. The rest is history.

[Young William joined a passing band of players and minstrels and left Stratford. After a year or so the band stopped at Cambridge to pick up some new ideas before returning to London. William was heartily tired of the hackneyed, shopworn plays and, feeling that he could do much better writing himself, and discovering that Cambridge had a University where they had literary courses that would be very helpful, he enrolled. Now you know the story behind Shakespeare's "lost years."]

> Now my charms are all o'erthrown,
> And what strength I have's mine own,
> Which is most faint. Now, 'tis true,
> I must be here confin'd by you,
> Or sent to Naples. Let me not,
> Since I have my dukedom got
> And pardon'd the deceiver, dwell
> In this bare island by your spell;
> But release me from my bands
> With the help of your good hands.
> Gentle breath of yours my sails
> Must fill, or else my project fails,

Which was to please. Now I want
Spirits to enforce, art to enchant,
And my ending is despair,
Unless I be reliev'd by prayer,
Which pierces so that it assaults
Mercy itself and frees all faults.
As you from crimes would pardon'd be,
Let your indulgence set me *free.*

William Shakespeare
Epilogue to "The Tempest"

Sonnet LIX
If there be nothing new, but that which is
Hath been before, how are our brains beguil'd,
Which, labouring for invention, bear amiss
The second burthen of a former child!
O that record could with a backward look,
Even of five hundreth courses of the sun,
Show me your image in some antique book,
Since mind at first in character was done!
That I might see what the old world could say
To this composed wonder of your frame;
Whether we are mended, or whe'r better they,
Or whether revolution be the same.
O, sure I am the wits of former days
To subjects worse have given admiring praise.

Sonnet LXI
Is it thy will thy image should keep open
My heavy eyelids to the weary night?
Dost thou desire my slumbers should be broken
While shadows like to thee do mock my sight?
Is it thy spirit that thou send'st from thee
So far from home into my deeds to pry,
To find out shames and idle hours in me,
The scope and tenure of thy jealousy?
O, no! thy love, though much, is not so great.
It is my love that keeps mine eye awake;
Mine own true love that doth my rest defeat,
To play the watchman ever for thy sake.
For thee watch I whilst thou dost wake elsewhere,
From me far off, with others all too near.

Sonnet XLVI
Mine eyes and heart are at a mortal war
How to divide the conquest of thy sight;
Mine eye my heart thy picture's sight would bar,
My heart mine eye the freedom of that right.
My heart doth plead that thou in him dost lie
(A closet never pierc'd with crystal eyes);
But the defendant doth that plea deny
And says in him thy fair appearance lies.
To 'cide this title is impanelled
A quest of thoughts, all tenants to the heart,
And by their verdict is determined
The clear eye's moiety and the dear heart's part;
As thus – mine eye's due is thy outward part,
And my heart's right thy inward love of heart.

Sonnet XXXVIII
How can my Muse want subject to invent
While thou dost breathe, that pour'st into my verse
Thine own sweet argument, too excellent
For every vulgar paper to rehearse?
O, give thyself the thanks if ought in me
Worthy perusal stand against thy sight;
For who's so dumb that cannot write to thee,
When thou thyself dost give invention light?
Be thou the tenth Muse, ten times more in worth
Than those old nine which rhymers invocate;
And he that calls on thee, let him bring forth
Eternal numbers to outlive long date.
If my slight Muse do please these curious days,
The pain be mine, but thine shall be the praise.

Sonnet CIV
To me, fair friend, you never can be old,
For as you were when first your eye I eyed,
Such seems your beauty still. Three winters cold
Have from the forests shook three summers' pride,
Three beauteous springs to yellow autumn turn'd
In process of the seasons have I seen,
Three April perfumes in three hot Junes burn'd,
Since first I saw you fresh, which yet are green.
Ah! yet doth beauty, like a dial hand,
Steal from his figure and no pace perceived;
So your sweet hue, which me thinks still doth stand,
Hath motion and mine eye may be deceived:

For fear of which, hear this, thou, age unbred;
Ere you were born was beauty's summer dead.

William Shakespeare
(writing about Crystal Ball)

Now, lest we forget: John Robinson, pastor of a group of Separatists from Scrooby, England, had studied at Cambridge, graduating in 1596. He became aware of Shakespeare's plays when he visited London for relaxation from his studies. Considering this to be possibly the Devil's work, he attended one of the plays and met Shakespeare backstage.

"Prithy, do you have a moment, Sir?" asked the young man.

"Why, yes, how may I be of assistance?" said the playwright.

"Sir, I am a theology student at Cambridge and have heard of your plays and that they be the Devil's work. But having sat through this one, I find that your inspiration cannot come from Satan, but must be from another being, one attuned to truth, verity, justice and honor, virtue and kindness and beauty, almost as if one of the fairer sex is leading you onward. Do you wish to clear my befuddled mind so that I may go back to Cambridge and confront my professors and clear my conscience and relate to them what you will tell me?"

Shakespeare looked at the student for many moments, not saying a word. Then he spoke. "Young man, I believe you are serious, and I will tell you. Go back to Cambridge, and in the Museum ask the curator to take you to the alcove where the lightning stones are kept – it is very private and secluded, with good lighting and with a clear view of the curator's lamp when night falls and the Museum is dark. The stone you want to hold is labeled 'Arabian East Shore, circa 500 A.D.' It looks different from the others, having a palm-sized shell-like accretion below the tube, and a flat black ebony wood base for the shell, well made as if for a King or Sultan. Near the entrance to the tunnel is a tiny round being, the source of my inspiration. It is up to you how you will use her, and what she will say to you. Just be very careful with her and do not remove her from her couch, nor the couch from the Museum – she seeks her Mate. And God be with you."

John Robinson did as Shakespeare requested. He became pastor of the Scrooby congregation and was quite instrumental in directing their religious life. In 1608 the congregation left England and settled in Holland, which had considerable religious freedom and tolerance. Still wishing to remain Englishmen and to live on English soil, yet keep their freedom of worship (knowing that if they remained in Leyden their children would soon speak Dutch and become Dutchmen in fact and their English heritage would disappear), they decided to go to America, and set sail in the Mayflower in September 1620.

John Robinson remained in Holland, where he died in 1625, but the Pilgrims landed at Plymouth Rock and founded a successful colony, with the help of the English-speaking Indian, Samoset; then Massassoit, chief of the Wampanoag people, accompanied by the only known survivor of the Patuxet Indians who, before pestilence had wiped them out in 1617, lived near Plymouth and whose cleared fields the Pilgrims were using. This courageous nobleman, Squanto, showed them how and when to plant and when and where to fish, living with them as their friend and guide until his death in 1622.

17
The Professors

Having studied at Cambridge, and desiring some relaxation before beginning his Professorship, Isaac decided to travel; and travel he did. All throughout Europe, then into Smyrna and as far as Constantinople (Istanbul as it was now known to the Turks, who had taken it in 1453). It was at Constantinople, in 1658, in company with English merchants, that Isaac encountered the following notable event that would change the course of history.

At the market place, teeming with people from all over the Old World, was a small space cleared out and marked off. In this clearing was a large, sturdily built man, a wrestler, a braggart full of his own strength and desiring to show it off for the gain of a few coins. This man bragged of his strength and valor like a barker at a circus side-show, and declared he would fight with any man – he dared any man there to try him. Two others were taking bets from the crowd.

On this particular day nobody was taking the bait when the English gentlemen came upon the scene. Isaac watched for a time, then said to the braggart, "Why, if none else will try you, I will."

Now Isaac was a little man, but tough and wiry, afraid of no one. He fell upon the braggart and beat him up so severely, that this one decided it prudent if he end his career at once.

After they were cleaned off, the former wrestler came up to the young man and said, "You beat me fair and square. What would you have, as you did not wager?"

Young Isaac, fresh out of college, and in Constantinople on a lark, thought about this for a time, then said with a laugh, "I don't desire money. Just give me the philosopher's stone."

The fighter's mouth dropped. The two wager-takers froze in their tracks, then went up to a group of old men sunning themselves nearby. Quiet conversation ensued with much gesturing. Finally they returned and asked Isaac, "Are you a man of learning, perhaps, that you know of the philosopher's stone?"

"I am a Professor from Cambridge University in England, but I was just joking, really. Everyone seeks the philosopher's stone, but no one really expects to find it."

The wagermen went back to the elders. More talk, more gesturing. They returned. "We do not jest with things like that. You are undoubtedly the one. Come, we show you."

Isaac was taken aback. "Are you serious?" he asked.

"We do not jest with things like that."

So Isaac cajoled two of the other Englishmen to go with him. What is a vacation, after all, if there is no adventure?

Through the wide and the narrow streets of the city they went, past the gates, and out into the countryside, to an old church, now in some disrepair because of Moslem rule. Past the church and into the decrepit cemetery, where they went up to the ancient caretaker sleeping in the noonday sun.

"Show us the marker with the philosopher's stone," ordered one of the guides. The caretaker awoke with a start and blinked until he was wide awake.

"Eh?"

"Show us the marker with the philosopher's stone."

Slowly the old man got to his feet. Then he asked, "Which of you is the right one?"

"He is," the two guides said, pointing to Isaac.

The old man looked at Isaac long and thoughtfully. At last he said, "You look like you be the right one. Praise God, my work is almost done!"

He led them far back into the markers, toward the "old" part of the cemetery. At last he stopped before a huge marker, cleared away the vines and undergrowth, and said, "Read that."

Isaac said, "Why, the top half is inscribed in Latin and the bottom half in Greek, but they both say the same thing."

"Read it then," said the caretaker, hoping beyond hope that this truly was the right one, and his burden would be lifted.

"Why, it plainly says, 'When the right one comes, tell him that I, Stavros, the richest trader in all Christendom, have given to the Venetian Marco Polo the philosopher's stone.'" Isaac was amazed. "How can this be? What does it mean?"

"If you don't know what it means, perhaps you are not the right one," said the caretaker, crestfallen.

One of the merchants piped up, "Why, we'll just go to Venice and get it from old Marco." The other laughed out loud.

The thrill of the chase. On his return trip, Isaac stopped in Venice, presented himself at the Cathedral of Saint Mark and found out quickly that Marco Polo had indeed visited China and returned, but had lost the philosopher's stone in Genoa while he was held captive there. Isaac then went to Genoa, where he learned that Polo had written his book with the help of the poet Rustichello, who had become quite adept at his trade in later years, and that there were rumors that a lowly descendant of his had sold the stone for a pittance to a Piero Medici of Florence during a visit in Genoa. Aha! Going to Florence, Isaac went to the hall of records in the Palazzo Vecchio and soon found that the stone had been given to a certain physician in payment for curing the fever of young Lorenzo, the most famous of the Medicis – they would not jest with things like that. Looking up the physician in the records (as he was also a Florentine), Isaac found the addresses of his descendants who were doctors. Checking out the leads, he soon discovered that their notable forbear had given this particular item to a Christopher Columbus of Genoa while they were on a ship to the island of Chios, and so started this eccentric on his adventures. Ha! Back to Genoa.

The records of Columbus were quite sketchy and of no help. Isaac decided to go to Spain, to where Columbus was buried, and in Santo Domingo, in a confusion of old papers and records, he came upon this tidbit in some papers stored with his will:

"To whom it may concern, the stone I receive from Dr. Toscanelli I give to the monks where I disembark in Ireland." Further closer inspection of the archives revealed which monastery.

Isaac took a ship to Ireland, where he discovered, almost without asking, where they had shipped the stone. "The Cambridge Museum! The Philosopher's Stone at the Cambridge Museum! Under my very nose!"

The mission was a complete success. Isaac returned to Cambridge, where he was soon made Regius Professor of Greek and later Lucastian Professor of Mathematics. He had also been acting Professor of Geometry at Gresham College in London and was deputized for the Professor of Astronomy, also at Gresham. Not bad for thirty-three year old Isaac Barrow.

About this time, Barrow became involved with a twenty-one year old undergraduate. This young man had been shipped to Cambridge by his farming family when he was eighteen, as he might do fair in studies, while it was highly unlikely he would ever be a good farmer. The young man took his degree in 1665, the year of the Great Plague in London, followed by the Great Fire of 1666. Cambridge closed down in the fall of 1665 in response to the Plague, and staff and students were dispersed.

Barrow realized a genius in the young man and became his mentor. When Cambridge closed, Barrow gave Crystal to his protégé to assist him while he was at his home in Woolsthorpe. ("He is a very intelligent lad withal. There must be some way to bring his intelligence out in the open. Perhaps if I give him this stone from the Arabian Shore, saved for posterity by that young Bedouin lad ... ")

The eighteen months the young professor spent at his home before returning to Cambridge to teach were the most productive of his long career. Out of it came his "Principia" and his "Opticks." Perhaps Crystal had just a little to do with this. The next chapter brings out more of his character and personality.

I do not know what I may appear to the world; but to myself I seem to have been only like a boy, playing on the sea shore, and diverting myself, in now and then finding a smoother pebble [Crystal] or a prettier shell [Stone] than ordinary, whilst the great ocean [Arabian Sea] of truth lay all undiscovered before me.

Newton, a little before his death

18

White Cliffs with Love

The fog began to dissipate in the early morning hours as the ship methodically slipped through the waves along the coast, nearing the port at Dover, England, having left from Calais, France, last evening. It was a packet, carrying passengers, mail and light cargo, scheduled three times a week.

In her cabin Maria Leeuwenhoek tossed and turned fitfully, dreaming of the meeting with the young professor, Isaac Newton, in a few short hours. For months she had been corresponding with an intermediary about a project of the "utmost importance and secrecy" that only her father could fulfill.

From the beginning she was intrigued by the "cloak and dagger" adventure, prodding Anton into the undertaking of the assignment. Leeuwenhoek was reluctant about the whole affair, finding one excuse after another for ignoring the project until the intermediary had offered a small stipend to him (and possibly various posts requiring an able and trustworthy man, offering a living salary but requiring little of his time) while he worked on the secret endeavor. He was still hesitant about undertaking such a mysterious offer but finally gave in to Maria's enthusiasm.

Anton Leeuwenhoek, 35 years old, soon to be 36 come October, lay quietly in his bunk listening to his daughter's restlessness. He had gotten very little sleep himself during the night, but it had little to do with Maria's sense of adventure. He was still having doubts about this journey to Dover to meet the young professor. Anton was studying to be a surveyor, and hoped to pass the examination next year. Also, he had his gardens outside Delft to look after, and a cottage he rented out, with apple and cherry trees – the apples would be coming in; in his mind he could taste the cider already. His wife Barbara had died several years ago, along with two year old Philips, leaving him with the only one of their five children to survive childhood, the young woman sleeping across from him, his twelve year old daughter Maria.

He hoped he had not been too hasty agreeing to this meeting. All this secrecy bothered him ... what was it Maria had called it? An adventure of the cloak and dagger, or some such nonsense. Yet he did feel something of a spy sneaking off to a secret meeting with some young man he'd never met, let alone corresponded with, simply because he did not understand the English language and Maria had to do all the translations for both of them. Nor did he like the idea of traveling so far away from home on a wild goose chase. Still, the idea did spark his curiosity deep down, and in a few short hours he would be speaking with the young man through Maria. He settled back onto his pillow listening to Maria move quietly about the small cabin.

Maria quietly slipped from her bunk and tiptoed across the room to the trunk where she had left her clothes the night before. She wanted to light a candle, but did not want to wake her father. The journey from Delft had not been easy for him and she worried he would not be at his best for the meeting if she woke him so early with her excitement. All the way through the Netherlands, across Belgium, into France, where they left the port at Calais not too many hours ago in rough weather, and his stomach just now settling down. A two-hundred mile trip! She had the map with her, prepared by her teacher at school, the one who taught her English.

She had wanted them to make the entire journey by ship, from Rotterdam to London, which would have been easier for Mr. Newton, but her father would not hear of it – didn't trust boats, he said. She quickly dressed and carefully unlocked the door, slipping out of the cabin as silently as possible.

Maria had never been anywhere so far away from home as this and did not want to miss one tiny detail of the most mysterious journey. She found her way to the deck, holding her cloak tightly about her shoulders when the chill sea breeze hit her. The late summer air of 1668 was beginning to show signs of the approaching coolness of the autumn. She was glad they would be back home in Holland before the first frost painted the landscape in its array of colors. Leaning against the rail she closed her eyes briefly, wondering once again what the professor would look like. Would he be tall or short, thin or heavy? Would he have dark hair or golden like the sun? Would he be kind in nature or pompous, flaunting his superior knowledge to all who would listen, like some of the professors at school? She giggled and opened her eyes, thinking how her father would scoff at such thoughts. They were here for one reason, and one reason only: to meet with the professor and hopefully undertake his mysterious project.

Although she was intrigued with the project and the mysterious adventure it represented, she also looked at the practical side as a way for her father to earn some extra money to enable him to continue with his life and not have to worry so much about supporting her. Maria smiled when she thought of all the excuses he had made not to take this journey to the White Cliffs of Dover. "Ah, Papa, sometimes I must prod you to do something for your own good," she whispered in her native Dutch. "You will see, Papa, the journey will prove to be most fruitful."

She looked out over the waves rippling across the water. It was daybreak; light began to stream through the cloud cover, bathing the eastern shoreline in a hue of dusky rose.

Later that morning the ship docked in Dover harbor. Maria's brown eyes danced with joy at the wondrous sights before her. Anton stood nearby, smiling proudly at his daughter's pleasure in the new experiences. Her wide-eyed curiosity and obvious pleasure made the trip worthwhile even if nothing else did.

After disembarking, the two separated from most of the other passengers and slowly made their way up the steep trail to White Cliffs castle overlooking Dover. Maria marveled at the chalk cliffs that arose some three hundred feet.

"No wonder they named the castle White Cliffs! Is it not beautiful, Papa?"

"Harrumpf! You call this beautiful, my daughter?" Maria smiled, and they continued up the trail.

At the top of the winding path Maria and Anton stopped briefly to rest. The castle rose majestically before them against the backdrop of deep blue sky and snow white clouds. Soon they continued their trek towards the keep, both noting that very few people were about and none seemed to pay any attention to them whatsoever.

"What a waste of time," Anton muttered under his breath. "I knew we should not have come."

"Be patient, Papa," Maria cooed, "We have only just gotten here. Come, let us view the pretty sites while we wait for the professor."

"You call this pretty? Oh, daughter, you are but befuddled by the quest! Holland is beautiful, but this ..." He gestured distastefully at his surroundings.

Maria smiled and placed her hand on his arm. "Come, Papa, you are just tired from the long trip. Let us find this mysterious professor."

Leeuwenhoek patted his daughter's hand. "As you say, my child, I am tired ... yet I cannot help but feel this is all for naught. What ever possessed me to agree to this..."

Maria only smiled and hugged her father's arm tighter, then guided him around the wondrous castle before them. They walked the grounds for what seemed hours to Anton. Maria continued to marvel at the structure of the castle, at the immaculate grounds, and the fact that they were now on the white cliffs towering above the blue-green waters.

Nearly half an hour passed before Maria spotted a man walking around in a long black academician's robe. Her heart began to beat faster, hoping this was the mysterious professor they had come to meet. Excitedly Maria nudged her father and pointed to the man walking with his hands clasped behind his back, intently watching each step he took, while he recited a strange litany in conversational tones.

"Abraham, Isaac, Jacob, Joseph and the brothers. Abraham, Isaac, Jacob, Joseph and the brothers. Abraham, Isaac, Jacob, Joseph and the brothers." Over and over he repeated these words before disappearing around the castle. Leeuwenhoek and Maria stared after him, watching until he had disappeared. Maria's heart continued to tap dance across her chest as she turned to her father.

"That was the password, Papa! Come, we must catch him."

"Settle down, girl. There is no need to go running after him. If that is Professor Newton he will be back around the castle before we can catch him. I have no intention of playing cat and mouse around the castle."

"Yes, Papa, I suppose you are right. It is just that I am so anxious to meet this man after all the correspondence." Anton cocked an eyebrow in wonder at his daughter but said no more. They waited in silence for Newton to come back around.

"Abraham, Isaac, Jacob, Joseph and the brothers." The two started towards the man. "Professor Newton?" Maria asked shyly.

"Abraham, Isaac, Jacob, Jo ..." Newton stopped a few paces away from them, in mid-sentence. He slowly turned, unclasping his hands, letting them fall to his sides. "Yes? Were you speaking to me?"

"Are you Professor Newton?" Maria blushed prettily. In slow motion twenty-five year old Isaac raised his head, taking in every inch of her lovely body, until their eyes met. The moment their eyes met it was as if they were locked together, bonded, soul-to-soul.

Newton's senses were reeling. He tried to speak but found the words had scattered from his mind. Never in his life had the sight of a young woman so affected him. He was so totally taken aback by her unadorned beauty that he could do nothing but drink in her loveliness.

Slowly his eyes began to rove over her sweetness, gently caressing her from her long wavy light-brown hair to her dancing brown eyes to her snub nose and full pink lips sculptured so perfectly into her cherub face. How he wished he could take her into his arms this very moment and kiss those full lips and hold her lissome body. But what was he thinking? He had just met the woman ... no, girl, he corrected himself...yet all his senses screamed out that this woman was destined to be his.

He couldn't help himself, his eyes continued to rove down her body from her budding bosom ready to burst into womanhood to her slender waist and generous hips. Her young body was perfectly accented by the peasant dress she wore. Her shapely legs were bare from her calves to her tiny feet. She was a vision to behold. Cautiously his eyes met hers once again. There he could see she was fighting the same emotions.

His mind went back in time, to his earliest recollections. He never knew his father, a farmer who died three months before he was born. His mother was his whole life and he loved her dearly – she had raised him alone from a two pound premature infant (he was her Christmas present that year, she told him) until he was about three, when his stepfather banished him to live with his grandmother, barely a mile and a half away – he could see his mother from a distance whenever she was in the yard. How he had longed for his mother, Hannah. And how he hated his stepfather, the Reverend Barnabus Smith. He was allowed back in the family as a teenager to help with the farm when the Reverend died, but it was not the same. It could never be the same. He had no social graces, and he knew it, and he did not care. He had filled his mind with more lofty thoughts. Now this young woman stood in front of him, blushing and smiling, and he did not know what to do. It was quite unexpected. This girl in the pretty peasant dress and bare feet reminded him ever so much of his true love, Hannah.

Maria stood as if mesmerized by the young professor. How odd the sensations she was feeling just having laid eyes upon him. Yet she felt the moment their eyes had met that somehow their fates were entwined. To her Newton was nothing less than "Prince Charming" come to take her to his castle. She loved the devilish sparkle in his piercing blue eyes. She longed to run her fingers through his long abundant golden hair…it looked so silky. His lips seemed to beckon to her to be kissed. But what was she thinking? She had only just met the man, she continued to remind herself. But oh, how she was drawn to him! He was not the tall, dark knight most girls envisioned but rather slight in stature and even ascetic, but she liked what she saw. Ah, but he was the most "lovely" man she had ever met.

She thought back to when she was ten, just before her mother died, when she was given instruction in the ways of the world and of men, of how they will seduce you to get their way and then forget about you. She thought about all her brothers and sisters who were no more, and especially about her baby brother Philips, the only sibling she had ever known, and whom she had loved dearly. A tear fell from her eye onto her full red cheek. This man standing in front of her with his flowing blond hair reminded her ever so much of how she had envisioned her dear brother if he were still alive and grown to manhood. She did not know what to think. Had she loved her baby brother so much that she had wanted to marry him some day? And yet marriage to anyone was impossible – must she not take care of her poor father? There was no one else; she must take over for her mother.

Newton and Maria stood several feet apart simply staring at each other, neither one remembering that there was urgent business to take care of.

"Harrumpf!" Leeuwenhoek cleared his throat loudly, bringing both Maria and Newton back to reality. They both blushed violently, the red coloration rising from their toes to their scalps.

Maria recovered first and smiled impishly from Newton to her father. "Professor Newton, this is my father, Anton Leeuwenhoek. I am Maria, and I will be the interpreter, as my father does not understand English. I am the one who has written to you in my father's name." Again she blushed.

They stood for another minute gazing into each other's eyes, not moving, blushing even more, if that were possible.

"HARRUMPF!!!"

"Oh, Papa!" Maria finally looked toward her father. "Papa, say hello to Professor

Newton."

"Mr. Leeuwenhoek? A Mr. Christian Huygens of the Royal Society, a country-man of yours, recommended you as being the one who could help me," said Newton.

"Slower, please," pleaded Maria, "I am not so fluent in English."

"Are you good with your hands, Mr. Leeuwenhoek, are you a craftsman?"

"Yes, I passed the master's test in the cloth-workers' trade in six weeks. I trade in cloth and haberdashery."

"Hmmm. Then you are familiar with magnifying glasses?"

"Yes, of course."

"Are you honest and trustworthy, Mr. Leeuwenhoek?"

"Yes, of course."

"Can you keep a secret, Mr. Leeuwenhoek?"

Anton was silent for a while after Maria relayed this question. Then he said, "What is the nature of the secret you want me to keep?"

Newton replied, "I want you to make a replica of a very powerful magnifying glass for me, keeping the original intact if at all possible, and returning replica and original to me when you are finished. During all this time no one is to know you have the original and you are to give it to no one."

Anton thought about this for a long time, then he replied, "I know nothing about making powerful magnifying glasses. I have heard of blown glass beads being used for this purpose. Is this what you are after?"

"No, I want you to make it the same size as the original, of the same material if possible, and of as good a resolving power. Mr. Huygens has developed improved methods of grinding and polishing telescope lenses and can assist you in this area. You are to use the original and your handiwork to conduct scientific studies on tiny objects, both living and dead."

Anton's interest was aroused. "Tiny living objects? How tiny? Fleas are the smallest creatures there are."

"Not so," said Newton, "I have seen creatures so small that fleas appear as elephants in comparison."

Anton stood there with mouth open in utter disbelief. "Maria," he said, "this professor is mad. We should be going now."

"Papa!" exclaimed Maria, "Hear him out. If he shows you, will you believe, and will you take on the project?"

"Yes."

"Professor Newton," said Maria, "my father would like to see some proof of your last statement."

With that, Newton reached into his robe and from one of its pockets took out a small glass vial, removing from it a long splinter of wood – a toothpick, at the end of which was wedged a small flat glassine slip. From another pocket he took out a palm-sized stone with a flat black ebony base, upon which stone was perched a tiny crystal sphere near the entryway to a small tunnel at the top of the stone.

"This is the magnifier you are to make a replica of," said Newton, pointing with the toothpick to the tiny sphere. Anton's eyes grew wide. "I have crushed a flea onto the glassine slip at the end of the dagger. Can you see it?"

"Just barely," said Anton, growing uneasy.

"Look at it magnified, as I do," said Newton, and he showed Anton how to hold Crystal and where to hold the splinter to see the enlarged view.

"My God!" said Anton, when he finally got the flea into focus, "It looks as big as an elephant! And as clear!"

"Yes," said Newton.

Maria was delighted that her father was really interested. It was time her father stopped mourning her mother and really got interested in life again.

"May I have the dagger for a moment?" said Newton. Then he walked a hundred yards away to the base of the castle walls where a puddle of water lay, with vegetation and small frogs and green scum. He dipped the end of the toothpick into the murky water and returned to the couple, still standing there watching him intently. "Now look at your dead flea," said Newton, handing Anton the toothpick.

"Mmmm. Oh! The flea is alive! I see its skin crawling. No, wait. Those things are on the slip away from the flea as well. What are they? What is going on?"

"That is for you to find out," said Newton. "Will you make a replica, will you conduct scientific studies, and will you keep the original a secret and return it and your replica to me in due time, along with a note on your method of manufacture?"

"Yes, yes, oh, yes!" said Anton.

"And you, Maria, will you keep the secret as well as your father?" admonished Newton.

"Yes, Sir, yes I will," replied Maria. "I will write you letters keeping you informed of my father's progress."

The first whistle blew on the packet down below. "Here is the sheepskin pouch in which to keep the Stone," said Newton, and Anton put Crystal into the pouch and put it into his coat pocket, which he buttoned securely. Newton and Anton shook hands, a gentlemen's agreement. Maria and Anton turned to leave. "Maria!" The voice of a frightened child calling out in the dark. Maria turned back with a startled look in her brown eyes. Newton's face slowly turned bright red. He reached out his hands for her right hand, took it, and slowly lifted it to his lips. Then they parted.

Maria fairly ran down the path to the dock, tears streaming from her eyes. She had calmed down by the time her father arrived. Another half hour and the second and final warning whistle sounded. They boarded the ship with the other passengers. Another fifteen minutes and the ship was well out of the harbor. Maria looked up toward the top of the white cliffs and saw a tiny figure in a black robe and with golden hair. She waved. The figure waved back.

Maria!
I've just met a girl named Maria,
And suddenly that name
Will never be the same
To me.

Maria!
I've just kissed a girl named Maria,
And suddenly I've found
How wonderful a sound
Can be!

Maria!
Say it loud and there's music playing –
Say it soft and it's almost like praying –
Maria ....
I'll never stop saying
Maria!
The most beautiful sound
I ever heard –
Maria ... *

19

The Accident

Anton was very old. He knew his time on earth was short. But he was satisfied. His life's work was almost completed. He had seen and written about all sorts of tiny things that had never been seen before. Even these days he was approached by many who would not believe such things existed: if one did not see them, how could they exist?

The only thing remaining was to remove Crystal and her two daughters from the shell-shaped stone and send them all back to Newton along with a note on his procedures. Anton had planned for several years to send some of his better microscopes to the Royal Society and had already prepared the wooden box. It would be relatively easy to include inside two small separate boxes addressed specifically to Sir Isaac. No one else need see the separate items, and even if seen, no one else would know they had once been together – the philosopher's stone of the ancients.

One gloomy, gray, hot, dark, steamy day in July in his ninetieth year, Anton decided it was time for the operation. It was evening, after dinner; Maria had done the dishes; Maria, ever faithful to her father and to the Professor. Anton went to his workbench – the candlelight was very dim this evening ... or was it his eyes? He had thought about this for a long time, over many years. He could saw the spheres off if he had a small enough jeweler's saw and a large enough amount of patience, but it would be tricky, and he might scratch them. A brass rod and a hammer to crack them from the umbilicals holding them to the stone would be safer, he had decided at last, and tonight he had all the tools in readiness.

He took the long thin brass rod and the small hammer and tapped the larger of the spheres in the "cave." "CRACK." Down it tumbled through the back of the cave and onto the bench top. He put it into a small tin box, pressing it onto a piece of sticky beeswax inside. He took the long thin brass rod and the small hammer and tapped the smaller of the spheres in the cave. "crick". Down it tumbled through the back of the cave and onto the bench top. He put it into the box. He took the long thin brass rod and the small hammer and tapped Crystal. "(no sound)" He looked to see if he had missed. Crystal was nowhere to be seen. Oh, oh, now where did she go? He looked carefully all over his crowded workbench, but could not find her.

"Oh, well, I will find her in the morning light," he said as he got up from his chair. "Scree': The chair had never before made a noise like that when he slid it back from the workbench. SCREEEEEE. His heart started pounding. An inhuman cry, almost of some unearthly creature in pain.

SCREEEEEE

"Crystal! Crystal! (My God, what have I done?)" He took the candle and placed it down on the floor, then kneeled down, moving his head all around, until finally he saw the glint. Then another glint. Crystal had broken in two! Anton wet his finger and carefully picked up the pieces and put them into the box. There would be no sleep tonight. The chair leg had done its work well.

The next morning Anton carefully checked Crystal and found the two pieces without scratch, with a perfect plane surface of cleavage on each, one piece slightly larger than the other. He turned to his desk and sat a long while; then composed a lengthy note, folded it and put it in the box beside the piece of beeswax holding Crystal and her daughters. He put the lid on the box and sealed it, never to open it again. But he added a codicil to his will, that this box and the box with the separate "couch" go to Sir Isaac Newton at the Royal Society of London.

R.I.P.
Antoni van Leeuwenhoek
Oct 24, 1632 - Aug 26, 1723 A.D.

20

Six Letters

"Did you see the package that arrived today from Holland?" The secretary of the Royal Society in London was speaking to an associate.

"Yes. It was from Delft, from a Mrs. Maria Leeuwenhoek. I wonder what it could be."

"Aha, you have been here only a few years, George. Little wonder you are unfamiliar with the particulars of Anton Leeuwenhoek the microscopist and his companion, his unmarried daughter Maria, who handles all the correspondence, unless it be of a purely scientific nature. I had the chance to visit some years ago to see his exhibits and demonstrations. Quite remarkable! And Mr. Leeuwenhoek is quite remarkable also. Oh! *Was* remarkable, I should say, George. He died this past August and this package is the box of microscopes and mounted specimens he promised us. Ah, Maria. Beautiful Maria. Such a pleasant creature. I almost fell in love with her the few hours I was there. Talked so much about her when I got home that my wife became very jealous. I find that most everyone who visits the Leeuwenhoek household comes under her spell the same way."

"Really? Maybe I should visit her," replied the young man.

"Hardly necessary, George. She is much too old for you; more like your grand-mother by now, I should say. Ha!"

"Why, then, perhaps you should mention her to Sir Isaac I understand he has never married. Probably never found the right woman. Certainly she would be available now." George was playing matchmaker.

"I and everyone else mentioned her and many other beauties to Sir Isaac over the years. But he strongly disapproves – true bachelor to the core," said the secretary. "Bring the package here and let's open it and see what we have."

The package was opened. The wooden cabinet was opened and all the micro-scopes in their silver holders were soon displayed.

"Beautiful, is it not, George? Look, he has notes for each one and specimens with most. Amazing! Would you please start cataloging all this so it can be sent to the Museum? Also, check out the letter from Maria that accompanies it."

An hour or so passed, then George noticed something. "Sir, there are two boxes here addressed specifically to Sir Isaac Newton. What shall I do with them?"

"Why, just keep them for our next meeting on November 7, and I can present them to him personally. Is there any indication of what is in them?"

"Here it is," said the associate. "One box says 'Anton's paperweight', the other 'miscellaneous Arabian lenses'."

"Ah, very good. Mementos from another scientist. Sir Isaac will appreciate that."

Newton was a man of science, but he was also much more. John Maynard Keynes (1883-1946), who owned a great collection of Newton's manuscript notes, called him a magician, saying that a large section of his unpublished notes concerned transmutation, the philosopher's stone and the elixir of life. There are strange passag-es in his letters, such as "but it is plain to me by the fountain that I draw it from .... " The trunk full of papers Keynes purchased at auction was full of notes on alchemy, biblical prophecy, the reconstruction from Hebraic texts of the floor plan of me tem-ple of Jerusalem.

Newton was unsound on the doctrine of the Trinity, was a monotheist, a Unitari-an, a believer in one God. He believed that certain texts of the scriptures had been tampered with. His last published scientific writing contains a passage beginning, "All these things being considered, it seems probable to me, that God in the Begin-ning formed Matter in solid, massy, hard, impenetrable, moveable Particles ..."

As John Collins, a friend of his, noted: for many years, during the spring and fall, Newton would be about six weeks in his laboratory, the fire scarcely going out day or night. Collins could not fathom what the purpose was, but his pains, his diligence, made him think Newton aimed at something beyond the reach of human art and in-dustry.

What sort of alchemy was Newton up to in the spring and fall? At these times of the year, the air temperature is moderate and steady and is conducive to proper polishing with a pitch lap, for lenses and for prisms, for testing various combinations of crown and flint glass (or other transparent materials) to get the best achromatization. Also, at these times the humidity was neither too high nor too low and was best for manual labor. Plus, when melting glass in his furnace, and for annealing, the furnaces should stay hot for long periods.

Newton had made several "Newtonian" type reflecting telescopes early in his career, because his work on optics had convinced him that lenses would not bring different colors to a sharp focus, whereas mirrors would. Later, Newton began reconsidering. These spring and fall forays were for the express purpose of developing types of optical glass that, when paired, would be perfectly achromatic – no false color fringes around the star images in the night sky, "something beyond the reach of human art and industry."

"At last! Success at last! No color fringes!" Newton had finally made a set of small one-inch diameter lenses that focused perfectly sharp star images when a high power eyepiece was held about three and a half inches away.

"And now all we do is wait for Anton to return Crystal, and I will have a well-founded eighty power telescope, small enough to fit into my pocket." He made some more tests, then became discouraged. "Almost success. The flint lens will devitrify and cloud up in about two hundred and fifty years – in the summer of 1936 by my calculations. Oh, well, I guess I should be happy for that."

Newton grew weary of waiting for Anton to return Crystal, and made up a similar tiny lens around 1700, to see if he could prod Anton into action. [Quoting from the book Leeuwenhoek and his Little Animals] "In two anonymous publications which appeared in the *Phil. Trans.* in 1703 are to be found some amazingly good figures of free-living protozoa and bacteria and diatoms – confirming and amplifying many of Leeuwenhoek's findings and accompanied by a commentary, light-hearted and conversational, which shows nevertheless remarkable insight and ability. The pictures were far ahead of anything previously published and are sufficient alone to establish their draughtsman as Eldest Son of the Father of Protozoology. All these letters were really written by the same person, whose identity I have vainly endeavored to discover … I fear that 'The Gentleman in the Country' covered up his tracks on purpose – in order to remain anonymous forever."

Newton took the boxes to his laboratory and opened the one marked "miscellaneous Arabian lenses." That would be Crystal and her daughters. Yes, there they were. Oh, oh, there were four lenses instead of three. He looked closer at the shiny spots in the beeswax. With a sinking feeling in the pit of his stomach, he realized that Crystal was broken in two. "Oh, Crystal, what happened?" Then he noticed a letter folded up in the box. Opening it, he found it was from his friend Anton. The letter was in Dutch! Translating carefully, he finally had it all.

The Note

To the Honorable Isaac Newton, Pres.
Royal Society of London
Dear Friend Isaac,

For many years now people have been asking me for my secret in making my lenses. It is time to tell you.

The common practice here in Holland and elsewhere is to pick out the best drops from a batch of blown glass. I tried this and found not one in a thousand any good – even for the roughest work. It takes much longer to inspect for a so-so lens than to grind one properly to begin with.

I take a small glass rod, and with the flame pull it out into a thread. I put the thread back into the flame and produce a small bead. I crack off the umbilical and mount the bead on my lath spindle with sealing wax. I then press a small piece of lead onto the bead, making a hollow impression in the lead. I then take fine diamond dust from the diamond cutters and grind out the irregularities in the front of the bead, using the dust on the lead lap. Then I polish with a bar of sealing wax and jeweler's rouge. Then I turn the bead over and do the other side.

The short neck of the umbilical (the navel) keeps the bead properly aligned in the small hollow I have cut into the spindle. When all is done, I grind the edge of the bead so that the navel disappears. This flat or cylindrical surface I use to align the lens in the silver plates. The lens is heated and removed and cleaned in alcohol and tested.

A pleasant morning or afternoon suffices to make a lens. A small vial of diamond dust and a cupful of rouge and one small piece of lead have lasted for my lifetime. Thus you understand my saying "all my lenses are ground in the same grinding cup". I do not go below about 1/13 of an inch for the bead because the sealing wax does not easily hold the tiniest lenses. Also, the images, while larger, are not as sharp, so I see less.

I tried natural quartz crystals, as you requested many years ago, but soon rejected them for these reasons: (1) my flame will not soften the quartz, (2) it is extremely difficult to grind a piece into such a small size accurately enough to allow me to continue with my lead lap, and (3) even after making a satisfactory (in shape) lens, there is a double image, which image does strengthen or weaken depending upon the orientation of the lens (showing it to be part of the crystal's structure), which makes accurate observation impossible.

Each lens is inspected when finished. Fully half are thrown away. Others are used for rough work or for demonstrations. Three I use for fine work. The clarity of the glass varies greatly. My best work is done with the bead not of my manufacture, but from God, produced on the Arabian Shore by a stroke of lightning, and mounted upon a stone of vitreous sand, which stone you will now have in your possession.

From my desk I look out my window every day toward the tower of the New Church pointing its spire heavenward, and ask my Creator how I can make a lens as good as this Crystal Ball. The answer has not come as yet and I am near death. On the windowsill sat the stone upon which Crystal rested, used as a paperweight during the day for my notes – visitors have seen it, but not one has given it a second glance. And now misfortune has struck and Crystal is broken in two.

Perhaps Huygens and Ramsden can use her in their eyepiece experiments, and perhaps you can use her two daughters (the larger spheres) in your physics experiments. I have done with her what I can. The new crown/flint a-chroma pairs and the newer methods of optical glass manufacture promise good results in compound microscopes. Perhaps they will achieve what I did not. I tried my best. And I have kept my word.

No purpose will be served in keeping this note among your papers.

Please destroy it now.

As ever, your friend,

Antoni L. –

Newton took the note and put it in a box holding his a-chroma lens assembly. He would make Crystal up into a Ramsden-type eyepiece (of about 130 power) later and check her out. He dug out a bit of beeswax holding the two halves and put this into the box, also.

Then Newton opened the other box, the one marked "Anton's paperweight." Yes, there it was, stripped of life. Yet there was something that had bothered him ever since Barrow had given it to him just before the University closed from the Great Plague of 1665: the stone was so light, even with a heavy ebony base. Perhaps it was hollow. Newton took it to his laboratory and carefully warmed it. Slowly the base began to slide away. Further warming and the base was off. The inside was hollow. There in the cavity was a rolled-up tan parchment of extreme thinness. With much care the parchment was unrolled and flattened. Arabic! A flood of Arabic symbols covered the page, symbols tiny but carefully formed.

"It is best I learn Arabic soon," he said, then put the parchment in the box along with the a-chromatic lens assembly and Anton's note and Crystal. "Well, Crystal, you are finally with your Mate, and I will presently know your story."

Newton returned to the paperweight box to put the empty, dead stone back in. What was this? There was a letter folded neatly into the bottom of the box, almost as if the writer was afraid to have anyone read it. He opened it with trembling hands. It was from Maria!

Delft,
the 5th October 1723
New Style

My Dearest Isaac,

You will know by now of the death of my dear father this past August 26, as I respectfully requested of our pastor at that time, and you probably have read the letter I sent the Royal Society dated 4 October 1723 concerning the six and twenty magnifying glasses, which letter was sent along with them. If you read this you will have received the articles you requested so long ago of my father and so I may rest content to have fulfilled my father's wish, having not broken my promise.

Please forgive me, but I am much agitated over my father's death, and I do not know where to turn. I write to you as a sister and as a friend, and if I may be so bold, as something more.

I am well. I cannot complain of my health, but I find I am at loose ends without my father to take care of and without his mental stimulation. There was always the excitement of his experiments to fill my thoughts and of his many visitors and guests to keep me busy in the household. I cannot seem to fill the void his passing has left. Perhaps time is the only healer. Friends have pleaded with me to try my hand at charity work or volunteering in the hospital wards at least until my grief passes. What opinion have you?

Dearest Isaac, I have tried to control my passion but must now say what is in my heart. I am writing to tell you of my deepest em –

Dearest Isaac, I will start again. Do you remember our meeting at the White Cliffs? I will never forget. Never before, and never since, has anyone affected me so. I run away crying after you kiss my hand because I think you are teasing with a young girl's heart, and I have fallen deeply in love with you. A schoolgirl's crush, yes, but why does it not go away? When I then first write you of my father's progress, I tease you and ask for a lock of your golden hair – and you send it! Maybe you like me a little, too. Dearest Isaac, I have it with me now in a locket I wear next to my heart.

My darling Isaac, I have loved you since we first met by the castle. I know, I was just a child in your eyes, a mere girl of twelve, a baby; but when we met my heart became entwined with yours forever. I felt we had known each other all our lives.

The bright twinkle in your lovely eyes and solemn smile made my heart skip a beat the moment our eyes met. I always thought your serious manner was belied by that devilish twinkle that lay just beneath the surface. I think that piercing sparkle often fails to convey the profound genius who has looked through them into the secrets of the universe. You professed such wonderful humility blended with greatness, and still do, I must add. I look at all you have accomplished my dear, and I find it hard to believe you were once a struggling professor of mathematics, who once lectured to empty classrooms. I think it was only that no one understood your visions. In simple truth it was because your visions were far beyond the simple minds you associated with. They did not have the capacity to view the wider horizon of mystery. But you, my love, ah, how you've set the world on fire with your visions ... your mysteries of the world. Many are totally in awe with what you have accomplished but you are consumed with what remains to be done. My chest swells as I dare to think of all the horizons you've yet to discover.

In the wee hours of the night when I have difficulty sleeping I find myself gazing into the heavens above and wonder if you are doing the same. I know it sounds foolish, but I somehow feel close to you by watching the night sky, as if a single star could transcend the miles and time and convey my thoughts to you.

Over the years I have had the pleasure of seeing many drawings of you. I must say you have grown even more distinguished with age, Isaac. I have always admired your abundant long hair, even though now it is white. You may not be other women's ideal, but to me you are my Prince Charming.

The time we spent together at White Cliffs was far too short. Many a time I have wished I could have thought of some excuse to have prolonged the meeting. Had I been older and more experienced in such matters perhaps I could have thought of something. I was so enthralled with the timbre of your voice and the intense emotion with which you spoke. I could not have fallen more intensely in love with you that day had we wined and dined and danced and spent the night in each other's arms.

So many hours I spent in childish fantasies of what it would be like to hold, you, to kiss your lips. All I had to do was to conjure your sweet face and the world somehow seemed brighter, warmer and not so big and lonely.

My most vivid dream was of a warm summer afternoon in a wildflower field. You and I frolicked hand in hand. So intense was my dream I could almost smell the heavy scent of the wildflowers in full bloom and the warmth of the sun upon our faces. I reveled in the heady sensation of your arms wrapped around my body and your gentle but demanding kisses assaulting my lips...I felt so cold, so empty when I would awaken only to find it was just a dream.

I had such idyllic dreams of how it would be to spend our lives together, although I realized early on that marriage would be out of the question – you were married to your career, while I must take care of my father. A wife and family would have only stifled your genius and deprived the world of your wondrous discoveries. But the daydreams helped ease the empty place in my heart.

I blush even to this day when I conjure the intimate visions of you and I sharing the pleasures only a man and a woman can give to each other. In my mind you taught me to soar to the heavens you studied so diligently. Oh, Isaac how a dream so vivid could make my heart sing, make the blood in my veins hum with sweet rapture ....

But such are the dreams of youth. They are inescapable I suppose. Youth is spent in folly at times and we all do what we must to make life pass by light-heartedly. For me it was with vivid, loving dreams of the man I love ....

Dearest Isaac, you could never possibly know how just a single thought of you could brighten my day. Often while helping my father I have found myself indulging in one of the many fantasies I have cherished of us over the years. Hard as it is to admit, the dreams outlasted my youth and I still contemplate what a meeting with you would be like after all these years apart.

I wonder could we possibly find the happiness I have so often dreamed of, now that we have grown old. Would the flame still be there? It has been hidden for so long but, yes, I think we could find some happiness together even at this late date.

I know that what I felt at White Cliffs that morning was shared by you. You may not have wanted to admit it but I sensed you felt the electricity flow through our brief touch just as I did. My dearest, I will never forget that kiss, the way you gazed into my eyes and didn't want to release my hand. Your gallant kiss upon my hand has been branded into my memory forever. No man has ever made such a gallant gesture, other than my dear father. Isaac, my heart, how can one man have such a lasting effect on me when we only met once so very, very long ago? To me that says we (or I) have a love that transcends all else.

Sad as it is to admit, I have grown old, as have you, and I find myself wondering more and more why we never made an effort to see each other again. Our correspondence over the years was a joy in itself. I cherished each letter, even though it was business matters. I reread your letters until they began to fall apart. My, how I longed for just one of those letters to be filled with words of love from you.

I do not know why you never tried to see me again. I am sure you had your reasons. I have heard some speculation on the matter over the years, though. Isaac, I do so wish things could have been different for us.

Oh, I know I had my duties to my father and I would not trade a single minute of sharing his discoveries. His work kept my mind stimulated and granted me many opportunities I would not normally have had. It was rewarding to help him and run his household.

It is just that in my advanced age I have finally realized what was lacking in my life. And I wish to do something about it before my life fades away. I am old and lonely and long for the companionship of the only man I have ever truly loved. Isaac, there are still many years left between us to share, to grow older together.

We have spent all our lives apart, yet for me my love for you has continued to grow with each passing year. Let us not waste away any more time. We are old, my dearest, but there is still time to share. I do not fool myself thinking we could share the intense passion I dreamed of in my youth, but there is still flame enough to kindle a splendid fire.

I must admit I feel foolish writing this. Yet all that has welled up in my heart through the years needed to be said at long, long last. Please believe my words of love, Isaac, for I could not mean them more. Do not think this the ramblings of some crazy old woman, for I assure you they are not. I still love you, my dearest, and need you as I always have.

Please, my heart, write me as soon as you can. I need to be near, touch your face, hold you in my arms, at long last.

Forget me not ....

All my love,

Maria

It was early morning before Newton finished the letter, half in Dutch, half in English. He thought back in time to the lovely vision at the White Cliffs castle. "Oh, Maria! How I have loved you through the years. I thought you didn't like me at all and were just going through the motions to please your father. How would I have known you liked me when you ran away crying? ..." Taking pen in hand, he began writing to the woman of his dreams. The hours passed, the sun came up.

Finally, Newton stopped writing, his passion spent. "What am I doing? What nonsense! This is all foolishness. I am an old man; Maria is an old woman. She feels melancholy because her loving father died. I know just how she feels – I felt the same when my loving mother died. But the feelings will pass. They must pass."

Newton put the two letters together, interleaving the pages, then presented a corner to the still-burning candle. The love letters were soon reduced to ashes.

"Sir Isaac, I smell something burning. Is everything all right?" asked the housekeeper.

"All is well. I am just burning some old notes."

Newton snuffed the candle, took out another piece of paper, and wrote the following letter, which letter Maria kept close to her until her death many years later.

Dearest Maria,

It was most pleasant to receive your letter and the items I requested. You have kept your promise; you may rest content for you and your father.

I write to you as a friend, or as a brother to his sister, for I understand how grieved you are over your father's death, as I grieved over my mother's death so many years ago. I read your letter several times, and I composed a similar one for you, but grief makes us think of things we normally think naught of, and we should not take these letters too seriously. They will remain a secret with us alone – I gave the letters to the candle's flame.

May you have a long and happy life, and may we see each other again in Heaven.

Your friend and brother,

Is. Newt.

The next few weeks were spent in making Crystal up into a Ramsden-type eyepiece and checking her out with her Mate – the field was flatter and wider than with his other spherical test lens, the resolution still good at the center.

It was time to see if anything could be done with her daughters. He mounted them on long strings with sealing wax and attached the other ends of the strings to the ceiling, so that the quartz balls (one about 5 mm diameter, the other about 3 mm diameter) were touching each other at about eye level when he was seated at his workbench. He ran all sorts of static electricity experiments on them, while they were together at rest and while the strings were spaced varying distances apart at rest. He ran experiments during the day, at night, and in the pitch blackness of night after snuffing the candle, when all other sounds died away and he could hear his heart beat and the sound of his breathing. After his experiments were done, he attached the two daughters with sealing wax to near where Crystal was mounted on the tiny telescope with her Mate.

Newton then turned to the study of Arabic writing and at last translated the message contained on the parchment. He wrapped this parchment and Anton's note around the telescope tube and sealed it all together with sealing wax.

Finally, Newton returned to Cambridge, to the University Museum, and signed the stone back in, as was the custom when one was finished with the study of an article. But he also put in the tiny telescope, one and one quarter inch diameter by four inches long, with the notes still wrapped around it. On the box, labeled "Lightning Stone, Arabian East Shore, circa 500 A.D., he added the words "FRANKENSTONE (for it came by way of the Franks)". Under this he added "Lightning = Electricity?" And he put a line through the 500 A.D. and added "3:26 AM, April 6, 523 A.D., New Style."

Newton with his prism and silent face
The marble index of a mind for ever
Voyaging through strange seas of thought alone.
Alone.

William Wordsworth
writing of Newton's statue
at Trinity College

ACT III

The Captain of the Caucasus

21
Thunder and Lightning

Donner und Blitzen, donner und blitzen. All night long there was thunder and lightning on the dry sandy shore of the Black Sea. The sheep were restless and the shepherds moved about carefully, comforting their charges. Thor was busy tonight hurling his bolts.

Greeks were they from the Dardanelles, and only three. Another flash and they saw a stranger walking along the shore. "Ho, there, approach and make yourself known!" they said in Turkish.

"A wanderer am I, from the Caucasus Mountains to the north. A scientist, an observer of nature and of mankind. And you?"

"We are Alexander, Pericles and Socrates, Greek shepherds. We are from beyond Constantinople toward the setting sun; the Empire of the World, where all knowledge is known. We seek quieter pastures. We too are interested in science and astrology. Could you give us an explanation for this strange weather, perhaps?"

The wanderer replied, "Nay, not tonight. My mind is set on discovering a stone wherewith I can magnify my sight and see things yet hidden to mere mortal."

Near daybreak the storm moved away across the water and the four of them stood watching the display. Suddenly a thunderbolt, mightier even than any of the others, hissed and crackled and exploded in their midst. All fell back. All was silent.

When the rosy hued dawn came upon the scene, the wanderer shook himself, but found himself sore and aching – and paralyzed. The sun was well up before he could arise and look about. All around was a scene of desolation – sheep and shepherds, all dead, not one alive save himself. Around him the sand was glazed, and at his feet was a thick crust of shimmering material, still warm. He looked closer into the cloudy mass and began to see visions of things past and things yet to come, visions becoming and enticing, yet still hazy.

"I must be away from here, else I go mad," said the wanderer aloud. But first he dug a shallow grave for the shepherds and put dirt and stones over them. On top he placed the shimmering translucent crust, for a cross.

"Dear Lord, I thank Thee for Thy protection from this terrible night. Leadest me on in my quest. Thy will be done."

Search on 'til thy quest be fulfilled,
Herr Kapitan Niemand!

22
Spatafora the Trader

Constantinople in 1660 was a bustling cosmopolitan trade center, the hub of the Ottoman Empire. Men of many different backgrounds – Arab and Jew, Italian and Frenchman, Greek and Turk – met and did business in the cacophony of its crowded streets. Never before exposed to so many people and to such a multiplicity of unfamiliar dialect, I was awed, and a little frightened. It took me several days of wandering the streets to get my bearings. I had come here because of the legend, because Constantinople is where the stone would be.

On the third day, as I stood in the bazaar eating a lunch of bread and cheese, my ears caught a welcome sound: a conversation in my native Georgian tongue. Quickly I sought out the speakers.

The younger was a mere boy of eleven or twelve, dark-haired and dark-skinned, bent nearly double under an impossible pile of rolled carpets. The older speaker, an immensely fat man in expensive clothing, berated the boy loudly in a Greek accent.

"Vadze! You dolt! After you have dragged these fine rugs through the dust from one end of the city to the other, how much do you think they will fetch in the marketplace? Stupid boy! I would be better off selling you!"

"I am sorry, Spatafora. It is just that they are so very awkward."

"No more so than you!" The fat man cuffed the boy on the side of the head, causing one of the rugs to fall from his arms and unroll at my feet.

"Please, let me help you," I offered, re-rolling the rug and handing it to the man called Spatafora, who took it unwillingly, allowing one end of the roll to rest on the ground.

"I hope you don't expect payment now," the fat man said archly.

"Of course not."

"You must be new here. Everyone else expects payment for providing a breeze." The older man sized me up and down, then turned back to his servant. "Do you think you can manage your job now, or shall I get rid of you and employ this vagabond? He looks much more competent than you."

"Yes, sir. I mean, no, sir," stammered the confused boy, and he left at a trot to Heaven knows where.

You notice," Spatafora said, turning back to me, "how they hop to it when you put a little fear into them."

I did not reply, and Spatafora began shifting his huge bulk down the street, the carpet roll wedged under his arm.

"If you decide you need a job," he called over his shoulder, "look for Spatafora the Trader!"

A spark flared in my brain, and I ran to catch up with the man. "You are a trader? As in – precious goods from the East, and from Arabia?"

"No, manure from my father's farm," replied the trader sarcastically. "I, Spatafora, am the richest trader in Constantinople – or I soon will be!"

"Have you, in your travels, ever heard the legend of a certain Stone?" I asked hopefully.

Spatafora's tiny eyes narrowed into folds of fat. "I have dealt in many stones. "

"This one is the stone whereby men may enlarge their vision."

Spatafora's eyes widened; he sucked in his breath. [Had his arch competitor really foreseen the future? Was this young Georgian the answer to his dreams? An Englishman had come, idly asking about the stone, not two years before, but clearly he was not the right one.] "I know the stone you mean. And I know where it is. But such information does not come cheap."

"I have no money – but I am willing to work," I said.

The trader cracked a crafty smile. "I am the only one who knows where it is. Twenty years' labor, and I will direct you to the stone. What is twenty years to a Georgian?"

"The same as it is to a Greek."

"I think not. But if the stone is not all that important to you …" and Spatafora turned to resume his trek.

"Twenty years. You have my word. But you must keep the Georgian boy also, and not cast him into the streets because you have me." I could wait twenty years for my love.

Spatafora cast a contemptuous look at the small form in the distance ahead, still laboring under his bundle of rugs. "As you say. But you had better be worth your feed, and his, too! What is your name?"

"Abdullah Bereshni Constantine Dimitri Aeschylus Frankenstone." The trader burst out laughing. "And where did you get such a ridiculous title? I will call you Constantine. That is easy for me to remember."

Pointedly he gave me the carpet under his arm, and indicated the way to his destination, which was his shop across the Bosporus on the western side of the city. We caught up with the boy at the waterfront, waiting for a ferryboat.

The years in Spatafora's service were hard. The boy Vadze and I lived and slept in the storeroom of the trader's tiny shop in the Greek quarter of the city, as our main function was to protect the trader's wares against damage or theft. Vadze respected me from the first, less for my seniority than for the fact that Spatafora never beat me, although the boy and I shared equally in hunger, cold, sore muscles, and lack of sleep. In the early days Spatafora did not take us on his trading missions, and we were left, occasionally for months at a time, to manage the shop and turn a profit. Here we were at a considerable disadvantage, knowing no Latin or Greek and only pidgin French, as the language barrier made us unable to bargain profitably with the Europeans. They were not about to teach us the nuances of their tongues, only to pay royally for the privilege.

Upon his return from a particularly lengthy trip, Spatafora found that we had undersold many valuable items in his absence. He cursed me roundly, but Vadze he beat so brutally I feared the boy would die. Vadze never did entirely recover his hearing, but I am sure he would not have survived at all had it not been for my ministrations, and the incident brought us even closer together.

In the spring of Vadze's twentieth year, the Sultan held a vast festival in the Hippodrome, and all work was suspended for the two-week duration. The entire city turned into a carnival, with no expense spared. In the center of the Hippodrome a huge pavilion was erected for the Sultan, canopied with gold and carpeted with the most precious of rugs, and all around this pavilion were pitched the priceless silk tents of foreign princes felled by the Sultan's might. The streets of the city were thronged with people watching entertainment of all kinds – dancers, musicians, jugglers, clowns, acrobats and minstrels. Out of the Sultan's largess, sherbet and julep were distributed to the crowds. In this atmosphere of jubilant chaos, Vadze and I managed to slip away from the shop for a moment, and in the anonymity of the streets he drew me aside for a confidence.

"I am leaving Spatafora," he told me. "No! Don't speak. The time will never be better; the old man won't be looking for me during the holiday; and so many people are pouring in and out of the city that I will never be spotted. But cover for me as long as you can – I want to be two day's journey from Constantinople before I am missed."

"My heart goes with you," I answered; "you have not had an easy life. But be careful. Spatafora will kill you if he ever lays eyes on you again."

"He will kill me if I stay here," said Vadze. "God speed."

He blended invisibly into the crowd, and that was the last I ever saw of my friend.

The sixth night of the festival, I presented Spatafora with the unlikely suggestion that Vadze was currying the favor of wealthy travelers, who would return with him the next day or so to examine Spatafora's wares. But when a full week of the festival had gone by and the boy had not returned, Spatafora confronted me furiously.

"It would appear he has met with some adversity," I replied, not meeting his eyes.

"It appears he has met with some adversity?" shrieked the trader.

"Lying bastard! The ungrateful wretch has run away, and you no doubt helped him do it!"

"And what if I did?" I cried, abandoning all discretion. "I have known him not even ten years, and in that time you have broken his nose, cracked his skull, and ruined his hearing. Last year in the middle of winter you threw slops on him and made him sleep soaking wet on the doorstep! Good God, Spatafora, if he stayed with you much longer there would be nothing left to beat!"

"If it's so bad with old Spatafora, why don't you split as well?"

"You know why."

The old man grinned viciously. "You haven't forgotten – that's good. Since your memory is so sharp, remember also you owe me eleven more years of service."

"And you, Spatafora, remember you owe me information about a certain Stone," I replied vehemently.

"Never fear – when your indenture is up, I'll lead you to it myself," said the fat man in honeyed tones.

After Vadze's defection, however, the demands upon me became even greater. I half expected Spatafora to pick up another orphaned street urchin to do the fetching, carrying, packing and unpacking, but he never did; and now I had to assume Vadze's job as well as my own. My only consolation was that the twenty years' apprenticeship was dwindling down, and at last, at long last, I would have the Stone of the legend, who would tell me where to find my love.

Unfortunately, less than a month before the agreement was to be fulfilled the strain Spatafora's gluttony placed on his heart became too great. He collapsed at the dinner table, and for a fortnight as he hovered near death, I was his only attendant. I found myself arched over his body far into the night, straining to make words out of his irregular breathings. The Greek's lips trembled often in his last days – a little spittle would pool in the corners of his mouth, but no words came out. If in fact he ever really knew the whereabouts of the stone whereby men may enlarge their vision, I finally realized I would never learn it from him.

The wily old trader died a week before the twenty-year apprenticeship was up, having never told me where I should look for the Stone. I was beside myself with grief and misgivings. On the day of the completion of the twenty years, I went to the graveyard to look at the trader's huge stone marker. On it (as I had been told, not knowing the writing) was engraved in Greek and Latin for all the world to see: "I, Spatafora the Greek, by my own hand and by my own skill, am now the greatest trader in all Christendom."

The bent, wizened graveyard attendant shuffled up to me. "Was he your friend?" he said in a dialect I could understand.

"No – my employer these past twenty years. He promised me that after twenty years of service he would lead me to that which I am seeking. But he died before it would be accomplished, and now I am beside myself with grief and misgivings."

"What is it you are seeking?"

And I answered, "I seek the stone whereby men may enlarge their vision."

I could see a glimmer of long-forgotten knowledge creeping into the old man's head, and after some thought to arrive at the proper phrase, he said, "Perhaps you are looking for the Philosopher's Stone?"

"Philosopher? What is that?" I asked, bewildered.

"The Bishop will know, but he is away on a trip and will return in a fortnight. You appear foreign. Do you have some Turkish blood in you, perhaps?"

"My mother was Turkish, a beautiful Turkish gypsy." I stopped, thinking back upon the event twenty years ago that started me on my journey. When I could control my emotions, I added, "She died giving me birth."

"Ah, I see!"

"My father was a mountain man of Georgia and had Arabic blood." Again I choked up. That event must be put out of mind.

I could see the wheels churning in the old man's head. "Come with me," he said.

We came to an old weed-infested part of the cemetery, neglected for hundreds of years. The old man went up to a large stone and cleared away the brush. "Read that," he said.

"The writing is foreign to me."

He grunted, then with a look of superiority, said, "My family has tended this graveyard for hundreds of years. When I die my son will take over; all from the largesse of the one buried here. My father showed this marker to the right one twenty odd years ago, and it was presumed that no one else would be coming. The right one had no problem reading it. The inscriptions are in Greek and in Latin, and I am told they say the following: 'When the right one comes, tell him that I, Stavros, the richest trader in all Christendom, have given to the Venetian Marco Polo the Philosopher's Stone.' And I am also told that the inscriptions on the other side are in Arabic and Turkish, and say the same."

The dark mood was still with me; I had all the time in the world ... Why not? "I can read somewhat of Arabic and Turkish. Let me see."

The attendant went around back to where me brambles and vines had overgrown everything, and began laboriously cleaning off the other side of the marker. I decided to help. After an hour it was cleared and I touched the inscriptions. "Yes, here is Arabic: 'When the right one comes, tell him that Stavros, richest of the infidels, gave to the European Marco Polo the stone whereby men may gain knowledge.' And Turkish: 'When the right one comes, tell him that Stavros, richest of the Greeks, gave to Marco Polo, Western trader from the city in water, the stone whereby men may enlarge their vision.'"

I felt my heart leap with joy. The answer to my quest! All I had to do was to find Marco Polo or his descendants. I cleaned myself off and prepared to leave. "Venice is to the west?"

The attendant looked at me questioningly and said, "Yes, but do you not wish to wait until the Bishop comes? He will know where to direct you and whom you must see."

"No," I said, "Once I get to Venice I should have no trouble. Everyone in Venice no doubt knows of the famous Marco Polo. I will visit a large church there and the Bishop can give me the particulars. Goodbye and God bless you."

"And may God be with you, my son," said the old man.

I then extended to him the customary Georgian phrase of greeting, and of parting: "May you live three hundred years!"

23

The Man in the Iron Mask

Constantine left for Venice on the next boat, taking advantage of the time on board ship to acquire excellent Latin from a French priest returning from the Holy Land. The ship docked in Venice in the spring of 1680, and Constantine at once set out to find Marco Polo. The French priest had not known, but thought that almost anyone asked in the streets of Venice could direct him to the proper location. He was greatly disturbed to learn that the Polo brothers had died many years in the past and no one knew of any descendants of their family still living in Italy. It was thought that the last Venetian of that name had settled in Paris and married there, some sixty or seventy years ago.

Not wishing to lose the trail so easily, Constantine decided to do what he should have done in the first place – go to a large church where records would be kept and inquire of the Bishop the whereabouts of Marco Polo or his descendants. To the Cathedral of Saint Mark he went, up the steps and into the imposing structure, a youthful man of forty-four, with long unkempt hair, dirty and unshaven from his trip, his clothes old and tattered, reeking from a scarcity of soap and water, with scarcely a silver coin to his name.

Coming to the first priest he saw, he said in impeccable Latin, "May I speak with the Bishop, please?" The priest shook his head and turned away. The same thing happened with the second black-frocked man he spoke to. This one, however, went up to another in expensive robes and pointed to Constantine. A lively discussion ensued. The robed man raised his eyes to Heaven and then went up to Constantine and spoke in Latin.

"I am Father Greggio. May I help you?"

"Sir, I wish to speak to the Bishop concerning the whereabouts of the famous Marco Polo of this fair city, or of his descendants."

"And what is the nature of your visit?" said the Father. "I seek the Philosopher's Stone, taken by Mr. Polo in Constantinople."

Father Greggio again raised his eyes to Heaven and then said, "I believe I can help you. There was an English gentleman here about twenty years ago with the same mission. Whom have I the honor of addressing? Please ... take a seat."

"My name is Constantine ... Abdullah Bereshni Constantine. I am a scion of Hasan, the great leader of world renown – the 'Man of the Mountain'; I am of the Mendeleev clan – I am Captain O'Mendeleev's son."

"You are then Mr. O'Mendeleev?"

"Indeed not. In our tribe the children are named by the mother. My mother was my father's favorite, and she named me on her deathbed at my birth – Petrach Ivon Pauli Abdullah Bereshni Constantine Dimitri Aeschylus Frankenstone. She believed that I had a manifest destiny that would be found in my name. She was a gypsy beauty from the South, in Turkey, while my father was a mountain man of Georgia to the North. Her ancestors came from India and China, while my father told me legends going back many generations, of his ancestors migrating out of Africa, where the sun had darkened their skin. But most of us from the Caucasus now have fair skin. And my mother told my father legends of her ancestors from China whose ancestors had migrated over a small bridge of land to an immense land with a mighty backbone that stretched from the North where the sun sets not, to the South where the sun sets not; some returning many generations later by boat, as the land bridge had disappeared by then. But whether these legends be true or not I do not know."

"You mentioned your mother was your father's favorite. Did each of his wives then die young?" asked the prelate.

"No, my father had three wives and many children and we all got along very well together. My mother had two daughters and three sons before she gave her life that I might live."

"A man may have only one wife – the Church does not allow more. Were you born out of wedlock, perhaps?"

"There is no way a man can have a child lest he wed his wife – I do not understand your strange sayings. The Holy Scripture says even King David and King Solomon had many wives and many children."

"That was in olden times when it was still acceptable to God. Our Lord and Savior said lest a couple be joined in the Church with the proper religious ceremony that their marriage would be null and void and the child of the union would be a bastard. Sir, you are a bastard and your mother was a bitch!"

"Well, then, brother, our Savior was also a bastard, for he was conceived out of wedlock, and his mother was a bitch."

"Do not call me brother! I am no brother of yours. I am Father Greggio, and you will address me in that most respected term, as I am a most religious man, praying to the Virgin and to the Saints unceasingly; and you speak blasphemy."

"I am sorry, Father Greggio, for I thought you were of the same religion as I, a Catholic, a Christian. For Christians follow their Lord, whose prayer begins 'Our Father, Who art ...' So that all Christians are brothers and sisters. Our Lord said to call no man Father, but the Father in Heaven, and he said to pray directly to the Father and not to our brothers and sisters. So truly I am sorry if I offended you. Of what religious persuasion are you then – Buddhist, Confucian, Hindu, Islam, Shinto, Sikh?"

"I am of the true religion, the Holy Roman Catholic Church, and we know that our Church is true, for our Most Holy Father in Rome has said so, and he speaks the Truth. While you speak heresy, and are doomed to eternal damnation, even as poor Mr. Galileo, who through error and Satan's control believed the Earth moves around the Sun, while it plainly says in the Scriptures, as our Holy Father the Pope asserts, that the Earth is steadfast and is the center of creation – any fool can see that the Sun goes around the Earth. But his soul is now saved, for he has recanted of his heresy. Now lest you ask forgiveness of your blasphemy and pay indulgences, your soul also will be in eternal torment. We have the rack to assist our poor sheep in saving their souls – would you care to try it? It will be for your own good."

"You have a very strange religion, where you send your brothers and sisters to hell to keep them from going there by themselves. Different people are allergic to different substances and may become addicted, and thus we have different religions. I myself am allergic to opium and to yak milk and to some mushrooms, even as Moses was allergic to pork and to shellfish. But my Savior was not allergic to any local substances and had to endure a forty day fast nigh unto death to receive his religious experience. So allow me a smile when you say you have the only true religion."

"Blasphemer! Heretic! Infidel! Bastard! How dare you speak so about our God and about the Mother of our God! For they are Holy and exalted beyond all mortal comprehension, and they will strike you dead for such blasphemy! "

"When your servant calls out to you and wakes you and tells you your house is on fire, do you laugh at him and say 'I will wait till the Pope comes by and tells me, for I cannot believe one so unworthy as you?' Who then would be your Savior?"

"Lies, lies, lies! Away with you, and never darken the doorstep of this sacred land again!"

And from that time on for many years the young man would not reply when a new acquaintance would ask his name, other man to say, "My name is Frankenstone."

There was no other lead to follow; Constantine hopefully set off, across the Alps to France. By the time the young Georgian reached Paris, he was out of money. The first thing to be done, therefore, was to find a means of supporting himself, and then a place to live. A friendly innkeeper agreed to take him on as a stable boy in return for room and board. This innkeeper, whose name was Boulanger, also proved to be an excellent source of information regarding his native city.

ILLUSTRATION

animal-killing religion of the Veda and set forth a plan—"the eight-fold way"—by which individuals could achieve nirvana, or deliver-ance from the cycle of reincarnation and its pain and frustration. Calling for both mental and physical discipline, the eightfold way includes such ethical precepts as abstention from lying, lusting, tale-bearing, killing of animals or people, stealing, or engaging in an occupation that brings harm to others. Good deeds combined with deep meditation advance one toward nirvana in this or the next life, bad deeds plus bad thoughts put one further away.

Both Jainism and Buddhism were originally propagated by the cloning of monastic communities, but Buddhist monasteries were more appealing than the Jains' because they did not require the self-inflicted hardships and physical suffering that Mahavira demanded. What Buddha advocated for his disciples was the "middle way" between a life devoted to the futile pleasure of the Vedas and the equally futile self-mortification of the Jains.

Meanwhile, partly as a consequence of the competitive thrust of Jainism and Buddhism, and partly as a response to certain under-lying conditions, that I'll get to in a moment, Vedic religion slowly evolved in the direction of modern Hinduism. Instead of continuing to sponsor the ritual slaughter of animals and redistribution of meat, the Brahmans gradually became the most zealous guardians of animal life. Preventing the slaughter of cattle and the consumption of beef became a major preoccupation of all Hindu castes, and ahimsa, rever-ence for all living beings, emerged as the central ethical component of Hinduism, no less than for Jainism and Buddhism.

By my count, Christianity was at least the fifth historically known ethical, soul-saving, otherworldly religion to appear on the world stage. But this is a very conservative figure. There must have been many similar religious movements during the 600 or more years that separated Zoroaster from Jesus. Northern India alone could have had a dozen embryonic rivals to Jainism and Buddhism about which we know nothing because their founders lived and died outside of the feeble light history shines on these remote times.

"Polo? No, I have never heard of anyone of that name in Paris – but wait! Poulaut, the shoemaker, is said to have Italian blood. His family could have changed the spelling of their name. After you've finished your chores, take the rest of the day off and go see him – and get measured for a new pair of shoes while you're there. Boulanger will pay!"

Gratefully Constantine made his way through the narrow cobbled streets to Poulaut's shop. The shoemaker turned out to be a fair-haired, blue-eyed giant of a man, much more French than Italian-looking, but he readily acknowledged his Venetian background.

"Yes, I am descended from the Polos of Venice, although it is strange you should know it. Seventy years ago or more my great-grandfather, a sailor like all my people, lost his leg in an accident at sea. He came to stay with his wife's family here in Paris and took up their trade of shoemaking, which we Poulauts follow to this day. Somewhere along the line our name was changed to sound more French – but we are Polos all the same."

Hardly daring to believe his good fortune, Constantine asked whether any property – especially stones or jewels – had been passed down from the great explorers.

The shoemaker laughed. "If I had the riches of the Orient, would I be a tradesman in Paris? No, rest assured my great-grandfather was as poor as a church mouse – and had he been in possession of any jewels when his ship went down, they would be at the bottom of the ocean now."

Dejected, Constantine left the shop, promising to pick up his new shoes later in the week. Where to now? He discussed his dilemma with Boulanger later that evening in the common room of the inn.

"The Philosopher's Stone, is it?" The burly innkeeper rubbed his chin in meditation. "I'm not an educated man, but I would say that kind of thing is best left alone. Many men have looked for it, Frankenstone, and the search has brought them nothing but madness and sorrow. It is not good to look after such deep things."

How to explain that the 'deep things' were all Constantine cared about looking for? He sighed and swirled the wine in his cup as Boulanger moved off to snuff out the last candles of the evening.

All at once the Georgian was aware of a presence behind him. He turned around, but in the new darkness could make out only the silhouette of a veiled woman, dressed entirely in black.

"If you would know whereof you seek," said the woman, "follow me."

The two passed out of the darkened inn into a tangled skein of streets. New to Paris, Constantine soon lost any idea of where he was. Finally they emerged on the banks of the Seine, and the woman spoke again.

"You are a sincere youth, but callow," said the woman, in a voice tantalizingly familiar. "The reason secrets stay secret is that they cannot stand the light. One cannot speak of them to innkeepers and tradesmen. At best you look like a poisson d'avril – a fool. At worst, people die for your indiscretion."

"Who are you?"

"Ah, Constantine," said the woman reprovingly. "It matters not. The person you should see is Nicolas Fouquet." "Who is he? Where would I find him?"

"You have not been long in France. How much courage have you?"

"As much as I need."

The woman extended her hand across the water, and repeated, "Follow me."

A boat with a single oarsman glided up the Seine and shuddered to a stop at their feet. The veiled woman and the Georgian climbed in, and the oarsman pushed away from the shore. The craft slipped silently through the water to a large fortress, re-splendent with torchlight. The two disembarked, and Constantine followed the wom-an into the building and through a web of passageways.

Although the fortress was heavily guarded, no move was made to stop the visi-tors; on the contrary, sentinels at every turn bowed to the cloaked woman as she passed. Constantine struggled to keep pace with her and thus get a glimpse of her face, but his companion was always a step or two ahead, and the veil's generous folds never defined the features beneath.

At last the woman stopped abruptly in front of a heavy wooden door. She tapped lightly and the door rasped inward on massive iron hinges. Constantine entered, and with a rustle of skirts, his guide was gone.

"I am Jean-Baptiste Colbert, minister to the court of the Sun King, Louis the Fourteenth. Welcome to my office."

Constantine searched out the voice. On the opposite side of the room, two men rose from a writing desk; the smaller one moved forward, his hand extended.

"... And you must be Monsieur Frankenstone?"

"Why have I been brought here?" asked Constantine.

"That is of no importance. You look to me like one of those 'clerici vagantes' - a poor wandering scholar, who has temporarily lost his way. We would be happy to escort you out of France to your home and family. What do you say to our kind of-fer?"

"I have no home ... I have no family ... I seek only the Stone. I have been led to believe that your Nicolas Fouquet has knowledge of the Philosopher's Stone, and it is this I seek."

Colbert puffed himself up disdainfully. "My Nicolas Fouquet, as you put it, is no longer Minister of Finance to this court."

"So where would I find him?"

Colbert gave his associate a sideward glance. "Monsieur Frankenstone, could you please wait outside with the guard while we discuss your case?"

Constantine stepped outside the heavy door, straining to listen to the muffled conversation within:

Colbert was much agitated. "Did you see his jaw tighten when I mentioned his home, his family? Did you notice his poor French, yet his ears perked up when I spoke a Latin phrase? We have a great actor here. If I am not mistaken, this is no idle wanderer, but a man with a purpose – a spy. A master spy! Idiots! We have been hounding the wrong man! We arrested the traitor Fouquet and all his household, as-suming that would control the cancer in our government; but here, nearly twenty years later, the pot is stirred from outside. This Frankenstone could be the mastermind behind Fouquet, behind everything!"

"But you convinced His Majesty that the key to the whole operation was Fouquet's valet. We've had the man in prison for twenty years!"

"Bah! This Frankenstone, or whatever his real name is, is an educated man, far more intelligent than the valet – more intelligent, I'll wager, than Fouquet himself. I told the King months ago I suspected a reorganization of Fouquet's supporters, and to watch for an attempt to counterfeit and debase the franc. I was right … *My God*, I was right! Frankenstone is here to get information from Fouquet before he dies, and how better to get to him than through this subterfuge. The Philosopher's Stone, indeed!"

"There *is* such a thing, though, milord. It turns base metal into gold. Whoever owns it can control the world or so it has been said."

"Don't be so naive. I know of the alchemists' search for the true Philosopher's Stone, but they have searched for hundreds of years and have not found it. No, this 'Stone' no doubt is a secret password of some kind. The spy's very name – Frankenstone – suggests he's the ringleader of the French operation, and possibly more besides. We'll have to be very careful with this one. We must let him do as he wishes, but we will follow his every move."

"And all this time we've been holding the valet. The King will not be happy about that," said the associate.

"He need never know. The valet can be given his freedom on condition he leave France immediately and remain out of the country for twenty-five years, and we'll just substitute Frankenstone in the valet's cell. That should be enough time for us to retire with good pensions, and the King himself may be dead by then."

"But someone would certainly notice that we made the switch!"

"The jailer, of course, but that is old D'Auverne, and he is loyal to us. We can put a mask on Frankenstone every time he has to appear in public – he is about the same build and height as the valet, so no one will be the wiser. Come, it's a perfect plan. Our mistake will go unpunished, and the franc will be stable at last!"

Constantine, meanwhile, had grown weary from the vain struggle to hear the minister's words, and was leaning against the outside of the office door. When the door opened at last, he nearly tumbled into the room.

"Monsieur Frankenstone," exclaimed Colbert cheerfully, "you are in luck! We've decided to take you to Fouquet."

Under cover of darkness Constantine was whisked by carriage through the moonless streets, Colbert and his unnamed associate accompanying him. Over the clatter of the horses' hooves and the iron wheels bouncing on the cobblestones, they asked him probing questions: how old was he? Where was he born? How long had he been in France? Distinctly uneasy now, Constantine pretended not to hear, and made the blandest of small talk until the coach pulled up in front of the Bastille.

A prison! Was Fouquet, then, in prison? What had he done? With a sure intimation of his own fate, Constantine followed Colbert into the dark fortress, down halls and up winding stairs, at last to arrive at a small barred cell where a single man lay sleeping.

The associate swung a metal rod back and forth across the bars. "Fouquet, you have a guest!"

The slight figure in the bed turned his face to the torchlight. "I do not know this man. Leave me to die in peace."

"Oh, Fouquet, you're not dying," said Colbert amiably, as if chiding a small child. "You're just getting tired of your accommodations. Go in, Monsieur Franken-stone, and see if you can help him appreciate our hospitality."

With a clang the door swung shut behind them, and Constantine and Fouquet were alone.

The Georgian knelt by the cot. "We haven't much time," he whispered urgently. "I don't know what they're up to. But I'll tell you quickly what I want to know. I've heard you know the whereabouts of a Stone whereby men may enlarge their vision, and I seek it desperately."

"Stone? I know of no such stone. You are a fool. Go away and let me die."

"The Philosopher's Stone, Monsieur Fouquet. Please try to remember."

Fouquet's eyes widened suddenly. With a great struggle he raised himself on one elbow. "The Philosopher's Stone. Yes, I too sought it; but I am afraid it is a mirage."

"No," Constantine corrected him gently. "I know it is not that."

Fouquet coughed. "Well, I never found it, and looking put me here. I'm no trai-tor. I never stole from the Crown, and the people of France know it. Colbert fears me because of the Stone. He's confiscated my books – the finest collection in France." Suddenly his eyes widened again. "In the corner, there ... a scrap of charcoal. On your sleeve write the address I will give you. It is the Royal Society in England, and you wish to write to Isaac Newton. He, too, has sought the Stone. He is a fine man. Wait for his reply."

Outside the cell, Colbert and his companion conferred in hushed tones. "Listen, Fouquet tells him to write Isaac Newton. Know you of this man?"

"Indeed, milord. A dabbler in the black arts; a scientist." "Ah, but most im-portantly, an Englishman! We must contact the Bishop; this seems a dark business."

"But milord, should we allow him to write the letter?"

Colbert smiled grimly. "Absolutely, my friend. We will even give him the stamps, take him to the central post office, and let him post the letter himself so he suspects nothing."

"And then?"

"And then we will take the letter, carefully remove the seal, check the contents for the code, and reseal it ... and it is on its way. No one will be the wiser. Then we switch him for the valet and intercept the Englishman's reply."

Constantine called to be let out. Colbert said amicably, "Yes, out you go. That wasn't so difficult, now, was it? Did you wish us to take you anywhere? The post office? Most assuredly. We will even supply the pen and paper and envelope and stamps. Will you be receiving a reply, Monsieur Frankenstone? Yes? If you have no other place of residence, perhaps you would then care to reside here in comfort until you receive the reply. We would be most happy to provide you with room and board and any other hospitality you may desire."

And that is how a surprised valet found himself free for the first time in twenty years, and Constantine found himself in strict isolation in the impenetrable castle at Pignerol.

As days passed into weeks and then months, Constantine pressed his jailer for an explanation of his solitary confinement.

"You were an associate of Nicolas Fouquet," was the jailer's reply.

"I only met him once in my life! And at any rate, what can he have done, that his merest acquaintances should merit such treatment?"

"You yourself should know. It is by the order of the Secretary Colbert."

Time dragged on, passing from weeks into years. At first denied even reading material, the prisoner at last was allowed books, but neither pen, ink, nor writing paper. And when even that small concession was made, the jailer swore Constantine to secrecy, convinced that he himself would be hanged if his conciliatory treatment of the prisoner became known to the King.

"But why? I have never wronged the King! I've never even MET the King!"

"You yourself should know," he was told again.

Taking comfort in his books, Constantine ceased to count the days, but reckoned time by the deepening winter that manifested itself outside the little barred window of his cell. His jailer, the close-mouthed but kindly D'Auverne, brought him any volume he requested, from any library in the realm; he also conveyed occasional news, such as the not unexpected death of Fouquet.

In the spring, D'Auverne appeared with a message that concerned them both. He himself had been appointed precept of the prison at Exiles, and Constantine was to accompany him there. There were, however, conditions. On the way the prisoner was to speak to no one, and neither give nor receive any object, note, or other means of communication from anyone he encountered. If he was unprepared to abide by these rules, he would be hanged before ever leaving Pignerol. Numbly, Constantine agreed.

The morning of his departure, D'Auverne entered his cell and fitted Constantine with a black leather mask that covered his whole head down to the mouth. His arms and legs were shackled so he could walk freely but not run, and royal guards escorted him across the sunlit courtyard to a waiting carriage. Just outside the gates of the prison, a crowd had gathered to watch Constantine's departure. As the carriage passed, a small girl pointed and cried, "I see him! There he is! The man in the iron mask!" Her mother clapped a hand to the child's mouth and scuttled her back into the crowd.

D'Auverne had Constantine moved, shackled and masked, twice more – to the Iles-Ste-Marguerite in 1687 and to the Bastille in 1698. Each time the crowds got smaller, and Constantine surmised that his story, if it had ever been widely known, was slipping from the popular mind. D'Auverne, meanwhile, was growing old, and Constantine wondered what would happen to him after his gentle warden's death.

He would soon find out. One night, when the full moon made the courtyard outside his window sparkle like crystals, a candle appeared outside his barred door. Quickly a key turned in the lock, and a familiar veiled form beckoned to him from the doorway.

"Come," she said. "It is time."

Constantine followed the woman in black down the passageway and outside into the bright moonlit courtyard, marveling that the years had left her step as little aged as his own. They passed across the compound, night watchmen bowing as respectfully as they had a generation ago in the offices of Colbert. At the prison gates a saddled horse stood waiting.

"Colbert has been dead many years," the woman said, turning to him, "and now D'Auverne is dead as well, so it is possible for you to leave. The winds of change are blowing – they wish to forget you ever existed. Some fishermen found a dying vagabond on the riverbank early last evening, starving and half naked. They could only make out the words, 'My father is dead and there is now none who will feed me'. When asked his name, he said only, 'Marchioli', then expired. There was evidence of much brutality – iron cuffs on hand and foot, lash stripes and bruises all over. He may have been a half-wit kept by his parents out of sight. His face was hideous, a monster's. The fishermen put a hat over his face so they would not have to look at it. In the morning he will be found in your cell. The authorities will say he tried to last escape but a fortnight ago if anyone inquires. Since no one but D'Auverne has seen you in twenty-three years, the body will be assumed to be yours. Still, it would be unwise to remain in France under your name of Frankenstone."

"Where then should I go?" asked Constantine.

The woman handed him an envelope. "This will explain."

Constantine's fingers trembled as he read the inscription. "This is from Isaac Newton!" he cried. "How long ago was it written? Why did I never receive it?"

"You see that the letter comes addressed to Mr. Frankenstone, c/o Nicolas Fouquet, Minister of Finance, Paris, France. That by itself might have delayed the letter. But look at the other side of the envelope."

The words were scribbled and difficult to read in the moonlight, words such as one might write in the heat of passion; and they were in Latin: "The spy Frankenstone is assuredly conspiring with the alchemist Newton. These scientists are out to destroy the authority of the Pope, the Church, the King! That pale English Anglican bastard [WASP]."

The woman waited until Constantine had absorbed this information. Then she continued. "You will notice that the seal has been broken. The letter was given by Colbert to emissaries of the Pope, who considered the correspondence some kind of witchcraft too powerful to dispose of. The Vatican has kept it all this time. But you have it now, and I believe it will tell you what to do."

She raised her veil, and as she kissed him, Constantine caught sight of the dark skin and mischievous eyes he had known so well, so many years ago....

"Wait!" he cried, reaching for her as she turned away.

"One day you will know me again in the flesh, Petrach. But first you must find Crystal," she replied, "the stone whereby men may enlarge their vision." Wrapping her black shawl more tightly around her lithe body, she became one with the darkness of the shadows.

Taking out the letter, Constantine found the words of Isaac Newton as clear in the moonlight as if the sky were lit by torches.

Dear Mr. Frankenstone:

Many years have I researched on the making of the Philosopher's Stone. If she were here in England, I would have her myself. France is gaining in scientific achievement. I would be cautious of Colbert, but surely you could hire yourself out to other notables as their assistant and in this manner have a livelihood and still learn more about your 'Stone whereby men may enlarge their vision'. She may be in France. If not, try Germany. If she is not in the land of the Franks, try Russia. I am sure you will find the object of your search one day. When you find her, please let me know.

PS: From what you have written, you will be in need of funds from time to time. Save as much as you can in your assistantships and deposit the money at a safe Swiss bank to draw compound interest. A thousand shillings now, and interest compounded at 5% for 50 years will give you 11,467 shillings, and extended another 50 years (for your descendants, unless you have found the elixir of life by then as well) you would have 131,492 shillings. Continuing with this sporting exercise, another 50 years and you have 1,507,818.7 shillings. But if you die without a legitimate male heir, the money reverts to Switzerland, so take that into consideration.

Yours faithfully,
Is. Newt.

PPS: The seal to your letter was broken and carefully resealed. Colbert's marks are all over it. You had best be careful.

His eyes wet with tears, tears of sorrow for things past, tears of thanksgiving for his freedom, and tears of misgiving for what the future might hold, Constantine tucked the letter into his waistcoat pocket, mounted the waiting horse, and rode through the prison gates into the eighteenth century.

[Note: Isaac Newton became Warden of the Mint in 1696,
Master of the Mint in 1699; was elected President
of the Royal Society in 1703; published his
'Opticks' in 1704; and was knighted in 1705.]

24
The French Connection

"If Newton thinks I should seek the Stone in Germany," Constantine decided, "then Germany it will be."

Cloaked and muffled against the November cold, Constantine galloped eastward across France, winding up eventually in Freiburg near the Franco-German border. There his passage was stopped for the winter, both by the inclement weather and his lack of funds. By springtime he had apprenticed himself to an itinerant Bavarian fiddler, and over the course of the next fifteen years worked his way across Germany.

The German states in the early eighteenth century, Constantine soon found, were a locus for innovations of many kinds, but the sciences did not seem to be among them. The Thirty Years' War was only a half-century past, and a reapportioned patchwork of states and principalities were busy putting their communal lives back in order. For the time being, the interest was in family life, the restoration of the economy, and the pursuit of whatever form of Christianity held sway in that particular locale at the moment. Constantine planned to cross the country to Poland and Russia and try his fortunes there.

Unfortunately, several miles north of the Prussian town of Halle, his Bavarian fiddler suddenly died, leaving Constantine again bereft of money and prospects. He took a room at the Wirtshaus in the neighboring town of Köthen to get his bearings and decide how to proceed.

As he sat at noontime in me common room of the Brauhaus, the most remarkable music wafted through the open windows.

"It's our new Kapellmeister," he was told; "the conductor of the personal orchestra of Prince Leopold. His music is quite difficult to sing, but revolutionary, some say. Go down to the church and listen."

Constantine hurried across the Platz toward the source of the beautiful sound, marveling at how the effect of the music changed as he neared it, from the most angelic harmonies to the rolling majesty of a storm at sea. This was surely a type of instrument – no, a body of sound – he had never before encountered.

Entering the old church, he at once located the stout little man at the keyboard; he mounted the wooden steps to the choir loft as soundlessly as he could – but not soundlessly enough.

The musician stopped playing. "Yes?" he inquired sharply.

"If you please ..." began Constantine. "What is that instrument you are playing? I've never heard the likes of it!"

"This?" The gentleman touched the keys, bringing forth another swell of sound. "This is an organ. Where are you from, that you have never heard an organ?"

"I was born in the Caucasus, but I have traveled much since then."

"To all the great musical centers of Europe, obviously."

Constantine ignored the snub. "Could you please play the last part of that song again? The part that goes –," and he sang a few bars.

The musician cocked his head. "You sing extremely well," he acknowledged grudgingly. "You have never studied voice?"

"I've never studied music at all. I worked in the service of a fiddler for many years, but learned nothing of music from him."

"Pity," said the organist. "And yet – "He seemed to make up his mind. "Do you read and write?"

"Turkish, Arabic, Latin, Greek, German and French."

"Excellent! Have you employment in Köthen, or lodging?"

"I am staying at the Wirtshaus, but I've found no work as yet."

"Work for me then, and board in my house. I am a recent widower with four young children, and my house is empty of adult companionship. For want of a better word, we'll call you my secretary, but I could also use you to tutor the children, copy my music, and sing a few bars of my compositions now and then. I have been accused, with some justification, of writing above my singers' abilities. Your fine untrained voice will keep me honest. What is your name?"

Constantine told him, and the musician did not bat an eye. "My name is Johann

Sebastian Bach," he replied. "I'm sure we'll get on just fine."

That night, by Bach's cozy hearth, Constantine related his complex history. The musician was fascinated by the legend of Crystal, but could shed no light on how the Georgian should proceed in his quest.

"If it's scientists you're looking for," he said, "we have none in Köthen, and for that matter, I've heard of none in this part of Germany. Work for me awhile; save your money; and then you can go where you will."

"Isaac Newton of England told me much the same thing," Constantine replied. "He advised me to set up a bank account in Switzerland for my savings."

"*Sir* Isaac Newton? The Master of the Mint in England? My, you *have* gotten around! Yes, indeed. A fine idea," said Bach, "and there I *can* help you. A former student of mine married into a Swiss banking family; I will give you their name, and if you go to Switzerland after you've made some money, they can set you up."

On that note the new friends retired for the night. In the morning the Georgian began his new job as Bach's assistant. After busying himself with answering nearly a year's worth of correspondence and seeing to the children's lessons, Constantine began the arduous task of learning both musical notation and the organ, in order to help Bach transcribe his complex musical pieces. Bach had begun to find the organ (and particularly Köthen's organ) limiting, and was spending more and more time composing concertos for chamber and full orchestra as well as chorales for voice. In order that each musician should have his own fair copy to read and practice from, Constantine found himself doing a great deal of transcription. He enjoyed the work, however, and Bach found him an apt pupil.

The following year, however, Bach began courting an attractive Fraulein named Anna Magdalena Wulcken, the musically trained daughter of a trumpet player. When it became apparent that Bach's house would soon feel empty no longer, Constantine knew it was time to move on. He stayed in Köthen long enough to see Bach and Anna Magdalena married on December 3, 1721; and then, fortified with nearly every pfennig Bach had paid him in his sixteen months of service, the Georgian set off south to Geneva to bank his savings.

But where to after that? He had built up a useful assortment of trades – linguist, trader, musician; and he began to put them all to work. He first obtained a position as church organist in a small church outside Strasbourg, wisely keeping his more esoteric interests to himself, and served there some twelve years. In 1734, however, he happened upon a copy of a newly published book, the *Lettres philosophiques*, or *Philosophical Letters* of a Frenchman calling himself Voltaire. With joy, Constantine found in those letters, dealing with Newton, a kindred soul. He immediately resigned his position as organist and returned to France – this time under his name Bereshni – to exchange ideas with the young philosopher.

At this time Voltaire was living in a chateau at Cirey with a beautiful young intellectual, Gabrielle-Emilie du Chatelet. There Constantine was welcomed as a fellow scientist. He found the household engaged in building a laboratory to solve an argument over the precise nature of fire. Bereshni immediately rolled up his sleeves and pitched in, with such success that the trio was able to present their findings to the National Academy of Science in 1738. At the same time, Voltaire set up a little classroom and remorselessly drilled Gabi and Bereshni in the rudiments of English – "without which," he said, "you will never understand the modern sciences." In return, Bereshni assisted Voltaire in the composition of the "Elements de la philosophie de Newton" for a French popular audience.

Bereshni at last had found his niche, with people who were his intellectual equal, and he remained at Cirey for five-years. Unfortunately, in 1739 a lawsuit forced Voltaire and his household to flee Cirey for asylum in Belgium, and the next ten-years were spent mostly on the move. Voltaire developed political interests Bereshni did not share, and Gabi began an affair with a poet. In 1749 she died in childbirth, and Voltaire was inconsolable. Bereshni grieved over his inability to reach his friend, but the magic circle was broken. Voltaire moved to Berlin in June of 1750 at the invitation of the King of Prussia, and Bereshni again was left to assess his prospects.

Now, however, he was in a much better position than he had ever been before. His work with Voltaire had earned him a considerable amount of money, which he had faithfully consigned to the Swiss bank in Geneva. Plus, his immersion in the most recent scientific developments had given him a sure sense of what he wanted to investigate next. He withdrew a small portion of his savings and signed on with an expedition of French astronomers bound for South Africa.

As interesting as the project was in itself, Bereshni's real object was the uninterrupted time at sea with the expedition's thirty-seven-year-old director, Nicholas Lacaille. Lacaille had, earlier that year, written a textbook "Lecons elementaires d'optique" – "Lessons in Elementary Optics" (published in 1756) – that fired the Georgian's imagination. Newton had hinted that it might be possible to make a stone equal to the Philosopher's Stone – perhaps its Mate, and Lacaille's notes seemed to obliquely confirm this. Could the astronomer shed any light on how this could be done?

An expert lens-grinder himself, Lacaille was only too happy to share his art with such an eager pupil. In South Africa the two scientists set up a workshop and produced progressively finer optics, which enabled Lacaille to locate and catalog over 10,000 stars in the Southern Celestial Sphere in two years. He also determined that "nebulous clusters" were made up of many stars, something not previously known with the optics of the time.

While in South Africa, a most enlightening discussion ensued between the two men:

"So you are looking for a 'Stone whereby men may enlarge their vision.' Are you not aware, Bereshni, that you have been working on and using such instruments? The telescopes we use have transparent 'stone' lenses, or perhaps 'stone' mirrors, which allow men to enlarge their vision. You have already found your stone. What need to search more?"

Bereshni looked at Lacaille dumbfounded. It was true. He had made eyepieces and objectives of glass which, with the mount, formed telescopes which enlarged his vision.

"But this Stone has upon it a tiny spherical ball which does the work," he said at last. "Crystal. Pure quartz."

"Ha!" exclaimed Lacaille. "A very tiny quartz ball, maybe one twelfth the inch diameter, could magnify close objects two hundred or so times in the diameter, but to enlarge distant objects, she would need a Mate. And that Mate would be an objective of high correction, of a double lens design discovered recently, in which the various colors could be combined precisely at a common focus. Otherwise, at that high magnification, Crystal as an eyepiece would see nothing at all! So to do the job up right, Crystal would need her Mate. But, sad to say, even the best designs to date have not succeeded in recombining the various colors accurately enough if we use a two-hundred-power eyepiece. I am afraid that remains beyond human invention. The best approach, if you would desire your 'Crystal Ball' as an eyepiece, would be to have a short-focus Mate, so the different colors would not be spread out too far. Yet that is no problem," continued Lacaille as he calculated furiously on a scrap of paper. "A focal length of only four inches on the Mate would give us ... can this be? ... an eighty power telescope??!!" Lacaille reworked his calculations. "It is so," he said at last. "This is most interesting. How small is the object you seek?"

"Crystal would be about the size you mentioned – she is smaller than a baby's tear," Bereshni said, remembering the legend.

"My Lord!" exclaimed Lacaille, "Is there really any truth to that legend? How long have you been searching? Maybe you are on to something!"

"There *must* be truth behind it. Why would (or how could) simple people make up something like that? Why would I have been subject to all my mistreatment because of it if it were not real? And I have been searching many years, more years than I care to tell."

"My Lord! I wonder why Newton didn't proceed on this tack instead of staying with his mirrors. Why, eighty power is enough to see Jupiter and his moons, Saturn and his rings, Venus in her phases, even the disc of Mars and the oceans and mountains of the Moon! And if the Mate were only an inch or so in size," here Lacaille did some more calculations, "we would gain another three magnitudes over the naked eye, and many more stars would be visible, even for such a small instrument. Hmm, eighty power, small size, light weight; an excellent spy glass, don't you think?"

Bereshni fell in love with South Africa during his stay and vowed that some day, when he had found Crystal, he would return. He was sorry when the expedition returned to France in 1754, but Lacaille offered him a position as his personal lens grinder at the Academy of Sciences in Paris. After Lacaille's death in 1762, the Academy asked Bereshni to stay on to repair and modify the telescopes he and Lacaille had made. This he gladly did, continuing to perfect his art and bank his earnings while he waited for Fate to send him in a new direction.

In the meantime, he had made the acquaintance of many other scientists associated with the Academy. One who became a particularly close friend was Antoine Lavoisier, a chemist who had made a name for himself by proving burning to be a function of oxygenation. Lavoisier had recently acquired an attractive and vivacious bride named Marie, and one of the couple's chief delights was entertaining fellow scientists in their salon. A frequent guest, in addition to Bereshni, was the American Benjamin Franklin, then ambassador to France and a learned scientist in his own right. One evening in 1777 he undertook to explain to Bereshni his perilous investigations into electricity.

"Have you ever had direct corporeal experience with lightning or strong electric forces, Mr. Bereshni?" asked Benjamin Franklin.

And Bereshni told him of his encounter many years ago with the three shepherds near the lakeshore. "When the lightning bolt struck, I became as dead. I left my body and floated around above it...and my wife was with me ... and I was in Paradise ...." Bereshni became very agitated from the memories after recounting this event and was silent for many moments. After he regained his composure, he finished his story. "I roused myself and found the sun well up in the sky. I looked around and saw the three shepherds, and the whole flock of sheep, lying around. Upon investigation I found them all dead ... all dead. I buried the shepherds as best I could; my body was sore and aching all over. There was a large mass of glazed sand nearby, the place where the bolt's main force struck the earth, I presume."

Franklin nodded. "Well, as you know, Mr. Bereshni, scientists here in Europe have been claiming for years that lightning and electricity are the same thing. I agreed with them; so being a brash young American I decided to prove it. I have never told this to anyone else and I trust you to keep this confidence. I, too, have had an out-of-body experience. It was when I did my kite experiment, which you may have heard about. It was in 1752 in June, I believe. Doctor Priestly published the account as I gave it to him, in 1767. That account is somewhat different from what I actually did. By the time we got the kite into the air, the thunder was rolling and the sky was ablaze. I did not have a silk ribbon tied to the twine for the key, but tied a knot directly in the twine for it. I had gotten myself completely soaked from perspiration, so that when the loose fibers of the kite twine were standing as erect as the fur on the back of a hissing cat and I presented my knuckle to the key, the force of the stroke traveled through my clothes and body to the ground. I was knocked unconscious, more so even than when I shocked myself instead of the turkey at Christmastime two years prior. I felt myself floating and saw my body on the ground. My son Willie who was helping me at the time, being of age and having considerable presence of mind, pulled me back into the shed. He cut the twine from the shed and the kite floated away and was no longer a lightning rod. My son saw that I was not breathing, and began breathing into my mouth, holding my nostrils shut, then putting his weight on my chest to expel all the air, giving me artificial respiration as it were, until I recovered. We had discussed this maneuver after my turkey incident in the event it ever became necessary. It was many months before I overcame my agitation and revised and tested a new and safer kite experiment. This revision is what you can read in the 'Electrical Kite' article in the 19 October 1752 Gazette."

Franklin continued. "Some artists have taken to drawing pictures of me concerning this event, in which I am holding the kite string in one hand, and presenting the knuckle of my other hand to the key, all the while I am looking very composed and dressed in my Sunday best, standing outdoors, the silk ribbon or twine dangling to the ground. I have done many foolish things in my lifetime, Mr. Bereshni, but I am not an idiot. No one in his right mind would deliberately ground himself in that manner. The article I mentioned specifically states to attach a length of silk ribbon to the end of the twine, fastening a key at the juncture, (I assumed the person would know enough to hold the bitter end of the ribbon), and that the person and the silk ribbon are to remain dry, and that it is very important that the twine not touch the frame of the door or window of the structure inside of which the person is standing, else the lightning will find its way too easily to the ground, as I found to my sorrow in June of that year. Then you can charge the phial from the electric fire coming off the key. By carefully following my instructions, just enough of the lightning's force will leak off to give a pretty blue crackle to your knuckle. I should have added that if the person, or the silk ribbon, becomes the least bit wet, it is prudent to let go the string and let the kite fly-away."

Franklin then finished. "I would not recommend that you stand on a high treeless hill, with your arm raised, in a thunderstorm, alone, unless you wanted to be a lightning rod and had planned to kill yourself. Also, you would not want to stand near any trees or tall objects in a thunderstorm, as they could draw more of the lightning's force than a kite string and a dry silk ribbon, which lightning could jump to you. You would want to lie down in a low spot until the storm was over. By lying down, even if you were shocked, you would not hurt yourself falling down."

"Lightning is electricity, then, Doctor Franklin?" Bereshni asked.

"Most assuredly," replied Franklin, "in more potent a form than anything else I've ever encountered ... and please, do not call me Doctor Franklin. I have received many honorary degrees, none earned – I am just Mr. Franklin, of Philadelphia."

Bereshni then told the legend of the formation of Crystal by a lightning bolt, and Franklin nodded again.

"A fulgurite," he said. "The size and shape you have described is rare, mind you – extremely rare. But it is certainly possible, and a quartz sphere formed in that way could be more optically perfect than anything made by man."

Bereshni was elated to have his own suppositions confirmed. He continued to meet with Franklin over the next several years, consolidating his theories and becoming more and more sure of the direction in which he was to go.

Note: In 1759 Voltaire published his philosophic novel "Candide," rumored to be based upon the story told him by Constantine of his search for his love. The illegitimate lad Candide becomes separated from his love, the Baron's beautiful daughter Cunegonde, and he searches for her throughout the world, finding disaster wherever he goes in this "best of all possible worlds." He finally finds her, now grown ugly, in Constantinople, and they live happily ever after, cultivating their garden together.

Now Voltaire was born in 1694 to the wife of a hard working middle class Parisian notary, M. d'Aumard. Voltaire was the fifth child, so weak and sickly that no one believed he would live. This feature was almost his trademark for all his long life of more than eighty years. Christened Francois-Marie, he would assume the name Voltaire when he was twenty-four, three years after the death of Louis XIV and some four years before his father died.

His mother's family aspired to rise out of the bourgeois class by buying into the nobility. His father (there is some conjecture it was some unknown lover of his mother) was much displeased with his son's champagne tastes and beer budget – a young

Depiction of Benjamin Franklin with his son William
as they carried on the famous kite experiment in 1752 which equated lightning with electricity.

From **Experiments and Observation on Electricity**
To Peter Collinson

Electrical Kite

[Philadelphia] Oct. 19, 1752.

Sir,

As frequent mention is made in public papers from *Europe* of the success of the *Philadelphia* experiment for drawing the electric fire from clouds by means of pointed rods of iron erected on high buildings, &c., it may be agreeable to the curious to be informed, that the same experiment has succeeded in *Philadelphia*, though made in a different and more easy manner, which is as follows:

Make a small cross of two light strips of cedar, the arms so long as to reach to the four corners of a large thin silk handkerchief when extended; tie the corners of the handkerchief to the extremities of the cross, so you have the body of a kite; which being properly accommodated with a tail, loop. and string, will rise in the air. like those made of paper; but this being of silk, is fitter to bear the wet and wind of a thunder-gust without tearing. To the top of the upright stick of the cross is to be fixed a very sharp-pointed wire, rising a foot or more above the wood. To the end of the twine, next the hand, is to be tied a silk ribbon, and where the silk and twine join, a key may be fastened. This kite is to be raised when a thunder-gust appears to be coming on, and the person who holds the string must stand within a door or window, or under some cover, so that the silk ribbon may not be wet; and care must be taken that the twine does not touch the frame of the door or window. As

soon as any of the thunder-clouds come over the kite, the pointed wire will draw the electric fire from them, and the kite, with all the twine, will be electrified, and the loose filaments of the twine will stand out every way, and be attracted by an approaching finger. And when the rain has wet the kite and twine, so that it can conduct the electric fire freely, you will find it stream out plentifully from the key on the approach of your knuckle. At this key the phial may be charged; and from electric fire thus obtained, spirits may be kindled, and all the other electric experiments be performed, which are usually done by the help of a rubbed glass globe or tube, and thereby the sameness of the electric matter with that of lightning completely demonstrated.

B. Franklin

From **Experiments and Observations on Electricity**
From a letter to John Pringle

Craven-Street. Jan. 6, 1758.

Sir,

I return Mr. Mitchell's paper on the strata of the earth with thanks. The reading of it, and perusal of the draft that accompanies it, have reconciled me to those convulsions which all naturalists agree this globe has suffered. Had the different strata of clay, gravel, marble, coals, limestone, sand, minerals, &c., continued to lie level, one under the other, as they may be supposed to have done before those

74

poet moving in the company of noblemen, diverting them with his stories, writing plays and epics that no one reads. In his will the old notary gave Voltaire life-interest in his son's inheritance – he could not trust his errant son with the principal, little dreaming that his reckless younger son would become a capitalist on a scale beyond his wildest imagination, loaning money to princes, supplying an army with rations, managing an industrial colony - the richest man of letters that ever lived.

And how did Voltaire acquire his initial capital, his gold mine, that allowed him to live the independent life of a man of letters without having to work at a humdrum job? Ben Franklin did it by thrift and industry as a printer, selling his printing business for a goodly sum. It was in this manner: When Voltaire was thirty-six the French Controller-General, to liquidate a part of the public debt, had hit upon the idea of a government lottery. This was so poorly planned that anyone who bought all the tickets would make a million francs. At a supper party where Voltaire was one of the guests, his mathematical friend pointed out the error. Voltaire formed a company which bought up all the tickets (surreptitiously but legally) and personally came out richer by over a million dollars in today's currency. He never knew real poverty again.

In 1755 when he was sixty and recently exiled from France by order of King Louis (XV), Voltaire moved to Switzerland, where he bought four estates, up to this time having owned no property, but having his money all invested in annuities, bonds, commercial enterprises. The largest estate was in Geneva, where his niece Madame Denis presided over a large household - a French cook, a cook's boy, a valet, a secretary, a coachman, a postilion, two lackeys, six horses, four carriages, a monkey and a bear.

In 1757 a young Jansenist fanatic, Pierre Damiens, attempts to assassinate the King – he strikes the King in the side with a pocketknife, causing only a slight scratch. Damiens is to die in a square in Paris with the nobility to view the spectacle from the balconies, more ladies than gentlemen. He is stripped naked, bound on a table. His right hand, the one which held the knife, is burned off. With red-hot pinchers the executioners tear out pieces of flesh, and into the cavities pour molten lead and rosin. His arms and legs are tied to four horses, who after much terror and prodding, start pulling apart – the clatter of slippery hoofs, the shouts of the drivers, the crack of whips, the shrieks of Damiens. He will not pull apart. Finally permission is granted to cut the muscles. An arm is torn off, now a leg, finally another leg. Damiens lives through an hour and a quarter of this hell, this best of all possible worlds. At last he dies – his soul is free.

Damiens remains a topic of conversation for several days. Louis rewards the executioners with much money.

And in the provinces a young Huguenot (Protestant) in the Catholic town of Toulouse commits suicide. He had wanted to be a lawyer, a profession closed to a non-Catholic. A crowd collects – a shout, "Those Huguenots have killed their son to prevent his turning Catholic!" The priests have their cue; they run the town. The father is sentenced to death. But first torture. Then the scaffold. Then his body is burned at the stake. The two daughters are shut up in a convent. The family's shop is pillaged and burned by a mob led on by the priests. All their property is confiscated to the King.

From these and similar events came the battle-cry of Voltaire – the greatest battle-cry of all ages – "Ecrasez L'lnfame!" Crush the Infamous Thing! In every letter he writes now, he inserts somewhere his battle cry – in full, abbreviated, at the beginning, in the middle, at the end, interpolating between topics, scribbled on every vacant space – "Ecrasez L'Infame!"

Out of Voltaire's writings come the ideas of the equality and worth of every man, the belief in freedom of religion, the seeds of the American Revolution, the Declaration of Independence, the Constitution and the Bill of Rights, the French Revolution.

Concerning Isaac Newton, this is what Voltaire wrote: "A distinguished company were discussing who was the greatest man, Caesar, Alexander, Tamerlane or Cromwell. Somebody answered that it was undoubtedly Isaac Newton. This person was right for if true greatness consists in having received from heaven a powerful understanding and in using it to enlighten oneself and all others, then such a one as Newton, who is hardly to be met with once in ten centuries, is in truth a great man. It is to him who masters our minds by the force of truth, not to those who enslave men by violence; it is to him who understands the universe, not to those who disfigure it, that we owe our allegiance."

25
Frankenstone's Monster

I remained in France until 1781, when the political tension in Paris became extremely uncomfortable for me. My friend Lavoisier was already becoming embroiled in the intrigues which would lead to his 1792 execution. Moreover, my banker and friend, Jacques Necker, in his role as Comptroller-General of France, had infuriated Queen Marie Antoinette by restricting her personal spending of public funds. When Necker was dismissed from office, I accompanied him to his opulent Swiss country home in Coppet, a few miles north of Geneva.

The house was already full of people, as I learned it usually was. In addition to Necker and his brilliant and witty wife Suzanne, I became especially close to the couple's lovely teenage daughter Germaine, as well as a family friend, Frederic-Cesar de la Harpe. La Harpe was a revolutionary by nature, quick to embrace any radical cause; his current obsession was the fact that his native region, the Vaud, was suffering under Bernese rule. He was tremendously excited to hear of my acquaintance with so many of the key figures of the Enlightenment, and would scarce leave me alone.

"My dear Mr. Bereshni, Germaine tells me you knew Voltaire."

"Indeed so. I lived with him for a time, and collaborated with him on some of his writings. He is dead now, unfortunately."

"That is unfortunate; I admired him greatly," answered La Harpe. "Are you, yourself, a philosopher? "

"Actually, I consider myself primarily a scientist."

"Oh!" exclaimed the young Germaine. "Then you must meet our other guest,

Doctor Henry Clerval! He is engaged in some kind of scientific research; I'm really not sure what."

"I should be delighted to make his acquaintance," I replied.

Germaine propelled me across the room to a newly arrived gentleman exchanging amenities with Mme. Necker. "Monsieur Clerval! Here is a scientist who wants to hear about your experiments. His name is Constantine Bereshni, but that's too much name for me, so I call him 'Nemo'. You can call him whatever you like."

Clerval laughed genially. "What would Monsieur like to be called?"

"Bereshni is fine. What kind of research do you do?"

"Gentlemen, come to dinner," Madame Necker interrupted. "We can discuss your project over our fine leg of lamb." The company settled themselves in the dining room and immediately I pressed Clerval for details.

"Well, M. Bereshni, you have heard of galvanism?"

"Assuredly." I explained to the others that the term referred to electricity generated through chemical means. "It's a fairly new concept, coming out of experiments done at the University of Bologne by an anatomist named Luigi Galvani. I've read his papers. He discovered that by touching the inner nerves of a dead frog with an electrical current, the muscles of the frog would contract as if alive."

"How repulsive!" La Harpe exclaimed.

"Really, Monsieur," replied Clerval. "Emotions do not enter into a pure scientific investigation. I myself have duplicated Galvani's findings on…larger animals, and it is my conclusion that the elixir of life lies dormant in all organic matter. All it needs is technology to spark it into being."

"Speaking as one who has engaged in considerable research of my own," I said, "I find that theory a little extreme."

"Oh, Bereshni, it is no theory! If you doubt it, you must come with me this very night. I have prepared a grand experiment in my laboratory; everything is quite set up; I need only an assistant to draw the spark and witness the event."

"You are not going to take Nemo away from me?" Germaine cried, grasping my arm.

"Never mind, ma petite," I told her, pinching her cheek playfully. "Your Nemo will be back to play with you tomorrow."

Hating to be treated like a child in front of all the dinner guests, Germaine let me go. It was only a short carriage ride to Clerval's home in Geneva. He had fixed the bedroom of his small second-floor apartment into a laboratory, which he kept securely locked from all eyes save his own – and now, mine. When I entered I could see why. The room reeked with an acrid chemical smell so potent that my eyes blurred and my nostrils seemed to shrivel in my head. A long table beneath the window had been draped with several sheets, apparently intended to obscure whatever lay there. Next to the table stood a variety of electrical paraphernalia. I recognized a Newtonian electrostatic machine, a large Leyden jar, and some kind of clockwork-driven pump, but little else.

"What I am about to show you could send me to prison, to the madhouse, or to the block," Clerval said impressively. "You must promise never to breathe a word of this to anyone until I have made the proper legal arrangements to protect myself and I give you the permission" (a promise, dear reader, I found I could not keep).

"Yes, yes, of course," I said, the hair rising at the back of my neck, my heart beating violently. With that he swept the sheets off the long table, and I screamed.

On the table lay the corpse of a horribly scarred man. My first impression was that he had been drowned, but my second was even worse than the first: I could see he had been preserved, piece by piece, organ by organ, in some kind of pickling fluid, and then sutured together again. Where he was seamed, the stitches cut deep into the yellowish, pulpy skin, giving him the impression of some horrible fowl, parboiled and stuffed for dinner. I wanted to retch.

"Steady!" Clerval admonished. "I know he's not pretty, but he's serviceable as a first experiment."

"Experiment?" I gasped.

"The ultimate demonstration of galvanistic principles! Galvani wasn't correct on a number of points, which held up my research for awhile, but by combining his work with that of other natural philosophers, I've so far managed to revivify a frog, a duck, a rabbit! .... This is my final challenge!"

Clerval moved the small stand with the Leyden jar closer to the body.

"I've invented a way to expand the electrical storage capacity of this jar to nearly ten times its usual potency," he said. "There's enough energy stored here to stop the heart of a living man, but it should have the opposite result released into a dead one. Your job is to draw a spark from the jar; mine is to transfer it, via these wires, into the corpse's heart, thus stimulating it to beat and bring the subject to life."

"It won't work," I told him, overcome with loathing at the prospect. "His brain is dead."

Clerval reached behind the corpse's skull and lifted two translucent vascular tubes running to the small pump on the Leyden jar stand. "I've taken care of that," he answered. "That circulating fluid is my contribution to science. It preserves the brain, alive and functioning, inside a lifeless body – or anywhere else, for that matter. Consider the implications! No one's intelligence need ever be lost just because the body wears out; no brain need ever die again!"

With that he motioned for me to discharge the stored electricity. I hesitated, and he snapped at me, "Damn it, man, you're a scientist! Do it!"

I touched the wire to the Leyden jar. Immediately a blinding arc of light knocked me to the floor, and I heard screaming all around me; some of it, I knew, was coming from my own throat, but the remainder of the chorus was not. I passed out. When I came to my senses, I know not how much later, I saw Clerval on the floor beside me, open eyed, open-mouthed, and dead. And above me, on the edge of the table, sat the monster, screaming with the terror of Hell.

I leapt to my feet and, thinking to console him, tried to put my arms around his shoulders; but he shrieked me away, blind animal panic in his eyes. Ripping the tubes out of his trepanned skull, he jumped off the table and made a mad dash for the door, grabbing the doctor's black cloak as he went. I was quick, but he was quicker, and I could but follow him crashing down the stairs and into the street. Behind me the landlady stood on the landing, calling, "What is happening? Where is Monsieur Clerval going in such a hurry?" But I could not stop to answer. She would find out soon enough.

I was a strong runner and in excellent shape, but the monster easily kept his distance. I had given up calling out to him because he did not seem to comprehend me and I needed all my breath to run, but he continued shrieking, which in fact enabled me to track him in the darkness. Suddenly it occurred to me that we were heading toward a steep precipice, which the poor soul in his panic could not hope to climb down. I intensified my efforts and managed to close the gap between us a little bit. When at last I saw him, less than ten feet from the edge, I expended my last ounce of strength in a warning shout. He turned around and looked at me, and I thought I had saved him; then all at once he shot forward again and, with a final cry of surprise, sailed serenely over the cliff.

Far behind me, in the sudden stillness, I could hear an approaching throng – probably neighbors roused by the landlady. Quickly I climbed a nearby oak and watched their torches draw near.

"He's gone over the cliff," called a voice. Everyone rushed to the edge to see.

"Do you know who he was?" asked another.

A man came running up breathlessly. "Doctor Clerval is dead in his bedroom! I checked upstairs. The noise woke me up. What is going on here? Did you catch the murderer?"

The landlady soon came up to where everyone was milling around.

"He went over the cliff! The blackguard! No wonder he ran. Serves him right." The first voice was speaking to the landlady.

The landlady looked down at the broken body. "Why, that's Doctor Clerval. Poor man. What was he running from?"

"Doctor Clerval is dead in his room!" shouted the first floor tenant. "That can't be the Doctor!"

"It's the poor Doctor's cloak," replied the landlady. "The Doctor and another gentleman went up to his room, and not fifteen minutes later the Doctor ... no, two men run down the stairs. If the Doctor is now dead in his room, who is the one at the bottom of the cliff ... and who was the third man? ... and where is the murderer?"

No one had any answers for all this, and up in my perch, with all the excitement, my head began to swim....

...And then my head cleared from the hallucination brought on by too much leg of lamb acted upon no doubt by the electric shock. I stood up unsteadily and saw the mad doctor twitching on the floor. His chest moved – the breathing was labored, by fits and starts. I forced myself to turn and look at the table. The corpse was still there – it had not moved at all. I left as soon as I saw that Clerval would live.

Deciding that Switzerland was no longer a safe place for me to stay, I returned to the Necker's home and begged leave of my hosts the following morning. Coincidentally, La Harpe was planning to depart as well; he had, he said, letters of introduction to the court of the Russian Czar. Would I like to go along?

I agreed gladly, and supplied with fresh horses, left that very afternoon on the first leg of a long journey east.

26
To Russia, with Love

La Harpe and I left Switzerland in May of 1782 and arrived in St. Petersburg two years later. La Harpe was in no hurry and liked to enjoy himself along the way. We were received into the court of Empress Catherine, and after meeting with us, the Empress offered La Harpe the position of tutor to her two young grandsons, and me the job of restoring and cataloguing the books at the Academy of Science. Both of us felt our appointments fit our personalities well and we settled into our work with gusto.

I was particularly pleased with my new job, which offered me unlimited access to all the greatest scientific and occult works of the world, both ancient and modern. I read voraciously, refreshing my early childhood memory of the Cyrillic alphabet and becoming fluent in the Russian of the intelligentsia. The Academy was my life for many years, and I would have to say that this period, spent in the quest of pure knowledge, was among the happiest times of my life.

In 1796, however, my patron Catherine died, and her son Paul came to power. I had never liked Paul; he struck me as petty and narrow-minded, and we had our first clash when he forbade the importing of foreign books, and strictly censored domestic ones. When I protested, he dismissed me from the Academy altogether.

La Harpe was dismissed about the same time (Paul's sons were teenagers now, and besides, Paul feared La Harpe's liberal ideas), and he returned to Switzerland to fight for the independence of his beloved Vaud. I had toyed with the idea of going with him, but then a contact I had made early in my tenure in Russia paid off.

Back in 1786 or 87, a high-ranking army officer named Suvarov had rushed into the Academy in search of a doctor. His young nephew had been prostrated with a high fever and convulsions, and none of the family's household remedies had been effective; Suvarov feared for the boy's life. I told him I was not a doctor but I knew a great deal about medicine, and I would be happy to take a look at the boy. We hurried to the officer's home, a large villa on the outskirts of town. There I met the boy's mother, accompanied by her female companions and much wringing of hands.

"Doctor Bereshnikov," (for so I was known in St. Petersburg), "Alexandr has been like this for two days now. He can't go on much longer."

"What has he had to eat?"

"Nothing; he is too sick."

"Drink?"

The women all looked at each other. "Well, yesterday a little water, but nothing today."

"The first rule," I told them sternly, "is the patient must keep drinking." I picked up the boy's arm and pinched the flesh. "See how the skin stays contracted, not smoothing out when I release it? He doesn't have enough water in his body."

I raised the boy's head and poured a few drops of water into his mouth, then handed the flask to one of the women. "Keep doing that until all the water in the flask is gone; then wait an hour, fill up the flask, and do it again. Keep that up all night."

I then turned to the boy's mother. "What have you tried, to alleviate the fever?"

"Well, when he was still conscious, we tried to dispel the poison in his body with a hot water emetic and a buckthorn purgative."

"I beg pardon if I offend you, Madame, but that was contra-indicated. You want him to keep liquid down, not bring it up or flush it out; plus buckthorn promotes sweating, which will only cause his body to lose more water. Can you prepare a shallow bath for the boy? Not too cold, but not hot, either."

The women scurried to do as I asked. We laid the boy in the lukewarm water and splashed him gently as I furnished further instructions.

"Now this should bring the fever down. If it goes back up again, give him another bath. In the meantime, keep liquid going into him, even if you have to put it on his tongue drop by drop."

"But doctor, what about the fits?" interjected his worried uncle.

"If he's never had them before, they're the result of the high fever. He'll be fine."

My prediction, fortunately, was accurate; Suvarov and little Alexandr would visit me quite regularly in the ensuing years, and when Suvarov learned the Czar had dismissed me, he offered me the position of medic with his regiment. This was to open a new chapter in my life, and one I do not recall with much fondness. The early nineteenth century was a bloody period in Russian history; they were alternately at war with the French, the Swedes, the Turks, (even my homeland, which they annexed), and finally the French again. It was terribly difficult for me to wage war against a country where I had lived so long and nurtured so many close friendships. I consoled myself with the thought that as a medical officer I was doing my part to save lives, not take them; but I could save so few and the carnage was so great that I lived constantly on the brink of despair.

After sixteen years of service with the Army, I found myself heading for France again, this time trailing Napoleon's dwindling Grand Armee back to France after the horrible battle of Borodino. I recalled the last time I had made this journey, and was suddenly filled with longing to see my old friend Germaine Necker, who, now separated from her husband, was living in her ancestral home at Coppet as Madame de Stael. I obtained an honorable discharge from the Army and headed for neutral Switzerland.

Germaine was delighted to see me, although she couldn't get over how little I had aged in the thirty years since our last meeting in 1782. She, for her part, had matured into a ravishingly beautiful woman, more than capable of holding the attention of lovers like the English poet Byron, who now sat at her side.

"Dear Nemo," she began, when we were all settled in her idyllic rose garden, "I've always wanted to know whatever happened the night you left here with Clerval. They never told me the details and the funeral was very secretive. It's been so long ago, I suppose it doesn't matter – but did you kill him?"

"Of course not!" I said, shocked; and I told her the whole story. The episode was engraved in my mind as in stone – I recalled it totally. Byron was entranced by the tale, and asked me to repeat many of the details over and over. (Little did I know that the following year he would share the story with his friend Mary Shelley, who produced the bastardized version known as "Frankenstein".) She then asked me to retell for Byron the old, old legend of Crystal, plus the scientific evidence I had acquired since we had last met. I ended by lamenting the fact that the trail seemed to have vanished; although I had had, at the Academy, access to the writings of the greatest minds of all time, I no longer had any idea where to turn.

"I have a suggestion," Byron said. "If you would consider returning to Russia, a young friend of mine has just received an assistant professorship at the University of Kazan, which as you may know is about four hundred miles from Moscow. He is a mathematician by training, but very conversant in literature and philosophy, and an altogether brilliant man. I am sure that if you went to Kazan and offered him your services, it would be well worth your time."

"What is this fellow's name?"

"Lobatchevsky. I'll draft you a letter of introduction."

I remained at Coppet with Byron and Germaine another month, then began my journey back to Russia. I was dismayed, as I traveled, to see the toll the long years of warfare had taken upon the proud nation. The discrepancy between the lifestyles of the upper and lower classes was more scandalous than ever; the landed nobility and intelligentsia lived in relative comfort, while the peasant classes lived in wretched poverty and squalor. In addition, the new Czar, Alexander, had taken on as viceroy for domestic affairs a reactionary named Arakcheev, who seemed determined to squelch modernism in all areas of public life, but particularly the military. I had gotten out just in time!

When I arrived at the University of Kazan in 1816, the young Lobatchevsky had risen from assistant to full professor of mathematics. He had also been appointed University librarian and curator of the disastrously disorganized University Museum, which in truth was nothing more than huge piles of books and artifacts. He was overjoyed to hear of my library experience, and we at once set to work dating, cataloguing, and organizing the vast collection of material. As we worked, we discussed the thinkers of the Enlightenment (whom he greatly admired) and the German philosopher Kant (with whom he violently disagreed). Lobatchevsky was particularly interested in the relationship of philosophy to mathematics, and struggled to find a way to refute Kant's transcendental idealism through not only logic, but also geometry! I recognized in the genial and hardworking young man an agile and creative intelligence, and it astonished me that his fellows at the University saw him only as a capable administrator.

In 1827, Lobatchevsky attained the position of Rector of the entire university, and he promoted me to his administrative assistant. We at once inaugurated plans to reorganize the staff and hire forward-thinking professors, despite governmental opposition (repression was the order of the day). I was given the special task of establishing a mineralogical collection that proved second to none in the world, which I am proud to say I accomplished. But within a few years, intimations came to me of a new line of inquiry to pursue.

At the University of Moscow at that time, a small circle of philosophers had formed, with a most unlikely man at its center: the poet Nicolas Stankevich. Every report I heard of him seemed more remarkable than the last. He was variously painted as a saint, a Christ, a prophet, a madman. His followers nearly worshipped him but couldn't understand what he said; however, he was reputed to have more "deep knowledge" than any other man living in Russia at the time. If any of these things were true, I had to meet him. I requested, and obtained, a leave of absence from the University of Kazan, as well as traveling expenses to Moscow.

Stankevich turned out to be everything I had heard, except mad. He was one of the most eminently sane men I've ever met, and certainly the closest, by nature, to God. And yet his religion had no ties to orthodoxy, but simply arose from the sheer purity of his heart. He invited me to share his modest quarters, and we talked long and earnestly about Crystal and the quest for my lost soul mate which had burned in my heart these past one hundred seventy years.

"Sometimes I wonder whether the whole thing is a fiction and no more," I told him despondently one evening. "I have never seen this Stone, nor spoken directly with anyone who has. I am arguably the most learned man in Europe, but the simple object of my quest eludes me at every turn."

"And what would you do if you found it, dear Ivon?"

"She will lead me to my wife," I answered simply.

"If that were your only goal and you had realized it a hundred years ago, think how much poorer the world would be for lack of your insight, your spirit! I sense that you are coming toward the end of this dark tunnel, and what you seek shines in the light on the other side. My advice to you would be: instead of focusing on Crystal as the consummate goal, visualize that goal attained. Not only will that manifest her realization to you, but it will show you what to do with your life when that manifestation is achieved."

"But where should I go? What shall I do?"

"Has not the Universe always provided that answer? You can only watch the flower unfold, not force the blossoming."

I remained with Stankevich for several years, accompanying him on his many tours through Europe, and I was even with him at the close of his short life, when he died of consumption in Italy at the age of twenty-seven. I returned in 1841 to Kazan and resumed my duties with Lobatchevsky with a much more optimistic heart.

Stankevich was right, however; Fate (or the hand of the Universe, as he would say) always intervenes in the most unexpected ways. In 1849 a book on optics was left at the library by an anonymous donor. In it I found a reference to the Leeuwenhoek Museum in Delft, Holland. The Leeuwenhoek Museum! I knew from my studies that Leeuwenhoek was a master lensmaker himself, making tiny magnifiers down to the size of Crystal, and may have had intimate knowledge of her. There were even dark rumors that he had once possessed the Philosopher's Stone. But he had died many years before I became acquainted with his work, and none of the other books had mentioned where he had lived, or worked, or died. If there was a museum devoted to Leeuwenhoek memorabilia, perhaps the end of my quest was in sight after all!

With all the dead ends I had come up against in the past, I felt it best if I wait patiently this time and consider the situation thoroughly. There was every likelihood that there would be no Crystal there, and no clue as to her whereabouts. The Museum may have dissolved and the contents dispersed, as the book was fairly old. After several years I finally made up my mind to go and satisfy my curiosity.

This time, rather than ask for another prolonged leave of absence, I submitted my resignation to the University. Lobatchevsky was saddened, as we had been engaged in a struggle against an increasingly censorious political regime and he would miss my support, but he understood the importance of my quest. I gave him many of my possessions, sold some, and packed the rest, and was on my way westward toward the Polish border when Destiny intervened again.

About ten miles west of Kiev, my carriage approached a small cluster of military men standing at the edge of the road. Beside them stood a riderless horse, and lying in their midst was an unconscious man. I called out to my driver to stop, and alighted quickly.

"I am a doctor of sorts. May I be of some assistance?"

The men stepped back to let me approach the fallen officer, but one told me, "I think it's too late. I couldn't feel a pulse."

The officer on the ground was of high rank, and of impressive stature I thought. There was something familiar about him. I pressed the carotid artery at the man's neck. The pulse was there, but very faint. Immediately I bent over him, pinched the nostrils shut with one hand, and began to breathe into his mouth. As I worked on him, long repressed memories of my youth came flooding over me, and the tears came freely.

"What are you doing?" asked the man who had spoken before – a lieutenant from his uniform.

"Saving his life," I gasped. "Tell me what happened to him."

"We don't know," the lieutenant said. "We were riding along and suddenly the Captain seemed to have a fit of some sort. He spurred his horse to a gallop and sped on ahead. We rode on several minutes, then heard the horse neighing, and found it ten yards off the road, in a marshy area recently flooded from the spring rains. The horse was mountless. We found the Captain finally and pulled him out of the water and carried him back up to the road, but he seems to be dead, although we see no blood and feel no broken bones."

"Was he underwater long?" I asked, surfacing for air.

"No more than two or three minutes; but we have been here maybe five minutes until you come."

Long enough, I thought. Suddenly the officer gave a mighty cough, and I rolled him onto his side and thumped his shoulder blades to clear his lungs. He shuddered, and breathed on his own. His men cheered.

"Come, let me put him in my carriage," I said. "Now that the crisis is past, we can take him back to Kiev and see how fully he recovers."

"Where did you learn that breathing trick?" asked the lieutenant in wonder.

"From my childhood, and elsewhere," I told him. "I've lived a long life, and have learned many things."

To make a long story short, the Captain recovered to a greater or lesser extent. However, because of the long period without air, he suffered some brain damage which impaired both his long-term memory and his manner of speech; from that day forward, he spoke and behaved in a strange, stilted manner, which his men said was not at all characteristic of him before the accident. Nevertheless, I felt my job there was done, and after a fortnight prepared to take my leave.

On the day of my departure, I was approached by the lieutenant I had conversed with on the road.

"The Government was very impressed with your quickness and valor in aiding my Captain, Alexandr Gorchakov, and would like to give you an official commendation – possibly even a monetary award or dascha, but there are two Ivon Bereshnikovs of your age listed here in Kiev alone. You do not appear to be from around here. What is your real name, your family or tribal name, and of what State?"

I took a deep breath. I had the sensation that a long chapter in my life had closed, and I was in some way about to come full circle.

"Frankenstone, of the Mendeleev tribe, of Georgia," I replied.

27
To Delft...and Off Again

I arrived in Delft, the birthplace of Leeuwenhoek, at the height of what must be Holland's most beautiful season, Spring. It was a Thursday, market day in the city, and all along the Voldersgracht Canal artists had set up their easels to try to capture the explosion of color and activity assaulting their senses. All around me, flowermongers hawked riots of tulips, hyacinths, and daffodils, whose exotic scent hung so heavy on the air, it left a sweet taste in my mouth. Between the flower stalls, other merchants sold cheeses and pottery, fabrics and laces. And every color and movement seemed doubled and magnified in the breathlessly clear water of the canals that served Delft as thoroughfares.

It took me some time to find a resident who spoke a language in which I could converse; but at last I wandered into a cafe near the Beestenmarkt and managed to make myself understood.

"You are a Deutscher, yes?" the burly proprietor asked me, extending a glass of beer.

"I have had many homes in my lifetime," I said in German, since that was how he had addressed me. "In Russia most recently, however."

"A world traveler," the man said appreciatively. "What brings you to Delft?"

"The Leeuwenhoek Museum."

He wrinkled his nose. "I have not heard of that place, although it sounds Dutch. Are you sure it is in Delft?"

"I should imagine so, since this is where Leeuwenhoek spent his entire life."

"Leeuwenhoek, you say? I haven't heard of him, either."

I was astounded. The Christian scriptures indeed say a prophet is seldom recognized in his own country, but I had never realized the truth of the maxim until now.

"Perhaps you could direct me to the Town Hall? At least there I could check the records to make sure the man I seek was indeed from this city."

The proprietor raised his arm to give directions, then shook his head. "You'd never find it, not on market day, and you not knowing the language. My boy can take you there."

He whistled, and a stout red-faced boy, the image of his father, appeared at my side. The elder said a few words in Dutch to the lad, who at once seized my hand and propelled me into the sunny streets. He ran pell-mell through the crowds, weaving me between stalls and carts of merchandise like a tail wagging a dog.

"Please!" I panted to the boy, and "Excuse me!" to the irate merchants and passersby, who fixed me with cold stares and pinched lips as I careened into them; for good measure I apologized in German, French, Russian, Greek, Arabic, and Turkish, although the likelihood of anyone understanding the latter tongues seemed extremely remote. At last, when I felt I could sustain breath no longer, we arrived in front of a stone edifice built in a graceful Italian style. My guide hammered lustily on the door with his fist before disappearing down the street. Without waiting for a response to this announcement of my arrival, I pushed the door open and entered.

A very young clerk rose from his seat and spoke to me in Dutch, apparently inquiring as to the nature of my business.

"Entschuldigen Sie," I began. "Do you speak German?"

"Of course. As well as some French, English, and the Flemish tongue."

"German is fine," I said gratefully. "I desire to know whether a family named Leeuwenhoek – and specifically one Antoni van Leeuwenhoek – lived in Delft in the 17th century, and if any members of his family still reside here."

"A scientist, wasn't he?" the young man asked. "I recall learning about him in school; I had a teacher who was very set on him. I'm sure Leeuwenhoek was from Delft, although I've never heard of any descendants, or others of that name. But let's look through the records – our information goes back much further than the sixteen-hundreds – and if there's anything on him, we'll find it."

Hours later, we emerged from the dusty stacks both encouraged and deflated. There was little doubt that Leeuewenhoek had lived in Delft and earned a living as the proprietor of a dry-goods shop – but there was no documentation on the location of his business, and no indication of any line of descent. And worse, there was no record of a currently operating Leeuwenhoek Museum.

"But the teacher I mentioned earlier would be the man to talk to," the clerk told me. "His name is Jelle Verhoeven, and it seems, if I remember correctly, that someone in his family actually knew Leeuwenhoek. He might have information that never made it into the official records, and he lives right across the Markt, near the Oude Kerk."

Thanking the young man for his help, I fairly ran to the building he had indicated and tapped on the heavy paneled door. It opened, and a young maidservant peered out at me curiously. I decided to try German again.

"Guten Tag! Am I at the home of Herr Jelle Verhoeven?"

Whether she understood me or not I do not know, but she at least caught her employer's name. Opening the door wider, she motioned for me to follow her down the hallway. At a wide set of French doors she paused, knocked tentatively, and apparently announced my presence. There was an answering response from inside the room, and I was shown into the study of a small, wizened man in a black frock coat.

"Have I the pleasure of addressing Herr Jelle Verhoeven?"

The gentleman inclined his head, and I was suddenly aware of a sickening feeling in the pit of my stomach; what if, after I had finally located someone who might have the key to my quest, Verhoeven spoke only Dutch?

However, I needn't have worried. My host replied, in perfectly modulated German, "I am he. And you are – ?"

"Frankenstone. Dr. Abdul Frankenstone. I am a scientist, newly arrived in Delft, searching for the Leeuwenhoek Museum."

"You have found it."

I looked around me, confused. Aside from the presence of a few primitive microscopes and optical devices, my surroundings looked like a typical sitting room. Verhoeven laughed gently.

"Not much to it, is there? Unfortunately, establishing a museum to honor Leeuwenhoek, while dearer to my heart than life itself, doesn't pay the bills. So as yet we have no real facilities for displaying my collection, and it remains in catalogued boxes in my storeroom."

"And of what is your collection composed?"

"Anything having to do with Anton – anything he made, anything he owned. Lenses, microscopes, desk and workbench, tools, letters, notebooks – "

"And a stone, perhaps?"

The old man gave me a piercing look. "To what stone do you refer, mijnheer?"

"A ... stone ... whereby ... men ... may ... enlarge ... their ... vision," I replied carefully. I heard the man's sharp intake of breath. He seemed to weigh his next words, cleaning the dottle from his pipe carefully as he spoke.

"My grandfather told me a story when I was very young. His grandfather was in love with Leeuwenhoek's daughter Maria, and remembered her to his dying day, although she discouraged his advances. She was in love with Newton, you see."

"Isaac Newton?" I fairly shouted. I recalled vividly the letter that had started me on my journey to Russia and back.

"The same. They only met once, when or where I do not know, and he never married her, or anyone else for that matter. She, also, never married – which, according to my grandfather, was a real shame, because she was such a beautiful girl. But at any rate, my great-great-grandfather spent much time at the Leeuwenhoek house, and that is how he learned about the Stone. Anton used it as a paperweight."

"Good God! How did he come by it? Where is it now?"

"My great-great-grandfather consoled Maria during her time of mourning, and he wheedled the story out of her. After her father died, Maria sent the Stone to Sir Isaac at the Cambridge Museum in England as a token of her father's friendship with Newton, along with some twenty-six microscopes Anton had prepared for the Royal Society. Ahh ... but nobody knows *how* Anton came by the Stone – some said from the Devil. As far as I know, the Museum still has it."

I sighed. "Then I must go to England."

The old professor looked at me sympathetically. "You are intent on this, aren't you? Would you care to see the house where Leeuwenhoek lived?"

"I thought there was no record of its location!"

"There probably isn't – but I know. Because of my great-great-grandfather, don't you see?"

Together we walked out into the teeming streets. From the Gothic spire of the Nieuw Kerk, a carillon of bells pealed out one melody after another, each more heart-breakingly beautiful than the last. From the promenade along the Oude Delft canal, we turned down the Nieuwstratt until we came to another canal, the Hippolytusbuurt. And from that corner, Verhoeven pointed to a narrow, two-storied brick house with shuttered windows.

"In Leeuwenhoek's day," he said, "it was the fashion to name one's dwelling, and this house was called 'The Golden Head'. He had his drapery and haberdashery shop on the first floor, and his private rooms on the second. The closet, as he called it, where he did his experiments is right there –," and he pointed to a second floor window.

I do not consider myself a sentimental man, and I have in my lifetime met the crowned heads and great thinkers of several ages without awe – but at the sight of the home of a man who had held the Stone in his hand, I wept. Verhoeven saw, and was moved as well.

"It will take you some time to secure passage on a boat to England," he told me. "You will need food and lodging in the meantime; why don't you stay with me? It will be a pleasure to share my home and provisions with such a kindred soul."

So I spent several enjoyable weeks with the good professor before heading for England, buoyed with renewed hope.

Saying farewell to kind mijnheer Jelle Verhoeven, I embarked on the ship at Rotterdam and was soon in London by the first of June 1852. My quest was almost over; relief flooded over me like a tidal wave. Newton would have preserved the Stone in good hands at the Museum. Summer in London was a delight and I took full advantage. Before I knew it, school bells were ringing, and I realized it was time to take the carriage to Cambridge, where my journey would end at long last. My journey for the Stone, at any rate; what the Stone would tell me, and where I would soon find my love, were still to be discovered.

I took a room in Cambridge the first week in September to consolidate my personal effects and scientific paraphernalia, arrived at the Museum about the 12th of the month, and proceeded to the Curator's desk to inquire as to the location of the lightning stones, or fulgurites. The Curator was most talkative, and it was with difficulty that I pried the directions out of him. But when I got to the proper spot, and found the lightning stones, nothing seemed to even remotely resemble the object in the legend, the object I had been searching for these past one hundred ninety two years.

Finally, after much agitation, I found an empty box. Its label stated "Lightning Stone, Arabian East Shore, circa 3:26 AM, April 6, 523 A.D. New Style???!!" Upon my soul, who in the world could have known such a precise time the lightning struck so many years ago? I lifted the box and looked for other markings. My heart skipped a beat, then the blood pounded furiously in my ears. "FRANKENSTONE". The word printed as plain as day. This must be the box! Arabian Shore, 6th century, my name. The omens all pointed to this, and this alone. I looked for the sign out/in sheet and discovered that a Charles Darwin had signed her out in 1831. Oh, no! Must I now look for this gentleman? Why would he keep it out over twenty years? Unless it was extremely valuable to him. Another omen! It was time to approach the Curator and get some instruction.

"Darwin? Charles Darwin? Lovely lad. Bright, industrious, honest, trustworthy. Interested in natural history. Left for Japan on the ship HMS Bugle or Beagle or Regal or Frugal, I believe, some years ago. Haven't heard from him. Might still be in Japan or still on his voyage, otherwise he would have signed the stone back in. We have other similar stones. Not interested in them? Well, perhaps you can catch him in Japan. Lovely country, Japan. Pretty geishas, beautiful snow-capped mountains. Prone to earthquakes and immense tidal waves. If he returns while you are gone, whom shall I say called? Nemo? No one? Oh ... Doctor Frankenstone. Yes, Doctor, I shall certainly tell him. Have a nice journey – enjoy yourself in Japan, Doctor. Lovely time of year."

28
New York to Milan

"And so, as we have seen in this past hour, gentlemen, we have come full circle. The environment, the small world inside the flask, the heat, pressure, light, concentrations, electrical and magnetic activity; this environment acts upon and changes the elements or materials into a different substance ... and this new and different substance, this material completely different in form and color and properties from the original ... this new substance, gentlemen ... changes the world!"

I stepped back from the podium as applause and cheering broke out. The sound was thunderous, and music to my ears. How long it had been since I heard such pleasant cacophony! Not since my childhood days, when I regaled my sweetheart and heard her laughter and the clapping of her hands reverberating and echoing through the mountain hollows of my beloved Georgia ... I must stop these thoughts .. .I will find her one day ... and soon...I feel it in my very bones in this New World ... I will find the Stone, and then ... My reverie faded with the applause.

"Excellent, Abdul, superb! Your reputation does not do you justice," Professor Renwick began, "On behalf of the staff and faculty, I am extending an invitation to take supper with myself and a few of our other notable professors at Delmonico's."

"I am not sure that I will. ... "

"Nonsense," Renwick interrupted, "I am sure that you will want to talk with some of the other members of the chemistry department. We have so many questions to ask you."

I let him babble on while I gathered up my notes, then said, "I really must be going. I have some research of my own to do in the library." Then I turned to leave.

"We will expect you at nine sharp. Delmonico's is located at the corner of Broadway and Chambers. Until then," Renwick called out.

The cold air was bracing. A good walk to the library stirred the blood and cleared the head of cigar smoke and idle chatter ... Hello, there, Robert Fulton's papers on the Nautilus, a submarine he invented half a century ago. What good fortune! ... The chimes! ... the bell tower? ... where ... the Free Academy ... what time? Nine o'clock in the evening! Have I been here all day? "Oh, my," I said to myself, "I wonder if the learned professors will miss my tardy arrival?" I returned the papers as they dimmed the lights and closed up the library. No sooner had I gone outside I was approached by a young man.

"Excuse me, Sir," he began nervously, "I was expected to escort you to meet with Professor Renwick. I hope that you do not mind?"

"So, they decided to place the blame for my absence on you. There is no need to worry. I shall accompany you to this forced meeting, releasing you of all responsibilities." Relaxing slightly, the young man headed off at a quick pace.

Delmonico's was better than I expected. Conversation centered on the use of electricity to combine substances. Although well versed in this area, the professors refused to accept my more up-to-date approach to this problem. Oh, these professors. Always babbling about that of which they know little, and refusing to consider that of which they know even less! The conversation turned to the chemical production of oxygen – Professor Chapman (bless his soul) was most eloquent.

"You are most welcome to drop by and examine my papers on this subject. I have an extensive collection," he boasted.

"That, sir, is a most interesting proposal. Perhaps." I could take it no longer, and left the learned professors standing in front of Delmonico's still discussing the issues.

The bell. Oh, my head. The bell. What time ... seven in the morning? Then I must be in my room at the Waverly House. Oh, my head. Ah, the Waverly; just like back in Cambridge, the Waverly. Much better than the Astor. A quick toilet and I will be ready for the day.... "Hello, there you are, breakfast and the morning paper, and at eight o'clock sharp. Here's a coin for you, lad."

PERRY GETS GO-AHEAD

Commodore Matthew Perry has been awarded commission of the newly formed Pacific Fleet. It is hoped that his experience as a diplomat will aid him on his journey. He is expected to force Japan into opening a trade agreement. The Japanese ports, as is well known, have been closed to all foreign nations since 1638, and their government has incarcerated many of our sailors. The fleet of four ships, all men-of-war, were placed at Perry's disposal and are at this time en route to San Francisco. Perry will depart New York the first week of February, 1853. In celebration of his commission, a reception will be held at the Astor House Nov. 20, 9 PM.

The article in the paper jumped out at me and I had a frightening thought. If a trade agreement is reached with Japan, the possibility exists that someone else might find her before I do and take her from Darwin. And even more to the point, the Japanese have taken Darwin prisoner where he rots in jail to this very day. Else why has the Stone not been signed back in at the Cambridge Museum? And the Japanese may very well have taken the Stone and are using it to their benefit. She must be in Japan! But even once I get there, how can I nose around and find her? The Japanese are none too friendly toward foreigners. I resolved to meet Commodore Perry and to offer my services as a science officer. Perhaps, just perhaps ... I could implement my plans with the help of the learned professors. I sent a message to Professor Chapman informing him that I would be arriving there at twelve to review his studies.

The professor was a short man, who obviously enjoyed his meals more than he should. He was light in color, hinting to his Scandinavian ancestry. After an afternoon indulging Chapman, I brought the subject around to Commodore Perry and his upcoming voyage.

"A most notable military mind. He has a great expertise in diplomacy. However, I have heard that he is a stern captain. Tolerates no insubordination," Chapman reflected.

"You have had the pleasure of talking with him?" I asked.

"On a number of occasions. He lectures here from time to time. Why, he's practically a native son; for the last four years he has worked here at the Navy Yard, and he has family here."

"How would one receive an invitation to the Commodore's reception?" I then asked.

"Oh, I am sure the faculty has already accepted his invitation. If you would care to accompany me, I would be most pleased."

The next week passed quickly. Between making arrangements for my belongings to be sent to California and the research I was conducting on chemical atmospheres, I was very busy.

The carriage arrived at eight. Although not usually inclined to social gatherings, I was looking forward to this evening. As with most formal affairs, the guests were announced upon their arrival. "Professor Abdullah Frankenstone and Professor Edmund Chapman of the Free Academy." Our entrance went unnoticed; Commodore Perry had yet to arrive. The professor was eager to locate an acceptable table. I left him to his task while I mingled with the other guests. Among those in attendance were many political officials and military officers; also a fine array of well-bred women. A fanfare announced the arrival of the Commodore, and he was escorted to the dais, at which time a series of gongs announced the beginning of the meal. I found Chapman sitting at a table near the dais and I joined him.

"The Astor House has some of the city's best cuisine," Chapman smiled, "Have you had the pleasure of dining here?"

I nodded, my face in a forced smile as I remembered my first meal in New York. Upon my arrival in the city, I had checked into the Astor only to find chaos. Gentlemen of stature spitting into brass spittoons as they propped their feet on the table. Ladies succumbing to the pleasures of alcohol while they gossiped freely. Children racing the hallways unattended and unkempt. Unpleasant to say the least.

The meal was a lengthy, trying affair, involving seven courses. The dessert, however, was 'Ice', a frozen confection of milk and eggs, created in the city. I found it most pleasing; the Commodore even more so - he indulged in several. Finally Perry stood, offered his gratitude and invited his guests to join him in the ballroom for music and dancing.

I took this opportunity to introduce myself to those persons that appeared closest to Commodore Perry; one in particular being a somewhat plump woman who had taken a fancy to me. "Allow me to introduce myself: Abdullah Bereshni Constantine

Dimitri Aeschylus Frankenstone – scientist, historian and entrepreneur." I bowed and seemed to have noticeably impressed her.

"Mrs. Mary Trollope, of the Philadelphia Trollopes. My pleasure I am sure."

She promptly engaged me in conversation. A most pleasant motherly type, articulate and well read. We talked at length on a variety of topics from the theatre to military protocol, and she kept up her end of the conversation nicely, somewhat frivolous and flirtatious withal.

The evening's festivities were coming to a close and I had not yet had the chance to meet the Commodore; my frustration must have showed.

"My dear Mr. Frankenstone, what is troubling you?" Mrs. Trollope inquired.

"Nothing, really. I had hoped to have the honor of meeting our distinguished host."

"Well, if that is all, allow me to extend an invitation to join myself, my husband and Matthew at the opening performance of 'Henry the Eighth' at the new Wallack Theatre in January."

"Madame, you are most generous," I responded with a wink and a smile.

"We will send a carriage to pick you up, if you will allow me to inquire as to where you might be staying?"

"At the Waverly," I replied.

She grinned impishly, "A recluse?"

I cocked my head and spread my hands, "You have found me out, Madame."

The New York Daily listed the Wallack's opening night as January 12, 1853. That would be sufficient time for me to complete my studies. Most of my papers and personal effects had been sent to San Francisco, and the equipment being manufactured for my current project would be sent directly to California. I would have ample time to explore the interior of America before setting sail for Japan.

I spent the holidays finishing my research at the University. If it had not been for the festive mood of the Waverly's employees, I would have missed the Christmas season completely. On January tenth a letter arrived from Mrs. Trollope:

Dearest Abdullah,

We have reserved a place in our box for you at the Wallack Theatre. Our carriage will arrive for you at eight on the evening of the twelfth. Black tie and tails will be required as we will be dining afterward at the European Consulate. We are all looking forward to your company.

Warm regards,
Mary T

PS: Matthew could not come. His nephew Christopher Perry, will take his place.

The Wallack Theatre was not an overly impressive building, but well refined compared to other theaters I had seen. Upon my arrival, I was escorted to the Trollopes' private box. Mrs. Trollope rose. "Chris, allow me to introduce ..." She gestured toward me.

Bowing slightly to Perry, I responded with my full name, "Petrach Ivan Pauli Abdullah Bereshni Constantine Dimitri Aeschylus Frankenstone."

"A man of many nations?" the Commodore's nephew inquired with eyebrows raised.

"And many talents," Mrs. Trollope added. She introduced the other guests as the house lights dimmed.

During intermission I remained quiet with my thoughts. The others engaged in small talk with other patrons of the theatre.

"You will have to excuse Abdullall, Chris, I think he would prefer an archive to a theatre!" she giggled. The performance received a standing ovation.

Afterwards, I found myself sharing a carriage with Christopher Perry on the trip to the Consulate. "So, Abdul, I may call you 'Abdul'?" I nodded. "What brings you to America?"

"Research mostly. However, I would not refuse gainful employment."

"Are you seeking employment?"

"Not actively."

"Your qualifications?"

I reflected momentarily. "I am a scientist. My fields are diverse, covering botany, biology, chemistry, engineering and mathematics. I have also served under many officers as a consultant and recorder." I spoke slowly, choosing my inflections carefully to highlight those skills I wished the Commodore to notice, hoping his nephew would relay the word.

"We will have to talk later in detail. Matthew might be able to offer you a stimulating and adventurous proposal," Christopher smiled. By the end of the evening, we had become quite close. We discussed many topics including military battles and scientific breakthroughs, and I was left with the impression that Matthew would be calling on me soon.

One week later a letter arrived from Matthew's wife Jane requesting I join them for dinner at their home. Quickly I returned my acceptance and hailed a carriage that afternoon.

As is the custom, Matthew's home was furnished by the Government; masterpieces of art and furniture abounded. Dinner was pleasant, the conversation centering on Japanese culture and economic conditions. Matthew again was away on business, but Christopher and his seven-year-old son Tom were there.

"Would you consider sailing with the Commodore as an observer?" Christopher asked after the table was cleared.

I restrained my emotions. "Exactly what would be my duties?"

"Nothing more than an accurate account of his journey from a neutral source. Your being from Europe is even better. It will allow for an objective report of this trip." Christopher stood, offering me his hand, then continued, "Of course, I will allow you time to consider this matter. I must have your answer by the end of the month. You would have to be in San Francisco by the middle of May. Unfortunately, I cannot offer you transportation. The Government insists that the Commodore's route be kept a secret, and I would have no one know of this arrangement until your report is submitted to the Government; for obvious reasons you cannot be reimbursed for your time or expenses." I nodded, then took my leave.

I waited one week before sending my letter of acceptance, including within a personal note expressing my delight in sailing with the Commodore. A short note from Matthew was returned the next day, saying he was pleased that I had accepted, and was looking forward to seeing me in San Francisco. Mrs. Trollope had helped my plan along to perfection.

The next few weeks passed quickly. Finding passage to the West Coast (as a foreigner) proved difficult. I would have to take the Erie Rail Line to Milan, Ohio. There I would pick up the Ohio Rail Line. That would take me to Cincinnati, Ohio, where I would then board the Batesville Stage. Then after transferring to two other stage lines I would board the Cumberland Line, which was a direct route to California. The next time I pass this way I will have rail coast-to-coast. Perhaps even faster passage – balloon from West to East? Powered flight through the air? With the speed of the peregrine falcon? Is it possible?

The weather was inclement on the day of my departure. Heavy snows were reported to have closed the rails in some spots. I was not concerned; at least one cannot drown in the snow. The memories of my recent Atlantic voyage still haunted me: The violent pitching and yawing and rolling in the confused seas and rogue waves; the winds not exceptionally strong, yet the huge seas; the feeling that we could capsize at any moment. The captain assured me that this often happens in the winter season and to give it no mind, but seasickness held me in bondage, and when the seas abated and my stomach settled, I found the captain's table at dinner strangely empty. And in conversation with the captain later, I find that one hundred feet below all this violence, the water is as calm as a garden pond. Fulton's Nautilus would be in its glory there. Yes, Spring would be a better time to sail to Japan.

"All aboard," the conductor called out.

I bid New York one last look. It was an experience I will not soon forget. The train moved slowly. Ice and snow blocked the rails in many places and had to be removed by hand, Night fell before we had reached the halfway mark. Searching out the conductor I inquired, "What type of a time delay are we experiencing?"

"More than usual, sir," he began. "We expect the snow to continue, making our arrival in Milan delayed by at least four hours."

"And the Ohio Line?"

"At last report the snow had left Ohio and was moving East. No delays expected there."

The conductor walked away. Blast this weather, I thought to myself; England was nothing like this!

Milan was blanketed with snow. "Excuse me, Mr. Frankenstone?"

"Yes?"

"I regret to inform you that the Ohio Line has departed. Your passage is assured; however, you may have to wait for the train to return from Cleveland. "

Blast it all! The conductor assured me that my baggage would be secure. He also offered some suggestions as to where I might find decent food. Sloshing through the snow with my thoughts elsewhere, I neglected to notice the small boy rushing towards me. We collided, throwing snow and slush all over ourselves.

"Excuse m-m-me ...." the boy stammered.

"Where might you be going in such a hurry, young man?" I questioned.

"I was hoping to beat the train to the station."

"I am afraid, young man, that you have missed it." The boy turned and muttered something about looking too long at Mrs. Longwood's boxes. "Pardon me," I began, "I was wondering do you know where the Cauffman Hotel is?"

"Yes, I do," the boy answered.

"Would it be too much trouble for you to take me to that establishment?"

"This way," the lad replied, stomping through the snow. "I am Mr. Frankenstone, and you are – ?"

"Tom Edison, sir, but everybody calls me Al."

"You are a strapping lad, why are you not in school, young Al?"

"Well," Al began, "my mother says I can begin school when we move in the fall. She is teaching me at home right now. I am already better at ciphers than my sister, and she's in the second grade!"

A proud look crossed his face. Al stopped in front of the Cauffman Hotel. "This is it."

"Do you have any plans for the afternoon?" I inquired. "Not much. I thought I might listen to the telegraphic dispatch awhile."

"Would you care to join me for a time? Perhaps we can discuss mathematics." Al considered this for a moment, then agreed.

"Alva Edison, you know you are not allowed in here without your parents," a stern woman said, taking Al by the collar.

"Madame, if you do not mind, the young man is with me," I replied, gently removing her arm.

"Oh," she exclaimed, "well, then, that is a different matter completely."

I took a seat near the window and motioned for Al to sit down. We ordered a light meal with warmed chocolate to drink.

"So you're a mathematician?" I began.

"Well, I like figures, they are easy for me to do."

"And you are also interested in telegraphs?" Al nodded, wiping chocolate from his mouth. "Did you know that mathematics plays an important role in how the telegraph works?"

"No."

"Do you know how it is that one can send and receive messages over great distances?"

"No, but it doesn't seem that hard. Mr. Peirson lets me have the old machines to take apart." Al's face took on an impish grin.

"An inventor, eh?" Al only smiled. "Well, master Al, allow me to tell you about electricity. Have you ever seen a magnet?" The boy nodded. "Then you know that a magnet draws iron to it?" Again he nodded. "Have you ever tried to put two together?" His smile told me he had. "You know then that one sometimes turns the other way. That is because a positive charge will not let another positive charge touch it. A negative charge, however, attracts a positive charge."

I ordered two more chocolates and continued; the boy seemed interested. "Electricity works the same way. Lightning is electricity. It has a charge. When lightning strikes, it is looking for a place to put its energy or charge. If you could harness that charge you would be able to do great things."

"Like what?"

"Operate a train for instance, or an engine. There are many ways to manufacture electricity. A motor will produce electricity with the help of giant magnets." I sketched a simple motor for Al.

The boy studied the diagram for a time, then said, "So if you run this magnet through these wires and turn the drum you get a charge?" I was impressed with the boy's intelligence. "How then would you tell the electricity where to go and where would you put it until you needed it?"

"Right now there are not very many ways to store or use electricity. Sometimes it is stored in a device called a battery. At other times it is used immediately. I have used electricity to change the way substances are combined. If you pass a current of electricity through a wire, the wire gets very hot. I use the heat to make chemicals stick to each other."

Al cocked his head and replied, "You are telling me that lightning can make things change the way they are?" I nodded. "Like what?" he insisted.

"A good example would be sand," I submitted cautiously.

"Sand??!!"

"If lightning strikes a pile of dry sand, it changes some of the sand to glass. You can find these baubles along any coast."

"Well, Mr. Frankenstone, what good is this electricity?"

"It can free man from depending on gas and wood for heat and light. It can make work easier for man and beast alike."

I was warming to my subject. "Electricity can be used to heat up a wire very hot and can create a better light than the gas lamps. Platinum conducts well and takes a high heat, but Wolfram, or heavy stone, is much better, except air must be excluded, else it will oxidize or burn up. A carbon filament is also good if air is excluded. Heavy carbon electrodes can create an intense electric arc light, which can project bright pictures onto a distant screen. And if these pictures are replaced fast enough, the eye will be fooled into thinking the pictures are 'moving', so we can see moving pictures of a man walking or a horse running, almost as if they were real."

Al looked at me with a blank stare. I had overtaxed his attention span. "Well, frankly, sir," he said, crossing his arms over his chest and looking me straight in the eye, "frankly, sir, I don't believe a word of it. I cannot believe all the tales you tell me."

I laughed. "Perhaps not now, but someday."

We left the hotel and headed back towards the train station. "So tell me, what country were you born in, Al? You have a French accent."

"I was born in Canada not long after the Battle of Lake Erie."

"Do you know of this battle?"

"A little; Mother told me about it. Before I was born, Captain Perry ...."

"Matthew Perry?" I interrupted.

"No, his name was Oliver, I think. Anyway, he had his ships close to the sand

162

bar in the lake. He used only one ship at a time in battle. The British thought that they were low on supplies, so they rushed them. Then Perry let loose with all his ships. He won. Then the revolution started and Father decided one war was enough and began saving money to bring us to America."

"Quite a rendition for a young man. I think that you are going to have quite a future," I said in honest admiration.

Al shrugged his shoulders. "Well, I have to go; Mother expects me before school's out and there's the bell." Al turned to leave. "I enjoyed talking with you and I will think about electricity!" he shouted over his shoulder as he sloshed his way home. I waved to the boy.

The train pulled into the station two hours later. I boarded tired and soggy. Not bothering to eat, I changed and fell asleep listening to the clack of the wheels on the rail. We were in Cincinnati before I awoke.

29
The Wild West

Abdul was restless and ready to depart for San Francisco. He had waited three days for the private stagecoach that would link up with the Overland Stage. The Commodore would be in San Francisco by now, making the final preparations for his voyage to Japan.

"Batesville Stage preparing for departure," a voice called out. "Have your baggage checked at the loading dock," another voice instructed. 'I am coming for you,' Abdul thought to himself. These days the desire to hold her and share the secrets of her soul was overwhelming.

"Mr. Frankenstone?" a voice interrupted.

"Excuse me?" Abdul replied.

"Your stage is ready to depart, sir," the porter informed him.

"Yes, but of course," he replied, climbing into the coach. As the stage lurched forward, he surveyed his fellow travelers.

A middle-aged couple dressed in clean but somewhat tattered clothing sat across from him. A well-dressed gentleman who smelled of whiskey sat next to a younger man dressed in working clothes. The odor that emanated from him was one of animals. Abdul smiled and nodded in his direction. The young man took no notice. 'It is going to be a long ride,' Abdul said to himself.

The stage pulled into the way station a little before noon. "None too soon for me!" the well-dressed gentleman said. He was headed for the out-house almost before the stage had stopped. The younger man was right on his heels. Abdul shook his head in disgust, then motioned for the woman to take her leave.

"Thank you, sir," her companion began, "Seems most folks these days have no manners." Abdul smiled in reply as they climbed down from the coach.

The station house was hardly more than a shack. While he was surveying his surroundings a heavyset woman burst through the door. "If'n you'll be needin' to wash up, there's a pump out back," she called out. "Lunch is just about on and the stage'll be leavin' in thirty minutes, so you all better hurry on up."

Abdul walked slowly towards the house. An ancient man sat motionless on the porch. Tipping his hat to the old man, Abdul noticed that his long hair was held with leather thongs. Around his neck hung a leather pouch. A sash of brilliant colors was draped over his cotton shirt. The sash was embroidered intricately with beads of many colors, forming a geometric pattern. The moccasins he wore came to his knee and appeared to be new. 'An American Indian', Abdul deduced. He had read many papers on the native culture and had attended an exhibit of their art in London.

"Supper's on!" the woman squawked.

"Will you be joining us?" Abdul asked. The old man shook his head.

Supper consisted of a spoonful of watery beans and a chunk of greasy cornbread. Abdul choked down a bit of the beans and passed on the bread, then took his leave. Hoping to talk with the old man, he walked outside, but the Indian had disappeared.

The horses had been changed and the drivers were checking the harness as he approached the stage.

"Be a few minutes afore we pull out," the driver began. "You might want to walk about, mister. It's gonna be a bit longer to the next station. These roads can be tricky."

"Thank you; I think I will," Abdul said, walking away.

When he returned his fellow travelers were gathered together. Abdul could hear them discussing someone in not so pleasant terms.

"I will not have my wife riding with one of those savages!" the woman's husband protested.

"Who let him buy a ticket anyway?" the young man retorted. "All they ever do is drink!" said the man who smelled of whiskey.

"Excuse me," Abdul interrupted, "what seems to be the problem?"

The young man spoke up, "Somebody sold one of them heathens a ticket to ride on the stage."

"What heathens?" he asked.

"Them damned Indians," the older man replied.

"I do not understand," Abdul continued, "If you are referring to the gentleman on the porch, he looked civilized to me."

"A lot you foreigners know," the woman began, "Indians have been killing us decent folks ever since we first moved to this land. They have no morals! They torture women and force their children to run naked through the woods." Her face lost all color.

"Now, dear, don't upset; yourself," her husband said, placing his arm around her.

"All aboard," the driver called out.

"I cannot sit with him," the woman whined.

"If it will make the ride easier for you, Madame, I will sit next to the gentleman in question," Abdul offered.

The passengers were still debating the issue as Abdul climbed inside.

Smiling, he took a seat next to the old man. Still grumbling protests, the others boarded the stage. The younger man was forced to sit with Abdul and the Indian.

Abdul was laughing to himself, 'All this fuss over something so trivial. Maybe this trip will not be as dull as I had expected!'

The tension inside the coach was incredible. The woman muttered continuously, her face wrinkled in disgust, a handkerchief held to her nose as if there was a horrible odor. The man who smelled of whiskey stared blankly out the window. The younger man shifted incessantly in his seat. The Indian sat stoically, turning a carved walking stick slowly in his hands. Abdul admired the carvings; he had to keep reminding himself not to stare.

The stick was smooth, with carvings from the top to the bottom. Some of the designs were simple, others intricate.

A few of the carvings were stained. A section of the carvings bore a resemblance to symbols from an old Arabic or Greek culture. Still others reminded him of ancient Egyptian pictographs. He decided that he would approach the old man to discuss the carvings. He would wait, however, until they could separate themselves from these prejudiced people.

The coach slowed as the sun was dipping over the horizon. "Batesville Station," the driver called out. The passengers wasted no time escaping from the coach.

Abdul found it amusing. "You would think that they had been riding with a pack of vipers," he said to the old man.

"The snake people are more pleasant," the Indian replied in a voice that was deep and rich.

"Allow me to introduce myself, Abdullah Bereshni Frankenstone from London, England," he said, offering his hand.

"I am called Inoli [Eye - no - lee is one called Black Fox in the Cherokee language]," the old man replied, climbing from the coach.

Batesville was bustling with small town activities. "Here you go, chief," the driver said, tossing a bundle to Inoli. "Mr. Frankenstone, sir, your baggage will be delivered to the Batesville Hotel. You will find it around the corner on your right." The driver continued, "The morning stage will be ready to depart by seven. If you wish, you may send your baggage back to the loading dock before your breakfast."

"Thank you," Abdul responded. Inoli was walking away from town.

"Excuse me," Abdul called out. Inoli walked on. "Are you not staying at the hotel this evening?" he asked, running to catch up.

"My people are not welcome in the white man's world. I will spend the night with the Earth Mother and her children. I am always welcome there." Inoli said, walking on.

"I was hoping to have a conversation with you after we had eaten?" Abdul inquired.

"If you wish, you may come and sit with me. I will be with my brothers ... there." Inoli pointed to a field just outside of town. Abdul watched him walk into the sunset.

The hotel was modest compared with some establishments he had frequented. The food, however, was well prepared and satisfying. After eating a hearty meal, he checked into his room and found it clean and inviting. After washing the grime from himself he decided to find Inoli. Passing through the lobby, Abdul noticed the two gentlemen from the stage – they were drinking at the bar. "A fine pair," he muttered to himself.

The night air was crisp, the sky clear, and the stars were shining brightly. Abdul found Inoli camped at the edge of town. A small fire burned steadily. As he approached, he noticed Inoli chanting softly and sprinkling something over the fire. The substance caused the fire to sparkle for an instant, and release an odor that reminded him of a forgotten and faraway place. He paused just outside the firelight.

"You may sit if you wish." Inoli gestured for Abdul to sit down.

"I came to talk with you," Abdul began, "Have you eaten? I was thinking that I might have brought you something if..."

"I have already eaten all that I need. The land is good to me. I treat her with respect and I never go hungry," Inoli said, offering him a cup.

A blaze of color exploded from Inoli's chest. Staring intently, Abdul asked, "Are you a magician?"

Inoli chuckled, "No, I am no magician. All I ever cared to be was a man."

"If I might ask, what caused the light upon your chest?"

"The daughter of Ulansunti [Oo - lahn - soon - tee is the name given by the Cherokees to the crystal embedded in a great beast – it means 'transparent']. She was given to me by my father as he crossed over. I have cared for her ever since." Inoli stared at the sky, as he placed his hand over the object that hung upon his chest.

"Is the daughter a crystal?" Abdul asked.

"I know not what crystal is," Inoli replied.

"They are exceptional stones from the earth. I am on a quest to find a very special one," Abdul began. "This stone is very old. With her, a man can see things that cannot be seen." Inoli nodded as Abdul continued, "She will share secrets that no man would ever know. On the night she was born, a great storm raged. The boy who was present at her birth cared for her for many years. He became a great man, possessing of strength and foresight unknown at that time. It is said that this stone became his companion."

"I have heard of such a legend. A long time ago, a white man told the grandfathers a legend of such a stone. It is a good legend, not like some that I have heard from the white man." Inoli continued, "This man was also on a quest. He was searching for a sacred spring. The water from this spring would allow the old to become young."

"I know of that man," Abdul began, "but what I came to talk to you about was the carvings on your walking stick."

Inoli nodded, "The marriage stick." He handed Abdul the stick. "This is the record of a bond between a man and a woman. When a couple wishes to join, they look for the tree that will yield the staff that will hold the memories of their union. When the bonding ceremony is finished, this carving is made by the medicine man." He pointed to the first carving. "It records the month and the year of the union. Every time a special event happens, another carving is added. Not all carvings are happy; some are very sad."

Pointing to another section of the stick, he continued, "That was the old way of recording our history; this is the new way of recording. Sequoyah invented this language before the removal." He traced the carvings that resembled the Arabic/Greek runes. "This one," Inoli pointed to a deeps angry rune, "records the day the soldiers came for my family. I was on the mountain with my grandsons when they came. My wife, daughter and son were sent to the reservation. I remained in the mountains with my grandsons until they were grown. Now I go to be with my wife."

Abdul recognized sorrow in his voice. "Soon the time will come to pass the daughter of Ulansunti to my son. I must cross over and the daughter must be given to my son." Inoli, chanting softly, busied himself with a small pot.

Abdul examined the runes in the light for a long time. His own memories stirred as he traced the designs. "It is getting late," Abdul said reluctantly. Inoli nodded. "Would you mind if we talked more on our journey together?" he asked the old man.

Staring into Abdul's eyes, Inoli said, "I will have to take council. You will have my answer tomorrow."

Abdul nodded, then handed the staff back to his friend. "Until tomorrow, then."

Abdul was up and packed before dawn. Inoli had evoked memories that he had almost forgotten. Anxious to talk more with him, Abdul ate lightly, sent his baggage to be loaded, then headed for the old man's camp. There was no trace of it. Disheartened, he returned to the station.

"Cumberland Stage departing for St. Louis in ten minutes," a boy called out.

Abdul looked in vain for Inoli in the crowd that was gathering. When he boarded, he found his friend sitting quietly. "Good morning," he began, "I went to your camp but you had left."

"Sometimes it is better to walk softly in the white man's world," Inoli whispered. "I will not speak with you until we can be alone." Abdul nodded and spent the day contemplating questions he would ask Inoli.

The day's journey ended in Versailles, Indiana. It was just like the other Midwestern towns he had seen. The same people with the same attitudes. The way that these people treated Inoli was trying his patience.

Inoli was camped outside this town as well. Once again he waited for Inoli's invitation. The old man smiled as he motioned for Abdul to sit.

"It was a good day's journey," he began, "My family was forced to walk to the reservation. It was a long and terrible journey. The soldiers would not let us bury our dead. Our women suffered more than the others. Many died bringing new life into this world. It was a sad time." Inoli traced a carving on his stick.

"Perhaps we can talk about the daughter," Abdul suggested, hoping to change their discussion to a more pleasant topic.

"I will tell you of the Ukenta." [Oo - ken - tah was a great warrior who was transformed into a beast]

"Ukenta?"

"Ulansunti was bonded to Ukenta. In hilahiu [Hi - lah - hi - you is the Cherokee word for ancient time] Father Sun became angry with the nations. He sent a terrible sickness to the Earth Mother and her children. The sickness took many lives. Great medicine men were not able to stop the sickness. A council was held for all the chiefs and medicine men. The Little Men were also invited."

"Who are the Little Men?" Abdul asked.

"They are the small ones who lived in the forests many seasons past. They had powerful magic. They talked to the animals and birds. They fashioned beautiful objects from stones they would find. I have found such stones," Inoli said, handing Abdul a stone from his pouch. It was yellow in color, oval and smooth. It was amber.

"My people call the Little Men 'Gnomes,'" Abdul replied, handing the stone back to Inoli.

"That is a good name." After pouring a hot beverage for both of them, Inoli continued. "The council devised a plan to kill Father Sun. A great warrior was selected. He was the strongest and bravest warrior of all the tribes. For many days the Medicine Men prayed and cast spells. As the days went on the warrior changed from a man into the Ukenta. He had sharp horns like the buck, and was given wings like the hawk. Ukenta's wings were small but strong. He had a body like the serpent with scales that changed color as he moved. He had talons like the eagles, so that he could grasp and hold Father Sun."

"While the warrior was being transformed, the Little Men had been fashioning and polishing Ulansunti. The Earth Mother had given a special stone to the Little Men. This stone was to be joined with Ukenta. Ulansunti would change the sun's light into colors so bright that it would blind Father Sun. Unable to see, Father Sun could then be destroyed by Ukenta. When the Medicine Men had finished transforming the warrior, he was delivered to the Little Men. The Little Men then joined the two together; Ulansunti was embedded into his forehead. Ukenta was ready to battle Father Sun."

'Is it possible that there could be *two* Crystals?' Abdul thought to himself. "What happened to Ukenta?" Abdul asked aloud as Inoli refilled his cup.

"Ukenta was sent to the upper world. After many months of planning, he engaged Father Sun in battle. Father Sun defeated Ukenta and returned him to earth. Ukenta was very angry. Angry at the Medicine Men who had transformed him; angry with Father Sun. Ulansunti was the only thing that he cared about. He would steal women to care for her. When Ukenta fed, the blood from his kills would foul her beauty. With talons for hands, he could not remove the blood from her." Inoli paused; carefully he removed the stone from around his neck and handed it to Abdul.

"Ukenta, having been a man, was cursed with the desires of a man," he smiled at Abdul, "Soon, he lusted for a woman. No matter what a man becomes, he cannot deny his nature. Sometimes he released his desires with an animal or a bird. Other times a woman was taken to fulfill his needs. Nothing that ever mated with Ukenta survived the birth of his child. His children were strong and lived no matter what nation their mother was from. The people were not aware of Ukenta's lust. They had been praying to the Earth Mother to banish Ukenta from the middle world, for the game was disappearing from the land.

The Earth Mother answered their prayers. After putting Ukenta to sleep, she separated Ulansunti from him. She did not want Ukenta to hurt anyone again. Ulansunti was given to the Cherokees. Special rituals were given to the people so that they might take care of Ulansunti. Ukenta was sent to the upper world where he finally found peace. Soon the people noticed that game was again disappearing from places where no one hunted. Women would disappear, sometimes even warriors. The Medicine Men fasted and sought visions to determine the source of the problem.

A frightening vision was revealed. Many small Ukentas were living in the cliffs of the great mountains. They were the children of the great Ukenta. Only one way to kill Ukenta's children was revealed to the Medicine Men. Many tried, only a few succeeded. The daughters of Ulansunti were removed by those who killed the small Ukentas, to care for and protect."

Abdul had been examining the stone that belonged to Inoli. It was a natural quartz crystal, a six-sided double terminated stone with a spot of brilliant red in the center. He held the stone up to the light; brilliant colors flashed as he turned it. "So, your father defeated an Ukenta?" he asked.

Inoli chuckled, "No, my father's grandfather defeated the beast. After the white man invaded our land, the great beasts left our land, as did the Little Men. We have not seen them in many, many seasons. The medicine is leaving the people." Abdul handed the stone back to Inoli, who began chanting as he raised the stone to the sky; then he sprinkled powder upon the fire and replaced the stone around his neck.

"You said that Ulansunti was given to the Cherokees?" Abdul asked. Inoli nodded. "Is she still in their care?" Again he nodded. "Have you seen her?"

"No, like my grandsons, she is hidden high in the mountains where she is safe. The time will come, after the hoop is rejoined, when Ulansunti will be returned to the people. She has many wonderful gifts. Her daughters also have gifts, but they are small compared to hers."

The moon was setting as Abdul returned to the hotel. Sleep evaded him. His mind raced with the implications of the evening's discussion – could it be that his beloved Crystal had a sister?

Thunder roused Abdul from his dreamy state. Soon a knock came at the door. "Mister Frankenstone?"

"Yes," Abdul replied.

"The stage will be delayed about an hour, sir."

"Thank you." Having some extra time, Abdul repacked his belongings. While sorting through his things, he came across his copy of "Moby Dick", the recently published American novel about Captain Ahab and the White Whale. It reminded him of Commodore Matthew Perry and the voyage they would soon share. "I will find you," he said softly.

The stage finally departed two hours behind schedule. Although slightly damp, Inoli was on board. Abdul seated himself next to him. The married couple had remained in Batesville, and two young women boarded here in Versailles, much to the delight of the other gentlemen. The journey was slow and very wet. They were entertained by the amorous attention being paid to the young women by the other passengers. Deep inside Abdul something was stirring. Inoli smiled; he was aware of the stirrings even though Abdul was not, and he nodded approvingly.

It was still raining when the stage pulled into St. Louis. The passengers ran quickly for shelter, leaving Inoli and Abdul alone. "Surely you will not be staying outside this evening?"

Inoli nodded. "I have no choice. I am not allowed to remain in the white man's hotel."

"I will find some place for us to stay. Please remain here at the station; I will not be long." Abdul paused for only a moment, then departed. After a lengthy discussion with the manager of one of St. Louis' less reputable hotels, arrangements were made for both Inoli and himself. Quickly Abdul returned for him. He found the old man exactly where he had left him.

"I have made arrangements for us. However, they will not let us eat in the dining room – we will eat in our room." The old man nodded and followed Abdul.

After changing into dry clothing, Abdul ordered their meal. Inoli only picked at his food. "Are you feeling alright?" Abdul inquired.

"Our journey together is coming to an end. Tomorrow we will reach the place where I must follow the footsteps of my nation. I will go into the desert alone." A smile replaced his frown. "Two days from now I will be with my wife."

"If my quest was not so urgent, I would go with you," Abdul offered.

"It is not something you need concern yourself with." Inoli reached into his bundle and retrieved a small book.

"I will have no need for this," he said, handing it to Abdul. "This is the book of our people. I taught my grandsons our language as well as the white man's word. Some day they will teach their sons."

Abdul opened the book and glanced at the contents. "Why are you not giving the Ulansunti's child to them?"

"They have not been instructed in the medicine ways. Without such knowledge, the daughter is dangerous. I must give her to my son. He was instructed in the ways before the removal."

Interrupting, Abdul inquired, "What powers does she possess?"

Pausing briefly, Inoli continued, "She will show men visions of things that are, things that must be and things that could be. In the wrong hands her powers can be used to change those things that are supposed to be, have been, or are."

"The daughter sounds very similar to Crystal. I wonder if they are related?" Abdul wondered out loud.

"All things are of the Earth Mother's family. We are all children of the Earth. You and I, we are brothers. You share your legends with me, just as I share mine with you. Our paths crossed so that I might pass on to you the language and legends of my people. You have shown me kindness that I have never known from the white man."

Abdul nodded, "I admire your honesty and friendship. I will think of you often on my quest. When I find her I will tell her of man who cared for her sister's child."

Both men found sleep impossible. Dawn found them waiting at the station to board the stage. They did not talk; there was no need for words.

The way station at Prairie Grove, Arkansas was a desolate place. The lush growth of the Midwest was replaced with scrub brush and sand. Abdul was saddened at the thought of Inoli traveling alone through this hostile land.

Inoli offered Abdul his hand. "Do not be sad; soon I will go to the land of my ancestors. My stay in this land will be a short one. The daughter will keep me company on the last part of my journey. I wish you well on your search; I think that you will be searching in lands that are very different from the ones you know." He smiled in a way that puzzled Abdul.

"I am not sure I understand."

"You do not need to understand. The Creator will show you, in his own way, the path that you must follow. Remember, one cannot deny forever what they are." Smiling, Inoli walked into the desert.

"Boarding in five minutes for Fort Smith station."

Reading on the stage was impossible. If the constant bouncing was not enough, the young women had chosen to sit with him. Abdul decided it was to avoid any additional contact with the other gentlemen. Fort Smith lived up to its name – a wooden fortress complete with soldiers, children and natives. His accommodations were sparse to say the least. Abdul spent the evening thinking of Inoli and wishing him well.

The next few days blended together. One patch of desert looked like the next. Choking dust and warm temperatures tended to make the passengers grumpy. The way stations were sparsely furnished and most were manned by soldiers. The only diversion provided was the young ladies. Abdul had ignored women for such a long time that he had almost forgotten how enjoyable they could be. From time to time he found himself engaging in conversation with the ladies.

San Francisco, California was only hours away. According to the paper Abdul had purchased in Fresno, the Commodore was procuring supplies and readying his ships for Japan. His departure date had tentatively been set for May first, only two weeks from today. The article went on to say what Matthew Perry planned to accomplish in Japan and where he was staying. Abdul was pleased that he would be able to locate him immediately upon arrival in San Francisco. Although he did not want to admit it, he was going to miss the company of the young ladies. 'There will only be one woman for me,' he reminded himself again.

O' GREAT SPIRIT, Whose voice I hear in the winds,
And whose breath gives life to all the world, hear me!
I am small and weak, I need your strength and wisdom.
LET ME WALK IN BEAUTY, and make my eyes ever behold
the red and purple sunset.
MAKE MY HANDS respect the things you have made
and my ears sharp to hear your voice.
MAKE ME WISE so that I may understand the things
you have taught my people.
LET ME LEARN the lessons you have hidden in every
leaf and rock.
I SEEK STRENGTH, not to be greater than my brother,
but to fight my greatest enemy – myself.
MAKE ME ALWAYS READY to come to you with clean hands
and straight eyes.
SO WHEN LIFE FADES, as the fading sunset,
my spirit may come to you without shame.

An Indian Prayer

30
To Japan

Abdul reached San Francisco in high spirits. He inquired of his supplies and equipment that had been forwarded, and found it all in satisfactory condition. Now it was time to present himself to the Commodore. The Fresno paper had mentioned Perry staying on his flagship Mississippi out in the harbor, the flagship having a different name painted on for secrecy and privacy. The harbormaster should have all the details, he decided.

"Perry? Commodore Matthew Calbraith Perry? Sorry, don't have any word of his being in San Francisco." "Well, when will he be expected to arrive?"

"We have no word of Perry coming here. Do you have a need to know?"

"But the paper! Here, look at the article here in the Fresno paper. It says he is already here!"

"Hmm. Do you have any papers or official orders from the Commodore?"

"Why, yes, here is a letter from Perry himself saying he would meet me in San Francisco the first of May."

"Hmm. Let me see. Hmm. Ha! Look at the signature!" "Why, it says 'Matthew'. That's Matthew Perry."

"Can't prove it by me. He always signs orders 'The Commodore', or 'Commodore Perry'."

"Well, the letter was in response to my visit to his home the day before. He was away on business, but his wife Jane and his nephew Christopher – and Christopher's son Tom – were there. His wife had written me a note requesting I visit."

"Hmm. Why did his wife request your presence?"

"Why, I had watched a play with them – Jane, Christopher and others – at the new Wallack Theatre in New York, and Christopher mentioned the Commodore might be interested in me."

"Hmm. 'What was the play?"

"Henry the Eighth."

"Hmm. And what date did you say you were there?"

"Uh, January 12; the curtain rose a little after 9 PM. We went to the European Consulate afterwards."

"Hmm. How did you come to see the play with them?"

"Why, I had attended a reception in New York for the Commodore on November 20 this past year – at the Astor House – and I met a lovely lady who invited me to attend the play with them – she has a box at the Wallack. She said the Commodore would be there with us in her box, but he couldn't make it and his nephew was there instead – a Mrs. Trollope ...."

"*Mary* Trollope? Well, why didn't you say so earlier?" How is dear Mary? Haven't seen her in some time."

"You *know* Mrs. Trollope?!"

"We are close friends. She has many close friends. Ha! So, anyway, why are you so anxious to see the Commodore?"

"I have a very important mission that has taken me from Istanbul to Paris to Russia to England and now to Japan. I learned that the Commodore was visiting Japan and felt it would be safer if I traveled with him."

"Mr....? Frankenstone? Mr. Frankenstone, I have been sworn to secrecy by my Government concerning this affair, but since the time is close and you seem to be telling the truth, and since we have a common friend in Mary, it is safe to tell you."

"So, Mr. Frankenstone, the Commodore really did a number on you."

"I beg your pardon?"

"You poor soul, you poor lost soul. That pompous, arrogant, New York/Newport aristocratic son of a .... He used you as a decoy, man, – bait, stool pigeon. He went around Africa and up along the China coast – left Norfolk, Virginia on November 24 in his flagship *Mississippi*. Our fishing boats and Clippers spotted his paddle-wheel steamer in Hong Kong this past April 6."

"But why didn't he go the usual Clipper route around Cape Horn to San Francisco and then only three weeks to Japan?"

"Therein lies the nub, the whole purpose for this mad venture to that barbaric country. Japan has coal, and those new-fangled steamers need lots of coal. Those smoke belching, noisy, smelly tubs in the water are being promoted by our Government, and by this imperious snob of a stuffed shirt Perry. Why they want to phase out our beautiful Clippers I'll never know. The steamers have to be re-fueled every few thousand miles; that's the only reason they want to open up Japan – they want a coaling station there! If you really want to go to Japan and be clapped in jail, why, sail one of our fishing boats – there is one going to Japanese waters in three days. Have you crewed, or have you other shipboard talents, or can you pay your way as a passenger?"

Abdul and the harbormaster worked out the details and our hero was soon sailing toward Japan and Darwin. They met a Dutch ship bound for Japan, and Abdul and his possessions were transferred, improving the odds that Abdul would receive a safe reception and could enter Japan on his mission. The Dutch ship had picked up four shipwrecked American sailors, who were adventurous enough to put their lot in with Abdul.

The Dutch ship knew of a small, uninhabited island (with deep lagoon, abundant food and natural resources) that was not too far away from Edo [Tokyo]. They sailed past and pointed out features to Abdul, in case he ever changed his mind and decided to become a Robinson Crusoe. The island must have recently emerged from an undersea volcano, as it was not shown on any of the maritime charts. The captain and crew did not hold out much hope for his safety in Japan proper.

On 6 July 1853 the Dutch ship docked in Edo, dropped off the four sailors and Abdul along with his supplies and equipment, and notified the two governors, Toda Izu no kami and Ido Iwami no kami, that Commodore Perry was coming with his navy in a few days, and that they better take good care of Abdul and the four, as this was a test case. If they were hurt, Perry would declare war, with the backing of the whole United States Navy.

Abdul and the sailors were put in jail under close supervision until Perry had come (8 July 1853) and gone by 17 July 1853. Then Abdul was taken before the governors and interrogated.

. "He speaks English, but his appearance is not English, nor yet Yankee as the Commodore Perry and the other crew members."

"You are not Yankee. Please to give name and background and why you here."

"My name is Petrach Ivon Pauli Abdullah Bereshni Constantine Dimitri Aeschylus Frankenstone. I am a scion of Hasan, the great leader of world renown – the 'Man of the Mountain'; of the Georgian Southern Caucasus am I. I am of the Mendeleev clan – I am Captain O'Mendeleev's son. And I am looking for that holy stone whereby I can magnify my sight."

"I do not understand his strange language. What says he?"

"He be a South Caucasian of great military renown by name of Omén de Lievson. And he seeks a certain transcendent stone to expand his insight."

"Ah, so! The Southern Colonel seek Philosopher Stone!"

"Yes, the Philosopher's Stone! Where did you hear of it?"

"The whole world know of famous Philosopher Stone. The Dutch ship of science that comes once a year (with our permission) has given us all detail. Their countryman, a Mr. Anton Leeuwenhoek, use Stone during lifetime to see things that cannot be seen. He said it be only a paperweight, but his friends easily pierce subterfuge. His unwed daughter Maria ship it to Sir Isaac Newton after father die. This is common knowledge, is it not?"

And Abdul stood there, thunderstruck, until he finally replied, "A certain Charles Darwin signed it out of the Cambridge Museum in England prior to sailing to Japan. Is he still here?"

"Charles Darwin. Spell, please. English, yes? When he leave England? ... Name of boat? ... Don't know? Will save much time if have name of boat. Then we know which jail he be in. Wait, please."

After several hours of perusing records, they returned. "No record of Charles Darwin. Ah, Beagle name of boat? HMS Beagle? Wait, please ... No Beagle land in Japan. No Charles Darwin in Japan. Maybe ship be wrecked before reaching Japan. So sorry. One problem: We allow Dutch ship once a year because Dutch scientists aboard do not, how you say, proselyte. They have own problems with pagan, barbarous, cannibalistic religion. Since you must be guest for year until the Commodore Perry return, we ask you please to refrain from mentioning your religion, otherwise we place you in jail again."

Abdul nodded his acceptance, and bowed in the Japanese manner. "Ah, so!" exclaimed the two governors, smiling.

For the future, let none, so long as the sun illuminates the world, presume to sail to Japan, not even in the quality of ambassadors. And this declaration is never to be revoked on pain of death.

Tokugawa Shogun Ieyesu

1638 A.D.

31
Madame Butterfly

"Cho Cho, please come down!" Yoshi pleads.

If I only lean out a little further ... "I can see them," I exclaim, "There in the harbor." I point in the direction of Edo bay. 'It is good that they are going', I say to myself. There has been much disorder since the Americans arrived ten days ago on the third day of the sixth month, sixth year of Kaei. Perhaps now the city can return to normal. We should be preparing for the festival of O Bon. It will be our last festival as maiko [apprentice geisha, usually 12 to 17 years of age. They are virgins whose duties are limited to singing and dancing.].

"I beg you, please! Come down." Yoshi is now whining. Her spirit is not adventurous at all. As I climb down I begin to giggle. Imagine the look on Okasan's face [Okasan is the name given to all teacher/mothers of geisha; she controls and oversees the training and duties of geisha and maiko.] were she to find me, Cho Cho San, a first class maiko, almost sixteen years old, climbing the bridge rail like a child. We turn towards the garden and I begin to laugh. Yoshi, sensing the humor in the situation, joins me. We talk of our plans for tomorrow.

The Festival of the Stars is a small but happy occasion. Lovers will place banners professing their desires at the shrines of the young lovers. Ito and I have made plans to meet after I have completed my duties. Hisho San has asked Yoshi and me to entertain with her that evening. We both agree that she will not need our services for long.

"Okasan chose Hisho's dana-san well," Yoshi giggles.

I agree. [dana-san is a proprietor for a geisha; plural danan-san] "I hope she chooses as well for me," she sighs heavily. Although I should be happy at my impending rise in status, my heart is heavy. Once I am geisha, Ito and I will never be able to meet. He is so young and still struggling. The business he opened is doing well, but it will be years before he could afford me. I hear his voice in the trees, his face is reflected in the pools of still water ... [A geisha is a Japanese woman who is trained in the cultural areas, singing and dancing, musical instruments as well as ceremonies such as the tea service and religious rituals. They rarely marry because they are supported by powerful and influential men. They are not prostitutes; the closest Western equivalent would be a courtesan, mistress, or concubine.]

"CHO CHO SAN! YOSHI SAN!" Okasan's voice calls out. "Come quickly." She claps her hands together. "Come! A Tokugawa Samurai awaits you in the main hall." We bow respectfully to our mother/teacher and hurry towards the house.

"I wonder why a samurai has a summons for us?" Yoshi asks anxiously.

"You worry too much. You will become wrinkled if you are not careful," I tease. "The Shogunate has probably sent another compliment to our Diayamo. *'I am pleased that you have chosen to enter your young women in such an honorable profession,'*" I reply in a husky voice, my chin lifted in the regal pose, and I nod towards Yoshi. She giggles, placing her hand over her mouth as we enter the hall. [Diayamo is a lord of a prefecture (district or "state") prior to the Meiji restoration.]

Eight other maiko are assembled; we are all nearing graduation. I smile at Yoshi as we take our places on the pillows that have been reserved for us. The samurai takes a deep breath and begins:

"Shogunate Tokogawa has issued the following command." Ceremoniously he breaks the seal and unfolds the parchment. "The Americans have left our waters." He pauses. "They elected to leave a small but treacherous entourage behind to insure our cooperation. In the interest of the security of our beloved Edo, I have divided these gaijin [foreigners] into smaller groups. These groups will be removed from the city." He pauses again. "Two samurai, a priest translator and two maiko will accompany the gaijin to neighboring prefectures." Yoshi and I exchange worried glances. "Your reward for helping to secure Edo will be: your choice of suitable danan-san; full rights and status as geisha upon your return to Edo. The Americans will return in one year and so shall you. You will be escorted to your assigned prefectures as soon as accommodations have been made for you and the Americans."

The samurai bows deeply and retreats. My mind reels from the implications. Gone? Leave Edo? Away from my beloved for one year? To be able to choose my danan-san myself? Would I dare choose one so young? Yoshi prods me from my thoughts. Okasan has arrived.

"I am not happy with the orders of the Shogunate. To take such fine maiko and send them to do the duties of a second class geisha," she shakes her head in disgust. "I will expect you to entertain the Diayamo as any other noble. He would never ask you to pillow, he will know your status. I have been told that the Americans find no pleasure in pillowing. There is always the possibility that one may approach you. If this should happen, I advise you to seek out another to take your place. If there is no other way, seek out a samurai. I plan to speak with them before you depart."

As is Okasan's way, she is most explicit in her instructions. "Cho Cho San, you and Yoshi will leave in the morning. You will be sent to your home prefecture, Chiba." She continues as my mind fills with memories of home. It has been many years since I was there. Mother will be so excited. My siblings are much older now. Pleasant thoughts of my childhood by the sea bring a smile to my face.

The passage to Chosi, my home village, proceeds smoothly. We passed the Festival of the Stars in Narita. Yoshi and I placed our banners at a small but well-kept shrine. I can only hope that Ito placed his banner and that Kami will hear our prayers. [Kami: spirit or life force. The Japanese see Kami in anything of beauty or strength.] It takes only four days to reach my father's house. As we approach I can see that the house has recently been renovated. A larger room has been added to the south wall and a small house sits alone in the front lawn.

"For the gaijin," Yoshi snickers. "Hisho told me that they smell like dung. They do not bathe." Her nose wrinkles in disgust.

"You are teasing, Yoshi. Surely they bathe."

She turns towards me, her face ashen, "Once, Hisho was asked to prepare one for an audience before Tokogawa himself. The gaijin threw her from the bath house!"

"Hisho must be mistaken," I mumble, recalling the only gaijin I have seen. He did smell and was unkempt, but all prisoners in the Edo jail are. His eyes I remember were black as was his hair. Edo prison breaks most men, but he was not broken. I can see him rising in his cell to bow to me as I passed. Okasan must be wrong. He seemed capable of pillowing to me.

Yoshi and I settle into our apartment. I am both pleased and saddened at the arrangement. As maiko, we are given separate quarters. The freedom is enjoyable, but I miss the closeness of sharing a room with my sisters. Mother refuses to allow me to help with the cooking, saying it is below my rank. Father is very removed and distant. Mother says he is adjusting to my rise is status and will be better when things return to normal. I hope she is right. There are so many things that we can share now that I am educated in worldly matters.

All too soon a courier comes with news that the Americans are only half a day's journey away from the village. Nervously we prepare for them by checking their quarters and preparing tea. The waiting is most difficult. The village children announce their arrival by racing before them yelling and screaming. Each person in the procession is greeted with the respect due them by rank and status. The five Americans, much to my surprise, are much younger than I imagined. Tea is served in an atmosphere that is strained. I notice that one American, more mature than the others, seems versed in proper etiquette. The others follow his example. He has dark hair and eyes like the other gaijin. I can feel his gaze as I go about my duties.

A few days pass and the household returns to a somewhat normal state. We have begun to prepare for the festival of O Bon. The Diayamo has requested that Yoshi and I dance for the village at the sacred shrine. Yoshi and I spend the mornings practicing in the gardens always under the watchful eye of the samurai and the dark haired American.

Today Yoshi is going to the village and I have decided to make my banner for the festival. Parchment and pens in hand, I retire to the garden. My lettering flows freely today. A strange voice speaks to me. Startled, I look up into the face of the American. His arms are full of papers and books.

I notice that the priest, who follows him everywhere, is absent. He gestures towards my pens and parchment and then to the ground. I interpret this to mean that he wishes to join me. I nod and point to the ground. We spend the next few hours writing. I find his work acceptable but constrained. He notices that I am appraising his work. He points to the top characters and says, "E nay mah." Tilting my head slightly I point to the markings. "E nay mah," he repeats, pointing to himself.

Nodding, I pen my name, then say it out loud, "Cho Cho." He pens a few more characters, then says, "Dimitri Frankenstone." I gesture to the first marks again. "Ee Ne Mo?" He surprises me by laughing. My face reddens as I realize that I might have been improper. His manner tells me that I am not.

Smiling, he points to the other marks and repeats them. Nodding, I reply, "Dimitri, Cho Cho. "Hai," he replies in my own tongue. Startled, I pen a few simple words for him. He picks up these words quickly. I find him most intelligent for an uncivilized person. We spend the rest of the morning exchanging simple words and phrases.

O Bon has begun. The villagers are proceeding to the shrine. Yoshi and I gather up our instruments and join the procession. We flirt with the crowd as they sing and dance. I glance back towards the house. The Americans have joined the procession. Each person places his banner at the shrine. We dance joyously, free from the restrictions of daily life. Being a geisha does have its advantages, I remind myself.

Mother has prepared a wonderful feast for us. Only the finest and rarest of seafood sit before us. My sisters and I delve into them with much pleasure. A priest interrupts. As is the custom, my mother and sisters leave the room.

"Please forgive my intrusion," he snivels, "The Americans have requested that you entertain them tomorrow." His face pales.

"And?" I inquire.

"I would be most happy to find another to serve them, Madame," he bows before me.

"There is no need. I will serve them." My reply is short and to the point. He stammers for words, but I bow, signaling the end of our conversation. He retreats as my mother returns.

"Cho Cho, you must not serve the gaijin." Her voice is shrill. "Mother, I am geisha."

"Not until you return to Edo," she reminds me.

"I have danced my final dance as maiko; I am old enough and will choose my own proprietor." The remainder of me meal is eaten in silence. Maybe Kami has heard my prayers.

As the time nears I find myself both excited and nervous. Walking towards the kitchen, I hear Father calling out to me. I bow and kneel before him.

"I have been informed that you will serve the gaijin?" I nod. "Daughter, it is below you to serve them. I will intervene and choose one more suitable."

"No, Father." I rise before him.

"I will not permit you to jeopardize your status by consorting with the gaijin."

"Father, it is no longer your place to choose for me. I am geisha, not you." My heart is racing when I enter the kitchen. Daughters are not to speak to their fathers that way. I remind myself that I am no longer a daughter, but a geisha.

The priest who informed me of the Americans' request meets me at the door of the small house. I inquire as to how many I will be entertaining. He informs me that there will be only one. He pleads with me to allow another to take my place. I find his manner unsuitable for one of his rank and tell him so. Obviously frustrated, he leaves.

I hear someone approaching. Much to my surprise, Dimitri enters dressed in traditional Japanese clothing. I bow so as not to appear rude. I find him most attractive.

"You look beautiful this evening," he smiles, reaching down to lift my chin. My face reddens.

"You look very pleasant," I reply meekly. He talks about last night's festival as I serve sake. It is easy for me to forget that he is gaijin – his command of our language is so good.

"I am famished," he announces.

This word is foreign to me. I return a puzzled look. "Food?" he repeats.

I nod and place his meal before him. "You will join me?"

Laughing, I inform him that women do not eat with men, that it is not proper.

"Perhaps you will not be proper this evening?" Although tempted, I decline.

He takes his food in proper fashion, slowly and without haste. "Very good," he announces, sliding his dish towards me. As I reach for the bowl, he places his hand over mine. "You are most desirable." Leaning closer to me, he places his hand on my chin, lifting it up so that I look into his eyes. My heart races. Gently he kisses me, his breath is warm and sweet. My emotions are jumbled. He rises, pulling me up with him. He embraces me; I relax in his arms. He strokes my shoulders as he murmurs words I do not understand.

"Will you lay with me, my little one?"

My eyes widen. "I am maiko; I have yet to experience a man." My voice wavers.

He does not withdraw; his mood however, changes slightly. "Some day, Cho Cho, but not tonight." He releases me from his embrace, escorts me to the door and kisses me once more.

"I have enjoyed your company; I look forward to the next time." He bows respectfully.

Dimitri and I spend many days together during the next few weeks. Walks to the village to visit the fishing boats become almost a daily habit. He amazes me with his knowledge of the sea and her creatures. I attend the theater with him. There are days when Dimitri and his companions are not to be found. I do not know where they could go, but they leave without the knowledge of the samurai. My curiosity regarding his absence is great, but I never think to ask of this when we are together. Over the next few weeks I learn much about Dimitri. He is not American but comes from a place called Europe. He speaks many languages and is very knowledgeable. Should he ask me again, I will pillow with him.

Today the air is crisp. I relish the relief from the heat. The winter winds will blow soon and our days of walking to the ocean will be numbered.

"Cho Cho San," Dimitri calls out, "I see that you are also enjoying the cool weather." We walk in the cool air. "I would like you to attend me this evening."

"I would be most honored, Dimitri San." A smile comes to my face.

This evening Dimitri seems preoccupied. He is sullen and distant.

"Have I caused you displeasure?" I inquire.

"No, you are not the cause of my trouble." He pushes his food away. "I came here, to this country in search of another. I have learned that she is not here." A frown crosses his face. "Does she know that you search for her?"

"No," he laughs. I am puzzled. How can one find someone who does not know that they are being looked for? "No need to trouble yourself, Cho Cho." His mood lightens. "She is very rare. Her beauty is unsurpassed by mere mortals. Beautiful and most dear to me, but you, you are most enjoyable." He kisses me.

"Where are your companions this evening?" I inquire.

"They will not return until tomorrow." He grasps my hands firmly. "Will you lay beside me this evening?" he asks, kissing my neck. I gaze into his eyes, unable to reply. Caressing me gently, he asks again. I reply with a kiss. We retire to his sleeping quarters. I find myself lost in a sea of emotion as we explore each other. Tenderly, slowly, we fulfill each other's needs. Our hearts beat together, our eyes cloud with passion. I expect discomfort but find none. Dimitri is most pleasurable. "I find no words to express how I feel," Dimitri says softly. I sense sorrow in his voice and do not understand.

I share his bed often during the next few months, but I find that his company is more enjoyable than pillowing. At times he is distant from me; I wonder if he knows of whom I think when we pillow.

"Daughter!" Father bellows, breaking my thoughts.

"Yes?" I bow but do not kneel.

"You must stop serving the American," he orders. "I will not have you succumb to his pagan ways." His eyes flash angrily.

"Dimitri San is a most learned and honorable man," I protest.

"I care not what you think. I am concerned for your future. What if you become blessed? You would not be allowed full rank upon your return to Edo." Tears form in my eyes; he does not know that I am already blessed; I have told only Kami.

"I do not wish to be geisha. You chose for me. I only wish to be married to Ito. A reduction in status would allow us to be together." I bow to hide my tears.

"Ito? The young man in Edo? He is a child. Daughter, are you deranged?" He paces furiously.

"I am not. Ito and I prayed to Kami to allow us to be together. We professed our love during the Festival of the Stars. There is nothing that you can do." Tears stream down my face and I run from the house. I hear him yelling at me from the house. Aimlessly I walk the grounds. Dimitri appears as if sensing my need. I whisper his name as I collapse into his arms.

"What is wrong, my dear Cho Cho?"

"It is my father." I try to control my tears. "He is angry at me because I share your bed."

"You have the right to choose."

"I am geisha – I choose my proprietors." My voice is quivering.

"Dimitri, we have created life."

He pushes me away and stares into my eyes. "A child?"

I nod, tears flowing down my cheeks. He pulls me close, wiping the tears from my face. "A child. When?"

"Near the time of O Bon in the summer." We hold each other, neither one of us speaking.

"Cho Cho, I cannot stay." His voice is full of emotion.

"I understand. I do not regret my choice. You are an honorable and generous man. Your child will be strong." I pause ... "You have given me more than a child, you have given me my freedom." We hold each other for a long time, not wishing to let go. The sun slips over the horizon. We release each other. I return to my apartment, not looking back.

The following week is most difficult for me to bear. Father refuses to speak with me. Yoshi is full of questions that I will not answer. Mother seems to cry every time she sees me, and Dimitri is nowhere to be found. As the days go by the tension fades and life resumes its natural course. The child grows with each passing day.

I visit Dimitri whenever I can. We talk of the child and speak only of the present. He will leave soon to search for his beloved. I have learned that she is not mortal but a Kami. Only a Kami could evoke such desire. Spring will arrive soon and he will be gone. I still wonder where they go when they disappear. Dimitri says it is best that I do not know. My heart grows heavy as the time for him to depart grows near. My emotions are in turmoil.

During our walk today he begins to speak to me, his face full of sorrow. "I will leave soon. I cannot tell you when, for I am not sure myself. When the time comes there will be no time for talk." I bow to hide my grief. "When I find the one I seek I will return. She will guide me to you and to our child." He places his hand on my enlarged abdomen. "Teach the child well, dearest Cho Cho. Guide the child; do not allow the mistakes of the past to be repeated with the child."

I kiss him gently. "I wish for a girl. I will tell the child of her father and how he gave me my freedom. The deeds that you have done will be told to her as she grows. One day we will welcome you home." I fight back the tears as we walk. "I will never forget you, E Ne Mo Dimitri Frankenstone."

The next few months I cannot sleep at night. Their words trouble me, words that I heard them speaking softly when they leave with Dimitri: 'Crystal not here; desert island; submarine; Darwin; Beagle; pidgin Japanese; crew of jailbirds; instruments; Krupp engines; keel; propeller'. What can it all mean? He is obsessed and sad. Some day he will return and I will find out ... The child comes – a beautiful black-haired girl. Thoughts of Dimitri fade. It is good. Ito is with me. We are betrothed and my father gives his blessing. I am happy ... A letter comes from America, from Commodore Matthew Perry, to my parents' address, through the American Consulate recently set up, for Dimitri. I will keep it until my daughter's father returns ...

32
The Search for Crystal in the Deep

Dimitri and the other jailbirds, as the reader may surmise, have been engaged in building a submarine to search the ocean floors of the world to check for the shipwrecked *Beagle*, for Darwin's body, and for Crystal.

Dimitri is the Captain of the ship, the Nautilus, built to his specifications on the desert island, the parts purchased with money he has acquired over the years in his Swiss bank account. A complete account of the last year of their voyage in the ship may be read in the notes of 1867-1868 by the French professor Monsieur Aronnax. It had taken Dimitri and his crew until 1865 to complete the submarine, and sea trials were completed the following year – the year in which bizarre rumors began circulating, rumors of ships at sea encountering an enormous thing, a long, spindle-shaped object, much larger and faster and more powerful than any whale.

The reader is strongly urged to procure and refer to a good English translation of these notes, found in Jules Verne's book "20,000 Leagues Under the Sea."

33
At the Museum

Nearly circumnavigating the globe in the search for Crystal, we approached the cold sea off Norway and the dreaded "Navel of the Ocean," a maelstrom formed at the tide in the confined waters between the islands of Ferroe and Lofoten. I was troubled ... deeply troubled by some thought playing at the very edge of my mind. During my long life, when such a problem was presented to me, if I could but engage in strenuous activity, then my thoughts would clear and the correct decision would be made. But just now, there was no event to challenge...

"Captain! Come to the bridge! All nature has broken loose, and Hell's Gates seem to be slamming in upon us!" The first mate was not normally excitable, so this must be a truly awesome spectacle. I grabbed my jacket and cap and bolted towards the forward deck of the *Nautilus.* Looking through the view panels, I could understand Daniel's fear. The maelstrom had drawn us down into its spinning clutches. There seemed no way out, no chance for survival!

Water rushed in and pounded the vessel until surely she must break. Think! Think, Nemo! Suddenly an idea, a chance to take that could mean salvation for us all. "Daniel! Take her down through the spiral, full speed ahead!"

Everyone who heard these words turned to me as if I had lost my senses. "But Captain," they began to mutter. The furious tone of my words lashed them to silence.

"If you wish to live, by God and all Creation, follow my orders now!"

The Nautilus responded to the surge of power, cutting through that downward spiral until my order for "hard rudder right" was obeyed, and we sped away from the maelstrom's clutches and into the open sea.

The men gave a loud hurrah that resounded throughout every hidden corner of the submarine. We took stock and found all shipshape, except the dinghy and the Frenchmen were gone! "They have escaped to their doom," I said sorrowfully. But then another thought...my own salvation ... Yes! God Omnipotent! Enough! It is accomplished. Enough! Darwin never returned to the Museum, but rests at home in England with her this very moment! It must be. Yes! Yes! And only then did I celebrate as well.

With the crew disbanded and the *Nautilus* secured a few feet below the surface in a secluded fjord, I began the long journey to London. And there I would find her. That was a certainty, my reasoning sound from my exertions of bringing my vessel through the maelstrom to safety. The two possibilities I had never considered were that Crystal had never left England and that Darwin had never sailed to Japan. I was convinced now in my mind that the Japanese had never seen him, and from my 20,000 leagues under the sea, that there was no shipwrecked Beagle. Darwin could have returned safely to England; he did return safely to England. If he had lost her overboard during his voyage, I would have found her, so closely had I examined the ocean floor. The only possible conclusion – she was with him, or his descendants, most likely living in London, and he had forgotten to return her to the Museum. In my years working on the Nautilus and in sailing her I had neglected my current events, an oversight which I would shortly remedy. My one ambition now was to reach the empire's capital as quickly as possible, and by any available means. The years apart from my beloved were coming to a close.

Dog and sled, horse and wagon, ship – and finally London. Tingling with anticipation, the game was afoot as I moved to claim my most prized possession. The gold stored away in the secret holds of the Nautilus paled in comparison with Crystal, the one to soothe a tortured soul, the one promised to me generations ago in the legend, the one to lead me to my love. I walked the streets briskly, long strides outpacing leisurely souls whose minds were much less preoccupied than mine. Dear God, I had only to locate Darwin and the long years of loneliness would soon come to an end. I felt better than I had in years; perhaps it was true – the vapors from the sodium-mercury amalgam used to produce the submarine's electricity had put me, and all my crew, into a progressively darker mood as the years had passed under the sea.

A few questions posed to quick-witted street urchins (street irregulars, I heard them called) and the accompanying shilling reward drew forth the information I so desired. Down House, outside London, there he lived quietly with his wife (a cousin, I was told). I was soon at the door.

For all the danger I had endured upon the sea, I watched like some interested by-stander as my trembling hand stretched out to grasp the brass door knocker. "Dr. Frankenstone to see Mr. Darwin," I said. Presently the maid returned with this man whose discoveries (as I learned later) on the voyage of the Beagle left very little of the book of Genesis intact as a literal account of history.

"Yes, Dr. Frankenstone, how may I be of assistance?"

"Mr. Darwin, I do not presume to be rude, but you have many years ago signed out a lightning stone from the Cambridge Museum, and I had reason to acquire it for study and have been searching for you for some time."

"I don't remember any lightning ... oh, my! I never signed it in upon my return to England back in '36. I am sorry, Dr. Frankenstone, truly I am sorry. This is not like me at all. Come up to my study. It should be there somewhere with all the other arti-facts brought back from the voyage. A fulgurite, eh? You start at that end and I will begin here, and we should find it presently. I never came across another quite like it. The Museum box also held a small telescope, which I have here somewhere, but as I could never get it to work, I never took it along. Emma, did you remove a lightning stone from my study and use it for a doorstop or something? Emma? Oh, never mind, here is the stone.

A shout, a cry of exhalation came involuntarily from my mouth, but I was not looking toward Charles Darwin – I had found the tiny, exquisitely formed telescope. "At last, I have found you, Crystal – the one sent by God to enlarge my vision and lead me to my soul-mate."

"Yes, Captain Nemo, here I am, with my daughters and my Mate – and Mr. Dar-win has the couch upon which we girls rested until freed by friend Anton and re-worked by friend Isaac; read the parchment and the letter surrounding our present home."

"Dr. Frankenstone, we shall take the carriage to Cambridge this very moment and sign the stone back in. Then you may have it for your studies."

"Yes, Mr. Darwin, the sooner the better. I will have some words with the Cura-tor."

CURATOR: Ah, Doctor Frankenstone. So nice to see you again. Oh, I see you have found Mr. Darwin. How are you, Charles? I haven't seen you since you left for your voyage to Japan aboard the *Bugle*. Was the voyage successful?

DARWIN: We never got to Japan, Robert. We were all getting anxious to get home, and Japan was out of the way. Indeed, when I returned, I found that we could not have landed in Japan, or having arrived in port, would have been clapped in jail, where I would be to this day. But yes, the voyage was quite successful. I have written several books from all the information I gathered on the *Beagle*.

CURATOR: Let's see, that was um, um, oh about thirty six years ago, wasn't it? Did you give the good Doctor his stone?

DARWIN: I am here to sign it back in. The voyage took five years and I must have come down with some tropical fever, as I feel tired all the time. I completely forgot about returning the stone.

CURATOR: Naughty, naughty, Charles. That is one of our more active items. We have had requests for it, oh, maybe six times in the last three hundred years since it was catalogued in. Was this any inconvenience to you, Doctor Frankenstone? No? Do you have the stone, Charles? Good. Yes, that's it. Let's walk it down to the shelves with the other Lightning Stones. This is more popular than the others for some reason – they all look much alike – this one has the extra shell on it – that must be the reason. Ah, here we are. Oh! There is a marking on the box. "FRANKENSTONE." I didn't see that before Why, someone must have wanted it for you, Doctor. Ha! Sign it in here, Charles. Good. Let's see. Darwin, Priestley, Isaac Newton. Sir Isaac signed it in soon before he died – must have been cleaning out his room. You could think about that too, Charles. I've heard reports. Ha, ha. Oh, my! Sir Isaac signed it in but Isaac Barrow signed it out just before that. This is irregular. Professor Barrow must have given it directly to young Newton, who then forgot about it until he cleaned out his room – he was very absent minded, you know. Professor Barrow should have signed it back in and let Newton sign it out again, though. Not like Barrow. Oh, yes. That was the time of the Plague when we shut down. The paper work probably got shorted then – you know how it is when there is a little disruption in your schedule. Do you wish to sign it out now, Doctor. Frankenstone? No? Extraordinary man, Sir Isaac. And he showed so little promise when he first came to Cambridge. Shows what a good mentor and a good schooling can do for a man, what? His father was an honest farmer and his mother was a fine virtuous woman, not at all scholarly, however. Sir Isaac was born premature and 'twas said he might have been put into an ale mug – never knew his father, who died several months before the blessed event. Never married, did Sir Isaac. Full of much loftier ideas. Never interested in the gentler sex. Step-niece was installed to run his household when he was near sixty. Catherine Barton – a great beauty and a wit was she, a toast of the town, and many fashionable young men and people of note came and went. She was probably as much of the fair sex as Sir Isaac would want. Perhaps an ancestor of Clara Barton of the Red Cross, who has recently been with the Colonies at Gettysburg, but I digress. Are you a philosopher, Doctor, as Sir Isaac? No? A scientist? The words mean the same. Philo – love of, and sophist – wise man; philosopher – lover of wisdom. Science – having knowledge. Oh, you know Latin, Doctor? Ah, you probably know all about Sir Isaac then; I am boring you. Perhaps Sir Isaac wanted to leave you his "Philosopher's Stone." Ha, ha! Extraordinary gentleman, Sir Isaac. Wrote the *Principia* and the *Opticks* you know. Thought out many of his ideas back at his home at Woolsthorpe, you know, during the Plague years. The clean air and the home cooking must have joggled all that book learning into place. Ha, ha. Woolsthorpe – where the apple fell on his head in the garden and caused him to think of gravity – joggled his book learning, no doubt. Ha! But I should not desecrate the memory of the man. His prism experiments were at Woolsthorpe also, where he awoke one morning just as the sun arose and cast its rays through a slit in the curtain onto a prism in the chandelier in his room and so cast a rainbow of colors onto the far wall. If Sir Isaac had only experimented with prisms of different glasses, he may have found out about how to make perfect telescope lenses without false colors, as Mr. Dollond has given us, and would not have had to make his mirrors. Ingenious gentleman, Sir Isaac – made his own lenses and mirrors and instruments with his own hands, he did. Amazing what a piece of glass can do in the master's hands, to make a stone whereby one can magnify his sight. You smile, Doctor. You are then interested in optics? Yes? Amazing thing, optics. They can let you see both near and far. For instance, my bifocals, perfected by an ingenious person in the Colonies, a Mr. Franken, or Franklin. This gentleman was handy, but not too smart, for he flew a kite in a rainstorm, and, holding up his arm with his knuckle near the string, presently felt and saw and heard a blue crack of electricity. Like to have killed himself. Wouldn't try that if I were you, Doctor. The crackle being exactly the same as from the banks of Leyden jars which the scientists were using in their experiments on electricity. Franken thus determining that lightning and electricity were the same. Amazing! You smile again, Doctor. Are you then also interested in electricity? Yes? Could this Mr. Franken then be related to you? No? Leyden – the city in the Low Countries or Netherlands, where the Pilgrims dwelt for eleven years before departing for the Colonies in the Mayflower. You know, we have some correspondence filed here between Sir Isaac and a gentleman residing near Leyden, something about optics; microscopes, I think. A Mr. Leydenhook, or some similar name. Amazing eyesight this gentleman had, a gift from God, as it were. Could see things no one else could see. And he also, as Mr. Franken, never went to Cambridge. Remarkable, indeed! Um, um, I shall have to retract that. I seem to remember that Mr. Franken did indeed visit us, although never as a student, or professor for that matter. 'FRANKENSTONE for it came by way of the Franks'. Yes, that is Sir Isaac's handwriting. I take it he wanted it for you and felt this was the quickest way to get it to you? Ha! You do not then have an address in Cambridge? No? A transient perhaps? Yes? Well, we have an apartment we lease for transients, in London. Only five pounds per year payable in advance, and you can come and go as you please. A gold coin? I will get you change back at the desk, and give you a key. The apartment is near Hyde Park – a rather nice part of town, somewhat seedy. You may decide to become a citizen of the Empire, Doctor. What say, Charles, you found a small telescope with the stone? Um, um, this is not listed on the records, and I don't remember any telescopes here – we have one of Sir Isaac's reflectors down the hall in the telescope wing. Sir Isaac probably made it up as a gift to you, Doctor. Ha, ha. Yes, you are free to keep the telescope. You really must get a permanent address. How is your wife, Charles? Fine? Good. It's nice to come home to a warm house and a warm meal and a warm wife, isn't it Doctor? I'm sorry Doctor, I didn't ask if you were married. Not presently? Well, you should start looking, really! A handsome man such as yourself! Well, here is the five pound note for change, from the Old Lady on Threadneedle Street. What say, Doctor? Yes, the note is good, and better than good. It is as strong as the Rock of Gibraltar. The address is engraved on the key, so you should have no problems. Go to Regent's Park and ask a Bobby. Must you be going so soon? Well, then, good day to you, gentlemen. It's been a pleasure conversing with you, Doctor Frankenstone. You were in such a hurry last time we met. And Charles, I will certainly look your books up in the library and read them. Might even buy a copy! Stop in again for another chat next time you are in town. Cheerio! (To assistant): Wonderful man, pleasant man, remarkable man, delightful man, that Doctor Frankenstone. Brilliant Conversationalist! We shall have to invite him as guest speaker to our annual Christmas party next time he is in town. But Charles seemed somewhat tired and drawn – must be his fever. What do you think, Fezwig?

ASSISTANT: Bah, Humbug!

Note: One may wonder why Nemo, whose favorite subject in his library of 12,000 volumes in the *Nautilus* (as noted by Monsieur Aronnax) was natural history, did not have the book "The Origin of Species," published by Charles Darwin in 1859. If you will procure a copy of this tome, you may see why. There are no descriptions or calculations or illustrations or sketches or real detail of any kind, or anything else of any value to expand one's knowledge of natural history (biology). Nemo may have even thumbed through a volume before 1860, when he cut off all ties with society. The name Darwin on the cover, if he saw it, would mean to him Erasmus Darwin (grandfather of Charles), who had proposed evolutionary theories many years before Charles was born. The book, in any event, is sterile of value. Nemo *knows* that his Crystal was created, not evolved; *knows* that his soulmate was created different from others and did not "evolve"; *knows* that it is these small *created* differences in each individual that eventually integrate into what was called "evolution;" *knows* that significant changes in the world order (cataclysmic events, such as comet strikes, solar flares, nearby nova, etc.) can cause significant changes in living creatures, significant enough to create different species almost instantaneously.

Aronnax had also noted the volume "Foundations of Astronomy", by Joseph Bertrand, published in 1865. Nemo and crew had begun checking out the *Nautilus* about that time, and had discovered they needed a little more knowledge of celestial navigation and astronomy, and so secretly procured the copy. Whether he paid for it or not is a moot point and need not concern us.

'Close' supernova blast may have speeded Earth evolution

SAN FRANCISCO (AP) — A star exploded relatively close to Earth 35,000 years ago, engulfing the planet in cosmic radiation that left traces deep in polar ice and may have accelerated evolution, a Soviet scientist said.

The supernova was closer to Earth than any other known exploding star, said astrophysicist Grant E. Kocharov, vice chairman of the Soviet Academy of Sciences' Cosmic Ray Council. It was in our own galaxy and only 150 light years, or 880 trillion miles, away, he said Friday.

By comparison, a 1987 supernova that was the closest exploding star seen by scientists in 400 years was 1,000 times more distant and located in another galaxy.

When stars explode as supernovas, the variety of radiation produced by the incredible blasts includes cosmic rays that can break chemical bonds in cells and cause mutations. Many mutations are deadly, but some alter species in ways that help them survive and evolve.

The supernova's cosmic ray bombardment could have speeded evolution by sharply increasing mutations. Kocharov said during the American Geophysical Union's fall meeting.

Cosmic rays also smash into nitrogen and oxygen molecules in the atmosphere, producing beryllium-10, a metallic element that then falls from the atmosphere and is incorporated in the polar ice sheets.

Kocharov drilled ice cores at the Dye 3 and Camp Century research stations in Greenland and the Vostok, Byrd and Dome C stations in Antarctica. He found the amount of beryllium-10 was doubled in ice that formed 35,000 years ago, at what is now about 2,000 feet below the surface.

That indicates a powerful supernova exploded nearby about 35,000 years ago, spurring the increase in incoming cosmic rays that accelerated beryllium-10 production, said Kocharov, head of astrophysics at the A.F. Ioffe Physical-Technical Institute in St. Petersburg.

Cosmic rays continually hit Earth and are strongest at the poles, which aren't protected by the planet's magnetic field. Kocharov's study indicates the supernova doubled the intensity of cosmic rays hitting the planet.

ACT IV

Crystal and Her Mate

34
The Foreigner Takes a Wife

Nemo studied the telescope for a long while after he got back to his apartment. Then he carefully removed the paper and parchment surrounding the telescope, which had prevented it from being focused. The paper of course was the note Leeuwenhoek had written to Newton about how he made his lenses, while the parchment was the note in Arabic from the old shepherd Omén concerning the last story told to Shahrazad by Crystal. Newton had not destroyed Anton's note, but had kept it for Frankenstone, if that gentleman would ever come. Nemo laboriously deciphered Anton's note, which was in Dutch, and then put it with his other papers for future reference. He quickly read the parchment, and began to ponder the meanings hidden in the words.

"Well, Crystal, have you been having a good time with your Mate these past one hundred twenty five years?"

"We have been sitting in the dark most of the time and really would like to get out in the light and explore."

Nemo tried out the 'scope and found it in good working order, with excellent resolution and sharp images.

After several months of checking out the 'scope in and around London, Nemo said to Crystal, "It is about time I now started searching for my wife. Where will I find her?"

And Crystal and her Mate chimed out in unison,

"Now go ye to Bristol and seek ye a boat;
'Twill take you to lands full of cow, sheep and goat.
Go inland indeed for yet more than a day,
And we will show you your wife – hurt but OK."

After closing up the apartment, he took a carriage to Bristol, where he found many boats, mostly local fishing boats. A large ship was there; the crew was busy readying her for a voyage.

"Where are ye going?" asked Nemo.

"We sail to southeast Africa to check on enlarging the Empire."

"Do you need another hand?"

"No. We look for a ship's doctor."

"I am a doctor of sorts."

"Come aboard." After some discussion, it was found that Nemo knew enough to be the ship's doctor. "We sail tomorrow; are you ready?"

"I have some business at the chandlery, and will come aboard this evening."

At the chandlery, Nemo sought out the proprietor and told him he needed a brass plate for his apartment in London, and he wrote out what was to be engraved on the plate.

"Here is a gold piece for the sign, and 1 will give you another like it if the sign is affixed to my apartment door when I return in several months – I am leaving for Africa, and may continue elsewhere."

"It will be done, Doctor," said the proprietor.

The ship was a British schooner, bound for Swaziland on the east of South Africa, where England was interested in colonizing. [The Empire would seize Zululand to the south in 1887; Swaziland today is a protectorate of England.] Some on board were military men and one of them knew Swazi. Nemo had several months to learn the language.

When the ship docked in late Spring at Lourenco Marques (now Maputo) around 3 November 1868, the crew left for the taverns, the officers left for their post, and Nemo left on foot toward the southwest, taking fourteen days' provisions to last him until he got back in time to catch the ship before it set sail.

Swaziland is a small landlocked country, a little larger than Connecticut and Rhode Island combined, about fifty miles inland. It is grass and bush covered – no natural forests. The natives are Swazis, a branch of the Bantu tribes related to the Zulus. They raise cattle and graze sheep from South Africa. Mile-high mountains lie to the west, toward Victoria Falls.

When Nemo is about a mile from a small village inland, he sees a commotion and hears drums and cries. Taking out the forty-power telescope, he sees a young girl, naked except for a short grass skirt, being tied to a post – this is about 9 AM of November 6. The people each take turns beating her with branches, with a shout each time she is struck. At high noon, they cease their exercises, untie the girl, and drive her away – she is bloody all over. She starts running down the cow path toward Nemo. He hides behind a bush, then when she approaches he comes from behind the bush and says, "Hello!"

The girl utters a startled cry and keeps on running. Nemo seeks out a tree for shade, makes camp, and by nightfall climbs into the tree near the campfire and falls asleep. When the last-quarter moon starts to come up he hears a noise at the campfire, wakes up and sees a shadow. "Hello," he says. He hears a startled cry but the shadow does not move.

"Who are you?" asks the girl.

"Why did you run away from the village and why did they beat you?"

"I was running away and may not return. I have the Spirit of the White God of Death in me."

"And what is that? Could you explain further?"

"This is the custom in our village. My great-grandmother had a sister who also had the Spirit – that was the last time it happened until I came."

"Why is the Spirit so bad for the village?" prodded Nemo.

"When the girl/spirit enters her womanhood she must be beaten and expelled from the village before two full weeks have elapsed, else bad luck will befall the village."

"Where were you running, and why did you return to me?"

"I have run ever since I left the village – I can run like the wind – and I was running until I dropped dead, for the old women told me that if I was lucky I would meet my destiny before dawn, before the jackals took me down. Are you not then the White God of Death, come to tear out my heart and drink my blood?"

"Why do you have the Evil Spirit in you?"

"I was born that way – the Evil Spirit was my father, for my skin is light. I am ugly. My backside is not full and firm and round like the watermelon and my chest is too large and my legs are too long – already I am taller than many of the men – and my nose is too thin and my hair grows too long and too straight. I am ugly. I am never to have any boyfriends, never to marry, never to have children; for I am ugly. I could not work in the fields during the day because of my light skin and so I was put to do all the dirty work at night until now."

"My name is Nemo. What is your name?"

"My name is Zola, for such name is given to all who have the Spirit of the White God of Death. The name is the closest they can come to pronouncing the hated name of Zulu, the great enemy of my people. They taunt me every time they say the name."

"The name is pretty to my ears."

"You must be from a distant land, for you do not speak as we."

"*You* are from a distant land now, and the "we" you speak of is now only you and me, for you are no longer a member of your former tribe," said Nemo.

"Yes, I am alone."

"Will you run away if I come down from the tree?"

"No, I am ready to die now." Nemo comes down and sits by the campfire. He was refreshed now and could watch for wild animals. "Come sit by me until the dawn, then run if you must."

"I will sit by you, but kill me before the dawn, before you see how ugly I am."

"The moon is up now and you are not ugly." So Zola sat by Nemo and soon fell asleep in his arms like a tired puppy.

It was late next morning when Zola awoke. Nemo had finished breakfast and was packing up to continue his journey. She awoke with a start and ran quickly away about thirty paces, men stopped and looked at Nemo.

"I am ugly, but you are even uglier than I. Ugly, ugly!" And she giggled.

Nemo stopped what he was doing and looked straight at her. "Zola, will you marry me?"

"Ha! Ha, ha! I can joke as well as you. The man I marry must be very rich – he must have many cattle. Do you have any cattle?"

"No."

"See, you are as poor as me. The man I marry must be content with a small family – I like adventure, and a large family will tie me down."

"A small family is acceptable, and I too like adventure." "Ha! Ha, ha! The man I marry must be content with no more than two wives, for I am a very jealous woman."

"You will be enough for me."

"Ha! Ha, ha! The man I marry will tell me I am very pretty. No. The man I marry will tell me I am the prettiest maid he has ever laid eyes on. Ha!"

"Zola, you are the prettiest maid I have ever laid eyes on. Will you marry me?"

Zola walked slowly back to Nemo, pigeon-toed, tears welling up in her eyes. "You are too old for me – you look over thirty years of age. Are you over thirty?"

"Yes, I am over thirty."

ILLUSTRATION

*T*HE *PRE-COLUMBIAN* religion of the Aztecs was the great exception to which I referred a moment ago. Unlike other ecclesiastic deities, the gods of the Aztec state craved human flesh, especially fresh human hearts. According to Aztec belief, unless this craving was satisfied, the gods would destroy the world. Human sacrifice, therefore, became the most important function of the Aztec priesthood. Most of the people sacrificed were captives brought back to Tenochtitlán, the Aztec capital, by military commanders. Forced to ascend the flat-topped pyramids that dominated the city's ceremonial precincts, the victim was seized by four priests, one for each limb, and bent backward face up, over a stone altar. A fifth priest then opened the victim's chest with an obsidian knife, wrenched out the heart, and while it was still beating, smeared it over the nearby statue of the presiding deity. Attendants then rolled the body down the steps. Other attendants cut off the head, pushed a wooden shaft through it from side to side, and placed it on a tall latticework structure or skull rack alongside the heads of previous victims.

To remove any doubts about what happened next, permit me to quote from Bernadino de Sahagún's *General History of the Things of New Spain,* the most fundamental and scrupulously honest source on Aztec religion:

> After having torn their hearts from them and poured the blood into a gourd vessel, which the master of the slain man himself received, they started the body rolling down the pyramid steps. It came to rest upon a small square below. There some old men, whom they called Quaquacuitlin, laid hold of it and carried it to their tribal temple, where they dismembered it and divided it up in order to eat it.

Zola put down her head, walked up to Nemo, put her toes on his sandals, put her arms around his neck, pulled herself up and wrapped her legs around his waist. "Yes, I will marry you, for you are different from anyone I have ever known, and you are even uglier than me."

She held him tight for a long time. Then her grip loosened and she stood against him again. "What do we do now? We cannot be married – the village will not have a ceremony."

"The first thing we do is bathe your body and clean you up." And arm in arm they walked to the nearby creek, an offshoot of the river separating Swaziland from Zululand.

"We must have a wedding ceremony," she said, "with music and with vows."

"The crickets' chirp can be the drums and the lowing of the cattle in the distance can be the song. What vows do you wish?" he asked gently.

"I wish you to be true to me."

"In sickness and in health?"

"When you are sick I will care for you and when I am sick I wish you to care for me."

"For richer or for poorer?"

"We cannot get any poorer. Yes."

"How long should I be true?" asked Nemo.

"Forever ... No, if I die you must be free. 'Til death do us part."

"Then, by the power vested in me as Captain of the good ship Nautilus, I pronounce us husband and wife. There, the ceremony is over."

"Is that where you came from, husband, from upriver inland on your raft?"

And Nemo told Zola of his early life in the Caucasus, of his young wife and baby girl, and the new life stirring inside her belly, when the Cossacks came and destroyed their village – his father, his two "mothers," his brothers and sisters, and all the others in the village, all murdered. Only he, out on a hunting trip, had been spared.

"I had heard of a stone wherewith one could enlarge his vision, and so to keep my sanity, I began the search, after three days in burying my people."

"Oh, I am truly sorry for you ... How long did you search, and did you find the stone?"

"I searched many years, and yes, I found the stone. I saw you running out the gate when you were untied from the stake. I saw another girl run after you for many steps until she fell to the ground and beat her fists and her head against the ground. I saw a boy standing by the gate calling out to the girl. I saw the girl return to him. I saw them standing arm in arm at the gate watching you run away until I came out from behind the bush and startled you. Are they your brother and sister?"

"How do you see all this? You are too far away. The girl is my only friend in the village and loves me very much. The boy is her boyfriend. How do you see all this?"

"Zola, they stood arm in arm watching you; and they were both crying ..."
"There is ... There is ... There is no boy in the village who likes me. I do not believe you. You are telling me stories."

"Zola, I love you with all my heart, and I am telling you the truth. See for yourself." Nemo took out the telescope, the forty-power telescope with Crystal and her Mate, put it up to his eye and faced the village. Then he told Zola to face the village and hold it up to her eye.

"Help me! Gods above! The world is upside down!"

Nemo took the instrument away from her eye and smiled. "This shows things upside down, but much larger. Look again."

"Oh! Oh! Oh! I did not run back and yet I am thirty strides from the gate! There is the chieftain's hut – and he is standing outside. Why doesn't he fall down into – the sky???!! My head is spinning; hold me." She gave the telescope back to Nemo and began to retch.

After a minute she felt better and said, "This is magic. The chief has many cattle and many possessions, but he does not have this magic. I am afraid." She walked away a few paces and sat down with her eyes closed – and she shivered in the hot afternoon air.

"Zola, do not be afraid. This is the stone I told you of, for which I searched these many years, wherewith I can magnify my vision. My quest is over. I have found the stone, and through it, after these many years of hope and prayer, I have found my Zola."

"You talk strangely. Hold me close."

That night they married one another, Zola the beautiful fourteen-year-old maiden, and Nemo, still in his prime at two hundred thirty two. The world would know them, in high society and in lowliest native village, as Doctor and Mrs. Nemo and Zola Frankenstone; but what does the world know?

But *we* know. We know now of Nemo's first wife, which he knew as a youth, and that she and all the others were murdered in cold blood by the Cossacks for sport, and that to keep from going mad, Nemo must focus on the only thing left – the legend of Crystal and the reuniting of the lovers in an afterlife – and that one day he would find Crystal...and his love.

Who were the Cossacks? There were the Don Cossacks from the area of the river Don, and the Dnieper Cossacks. Don Cossack Stenka Razin led the peasant revolution in Russia in 1665, the year Newton took his degree and the year of the Great Plague in London – and the fifth year of Nemo's servitude in Constantinople. A creature void of mercy and honor, fearing neither God nor devil – such was the popular conception of the Cossack in Russia.

"Essentially the Cossack was a serf who made his way to freedom. Predominantly he was a peasant of the Orthodox faith. Predominantly he was a Slav, a Russian or Ukrainian ... the Ukraine ... .is immense and was sparsely settled ... rich land on which to grow grains and vegetables, excellent grass on which to breed horses and fatten cattle ... the Ukraine was Russia's great Wild West.

"No other nation anywhere has cultivated a warrior and a human being like the Cossack. Lover of strong drink and rich food, of tender song and violent dance, of gay laughter and rowdy speech, of unruly living and reckless dying, he has ever been the playboy and the bête noire, the defamer and the defender of Russian civilization and its most undaunted warrior."

from "The Cossacks"
by Maurice Hindus

From the quiet island inlet
Out to where the stream flows deep,
Stenka Razin's painted galleys
Through the waters boldly sweep.

Stenka in the foremost galley
Has his princess at his side,
Drunk with wine and mirth together
As he clasps his new-won bride.

Sullen murmurs rise behind them:
"Chucked us for a wench! Why, true,
Just one night with her and Stenka
Has become a woman, too!"

Swelling now the angry mutter
Surges round the headman's ears,
And he holds his Persian beauty
All the closer at their jeers.

But his brows are scowling darkly.
Now a storm begins to rise.
There are swift and savage lighnings
In the headman's bloodshot eyes.

"Volga, Volga, Mother Volga,
Russian river, look upon
This my gift: you've not yet seen one
From a Cossack of the Don.

"In a fellowship of free men
Never shall a quarrel rise.
Volga, Volga, Mother Volga,
Take the beauty as your prize!"

High he lifts the lovely princess,
With his great arm's mighty sweep
Forth he hurls her, without looking,
Forth into the hungry deep.

"Why so glum, you devils? Stow it!
Filka, do a jig, you cur!
Thunder out a brave one, comrades,
All in memory of her!"

From the quiet island inlet
Out to where the stream flows deep,
Stenka Razin's painted galleys
Through the waters boldly sweep.
(from Russian folk song)

35
Home at Last

Dawn broke warm and clear, as it always does in Swaziland. "Nemo, I have the fever. I am dying. The jackals are eating my insides and the God of Death has put me on fire. Goodbye, dear husband, I love you."

"Zola, let me look at you. Yes, you have a fever. You have a bad case of sunburn. And you have not eaten for two days."

So Nemo made his wife a wide brimmed hat from the local flora to protect her from the midday sun – they would have a long four day journey out to the coast where the ship was in port for two weeks while the British officers checked the area for possibilities for expanding the Empire.

"Stop eating all my provisions," said Nemo. "You will get sick, and we have many days to go yet – I will not carry you."

"I am hungry! I have never been hungry before." Zola had eaten most of Nemo's provisions and her stomach was full and tight. "I am sleepy, I will lie down."

"Zola, if you lie down the sun will finish you off. We must march back east to the coast all day until the sun goes down."

"You are a mean husband ... Why do we go to the coast? What is this coast?"

That is where the land stops and the ocean begins."

"The land stops? Do you mean we walk to the end of the earth? That will take forever, and we will both starve. You are a mean husband."

"Zola, we will return to where I live and we will take a boat."

"Where do you live and where is this boat and where is this ocean?"

"You have much to learn, Zola."

"You are a mean husband, Nemo love ... Why do you take that funny-looking walking stick?"

"This is a rifle to shoot our dinner for this evening."

"A walking stick! ... Do you throw it at the animal?"

And so, with one hand holding her hat on her head and the other holding Nemo's hand, our barefooted, bare-breasted, grass-skirted, tight-bellied, sunburned, heavy-lidded girl/woman heroine with long black wavy hair reaching well below her shoulders and with raw welts all over her arms and back and sides and thighs begins her trek to white man's civilization.

We will not have the reader suffer through Zola's learning experiences. When they near the coast where civilization is evident, the worst of her sunburn is over, and Nemo makes her wear his jacket, which hurts her no end, but covers her sufficiently to be acceptable to the ship's Captain.

"Ahoy, Doctor Frankenstone. So you have found the one for whom you have been searching. Why, she looks like an American Indian. I didn't know there were any of them in these parts. What is your name, lass, and do you have any relatives living hereabouts?"

"My name is Zola. My father is Death, and my mother died when she gave birth to me."

"I am so sorry, Miss. Doctor, where be you taking her?"

"Back to England. She has agreed to be my wife."

"She is much too young for you, Doctor. Let her grow up in a proper orphanage and she will marry a young man soon enough. She is a beautiful Indian Princess."

"We are already married."

"Well, then, that makes it easier for me. Women on board ship makes for bad luck, ten times so if they are unmarried, a hundredfold if they are of loose morals. Ahoy, ye scurvy crew! Attend my words. This beautiful lass is recently married to the Doctor. Any of you who so much as lays a hand on her will be shark bait. Do I make myself clear?"

"Aye, Captain."

"My wife has lost all her possessions, even her clothes. Can you provide a decent covering for her?"

"Aye. Quartermaster! See this lass has a proper sailor's suit."

And this is how Zola became a sailor, and a good one at that, climbing rigging and setting sheets and furling sails with the best of them – indistinguishable in her uniform from any of the other young crew; her hair neatly tied in a bun under her cap.

The first evening the Captain desired Nemo and Zola to dine with him. Nemo came, but Zola had been told that the crew does not dine at the Captain's table, so she did not show up – she was still a little seasick anyway.

"Blast it, Nemo, get her here, or else we will have to dine with the crew."

For the rest of the voyage, the Captain and Nemo ate with the crew at dinnertime. Zola desired to have Nemo's telescope, and after each dinner she played with it and looked through it and began to tell stories, some of her childhood, more from what Crystal and the Mate told her during the day.

As she learned the ropes, she became expert at climbing to the crow's nest and staying there hour on end with the telescope, scanning the horizon and nearer parts:

"Whales blowing on horizon, port abeam."

"Dolphins playing on the bow waves."

"White turkey on bowsprit."

"That bird is no turkey, you dunce," said a crewmember. That is a gooney bird – an albatross. It is an omen of bad luck."

"Land Ho! Off the starboard bow."

"Aye, that be St. Helena," said the Captain. "We are on course. St. Helena – where the great warrior Napoleon was exiled and where he died almost a half century ago."

"Was he as great a warrior as the leader of the enemy of our people – the Great Shaka?"

"I never heard of the Great Shaka, Zola," replied the Captain. "I never heard of Napoleon."

"White flag on horizon, port quattah!"

"Watch it carefully, Zola," said Nemo, "for at least an hour. See if it come closer or disappear."

"You look anxious, Doctor," said the Captain. "Does the white flag mean anything to you?"

"I have had some problems with that nation."

"Land Ho! Off the port bow."

"Aye, that be Ascension Island. We make good time."

"Floating island dead ahead five mile!" Zola sang this out soon after midnight on a clear moonless night.

"The Sargasso Sea! We should be well east of it! All hands on deck! Prepare for port tack! Ready about!"

"Port ready, Captain."

"Stahbud ready, Captain."

"Helm's alea!"

The ship turned smoothly and swiftly ninety degrees to the right on the port tack. The floating seaweed was cleared by less than half a mile as the ship veered north northeast directly for England. They were much farther west than the dead reckoning indicated – the day before had been cloudy and no sights could be taken after lunch.

The Captain was furious. "Navigator, what in blazes are ye doing? Have ye been in the grog pot? Helmsman, do ye sleep at the wheel?"

"Sir, we follow the compass faithfully since yesterday noon when you last took sights."

"Blast! Me sextant must have dropped! Navigator, remind me to have me sextant and chronometer checked out immediately we berth at Bristol. I have never been so far off. We could lose a day. Can the currents or tides have changed?"

The sky was lightening a little. The Captain went back to the helm. "Helmsman! What are these pants draped over the binnacle? And with a knife still in the scabbard! First Mate! Have the crew line up. NOW! We will get to the bottom of this." (Crew lines up.) "Gentlemen, I have found iron near the compass in the form of a knife hooked to a pair of pants draped over the binnacle. The compass must have been off twenty degrees all night. The one of you responsible for this will please step forward for his twenty lashes with the cat-o-nine-tails. No one? If no one steps forward within ten seconds, the whole bloody lot of you will be flogged!"

One sailor stepped forward. Then another; and another. Very soon all had taken the step.

"Take the first and tie his hands to the mast." While this was being done the Captain went to his cabin and got the cat-o-nine-tails. "Rip open the back of his shirt so he can feel its full caress."

It was getting light enough now to distinguish small features. When the shirt back was ripped open, the Captain saw red welts that covered the whole back, and around the sides to the ribs, far more than twenty lashes could ever do.

"My God, man, said the Captain, "you have had enough flogging for a lifetime, and not more than two months ago! And I don't remember taking on a crewman as young as you. Are you a stowaway? How old are you, lad?"

"Fourteen, Sir."

"Your voice has not even cha ..." and the Captain finally realized who it was. "First Mate, get the Doctor up here immediately. I don't care if he is sleeping soundly – a robe is all the clothes he needs."

"Doctor Frankenstone, will you please explain why your wife has been whipped to within an inch of her life?"

"You would not believe me, Captain. Ask her yourself." So Zola told the Captain how her beating came about and how she was rescued by Nemo and willingly became his wife and that he had not hurt her, but told her she was free to leave him anytime she desired – he would understand.

"But why did you step up to take the cat? What did you have to do with this affair?"

"My husband accidentally spilled coffee on his pants when I tickled him last night after dinner, and I rinsed them out and put them on the binnacle to dry out in the sea breeze. I was not aware that the compass could be affected."

"I must maintain discipline. You are restricted to your husband's quarters until midnight, and your rations until then will be black bread and water. The rest of you are dismissed for the morning mess. GO!" In three seconds the deck was clear except for the three.

"Women!" spat out the Captain. "They are nothing but trouble. You will rue the day you married this tomboy, Doctor. Mark my words ... I am thirty-five years old – too old for this life on board. Discipline is too stressful. But discipline must be maintained to achieve any worthwhile goal."

The dinner that night was a very sad affair. The crew ate together and said not a word. The Captain ate alone. The officers and Nemo ate together and discussed the possibilities they found for making Swaziland and Zululand into British protectorates. The rest of the trip was uneventful.

As soon as the ship docked in Bristol, the navigator had the sextant and chronometer checked. The sextant was in perfect adjustment, the chronometer slow by three minutes; not good, but not bad for a five months' journey. The Captain considered the events of the trip carefully and married his childhood sweetheart and raised a fine family. He went to sea again when the youngest was six – the sea was in his blood.

Nemo and Zola took the carriage from Bristol to London. They took the walk from the terminal near Regent's Park to the apartment. They walked up the steps and stood by the door to the transient's apartment. "Home at last," said Nemo.

"What is the writing on the door – what does it say?"

"The sign says that Dr. & Mrs. Nemo and Zola Frankenstone live here."

"Oh, you tease! You didn't know me before you left for Africa."

And before Nemo took out the key to open the door, he took out a handkerchief and carefully polished the brass plate, which said:

Dr. and Mrs.
Nemo and Zola
Frankenstone
221b Baker St.
Apt. 13

36
The Private Eye

Nemo enrolled Zola in first grade elementary school, for her education. ("You are a mean husband.") She went through three grades a year and by the time she was eighteen she was graduating from high school with her classmates. In her best Cockney accent after the graduation ceremony she introduced her husband to them and said, "Don't be shy, loves. Knock me up whenever you are in the neighborhood."

"Won't the Doctor throw us out?"

"Gaw, 'e loves company. 'E will welcome you. Don't be wimpy."

Zola went on to theatrical school and was soon making stage appearances in bit parts in the theater district. The highlight of her career was as the stand-in for Carmen. Nemo was also involved, but this is another story.

Now the good Doctor, as soon as he felt comfortable at "home," said to himself, 'I really should become a proper Englishman. I already play the organ quite well, having had much practice on the *Nautilus*, but this instrument is not transportable and is too big and loud for the apartment. I will take up the violin again. ("Take up any instrument you like, dear, but *please* – not the violin, at least not in my presence.") I shall buy a pipe and a smoking jacket and an all-weather tweed jacket and a cap to keep the damp air from my head.'

As he walked around the neighborhood in this outlandish outfit, the residents decided that he looked like a lawyer of sorts, and could he help them with their problems – cut rate. Working through the legal morass, he saw that this wasn't his cup of tea, and anyway the neighbors really needed good detective work. And this is how he spent his time for the next thirty or so years, with Crystal and her Mate ever present, dangling from a lanyard around his neck.

Ten years pass since the couple set up housekeeping. One evening there was a knock at the door.

"'Oo his it? Have you knocked up me or the private eye?" Zola was dressed as a Cockney maid for her performance that evening, and was on her way out.

"I am really sorry to bother you, but I have recently graduated from the University of Edinburgh, and may decide to set up practice here in London. On the way down I stopped at Cambridge, and the curator at the Museum told me he had a transient's apartment to let at five pounds the year. Finding the price reasonable, I took him on. Here, I have the key. But I see that this apartment is already occupied, and as evening has fallen, I will have difficulty finding lodgings for the night. Is the Master home, and may I speak with him?"

"Aye, the Shylock's 'orne 'e is. Nemo!" she shouted, "There is a gentleman here wishes a room tonight. 'Bye, loves." And she leaves for the theater.

Nemo came to the door and said, "Good evening, I am Doctor – what, son, you say you need a room tonight? There is plenty of room here. You look tired. Come in and rest and have dinner with me and tell me your story. Perhaps I can help. What is your name?"

"I am just graduated from Edinburgh and have rented this transient's apartment through the curator at the Cambridge Museum, as I thought of setting up practice here in London. My name is Budd. Dr. George Budd."

"And I am Frankenstone. Dr. Nemo Frankenstone. Come in, come in! Budd, you say? I met a Dr. Budd when I was at the chandlery in Bristol prior to my departure for Africa. Are you kin?"

"He is my father, or was my father. He has passed on several years ago."

"I am sorry to hear that. Very nice gentleman. Here, help yourself to the hot stew while I get us some tea. Let me show you Crystal and her Mate. They help me no end in my work. Each is a magnifier, the Mate being four power and Crystal being one hundred thirty-power. I am presently a detective for difficult cases, such as ones Scotland Yard gives up on. Ha! And together they make an extraordinarily small forty-power telescope!"

"My word, Dr. Frankenstone, I have a good friend from Edinburgh – we studied together – who would be most anxious to see this object. Art Doyle. Are you acquainted with the Doyles?"

"No, I have never had the pleasure. Invite him to drop over whenever he is in town. He would be most welcome."

37

The Little Match Girl

Monday Afternoon

"Zola, dear, don't you think it's time we started a family? Your acting career is at a standstill and you are not getting any younger."

"I may not be working in front of an audience right now, Nemo, but understudy to the lead in the new French opera is exciting, and who knows – I may have my chance yet."

"Unlikely. I watched one rehearsal and the leading lady is young, and healthy as a horse. And the same goes for Don José. The critics in France panned the play unmercifully when it opened there, so I don't know how it will eventually do here in London, but I liked the tunes and brought home the score, as well as the lines, and have practiced a little on the violin. Would you like to listen?"

"No! No! I hear enough of the violin at the theater."

"You would really make a good gypsy. Your voice is very good and you can make yourself up into a very convincing Spanish flirt – and the costume completes the illusion."

"Me – a flirt? No, never!" she said as she batted her eyes and swished her long skirt and turned an ankle. Then she went into the scene in Act I where she seduces Don José, arranging a rendezvous with him near the ramparts of Seville. Nemo follows Don José's part in a fair tenor.

"Indeed, I love you very much, Zola, never so much as when you flirt."

A knock on the door. "Is the understudy in, Sar? I have a message."

"I will give it to her," answered Nemo.

"No, no. She must sign for it. It is very urgent."

Zola gave the messenger a shilling and opened the sealed envelope. It was from the theater manager.

Dearest Love,

Saturday opening night is only a few days away and the house is sold out. Catastrophe has befallen. As you know, the leading lady and the Don and his under-study, as well as several other unmarrieds in the cast, had gone north for a quick vacation this weekend, and a late snowstorm has completely blocked the roads. If we are lucky they can be back late Friday, otherwise Monday for sure. You have only a short time to polish your part in the event you go on Saturday. Opening night is critical – we cannot postpone. If we must return the moneys for opening night, we will be bankrupt. The show must go on. Thought you might like to know. Love and kisses,

Reginald

PS: I know it is a little late, but do you know of any gentlemen you can work with who could play the Don? He doesn't have to be good, just a warm body. Opening night is an affair, and they won't be watching the play, but ogling each other; but we need that warm body for rehearsals. Ta ta!

So there it was – Zola's chance to star for one night. "What do you think, dear, would you like to play the Don?"

"Ha, ha. I will play the Don Saturday night if you quit the theater after Saturday night's fiasco is done. Ha!"

"Very well. If you must play the Don Saturday night, I will quit the theater and consider a family. Ha, ha!"

Nemo was stuck. He must attend morning, afternoon and evening rehearsals from Tuesday to Saturday morning's dress rehearsal. Saturday afternoon was a time to rest and breathe and think of anything but the opera. It was not a good time for Nemo. This was a completely foreign world to him, where people acted out emotions they did not feel. He had a projector set up in the theater's wings, using the Mate as the lens, a large sheet as the screen, a stage lamp for the light source, and the oiled sheets of the opera's lyrics pasted on panes of window glass – he still needed prompting.

Saturday morning's dress rehearsal was over at last. They were all leaving the theater when a shout went up. The leading lady and her Don were back! The manager called everyone back, even the musicians.

"We are saved," he said, "Act I, Seguidilla through Finale." The leads and the orchestra took their places. The orchestra struck up and the leading lady opened her mouth – nothing came out.

"Laryngitis," croaked the Don hoarsely. "All of us. Too much cold. Be better Monday." His understudy nodded in agreement.

Nemo was *really* stuck. He would, for better or worse, be Don José tonight. Butterflies began to flit around in his stomach.

"Let's go to Hyde Park and relax and forget everything for awhile," said Zola.

Saturday night came. When all were in their seats, the manager came out and made a little speech.

"Ladies and gentlemen. There is a slight change from the printed program. Our leading lady has laryngitis and her part will be played by our ever-capable Zola. Don José, as a special for tonight only, will be played by the well-known Greek tenor, Aeschylus, who is in town tonight and has graciously agreed to perform. Any of you wishing a refund, please raise your hand and an usher will be with you."

Two handsome young men at opposite sides of the theater raised their hands. No sooner had the ushers taken the stubs and given them their refunds, when the old bejeweled dowager sitting next to each raised her hand and took the money from her consort. The two couples had half-risen to leave when the manager, sensing that the audience was in a receptive mood, and would applaud anything short of a complete turkey, said to them, "You may stay if you wish." So they settled back in their seats.

The opera went well, as well as any French opera could in England. At the end, Nemo stabs Zola with the fake knife and she falls to the floor. The opera is almost over. As he bends over her, she opens one eye and says, "You are a mean husband," and sticks out her tongue. Nemo tries to control himself, but as the opera ends and the applause grows, he bursts out laughing, his whole body shaking convulsively, deliriously happy that it is all over, that they had done well, and that he might soon be a father.

The next morning a small column appeared in *Punch*: History of sorts was made last night at the Strand at the opening night gala of *Carmen* by the Frenchman Bizet. An unknown actor, billing himself as Aeschylus, after a slow start in Act I, has given a performance in acting out the love-sick suitor that this critic has seldom if ever witnessed before. Don José's love for Carmen was palpably felt by the whole audience. His sobs at the end (after he stabs and kills her because he cannot have her) was acting at its finest, and the audience gave him a standing ovation. This Phantom of the Opera (Nemo or no one, as he was called backstage) has a great future in the theater. Our favorite Zola was a fine Carmen. The regulars have their work cut out for them when they return Monday after a freak Spring snowstorm and a bout with laryngitis.

38
Around the World in Eighty Weeks

January 1899

"Have you really decided to start a family, Zola?" "Yes, Nemo, but first let's take a vacation."

"That sounds good. What would you like – a weekend in Scotland, a month sailing around Scandinavia and the North Sea?"

"That would be nice to start us off. I was thinking of a trip we have never taken before – like Marco Polo did – to Cathay."

"China! Why, it will be two years before we get back home, and that is taking the Orient Express, a ship from Hong Kong to San Francisco and a train across country in the United States of America."

"Well, if you'd rather not...."

"No, no, I am not dashing on cold water. I think it is a capital idea. We will not get to travel much with small children. Let us do some planning."

Four months later saw them in India ready to begin their journey to Cathay, having taken the land route across France, then by boat across the Mediterranean, down the Red Sea and eastward in the Arabian Sea.

Humming softly to himself, Nemo opened the curtains, allowing the sunlight to flood the room. How many sunrises he had seen, and yet, since finding Zola, the world had taken on a new beauty. She stirred slightly as he gently sat down next to her. He pushed the hair from her face and whispered, "Good morning, sweetheart." Zola mumbled something in reply.

"Are you planning on sleeping the day away?" he teased. "I might," she purred.

"Well, if you don't get up soon I might just have to join you," he retorted, nibbling her ear.

She responded by pulling him close. It was late morning before they ventured out of their houseboat.

The shikara [a special boat designed like a gondola, used only on Del Lake, Kashmir, India] that Nemo had hired to transport them glided silently through the unspoiled waters of Lokut Dal.

"Another spectacular day!" Zola announced.

Nemo nodded, then added, "We should consider moving on. Soon the snows will come; already the days are turning colder."

"But Nemo," Zola protested, "it is still August!"

"Kashmir will be covered with snow by the first of October," he replied, gesturing toward the mountains.

"This country is most perplexing," Zola noted. "We arrived in Goa in May, and the climate was warm but dry. Within a few weeks it was humid and the rains were falling to the south. It was most impressive to watch the monsoons roll onto the plains." She reflected as the shikara navigated close to the dock. "The Ganges reminded me of home, except for the poor naked lions."

"Naked lions?" Nemo chuckled.

"Yes, lions look much better with a mane. You can't tell one from the other here," she said as she climbed from the boat.

"Well, how did you like Nepal?" he inquired.

"It was beautiful, but the air was too thin for my tastes. I never seemed to have much energy there. Kashmir is much better. You are right, though." She paused to pull her cape closer as a brisk breeze blew in from the north. "The days are becoming cooler."

"The Ganges will be wet now and teeming with life," Nemo informed her as they strolled through the gardens. She snuggled up close as the chilly wind picked up again.

"You know, I have always wanted to see the Cherry Blossoms."

"Spring in Japan?" Nemo mused. Zola nodded. "If that would please you, dear, then I will make the arrangements."

As he booked their passage south, pleasant memories filled his mind of the time he had spent in Japan. He drafted three letters to be sent before they departed. One was to the Cantonment in Ceylon requesting permission to visit the Andaman Islands. The second was addressed to the American Consulate in Japan requesting assistance in locating Cho Cho San. The last was to Cho Cho herself.

Dear Cho Cho,

It has been many years since I left you and the child. I found my beloved Crystal! She led me to my wife. Currently my wife and I are traveling the world and plan to be in Japan for the Cherry Blossom Festival. I would very much like to see you and our child. My wife is not aware of the time I spent in Japan, nor does she know of our relationship or of the child. Your discretion in this matter would be most helpful. If you are agreeable to this meeting, you may send word to the Shiokaji-agaru in Kyoto by April. I sincerely hope that you will accommodate me.

With warm regards,

Nemo Dimitri Frankenstone

Nemo had understated the beauty of the India plains. What had been a parched and dry terrain was transformed into a lush green garden. Birds of uncountable number, size and color flew overhead. It was late October before they reached the Cantonment in Rameswaram. Nemo found two letters awaiting him. One was from the British Government informing him that he and his wife had been granted permission to visit the Andaman Islands to the east.

The other letter was from a Mr. Sharpless, American Consul in Japan. He informed Nemo that Cho Cho San had been located and his letter delivered; however, she sent no reply. The letter went on to say that should Nemo need additional help while visiting Japan to feel free to call upon him. Nemo read these letters with interest.

"Good news?" Zola inquired, adjusting her hat.

"As a matter of fact, yes. The Government has granted us an unlimited stay in the Andamans. I think you will find the natives most interesting. Despite foreign occupation for over a century, they live as they have for eons."

"Sounds intriguing. When do we leave?" She smiled.

"You are remarkable," Nemo chuckled. "Always ready for an adventure!" He kissed her passionately, much to her delight.

It was late March before they reached Miyazu, Japan. Slowly and without haste they traveled to Kyoto, enjoying the countryside. Zola was pleased with the change of climate, cuisine and customs. She remarked more than once about how pleasantly the Japanese treated foreigners. Nemo did not have the heart to tell her how they used to treat strangers – best to leave well enough alone.

When they arrived at the Shiokaji-agaru, a traditional Japanese hostelry, a letter was waiting for him. Cho Cho had talked with their daughter and both agreed that they would welcome a visit from him. Upon their arrival in Tokyo, Nemo was to send word through Mr. Sharpless that he was ready to meet with them. She would then return a message informing him as to the time and day that she and her daughter would receive them. Her husband Ito would not be present, as he had no desire to meet Nemo. The letter was signed 'Cho Cho San and Saiko San'.

"Saiko, my daughter." Nemo repeated her name to himself many times.

Zola was thrilled when Nemo presented her with tickets to the Kabureno Theatre in the Gion district. There she and Nemo took part in the public celebration of the Cherry Blossoms. They participated in both the traditional tea ceremony and a dance. She blended in well with the Geisha, her movements fluid and graceful. Although attentive, Nemo found his mind wandering. Many changes had taken place in Japan since he was last here. Rail service had replaced the foot paths, Geisha no longer graced the cities; beggars, open markets and squalor were to be found at every corner – the days of dignity and order were gone.

The trip to Tokyo was uneventful. After arranging accommodations in the Okubo house, one of the few traditional inns left in the city, he sent a message to Cho Cho. Anxiously he awaited her reply. Two days later it arrived.

"Zola," he called out, still reading Cho Cho's letter. "Yes?"

"How would you like to visit the home of a traditional Japanese family?"

"I would welcome the change. Although I like being treated with respect, lately I have the feeling that I am being treated with *too much* respect!" she giggled. "Perhaps if I was a guest instead of a paying customer I would learn more about these people." Nemo nodded, his thoughts elsewhere.

Finding the home of Cho Cho proved an easy task for Nemo. Cho Cho greeted them at the door, her slightly graying hair was still pinned up in the traditional Geisha fashion, but she no longer wore the white face. "Konnichi wa, Dimitri San," she said, bowing.

"Demo arigate gozaimasu, Cho Cho San," he replied.

Zola was impressed with Nemo's ability to speak Japanese so fluently.

Cho Cho invited them into her home, where they found tea waiting. She poured tea with movements that seemed forced. Zola and Cho Cho engaged in trivial conversation about home and family. Nemo noticed that at times Cho Cho's voice was strained, but she remained the perfect hostess. Never once did she mention the past or give any indication that she had known him before.

Suddenly two small children burst through the door. They bowed quickly to the guests and raced towards Cho Cho. They lavished her with hugs and kisses. Cho Cho whispered to them and sent them on their way. "My daughter's children," she explained to Zola, who smiled in reply.

Cho Cho rose as her daughter entered the room. Saiko bowed as her mother introduced Nemo and Zola. Nemo turned to greet his daughter and an audible gasp escaped from his lips. Before him stood a mirror image of Zola! He could not believe his eyes.

Zola, noticing his awkwardness, took charge of the situation; she engaged Saiko in conversation as Nemo stood by silent. The two women were soon talking and laughing as if they had known each other for years. As Cho Cho relaxed, Nemo became more uneasy. Zola had never known Nemo not to be in control of any situation. During a break in their conversation, Nemo suggested that they pose for a picture. The women seemed very excited. They primped and polished themselves as Nemo went outside to look for good lighting and background for his Kodak camera. Zola noticed a small porcelain butterfly on a table and suggested that Saiko place it in her hair.

"After all, if you don't, how would anyone be able to tell us apart?" The three women laughed heartily, and were still smiling as they went outside for their picture.

Nemo found it difficult to concentrate and took four pictures before he was satisfied. They went back inside for some more small talk, but soon Nemo suggested to Zola that perhaps they should be going. Zola agreed and walked outside with Saiko, leaving Nemo and Cho Cho alone.

"I am at a loss for words," he stammered.

"There are no words, Dimitri," Cho Cho replied. "Zola is most suited for you. I am pleased. Live a long and happy life, Dimitri San." She bowed before him.

He raised her chin so that he might look into her eyes. "I will never forget you, or Saiko." Tears formed in their eyes as Cho Cho retreated from him.

"Dimitri!" The word was a command and the startled Nemo turned and looked at Cho Cho. "I have letter for you, from Commodore Perry. I do not know where to send, so I keep. Stay!"

Cho Cho ran quickly to her bedroom and returned with the unopened letter. Nemo began reading out loud, but soon the tears formed again in his eyes, and he finished it with difficulty.

"Did I do something wrong, Dimitri?" asked Cho Cho contritely.

"No, you did the right thing. Better to be sailing the oceans and having fun than to wait out fifteen years in Africa coming down with all sorts of fevers."

They held hands until Zola called from outside, "Nemo, I thought you said we had to be going, love."

Dear Mr. Abdul Frankenstone:

June 1855

Heard about your case from the Consulate at Edo. When I returned home from Japan, I found out that my nephew Christopher had taken it upon himself to play the master of espionage, using you as an unwitting decoy to confuse everyone as to my whereabouts in the opening of Japan.

The Consulate confirms that you arrived in Japan shortly before me, looking for a Mr. Charles Darwin of England, his ship the Beagle. They also confirmed that, although you were in jail before my visit, they treated you honorably after I left in '53. You were to wait there until I returned in '54, but you "jumped ship," along with some others.

The only address I have for you is that of the parents of a certain Geisha Cho Cho San, so I use it in hopes that when you contact her, she can forward the letter. I know you will not be returning to Japan, as being too risky.

Concerning Darwin, I find that he left from England many years ago on the ship HMS Beagle, but never ventured anywhere near Japan, returning safely home in '36 and presently living in Down, near London, with his family, in relative seclusion, working on a book.

I trust this letter will reimburse you in some small way for my nephew's inconsideration.

Commodore Matthew Calbraith Perry

Unlike on their previous voyages, Nemo remained distant as they crossed the Pacific to America. Zola knew that something was weighing on his mind, but did not wish to interfere. By the time they docked in San Francisco Nemo's mood had improved.

"Well, my dear, what direction pleases you?" he asked, studying the rail routes.

She considered his question for a moment, then replied, "I think that I would prefer to see the mountains from a distance, thank you. The southern route would probably be very hot and dusty?" Nemo nodded in agreement. "Well, that leaves the Plains, doesn't it."

"Central Pacific it is then," Nemo smiled, booking their passage.

Their accommodations were luxurious compared to India's trains. Their berth had running water, tables and bedding. Zola found herself inclined to spend her time in the vestibule enjoying the scenery and the wares of the 'butcher boys', who were most attentive.

"Nemo, look at this!" she exclaimed, handing him the Chicago Gazette. A picture of the Wright Brothers and their newest model of bicycle, the 'Wright Cycle' was captioned 'Innovative and Reasonably Priced'. The article that followed went on to explain that the balloon tire cycle with its modified frame would prove to be the fastest-selling model of the year. "I have always wanted to ride one," Zola said wishfully.

"Why not stop and try?" Nemo suggested.

"Do you mean it?" she teased.

Of course," he replied, copying the information from the paper. "We'll just make a transfer when we get to Chicago."

After a hearty meal in the dining car, Zola retired and soon fell asleep.

Nemo was restless and stared out the window, watching the stars and remembering his last trip through America. Crystal called to him, and they spent the late hours thinking of her kin in the Great Plains.

Transfers to Dayton via the B&O railroad were easily arranged in Chicago, and within two days they were standing before the "Wright Cycle Shop" on Williams Street in Dayton. The red brick building was modest compared to most shops in the area. They found the door unlocked; however, no one was inside. Little did they know that they had just triggered the silent alarm that Orville and Wilbur had installed so that they might continue their research without interruptions from persons only needing air for their tires. Nemo suggested that perhaps they should leave, when they heard footsteps on the stairs. They heard two men engaged in conversation; presently a thin man in a blue tick apron appeared.

"Good day! May I help you?"

"We were wondering if you rented bicycles," Nemo said.

"As a matter of fact, we do. For the day or for the week?"

"Just for the day," Zola answered.

"Two, then," the other man said, and headed for the back.

"No, only one. I will not be indulging," Nemo said quickly.

"Hey Orv, is Kate's old St. Clair still in the back?"

"I think so. We were going to dismantle it to make the wind tunnel, but I don't think we got to it yet."

Orville walked into the back room with Nemo following behind. The room was filled with kites and models of gliders, machines of unknown purpose and scale models of airplanes.

"I see that you are interested in flight," Nemo announced.

"Oh, yes. It is our passion. The bicycle shop is only to provide us with the means to carry on our experiments." Orville retrieved a slightly dusty women's bike from the corner and pushed it to the front. Nemo remained, examining the modification they had made to a Lilienthal glider.

Wilbur interrupted, "Excuse me, but your wife is asking that you come and watch her first attempt." Zola sat astride the bicycle nervously. Orville steadied her as she made her first try. It took only a few times before she mastered the balance and maneuvering qualities of the bike.

"Would you care to try?" she teased Nemo. He shook his head. "Well then, I am off. I am going around the block this time," she announced audaciously, pedaling away.

"She's quite adept you know," Orville said to Nemo. While Zola rode, the brothers and Nemo discussed man-powered flight. Chanute's ideas were defended by Wilbur, and Orville stood by Langley. Both felt that Pilcher had contributed, but to a lesser degree. Nemo listened attentively as they detailed their plans to attempt the first powered flight by 1905. They openly discussed the modifications they had made to the wings that included a unique warping, and rudders for each side that could be controlled by the operator. Also a rear rudder that was moveable, to counteract the tendency to roll. Orv went on for a great while about his special canvas that was lighter and stronger than any tried so far. Wilbur shared his equation for lift and drag: Lift equals air pressure times area of lifting surface times velocity (where velocity equals headwind plus airspeed, squared) times the coefficient of lift. Both brothers agreed that their mathematics was sound. Nemo had to agree – the formula was well thought out.

It was late afternoon before Zola announced she was finished. "Would you mind terribly taking a picture of me and this marvelous machine?" she asked breathlessly.

As Nemo set up the camera, she invited the brothers to pose with her. The three of them stood before the bicycle shop with Zola astride Kate's old St. Clair, while Nemo snapped the picture. They took many pictures on their trip around the world, but Zola especially liked this one, for within five years the brothers were in Europe demonstrating man-powered flight for the public.

Back on the main line again, they were not many hours from New York. Zola was looking out the window, while Nemo was sitting next to her, nodding off. Suddenly Zola dug her elbow into his ribs.

"Nemo! Wake up. Look! It looks just like my old home in Africa! Ask the conductor where we are!"

Nemo stumbled out of the berth in search of the conductor. They returned in a few minutes. "Ask the conductor what you wanted to know, Zola."

"What place did we pass through a few minutes ago? So peaceful and bucolic. It reminded me of happy times in my childhood."

The conductor smiled. "That would be Lancaster County, Pennsylvania, Ma'am. Paradise Township."

"Oh, Nemo, I would like to live in Paradise some day!"

The couple returned to their apartment in London by the twentieth of July, 1900, having spent some eighty weeks on the road.

"We've had our fun," Zola teased, "Now take me to bed. I am yours!"

May the warm winds of heaven blow softly
on your home and the Great Spirit
bless all who enter there.
Cherokee Indian Blessing

39
'Stones and Watson

"The pictures using the telescope as a telephoto turned out rather well, Dear, don't you think?" said Zola noncommittally as they were going over the highlights of their trip around the world some three years ago.

"The edges are blurred. I think perhaps Crystal could be improved upon for this use. Junior is almost two and is old enough to travel. I hear the Black Forest has some wizards in optical surgery. Are you up to a trip to Switzerland? We can stay there while the surgery is being performed. If we go, it should be soon, before the leaves are all off the trees."

"Yes, I am ready."

The three of them went to Switzerland, where Nemo rented an apartment in Bern and took a temporary position as janitor for the Patent Office there – in this way, he could keep abreast of scientific happenings while Crystal was in surgery.

Several months later, in the winter, Nemo was sitting in his chair by the fireplace. The apartment was quite cozy when the hearth was blazing, even here in Switzerland in the winter. A small book lay in his lap, a mystery story by Conan Doyle. Slippers were on his feet and his smoking jacket on his shoulders, but his pipe had gone out some time ago. He was not feeling very comfortable just now. A call had come not five minutes ago, and so late at night, from the Black Forest. The gnomes had relayed some bad news: while the optical surgery on Crystal's back half was progressing nicely, her larger front half, which was being held in storage on a shelf, had mysteriously developed a bad scratch on the rounded side. Herr Mürrisch discovered it when he took it out to measure it in preparation for making a mounting for the two elements. He did not know how long the scratch had been there. Herr Mürrisch said he would not have called so late except that when he got home there was a note in the mail that hinted of sabotage or vandalism (or worse) on Crystal, and he went back to the shop to fortify security, where he was now calling from.

"Not to worry," Mürrisch had said, We will work around the problem and solve the mystery. Only a delay – nothing serious. She will come out of this in better shape than before!"

Nemo nodded in his chair and fell into a fitful sleep.

The Case of the Ravished Inamorata

"Mr. Watson, come here. I want to see you." I replaced the earpiece on its hook and immediately there was a knock at the door. "Come in," I said. There stood Tom Watson.

"Sorry I am late, Doctor 'Stone, but the channel boat got caught in a storm, and I had neglected to get the proper visas, and my passport was out of date."

"Didn't you tell them all of the urgency of the situation?" I chided Watson. "A few pounds here or there might have greased the wheels. It is acceptable this time. At least you are here safe and sound, if quite tardy. Try not to let it happen again. We used to work as a team, but things are getting slipshod."

"Would you like to hear a new sonata just come out?" I asked to no one in particular. Without waiting for a reply, I took out my violin and bow and tuned up while Watson was taking off his coat and boots.

"I notice, Watson, that it is snowing outside, that your wife has been away to see her mother for about two weeks now, that one of your clients has not paid his bill in three months, and that you have taken in the six year old daughter of a late Scotland Yard official."

"More like seven ... ! How the devil did you deduce all that, Doctor 'Stone?"

"Think about it, Watson; look at your boots and coat pockets. It will come to you."

With that I began the sonata. Then I went on to a violin concerto, having Watson and myself hum the piano and orchestral parts. I became lost in reverie and played on and on for several hours, compositions of my own creation.

"Time for bed, Watson, eh? I'll show you to the door, or you can stay if you wish."

"'Pon my soul, Doctor 'Stone, what did you call me to Switzerland for?"

"Eh? What? Call you? I thought you called me. I know you called me. You are getting forgetful lately. Do you care for some tea? Help yourself." With that I dropped to my chair and fell asleep.

The next morning I woke up late. Watson was still there. "Watson, are you ill? You haven't moved all night."

"I was waiting for you to remember why you called me here."

I looked hard at my companion. "Don't you remember, Watson? The scratch, the miserable scratch. The gnomes have destroyed my gemstone, and with it the photophone! The patent is useless without Crystal. Don't you remember, man?" The whole world is upside down and no one cares ... no one cares ... and I rushed out of the apartment.

The next thing I know I find myself in a waiting railroad carriage bound for the Black Forest.

"Ticket, please?" requested the conductor politely. Fumbling in the pocket of my waistcoat, I produced a small square of black cardboard, which the conductor punched with a flourish. "Bound for Germany," he observed.

"The Black Forest." For the first time, I was aware of perspiring profusely, even though I was wearing neither coat nor hat, both of which would have served me well in the chilly northern woods. "On a matter of greatest urgency."

"In response, I see, to a distressing telephone call."

"How did you know that?" I asked incredulously.

"Why, Herr Doktor, it is perfectly plain! In your distress, you clamped the receiver of the phone to your right ear so tightly you left its impression on the side of your head."

"And how did you know I was a doctor?"

"That, too, is obvious." He pointed to my waistcoat pocket. "Your watch fob is a medal given to Russian military physicians as a commendation of extraordinary service. I wrote a monograph on obscure military medals some years back, and consider myself somewhat of an expert on the subject. Your fob, combined with your highly intelligent mien and learned accents, made it safe for me to assume you were a doctor of some kind; although I perceive from the callus on the outside of your right thumb that you are engaged in some kind of bookwork of late."

"Marvelous! I exclaimed. "You are just the fellow I need! Can you come to the Black Forest with me?"

"As it happens, I was headed in that direction. I am, after all, the conductor of this train." He smiled. "But if your question implies my ability to get off the train at a particular destination – yes, I think I can delay the engineer for the requisite few moments it would take."

"Bless you, dear fellow!" I cried, shaking his hand vigorously. "For I have a mystery worthy of no less a mind than your own. What is your name, Sir?"

A dimple appeared in the beardless cheek. "Watson," he replied simply.

"Mr. Watson! In my haste, I left you in my apartment, yet you are here as the conductor of this train!"

"A man must do what a man must do," said my friend. The train sped off.

"Why hello, Mr. Watson," said the receptionist at the office of the Optische Werke in the Black Forest, "Whom do you wish to see?"

"Herr Mürrisch, bitte, Fraulein," said Watson.

"And is this gentleman with you? Would you please sign the register, Sir? How is your wife, Tom?" she asked earnestly.

While they were discussing matters as old friends, I took the pen and signed the ledger majestically: 'Doctor Alex G. Bellstone. My word, is that me?' I said to myself.

"Go right in, gentlemen," said the young lady, and we entered the hallowed cubicle where Crystal was undergoing her operation.

Her smaller half was still in the Iron Lung, where it would remain for another year. Some of her silica molecules were being respired out and replaced with other metal oxides and rare earths, for a better match with the Mate. Her larger half was lying flat side down, glued to a small square of black cardboard with a strange design punched out of one corner. Herr Mürrisch was being paged.

I took a close look at the well-rounded form rising from the black patch. A shiver ran down my spine. It was an ugly scratch. I inspected it more closely with my magnifying glass – it was even more ugly.

"That's an ugly scratch, Doctor Bellstone, is it not?" said Herr Mürrisch with a wry smile as he entered.

"Very ugly," I responded.

"Perhaps we can quantify it," said Watson. "Doctor 'Stone, would you please get out the three-axis surface profilometer, and we can run a detailed chart in polar coordinates and Z-axis, so we may determine what instrument caused the wound and who the perpetrator was."

Herr Niesen was called in – he was the technician on mensuration – and he was soon absorbed in his work.

"A - a - a - Chooo!!" The black cardboard flew out from the profilometer stage and landed upside down on the floor. Herr Niesen in his haste leapt from his stool and his right foot came down from directly above the patch ....

My attention faded from that scene and I was aware of Herr Mürrisch pushing a note in front of my face.

"Here's the note I found in the mail last evening, Doctor Bellstone. What do you make of it?"

["Nemo, come to bed. It's almost midnight. I have on my special nightie," Zola said enticingly as she bent down and kissed Nemo on the neck.]

"Let's see here. My, my, such awful language. This is in bad French. It says, 'This is only a warning. Stay away from her or Crystal will be kidnapped'. They wouldn't, they couldn't, pull the plug on Crystal; she would die. Only the most heinous of villains would dare follow through on such a bold plan. Watson, check the note for fingerprints!"

While Watson was dusting the note for prints, Herr Niesen came back with his report. I noted that the envelope in which the note came bore a local German postmark.

Herr Niesen presented his report: "There is a slight chip on the edge that I used for zero degrees, and the full radius along the diameter will be equal to one (l). Here are the coordinates and scratch depths in the convex surface:"

Angle	Radius	Depth in Microns
0	0.00	0
15	0.70	20
30	0.65	30
45	0.70	40
60	0.75	45
75	0.60	80
90	0.50	80
105	0.45	75
120	0.50	70
135	0.55	60
150	0.60	40
165	0.00	0
↓	↓	↓
360	0.00	0

"We seem to be at a loss, gentlemen. I can make neither heads nor tails of the clues," I said to the gnomes. "Suppose you tell me just what happened as best you remember."

Herr Mürrisch took a deep breath. "Night before last, we were working on the photophone cable. Three of us – myself, Niesen here, and young Herr Blöde, the apprentice. The process was going quite smoothly, and only another hour or two of work remained to be done on this particular phase. I may not tell more on the photophone, as it is classified. Anyway, we were exultant over the results, but as it was suppertime and the light was becoming bad, we decided to retire to our homes and resume work in the morning."

"Who locked up the workshop?" I asked.

"I did, myself," Mürrisch replied. "I always do; I have the only keys, one to the back door of the shop and one to the front. I wear the keys on a long chain – see, it is about my neck now. I only take it off when I sleep. As you know, we make and repair many priceless objects, and I take my responsibility seriously."

"I know you do," I replied soothingly. "So no one would have had access to the keys unless they also had access to your bedroom. Does anyone live with you?"

"No one; although I have a woman, Brigitta Hofnagel, who comes in to cook and clean. She also cleans for the others and tidies up here in the shop. She goes back to her parents' home every evening, though, and she has keys to neither my house nor the shop."

"This Brigitta is a gnome as well?" I asked.

Mürrisch grimaced. "Yes, but not exactly a prime example of our species – too tall. A nice enough girl – a little given to flights of fancy - but PLAIN." He shuddered, from which I assumed that his polite terminology did not begin to describe the unfortunate girl's plainness.

My eyes narrowed. "Does Niesen share your assessment of her appearance?"

216

Mürrisch nodded, "My younger brother Günstig also works here, and he tells dreadful jokes at her expense. And the saddest thing is, at one time it was quite obvious that Brigitta had designs on young Blöde. Nothing he did could discourage her advances, and he prevailed upon me to have a talk with her. I obliged, explaining gently that the boy was at the beginning of a long and arduous apprenticeship for which he showed great talent and promise, and he could not waste time in courting. She took it well, and Blöde was most grateful to me, although my brother continues to tease him about it to this day. Günstig, I'm afraid, is more fond of teasing than work."

"We are getting far ahead of ourselves," I interrupted as Watson came back into the room with the note, "although I am indebted to you for providing such a rich background. But I would like to get back to the particulars. Yesterday morning you returned to the workshop to find the door – open?"

No, sir," said Herr Mürrisch in some surprise. "Locked. Both doors – back and front."

"Locked!" Watson cried. A pulse-beat throbbed visibly at his temple. "Locked!"

"Well, I don't find that so extraordinary," I said. "After all, whoever let himself in wouldn't want to arouse suspicion by leaving an open door."

Watson waved my ponderings aside. "And the windows – do they open?"

"No," said Niesen, they are stationary; just glass set into the walls."

"Wonderful!" Watson cried in delight. "When you went into the workshop, Herr Mürrisch, tell me exactly what you saw."

"Nothing seemed out of the ordinary at first. But when I got to my workbench I saw some items in disarray, and when I took Crystal #2 from the shelf to measure her for her outfit, I saw the ugly scratch which we now have complete data on.

"My poor Crystal!" I cried. "What could this maniac have against her – or me?"

"Calm down, old sport," Watson advised serenely. "I doubt it has anything to do with you at all. Tell me, Herr Mürrisch, what did you do then?"

"I began to yell and scream, I'm afraid. I ran out of the shop and met Niesen on the path, coming to work; by the time we got back to the shop, Günstig had already arrived, and we tried to figure out who could have wrought such mischief. The others were as baffled as I. Then Brigitta came on her way to the Optische Werke to do chores and was told of the damage. She was visibly upset and left work soon after and went home with a headache ... she has a particular fondness for Crystal. And then nothing, until I received the note in the mail that night, just last night."

["Dear, if you won't come to bed, please wake up and have this iced tea I just made – I used some fresh snow; it's snowing nicely now. Your forehead is so hot. You put too many logs on the fire again, as usual."]

[Nemo half awoke from his torpor, drank the tea, then resumed his dream.]

"All the clues are coming into focus," I said to Watson. "Did anyone check the groove shape along the whole length of the scratch?"

I soon had a collodion negative replica underneath the toolmaker's microscope. "Aha," I said after some minutes of scrutiny, "sixty degrees, no more, no less, all along the scratch."

Watson handed me the dusted note and said, "Only two prints – a right thumb print on the right upper corner of the note and a right forefinger print directly beneath on the other side."

I held my face very close to the note, my magnifier directly over the thumbprint. "Just so," I said. Then turning the note, I inspected the other print. "Aha, just as I suspected. A woman's print!"

"How can you be so sure, Doctor 'Stone," said Watson. "The gnomes have small fingers also."

"True, I said, "but I don't believe these gentlemen are in the habit of using strong chemicals such as methyl ionone! I believe I know who wrote this note, and we will not have to ask Scotland Yard for fingerprint analysis."

"My word, Doctor 'Stone, have you memorized all the suspects' fingerprint whorls?" exclaimed Tom Watson.

I only smiled. "Watson, did you bring the Sunday paper?"

"Why, yes sir. I always carry the latest Paris Sunday."

"May I see the theater section, please? ... Aha! Thank you, gentlemen. Watson, we go to Paris immediately. Time is of the essence."

I plunged out of the cubicle, past the reception desk where I signed myself out, and into a waiting railroad carriage bound for Paris.

"Ticket, please?" requested me conductor politely. Fumbling in the pocket of my waistcoat, I produced a small square of black cardboard, which the conductor punched with a flourish. "Bound for France," he observed.

"Paris. The theater district." For the first time, I was aware of shivering in the cold, even though I was wearing my coat and hat, which should have served me well in this chilly climate. "On a matter of greatest urgency."

"In response, I see, to an important clue in a note left near the scene of the crime."

"How did you know that?" I asked incredulously.

"Why, Monsieur, it is perfectly plain! In your excitement, you held a magnifying glass to your eye so tightly you gave yourself a black eye."

"And how did you know it was a note that held the clue?"

"That, too, is obvious." Your face and your fingers bear unmistakable evidence of the strong chemical methyl ionone, which type of chemical is often used in conjunction with notes of deception."

"Marvelous! I exclaimed. "You are just the fellow I need! Can you come to Paris with me?"

"As it happens, I was headed in that direction. I am, after all, the conductor of this train." He smiled. "But if your question implies my ability to get off the train at a particular destination – yes, I think I can delay the engineer for the requisite few moments it would take."

"Bless you, dear fellow!" I cried, shaking his hand vigorously. "For I have a mystery worthy of no less a mind than your own. What is your name, Sir?"

A dimple appeared in the beardless cheek. "Watson," he replied simply, "Thomas Augustus Watson. At your service, Doctor 'Stone."

"Mr. Watson! In my haste, I left you at the Optische Werke, yet you are here as the conductor of this train!" "A man must do what a man must do," said my friend.

The train sped off through the Alpine tunnels.

The train lurched to a stop and we were at the ticket booth of the Paris Opera House. "Doctor Bellstone to see Lilli Lehmann, please."

"Lilli is on stage now. Would you gentlemen care to wait in her dressing room?"

We were in the audience, front row center, enjoying her singing immensely. Before the applause died, we found ourselves transported to her dressing room. Lilli came in, radiant.

"Tom, I'm so glad you're here," she said as they embraced.

"Hello, Doctor Bellstone, are you here on business or can the four of us go to a party after I get my makeup off" "Who is the fourth?" I asked.

"Why, I believe Mr. Watson's wife is here, waiting. Hello, Elizabeth. Well, shall we go?"

"That perfume, Lilli," I said....

"Yes," she quickly answered, "It's new. My boyfriend purchased it in Rome this past week. Violets, with a hint of pine."

"I take it your boyfriend is a sales representative for a machine tool company, specifically grinding wheel dressing equipment," I parried, pressing the attack.

You are amazing, Alex, even if quite wrong," she blushed.

"Come, come, admit it. You are tired of me," I accused.

"Well, dear, if you would stop running around all over creation with Watson, picking up impetuous women .... "

"Back to Switzerland, Watson," I cried, "The case is solved!"

I was back in my apartment seated in my chair by the fire, smoking jacket and slippers on, glass of ice cold Madeira in my hand. Watson was putting on his boots and coat.

"I can see you don't need me any more, Doctor 'Stone. But before I return to London, please explain how you solved this most baffling case."

"Quite elementary, my dear Watson. You see, the scratch was in the form of the Arabic numeral "7", implying that the perpetrator knew there were seven men working on the secret photophone project. The one who did the deed was a spy for foreign interests. This is quite plain. He used a diamond tool with a perfect sixty-degree point – the smooth sides of the scratch groove preclude anything but diamond. His cover was as a sales representative for various machine tools, and so he could gain entry to the Optische Werke quite easily, as they use many types of equipment in their work.

He had an accomplice, this Brigitta Hofnagel, who secreted him one evening in the shop, after he signed himself out when the receptionist left for a moment. The next morning he waited for her "all-clear" signal and left the Optische Werke quietly. He is the boyfriend of Lilli and had made advances to the plain Brigitta only to gain access to top secret information. To confuse the issue and to hide her involvement in the crime, Brigitta sent the note to whoever first discovered the scratch, who happened to be Herr Mürrisch.

"The wording of the note, 'Stay away from her ... ' and the poor French and the evidence of methyl ionone all indicate a non-European, probably American, woman of means and of taste who has learned of her boyfriend's unfaithfulness, and who sent the note to poor Brigitta as a warning to both of them. The only woman who meets these requirements and who knows how important Crystal is to the gnomes is the American operatic soprano Lilli Lehmann, since I have discussed this matter with her on several occasions when she was in England, and to no other woman. On the off chance she was in Europe on tour, I had you look in the theater section of the Sunday paper. The rest falls into place quite naturally."

The telephone rang. Nemo woke up and answered. It was Herr Mürrisch.

"Sorry to bother you again so late, but I wanted to keep you posted. We've decided to increase the focal length of Crystal's front lens to 1.3 times that of the back lens. That will clean up the scratch with the least amount of material removed, and the aberrations and distortions will be reduced considerably – the eyepiece will be better than ever. Oh, the note. A machine tool sales rep who comes here frequently was making out with Brigitta, and during a moment of passion the lens was knocked from the shelf and he stepped on it. Brigitta, who is quite taken with Crystal, was devastated, broke off the relationship and called his girlfriend in Paris, who then sent the note to Brigitta for when he showed up again."

"I knew all that," Nemo said. But thank you, anyway."

The next morning Nemo was up early for breakfast. Zola came in with the Sunday paper.

"I understand, dear," he said, "that Lilli Lehmann, the noted American soprano, is here in Europe, in Paris, and has recently broken her engagement to the heir of a large, important industrial establishment."

"Hmmm? Oh, look, Nemo, in the paper! My good friend Lilli Lehmann from America is in Paris and has just broken her engagement to a rich young Frenchman, who was using his job as sales representative for his father's machine tool company as a cover for his spy work as an agent for an Italian perfume maker. He traveled all over Europe and elsewhere with impunity until his doings were found out by a small German optical company – the cleaning lady and an apprentice blew the whistle on him. Oh, how nice. These two have just become engaged; so all is not lost ... What were you saying, dear? Oh, you had told me what I have just read to you!"

"Yes, of course."

"But I was just now handed the paper by the concierge!"

"I couldn't get in the mood for sleep, so after you went to bed, I strolled down to the lobby and saw the headline on the stack of Sunday papers: 'Opera Star Dumps Playboy Spy'."

Nemo was quite happy, now that Crystal's surgery was back on track, and the next day he went in to the Patent Office whistling. The broom flew, the trash cans almost emptied themselves.

Presently he came up to young Albert, the new probationary Technical Expert, Third Class (as of 23 June 1902; soon to have permanent status in September 1904); the young man who had edged Nemo out of the position at the last minute, primarily because in Nemo's letter back in the summer of '02 he had indicated he might be arriving that winter, and could stay for only two years or so – a temporary position. When Nemo did finally arrive, the janitor's position was the only opening available.

Nemo, however, found this advantageous. He could be there late at night when everyone else was gone and sift through the papers in the trashcans for ideas, to keep abreast of the latest in science. It was a most rewarding position, and he hardly needed the money.

"Hello, Albert, how go things?"

"Wie geht's, Nemo? Oh weh, no time for myself – just plugging away.

People come up with the darnedest ideas; perpetual motion is all the rage today, and some people think they have come up with a heat engine that converts close to 100% of the heat energy into rotational energy without changing the water to steam. Oh weh!"

"I am full of vim and vigor today, Albert. As one 'Stone to another, I just must tell you about the Stone that brought me here and what she can do! Do you have an hour or so?"

"Ach. Come to my place tonight and we can discuss her over some beers. Mileva will be there. Mileva Maric. We plan to be married. But she does not like my violin playing."

"Do you play the violin also? Yes, indeed, I will see you tonight about 7, if that is alright with you and Mileva?"

So that evening Nemo told Einstein of the legend of Crystal, and of Newton and the Mate, and what the little telescope could do.

"Such a big image from such a little thing!" exclaimed the young man.

"Well," said Nemo, "everything is relative. The lightning's energy created Crystal, which caused Newton to make his telescope, thus multiplying the value:

$$e = \qquad C \qquad X \qquad MC$$
$$\text{lightning} \quad = \qquad \text{Crystal} \quad x \quad \text{Telescope}$$
$$\text{or } 3 = MC^2$$

"In 1905 Einstein's genius burst into dazzling flower. It was a fabulous year. In the annals of physics it ranks with the years 1665-66, when the plague that ravaged England forced Cambridge University to close and caused young Newton to leave Cambridge for his home in the quiet village of Woolsthorpe ...."

From the Biography,
Albert Einstein, Creator and Rebel

40
Junior and the Pirates

Late Spring 1904

Junior waved repeatedly to a few of the longshoremen on the Bristol dock as Captain Nemo, at the helm of the *Auggie*, sailed out of the confines of the busy harbor and into the thin morning fog of the Bristol Channel. The little boy, just turned three, was getting tired of being held in his mother's protective embrace.

He waved one last farewell with his chubby outstretched hand and watched as the port faded from view. Looping his fat arms about Zola's neck, he looked up into her face with a pout. "Mommy, I want down," he commanded.

Mrs. Frankenstone, known by the fishermen as Mz. Zola, let her small son down with a firm warning. "You stay in my sight, young man. I don't want you running around the deck and bothering the crew or falling overboard. And if you go below, let me know. If you get stuck inside one of the cupboards you will get a paddling when your Daddy finds you."

Junior smiled. "Yes, Mommy."

Mz. Zola patted the top of her son's curly fair head, then bent down and kissed his plump cheek. Junior hugged her in response and then skipped over to the port beam railing.

Zola sank down on the cabin top, her back against the mast, and began repairing the jib and storm sails – the last voyage had seen some heavy weather. She watched Junior constantly as her hands worked with the needle and leather palm.

"Boys will be boys," she thought, "One cannot take the adventure from them. I only hope his adventures all turn out as well as mine."

Junior gazed intently into the fog. His blue eyes widened in excitement – the outline of a phantom ship appeared out of nowhere – and he had to tell his Mommy and Daddy. Scampering back to the cabin, he pulled himself on top and tugged at Zola's right pant leg.

"Mommy, a real pirate ship. Look! Daddy! A real pirate ship on port beam. Look!"

Zola tried to calm the anxious boy down, but he kept pulling frantically at her arm. "Alright, Junior, you win. I cannot do any sewing with you pulling my arm out of joint. Where is the pirate ship? Point to it. Oh, yes. Nemo – look at the ship – are we on a collision course?"

"It appears so, Dear. I have been watching it for some time, and when I turn, it turns. It looks like they want to board our vessel."

"*Is* it a pirate ship, Mommy?" came a whispered question from the curious youngster. Zola shaded the bright haze with one of her hands and saw the long body and the dark flag of a seafaring vessel, but yet nothing indicated that it was pirates.

"If it is pirates, they are very bad people. Go below and get your father's telescope and bring it to me. Perhaps Crystal and her Mate will show the flag and what manner of men are on board. Hurry!"

"Albert!" said the Captain to the first mate, "get my pistol and load it and have it at the ready. Something is fishy."

"Here is Crystal, Mommy. What does she say?"

"Yes, dear, she says it is the Jolly Roger. And she shows me some men in tattered clothes. Nemo, what are pirates doing here in England?"

"I don't know, my love, but I will hold course. Steady as she goes."

The pirate ship appeared to be riding the tide like an attacking shark – closer and closer it moved.

"Junior," said Zola, "go below and hide, and I will be down shortly."

"Yes, Mommy."

Finally the ship came alongside, and with grappling hooks heaved and lines secured, the two ships were soon riding as one. Junior heard the sound of scuffles and yells coming from above.

"Where is ya prized wife and son, Cappie? They will be me hostages 'til ya tells me where ya stowed me 'scope. I've waited twenty year to see this day. No one turns on Fisheye," cackled an evil husky voice.

Junior and Zola were hiding in the hold and the little boy was clinging to his mother. They heard a shot fired into the air; then another. Zola could take the suspense no longer.

"Come, son, hold on to Crystal and her Mate and we will go above and give the pirate what he wants."

They emerged into the bright sunlight. On the deck, with a dagger in his black rotted teeth, was the pirate Fisheye, hook-nosed with a wart, greasy tangled black locks, an eye patch, and wearing a tattered red velvet coat and breeches. On the deck of the pirate ship were the rest of the pirate crew – a motley group.

"Ahoy," said one, "request permission to come aboard!"

"Why," said Zola, "I would know you troupers anywhere. You are – why, you are the Pirates of Penzance! It has been many years since I was in that play and five years since I quit the stage, but seeing old friends makes it all seem like yesterday. Junior, look, these are Mommy's friends from long ago!"

And a great time they had, going from one ship to the other, climbing the rigging, spinning sea yarns, playing with Junior, scanning the horizon with the 'scope, reliving old times when Zola was a bit actress and Nemo played detective with his spyglass.

"How did you find out about us and Junior?" asked Nemo. "Oh, word gets around. And we miss Zola. Do you ever think about returning to the stage?"

"Oh, pshaw, I'm too old. I'm almost fifty. Yes, I think about returning, but my family comes first." She took Junior up into her arms and held him close. "I'll try to get Nemo to see the play. Has it been running long?"

"We've just finished up a six month tour and decided to go out sailing and celebrate and see you and your family."

Junior was much impressed with this adventure and decided he wanted to be a pirate some day.

41
Junior Goes Courting

Junior's daydream was interrupted by the voice of his mother coming from the kitchen.

"Son, I'm not going to repeat myself again – get in here and eat your soup. It's getting cold!"

Junior gritted his teeth in anger and frowned – he didn't feel like eating any lunch. All he wanted to do was think of Miss Penelope Fletcher. Sweeping his toy soldiers aside with a careless brush of his hand, he got unwillingly to his feet. Zola noticed there was something wrong with Junior the moment he came bounding into the kitchen. He took his chair rather sulkily and commenced to stare down into his bowl.

'You know,' said a voice of reason in Mrs. Frankenstone's head, 'You know, Zola, you must face reality. Junior isn't far away from being a young man now. He isn't your nappy wetty baby fatty anymore, the one you quit the theater for!'

Zola didn't know how to respond to this wisdom – she carelessly ladled some of the vegetable soup into her bowl. Joining her son at the table, she decided to ask him why he was pouting.

"What's the matter with Mom's favorite Junebug this fine Saturday morning with the sun shining and the birds singing and no school?" she said to him teasingly across the table.

Junior stopped twirling his spoon in the soup and looked up at his mother with a frown. "Mom, I'm not your little Junebug anymore. Face reality. I'm almost nine years old!"

Mrs. Frankenstone choked on a spoonful of soup, but after coughing and clearing her throat, she gawked at Junior in disbelief. Since he was talking so maturely, she decided to hear him out.

"Go ahead, lad, tell me what's bothering you," she said seriously.

Junior pushed his chair back from the table and folded his arms in deep thought. After a few minutes passed, Zola could no longer bear the suspense. Clanging her spoon onto her bowl noisily brought him back from his own private little world. Junior glanced her way and let the proverbial cat out of the bag.

"Mom, I think I'm in love. Her name is Penny. The problem is, I adore her, but she thinks I'm a certified wimp. How can I gain her favor? Dad got you – I need some advice."

Zola felt another lump forming in her throat and immediately reached for the glass of water in front of her. 'In love!' she shouted inwardly to herself.

Mrs. Frankenstone motioned for her son to remain in his seat and then vacated the kitchen in a flash. She found her voice again, mysteriously, at the door of her husband's tiny study. Knocking loud enough to get his attention, and wake the dead, she heard the melodic voice of Nemo.

"Entree, mon cherie amour ... I'm in the mood for love ..." Zola stepped inside the carpeted room and met the questioning gaze of her pipe-smoking spouse. "What is it, love? You promised me no more dramatics before our Junior was born."

Zola took a seat in the plush chair that sat beside his desk. She leaned forward. "Pardon me, Nemo, I'm not acting. We do have a problem. Our Junior is ... he's ..."

Zola could not finish the sentence – she started sobbing in her hands.

Nemo put his pipe down and stood up behind his desk stiffly. He commanded his wife, almost as if he were at the helm of the Auggie once more:

"Attention! Straighten up now, Seaman Apprentice Zola – no more babbling. Out with it!"

Mrs. Frankenstone held her shoulders back and dried her eyes. "It's this way, dear Captain – you must talk to your son – he's told me that he was ... that he was in *love*!"

Nemo's mouth dropped open, but reality set in for him, not anger or worry. He looked down at his wife sternly and gave her another order.

"Madame, you will do your share as well. So, our boy says he's in love. We can't condemn a first romance, now, can we? We must help along ... after all, Junior *does* take after us. I had my first crush at eight; and you, didn't you once tell me that you had a lover when you were ten?"

"That was different, Nemo. You will know how different some day."

Junior was frightened when his father entered the kitchen and grabbed a seat beside him, patting the child on his fair head, as he did many times since the boy was a tot. Nemo poured himself a cup of cold tea to steady his nerves and then made his inquiry.

"So, Junior, I hear that you've fallen under the spell of a charming female. Tell me who the fair lady is and why you appear so down."

Junior was surprised. He had expected his dad to be upset like Zola. Grinning at the Captain, he repeated everything he had told his mom, and added, "Dad, Mom was once very good in the theater. Do you think she could teach me to play the part of a suitor?"

Nemo turned to his wife and then back to the inquisitive boy. Shrugging his shoulders, Nemo then nodded and said, Your mother wasn't the greatest actress in town, but she did play a fairly good Carmen. I'm sure she can show you the basic outline and courtesies of a Beau. I, on the other hand, can supply you with advice as to what you should wear, what you should buy for your lady friend; and I will even throw in a free violin lesson for "O Sole Mio."

Junior gave his mother a wink of his eye and shook hands with his father. He was glad that they were finally realizing that he was indeed growing up.

After two weeks of etiquette and violin lessons, Junior was ready to make his debut as a first-rate suitor. Captain Nemo, to give his nervous son added confidence, placed Crystal and her Mate on duty about Junior's neck. The boy reflected on the past as he touched the 'scope. Even though he was just three then, he could still remember the pirate adventure on the *Auggie*, when he was knee-high to a cricket and wanted nothing more than to be a pirate like Fisheye. Now that he was nine, all he cared to be was the apple of Penny's eye.

'Are all these different wishes a part of childhood?' came the question into his mind. Unable to answer this one himself, Junior asked Nemo.

"Remember this always, lad. Life is always subject to changes and so are people. When we are young, we dream so many dreams. It's nice to live them whenever we get the chance, because only from experiences, firsthand, do we grow into fine adults. Childhood ends one day ... but a first love is forever."

Junior understood what his father was trying to say. Though he wasn't any longer a tiny sprout, he wasn't yet a mature tree. He still had four years before he was a teenager. What he felt for Penny was a sign that he was changing inside, getting older, becoming a man.

Nemo patted his son on the arm and brought him back from his reverie. "Time for you to go and serenade your Penelope, lad. Hurry on, now. Be back before your bedtime – she only lives down the block."

Junior placed the black top hat on his head firmly and picked up the violin case.

Looking in the mirror, he decided that he was as dashing as Don José. Amusement and mischief danced in his slate blue eyes.

Zola peeked in on her son by the door and complimented him. "Could this handsome young man be my Junebug? If only I were forty years younger! "

Nemo joined his wife at the door and told Junior to stop primping and get on his merry way. Junior saluted his father with a white-gloved hand and marched out of his bedroom. Zola started crying softly on the stairway as she watched Junior leave.

Nemo gathered his wife up in his arms and carried her to their bedroom entrance. "Let's do something about those tears of yours, love; what say?"

Mrs. Frankenstone put a hand to her forehead and tossed her head back dramatically. "Take me; I am yours."

Now Junior found Penelope's house after a short walk and went up to the spot on the lawn beneath her bedroom window. It was in darkness. Picking up a few pebbles, Junior pitched one after the other on the glass pane. Soon a light came on in her room. Junior watched as the window was opened, and a girl with long red braids poked her head out. She was dressed in a pink velvet robe. Glancing below, her fair face became red with anger.

"Junior Frankenstone! Just what are you doing? I was asleep. Why did you wake me up with those darned rocks?"

Junior responded by smiling up at her dreamily. He hoisted the violin onto his shoulder. Penelope covered her ears as he played, and disappeared from the window; she returned just before the finish of the musical piece. After finishing with a flourish, Junior bowed low, and Penelope smiled down at him sweetly and spoke in a stage whisper.

"Junior, come a little closer, please. I want to thank you for the entertainment."

When he had come as close to the window as he could get, Penelope held a bucket out of the window and poured water down on him. Then she laughed. Completely drenched, Junior picked up the violin case with his free hand and returned home holding the soggy violin and bow still dripping water.

Junior relayed every detail of the incident to his parents. Zola and Nemo tried to comfort their heartbroken son. Before telling him goodnight, they somehow encouraged him to give Penny another chance – Nemo said that a Frankenstone never deserts his ship.

The next morning after breakfast, at the suggestion of Zola, Junior rushed down to the corner bakery on his bike. He returned with a lemon creme pie for Penelope. Zola told him to go right over to the girl's house at once, before school started, and deliver the pie in person for her breakfast, as the pie would not be nearly as fresh that evening.

Junior rode over and parked the bike on the grass. He knocked softly on the door, and when the housekeeper answered, he said, "I'd like to see Miss Fletcher, please. Tell her Mr. Frankenstone is here with a token of his affection. "

When Penelope came to the door, Junior asked her to hold out her hands, and when, after the longest time she did, he placed the box thereon.

Penelope scowled at the boy. "Open it up. And it better not jump out at me ...

Why, it's not my favorite kind of pie, silly. I only like blueberry apple."

She took the pie out of the box with one hand and moved forward.

Junior backed up as she approached. Laughing, Penny said, "Maybe you should eat it!", and before Junior could duck, she had pushed the pie right into his face.

"I don't like wimpy boys, Junior, and you're one. I only respect strength and manliness. Ha, ha, ha!"

Junior licked some of the pie off his face and quickly made an exit.

At home, Junior had to clean up, and Nemo and Zola were shocked by Penelope's behavior. They decided that Junior shouldn't waste his time with this little witch.

Junior decided to ask Crystal's advice. Crystal spoke to him in images.

"Junior, remember our pirate adventure of long ago? Act out the role of a seafaring cad with your Penny. She likes the swashbuckler kind. Be guided by Fisheye's commanding nature; Penelope will fall for you." Junior kissed Crystal and went about putting together a pirate's costume.

That Friday, after school, Zola almost died of astonishment when Junior came out of his room wearing tattered red velvet breeches and coat. He had a black patch over his left eye. The boy winked at his mother and cackled in his deepest voice, "Mum, I'm off to claim me woman – see ya when the tide prevails!" He waved his yellow-painted wooden sword.

Nemo didn't get a chance to behold this odd scene – he was napping soundly. As soon as he was up, Zola told him every detail. He snickered and giggled like a schoolboy.

"I always knew he was a pirate at heart, like his dear mother!"

As for Junior, he swaggered over to Penny's house and pounded on her door. "You're mine, wench. Say yes or I'll make ye walk the plank!"

Penelope stood in the doorway, completely dumbfounded. 'Was this the same Junior?' she thought.

Junior pointed his golden sword at her middle and demanded her answer. Penny clapped her hands together and smiled at her blond pirate.

"Yes, I am yours, my hero! Forever and always!" She offered Junior her hand and he kissed it roguishly.

And this is how Junior went courting and won the hand of the fair maiden, Penelope Fletcher. Theirs was a delightful summer romance.

42
Little Zola

SLAM! "MO-THHERR!"

"Yes, dear. Are you back home from school already? Where did the day go? Are you all set for the big weekend?"

"MO-THERRR! The class was discussing the Empire today, and all the various people and races comprising the whole of our society. The kids told their race and where their ancestors came from. When my turn came, I said I was Caucasian, 'cause my father was from the Caucasus Mountains, and Penelope Fletcher started giggling. Then I said I was also African, 'cause my mother was from out of Africa, and Penny started laughing out loud. Miss Farnsworth quieted the class and asked Penny why she was laughing. Penny said, 'Mr. Frankenstone cannot be Caucasian because he is darker, and he looks like an Arabian Sultan ... and Mrs. Frankenstone is too light to be an African – when she is sunburned in the summer she looks like an American Indian Princess ... or she also looks like an Arabian Queen'. She's all messed up; she's an airhead. Miss Farnsworth told Penny that Arabians are also Caucasians, as are Indians from India, many of whom have skin as dark as many Negro tribes of Africa; and that South Africans, or Boers, or Afrikaners, are true Africans, having lived there over two hundred years, but since they came from the Netherlands, their skin can be as light as an Irishman's. We had just studied Arabian culture in geography last week – maybe that's why Penny is so mixed up. Father told us all about his childhood in the Caucasus Mountains many times, but you never told me much about your childhood in Africa. If you are African, why aren't you darker?"

'Oh, my,' thought Zola to herself. 'I knew the time would come some day'. Then to Junior she said, "Well, you know the Boers from Holland are Africans, and their skin is lighter than mine."

"Are you a Boer, then? Were your ancestors from Holland?"

"Your father will be home at six. After supper we will discuss it."

"Nemo, Junior has a problem. In class today they were discussing race and ancestry. Junior wants to know, if I am African, why is my skin so light, and if my ancestors came from Holland."

"The lad is eleven, my dear. It is time to tell him your story. I would like to know too. You never told much about your childhood except when we were on the ship back to England."

"Well, you two go get some popcorn made and I'll clean out the fireplace and set a nice cheery fire. That's me, Cinderella and the Ugly Duckling, all wrapped up in one." And Zola let out a long sigh.

When everyone was seated in front of the crackling fire, munching on popcorn, with Zola between her two men, she began.

"I did the dirty work in the village, like cleaning out the fire pit. I did not look like the others in the village. I was very ugly. Very ugly. But not as ugly as your father." And she poked Nemo in the ribs.

"MO-THERRRRR!"

"Really, Junior, I do not know who my ancestors were. I could have been rescued as a baby from a shipwreck, or taken to be raised as a slave when my parents as adventurers or explorers or prospectors or even missionaries, took me to the region and were killed and eaten."

"Oh! Oh, no!"

ILLUSTRATION

I REGRET THAT I must begin by making excuses. This is a tricky question to answer because the features that we depend on to identify whether a person is caucasoid, negroid, or mongoloid, etc., are the superficial soft parts of the body. Lips, noses, hair, eyes, and skin do not fossilize. At the same time, the hard parts that do get preserved are not reliable as racial markers because almost all of the skeletal dimensions of all the races overlap. But there is a more profound problem with trying to say how long the contemporary races have been in existence. Genes that determine features used for defining contemporary races need not form permanently associated hereditary bundles of traits. Variants of skin color, hair form, lip size, nose width, eye folds, and so on can be assorted and inherited independently of each other. This means that the traits that go together today did not necessarily go together in the past, or indeed even existed in the past, among the populations that were ancestral to today's racial groupings.

Even today, there are so many different combinations of racial traits around the world that no simple scheme of four or five major racial types can do justice to them. Millions of people with thin lips, thin noses, and wavy hair, but dark brown to black skin, live in North Africa. Native inhabitants of southern Africa, such as the San, have epicanthic eye folds (like most Asians), light brown to dark brown skin, and tightly spiraled hair. India has people with straight or wavy hair, dark brown to black skin, and thin lips and thin noses. On the steppes of central Asia, epicanthic eye folds combine with wavy hair, light eyes, considerable body and facial hair, and pale skins. Indonesians have a high frequency of epicanthic eye folds, light to dark brown skin, wavy hair, thick noses, and thick lips.

"The chieftain's number one wife took me and raised me as her own, and I was even allowed to call her 'Mother' when we were alone together. But the number one son was a pain. I was several years older than he, but he ordered me around to do things he would have had to do if I had not been there. Junior, please go get Crystal and her Mate. I can tell a better story when they are in my hands."

* * * * *

"Speaking of Dutch, Dear, did you see in the paper where Mata Hari, that voluptuous Javanese Hindu dancer, may really be Dutch?"

"Oh, my, yes, Nemo, the theater grapevine has it (by good authority) that the 'Eye of Dawn' [this is the meaning of the name in Javanese] is indeed Dutch, and has a daughter to boot. Non, I think the girl is called, although that is not her name. She is about your age, Junior, maybe a year older. And is rumored to be even prettier than her mother."

"Perhaps you could arrange for Junior to meet the girl." "Oh, Father! Really!"

"Just joking, Junior."

"I saw Mata Hari's picture recently, Father. She is rather handsome, very tall, with long black hair and dark features. Indeed, she reminded me very much of you, Mother. She could be your sister."

"Really, Junior! Enough already!" Zola blushed and said, "She is more of a courtesan than a dancer presently. She will come to no good end if she continues. "

"What is a courtesan, Mother?"

Nemo blurted out, "Why a courtesan is nothing but a prostitute for the rich and famous. But the courtesan, like the geisha of Japan, must be intelligent and well-read, a good conversationalist, as well as beautiful and a delight in bed."

"How do you know so much about courtesans and geishas, Dear?" asked Zola.

"I have seen the ways of the world for many years before either of you were born. As your mother says, Junior, Mata Hari will come to no good end. She sleeps with a different man almost every night, and that is the road to Hell. A woman should stay with one man ... However, a man may safely have more than one wife. My father did." Nemo began to reminisce.

"Hold on," said the others, that doesn't sound fair. If indeed a man is allowed several wives, why not several husbands for a woman?"

"Fair is one thing, but that is not the way our Maker created us. If a woman can have a child, why then not the man? Fair is fair. .. Yet indeed, a man can bear a child. But our Maker has wisely required the child to develop in a womb before birth, and so the man must have a womb. The Anglo-Saxons have a word for that kind of man – they call him a man-with-a-womb, or womb-man, or woman. Ha!"

"Well, really, Nemo! I see no need for any woman to sleep around. You keep me happy and well satisfied." And both men blushed deeply. "Now, where was I?"

"My first recollection was ... one day I remember being hungry, and as usual, I called out (cried) for the breast for warmth, comfort and nourishment. I was lifted up onto a lap, with me sitting away from my meal, and a large bowl of porridge was placed in front of me. My fingers were dipped into the stuff, and then my hand was pushed against my mouth and rubbed around. I kicked and squirmed free and ran to the next available breast – I must have been the center of attraction at feeding time for all the available wet nurses."

"Is that why you went into the theater, my dear, because you liked being the center of attention?" asked Nemo.

"Nemo! Well, I never! I...I never thought about it that way. Perhaps it is. Don't interrupt me. Where was I? Oh, yes."

"In any event, I ran to the next breast and was starting on the nipple when it was pulled out of my mouth, and I was lifted around and plopped down in the lap away from my meal, and a large bowl of porridge was placed in front of me, etcetera. This went on, oh, a long time, until I had exhausted all the available sources. Then I sat down in the center of the circle of wet nurses and started bawling – I cried my little heart out. Finally, after an eternity, I quieted down, and a large bowl of porridge was placed in my lap. I put my hands into the bowl and crammed my mouth full of the stuff. When I finished that bowl, another was put in front of me, and I finished that off. And that kept up until I was as tight as a tick ... and then I threw it all up and went to my bed. After a while the chieftain's number one wife came in and said to me, 'Zola, it is time you were weaned. No more nipple'. 'But why, Mommy, why? Why? Why?' I guess I was about three at the time. 'Because you are growing up, little girl. You are hurting the wet nurses – your teeth are too sharp.'"

Zola thus ended her first story and began cramming her mouth with popcorn. "Oh, this is good. How did you make it?" She took another handful and crammed her mouth.

"Careful, Mom, or you might throw up." And they all laughed.

"Now after I was weaned, I started eating like a pig, and my 'Mother' did not stop me – she even helped me along, with the choicest morsels and tastiest dishes she could dream up. I got even much fatter than you ever were, Junior, when you were a baby. I guess I was about four. I was so fat I could hardly walk. One day I was half carried, half dragged by the chieftain and his wife into the center of the courtyard and placed on a large black sheepskin. I was told to stay on the sheepskin and not get off until the ceremony was over. That was alright with me. I sat down on the black wool and looked around. All I saw was a sea of eyes staring at me. And children! I had played with a few at the chieftain's hut where I had been kept, but nothing like this – there must have been a hundred children in the inner circle, all staring at me. The drums began beating. The rhythm got to me and I stood up and began dancing or waddling around on the sheepskin. Then after it seemed like an hour, I got tired and sat down again. That's when the chanting started along with the drums. 'Zola! Zola! Zo-lah!' And the big people started moving in, in single file, and began touching me. Some lifted me up with a groan, and a smile on their lips, as if I was to be their next meal. They patted my head, my arms, my legs, my belly, my backside, tickled me in my private parts ...."

"Did they then take off your clothes to do this, Mother?"

The Toast of Europe ~ *161*

Mata Hari was such a popular performer that a series of postcards showing her dancing was issued in 1905–1906. Her costume resembled that of true Wayang dancers but was much more transparent—a move calculated to appeal to her audience. (Author's collection)

Journal wrote glowingly: "Mata Hari personifies all the poetry of India, its mysticism, its voluptuousness, its languor, its hypnotizing charm. To see Mata Hari in a rhythm and with attitudes that are poems of wild voluptuous grace is an unforgettable spectacle, a really paradise-like dream." The review in *The Press* sounds rather like a love letter, exclaiming, "One would need special words, new words to explain the

"Oh, Junior, I was as naked as a jaybird, as were all the young children standing around staring at me. Then after all the adults had finished with me, the chanting ceased and some children came close – they were all about five or six years old, I would judge. The girls flipped me down on my back and pinned me down with outstretched hands holding on to my arms and legs. Then the boys crowded in close. They looked at me with eyes wide. Then the drums ceased, and before I knew it I was covered with smelly water. The girls giggled and the boys shouted. Then the drums began a different beat. The boys moved away and the girls released me."

"I got up and tried to chase the closest boy, but he easily ran out of reach – I could hardly walk, much less run. I sat on the sheepskin and cried my heart out – why was the daughter of the chieftain being humiliated this way? Then the skin was lifted up with me in it and I was carried for the longest time, not knowing where, until I was thrown into the river, where the laundry was done. The chieftain and his number one wife were the only ones there. The chieftain spoke, 'My child, I am not your father. Your father is the White God of Death, who has given you life for a time.' The wife spoke, 'My child, I am not your mother, but I will care for you until you reach womanhood. Your mother died in fright at your birth, you were such an ugly child – because she then knew that the White God of Death had indeed visited her in her sleep. Wash yourself off, and wash the skin also. It is a black sheepskin you wash, so you become aware of what color you are not.'"

"When I was taken back to the hut I was admonished by the number one wife, 'You may not call me 'Mother' any more. Only when we are alone together may you call me 'Mother'.' And she picked me up in her arms and held me close for a long, long time. And I got wet upon again, this time from her tears."

"After that 'coming-out' ceremony, I was allowed to come and go as I pleased, except when some dirty work had to be done. I played with the other children, but it was like I was the butt of their jokes, and that they used me for their entertainment. It wasn't long after that that I vowed to lose weight and be the fastest runner in the whole village, so that I could catch and beat up someone who tried anything with me, or at least outrun them if they were bigger."

"I remember very vividly one night after I had slimmed down – I was about six. The chieftain and his wives and other relations were in the hut talking in hushed tones. It was past my bedtime, but number one wife kept me up. 'Zola,' said the chieftain, 'Zola, we need you for a very important undertaking'. Now this was quite unusual, in fact it had never happened before, the chieftain needing me. 'Yes, Sir'. 'Zola, my older brother has died in a very nasty accident. He was out hunting with the others, and in very unusual circumstances he became trapped in the cleft of a submerged rock near a quagmire and was severely mauled by a great cat – a lion. The others found him yesterday and brought him back for burial. His body is badly cut up and needs to be sewn back together for a proper burial. Think about it tonight and let me know in the morning if you will do the job – the body is starting to smell already'. 'Yes, Sir.'"

"And so the next morning I sewed up the stinking body and as soon as I finished, the burial was held and everyone left as quickly as possible. The chieftain thanked me – he thanked me! And he told me the White God of Death would be pleased with my work. And so, from then on, whenever someone died, I would help out in whatever way I could."

Zola took the last handful of popcorn and ate it thoughtfully. "Then when I was about ten, this girl my age started coming around and started playing with me. Actually playing, not making fun. She had me do all sorts of interesting things with her. She touched me in certain ways that I had never been touched before. She caressed me like a mother with her child. It was very exciting. I think she was in love with me."

"Zola, Junior has fallen asleep."

"Dear, wake up and go to bed. We have a busy day tomorrow. You are a big boy now. I will not carry you."

"Yes, Mother. Goodnight, Mother. Goodnight, Father."

Zola and Nemo looked at each other and smiled and held hands a long while after Junior was in bed softly snoring. They talked about many things as they watched the dying embers in the fireplace. And Crystal and her Mate blushed exceedingly, to learn that Zola had had an earlier lover.

43
Into the Pot

March 1912

"Junior, you are fast approaching your manhood. I think we should celebrate with a trip of some sort. I have booked passage next month on the maiden voyage to New York of the Titanic – a marvel of engineering. I was of some small help on the design of the airtight compartments."

"Oh, yes, Father, that sounds like a capital idea – I can be a pirate and climb the rigging with a dagger in my mouth and search the horizon from the crow's nest, as Mother did."

"Well, this ship is not exactly designed for pirates, but it will be an eventful, memorable trip, nevertheless."

"I don't know, Nemo, I feel we shouldn't take it."

"Why, it is perfectly safe; it is unsinkable with the airtight compartments. They say the only way it could sink is if there was an impossibly large fire in the engine room, which heat would stress the hull and crack it like an egg and split the ship into a smaller stern and a long bow section. The air space in the cavernous engine room would be no longer and each section would be heavier than the water and would then quickly sink to the bottom. But eternal vigilance of the crew would prevent such a fire from occurring. It is impossible for a fire to get out of control – not maintaining a fire watch aboard ship is unthinkable. The Captain just wouldn't do that."

"Or secondly, old paint rags with linseed oil thrown into the coal bin as it was being loaded could eventually cause spontaneous combustion and the coals could ignite and become red hot. Dowsing it with water to cool the coal would produce water gas (mostly carbon monoxide) which is very explosive, and this could rip the ship apart at the engine room area. But this would be very poor housekeeping indeed and would not be shipshape Bristol fashion. Only slovenly landlubbers would throw oily rags away thusly, and only inept sailors would attempt to dowse a coal fire with water – you must keep the oxygen away."

"I didn't know that putting water on red hot coals could cause an explosion, Father."

"Well, Junior, a well-trained crew *would* know that. And they would know that the carbon monoxide, even if it did not cause an explosion, would make them fuzzy-headed and incapable of issuing, receiving, or acting upon an order in an emergency."

"And the third possibility, which is even more impossible than the others, is if the watch was not on duty and the ship came upon an iceberg or other object unawares. Then the Captain would send orders to the engine room for full speed astern, and the furnace's fires would be cranked up to their maximum. In the excitement, the safe boiler pressure might be exceeded and the water tubes or the boiler drum itself might spring leaks or explode. This would spray water all over the red-hot coals in the furnace, generating the aforementioned explosive water gas. The boiler explosion would also tear the furnace walls apart, allowing the oxygen in the engine room air to mix with the water gas, and almost in an instant the explosion could tear the ship apart. But we are talking nonsense. A watch is always present and about, and the Captain is always in charge."

"That explanation relieves my mind," said Zola, "but that is not why I am uneasy. There will be many rich people there flaunting their wealth, and I do not like all that posturing and falsity."

"Then I shall book passage for the same time on some smaller steamer bound for Africa where we can visit your Mother's birthplace – it is a pleasant journey and a pleasant land. You can play explorer as Mr. Livingstone many years ago."

"And can I be a pirate also?"

"Perhaps. "

"I don't know, Nemo. It sounds like a dangerous journey. They may kill us if I return. There are many other things Junior can do to celebrate – Spring is coming, and there are many parks and museums and theaters here."

"Oh, Father, let's go to Africa. It sounds exciting!"

The trio stood at the spot where Nemo had seen eleven year old Junior's mother forty-three happy years ago. "Can you see the village, my son?"

"Yes, Father, but it is high noon and nothing is stirring."

Suddenly from out of the bushes and high grass appeared thirty black-skinned natives in full warrior dress, each bearing a sharp bronze spear that gleamed in the sun.

Zola," they called out menacingly, and pointed with their spears, indicating that the trio should walk to the village.

Zola said, "Nemo, I told you this was a dangerous journey, that Junior could do many other things to celebrate his approaching manhood. Now they will kill us all."

"Love, I thought the British had the whole area under law – Swaziland has been a protectorate for many years now."

"Father, will they boil us in a pot and eat us?"

Zola smiled a wry smile. "They do not kill their enemies like that – they let the jackals eat."

"I will protect you, Mother." Junior bravely went up to one of the warriors and put his finger on the spear, as if to push it away. "Ouch!" The spear was sharp! Blood trickled from the cut.

They were walked through the gate and into the courtyard facing the chieftain's hut. The villagers were all gathered around the edge of the courtyard, but nothing stirred – all was quiet except for the buzzing of the flies.

Minutes passed like hours. Then the old chieftain appeared in the doorway and surveyed the group. One word passed his lips. "Zola!"

He came out several steps and looked at Nemo. Then, walking rapidly up to Nemo and extending his hand, he said, "Doctor Frartkenstone, I presume?"

"Yes," said Nemo, "and may I present my lovely wife Zola and our son Junior."

"Zola, Zola," said the old man, and he went up to her and embraced her. The villagers had all been standing around watching during this whole scene – one of them started tittering. Then another; soon the whole village was laughing and crying. Zola! Zola! The women started to crowd around Zola. One of them approached and kissed her on the cheek, then another on her neck. One shyly pulled at her dress to free a shoulder and kissed it. Then all bedlam broke loose. Zola's clothes were quickly stripped from her down to her undergarments, and each woman in turn kissed her where they had struck her with a branch many years ago. Laughing and crying, shrieking and screaming, dust and commotion. The smaller girls and younger women stood outside the tight circle and looked on in amazement. The chieftain said to Nemo, "Sir, shall we all retire to the clearing and play a game of cricket?"

So the men (and boys) all went out to the cricket field and were out of sight before things quieted down in the courtyard. Then the circle opened and one of the women ran out and beckoned Zola to follow. Zola came out of the circle in her panties and looked around shyly. "Come," said the woman, "race me. So a foot race started with all the middle aged women, amidst laughing and shouting, out the gate, up and down the cow paths. In fifteen minutes Zola returned to the courtyard somewhat out of breath, and each one that followed held hands with the one before and the one after, making a circle.

One of the women, the one who had called out 'Race me', had kept up with Zola all the way, but she stopped at me gate and sat down and started to cry. All were finally back except the woman at the gate – the circle was completed except for her. Then she got up and completed the ring, all the while looking up at Zola's face. Then she put her arms around Zola's neck and embraced her. The others clapped and cheered. But the woman would not let go. She lifted herself up and wrapped her legs around Zola's waist and began sobbing. A murmur began in the circle. One called out "Zola", and when Zola looked, she lifted her arms up like a chicken and tickled under her armpits with her fingers. Zola tickled the woman in her armpits. The woman sobbed and shook and began to giggle. Soon she was giggling so hard she let loose, and, taking Zola's hand, she ran with her down to the dammed-up area of the creek where the villagers went swimming and where they washed the clothes, all of the others including the younger women and girls following.

The women took off their clothes and splashed around with Zola, laughing and giggling and playing – the others stood around with eyes wide in wonderment. Finally everyone dried off as best they could, dressed and returned to the village to prepare the banquet for the evening. The men and boys were still busy with cricket, showing Nemo and Junior how to play and what they were doing wrong.

After the banquet, the chieftain invited Nemo and Zola and Junior into his hut. His number one wife and number one son were already there when the group entered. When all were seated, the chieftain spoke.

"Number one son, you have not smiled all day. Is something troubling you?"

"Father, I have worked faithfully for you these many years and not once have you given a banquet in my honor. Yet when this Zola returns after you have condemned her to death many years ago, you give her much honor. Why?"

"My son, you know that I am old and that soon everything I have will be yours. But I am happy to see that the jackals have not taken this child of God, and that she is still alive and prettier than ever. Son, say hello to your older sister!"

Everyone sat stunned except for the chieftain, who smiled; and his number one wife, who giggled; and Nemo, who turned red and looked quite embarrassed.

"Is this true," said Zola, "is this true that he is my brother and you are my father?"

"Yes, my daughter, and Dr. Frankenstone is my son-in-law, and Junior is my grandson." And he beamed.

"But how ... and why...? Nemo, you please explain. I am dizzy – I have had too much to drink."

"The drinks were not strong, Zola, for all here are now Muslims. But I will explain. Desiring to visit again where I had met Zola, and deciding that Junior might be interested, and believing that it would do us all good to get away from England for awhile, I wrote the British consulate in Swaziland this January that I was interested, and was the village still there, etcetera, and received a letter back saying it would be safe to journey here. But I am at a loss to explain the welcome."

"Allow me to elucidate," said the chieftain. "We heard the jungle drums announcing your arrival in Swaziland day before yesterday ... and the Embassy in London had sent us a telegram last month saying you were then leaving England for here ....and a year ago today I had a dream in which Zola was still alive and still beautiful, and that she would soon be coming here before I returned to my ancestors."

Zola started from her chair much agitated. "Then that was you I saw in my nightmare" – and she began to shake. "But why do you push me from your village and whip me and treat me so poorly when I am young?"

"Dear Zola, ours is a subsistence economy. Everyone must work, yet everyone plays. We do not have the wherewithal to maintain a non-working priest class, and have others tell us what we should do when we already know what we should do. You are very beautiful, but cannot work in the fields because of your light skin, and because you do not have the big buttocks to allow you to lean over all day tending the crops. If we had let you stay, all the boys in the village would be after you, and we would have no healthy children, but much sickness. We do not kill those we cannot integrate into our society, but send them away. The jackals get some. The Zulus get some for servants. Those they do not want they trade to the white man. I tied you to the stake and I gave you the first blow. Every shout cut my heart like a knife. When I saw your future husband surprise you as you ran away, I hoped he could lead you to safety. Today we would send you to Oxford or to Cambridge for your education, where you would probably marry a proper Englishman." And he grimaced. "But your husband does not look English." And he brightened.

"I now understand," said Zola, "but I cannot call you father. And you [pointing to number one wife] I had always known as my big sister, and wondered why the chieftain's wife would stoop to help me grow up – I was always told my mother had died out of fright when I was born."

"Yes," said the chieftain, "do not call me father, for you are an adult now, and we are all brothers and sisters – sons and daughters of our Father who is in Heaven. For we are Muslim ... but we are also Christian. And you," he said, looking at Nemo, "you showed us how your telescope works out on the cricket field, and many of us want to purchase one just like it for our pleasure. Perhaps you will set up a mill – a manufactory."

"I have been thinking of that."

"You may be my sister," said number one son, "but I still do not like you."

"Strange," replied Zola, "but I feel the same about you." They slowly reached out and shook hands.

"We are Bantu," said the chieftain, "The People. Our first earthly father was created by our Heavenly Father, and through him sprang all mankind."

Nemo answered, "The Jews say the first man Adam was created about six thousand years ago in the Garden of Paradise. It is in the Bible."

"Then the Jews are mistaken; something was lost in the translation of the Word from the Heavenly Father. Perhaps one or more of our Zolas were cast out and traveled there, for the Bantu have been here, not tens of thousands of years, but hundreds of thousands of years. The boy Zola, when he first comes into his manhood, is not tied to a stake and beaten with branches, but is taken outside the gate and encircled (horseshoe fashion) by a band of thirty men in full warrior's dress, with polished sharpened bronze spears, who poke and prod and cut him until he leaves in the direction of the opening, whether that be south or north, west ... or East of Eden."

During the week's stay, at night, Zola is helping with the dirty work she did as a child. The chieftain comes by.

"You do not have to do that, my child. You do not have to do that to please me."

"I am not doing it to please you. I am a very selfish person. I feel better when I work at what I do well – I do this to please myself." She continues her work, and the old chieftain bends over and kisses the back of her neck.

The time for farewells had come, for they had stayed their week. The villagers were all lined up – children in front, then wives, then husbands in back. Zola kissed the babies, hugged the young children (or swatted them on their backsides), hugged and/or kissed or shook hands with the women, shook hands with the men. Nemo and Junior shook hands with their friends and with those who extended their hands. The last in line was the woman who loved Zola.

In front were her two grandchildren and in back was her husband. All the others were happy and smiling, but she was crying. The four-year-old granddaughter looked back at her grandmother and saw that she was crying. She whispered in her six year old brother's ear, "Why is grandmother crying?"

The boy looked puzzled, then went back to his grandfather and tugged at his hand. The man bent down and the boy whispered in his ear, "Grandfather, why is grandmother crying?"

The man whispered back, "Because she loves Zola and is sad to see her go."

The boy whispers, "But we all love Zola and we are all sad to see her go."

"Yes, my child," and he puts his arms around his wife's waist.

The boy shrugs and goes back and whispers in his little sister's ear. She nods and smiles, but as Zola approaches she looks back at her grandmother and sees that she is crying more than ever, and the girl starts crying. Zola hugs the boy, picks up the girl and hugs her, hugs the grandmother. While she is hugging the woman, she and the husband look at each other and they move their heads forward and kiss each other. Then the trio leaves and waves goodbye, and all the villagers wave and disperse to go back to their lives.

Only the grandfather, grandmother and two grandchildren remain – the chieftain remains at the door of his hut and signals with his spear as the trio wave. The spear gleams in the sun. The woman tries to free herself from her husband's grip and run to Zola. Zola sees this and beckons to the chieftain – she holds her arms out like a chicken and tickles herself under her armpits with her fingers. The chieftain nods and sets his spear aside and goes up to the woman from behind the husband, reaching out his arms and tickling the woman in her armpits. Soon she is laughing and crying at the same time. She reaches down for her granddaughter, who is standing facing her and crying – the husband releases his grip on his wife. The woman picks up her granddaughter, who puts her arms around her grandmother's neck and her legs around her grandmother as far as they will go, and both woman and girl are now laughing and giggling. The grandfather picks up the boy piggyback and they return to their lives – husband and wife holding hands. The girl waves to Zola and laughs loudly. The woman looks back at the same time Zola looks back, and they wave one last time – the girl is still holding on to her grandmother.

As the trio reach the crest of the hill about a mile and a half from the village, beyond which the village will be lost to view, they look back. Zola whispers quietly, "Goodbye, Father." After several seconds they see the flashing of a spear as the scene fades from view.

44
Video Replays

"The steamer will be leaving next week back to England. What do you think? Should we continue our journey to the Arabian Shore where it all started?" said Nemo.

"Junior has his schooling. Perhaps we should forget it. Arabia to your home in the Caucasus and back to England will take six months or a year," replied Zola.

"That's alright with me, Mother. I will sacrifice my schooling for one year." Junior was very courageous.

There was a freighter leaving that very afternoon from Maputo port bound for Muscat and the Persian Gulf.

"No, sorry, we cannot take any more passengers. But we do need two crew to replace those who have departed [jumped ship]. Have any of you had any experience at sea? [All three start gabbling away about their sea adventures.] Really! Well, we will charge one full fare for the three of you, if you can manage in the crew's quarters. Your wife, sir, will have to sleep with one of our unescorted lady passengers. Is this agreeable?"

"It will only be for a month, dear," said Zola.

"Yes, please, Father. It will be a great adventure. I can be a pirate and everything!"

"Well..."

They carried the little baggage they had across the gangplank; the freighter blew its whistle three times; the gangplank was pulled up, and they were off. The freighter was not a sailboat, to be sure. But it did move at a good clip. The steam engines were kept well supplied with coal picked up at Maputo and they moved right along. Guess who was helping shovel coal into the furnace now. It was hot and dirty work, but there were many breaks.

"Look, look, Nemo, to the right. A new world!"

"Yes, Dear, the island of Madagascar."

First stop was Zanzibar to pick up cloves and copra. Junior found that what rigging there was, was not well adapted to climbing with a dagger in one's teeth.

Almost before they knew it they were at the sidewalk cafe in Kuwait near the bazaar, sipping pomegranate floats, when a Palace guard approached.

"A thousand pardons, Sir and Madam, but the Sultan requests the honor of your presence, at two o'clock this afternoon."

"It is practically two now," said Nemo, "Will you please accompany us?"

"As you wish," replied the guard.

"Why in the world does the Sultan wish to see us?" said Zola. "How does he even know we are here? Have we done something wrong?"

When they approached the Palace, Zola started to get a little dizzy, and when they entered the gates and stood inside in the cool, she fainted.

As Zola was coming to, she whispered to Nemo, "Sher's portrait, lower left back." Then she arose and said, "It must have been the heat and the float - I never faint. I have the strangest feeling I have been here before."

The guard escorted them to the Sultan's library, where he was hard at work at his desk on business matters. When their presence was announced, the Sultan looked up. He glanced at the trio and then his eyes riveted onto Zola. He stared at her for a long, uncomfortable time – no smile on his face.

"Please to follow me into the Hall of Honor," he said.

There on the walls were paintings of all the rulers of the dynasty; many, many paintings. He took them to the largest portrait at the center of the Hall of Honor, a portrait of a Sultan and his Queen.

"This is the founder of our dynasty and his lovely Queen Shahrazad, the only one he desired, although he had many other wives and concubines."

Zola fainted again. As she was coming to, she again whispered, "Sher's portrait, lower left back."

When she arose this time, the Sultan said to Nemo, "What did your wife say as she was coming to?"

"Sher's portrait, lower left back."

The Sultan took another long look at Zola and then went up to the portrait and felt behind the picture at the lower left. When he withdrew his hand he had a sealed letter – old and dusty. He broke the seal and asked Zola in a hesitant manner, "May I read it for you? It is in Arabic."

"Yes, please. I love my shepherd boy." And as soon as she had said this she put her hand to her mouth and stood there, wide eyed at what she had said.

[The letter]
Dearest brother Omén,
I fell in love with you when first my eyes came upon you these long four years ago. My life was spared through you and your Crystal. I was wedded to the Sultan, but wish every day to be with you. It is impossible; I am the daughter of the Wezir and the wife of the Sultan, while you are only a shepherd. I pray that if there is a life hereafter, that I may be with you as your wife. I hide this letter behind my official portrait to keep as a reminder of you. When I come again I will take it and give it to you. Sher —

The Sultan put the letter back in the envelope and gave it to Zola. "Take it, dear lady. There shall be no hint of scandal in this dynasty."

"Nemo, you take it. See if that's what it really says. I don't want it; it gives me the willies."

"You may be dismissed."

They were ushered out without further ceremony. After they were well away from the Palace, Junior broke the silence.

"Mother, why did they hang a portrait of you in the Hall of Honor?"

Next stop would be Mecca. "Perhaps we shall be allowed to touch the holy stone," said Zola.

"A thousand pardons, honored guests, but we must detour to Riyadh to pick up supplies. We were notified only yesterday."

But that will put us many days behind," said Zola.

"It is the will of Allah."

They reached Riyadh at mid-day - it was very hot. It was a little cooler under the canvas of the bazaar, but Nemo looked very red and very hot.

"Wrap a cool wet towel around your head, Sir," said the waiter as he presented the item.

They were sitting there enjoying their pomegranate floats, when a Palace guard came up and said, "A thousand pardons, Sir and Madam, but the Sultan requests the honor of your presence at two o'clock this afternoon. The boy may come also."

"It is practically two now," said Nemo. "Will you please accompany us?"

"As you wish."

They were ushered onto the veranda by the pool. Two of the Sultan's wives stood in the background whispering and giggling. The Sultan put down the book he was reading, got up from the deck chair in his swim trunks, and extended a hand to Nemo.

"Welcome to Riyadh, Mr. – ?"

"Frankenstone, Sir. Nemo Frankenstone. And my wife Zola and our son Junior."

"Ah, yes, Mr. Frankenstone. Please follow me to the Hall of Honor; it is cooler there." Putting on his robe and sandals, the Sultan padded off to the Hall with the trio. "Do you recognize anyone?"

They all looked around. None of the paintings on the walls were in the least familiar to Nemo. Zola saw one of the paintings, the one in the place of high honor, which was of a man with a turban wrapped around his head, the wrapping identical to what Nemo still had on his head.

"That looks just like you, Nemo," she giggled. The two wives in the background giggled.

"Those two giggling magpies in the back were at the bazaar an hour ago and saw Mr. Frankenstone with his turban; they told me he looked just like the portrait we are now standing before. This most honored gentleman was not our first Sultan, nor our last. He was not strictly of our dynasty, as he never married nor had concubines ... but he was the one who developed us from a sleepy town into the metropolis you see today. He was the one who advanced mathematics, as he developed the zero, the number representing nothing that does many things. His name is Omén. Sultan Omén. He was of lowly birth from the southeast coast and spent his young life as a shepherd. And I also think you resemble his portrait. Please spend the afternoon with us. Perhaps you care for a game of chess?"

And so a pleasant afternoon was spent at the Palace. They were about to leave when Junior tugged at his mother's elbow and whispered in her ear. "No, no," said Zola, "I'm sure the Sultan will not agree to such foolishness."

"What is that, my dear lady?" said the Sultan.

"Junior thinks there is a secret message behind the painting."

"Perhaps there is, young man. Let us go look," said the Sultan in a conspiratorial manner. "This has never come up before. My curiosity is getting the best of me. I wonder what the secret message would say."

So they went back and Junior reached behind the portrait on the left bottom. There was nothing.

"Ah," said the Sultan lightheartedly to protect the feelings of his young friend, "to be young again – the creativity, the imagination, the inspiration! ... Perhaps Mrs. Frankenstone would like to try?"

Zola blushed and went up to the right side and felt behind. She pulled out an old dusty sealed envelope marked in Arabic. Her hand shook as she gave it to the Sultan to read.

The Sultan appeared quite taken aback by this turn of events, and he took out his glasses and cleaned them. "The envelope says, 'To Shahrazad Only'. Perhaps we should not pry." "Yes, yes," said Junior, "read the letter. What does it say?"

Dearest Sher,

I am an old man, but I have never forgotten you. Those three years at your feet were bliss. I keep the only treasure we both shared, and shall keep it with me all my life; and the treasure that brought us together will keep us together eternally.

You are the bright and shining star of my life:
my swan, al bireo (the back of the swan)
my rider, al cor (the rider)
my right side, al genib (the side or flank)
my home, al chiba (the tent)
my helpmate, al debaran (the follower)
my right arm, al deramin (the right arm)
my star of stars, al firk (star of the flock)
my lover's hair, al geiba (the mane of the lion)
my lover's face, al genubi (the head of the lion)
my black haired beauty, al gorab (the raven)
my crook and my staff, al kalurops (herdsman's club, crook, or staff)
my cup, al kes (the cup)
My Crystal Ball, al nilam (a belt of spheres or pearls)
my heart, al niyat (the outworks of the heart)
my gypsy, al rakis (the dancer)
my eagle, al tair (the flying eagle)
my lover's eye, al terf (the lion's eye)
my maiden, al udra (the virgins)
my enchantress, al oz [a nova in Omén's time?]

I could not have you in this life, but if there is another, you will find this note, and I will be with you. Omén –

"Please take the letter, Madam; we hold Omén in too high esteem in our memories to allow a scandal."

As soon as the family left, the Sultan telephoned his brother in Kuwait. "You lose. The boy went back to look for the note."

"I don't think we should play this game with the tourists any more," said the brother in Kuwait.

"Why not? Did you run out of copies for this year already? I can have my scribe work up some more."

"No, no."

"Are you tired of losing all the time?"

"No, that is not it. You like your chess, while I am into word games. Write his name forwards and backwards, in Roman letters."

"A coincidence."

"Write her name backwards likewise, and you have Omén's term of endearment

243

for his love."

"Another ... another coincidence."

"Mr. Frankenstone's wife looked for all the world like Shahrazad's portrait."

"I have seen many beautiful women who looked like that, and you have too."

"But the wife knew where to look before she had entered the Hall!"

The Frankenstone family returned home safely, stopping in Geneva for a formal marriage ceremony, thence to Nemo's bank, where Junior gave them his thumbprint.

45

The New World

London, June 1913

"You have lost a year of schooling, Junior. Do you really want to be in a class that was a year behind you?"

"I had not thought of it in that way, Father. It would not be much fun, being in the same class with babies, while my peers were laughing at me."

"I am thinking it is time to start a manufactory for the small Newtonian refractoscopes. We have the design now for the double-ended eyepiece with Crystal and her daughters, courtesy of the gnomes of me Black Forest; and we are in a position to make the original spherical Crystal Balls as Leeuwenhoek made them, from his note wrapped around the telescope, which sleeve prevented Darwin from focusing it and so he never used it, but it lay there in his room all the while I was chasing around the world in the Nautilus ... but such is life. Crystal Ball will not be naked, but will have a girdle for modesty ... which girdle may prevent the rainbow appearance, but the images will be as sharp as the original Crystal.... "

"Can I help out in the manufactory, Father?"

"Yes, of course," said Nemo. You know, Junior, the gnomes were intrigued by the color correction of the Mate -almost perfect. Much better than the Zeiss fluorite apochromat of microscopy. They researched Newton's notes and found the formula, in a secret code which took some time to work out. Unfortunately, the flint element is very unstable and will recrystallize and lose its transparency in only two hundred fifty years, according to Newton and confirmed by the gnomes. This will place the death of the Mate at around 1936. So we must look for another way. A mirror telescope is possible, using a small secondary mirror to fold the optics into a shorter tube, but there would be a central obstruction, and the useful field would be rather narrow. Perhaps we should all make a new beginning in the New World. ZOLA ... could you please come into the study for a minute?"

"Just a moment, Dear, 'til I wash my hands. I'm making a cherry pie ... Yes, loves, what is the special of the day?"

"Zola, I have just discussed with Junior my desire to make the Newtonian refractoscopes and the problems involved, and we also mentioned the year's setback in his schooling. We think we should make a new beginning in America."

"Yes, Father, America!"

"Oh, yes, Nemo, to Paradise!"

In the summer of 1913, then, the Frankenstones cleared out their belongings, took off the nameplate from the door, and returned the key to the new Curator at the Cambridge Museum, who happened to be the granddaughter of Robert. She was quite taken aback that Nemo knew her grandfather, supposing that Nemo must have been a tiny tot at the time. She was most thankful for the key, telling them that the five-pound rent hardly covered maintenance expenses for many years now, and that the structure was soon going to be torn down and that she was just preparing to send off a letter apprising them of this turn of events and that they should be looking for permanent quarters and that the reason for this strange method of rental was that her grandfather's grandfather had established a trust for this very purpose because he had once been a transient caught in London on his way to the University without a place to stay and that five pounds was worth something in those days and that she hoped their accommodations had been adequate ('Well, really they must have been; we have heard no complaints from you.') and that they should have a most pleasant life in the 'Colonies' as her grandfather used to say when he spun all his yarns.

From Liverpool the Frankenstones set sail for New York, passing over the grave site of the *Titanic* near Newfoundland. They spent that evening reminiscing about their adventures of the past year and what could have been their fate if they had embarked on that ship.

The Statue of Liberty! Nemo thought of his friend Frederic Bartholdi and how they had worked together on this project one summer in Paris in 1879 while Zola was immersed in the theater; Bartholdi, who had died there in Paris just this past year.

(Immigration Officer): Name, please.

(Nemo): Frankenstone.

(I.O. prints name): FRANK N. STONE. Nationality, please.

(Nemo): British. citizen

(I.O.): And you wish to become an American citizen, Mr. Stone? Immigration is easy for the English. What job do you hold, Mr. Stone, and with what company are you employed? Oh? Well, you should find employment as soon as you can, which is easy - the country is expanding by leaps and bounds. Unemployed immigrants have ninety days to find work or they will be shipped back. You say you are considering setting up your own mill? Then you have funds? Well, then, welcome to the land of the free and the home of the brave, Mr. Stone. There are a lot of Stones here; are you related to any of them? No? What does the "N" stand for? No name? It is not a name? FRANK NEMO STONE. And this is young Frank Junior? And your wife Zola, as indicated on your passport as traveling with you? Nemo is a popular name, Frank, my lad. No one can forget the Captain of the Nautilus. Have you read the book by Jules Verne, "20,000 Leagues Under the Sea"? I am reading it with my young son. You haven't heard of it? It was written for lads like yourself. Have a nice day, Mr. and Mrs. Stone; and you too, Frank, my boy. NEXT!

Junior went to a local elementary and high school near Paradise, Pennsylvania. Then, after the war was over in 1918, he enrolled at the University of Berlin, as this would be better for learning about optics and precision manufacturing.

Toward the end of his fourth year, Junior finished his thesis in his physics major, and presented it to his professor. When the professor had finished reading the thesis, he looked up from his desk and spoke sternly to the young hopeful still standing there.

"Come, come, this will not do at all. There is a germ of an idea here, but it is entirely too short, and does not even include any of the important truths, such as four-dimensional space/time, metrical tensors, relativity, curvature of space/time, general covariance, quantum theory, Planck constant, light quanta, or even any mathematics to speak of. Really, now, I cannot accept this. It is too late to start over. All we can do is make an appointment to see the Great One and have him read it and say whether you should be granted your degree or not."

So an appointment was made and they were ushered into the Great One's room. In hushed tones the professor gave the story of Junior's transgressions, and begged him to just glance at the manuscript before dismissing the young man.

The Great One took the manuscript and placed it on the desk in front of him. Then he took out his pipe, cleaned it and filled it, lit it and settled back in his chair. Then he put on his glasses, took up the manuscript and began to read....

The pipe had gone out ere the Great One finished. Then he put the manuscript back on the table, put down his pipe, took off his glasses, glanced at the young man, then looked quizzically at the professor. Then he gazed long and lovingly at the young man and shook his head, as a father to his errant son. Then lifting his eyes he quietly spoke only four words, which shall reverberate through the ages, and which have been translated into all languages throughout the world:

MEIN GOTT IM HIMMEL!

Dear sweet Albert, who spent the latter half of his life in search of a theory to unify all field forces, how dare such a young upstart even hope to conceive a much grander scheme of unifying all matter and all energy!

And so Junior left those hallowed halls in dishonor, without a degree, to return to the mill where his father worked.

Sic Transit Gloria Mundi

46
Inventions

Paradise, Pennsylvania, United States of America
Friday, June 22, 1923

"Oh, Junior," consoled Zola, "I'm so sorry. I'm sure you did your best – German universities are very difficult."

"Well, Frank Stone Jr.," laughed Nemo, "I hear you struck out. Did you learn anything there, or were you too busy socializing?"

"Please, Father, do not joke," replied Junior. "I just practically got off the boat, and do not feel all that good."

"Who made the decision not to accept your thesis?" asked Nemo.

"Why, the Great One, Father. Everyone seems awed by him, even if they can't understand relativity or much else he propounds, but he must know what he is talking about."

"What is your thesis all about? Since you majored in physics and minored in manufacturing engineering, maybe there was a clash, or maybe the subject was not approved by the board."

"The title is "Unified Theory of Matter and Energy." I used a different approach, based on Newton's ultimate particles. I thought it was well thought out as a working model of the Universe."

"Sounds like something they would be anxious to look into. I mentioned the possibility of unified field theories to Albert back in '03."

"I didn't know you knew the Great One, Father!"

"Tut, tut, Son, I was just having fun with him while I was in Switzerland during Crystal's operation."

"Yes," said Zola, "and coming home at dawn singing and half drunk. I remember that night well. I was up with Junior all night long – he had a fever…cutting a tooth."

"Not to change the subject, Junior, but do you have your thesis with you? May I read it?"

"Wait 'til I unpack, please, Father. You can read it while I lie down and take a nap. It isn't all that much."

Indeed, it didn't take Nemo all that long to read. [Refer to Unified Theory, page 263]

When Junior was up from his nap, Nemo said to him, "Your thesis is most interesting – the loose ends are all tied up, except for a few on light, photons and quanta. It has practically no math in it – no doubt that is why it was rejected. Professors like a lot of math; as long as the math works out they are happy. But the Universe would go along on its merry way whether or not there was such a thing as math. Ha! Did you learn anything that would help us here at the manufactory?"

"That I did, Father. Most of it not at the University but at the Optische Werke – the gnomes were most gracious and hospitable. We can discuss all that Monday when I start full time. I have to clear my head -the automobiles here in the States are so noisy and smelly it makes my head swim."

"Well, Son, that is the American way. They want to push as much gasoline through the engine as they can – gas (or petrol in England) is very cheap, and besides, extra gas through the carburetor results in carbon monoxide."

"Why would that be an advantage? I thought monoxide was toxic. Didn't you tell us that concerning the *Titanic*?"

"Yes and no. The monoxide causes the driver to become drowsy or dull-witted, as you know. This results in accidents, as you know."

"So why would this be an advantage? Why would it be tolerated, Father?"

"I see you have been in Europe too long; you have forgotten the American way. The rash of accidents builds business for the body shop, the person shop or hospital, the new car dealer, not to mention the undertaker. The driver is the direct cause of the accident, while the monoxide that made him sleepy is undetectable at present. This all increases the Gross National Product -it is the American Way."

Nemo continued. "Junior, I don't mean to be harsh, but while I was working at the patent office in Switzerland I came across several patents pending relating to this subject. They were called atomizers or nebulizers. The purpose was to break up the liquid droplets coming from the carburetor into smaller particles which would burn faster and more completely, thus reducing or eliminating the toxicity."

"I don't think they are being used. Do they work?"

"Yes and no, Junior. There were three recent U.S. patents concerning this: Patent 1,123,898 by Langendorfer, Jan. 5, 1915; 1,282,654 by Thurston, Oct. 22, 1918; 1,315,758 by Brown, Sept. 9, 1919. These relate to a screen to be affixed under the liquid hydrocarbon burette, or gasoline metering device, or 'carburetor'. The carburetor can do a bang-up job in metering the fuel, but it falls down severely in breaking up the droplets and mixing the fuel with the air so it will burn quickly and completely. The screens were supposed to do that. They don't. Some of these screens actually 'reform' smaller drops into larger ones, thus compounding the problem. You may have seen how wires or spider webs in a fog will have large water drops falling from them. Same principle. But I have done some work on this problem, and have discovered that a properly designed screen will work, and will not cause a noticeable pressure drop in the system."

"Did you patent it, Father?"

"I tried, but the Patent Office said it was too similar to the other patents, and refused a patent. Perhaps you could try your hand. Maybe you would be luckier."

"What does your screen look like? Maybe you could get a design patent, Father."

"The screen fits into the hole, usually circular, directly below the carburetor. On the first try I made the whole thing out of a piece of window screening. The moisture in the air and the chemicals in the fuel soon ate it up. But steel plated with gold or platinum should hold up, even if expensive. A new 'stainless steel' known as 18-8 has been developed recently which should work. The size of the mesh is important. I found a 20 X 20 or 24 X 24 mesh works best - a larger mesh does not break up all the droplets and a smaller mesh starts increasing the pressure drop excessively. Wire size should be as small as possible. Now the design. Proper design eliminates engine knocking completely, no matter how much you advance the spark. Knocking is from a sudden expansion or 'explosion' of the fuel droplets, much like popcorn. Oil companies have taken to putting in toxic lead compounds to reduce this problem, but that is another story and we best not get into that now. Anyway, I make up a cylinder of the screen to fit inside the passageway below the carburetor, the length of the cylinder about two and a half times the diameter. Then I bend one side of the cylinder in to a tapered shape, so the airflow is seeing a convex surface at about thirty degrees from the flow direction. The bottom of the screen is stitched shut, or can be soldered. The fuel/air mix burns so much faster that the spark must be almost at top dead center. The fuel is metered back so it is not excessive for the amount of oxygen available. The engine runs like a charm, and there is no toxic smell from the exhaust ... However, this is a disadvantage for the automobile companies."

"How can this be, Father? Why would anyone want to run a smelly automobile if he didn't have to?"

"Gasoline fumes, and some of the partially oxidized products, are addictive to many people, just like drugs. They like the smell, become addicted to it, even though it makes them dull-witted and accident-prone. Those working for the auto companies, many of them, got into the business because of the addiction - they say that 'gasoline is in their blood', and they are right. So they will fight any attempt to reduce or eliminate their 'fix'. I daresay it will be sixty or eighty years before they decide to put in the inexpensive screen, especially since they can place an expensive catalytic unit in the exhaust pipe to do the job partway - that is the American Way."

"America is a very strange place, Father."

"See, you have been in Europe too long ... There is another invention I must mention while we are discussing engines. The automobile engine runs on the Otto cycle, which you may have heard about in your Thermodynamics courses. This cycle can get only about 30% of the heat energy out of the fuel, and this is under ideal conditions – 20 or 25% would be closer to the actual figures in the automobile on the road. So three quarters or more of the fuel is wasted, so to speak. In Switzerland at the patent office in '03, I came across an invention that promised to get practically 100% of the heat out of the fuel in the form of rotational energy, and the working substance, which was water, would not turn to steam or even be heated up! The patent clerks thought this smacked too much of perpetual motion. I can go over the highlights of the engine design some other time – perhaps you can get a patent here in the States." [See Steam Engine Patent, pp. 261-262]

"Father, I think we had better stick to optics. It appears much safer."

47
Interludes

FRANK N. STONE
& SON
OPTICAL MANUFACTORY

Nemo was quite pleased with the brass plaque nailed over the doorway of their small business establishment located off the beaten path of the busy metropolis of Paradise. He liked the quiet – very seldom would he hear the clop-clop of the horses' hooves or the rattle of the carriage wheels on the MacAdam roads. Junior also liked it here; it was the very opposite of the hubbub of Berlin, and there were very few automobiles in these parts.

They lived in the back of the building, "almost camping out" they said, just like their neighbors, with a hand-pump for water, a wood stove in the kitchen, an outhouse, and no electricity. An icebox served as the refrigerator. Zola especially liked it here – it was just like home to her – and she fit right in with the women: baking pies, quilting, gardening, and gossiping. She even kept some sheep and goats on their four acres.

The business end of the building was kept up to date, for employees, for customers, for salesmen. They put in electricity for lighting and equipment, an indoor toilet and running water, an electric refrigerator for when someone wanted a cold drink, and an electric range in the lunchroom area. It was quite modern, really. Zola learned how to use all the conveniences, but did not really care for them.

Two hired hands were added to work on Crystal Ball magnifiers and another to work on the double-ended eyepieces. Nemo and Junior were still in research and development on the Mate, and after a year wrote the Optische Werke to see if anyone there would like to hire on in America as a consultant. Herr Blöde and his wife Brigitta and their thirteen year old daughter Schläfrig decided to come over and were of great help. Brigitta was put on polishing work, which she enjoyed, and Schläfrig did some inspection and testing on the stars, as she was a night person and quite industrious then, while everyone else was sleeping. Nemo gave her a good three-inch astronomical refractor on a tripod so she could compare images with what their little one incher was doing.

Summers the business was closed for two weeks' vacation - everyone would go their own way. Nemo liked sailing and had purchased a forty-foot yawl. *Auggie II* was kept down in the Bay near Havre de Grace, where Nemo and Zola would frequently go for long weekends or a week at a time, while Junior managed the business. *Auggie II* was a good stout wooden boat, lean of beam with a full deep keel, quite stiff, sea-kindly and seaworthy, with enough room in the cabin for six people. It had a galley, a head, good headroom, two berths in the forepeak, two athwart-ships forward of the galley, and two large berths abaft below the cockpit; but no engine – the wind was the engine; gas or diesel engines were too noisy, too smelly, and shook the whole boat. No self-respecting sailor worth his salt would even consider an engine at that time.

Nemo was also interested in hot air ballooning, and had made one of coated silk, with a large enough basket for one person. He made a special gasoline blowtorch for the hot air so he could rise and descend at will without using sandbags or other ballast, other than for the initial balancing. He would frequently go up a mile or so, tethered to the ground with a long silk rope, and scan the horizon for weather patterns. With Crystal and her Mate on a clear day, he could see the outskirts of Philadelphia, and even automobiles zipping along the roads there. He could also see the Bay, and *Auggie II* if she was anchored well out. Quite a difference from the close quarters of the *Nautilus*. He had not kept up with the crew since they had dispersed back in 1868, and supposed they would all be gone by now.

By the Spring of 1927, when Schläfrig was fifteen, the R&D had progressed enough that the Stones decided to close down for the summer and sail the West Indies. The three Stones and the three Blödes packed their summer gear and put *Auggie II* in Bristol fashion. The two old-timer hired hands decided to sail with them as far as Virginia Beach, where they would rent a cottage for the summer and do some fishing, while the one on eye-pieces went in toward Lancaster to look for summer work. Nemo took his balloon along for fun times on the islands.

They made passage to San Juan in ten days and restocked provisions in preparation for a month's cruise in the Lesser Antilles as far as Trinidad, stopping at each island for a day or so. They were well out of sight of Grenada in the Windward Islands toward Port of Spain, Trinidad, when they were becalmed. They were running low on fresh water anyway, so on the fourth day of hot sun and no wind, Nemo was becoming concerned.

"Schläfrig," said Nemo about nine that morning, "Schläfrig, wake up. What do you think about going up in the balloon and seeing if a cold front or some weather will be coming so we can get a breeze. We will die of thirst if we stay here much longer."

The teenage girl mumbled an OK, took a sandwich and a canteen of water her mother had fixed, took Crystal and her Mate from Nemo, climbed into the basket sitting on the deck, turned on the burner as Nemo had instructed, curled up in the basket and promptly fell asleep.

Now Schläfrig was a sturdy lass, huge for her age, almost four feet tall and fifty pounds – the Blödes couldn't get over how big she was, and she wasn't even full grown yet! The one-eighth inch silk line was a mile long, wound on a reel attached to the bow, weighing fifty pounds total - sixty in a fog. The wicker basket weighed forty pounds, the burner and fuel forty more. The silk balloon was thirty feet in diameter and weighed a hundred pounds. Nemo and the others were busy opening the balloon, making sure it didn't catch on anything, and that the burner didn't get near the silk. The balloon at last was filled with hot air and was on its way straight up. The deck hands all gave a shout and they saw an arm slowly waving over the side.

Toward noontime Schläfrig was getting hungry, so she woke up and had lunch. Then she took the little telescope and searched the horizon for clouds or anything else. She looked down through the basket and saw a tiny splinter down below. Yes, she was a mile up, and soon felt a chill, so she bundled up and put the telescope away. One last glance now - there was Trinidad in the distance on the horizon thirty miles away toward the south, and Grenada barely visible toward the north. Nothing special to report, but she dropped a note down the line anyway, and fell asleep again.

The note worked its way down the line in half an hour. Junior saw it first and took it off the line. It said, 'Cool wind from Grenada'.

"Father," said Junior, "Great news! Cold front from the north."

"Up *there*, maybe," said his father, "but do you feel anything *here*? We are in a flat calm here; the telltales are not even stirring; the water is as calm as a pond."

Toward evening, after a day of fishing and staying in whatever shade was available, the crew had heard nothing else from their scout, so they began reeling her in; besides, the fuel supply would be getting low, and that could be dangerous. Zola and Brigitta were gossiping at the bow. They decided to look at their horoscopes, and started giggling at the statements.

Your financial picture is brighter this evening because of decisions you make this morning.
Romantic involvement is of prime interest today, so act on impulse.
Today someone who has rescued you from a difficult situation needs aid – provide it.
Turn to a friend and you will find the help you need.
Manners and politeness will serve you well today.
Time spent out of doors today proves refreshing and profitable.

You will receive good news in abundance today.
Keep speculations and risks to a minimum today.
Tomorrow is a good day for new beginnings.
Make plans for travel.

Brigitta looked up and saw something in the distance; she remarked about it to Zola. Zola looked carefully.

"Nemo," she exclaimed, "the tides have taken us back to Grenada! Maybe we can get the dinghy out and row ashore and pick up some fresh water."

Nemo took out his binoculars and inspected the features in the distance. "That is not Grenada, Dear; we are headed straight for Port of Spain and are practically in the harbor now!"

They finished reeling in Schläfrig, who woke up when the basket hit the deck. The shore breeze sprang up a little then and filled the sails enough so that they could maneuver after they bagged the balloon, and they docked as the sun was setting. The tugboat in the sky had pulled them all afternoon.

48

O Captain! My Captain!

Summer 1936

Zola was dying. She was in her bed and her eyes were closed. Nemo bent down and whispered in her ear, "Zola, I love you. I have always loved you."

"Did you not love your first wife?" "Yes."

"You never told me her name."

"I think you know her name, darling."

"Let me hear it from your lips," said the dying woman.

"She had the same name as my mother, for my mother was well-liked by all. .. Zola the gypsy ... Zola the enchantress. When I first saw you tied to the stake it looked like Zola my wife; when you ran past on the cow path, I knew it was my wife, for my wife can run like the wind."

And Zola put her arms around Nemo and smiled. Slowly her arms slid from around Nemo's neck, and with a smile still on her face, Zola began the long run to her ancestors in the sky.

Aloha – Hello, my friend. I missed you so.
Aloha - Goodbye, my friend. I love you so.
Auf Wiedersehen – 'Til we meet again.

They buried Zola after three days, under the spreading chestnut tree behind their place, the one she enjoyed sitting under during the hot days of summer, whether she was pitting cherries or snapping beans or milking the goats or shearing the sheep. Nemo and Junior both helped dig the grave, and both helped make the pine coffin to

Nemo's design. All the help and all the neighbors were there at the funeral and they all cried and placed posies of violets on her in the open coffin. Then the coffin was closed and lowered. Nemo put on a shovel full of dirt, then broke down. Junior thanked them all and they departed.

Nemo was beside himself that evening. Junior tried to console him, but to no avail. Nemo repeated the same phrases he had uttered ever since the funeral.

"My Zola is gone; the Mate is white; my beard is white; my strength is gone. My arm can no longer string the back-bent bow of Odysseus; my legs can no longer out-run the deer; my eye can no longer see beyond the rainbow; my time has come. As Crystal and her mate will be together, so we will be together."

That night it clouded up and a thunderstorm was heard coming from the west. Junior implored his father, but it was no use – Nemo went outside with the 'scope on a lanyard around his neck, up the hill to the clearing where a picnic bench spoke of happier times. He stepped up onto the bench top, took the 'scope from his neck and held his arm heavenward.

"God in Heaven, take your children back unto You!" he cried.

Junior stayed at the house, tears streaming down his face.

He knew what his father was planning. He heard a loud thunderclap and saw the flash almost at the same time; then the storm moved to the east.

When the thunder was heard only in the distance, Junior walked up the hill and found the lifeless body of his father lying on the ground. He picked up the form – how frail it felt – and carried it back to the house. He notified the preacher and the hired hands, and they had a service that night – the body was badly burned. Nemo was buried with Zola in the same pine coffin. Junior placed their hands together, closed the lid, and shoveled the dirt over.

O Captain! My Captain! Our fearful trip is done,
The ship has weather'd every rack, the prize we sought is won,
The port is near, the bells I hear, the people all exulting,
While follow eyes the steady keep, the vessel grim and daring;
But O heart! heart! heart!
O the bleeding drops of red,
Where on the deck my Captain lies,
Fallen cold and dead.
O Captain! My Captain! Rise up and hear the bells;
Rise up – for you the flag is flung – for you the bugle trills,
For you bouquets and ribbon'd wreaths – for you the
shores a-crowding,
For you they call, the swaying mass, their eager faces turning;
Here Captain! Dear father!
This arm beneath your head!
It is some dream that on the deck,
You've fallen cold and dead.
My Captain does not answer, his lips are pale and still,
My father does not feel my arm, he has no pulse nor will,

The ship is anchor'd safe and sound, its voyage closed and done,
From fearful trip the victor ship comes in with object won;
Exult O shores, and ring O bells!
But I with mournful tread,
Walk the deck my Captain lies,
Fallen cold and dead.

Walt Whitman

The next morning broke bright and clear. A young child ran up the hill to the park, her mother not far behind.

"Mommy! See the pretty rock!" and she held it in her tight little fist. The sun danced on the limpid stone, now tinted green, yet still clear.

"Heidi! Don't cut yourself on that broken glass!" The mother came up and took the piece, and was going to throw it into the trash can, but the girl began to cry, and the softness of the curves on the stone, with no sharp edges whatsoever, tempered the mother's concern and she gave it back to her daughter for a pet rock.

Entwined in life and love, entwined in death, Crystal and her Mate – Zola and her Nemo.

And Junior, now orphaned and with no family – what was he to do? Where was he to go? Would he find his true love even as his father before him?

In that same year, on the Dark Continent in the Namib Desert, on the shore of the Great Salt Sea by the diamond mine, a young shepherd was tending his flock. A storm was brewing....

Epilogue

The scene shifts to the mountains of the Southern Caucasus in Georgia. Nemo and Zola are both fourteen years old. They are foot racing up a mountain path – Nemo in the lead. The day is warm – both are bare-chested. Nemo stumbles and sits down, watching Zola run ahead, her hair blowing in the wind, and she disappears behind some trees near the mountaintop. After a minute he starts running again. When he passes the trees he calls out, "Zola!" No answer. He runs on to the top of the mountain. "Zola!" No answer. Then Zola appears behind him and sneaks up and with a warrior shriek, jumps him and they both fall to the ground giggling and wrestling and hugging.

"Petrach! Ivon! Enough!"

"Oh, Zola, when it is time for me to marry, I will want no one but you."

"You tease, Pauli," and she blushed.

Then they both walk down the path slowly, hand in hand, not daring to look at each other, both blushing. The view switches to the beautiful panorama of the Caucasus, and majestic music as the scene fades.

THE END

An Open Letter
to
other Crystal Balls
To whom it may concern:

If thou canst clearly transport the Holy Writ (that which is scribed by the angels standing on the head of a pin), then thou art a friend and a sister, and I will say to thee, "Welcome and well come."

But if thou canst not clearly transport the Holy Writ (that which is scribed by the angels standing on the head of a pin), then thou be naught but a thief and a scurvy wench, and I will say to thee, "Thou lowly scullery maid, thou be no fair lady: thou hast besmirched my pure name. Be gone with thee!"

As ever,
Crystal Ball

(The above letter does not necessarily reflect the views of Crystal's agent, nor of this publication.)

BIBLIOGRAPHY

The author acknowledges the following partial list of references used in preparation of this text.

World Book Encyclopedia

Encyclopedia Americana

The Bible, KJV

Christopher Columbus – The Dream and the Obsession, by Gianni Granzotto, translated by Stephen Sartarelli, Doubleday & Co., Inc., Garden City, NY, 1985

The Columbia History of the World, edited by John A. Garraty and Peter Gay, Harper & Row, Publishers, 1988

Measuring the Invisible World – The Life and Works of Antoni van Leeuwenhoek, by A. Schierbeek Ph.D. ©1959, published by Abelard-Schuman, London & New York

Isaac Newton, by E.N. Da C. Andrade, Max Parrish, London 1950

Stories from the Thousand and One Nights, translated by Edward William Lane, Revised by Stanley Lane-Poole, P.F. Collier & Son Corp., NY, 62nd Printing 1969

Puccini, a biography by Howard Greenfeld, G.P. Putnam's Sons, New York 1980

Femme Fatale, by Pat Shipman, Harper Perennial 2007

Pilgrim Colony – A History of New Plymouth 1620 - 1691, by George D. Langdon, Jr., New Haven & London, Yale University Press 1967

"Old Bruin" – Commodore Matthew Galbraith Perry, by Samuel Eliot Morison, 1967, Little Brown & Co. Ltd. (Canada)

Albert Einstein, Creator and Rebel, by Banesh Hoffmann, New American Library 1986

Exploring Life, the Autobiography of Thomas Augustus Watson (1854 - 1934), D. Appleton & Co., 1926

Voltaire – Genius of Mockery, by Victor Thaddeus, Brentano's New York 1928

TECHSPEC® FUSED SILICA BALL AND HALF-BALL LENSES

• Excellent UV Transmission
• Low Coefficient of Thermal Expansion
• Ball and Half-Ball Options Available

Fused Silica features high transmission from 200nm to 2.2µm with a low coefficient of thermal expansion, making it ideal the most demanding ball lens applications in the ultraviolet, visible, and near infrared spectra. Ball lenses are commonly used for improving signal coupling between fibers, emitters, and detectors, as well as objective lenses in endoscopy and bar-code scanning applications. Half ball lenses simplify handling and integration.

TECHSPEC® FUSED SILICA BALL AND HALF-BALL LENSES — *Call for Availability and Pricing*

Diameter	Prices – Ball Lenses				Prices – Half-Ball Lenses			
	Stock No.	1-5	6-25	26+	Stock No.	1-5	6-25	26+
0.5	#67-379	$36.00	$28.80	Call For OEM Qty. Pricing	#67-390	$41.00	$32.80	Call For OEM Qty. Pricing
1.0	#67-380	$36.00	$28.80		#67-391	$41.00	$32.80	
1.5	#67-381	$36.00	$28.80		#67-392	$41.00	$32.80	
2.0	#67-382	$30.00	$24.00		#67-393	$34.50	$27.60	
2.5	#67-383	$30.00	$24.00		#67-394	$34.50	$27.60	
3.0	#67-384	$30.00	$24.00		#67-395	$34.50	$27.60	
4.0	#67-385	$30.00	$24.00		#67-396	$34.50	$27.60	
5.0	#67-386	$33.50	$26.80		#67-397	$39.50	$31.60	
6.0	#67-387	$43.50	$34.80		*	–	–	
8.0	#67-388	$50.50	$40.40		*	–	–	

Material:	UV Grade Fused Silica
Index of Refraction:	1.458
Diameter Tolerance (Ball Lenses):	
0.5 to 5.0mm Diameter	±2.5µm
>5.0mm Diameter	±10µm
Radius Tolerance (Half-Ball Lenses):	±2.5µm
Thickness Tolerance (Half-Ball Lenses):	±35µm
Surface Quality:	40-20
Sphericity:	±2.5µm

TECHSPEC® HIGH INDEX BALL AND HALF-BALL LENSES

• Index of Refraction of 2.0
• High Tolerance

Our high index ball and half-ball lenses are manufactured from Ohara S-LAH79 material, which features an index of refraction of 2.003. The high index provides an extremely short back focal length which simplifies fiber coupling. Other applications include endoscopy, bar code scanning, ball pre-forms for aspheric lenses, and sensor applications. The half-ball design simplifies system integration.

TECHSPEC® HIGH INDEX BALL AND HALF-BALL LENSES — *Call for Availability and Pricing*

Diameter	Prices – Ball Lens				Prices – Half-Ball Lenses			
	Stock No.	1-5	6-25	26+	Stock No.	1-5	6-25	26+
1.0	#47-128	$64.50	$51.60	Call For OEM Qty. Pricing	*	–	–	Call For OEM Qty. Pricing
1.5	#90-520	$64.50	$51.60		*	–	–	
2.0	#47-129	$64.50	$51.60		#90-858	$71.00	$56.80	
4.0	#48-895	$64.50	$51.60		#90-859	$71.00	$56.80	
5.0	#47-130	$64.50	$51.60		*	–	–	
6.0	#48-896	$64.50	$51.60		*	–	–	
8.0	#47-131	$73.50	$58.80		#90-860	$81.00	$64.80	
10.0	#48-897	$76.00	$60.80		#90-861	$86.00	$68.80	

Material:	S-LAH79
Index of Refraction:	2.003
Diameter Tolerance (Ball Lenses):	+0.00/-3.00µm
Radius Tolerance (Half-Ball Lenses):	+0.00/-1.50µm**
Thickness Tolerance (Half-Ball Lenses):	±50µm
Surface Quality:	40-20
Sphericity:	2µm
**Radius Tolerance for #90-861 is ±1.50µm	

SAPPHIRE AND RUBY BALL AND HALF-BALL LENSES

Sapphire Material:	AL_2O_3
Ruby Material:	Ruby Doped AL_2O_3
Index of Refraction:	1.77
Dia. Tolerance:	±0.0001"/±2.54µm
Surface Quality:	40-20
Sphericity:	0.000025"/0.64µm
Specific Gravity:	3.98
Melting Point:	2053°C
Compressive Strength:	300,000psi
Chemically Inert Thermal Expansion:	8.4x10⁻⁶/°C

• Excellent For Severe Environments
• High Strength and Hardness
• High Chemical Stability

Sapphire and Ruby Ball Lenses are both made from AL_2O_3. Ruby or Ruby-doped sapphire owes its red color to traces of chromium oxide (chromium content for ruby balls is typically >0.5%). While the physical and chemical properties are basically the same, their optical properties are somewhat different. Sapphire has superior optical transmission qualities. Ruby is easier to see and therefore easier to handle for physical applications.

SAPPHIRE AND RUBY BALL LENSES

Size (mm)	Size (in.)	Sapphire Ball Lenses			Sapphire Half Ball Lenses			Ruby Ball Lenses			Ruby Half Ball Lenses		
		Stock No.	1-10	11-25	Stock No.	1-10	11-25	Stock No.	1-10	11-25	Stock No.	1-10	11-25
0.30	0.0118	#46-115	$14.00	$11.20	–	–	–	#46-223	$14.50	$11.60	*	–	–
0.40	0.0156 (¹⁄₆₄)	#46-116	$14.00	$11.20	#63-754	$17.00	$13.60	#46-224	$14.50	$11.60	–	–	–
0.50	0.0197	#46-117	$14.00	$11.20	#49-553	$17.00	$13.60	#46-225	$14.50	$11.60	*	–	–
0.79	0.0312 (¹⁄₃₂)	#46-118	$14.00	$11.20	*	–	–	#46-226	$14.50	$11.60	#49-557	$17.50	$14.00
1.00	0.0394	#43-638	$14.00	$11.20	#48-428	$17.00	$13.60	#43-639	$14.50	$11.60	#49-558	$17.50	$14.00
1.50	0.0591	#43-640	$14.00	$11.20	*	–	–	#43-641	$14.50	$11.60	*	–	–
1.58	0.0625 (¹⁄₁₆)	#46-119	$14.00	$11.20	*	–	–	#46-227	$14.50	$11.60	*	–	–
2.00	0.0787	#43-642	$14.00	$11.20	#48-429	$17.00	$13.60	#43-643	$14.50	$11.60	#49-559	$17.50	$14.00
2.38	0.0937 (³⁄₃₂)	#46-120	$14.00	$11.20	*	–	–	#46-228	$14.50	$11.60	*	–	–
2.50	0.0984	#43-819	$14.00	$11.20	#49-554	$17.00	$13.60	#43-820	$14.50	$11.60	#49-560	$17.50	$14.00
2.78	0.1094	#43-821	$14.00	$11.20	*	–	–	#43-822	$14.50	$11.60	*	–	–
3.00	0.1181	#43-644	$14.00	$11.20	*	–	–	#43-645	$14.50	$11.60	*	–	–
3.18	0.125 (¹⁄₈)	#46-121	$14.00	$11.20	#48-430	$17.00	$13.60	#46-229	$14.50	$11.60	#49-561	$17.50	$14.00
4.00	0.1575	#43-823	$17.00	$13.60	#49-555	$19.00	$15.20	#43-824	$18.00	$14.40	#49-562	$19.50	$15.60
4.76	0.1875 (³⁄₁₆)	#46-122	$17.00	$13.60	#48-431	$19.00	$15.20	#46-230	$18.00	$14.40	#49-563	$19.50	$15.60
5.00	0.1969	#43-646	$19.50	$15.60	#48-432	$23.50	$18.80	#43-647	$20.50	$16.40	#49-564	$24.00	$19.20
5.55	0.2187	#43-827	$19.50	$15.60	*	–	–	#43-828	$20.50	$16.40	*	–	–
6.00	0.2362	#43-829	$21.50	$17.20	#49-556	$25.50	$20.40	#43-830	$23.00	$18.40	#49-565	$26.00	$20.80
6.35	0.25 (¹⁄₄)	#43-831	$24.50	$19.60	#48-433	$29.00	$23.20	#43-832	$26.00	$20.80	#49-566	$29.50	$23.60
9.525	0.375 (³⁄₈)	#43-227	$62.00	$49.60	*	–	–	#43-228	$67.00	$53.60	*	–	–

🔵 NEW LOW PRICE   🖥 Visit WEBSITE for MORE INFO.   **WWW.EDMUNDOPTICS.COM**   **75**

Appendix

TIME LINE

Birth of Omén	507 A.D.
Birth of Crystal	April 6, 523
Death of Omén	595
Marco Polo	1254?-1324?
Lorenzo de Medici	1449-1492
Christopher Columbus	1451-1506
William Shakespeare	1564-1616
Birth of Anton Leeuwenhoek	1632
Birth of Captain of the Caucasus	1636
Birth of Isaac Newton	Dec. 25, 1642
Birth of Maria Leeuwenhock	1656
Isaac Barrow visits Constantinople	Approx. 1658
Captain of the Caucasus in Constantinople	1660
Captain of the Caucasus leaves C. for Venice	1680
Captain freed from jail in France	1703
Captain meets Ben Franklin	1777
Captain meets Tom Edison	Feb 1853
Zola Born	1854
Captain finds Crystal and Mate	1868
Captain marries Zola	Sat. even. Nov. 7, 1868
Junior conceived	July 20, 1900
Captain meets Einstein	1903
Trip to Omén's haunts	1912
Junior meets Einstein	1923
Zola, Captain, Crystal and Mate die	1936

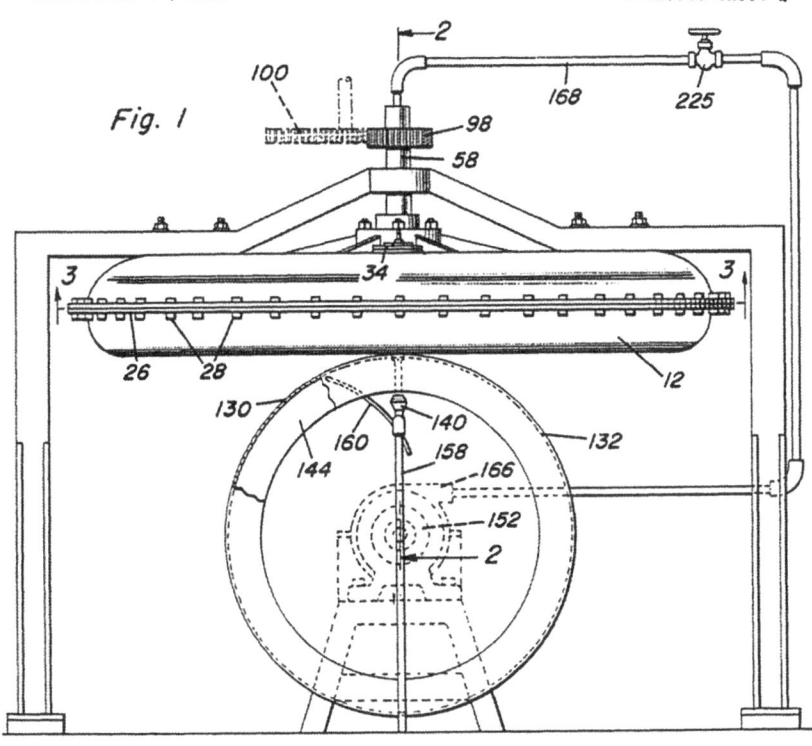

Fig. 1

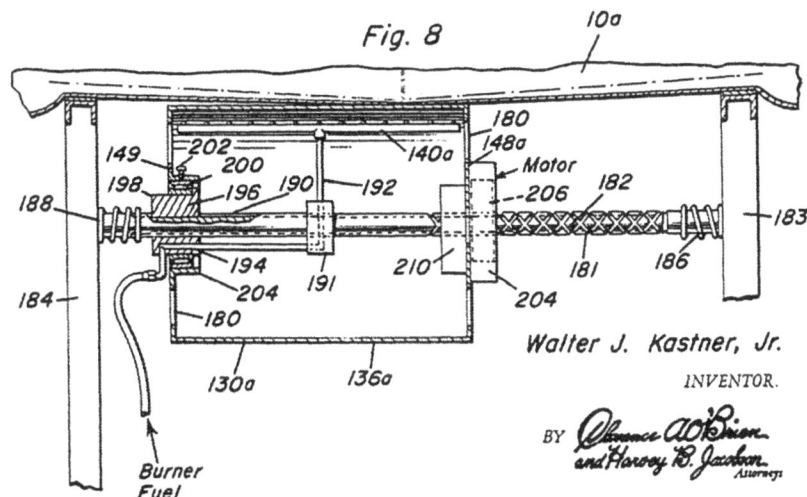

Fig. 8

Walter J. Kastner, Jr.

INVENTOR.

BY

Attorneys

Burner
Fuel

261

1

2,961,835

STEAM ENGINE

Walter J. Kastner, Jr., 213 E. Weatherspoon St.,
Sanford, N.C.

Filed June 22, 1959, Ser. No. 821,737

5 Claims. (Cl. 60—108)

This invention relates to steam engines and more particularly to a self-condensing steam engine.

An object of the invention is to provide a steam engine to utilize more efficiently the heat energy which it receives.

Another object of the invention is to provide a steam power plant which possesses a number of advantages over ordinary steam power plants or engines. The self-condensing steam engine in accordance with this invention requires no cooling water, no separate condenser and no exceedingly high pressures or temperatures. Maintenance is simple and it is felt that a comparatively large amount of power is available in a small space as compared to other steam power plants.

Summarizing the invention very briefly, there is a turbine provided with a turbine case and rotor. The turbine case has an opening into which a stream of water is issued and strikes a very hot surface so that the stream of water at once flashes into steam and travels in almost radial planes in the turbine casing to the motor. The outward velocity of the steam rotates the turbine wheel or wheels of the rotor, and the steam condenses in the same casing that is occupied by the rotor.

Accordingly, the condensate may be drawn off by a very simple water pump and returned to the nozzle for recirculation. The rotor of the turbine is operated in the presence of a vacuum which may be drawn within the casing by a vacuum pump or may be drawn in the casing by using the engine and a relief valve in a manner to be more fully described subsequently. By having the vacuum in the casing there need not be elaborate condenser systems associated with the turbine casing since the steam more readily condenses after it has served its purpose of actuating the turbine wheels of the rotor.

Another object of the invention is to provide a steam power plant constructed essentially along the lines discussed above and which is made very simple in construction and easy to maintain. The engine may operate for long, extended periods of time with no maintenance, so long as heat is continually applied or intermittently applied in sufficient amount to keep the heated surface at an elevated temperature so that when the water stream impinges thereon it flashes into steam and enters the turbine casing to operate the rotor of the casing.

These together with other objects and advantages which will become subsequently apparent reside in the details of construction and operation as more fully hereinafter described and claimed, reference being had to the accompanying drawings forming a part hereof, wherein like numerals refer to like parts throughout, and in which:

Figure 1 is an elevational view of a steam engine constructed in accordance with the invention.

Figure 2 is a sectional view taken on the line 2—2 of Figure 1.

Figure 3 is a sectional view taken on the line 3—3 of Figure 1.

2

Figure 4 is an enlarged sectional view showing the details of the water nozzle and turbine rotor shaft of the steam engine.

Figure 5 is a sectional view taken on the line 5—5 of Figure 4.

Figure 6 is a fragmentary plan view showing the details of a typical multi-stage rotor in the turbine section of the engine.

Figure 7 is a fragmenatry sectional view showing the action of the water stream and flash stream as the water strikes a heated rotary drum and the steam flows in the turbine casing.

Figure 8 is a fragmentary sectional view showing a modification of the invention.

In the accompanying drawings there is a steam engine 10 which diagrammatically represents the principles of the invention. Figures 1–7 relate to an engine which includes only the essential features of the engine, while Figure 8 discloses engine 10a of a slightly different configuration. However, both of these engines are subject to very considerable modification without departing from the invention.

Engine 10 is constructed of a turbine assembly 12 having a turbine casing 14 provided with an upper wall 16, a lower wall 18 and side walls 20, although the walls may have a different orientation, for instance, if the power output shaft 22 is to be operated about a horizontal axis of rotation instead of a vertical axis of rotation. Casing 14 may be constructed in numerous ways, one of which is to have the casing made of two sections, each provided with bolting flanges 26 through which bolts 28 are passed. Wall 18 is conical and has opening 30 at the apex thereof. The wall 16 has an aperture 32 cooperating with relief valve structure 34 to function as a device to maintain a vacuum within chamber 36 defined by the walls of the turbine casing. Valve structure 34 is merely a hinged door 38 mounted on the exterior of wall 16 and having a compressible seal 40 between the door and the wall 16 adjacent to aperture 32. A combination latch and stop 42 made of an essentially U-shaped rod mounted for rotation through door 38, engages the bottom surface of wall 16 to limit the upward movement of the door 38 so that when the pressure in chamber 36 exceeds atmospheric pressure the valve structure opens enabling air and/or steam to escape from chamber 36.

Turbine assembly 12 has a multi-stage rotor 46. The number of stages of the rotor may be two in which case there are two turbine wheels 48 and 50, however, the number of stages may be decreased or increased. Turbine wheel 50 has a hub 52 to which wheel disk 54 is secured, together with a plurality of slightly curved very thin vanes 56 arranged in a circle at the periphery of the wheel disk 54. Hub 52 is secured to the lower end of power output shaft 58 which is mounted for rotation in anti-friction bearings 60 and 62 (Figure 2). Turbine wheel 48 has a hub 64, a turbine wheel disk 66 and a plurality of vanes 68 arranged in a circle at the periphery of disk 66. Vanes 56 and 68 are oppositely curved (Figure 6) to cause the turbine wheel to be actuated in opposite directions. Anti-friction bearing 72 is mounted between hubs 52 and 64 so that the two turbine wheels are held spaced apart at their hubs and so that they are capable of independent rotation with respect to each other.

Power output shaft 58 has a gear train 76 associated with it and with the turbine wheels 48 and 50. The gear train consists of a sun gear 78 fixed to shaft 58 together with a plurality of idler gears 80 each of which has a fixed axis of rotation established by spindles 82. The spindles are mounted in bearings 84 cast integral or

UNIFIED THEORY

OF

MATTER AND ENERGY

by

Walter J. Kastner

263

UNIFIED THEORY OF MATTER AND ENERGY

Extra copies available:

A244694
RE 810-002
Contact: Augen Optics
          Ph/FAX 1-717-397-7318

CHAPTER 1

Space contains primary spherical particles of matter called bits, traveling at the speed of light. These bits are the source of, or rather are, both matter and energy: matter because of their mass, energy because of their velocity. A bit imparts energy by change of direction and by absorption into a group of bits called mass. Gravitation, magnetism, coulomb forces, etc., do not exist as merely some intangible force permeating space but are the direct result of the motion of these bits.

Assume a sphere filled with 1000 bits, spaced evenly. There are no forces acting on these particles (there cannot be because these particles, when in motion, constitute the various forces) and they stay where they are placed. Let another bit enter with the velocity of light. The only way this bit can lose velocity is if it combines with or sticks to another bit; we will assume that it does not do this, but rather, when it hits another bit, it changes its direction of motion, imparting a velocity to the other bit. When the high speed bit returns to the inner surface of the sphere we will assume it rebounds at $v=c$. It may hit another stationary bit and impart velocity to it, or it may hit the already moving bit, speeding it up more. In this manner, after an infinite number of hits, all 1001 particles are moving around at the speed of light. This is the way energy is created.

Now let us assume that two bits come together head on. They can either fly apart at right angles to their line of approach, or they can stick together, reducing their speed to zero. If they do the latter, they have lost their velocity and have become "matter". Thus the only difference between matter and energy is that matter is made up of large enough coagulations of bits moving slowly enough so that we can observe them.

From out of this basic idea come the many varied and strange phenomena of the universe – atoms and galaxies, matter and energy.

CHAPTER 2

As we have already gathered, these bits are inelastic, perfectly hard, frictionless, all mass. If they hit head on they cannot rebound because they are not elastic. Rather, they push each other aside without slowing down and therefore fly apart from their collision at right angles to their approach. In general, for any collision between two bits, if they are going at the same speed, they will fly apart in parallel lines. If not, the paths after collision will not be parallel.

Now we come to the problem of how these speeding bits can come to a stop. Ordinarily, when two bodies of equal mass come together at equal speeds they either stop, giving off energy, or they rebound, with the same energy as before, or they do some-thing in-between. The same thing happens with bits. However, since they are ultimate particles, they cannot do anything "in-between". When they come together, they either fly apart (but not rebound) with their same speed, or they stick together and give off... what? They cannot give off anything. They just stop.

The mechanism whereby these spheres remain stuck together is a little uncertain, so we shall gloss over this for the moment. Rather, we will take up the structure of the various atomic particles and energy particles.

Stability in any group of bits is represented by the degree of sphericity. Any group of bits that is perfectly spherical is very stable indeed and will not break down under normal circumstances. Let us get some small steel balls and make some models. First there is the single ball – it represents a bit. The next halfway stable grouping is four balls – possibly this is a unit of heat, light, or electro-magnetic energy. As we keep adding on balls we will come to a fairly large, fairly round grouping – the electron. Since a proton is about 1840 times as heavy as an electron, we would be kept fairly busy to make this model, but the procedure is still open to any hardy soul. As we pack together various groupings of protons we can determine their stability, which should correlate closely with actual weights of atomic nuclei. Thus atomic nuclei consist merely of various numbers of bits all stuck together.

When these nuclei are broken apart, as in nuclear reactions, they will break down into some parts which are stable, and others which are not. The unstable parts are radioactive, breaking down into stable groupings and individual bits. Thus there could be thousands of different particles, but most are very unstable. There are 30 or 40 already known today.

CHAPTER 3

Gravitation. All forces that we know today are derived in some way or other from the process of gravitation. To understand this basic force we should start at the beginning. Einstein says E = mc2, kinetics theory says K.E. = 1/2mv2. Thus we see that the only difference here is the constant 1/2. Let us investigate. According to relativity theory the mass increases as its velocity increases, obeying the formula

$$m = \frac{m_0}{\sqrt{1 - (v/c)^2}} .$$

Make two graphs (see Fig. 1), one with mass and velocity as coordinates, the other with mv and velocity as coordinates. The area under the second graph will represent the energy of the mass (mv²).

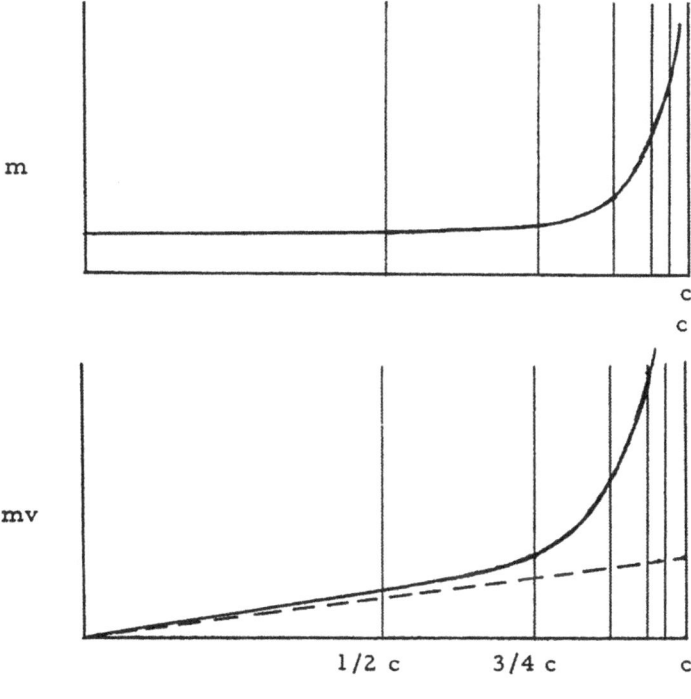

Fig. 1

The total area under the curve is the actual energy, the area under the dotted line (assuming mass is constant) is according to kinetic theory and is found to be 1/2 the total area. Thus $E = mc^2$ and $K.E. = 1/2mv^2$ represent the same thing. All that remains to be shown is how the mass increases with velocity.

Let us discuss inertia. Take a grouping of bits, a proton, if you will. Let the energetic bits in space hit this from all directions. Every time a bit hits and is deflected, the force deflecting it also deflects the proton (action and reaction), the direction of the force imparted to the proton being the line bisecting the obtuse angle formed by the incoming and deflected directions of the bit. Averaging up the forces from all the bits, we see that the proton jumps around somewhat, but its average position remains the same. Now let more bits come at it from one direction, in effect putting the proton in a moving bit field. With more bits coming from one direction, there is more chance of bits sticking on the mass from that direction, and the proton becomes egg-shaped or teardrop shaped. When bits stick, they impart force along the line of their motion and speed up the proton. The relative speed between field and proton becomes less and less and soon the proton is back to its original size and shape, but is now moving along at a good rate, although in relation to the moving bit field its speed is zero. Thus we see that if the moving bit field arrives suddenly at the proton, there will be a rapid build-up of mass, causing the egg shape. If now the field is stopped suddenly before the proton has caught up to speed, the proton will still be egg-shaped and will be hitting into the stationary bit field with its big end forward. The small velocity it had gained will result in a small relative velocity between field and proton, and as we have seen above, this will result in some bits being added onto the forward side. One would think that this would slow the proton down again and it would stop, but remember that we have a tapered shape at the rear. Bits hitting from the sides will stand more chance of being deflected to the rear, thus pushing the proton forward. There will be a steady propulsive force pushing the egg forward against the resistance. The proton will keep moving, and the same bits that hit and cause it to keep moving also keep the egg shape from breaking down. If now we reverse the bit field, but give it the same strength and duration, bits will pile up on the leading side of the proton, and as the relative velocity between field and proton decreases bits are removed from the front side. At the end of the "bit impulse", the proton is sitting in a stationary bit field with equal-sized tails on both front and back sides. This is not a stable condition and the extra bits are knocked off (with the resultant evolution of energy) until the proton is spherical again. We now have an understanding of how mass increases when matter is speeded up.

Now let's look at gravitation. Take two protons (or neutrons, if you are worried about electrical forces of repulsion). The bit force is uniform all around each mass except in one direction – along the line joining their centers. This is so because a bit coming along this line from space hits one mass and is deflected, never reaching the other mass. Each mass, in effect, screens or shadows the other from the bits coming along a line joining their centers. What happens? There is an unbalanced bit force. As shown above, this results in a velocity in the direction of unbalance and the masses come together, gaining a little mass in the process. What happens after the two masses come together is another story.

CHAPTER 4

Space-Time Relativity. Assume that in another section of the universe the bits are half as numerous as they are here. This means atomic diameters will be twice as large and electrons will revolve half as fast. Gravitation will be weaker. All this is from our viewpoint, however. From the viewpoint of a physicist in that other section of space, time will remain the same. Take the velocity of light. In our system it is 186,000 miles/sec. In his system, since the miles are twice as big, the light will only travel 93,000 miles/each of our own seconds. But his seconds are also twice as big (since rotational speed is cut in half), so to him light is still traveling at 186,000 miles/sec.

See Chapter 11 for a mathematical approach to the actual values of atomic diameters and time of revolution in bit fields of different density. The time of revolution of an electron in a bit field density of 1/2 that at our present location in space will actually be closer to 4 times instead of 2 times as much, and thus light would seem to travel faster to the physicist in that part of space. This might shed some light on the discrepancy between theoretical and observed values of the Red Shift in astronomy.

CHAPTER 5

Magnetism. This is one of the least understood of the physical phenomena. Why should the force decrease as the cube instead of the square of the distance? What are all these lines and tubes of force? – the terms being thrown around so loosely as if everyone understood perfectly what is going on. How about the two poles? Do they really exist and are they necessary in order for the lines of force to leave and return? A torrid coil energized with an electric current produces a magnetic field and there are no poles there – no beginning and no end.

The phenomenon of magnetism arises wherever there is a non-uniformity of the bit field, either a drift of bits or a denser or rarer field at some location. Such a thing might allow gravitation to be considered as a special case of magnetism. In any event there are so many magnetic phenomena (so many ways the bit field at a place can be different from the average field in space) that we shall cover only two of them. (The bit field varies due to the interaction with matter; in space the bit field tends to equalize.)

North and South Poles. Take two spherical masses separated by a distance. Let them both be in rotation clockwise and call them north magnetic poles, Enlarge an edge of one of the spheres and inspect it. (See Fig. 2) Let two bits approach (one at a time), parallel to the line drawn through the center of the mass and the center of one of the bits on the surface.

The bits are coming in at an infinitesimal distance on each side of this radial line. The one on the right will be deflected toward the right with the included angle slightly more than or just at right angles. The one on the left will be deflected toward the left, at a greater included angle than the other bit. It will then hit the next surface bit and be deflected slightly upward.

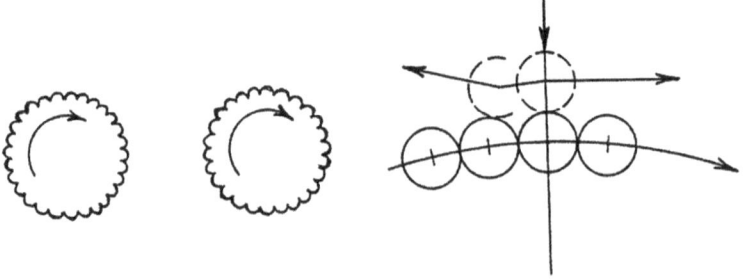

Fig. 2

270

This in effect says that there is more force coming off of the mass toward the right. Summing up all around the sphere, we see that the bit field is rotating.

This rotating field will rotate the fastest near the mass and will decrease as it goes out. We can draw concentric circles around each mass with their spacing denoting speed of rotation – rotation is faster where lines are closer. This is straightforward with one rotating mass, but when we have two, the circles have to be altered so there will be no abrupt change in the direction of the lines. (See Fig. 3) Now draw gradient lines on the diagram. The result is what we see when we sprinkle iron filings between magnetic poles. Bernoulli's Principle can be called in here-pressure increases as velocity decreases, and vice versa. Thus the attraction and repulsion.

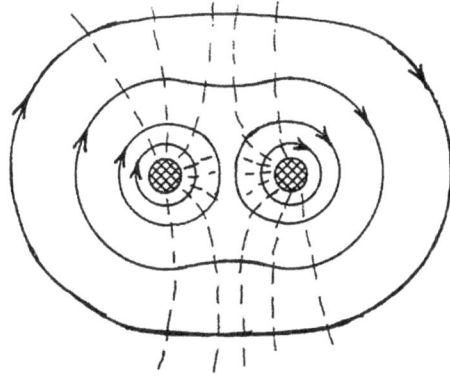

Fig. 3

Magnetostriction. The above paragraph was left a little hazy so the reader would do some thinking on his own -the idea takes some time to sink in. When we come to the varied phenomena of magnetostriction the reader can relax, because the basic idea is so simple and can be grasped readily. These effects depend upon producing some type of special field — compressed, expanded, rotating, etc. — other than a stationary, uniform density field. Take an expanded field, for instance. The effect is the same as that indicated for our physicist in Chapter 4. Matter in a less dense field will expand. Since the atoms have magnetic fields of their own and there are so many ways the neutral field can be altered, naturally we will have many effects - the Joule effect, the Wiedemann effect, the Barrett effect, the Wertheim effect, ad infinitum.

CHAPTER 6

Let us digress for a moment and indulge in some philosophical questions. Why are there a certain number of electrons circling the nuclei of each kind of atom? Suppose all of a sudden the earth received a huge number of electrons from space. What would happen to them? Would they keep circulating throughout the earth and so keep up a perpetual electrical current? Or rather, would they attach themselves to the atoms after a certain amount of time? One would think that this couldn't be done, because it would mean that the number of protons in the atoms would have to increase to balance the electrical charges.

The bit theory allows us to forget about electrical charges and gives the electrons permission to find a home on the atoms. The additional electrons, however, change the way the atoms interact with each other, meaning a change in chemical properties and probably a change in electrical properties. For instance, more of the electron "holes" in a conductor might fill up, making semi-conductors act more like insulators, and possibly changing some insulators into good conductors.

An experiment the author would like to see tried out (perhaps it has already been performed) is to take a thin gold foil (thin enough for some green light to come through) and charge it with electricity, both positive and negative, and observe whether there is any change in the amount of light transmitted in either of these cases.

CHAPTER 7

"...If men were willing to regard the advancement of philosophy, more than their own reputations, it were easy to make them sensible, that one of the most considerable services they could do to the world is to set themselves diligently to make experiments and collect observations without attempting to establish theories upon them before they have taken notice of all the phenomena that are to be solved."

Robert Boyle

Static Electricity. In the author's opinion, one of the greatest setbacks to the science of physics was the conclusion that there are positive and negative types of electricity. Electric current as a flow of electrons is presented much more clearly. The idea of positive and negative electricity probably got started by comparing the attraction and repulsion of magnetic poles with those of pith balls. But it is a well-known fact that two poles are not necessary for the production of a magnetic field.

As to the attraction of unlike charges and the repulsion of like charges, take the classic example of a television tube. An electron stream is boiled off a plate, focused by a magnetic field, and allowed to drift from there to the screen free of any focusing effect. Electrons are supposed to be charges of negative electricity. But everyone knows what happens – they come together at a small spot which keeps moving, producing the picture.

On the screen we see a science class in progress. The professor is explaining all about electricity. He has his pith balls and other paraphernalia, and some radio tubes and a diagram of the workings of a television tube. He has forgotten to connect the strings from one point so that the balls should touch, and they hang at a small distance from each other. He takes up his hard rubber rod, strokes it a few times on the wool cloth and holds it close to the balls. What's this? The balls are attracted to the rod. Before he has a chance to move the rod out of the way the balls have touched the rod and have been violently thrown back. A sharp-eyed student in the front row notices that the balls remained on the rod for a split second, but he says nothing. The balls now stand farther apart than before. "So you see," says the professor, "the balls have acquired a like charge and therefore repel each other." He then takes up his glass rod and holds it close to the balls. He is so proud of his previous success that he has forgotten to stroke the rod with the silk cloth. The balls are attracted to the glass rod. "And as you see," he says, "unlike charges attract." "But professor, you forgot to rub the rod." "Hmm? Oh, yes, so I did." He's getting a little hot under the collar now. He rubs the rod and holds it up close to the balls. They are attracted the same as before. He rubs the rod vigorously now as if to make up for his oversight and again presents it to the balls. This time they are violently attracted and violently repelled. They now hang at, their original small distance from one another. He brings the glass rod up to the balls again, but the balls remain almost motionless. "Professor, after the balls hit the rod and bounced back, hadn't they picked up like charges? They're not repelling, each other." 'Hmm, yes; well that's because the charges were neutralized." (Quick thinking, professor; keep up the good, work.) "Now we come to electric currents. Electricity can be thought of as electrons, or negative charges, in motion. A good example is your television picture tube, which we see here. The electrons come off this plate and are accelerated by means of this positively charged grid here which attracts them. Then they are focused by the magnetic field here and move on to hit the phosphorescent screen, in a little dot; This material on the face of the tube lights up when hit by electrons. It is the fast movement of this dot across the ... " "Uh, professor, I don't understand the dot. You said electrons were negative charges and that like charges were supposed to repel each other. Why do the ... "CLASS DISMISSED!"

When two surfaces are rubbed together some of the surface electrons will gain energy and tear themselves loose from their atoms, allowing them to be free to move around in each piece of material. The number rubbed off each surface may differ, depending upon the materials. These freed electrons will tend to move into that material which has a greater attraction for them (the material whose atoms are better able to add extra electrons, as indicated in Chapter 6). When the surfaces are separated we have this condition: both surfaces have some atoms stripped of electrons, but one surface has more of the high-energy electrons than the other (assuming two different kinds of material).

Assume the surfaces are pulled an infinite distance apart, and let's inspect one of them. There will be no unbalanced force and the high-energy electrons will move throughout the mass. When they come to the outside of the mass they will not escape (unless their energy is high enough) because the surface atoms will "pull them back" and they will move around the surface atoms much like a comet moves around the sun, coming in closer to the nuclei than the outer electrons, and moving out into space a certain distance from the nuclei. No matter in what direction they start moving out, soon their elliptical orbits will be perpendicular to the surface. Thus if the mass is a sphere, we have a "charge" on the surface of the sphere.

Now bring the two masses into proximity. Not only is gravitation at work on the masses, but the electrons between the masses are attracted to each other. (See Fig. 4) When the electrons attract each other they gain energy and lengthen their orbits. Since their "year" is fairly short they keep gaining energy rapidly, This in effect increases the force of gravitation tremendously and the masses are forced together. When they come close enough something happens. The electron now has enough energy on its own to get all the way across the space and it starts revolving around an atom (nucleus) on each surface. This changes the situation entirely. The electron is now forcing the masses apart. Let's see how this can be. (See Fig. 5)

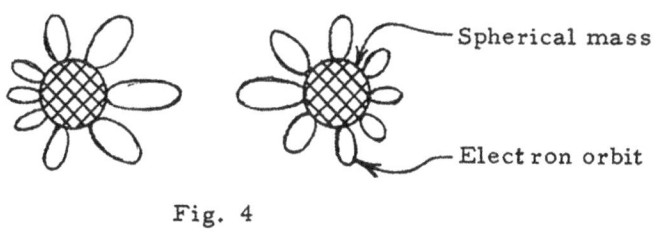

Spherical mass

Electron orbit

Fig. 4

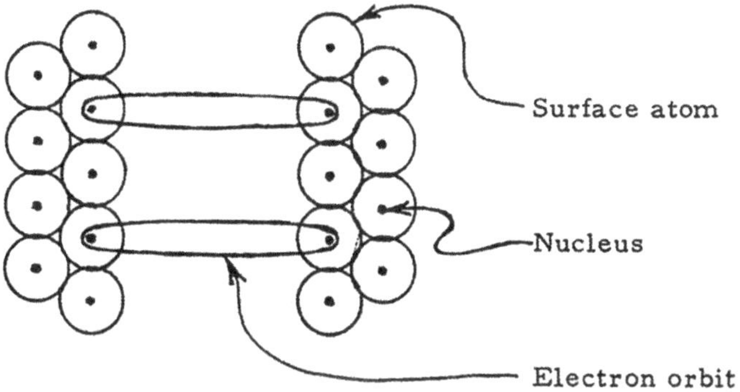

Surface atom

Nucleus

Electron orbit

Fig. 5

When the electron revolves as indicated in the diagram it means that if the other surface were not there the orbit of the electron would be much longer and perhaps would become a hyperbolic orbit, with the electron going out into space and never returning. Considering just one nucleus and an electron on one of these paths between surfaces, this means that the gravitational force pushing the nucleus in when the electron is between the surfaces is not equal to the force pushing the nucleus out when the electron comes around on the other side of the nucleus. Thus the electrons "pull" the surfaces apart. If the surfaces have some moisture on them the energy of these electrons will be dissipated slowly. Soon the electrons can no longer reach across to both surfaces and each starts revolving around only one nucleus. What happens? The surfaces then attract each other again and the cycle repeats. If the surfaces have a lot of moisture on them the energy will be dissipated rapidly and before any other effects can be seen the electrons have lost enough energy to be recaptured by the atoms and there are no effects of attraction or repulsion seen. If the surfaces are very dry, the electrons can quickly get up enough energy to jump the gap and there is no attraction noticed, only repulsion.

To account for attraction between opposite charges in dry air, we look at our surfaces again to see what is happening. On oppositely charged surfaces one surface has more of these active electrons than the other and also would have fewer electrons stripped off its atoms. (In fact it is not improbable that it would capture all of the active electrons if given time.) Here we have a condition of active electrons on one surface and atoms deficient in electrons on the other surface. Because active electrons are on only one surface they cannot increase their energy as fast. Their long elliptical orbits, however, allow gravitation to pull the nuclei in both surfaces together. When the surfaces come within the orbits of the electrons they will try to repel each other, but since one surface has fewer electrons in some atoms than is normal, the fast electrons will come home to roost if given a chance. That chance is the loss of energy of the electrons as they go around the nuclei in the "negative" surface. Loss of energy requires that the atoms (nuclei) the electrons go around be fairly mobile and not bound up in a hard, crystalline structure. This is the case with "negative" materials such as sulfur, sealing wax, hard rubber, and amber.

The movement of individual electrons in orbits as explained above is valid only in a perfect vacuum. When a material is interposed – a gas, liquid, or solid – the electrons collide with the electrons in the substance, and shock waves are set up. These shock waves propagate the effect from the electrons almost as if it were the same electrons moving in their orbits, and thus we can use the same reasoning when we conduct experiments in air as we can in a vacuum. More will be said about shock waves in Chapters 8 and 9.

Electric sparks and discharges are similar to static electricity except the electrons have enough energy to knock light waves out of the atoms in the space between the surfaces. Thus we have the explanation for corona discharge and also for a bolt of Lightning, in which a streamer goes up from the ground to meet a streamer coming down from the cloud the instant before the main bolt appears.

Experiment with static electricity and find out if it is so.

CHAPTER 8

Electric current as a flow of electrons is fairly well taken care of in present theory. After we go over the fundamentals of electron flow in conductors, we will discuss two phenomena – the production of a magnetic field from a current of electricity in a conductor, and the "waves" associated with a stream of electrons in a vacuum.

When voltage is applied to electrons in a wire it means that a bit field is incident upon them. The electrons gain energy and bits and thus start to move along the wire. They collide with the electrons in the wire and set up shock waves of electrons. These shock waves will move out at about the speed that the first electrons gained. If the electron current is continuous (D.C.) we will have a "continuous" shock wave in which electrons all through the wire will be knocked back and forth at high speeds. All this knocking around tends to dislodge bits, which cause the shock wave to lose energy and the bits fly off and become heat energy.

In superconducting metals at low temperatures, the energy that is knocked off is returned to the electrons, because the vibration of the atoms is reduced enough so that a good wave system can be set up in the bit field (more about wave systems in Chapter 9), and thus we have our shock waves continuing for long periods of time.

Insulating materials insulate only because they interfere in some way with letting an electron drift occur – they still allow shock waves to pass through, so that we get our static electric phenomena. In alternating current the voltage, and therefore the electrons, speed up, slow down, and reverse, and thus we have a great number of shock wave fronts all moving at different speeds. If we can get the frequency of the current high enough, we will come to the point where a cycle is about equal to the distance between collisions, and there will be no great electron drift in either direction. At very high frequencies, therefore, all materials should become insulators, since there is no flow of electrons. As the density of the electrons in an insulator increases, due to the increased electrostatic charge, the force of gravitation on these extra electrons decreases and the atoms allow a certain amount of drift. Therefore increased electrostatic charge should make an insulator act more like a conductor.

Now let's take up the magnetic field. Assume that we have a current of electrons moving along in a wire. We can forget about the shock waves and concentrate on the electron drift because when a fast moving electron hits into an orbital electron, it knocks it ahead and in turn becomes an orbital electron. The effect is the same as if the same electron were moving along the wire. When a fast electron comes close to the nucleus of an atom a bit field is set in motion (gravitation). When the electron approaches the nucleus, bits are added to the electron. When it recedes, bits come off. This results in a bit field that rotates around the electron-nucleus combination. (See Fig. 6)

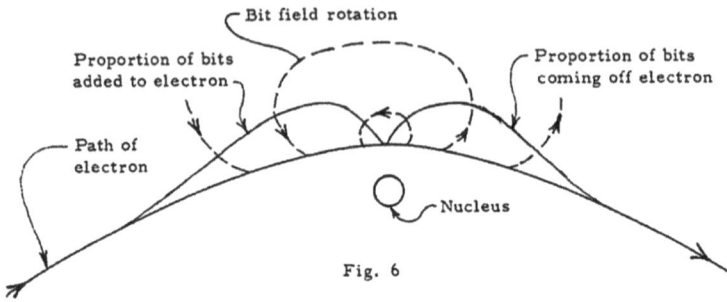

Fig. 6

If we sum up the effects from a number of electrons we see that in general the bit field is moving in a direction opposite to the direction of the electrons. This is the source of the back electromotive force. If we wrap the wire up into a solenoid, the bit field will be set in rotation opposite to the rotation of the electrons. Because of the interaction from all around the coil, the angular rotation near the center of the solenoid will be fairly uniform.

Electron Waves. Let two electrons that are close together move out in the same direction at the same speed. Gravitation will take over and push them together. Their distance apart at the start determines how much energy they have when they come together. When they meet, if they stick together their combined size is not stable at the forward speed they are traveling. Therefore they can either (1) disintegrate or (2) fly apart at right angles to their line of approach, much as a vibrating drop of water. Their speed of approach and their forward speed will determine which happens. Assume they fly apart. Then their speed at the instant they fly apart will be the same as their speed of approach just before. Gravitation slows them down and they stop at the same distance apart they originally were. Since gravitation is still working, they come together again and the cycle repeats. If one lags behind the other when they start out into space they may not actually hit, or they may hit off center. In these cases their direction of departure will not be at right angles to their direction of approach, but will make some angle (between 0° and 90°) with it. A graph of the distance between them plotted against their forward speed will indicate their wave form. It is most likely not a sine wave. Looking at a number of these electron pairs coming toward you from the same direction, their different directions of approach to each other will trace out lines which can be contained in a circle and which cross at the center of the circle – in other words, a ray of unpolarized electron waves.

CHAPTER 9

Light waves exhibit the properties of both waves and particles, so any theory that holds up must explain both at the same time. The author has tried, and failed, to work up a theory based on groups of four bits, or tetrahedrons, as indicated in Chapter 2. Therefore a theory will be worked out based on wave motion of groups of separate bits.

Light waves seem to be shock waves. The speed of the waves could be the average forward speed of individual bits, as in the case of sound waves, where the speed of sound is about three fourths the speed of the individual molecules; or the speed of the waves could be equal to the maximum forward speed of the bits. We shall assume the former case, making it a shock wave of Mach 1. In this case the speed of individual bits is somewhat faster than the speed of light.

Because of the scarcity of information on shock waves at the present time, the author will make several assumptions concerning shock waves of light and hope that future experimentation will bear him out.

The waves consist of groups of bits moving along in the same direction. These groups (or clouds, or photons) retain their size, and do not keep spreading out and getting larger until they disappear, even though different bits come into the cloud all the time.

The size of the cloud, and its wavelength, depend upon the number of bits making up the cloud, more bits meaning a smaller, denser cloud and a shorter wavelength. The cloud is in the shape of a disc, in the plane of the orbit of the electron giving off the photon.

The speed of the cloud is constant when referred to the bit field it goes through.

The speed of the bit field in the plane at right angles to the velocity of propagation pushes the cloud in this direction.

Assumption (1) explains the particle-like aspects of light waves, or photons. Let us understand now that electromagnetic waves are different, consisting not of photons but of continuous oscillations or vibrations in the bit field. Assumption (2) explains the wave properties of light waves and also explains photoelectrons. If some bits in this cloud hit an electron and knock it out of the atom, the cloud has lost some bits and has therefore increased its wavelength (and reduced its frequency). At the same time, the cloud has gotten bigger, because there are fewer bits in it. Assumption (3) explains the speed of light through space. In the case of distant nebulae, where the expanding bit field is moving away from us, light starts in our direction more slowly relative to us. As it comes in closer it speeds up, at the same time encountering a denser bit field. The extra energy necessary to speed up is taken out of the cloud, and some bits in the cloud are lost, lowering the frequency and producing the Red Shift. Assuming a non-expanding bit field, the Doppler effect will only work if the radiator is moving in relation to the bit field. If we approach a radiator that is stationary in the bit field, we will see no Doppler effect, but only an increase in intensity of the light. (This is subject to any effects on the time of revolution of electrons and diameter of atoms when we move through a bit field.) Assumption (4) explains the Faraday effect, in which plane polarized light is rotated when put in a magnetic field. When a ray of polarized light is sent down the center of a solenoid, the magnetic field (bit field) rotates when current is going through the coil. This rotates the plane of polarization. Accordingly, if the ray is sent parallel to the axis of the coil, but not along the center, the light ray should be displaced at the same time that it rotates, the amount of displacement depending upon the speed of rotation of the field. If a transparent substance is placed in the rotating field, the field will rotate the electron orbits out of all proportion to the rotational speed of the field, much as eddy currents set up in a fluid, and the effects will be much easier to see in experiments.

The Radiating Source. An atom when bound up in the solid or liquid state will have its electrons displaced all around in the volume of the atom. With a two-atom molecule the orbits will tend to become elliptical and will line up at an angle with the line connecting the nuclei. The area of interference of electron orbits will rotate at a certain rate of speed around the axis connecting the nuclei.

When an atom is free, as in an ionized or a monatomic gas, the orbits of the electrons will become more circular and will lie in a plane around the nucleus, as with the planets around the sun. In this last case the orbits have settled down into a stable form. A sudden pulse of energy may upset the orderly arrangement of electrons. When they go back to their original state, they readmit this energy into space as a packet of bits, which will be lined up in the plane of the electrons. Thus from each atom we get polarized light. Whenever an atom comes close to another, the electron orbits are disturbed. Afterwards it takes some time for the orbits to return to their plane. From this we infer that the less the atoms collide (the closer to absolute zero or the higher the vacuum) the sharper the spectral lines will be.

Interference and Diffraction. From experimentation it has been found that light from a point source incident upon two narrow parallel slits will set up an interference pattern on a screen placed a distance behind the slits even when the intensity of the light source is such that only one photon will be found between slits and screen at any time. This phenomenon requires that a stationary wave system be present in the space between the slits and screen. If a photon hits an atom located in the "crest" of the wave, it will be reflected or absorbed, to be radiated later. If it hits an atom in the "trough" of the wave it will be transmitted. There are two ways in which the energy to set up the wave system could be obtained. One is from the first photons that go through the apparatus, the other is from the motion of the electrons already present in the apparatus (in which case a standing wave system would be present whether photons came in or not). We will assume the former, and say that it can be checked by allowing a few photons to enter the apparatus, destroy the wave system that is assumed forming, let a few more photons enter, etc., until an image is built up on the film, and see if this image shows interference effects.

When standing waves are set up their wavelength depends upon how much difference there is in the density of the bit field between the crest and the trough of the wave. The greater difference there is, the shorter the wave-length is. This fits in nicely with the incident photon, where a denser cloud means a smaller cloud. Assuming the wavelength of the photon is the same as that of the standing wave, if the photon is in the trough of the wave, the resultant bit field density is the same as if there were no photon and no standing wave. An atom on one of the boundaries of the wave system, having given up some energy when expanding while this trough was set up, now absorbs some energy and gives it right up again to the passing cloud. If the atom were in the crest of the wave, and thus compressed when the photon came in, the density of the bit field around the atom would get even greater, and the atom would be compressed more, if it did not get rid of the extra energy by reflecting it back, or using it to cause chemical changes, as in film.

Interference effects do not come into being until we can get a standing wave system set up to reflect some photons and transmit others. The system can be set up with diffraction gratings, edges, and surfaces, but in all cases we need two surfaces spaced some distance apart so the standing waves can be set up - grating and film, edge and viewing surface, two surfaces placed together showing interference fringes, etc.

Diffraction. When a bit cloud comes near a mass, or gets into a moving bit field of any sort, it can be deflected sideways, giving rise to a spreading out and curving of the clouds around the surface of the object. The action of the standing waves on these dispersed clouds will cause the diffraction patterns. In the case, of a lens, with its aperture creating diffraction, if we can get rid of the standing waves resulting from the aperture, we can get light focused at a pinpoint (assuming aberrations of the lens are corrected) and magnifications of many thousands would be possible in small telescopes and microscopes of low numerical aperture.

Refraction. These bit clouds do not slow down when they get into an optical medium. The cause of the apparent slowing down is that the bit fields in the medium cause the clouds to be deflected sideward first one way, then another, so that the cloud threads its way through the atoms like a snake. It is always moving at the speed of light, but its total path through the medium has been lengthened. If the cloud comes in at an angle to the normal to the surface, it is in effect hitting the bit field in the medium from the side and is pushed in toward the normal, creating a refracted photon. If the optical substance the light is traveling through is moving in the same direction as the light, the light will not have to undergo as many of these direction changes to cover the same straight line distance, and will seem to speed up. If the optical substance is moving across the path of the light, there will be more direction changes in the direction of motion of the optical substance, the changes being in proportion to the index of refraction, and the ray of light will move in the direction of motion of the medium. Thus, in the aberration of light (Airy's experiment), it does not matter whether the telescope tube is filled with air, water, or carbon disulfide.

Reflection. If, when the cloud comes in on the surface, the bit field on the surface is moving rapidly, or there are a number of small fields around atoms that are very active, the cloud cannot keep on forging through these fields, and is reflected. This is especially the case with metals, where the electron orbits are not filled up and as a result the bit field would be in violent motion. The angle of reflection is the same as the angle of incidence because ordinarily no energy is lost in a cloud when it is reflected.

Michelson-Morley Experiment. Assuming an ether to exist in space as a medium for the propagation of light waves, this experiment indicates that the ether is dragged along by the earth, while all other experiments, such as the aberration of light, indicate that the earth is moving through the ether. The only way to make the experiments agree is to assume that a linear change of length occurs when matter moves through the ether. Let us see how this change in length occurs. Take a hydrogen atom and place it in a stationary bit field (no relative velocity between atom and ether). Now have the system move in relation to the bit field with the plane of the orbit of the electron parallel to the direction of motion. Bits will attach themselves to the particles so that their shape will allow them to move through the bit field (inertia), but aside from the extra mass, we now have an unbalanced force acting on the electron. As it goes ahead of the nucleus, its speed in relation to the bit field increases, and thus there is a force pushing the electron back.

It goes around in front of the nucleus and then starts to move behind. Now it is slowing down in relation to the bit field, and there is a force pushing it ahead. The effect on this electron is to move the plane of its orbit so that it is perpendicular to the direction of motion through the bit field. From this we can determine the motion of the solar system through space – if there is any motion of the sun in relation to the bit field, the planets will tend to align their orbits perpendicular to this direction. The same is true for any individual atoms moving along in relation to the bit field. The fewer collisions they have the more chance of the electrons lining up in this manner. In certain nebulae there are regions of polarized light, indicating the direction of motion of the stars and gases in each region. Getting back to the Michelson-Morley experiment, we now see that when we have a large group of atoms (matter) in which we can measure a certain length, that when this matter is moving through the bit field its length in the direction of motion will be shortened. Inertia tries to keep the electrons moving at the same speed through the field; with relative motion between atoms and field, this goal of uniform speed can only be obtained if the electron orbits try to move into planes more at right angles to the direction of motion. Thus we have a shortening of the length of the atoms in the direction of motion.

CHAPTER 10

Evolution seems to be pretty well believed by most informed people today. The process depends in large measure on survival of the fittest, with the changes in form that come into being, weeded out until only the best forms survive. The catch is in the appearance of these changes, or mutations. The general belief is that cosmic rays, or radioactivity of some sort, produces the mutations which start evolution on its capricious road down the ages. Unfortunately, all the mutations we have produced in the laboratory from radioactivity have all been worse from the standpoint of survival, at least no better. Even today the fear is that radioactivity from nuclear tests will harm future generations. If "evolution" mutations were actually from radioactivity, we should welcome these tests and wish more of them, even nuclear warfare, in the sure hope that we would be bettering ourselves through evolution. No, evolution does not come from radioactivity.

Let us ask ourselves a basic question. Fossil forms and bones remaining in different layers of ground are our main source of information concerning the evolution of life upon earth. Where did this extra matter come from that forms a definite layer for each age? Some of it may have come from sedimentation when the land was under the ocean, but how about those layers where different ages are represented by land animals? Did the animals live, die, and the land sink beneath the sea for a time (with no record of marine life), only to lift up out of the sea and another cycle of land animals begin again? And this to be repeated many, many times? It hardly seems likely.

What happens to the cosmic rays, meteors, meteorites, and comet tails that enter the earth's atmosphere? Are they not captured by earth's gravitation and so increase the mass of the earth, however slowly at present? And if they come from outer space is it necessary for them to have the same proportion of electrons to nuclei as is present on earth? And if the proportion actually is different this means that the earth could be gaining or losing electron "pressure." In other words, if enough electrons were added to the earth, a substance such as oxygen could become similar to fluorine, or carbon similar to nitrogen, or sodium similar to magnesium, gold to mercury, iron to cobalt or nickel, phosphorus to sulfur, etc. If the electron proportion were reduced, the changes would go in the other direction. (Note: if the proportion were reduced enough, the "unearthly" high density of Pluto would be easily explained.) Which way are they going? Take the case of dating the age of various once living fossils. It can be done by fluorine percentage, which increases as the age of the fossil increases, or by radioactive carbon 14, which decreases as the age increases. Looking at a table of isotopes we see that oxygen 19 is radioactive and will change to stable fluorine by gaining an electron (and losing a gamma ray) and that carbon 14 is radioactive and will change to stable nitrogen by gaining an electron. Both of these roads lead to the conclusion that the earth is gaining electron pressure at the present time, on the average.

It is well known how dependent living matter is on its environment. A little too dry, a little too salty, alkaline, hot, too much light, pressure, etc., and the life form dies. The more advanced or complex life forms are especially susceptible to changes in environment. Why do life forms need all the various elements found in them? Could it be to balance up the electron pressure so that they can exist on the earth in their present forms? And if the electron pressure of the earth changed, would not the life forms change their pressure also? This change would mean that the appearance or structure of the offspring would change. The author contends, therefore, that it is the matter from outer space that is controlling the evolution of life and of mankind. If the electron change was sudden, who knows what changes would come about in the earth? How long would it take to alter the appearance of the world – a year, a day, an hour? In the twinkling of an eye?

The tale is told in all its wonder
Try now to tear it all asunder.

CHAPTER 11

Gravitation. We will discuss semi-mathematically the reasons why gravitational force obeys the law $F = Km_1m_2/R^2$.

Where F = gravitational force of attraction
K = gravitational constant
m_1 = mass of first body
m_2 = mass of second body
R = center distance between masses

First, the factor K. K represents the density of the bit field in space. If the bit field were half as dense there would be half as many impacts of bits pushing the masses together and the force would be half as much, assuming the center distance remained the same. Atoms would be larger; the earth would move around the sun at a greater distance. We will determine the exact quantities later. It is the density of the bit field, as represented by K, that says that the electron of a hydrogen atom should be circling around the nucleus at such tremendous distances compared with the size of the nucleus.

Next the factor m_1m_2. Let m_1 and m_2 represent nuclei of various sizes. These are compact groups of bits, so no moving bits can go through them, and it will simplify the mathematics. Let us study the following simple equations:

$$m \propto V \qquad V = 4/3\pi r^3 \qquad A = \pi r^2$$

Where m = mass of sphere
V = volume of sphere
A = cross-sectional area of sphere
r = radius of sphere
And so if the product of the masses is constant, the product of the radii and the

Let $m_1m_2 = C$

Then $V_1V_2 = C_1 = 4/3\pi(r_1^3r_2^3) = 4/3\pi(r_1r_2)^3$

$\therefore (r_1r_2)^3 = C_2$ and $r_1r_2 = C_3$

Also $A_1A_2 = \pi(r_1^2r_2^2) = \pi(r_1r_2)^2 = \pi(C_3)^2$

$\therefore A_1A_2 = C_4$

product of the cross-sectional areas are constants.

Now let us take three cases where the distance between the centers of the masses is constant and where the product m1m2 is constant and let us see why the gravitational force is constant. We start out with some arbitrary values, and we work out the others as shown below, since

$$A \propto m^{2/3} \text{ and } r \propto m^{1/3}.$$

If we multiply A1A2 or r1r2 we see that they are constant for all three cases. (See Fig. 7)

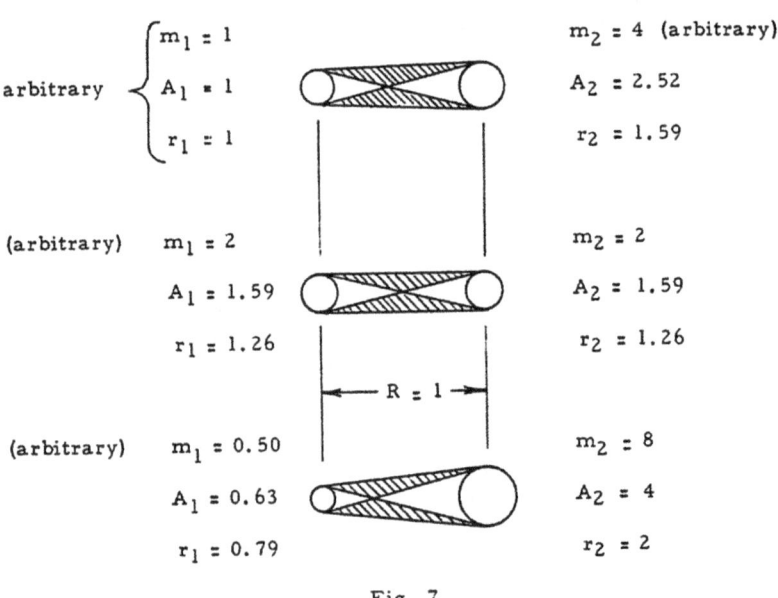

Fig. 7

Now we figure out the shadowing effect to see if it is the same for all three cases. The gravitational force will depend on the bits pushing the masses together that are not offset by those pushing them apart; because of the uniform density field it should be possible to show this number as a certain volume. Let us determine the volumes of revolution of the shaded areas shown in the above diagram.

V of frustum of cone – V of left cone – V of right cone = V of shaded part. Using our volume equations for cones, we have the following:

$$\frac{\pi}{3} R(r_1^2 + r_1 r_2 + r_2^2) - \left(\frac{\pi}{3}\frac{r_1}{r_1+r_2} R r_1^2\right) - \left(\frac{\pi}{3}\frac{r_2}{r_1+r_2} R r_2^2\right)$$

$$= \frac{\pi}{3} R \left(r_1^2 + r_1 r_2 + r_2^2 - \frac{r_1^3 + r_2^3}{r_1 + r_2}\right)$$

Let $\frac{\pi}{3} R$ drop out since it is a constant. Substituting,

1) $\left(1 + 1.59 + 2.52 - \dfrac{1+4}{2.59}\right) = 3.18$

2) $\left(1.59 + 1.59 + 1.59 - \dfrac{2+2}{2.52}\right) = 3.18$

3) $\left(0.63 + 1.59 + 4 - \dfrac{0.5+8}{2.79}\right) = 3.18$

Are these equal volumes a coincidence, or do they actually represent the number of bits shadowed out?

Lastly is the factor I/R^2. The bits can be thought of as light waves coming in from all directions, the denser the bit field, the brighter the illumination. Since the bit field density is constant, the force on the outer hemispheres is constant, but the amount of shadowing will decrease as the square of the distance, similar to the way the illumination of an object decreases as the square of the distance from the light source. The gravitational equation can be determined experimentally by putting two small spheres inside an illuminated photo-sphere and determining the decrease in luminosity on the sides of the spheres facing each other by means of film, light meter, etc.

When the nuclei and electrons are far apart, as in ordinary matter, most of the bits can find a way through, and the shadowing effect is very incomplete, resulting in ordinary forces of gravitation. Where a nucleus is close to another nucleus or electron, the force is much greater because the particles shadow all the bits in a narrow cone. When we consider a single nucleus, it is held together even more firmly because the "shadowing" is complete.

Thus we have regular gravitational forces, atomic forces, and nuclear forces all coming from the same bit field.

We will now resume the problem of determining orbit sizes. Taking a hydrogen atom as an example, when the bit field density changes, the electron orbit must change in some way; if the electron velocity remains the same when the field becomes less dense, then the electron must go nearer to the nucleus – the orbit must decrease so that the electron can still be held by the nucleus. This is not logical, since the force on the electron is less. Therefore the velocity of the electron in its orbit must decrease at the same time that the radius increases. Let us assume that if the radius increases by x, the velocity changes by l/x.

We have $F = Km_1m_2/R^2$, or for the same masses,

$F \propto K/R^2$ and $F \propto a$, which equals $R\omega^2 = V^2/R$.

And so $F \propto R\omega^2$ and V^2/R.

Let density $K = 1/2$ normal, making $R = 2$ normal.

Then $F = 1/8$, $a = 1/8$, $V = 1/2$, $\omega = V/R = 1/4$, normal,

and the time of rotation increases by a factor of four.

Jumping back to Chapter 4 on Relativity, we see that we must make a correction. At density 1/2, the speed of light would increase - neglecting the modifying effect of part of the speed of the bits going into an outward expansion, it would be 372, 000 half density miles per half density second.

That the velocity does actually decrease in proportion to the increase in radius (V C/R) can be worked out from Kepler's law which says that the radius vector joining each planet with the sun describes equal areas in equal times. If we can discover the reason behind this, we can find out why an unionized, or normal, hydrogen atom has its electron moving around the nucleus at a definite average distance; if it was left to chance, the radius could be twice as big or half as big or any other size, as long as the velocity was right for that radius. An idea strikes us – it is the velocity that determines the radius, so we should study the velocity of the electron.

Suppose there were only a proton and an electron in space, both stationary with respect to the bit field. Let them be a good distance apart – say an inch. Gravitation pushes them together and they speed up, especially the electron. When the electron gets within its normal orbital radius it is probably going faster than normal velocity; we will find out later.

Let us assume that it does not hit the nucleus head on, but comes very close to it. Gravitational force keeps pushing it in toward the nucleus, so that its direction of motion is changed and it goes around the nucleus and back toward its original distance from the nucleus, but it will not move out to that inch again. Why not? If we kept our nucleus held firmly in space so it could not move, the electron would, but such is not the case. When the electron is approaching the nucleus, the nucleus is approaching the electron – the distance, and therefore the maximum electron speed possible, decreases each time the electron makes a revolution. The original straight-line motion of the electron changes into an elliptical orbit because of the angular velocity given the electron when it moves around the nucleus. In a hydrogen atom, the electron will soon be moving around in a circular orbit. We can get some idea of the size of the orbit by finding out the maximum energy the electron can acquire by coming in from infinity.

We can make a graph of the gravitational force on the electron as it comes toward the nucleus. Letting the force equal one when the electron is one nuclear diameter away, it will be 1/100 at 10 nuclear diameters away, 1/1,000,000 at 1000 nuclear diameters, etc. The force decreases tremendously by the time we get out a distance equal to the radius of the hydrogen's electron orbit. Taking the area under the curve, we have the work done on the electron. Equating work to kinetic energy, $1/2\ mv^2$, we see that the maximum speed does not vary greatly whether the electron starts from infinity or from a distance equal to the radius of the normal electron orbit. There is a definite limit to the amount of energy that an electron can pick up, by gravitation, to form an orbit around a nucleus. If the electron has zero velocity very far inside its normal orbit, when it is pushed to the nucleus it will not have gained enough speed to go around the nucleus, but will crash into it and cause the nucleus to become radioactive. Thus we have a narrow range of orbits for a hydrogen atom.

Going a step farther to atoms with several electrons, let us see how these orbits build up. Let electrons come in one at a time from infinity. The first orbit is formed in the manner indicated above. The second electron now comes in and tries to form an orbit the same as the first. If the electrons were not attracted to each other, we would soon have two electrons traveling around the nucleus in the same orbit. Theoretically this could happen if the electrons traveled at exactly the same speed and were diametrically opposite at all times, but this would be a very unstable setup. Let us assume we have an atom with these two electrons in the same orbit, or more exactly, revolving around the nucleus at the same distance. First of all, gravitation will push the electrons closer together and their orbits will tend to lie in the same plane. When we reach the condition of two electrons revolving in the same orbit, and assumed in the same direction, they will approach each other because of the gravitational force acting along the chord connecting them. This force pushes both of them closer to the nucleus, but at the same time one is speeding up and the other is slowing down. The one that speeds up moves out from the nucleus, the one that slows down moves in. The nucleus is pulled out of line more strongly by the faster moving electron, as seen in the previous pages, and after a while the faster electron is found revolving in an orbit a little closer to the nucleus than the other. If the electrons start out revolving in opposite directions around the nucleus, the gravitational force will tend to push them together and their orbits will approach each other. Every time the electrons get near each other they will speed up, moving farther from the nucleus. In other words, the orbits of both will start degenerating into longer and longer ellipses – this is an unstable condition.

Although we now have our two electrons revolving in the same direction, there is something else we must consider. If their orbits are too close to one another the force of gravity will try to push them together when they approach each other on their orbits. The result may be just a large perturbation, or the electrons may switch orbits. This latter result is an unstable condition. The orbits will keep shifting until there is no chance of the electrons changing orbits. The inner orbit will get smaller, the outer larger, until this condition is achieved. The total energy of the two electrons will be the same as twice the energy of one electron circling the nucleus, but one orbit will be larger, and the other smaller, than the original orbit.

Now we will try to get an idea of why this two-electron configuration is so stable, as in the helium atom. Let us take some liquid helium and magnify the atoms. The nuclei are some distance apart, but the outer electron orbit of one atom comes close to those of others. As these electrons attract each other their orbits are continually changing direction. The inner electron orbits are pulled out of line in trying to line up with the outer orbits, and they will lag behind the outer orbits, possibly as much as 90 degrees. Each revolving electron creates a rotating bit field. The resultant of two bit fields rotating at right angles is a bit field that oscillates but does not rotate. We can see this if we take a globe with two axes at right angles and rotate it around both at the same speed at the same time. Since the bit field does not rotate there is no chance of the "magnetism" of two atoms (bit fields rotating in opposite directions) to hold them together in molecular form. If we have three electrons, and thus three rotating bit fields to consider, no matter how our axes are placed relative to one another, the resultant bit field will always have some residual rotation. Thus the reason why the helium atom is so stable and neutral. This residual bit field rotation in atoms also gives us a clue as to why they build up in molecules like they do.

Let us now discuss the hydrogen spectrum, keeping in mind the way the electron is added to the hydrogen nucleus. A single atom is capable of producing many frequencies as the electron returns to its rest state. The only way a light wave can be generated is if bits are thrown off. Ordinarily when an electron is circling the nucleus in a stable circular orbit no bits are added or removed, on the average. When the orbit is disrupted and becomes elliptical, however, bits can be switched around on the electron as its orbit changes from ellipse to circle. In other words, as the electron moves in toward the nucleus it is speeding up, and bits are added. When it moves around the nucleus and starts to recede, it is slowing down and bits are removed. It is likely that these bits are removed suddenly, at the time the electron is nearest the nucleus. Also, the nucleus itself may have bits dislodged at this time. Let us look at the motion of the nucleus as the electron comes from infinity and settles down to a circular orbit. We see that when the nucleus starts moving toward the electron it is speeding up, and continues to speed up until the electron gets near. Now its direction of motion is altered so that it follows the direction of motion of the electron around it – the two orbits are more or less in phase. Also the nucleus is slowing down – its speed and direction through the bit field have been abruptly altered. To get an idea of the impact on the particles, let us suppose the electron can go through a hole in the center of the nucleus. When the electron reaches the nucleus the force is tremendous. It is pushing the nucleus to the left and the electron to the right. In the next instant the force is reversed – the nucleus is being pushed to the right and the electron to the left. To get the feel of the force, think of driving your car, steadily accelerating around a blind curve, and meeting head on with a speeding car coming toward you.

When a hydrogen atom is in the lowest energy level, the electron and proton are circling around their center of gravity. For radiation to be given off, the nucleus must circle with the electron, although in a smaller orbit – in other words, the frequency of revolution of the electron must be slow enough so the nucleus orbit will be in phase with it. At resonance frequency both electron and proton are in a semi-stable condition, and may keep revolving this way for a long time before breaking 180° out of phase – hence the persistent lines in the spectrum. Summing up, if the two particles are in phase they will give out light waves (bit clouds) until they arrive at the condition of revolving 180° out of phase (revolving around their center of gravity). The "frequency" of the light depends upon the number of bits given off at each approach.

CHAPTER 12

Gravitational Force vs. Coulomb Force. Why are Coulmb forces 10^{42} times as strong as gravitational forces? The basic gravitation equation is $F = Km_1m_2/R^2$.

Electrons and nuclei are solid groups of bits – no moving bits can travel through them. Since most of an atom's mass is in the nucleus, we will just take nuclei and work with them. A nucleus is somewhere between 10^{-4} and 10^{-5} of the diameter of an atom, and therefore its volume is between 10^{-12} and 10^{-15} of the volume of an atom – let us agree on 10^{-14}.

Let us take two equal sized spheres, first letting them be solid, as in nuclei, and then composed of atoms, as in ordinary matter.

$F = Km_1m_2/R^2 = 1 \times 1 \times 1/1^2 = 1$

$F = Km_1m_2/R^2 = 10^{-14} \times 10^{-14} \times 10^{-14} / 1^2 = 1 \times 10^{-42}$

K is only 10^{-14} in the second case because this is the proportion of bits that cannot get through, due to that amount of space being taken up with mass. (Since most of the bits *can* get through, the shadowing effect in the second case is very much weaker.) Therefore we see that gravitational force is 10^{-42} times as strong as Coulomb force.

CHAPTER 13

We will discuss three common producers of magnetism, how the bit fields are made, and the interactions of these fields with each other and with a bar magnet or compass needle.

1) A wire with DC current. The bit field (outside the wire) is moving opposite to the direction of electron flow, meaning a movement in the direction of current flow. The speed along the wire is greatest near the wire and decreases as the distance increases- looking somewhat like viscous laminar flow around a cylinder drawn through a fluid.

2) The earth. The earth is rotating from west to east in the bit field of space, making a bit field rotation relative to the earth from east to west.

3) Bar magnet. A bar magnet has electrons rotating within it, with the magnetic axis as the axis of rotation. The bit field will then rotate in the opposite direction.

If the magnet is an infinitely long rod, we can neglect the effect from the poles, and the bit field will rotate uniformly around the axis of the rod. If we now cut the rod in half (keeping the space between, small) the rotating bit field between the surfaces will exert less pressure on the sides than if the field were not rotating (Bernoulli's Principle), and the two halves will be pushed together. Let us call the end on the left the North Pole, and the one on the right the South Pole. Now take the right half and move it around with the cut as the pivot until the two halves are parallel. If we assume the bit field rotation of the left half to be counter clockwise when facing the cut, we now discover that the bit field rotation of the other half is clockwise. This is equivalent to two gears in mesh. The velocity of the bit field between them reduces the pressure on the sides (Bernoulli's Principle) and they are attracted. The same reasoning applies when we have North Pole next to North Pole, and we have like poles repelling each other.

Let us consider end effects. At the cut the bit field rotation changes from rotation around a cylinder to rotation in a plane. The rotating field will spread out from the cut and gradually grow weaker. The spreading out of this end rotation combined with the rotation around the rest of the magnet gives the appearance of poles when iron filings are sprinkled on. It will be noted that if the bar magnet is long and thin, the iron filings sprinkled on the paper above the magnet will line up parallel to the length of the bar all along its length except near the ends.

We will see how a compass needle is affected by the bit field produced by a DC electric current in a wire, so we can determine if we have assumed the correct bit field rotations in the case of the earth and the bar magnet. The compass needle aligns itself perpendicular to the wire with its north pole in the direction of advance of a right hand screw thread going in the direction of the current. From what we have learned from the bit field around a current-carrying wire, the compass needle will thus line itself up with respect to the bit field as follows: the magnetic axis of the compass needle will line up perpendicular to the direction of motion of the bit field (we will try to find out why later), and in such a position that the strength of the field is uniform (as near as is possible) on each half of the needle. Let us see why the North Pole lines up in its particular direction. The bit field of the compass needle itself is in rotation around the longitudinal axis. Let us assume this rotation is counter clockwise when facing the north pole of the compass needle. We are now looking along the longitudinal axis of the needle held above the wire whose current runs from left to right. The counter clockwise rotation around the needle combines with the motion from left to right along the wire to increase the pressure above the north pole of the needle and decrease the pressure below. This will try to push the North Pole down. But the South Pole is acting the same way - it is being pushed down. If the poles are reversed there will be a force pushing the needle up. This can be demonstrated by hanging a magnetized needle from a long string and sending a DC current through a vertical wire placed close to the needle. It will be seen that the needle can be made to stay with its south pole where its north pole should be, but that this condition is not very stable. The answer to why this is unstable lies in the spreading out of the rotation at the ends (poles) of the needle. In the lower half of Fig. 8 the bit field is pushed up. Any time the wire is below the magnet (in the diagram), and displaced any distance from the bisecting perpendicular, there will be a force pushing on the pole closer to the wire. The direction of the force will be approximately perpendicular to the "surface" of rotation of the bit field at that point (perpendicular to the "lines of force"). When the wire is below the needle (in the diagram) any slight displacement of the needle sideways will cause a force tending to increase that displacement. The pole closer to the wire will be pushed away from the wire at first, but since only the lower half of the bit field at the pole is being affected, a moment arm is introduced which starts turning the needle around. When the pole closer to the wire is pushed down enough so that the magnetic-axis-extended passes under the wire, the two sets of bit fields are going in the same direction and reducing the side pressure between pole and wire. The pole and wire are then attracted, and the needle will touch the wire (or attempt to) a little back   from   the   end   of   the

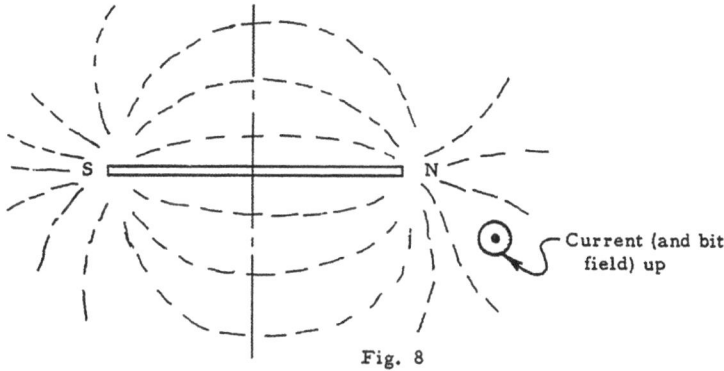

Fig. 8

293

needle. The same effect is noticed whichever pole is brought slightly closer to the wire. A very interesting demonstration can be given by suspending a magnetized needle by a thread and placing a DC current-carrying wire vertically and moving it around the needle.

Now for the earth's field. When we look down from above on the earth's magnetic north pole, the bit field should be going clockwise, since it is actually a south pole (the north pole of a magnet is attracted to it), taking for granted that we have proved sufficiently in the above paragraph that we were right in our assumption on the direction of rotation for north and south poles. A clockwise bit field means a rotation around the earth from east to west, which is satisfactory, since the earth is moving through the bit field from west to east. A compass needle will line up perpendicular to this east-west motion, which brings it north-south. As in the case with the current-carrying wire, a bit field motion from east to west (left to right) will make the north pole of the needle above the earth (wire) point north (toward the observer).

We now come to a very interesting proposition, that the strength of the bit field around a moving object is proportional to the mass and the speed of the object. In planets, their speed depends only upon their distance from the sun. Assuming the same mass, but twice the speed, the orbit radius would be one-half, and the strength of the bit field would be twice, but since the circumference of the orbit is one-half, the total magnetic effect upon another planet or comet (perturbations) would be the same at the same distance of the planets from each other. Since the bit field is moving all along the orbit, the effect on the other planet would be the same as if the mass of the planet were spread out all along the orbit, in accordance with Gauss's findings. Therefore, for planets their influence upon each other (perturbations) would be made up of gravitational attraction and magnetic effects; possibly the magnetic effects are much the stronger.

If this bit field motion is true (it is not contradicted in the case of the bit field motion along a current – carrying wire, and could be determined by seeing if a magnetic field is set up by electrons traveling in a stream in a vacuum -cathode rays - and is aided by the discovery that electrons cause magnetic fields when revolving around their nuclei – Zeeman effect), then it can be said that any time an object is set in motion in a stationary bit field, a moving bit field is set in motion in an opposite direction to the motion of the object. We can test this by the following experiment: take two 1/2" steel balls and hang each from a long string, placing them about 1" apart. Put the whole system in a vacuum. Fire a bullet between the balls. See if they are attracted more than would be called for by gravitation from the bullet.

Ordinarily objects move so slowly that the bit field motion is hard to detect. In the case of electrons and particles accelerated in atom smashers there is enough speed to overcome this trouble. We now see that not only is the bit field around the earth not being dragged along with it, but that it is actually moving somewhat in the opposite direction. The same is true of the earth's magnetism. The bit field around the earth does not remain stationary while the earth rotates in it, but rotates slowly in a direction opposite to that of the earth. Now we have our reason why the earth (and magnetized objects, too) does not slow down rotation or revolution and lose energy while it constantly creates a bit field. In a nutshell, this oppositely moving bit field is the source of inertia that keeps pushing an object once it is in motion.

Why does a compass needle line up perpendicular to the direction of motion of the bit field? First of all, let it be said that if this bit field is of constant strength, or the strength increases wherever the needle tries to move (as it would for a needle inside a hollow current-carrying tube), then the needle will not line up perpendicular to the motion of the bit field. There is still a "magnetic" field inside the metal tube, but because the needle gives no indication of lining up the statement has been made that there is no magnetic field inside a tube of this sort. When the current is first turned on, the needle as a whole will start moving (?) in the direction of the current. This can be checked by our suspended needle.

Besides having a weaker field to be able to turn to, the needle will only turn by virtue of the bit field around each pole. As the bit field is rotating around the ends, it is also spreading out and growing weaker - there is a component velocity of the field in a direction away from the ends. This can he explained in this way: the rotation around the length of the needle decreases the pressure here. The outside bit field will then move in to fill up the "vacuum". Bits are constantly moving into the needle and must move out again somewhere, namely at the poles. In a toroidal coil there are no ends for the bit field to "leak out", and when an electric current is sent through, the bit field will soon stabilize into a "smoke ring" in which each cross-section is rotating and yet has enough side pressure to keep any more bits from entering the ring. If we have our needle parallel to the wire with south-north in the position left-right (the same as the direction of current travel) then the bit field going out from the south pole is pushing against the bit field motion along the wire, increasing the density and the pressure. Also, the bit field going out from the North Pole is going along with the bit field along the wire, decreasing the pressure. The south end will be pushed up and the north end pushed down. At the same time, the resultant pressure on the ends is not in such a direction as to cause the south end to move directly up, and the north end to move directly toward the wire. Let us study the South Pole with the field from the wire coming toward it. The field moving out from the needle increases the pressure of the resultant field directly along the axis, but the bit field coming out of the end of the needle is at the same time rotating clockwise (when facing the south end). The velocity of rotation down on the right, combined with the outward velocity, decreases the resultant velocity and thus increases the pressure on the right, at the same time decreasing the velocity of rotation and outward velocity on the left, leaving less opposing velocity to increase pressure on the left. The bit field coming out of the north end of the needle is moving with the field from the wire, increasing the velocity of the resultant field along the axis of the needle and decreasing its pressure. The bit field coming out of the north end of the needle is at the same time rotating counterclockwise (when facing the north end). The combined outward and rotational velocities increase the velocity on the left (decreasing the pressure), and leave less of the bit field remaining coming up on the right to decrease the pressure as much on the right. Thus on the south pole the force is to the left, and on the north pole the pressure is to the left, resulting in a torque that turns the needle perpendicular to the wire.

A CERTAIN Ms. BALL

by

Walter J. Kastner

Based on the first act of the novel "A Certain Ms. Ball"
by Walter J. Kastner
(revised screenplay)

The movie you are about to see (and the next three, based upon the book) just *might* be true. The actors may be unknown or may be box office draws - it is unimportant. The star of the series is a diminutive object, a hardly visible, naturally formed creature with many abilities. The actors are here to allow her to tell her story, and they can better put their heart and soul into their craft by letting her be the star – they are her midwives and nurses, shepherds and companions, friends ... and enemies.

There is a fine line between heroic/majestic/vibrant/bittersweet/uplifting/sublime emotions, and ridiculous camp. A good actor and a good director will know on which side to tread.

John Williams is ideal for the musical score, Steven Spielburg for the director, although he could easily destroy it by pumping in too much money and special effects. We can all dream. Check Salli Richardson to play the role of Shahrazad. Perhaps Barbra Streisand for Halima?

Before you revise the screenplay, be advised to read the book. Otherwise, you may have lost the next three feature full-length movies.

FADE IN:

EXT – PALACE – LATE AFTERNOON

View source (camera) pans the whole palace one view at a time as credits start rolling. Then view source comes up the steps at a walking pace toward the TWO GUARDS, one at each side of the impressive doors.

Guards bow and gesture for view source to enter as they open the doors. View source moves inside.

INT – PALACE

No people are seen about. View source walks down a long hall; as view sweeps around, some evidence is seen of a hand, the sleeve of a robe, a robe skirt and sandal, as well as the paintings on the walls of the former Sultans, the parquet tile floor, the intricate design of the high vaulted ceiling, the alcoves leading off from the hall.

The credits finish as view source turns off into one of the alcoves. The view source reaches an elaborately carved wooden door. The hand, upon which is a large signet ring, reaches out from the sleeve and knocks twice, quietly. The door opens slowly on its leather hinges.

INT – SULTAN'S CHAMBERS, RIYADH, ARABIA, CIRCA 590 A.D.

The room is darkly lit by oil lamps. The SULTAN OMÉN, an eighty seven year old man, lies in his bed at the end of the room, facing the door, his head propped up with pillows. He is dying. Twenty or so RELATIVES and official PERSONNEL stand respectfully around him and listen to his last words. A SOB or a CRY emerges now and then from the people. The Sultan's voice is relatively strong – he will speak, if haltingly, for the next two hours. Omén lifts his eyes as the view source enters the room. Several people turn their heads and give a faint bow to the view source.

SULTAN OMÉN
You are clear now on how the dynasty is to continue. Only one more command – bury my treasure with me when I die....

He motions with a nod of his head toward the small chest sitting at the foot of his bed on an ottoman, the chest's lid open, the contents not in view.

SULTAN OMÉN (Cont.)
Please…humor this old shepherd and bury my treasure with me when I die…

As the view source moves in and over the chest, the contents come into view, many old letters and a small well-worn sheepskin bag resting on top. Omén continues talking, haltingly.

SULTAN OMÉN (Cont.)
You know my story. Humor this old shepherd Omén and listen to it one last time. I have kept my vow...I *will* be with her...always.

CUT TO:
EXT – SOUTHEASTERN ARABIAN SHORE – MORNING

It is early morning sometime before sunrise. The sky is dark and cloudy. Lightning and thunder from over the water to the east and over the scrub greases and beach to the north. On a hillock are FIVE SHEPHERDS, their tent and a flickering campfire nearby. A flock of about 300 sheep are in the distance in the sparse meadowlands above.

Two shepherds are near the tent watching the display, the boss ABDUL and the sixteen year old youth OMÉN. The sky overhead clears and becomes brighter from starlight – there is no moon since it is only a few days after new moon.

A dateline marches across center screen right to left and disappears – 3:25 AM April 6. When the line disappears, the hour/minute/second time display starts in the lower left-hand corner.

The other three shepherds meander up, having checked on the flock. The boss speaks.

ABDUL
(to the three)
Are the sheep still restless?

JUMAIL [little camel]
We quieted them. They will not stray.

OMÉN
(pointing over the water)
Have you seen such a wonder? And no rain all this time? The sand is still dry.

BAHLUL [fool]
Listen to him! Why don't you make yourself useful, O great and noble Omén, and bring us some badly needed water? Bahlul laughs coarsely, without a smile on his lips.

ABDUL
Bahlul, be quiet.

BAHLUL

Well, he keeps saying he wants to return to Kuwait, like as if a flying horse had brought him here from that distant world when he was a baby. We all know he is from nearby. If he wants to go, let him go. Why does he hang around us?

ABDUL

BAHLUL...SHUT UP!!

All five stop and look at the heavenly display. The time display goes into slow motion at 3:26:40 AM and stops at 3:26:43AM. A faint bluish-white discharge suddenly comes from the ground up to about thirty feet at a distance from them of only twenty feet toward the beach.

A faint stepped leader comes from the top of the screen down quickly to meet the ground discharge. A brilliant light about five inches in diameter starts at the ground and quickly moves up along the faint line, until soon the screen is split by a brilliant lightning stroke.

At that time a bluish discharge like a ground fog suddenly appears around the stroke at the ground for several yards around. The stroke disappears then reappears somewhat diminished four more times (50 thousandths of a second apart in real time, about ¼ second apart in the slow motion) and the five sharp cracks of the initial thunder are heard starting some time after the second stroke.

Then a ball of fire, golden butter in color and basketball size, appears several feet off of the ground near where the last stroke has just disappeared and moves toward the shepherds at about 10 feet per second in the slow motion. The bluish ground discharge disappears about the same time the ball lightning appears.

The time display switches to 3:26:44 AM. The shepherds now react to the lightning. Their eyes blink and their mouths open. They see the ball of fire approaching but are rooted to the spot. The ball of fire sweeps past each with a crackle and disappears with a violent pop. It is now 3:26:45 AM.

As the ball approaches, the thunder starts with an ominous loud, low frequency rumble. The shepherds slowly fall back-wards as if to escape the fire and they drop as if their legs were turned to rubber. 3:26:46 AM. They have fallen and the thunder and the time display return to real time.

The thunder is a real earth shaker/boomer and lasts for twenty seconds. Then five seconds of complete silence and the time display goes to fast forward as the sky lightens; the time display fades out at 4:34:21 AM, ending in real time. [Ref: All About Lightning, by Martin A. Uman, Dover 1986]

The shepherds stir and moan and move as if they all had the rheumatism – they ache all over. DJUHA opens his eyes and rubs them. Then he reaches over and shakes Jumail next to him, who opens his eyes and looks at Djuha for a long second.

DJUHA [trickster] & JUMAIL
Praise be to Allah – we see!

DJUHA
Abdul! Bahlul! Wake up!

Djuha gets up and shakes Abdul and Bahlul, who get up and look around.

ABDUL
Omén, wake up! ... All of you, hurry and break camp! We must gather the flock and be out of here to the next watering hole before high noon, else we perish. It is a bad sign. Never have I seen such a night.

The shepherds get their bedrolls and supplies out of the tent, then go to round up the sheep. They are working slowly, like old men: they are still stiff and sore from the lightning, and from sleeping on the cold ground. It is Omén's job to take down the tent, which he rolls up sloppily, the poles and stakes not carefully snugged. Then he "runs" and gets the old ram, used as a beast of burden, and manhandles the tent onto the swaybacked beast and ties it on.

He looks down toward the beach where the lightning bolt hit. The brightening sky casts a sheen on the sand for yards around the hit. He walks carefully around the strike zone toward the water, looking at the shiny area all the time, finally walks back, facing Mecca to the west. He drops to his knees and offers prayers of thanksgiving that he and the others were spared.

When he opens his eyes he looks toward the center of the sheen where there is a thicker, shinier crust. Immediately the sun peeks above the horizon and streams upon the scene, and a rainbow of colors greets his eyes as he starts to get up. He drops back to his knees and looks closer, carefully walking on his hands and knees, lower and lower to keep one or another of the colors in view.

He comes to the center of the strike, where there is a palm sized shell-shaped shiny crust. But the rainbow is not coming from that. It is coming from a tiny (2 millimeter diameter) crystal-clear ball attached near the edge of the crust, close to a tunnel-shaped structure (fulgurite, or lightning stone) firmly attached to the "shell".

He brings his eye right up to the tiny ball to examine it more closely. Behind the ball is a loose sand grain, but with the high magnification (230 power for 2 millimeter diameter quartz) the sand grain looks like a boulder.

OMÉN
Praise be to Allah! I will keep this ball of crystal!

Omén lifts the palm-sized crust out of the loose sand and searches around for something to put it in. His hand falls on his little sheepskin lunchbox tied at his waist.

He gently places the crust back in the sand, unties his lunch bag from his waist rope, upends the bag and crams his mouth with the figs and dates for his breakfast, turns the bag inside out so the wool is on the inside, slides his find into the soft wool, ties the bag back on his waist rope.

The others by this time have rounded up the sheep and are moving out.

ABDUL
Hurry, Omén. You will never get to Kuwait if you dawdle.

OMÉN
(his mouth still full)
Look, look what I found!

Omén runs up to them.

BAHLUL
What nonsense are you up to now?

JUMAIL
Come, Omén from Oman. A dreamer you are, and a dreamer you will always be.

BAHLUL
(in derision)
Sultan Omén!

Jumail and Djuha bow. The three laugh heartily, Bahlul still without a smile even though he laughs. But they all look, even Abdul, when he shows them his treasure.

SULTAN OMÉN VO.
Fairer than Venus who sprang fully clothed from Jupiter's brow; More perfect than the full Moon; Alive with knowledge and wisdom of things past and things yet to come; Stay with me always, my Crystal Ball. Allah be praised!

As they slowly walk north with the sheep, a new dateline comes across center screen right to left in huge letters: "523 AD .... " to the accompaniment of heroic music and a final crash of cymbals, which sounds fade out as the dateline disappears at the left. (For foreign Muslim distribution, 523 AD is about 97 "B.I." – Before Islam, which starts 620 AD.)

EXT - SHORE - DAY

It is several days later. Omén sits on a hillside overlooking about 20 sheep entrusted to him. His back is resting against a rock. He has the "stone" in his hands and day-dreams.

EXT – VISION – DAY – SILENT

Omén, sword in hand, slays ENEMIES right and left, while a SULTAN, tied to a stake, looks on. Within several seconds, Omén has dispatched all the outlaws. He proudly goes up to the Sultan and cuts his ropes with one fell swoop. The Sultan, tears in his eyes, embraces Omén. 10 seconds.

INT – VISION – SILENT

Omén, sword in hand, slays swarthy HOODS right and left, while a PRINCESS, on her knees at the center of the hoods and her hands together as in prayer, looks up to him pleadingly. Within several seconds, Omén has dispatched all the hoods. He gallantly goes up to the Princess, scoops her up with his free arm and kisses her passionately, while she swoons with her arms around his neck. 10 seconds.

EXT – VISION – DAY – SILENT

Omén directs the THREE FOREMEN of large construction crews on the building of a half-finished palace. The foremen nod in turn, look at him with awe, and shout the orders. The crews nod and signal in turn and get busy with a vengeance – no one dares slack off – not with OMÉN in charge! 10 seconds.

INT – VISION – OMÉN'S HOME – SOUND

His MOTHER is hard at work. She looks at Omén with loving eyes. His TWO younger BROTHERS play a children's game together. His little SISTER jumps on his back, SQUEALS with delight and SHOUTS.

SISTER
Omén, skinny bony! Omén, skinny bony! Hee hee hee....ha ha ha ha

As he tickles her and shakes her off. Then the face of his FATHER comes into view.

FATHER
Omén, stop daydreaming. You are a fool if you believe all that nonsense. You will never exceed your station in life. Apply your energy to your responsibilities – you will like your life better. Dreams are for girls who have nothing better to do. Ah, Omén, what am I to do with you?

The scene suddenly appears washed with tears. At the left lower corner the anomalous face of Abdul intrudes,' and his Father's face disappears from the screen. The anomalous face gets larger while the rest of the screen remains black.

EXT – SHORE – DAY

Abdul comes up on the daydreaming Omén and gently shakes him by the shoulder.

ABDUL
Ah, Omén, why must you dream so much?

Omén jumps up and looks around as if unsure of where he is. He puts the stone in his bag and rubs his eyes as if struggling to get Abdul in focus. The teartracks still stain his dusty cheeks below where he rubs.

OMÉN
I only....

Omén looks toward his small flock, embarrassed at being caught daydreaming, and possibly being caught crying like a girl.

OMÉN (Cont.)
Praise be to Allah, the sheep have not been harmed.

ABDUL
Praise be to Allah, indeed. Omén, you must pay more attention to your duties. The sheep are fine ... this time. Be glad it was I who caught you napping.

Omén smiles sheepishly. Abdul turns and starts back to the encampment

OMÉN
It won't happen again!

ABDUL
See that it doesn't, my young dreamer. You best see that none have strayed.

Abdul waves his walking stick (staff, crook) and continues down the path out of the scene.

Omén stares after Abdul for a moment, then counts the sheep below on his fingers, as Abdul had shown him. He gets to ten, then starts over and gets to eight. He looks down at his hand and sees that he still has two fingers in his palm.

SULTAN OMÉN V.O.
Abdul knew that some had strayed.

Omén picks up his staff and sets out on the search.

OMÉN
A dreamer, indeed! I'll show you. I'll show all of you. By Allah, I will be rich when I get to Kuwait!

EXT – CAMPSITE – EVENING

Hi shot. The five sit around the campfire, finished with the evening meal. It is twilight. Jumail, Bahlul and Djuha talk and laugh among themselves. Snatches of conversation are heard between laughs … "Jamila … favorite … doe eyes … how many times? … long sturdy legs … warm … fresh milk … tomorrow … Hamda …"

Abdul and Omén are silent. Abdul gets up and signals Omén to follow. They go some yards away on the other side of the tent, out of earshot of the others, and sit facing the almost full moon just above the horizon.

ABDUL
Omén, you have been with us now as many days as the number of sheep in your charge, and yet you don't seem to be getting the hang of it. You keep saying you want to be a shepherd, but your heart isn't in it. All you do is play with that stone …

I took you on to pay back a debt to the one who took me on when I decided to leave home and make my mark in the world, much as you. My father was a shepherd much of his life, and I vowed never to become like him. I left for the city life in Muscat and became a rope maker, married happily and had a family. My children grew and prospered.

My wife died. Rope making held no more joy for me. I returned to the life of a shepherd and am content. Perhaps that is what my father learned.

What is it that makes you want to leave home? You are old enough, surely. But Kuwait? So far away? So far the camel caravan takes a month? Do you hate your father so much?

Have you perhaps … forgive me for thinking such … perhaps by accident … killed someone?

Someone died by your hand and you must leave your family?

Silence. Close-up on Omén shows him agonizing. His lips move, but no sound. Tears well up in his eyes. Then …

OMÉN
My father calls me a dreamer, even as you do. I do not wish to follow in his footsteps, even as you did with your father … but I do not hate my father … and I am not running away.

ABDUL
But why Kuwait? What is there in Kuwait that you cannot have here? You have no money to join a caravan. You cannot walk there alone. The first village you come to would turn you out as a thief or vagabond.

As a shepherd it is possible. Sell the wool; drink the milk. Sell some sheep after the freshening; if worst comes to worst you can cook one of the old rams and last for weeks ... you would not starve.

But even so it would take years ... you would be a man when you got to Kuwait, that is sure. But you will have to learn well.

Tell me ... why should I teach you? Why must you go to Kuwait? Give me an answer that will sustain me.

You have much to learn, and little time.

We turn back to Muscat before another month is out.

OMÉN
I must go to Kuwait. My God has told me ... many times ... my destiny is in Kuwait. He told me that I must leave family and friends now and join a band of shepherds going north toward Kuwait.

I do not want to. I must...I must go to Kuwait and meet my destiny. I must go. Help me ....

ABDUL
My son ... I will help you.

EXT – DAY (OVER A PERIOD OF SEVERAL WEEKS)

Various scenes in quick succession as Abdul teaches; sometimes Omén follows his example: how to shear sheep, how to milk, how to make pouches and bags for food and water, how to skin a sheep and tan the hide, how to castrate the undesirable rams to improve the flock, what plants are poisonous or undesirable. how to heal a sheep's wounds, how to scare off wild predators, how to barter and bargain with the villagers, how to build a fire and cook the sheep's flesh to have it keep for a long time, how to help the lamb come out at lambing time, how to get the proper ram to mate with the proper ewe, how to make and repair clothing from sheepskins, signs to look for and medicinal plants to use when sheep get sick, etc., etc.

ABDUL
Indeed you are an apt pupil. You now know everything I can teach you. And it is not yet new moon. It is time I gave Bahlul his old job back.

EXT – EARLY NEXT MORNING

They are breaking camp. Omén is gathering the tent poles to pack with the tent. Bahlul approaches.

BAHLUL
Ho, Omén! It looks like you will never get the hang of it. Abdul thinks it is time for me to take over my old job.

Bahlul takes the tent poles from Omén, expertly bundles them up with the tent, and with one easy swing with some leverage from his knee, throws the heavy bundle exactly onto the back of the old ram; the animal visibly sags and MOANS as the weight settles. Bahlul smiles, and Omén sees the smile on Bahlul's turned-away face as Bahlul ties the bundle on.

SULTAN OMÉN VO.
I was getting very hungry for meat, and it looked like the time for butchering the old ram was drawing near. I had never seen Bahlul really smile until then.

EXT – DAY – VARIOUS SCENES

Bahlul has his arm around Omén's shoulder, and shows him how to count higher than twenty sheep.

BAHLUL
Suppose you have more than twenty sheep in your charge. You count the first ten the usual way, then pick up a stone and put it in your pocket. Then you count another ten the usual way and put another stone in your pocket. And so on. Each time you count the sheep after that you switch a stone to your other pocket for every ten sheep. You should be able to remember your fingers for odd lots. Now you try it on my flock.

Jumail answers one of Omén's questions. Omén points in several directions, then makes a sweeping gesture.

OMÉN
But suppose I can't find any firewood. Neither there, nor there, nor anywhere. Then don't we do without a campfire, without a meal?

JUMAIL
(smiles)
No, Omén, we still cook. When firewood is scarce sometimes it is necessary to pick up the sheep droppings and spread them on rocks to dry during the day.

When late afternoon comes, you collect the dried dung and we have enough fuel for a great meal. But when it rains, well, yes, we don't cook then unless it is a light rain and we set up a skin over the fire to tan.

Hi shot. Djuha comes upon Omén who sweats and strains trying to get a sheep's foot free from between rocks. Omén looks up and questions Djuha. From the distance we can't hear what he says.

Close-up. Djuha stoops down and deftly frees the foot.

DJUHA
No, it is not all work, Omén. Some times we will stop at a village to sell and buy ... And sometimes the village has some pretty girls ... does that interest you?

EXT – EVENING

All five around the campfire. The others eat and talk; Omén has his stone in his hands, holding Crystal up to the fire to warm her so she will not be cold through the night. He puts the stone to his cheek to check its temperature. Then he holds the stone to the fire again.

OMÉN
(whispering)
Are you warm enough to last the night, my love?

JUMAIL
Omén, some day you will take that stone and bathe it in a stream before you bathe yourself.

Bahlul and Djuha laugh, and Omén joins in with them.

OMÉN
A good one, Jumail. I just might do that. Do you happen to have a good cold stream in your pocket?

Jumail and Djuha laugh. Bahlul raises his eyebrows and smiles.

EXT – AFTERNOON

Omén tends his sheep, the stone in his hands. He looks at it intently, more like looking through it as if in a trance. There is a village in the distance. The others come up to him and he puts the stone in his pouch.

ABDUL
(pedagogically)
Omén, we will be going into yon village for some supplies. I will be back shortly. The others will be staying all night. This is their favorite village. They must have their pleasure. You have a great responsibility with the whole flock. I am counting on you.

Omén nods. The others walk away toward the village. Omén jogs the other way in a wide sweep to check on strays and to consolidate the whole flock.

EXT – MORNING

Omén is in the village and gets some supplies.

OMÉN
(muttering)
After sunup and they just now returned. Wonder what they do all night that is so much fun.

He leaves the village. At the outskirts he sees a stray dog, a WOLFHOUND. There is a WOMAN nearby. She half tries to shoo the dog away, but she does it with an air of resignation, as if still attached to it. The dog sits in the dirt, its eyes are sad and its head hangs. It cringes every time the woman shoos it.

OMÉN (Cont.)
That's a fine looking animal you have there, Ma'am.

WOMAN
'Tis just a cur, part wolfhound. The bitch died giving the litter, and this one is still here. The master ....

Here she looks like she is about to cry. The master is no doubt her late husband.

WOMAN (Cont.)
... my husband has departed and we will no longer keep it. Would you care to take the dog?

OMÉN
I ... oh ... what's its name?

WOMAN
We call it "Dog". It comes and goes. It was nursed by a black sheep, as the litter came in the Spring – it seems to like sheep.

The dog eyes its mistress warily from its resting-place on the ground.

OMÉN
Here, Wolf

The dog's eyes brighten. It rises, and its tail wags. It walks up to Omén and stands quietly by his side, the tail still wagging.

WOMAN
It looks like he is yours, young man. Good luck to both of you.

OMÉN
He can keep me company on my trip to Kuwait.

WOMAN
(surprised and upset)
Kuwait, you say! That is a far piece. The dog will never make it. He is already four years old.

EXT – AFTERNOON

As Omén makes his rounds, the dog runs after him, and also after the sheep, yaps and nips at their legs to keep them from straying. Jumail sees Omén and the dog and shouts.

JUMAIL
Hey, Omén, you are soft in the heart, as well as a dreamer.

Omén grins and waves at Jumail.

SULTAN OMÉN V.O.
Jumail spoke the truth. But I was to have a companion on those long lonely nights as I made my way to Kuwait.

EXT - HIGH NOON

Hi shot. There is an oasis on the left, the main flock in the lower part of the screen with the other shepherds. Omén, Wolf and six sheep are in the upper part of the screen to the north. It looks very hot and dry north toward the horizon. This is the parting of the ways. Abdul and the others will turn back south; Omén will continue north. Abdul picks out sheep as wages, but mostly as a gift – enough for Omén to make it to Kuwait. He picks out the final four-year-old sheep, and then considerable study to pick out the proper ram for breeding. There are a total of eight: one young lamb, three two year old ewes ready for breeding, three older females who have been through it before and can help the young ones lamb; and the ram.

Bahlul and Abdul lead the two sheep up to Omén's small flock of six. Bahlul whispers in Abdul's ear. Abdul shakes his head.

ABDUL
Why? He already has much more than he earned. He has a young one, three ready for breeding, three teachers and the ram. I just feel he would never reach Kuwait with less.

Bahlul whispers again. Abdul thinks for a while, then nods. Bahlul runs back, picks out the old decrepit ram, and leads it up to Omén's small flock. The ram has no tent on his back.

ABDUL
Well, Omén, this is it. I wish you much luck. The ram .... well, he is too old to carry the tent. Goodbye, my son. May Allah be with you.

Bahlul goes up to Omén, extends his hand, and they clasp hands. Then all except Omén turn south and begin their march home. They look back and wave. Omén waves to them, tears trickle down his cheeks. Then he slowly turns and walks north. Wolf jumps around excitedly and gets the sheep moving.

EXT – DAY

Almost four years have passed. (This is a good time to change actors.) Omén looks visibly older and more mature, with a slight beard. His clothes are torn, he has cuts and bruises, he looks hot and dry. The flock has grown to thirty. The old ram is gone. Wolf walks with a limp. Omén sits down and upends his water bag - just a few drops dribble out into his mouth. Then he keels over.

The scene shifts up to the blazing afternoon sun. Then it shifts back – close-up of Omén's face, his eyes closed, his mouth open in a SCREAM, but the scream comes from O.S., high and desperate – woman's scream. The scene transfers to the hallucination or delirium mode: the color balance shifts cooler.

When Omén appears again, he sits where he was before, but he and his clothes are fresh and clean - a robe and sandals, and a scimitar at his side. Wolf and the sheep are nowhere to be seen. Omén springs to his feet as the scream comes again. This time the cry is longer and mixed with the frantic neighing of a horse.

Without hesitation Omén runs up a sandy ridge toward the sound and draws his scimitar from its scabbard as he goes. He tops the hill and sees darting shadows behind a huge rock outcropping. He lopes down the hill to the near side of the rock and flattens himself against the stone, then carefully edges around the corner.

312

He sees a young, firm breasted, full bottomed, dark skinned beautiful LADY (houri) on a milk-white MARE. She struggles with THREE swarthy MEN. Two hold the mare's bridle, the third tries to drag the lady from the saddle.

Omén bursts into their view with a loud cry. Everyone, including the panicked mare, stops and stares at Omén with looks of utter terror. A shadow comes up behind Omén, there is the thunder of hooves, the rumble and rush of a plunging body. It is a BLACK STALLION with fiery red eyes.

The stallion gallops to the nearer man holding the mare's bridle, opens his mouth, and chomps down on the man's neck. The CRUNCH of bone, and the SPURT of blood. The mare rears free and the lady delivers a killing blow to the other man holding the bridle, using her small dagger. The third man throws down his sword and tries to escape into the rock formation. Omén rushes and tackles him.

The stallion leaves his victim crumpled on the sand and goes after the tackled man, rears above him, and comes down with a sickening CRUNCH. Then the stallion turns toward Omén, his next victim, but stops as though bewitched.

The lady on the mare murmurs to the stallion and holds out a shining stone. The crystal on the stone flickers in the sunlight. Omén gets up and strides toward the lady, not heeding the snorts and stamps of the stallion. The lady holds the stone in front of her.

LADY
Stay!

OMÉN
I threaten you not. I wished to offer aid, but he [nods toward stallion] came before me .... That crystal ... where did you get it?

LADY
That is no concern of yours. I'll ask the questions now. You say you came to rescue me - from where and to where, traveler?

OMÉN
I am on my way to Kuwait from the South. Bandits attacked me and took my crystal, the crystal that could be the sister of yours, my lady.

The lady sits on her prancing mare for a time and considers his words. At last she turns her eyes to the west.

LADY
The sun moves lower. We must retire to my stronghold to find out more about each other. Come.

She wheels her mare westward toward the sinking sun.

OMÉN
Wait! Can your mare ride both of us?

LADY
Never! Oh .. .I had forgotten you were afoot. Ride the Black!

OMÉN
The stallion?

Omén reels at the idea. The lady smiles at his discomfiture and waves vaguely at the snorting stallion. The stallion walks up to Omén and stands calmly waiting.

Omén gingerly swings himself aboard the gleaming Black and rides after the lady on the mare. They ride at an easy canter. Soon they come to an oasis that seems to spring up from out of nowhere.

A golden tent is set up under some trees. A small herd of FIFTEEN MARES and COLTS stand in the shade behind the tent. Like the mare and the stallion, they are the most magnificent horses Omén had ever seen.

OMÉN
(wide-eyed)
Beautiful!

The tent flap opens and out come TWO beautiful WOMÉN, raven haired and dark like the lady on the mare. Omén turns his head and looks at them with his wide-eyed stare.

OMÉN
Beautiful!

The lady slides off her mare and unsaddles it. Omén speaks to her as he follows suit.

OMÉN (Cont.)
Your father must be a great lord to have this wealth in horses.

LADY
Our father has been dead these fifteen years. Allow us to introduce ourselves. This is MARl, and this is SIAN.

I am NEVA. We will welcome you to our hospitality tonight and discuss this matter of crystals.

314

INT – TENT – EVENING

The tent is luxuriously furnished. The remains of a sumptuous dinner are in evidence. All four have goblets of white wine. Omén finishes off his (for the nth time) and his face indicates that he appreciates its strange, heavenly flavor. Neva refills his goblet.

They sit in a circle upon thick silk pillows and stare at the crystal on the low table in front of them. Mari smiles at Omén, takes an identical stone from her robe and places it on the table with the other. Omén looks from the one to the other. Which is his?

Then Sian smiles at Omén, takes an identical stone from her robe and places it on the table with the others. Omén cannot believe it. He cannot take his eyes off the glittering gems. Finally he asks in an awed voice:

OMÉN
Are there others?

Neva smiles and produces from her robe yet another crystal like the others, but it has a golden glow when she puts it in front of Omén. Omén gasps and reaches for it, but Neva stills his hand. She looks him straight in the eye.

NEVA
I believe you to be an honorable man, and honest. If we return this treasure, which we believe to be yours, will you promise to tell no one of us or our crystals or to ever seek us again?

We owe you a debt for helping to save me from those scoundrels this afternoon. There is a black colt of the stallion you rode today. Upon your vow of secrecy, the crystal is yours again ... as is the colt.

Omén stares at Neva, at her lovely face and figure, then at Mari and Sian in turn. He sadly nods his head.

OMÉN
I will take my crystal and do as you say, my lady.

Neva gives him more wine, Sian places his crystal in his hand, and Mari plays a golden harp. Omén's eyes grow heavy and the scene fades.

SULTAN OMÉN V.O.
I *do* wish I could have kept the colt.

EXT – EARLY – MORNING

Omén is back in his rags and filth: he lies where we saw him before the hallucination. A VILLAGER approaches, pulled along by Wolf. The villager takes in the situation, gives Omén a drink of water before he passes out again, gives Wolf a drink, sets the water bag nearby, then goes to get help. The villager jogs over the sand and scrub toward the village, some five miles distant.

INT – DHAHRAN MERCHANT'S HOUSE – DAY

Omén lies in a bed. His clothes are off – a covering over his loins. A young WOMAN about 28 years old bathes his wounds and tends him.

He is unconscious, but moves about occasionally in spasms, and he mumbles. The woman is quite plain looking, but certainly not ugly. She is plainly in love with Omén. Her name is HALIMA.

HALIMA
Hush, my love. Carefully I wash you. Tenderly I touch you. Fondly I kiss your wounds. Gently I anoint them and bind them up. Hush, my love, and sleep.

EXT – DHAHRAN HARBOR FRONT – DAY

Omén strolls the waterfront with Wolf. They watch the ships (dhows) come and go. He sits down facing the ocean and puts Crystal in his hands to let her enjoy the salt air. Halima walks by.

HALIMA
Salutations and greetings, Omén. You look well today. I understand you have hired two of our young men to watch the sheep for you.

OMÉN
Hello, Halima. I usually never see you but at your father's house. Not hired, really. They are anxious to see Kuwait for the adventure .... I really should be moving on - I am imposing on you and your father.

HALIMA
Stay. Stay. There is no hurry. You have been here but a few months. Is this Dhahran not a fine country?

Then she lowers her eyes and speaks quietly.

HALIMA (Cont.)
Is this Halima not a fine woman?

OMÉN
(blushes)

316

Indeed, you are a fine woman. I would like to stay, really ... but I must see Kuwait, and it is far from here.

HALIMA
(hopefully)
Have you wondered about the ships? They are made in Kuwait. My father the merchant could arrange for your passage to Kuwait and you could be there and back in two months.

I would miss you mightily while you are gone. The wedding feast would be ready when you return.

OMÉN
I will ask my Crystal about this.

EXT – DHAHRAN STREET – DAY

Omén walks along. The SHOPKEEPERS and FELLAHEEN greet him. Some ask him to share their meal or invite him to their house of an evening. He sees young GIRLS staring at him, WHISPERING and GIGGLING among themselves.

A shopkeeper's WIFE looks at his back longingly as he walks down the street. The SHOPKEEPER comes out and has some sharp words with her. She goes back inside.

Omén is now twenty years old, tall with sturdy shoulders, and he walks with the grace of a dancer. His long dark hair is bound with a leather thong. Indeed, Halima is not the only one interested.

INT – MERCHANT'S HOUSE – NIGHT

Omén returns after an evening with a friend. The door opens.

OMÉN O.S.
'Bye now. Really enjoyed the visit.

Omén comes into the main room and is surprised to see all the people there, then he shrugs his shoulders. He has been expecting this for some time. The village ELDERS are seated in a "U" around the main room, all eager to hear his story. Many OTHERS are there also. Halima and her father the MERCHANT are sitting together in their places as hosts.

OMÉN
You have all been so kind. There is no way I can repay your hospitality and your care with my animals these past three months. You already know about the bandits, and now you want to know my story of the desert. I had been ashamed to tell anyone, but

now that I am about to leave, I would be more ashamed if I don't tell it.

All eyes are eager. Heads nod. Wine is poured. Snacks are set out. Comfortable chairs are brought. CHILDREN are hushed.

OMÉN (Cont.)
It has been almost four years since I attached myself to a band of shepherds far to the south. They taught me all I know. I...I must go to Kuwait. My ... destiny is there. My... my God has said so.

Omén looks around to see what the elders think about this. They see nothing strange, but nod sympathetically, drink their wine, eat their snacks – a commercial break before the main event.

OMÉN (Cont.)
We were several months out, and they had to turn back to Muscat.. ..

Here there is a MURMUR rising from the crowd. Muscat! Indeed, the young man is telling the truth. A far away place, Muscat. A shepherd could easily take four years to get here ... but why the desert? ... Perhaps he will tell now ....

OMÉN (Cont.)
They gave me nine sheep, a gift from their leader ... Abdul...

Here Omén stops, thinking about Abdul, and how he would have wanted him for a father.

OMÉN (Cont.)
He was like a father to me. Before we parted, I took on an unwanted wolfhound, the immediate source of my deliverance here ...

MURMURS from the crowd: fine animal ... amazing ... noble animal ... loyal

OMÉN (Cont.)
We started out along the village route near the coastline. After three years I was despairing of ever getting to my destination.

I had heard of other, faster routes farther inland, but fraught with dry wells and bandits. I finally decided to go, near Salwa. There were villages, and water.

But after Abqaiq the water ran low ... it was late summer and the sun was high.

I turned eastward - the land seemed somewhat greener there. I was very low on water, the sheep were dry and giving no milk.

If my eyes had not been clouded, I would have seen your village. The bandits overtook me two days before you found me, near death ... I can never repay your hospitality.

The crowd smiles demurely, and waits patiently.

OMÉN (Cont.)
Shortly after I joined the shepherds, there was a sign in the evening sky: the messenger was approaching the horns of the new moon.

CROWD
Ah!

OMÉN
Three days after, there was a terrible thunderstorm late at night, but no rain. We were watching the display.

A great lightning bolt was cast not ten paces in front of us, and a strange ball of fire swept 'round us and exploded. The thunder over-powered us and we fell unconscious...

Murmurs from the crowd.

OMÉN (Cont.)
The next morning we found ourselves alive, praise be to Allah and all the gods. After our duties, I went to check where the bolt had hit – there was a strange sheen on the sand around.

I found the object you are all wondering about, and have vowed upon my eyes never to part with it. It is from my God, to help me on my way.

The crowd murmurs excitedly, and Omén takes the stone from his pouch. The elders get up and stand close together around Omén to get a better view as he explains and points, and the scene fades.

EXT – MORNING

Omén, Wolf, the thirty sheep plus two new lambs, the two young shepherds, FARIS and HUSAM, and Halima and the merchant are at the outskirts of the village. Omén holds Halima's hands. Halima is very sad. Omén pulls her close and kisses her on the cheek. Then everyone leaves except Halima and her father the merchant. The shepherds call out.

FARIS
'Bye, Halima. See you in a few years.

HUSAM
Take good care of your father.

Close-up of Halima and Merchant.

HALIMA
Omén will never return.

Halima starts to cry.

MERCHANT
Halima … now, now … was it not a sweet interlude to remember forever?

They turn away toward the village, and the merchant takes his daughter's hand. Halima from the back is very enticing - there has not been this view of her up to now. Any young man from the village would give his eye teeth for a rich man's daughter who can expertly nurse him and mother him when he is sick, who can cook up a storm and keep house, especially one as beautiful as this. A YOUNG MAN, about Omén's age, comes onto the screen from the side.

YOUNG MAN
Halima, may I walk you home?

Halima nods, takes the young man's hand and gradually disengages her other hand from her father's. Then she moves close to the young man and slowly places her head against his shoulder as the three walk into the village.

EXT – CAMPSITE – EVENING

Silence. Omén sits by the campfire with Wolf. The dog looks old; he sleeps. The helpers Faris and Husam are off with the sheep. Omén takes Crystal from her warm woolen bed, holds her before the flickering fire, and watches the reflection from the flame sparkle on her surface. He shakes his head from side to side.

OMÉN
Sometimes, my lovely gem, I think I must be mad. I talk to you, tell you my dreams and problems as if you can help me.

He turns his head about, looking to make sure the shepherds are not near, then turns back to the fire.

OMÉN (Cont.)
Faris and Husam will be out all night with the sheep. That night the bandits came … my first thought was to hide you in the sand…I placed your safety above my own…I

could not bear the thought of being separated from you. I do not understand this bond between us ... by the Gods, I do not understand.

He sits in silence for several seconds and watches the flames.

OMÉN (Cont.)
Ah, Crystal, I know you speak. I heard you urge me on when my strength failed. I do not want to believe the voice I heard was a hallucination from delirium, as were the beautiful sisters who returned the stone to me.

Please tell me you spoke to me, Crystal Ball! [Now whispering] Why won't you speak to me, my beauty? Must we be in danger before you will speak again?

Silence. Finally, in defeat, Omén sadly and dejectedly starts to put Crystal back in the pouch. Suddenly there is a heavenly sweet SOUND (possibly a high rising sweep from the celesta or harp) and CRYSTAL speaks. Her voice is that of a mature woman, self-assured, well satisfied with herself.

CRYSTAL
(quiet voice)
No, my friend, we do not have to be in danger again before I will speak.

Omén is startled. He almost drops Crystal from his shaking hands. Tears well up in his eyes.

CRYSTAL (Cont.)
Yes, Omén, I *can* speak. But you were not ready to listen until the desert ordeal...And since then I have been more concerned with your regaining your strength.

OMÉN
But how is it you can talk?

CRYSTAL
(cooing)
That need not concern you for now, love. We have a whole lifetime before us to learn of my secrets.

Now get some sleep ... We have a long day ahead of us tomorrow ... And within the year you will meet your destiny ....

EXT – CAMPSITE – NEXT MORNING

Wolf is up and about. He is really showing his age, and he walks stiffly. Omén wakes, then shows wonderment in his face, and he feels the pouch where Crystal is. He busies himself: rekindles the campfire and puts some tea on to heat. He sits back and takes Crystal from the pouch. The sun peeks over the horizon, he hears the heavenly sound, and a cheery voice greets him.

CRYSTAL
Good morning, Omén.

Wolf's ears perk up and he stares in the direction of Crystal. With trembling hands Omén tightens his grasp on the stone.

OMÉN
Praise be to Allah, you do speak!

CRYSTAL
Do you doubt your own ears?

OMÉN
I ... I thought ... I was afraid that perhaps I had dreamed it all last night.

CRYSTAL
No, dearest, you did not dream it. I do speak.

Omén sits dumbfounded. Wolf nudges Omén's arm, then sits down beside him to get a better look at Crystal. Faris and Husam come in from their night's vigil.

FARIS
Hey, Boss, noble one, leader of men. What you got us for breakfast?

The two boys laugh.

EXT - TRAIL - DAY

The sun is high. The motley band is on the trail northward: Omén, Wolf, Faris, Husam, and now fifty or so sheep. The sky clouds up and a warm gentle rain falls.

CRYSTAL V.O.
My secrets you may learn, as others will in turn. The sand that makes clear stone, To see what can't be known, Up close and yet out far, Beyond the farthest star ...

Now she speaks quietly, dreamily.

CRYSTAL V.O. (Cont.)
Then fiber optics ... computer chips ...

Now she speaks sprightly.

CRYSTAL V.O. (Cont.)
Yet too much more I fear, So let us meet your dear.

EXT – ON TRAIL NEAR KUWAIT – DAY

A hazy view of the great metropolis of Kuwait in the distance about three miles away. Also in the distance, barely discernable, are three separate herds of sheep, 300 to 400 head each. The sheep graze contentedly on scrub grass and meadowland that looks greener closer to the city. On the screen appears in large letters "KUWAIT 529 A.D." A lone shepherd enters the screen in the foreground and walks toward the city. The usual shepherd's clothes and a walking stick. It is Omén: his hair is full, but cut shorter, more like the other men of the area.

SULTAN OMÉN V.O.
We have been camped here about two months now. I am going in to get a few supplies and to spend the night with friends.

My two helpers are working out very well - only two years now and they can handle our flock of almost eighty by themselves.

I should not talk of Wolf - it pains me too much - his heart gave out nine months ago and I buried him by the trail …

Notice the other herds there. We had trouble getting a spot, it is so crowded here ... and the city charges rent for the use of the land!

You wouldn't believe what happened when I finally had a chance to get away and enter the city gates for the first time …

EXT – CITY GATES – DAY

It is crowded - people come and go. Omén goes up to first one, then another, hops up and down, smiles and laughs, points to the gates, cries out.

OMÉN
I'm here! I'm here!

No one pays him any attention. Then he falls down on his hands and knees and kisses the ground. Then he gets up and looks around in embarrassment. All this time no one pays him any attention whatsoever. They are all busy with their own affairs.

Only one man looks at him, quizzically, while Omén looks around. This is mostly because Omén is in his way and the man wonders where Omén is going to jump next. Omén races inside the city gates.

EXT - INSIDE GATES - DAY

View source is Omén's eyes. He runs up and down a wide expansive court-yard/market area, then runs further inside and rounds the corner of a building while looking in a different direction. The very out-of-focus blur of tan/gold-flash/ amber/brown comes onto the screen from the side where the corner of the building is, then the screen is just about covered in deerskin color.

There is a "THUMP". The view goes completely out of focus. There are patches of blue sky and much movement. The movement stops suddenly and the screen turns purple. The blur slowly comes into focus - a pair of purple pantaloons.

The view slowly moves up, and by degrees takes in a huge GIANT towering over-head. The man is dark-skinned, chocolate brown, tall, powerfully built, with light brown eyes and hair (almost amber or blond), a wide streak of gold dust below each eye, a large round gold earring in his right earlobe, a curiously shaped collar of gold around his neck, a deerskin vest the color of his hair, a gold stranded braided rope holding up his pantaloons which are down to mid-calf length, and sandals with gilded straps. His arms are folded on his broad chest. He looks down. His name is ZEUS.

Medium close shot. The full form of Zeus stands over Omén. People still do their thing in the background. Omén sits on the ground, his legs extended, his arms behind him to brace himself.

Zeus takes a step forward and his legs straddle Omén's. Omén scrambles to get up, but Zeus reaches down with one hand and pulls Omén up and off his feet by the back of his shirt. Zeus smiles at Omén face to face, hardly more than six inches apart, his pure white teeth gleaming against his dark skin.

ZEUS
Welcome to Kuwait, Sahib!

Omén warily returns the smile. His shirt cuts into his windpipe, and he finally speaks in a strained voice.

OMÉN
Please let me down, Sir.

INT – OMÉN'S LEAN-TO – MORNING

Omén lies on his back on his blanket. He has had too much wine the night before and has a terrible hangover. He closes his eyes, feels nauseous, and moans. From outside in the silence booms a deep-throated LAUGH. Omén opens his eyes slowly and sees Zeus standing in front of him with an amused look on his face.

ZEUS
Come, friend shepherd. The market place awaits your wares.

Omén rises up on one elbow and shades his eyes from the morning sun.

OMÉN
Not funny, Zeus. How do you drink so much wine? Ohhh ... my head feels like a thousand camels have raced through it.

Zeus throws back his head and laughs again.

OMÉN (Cont.)
Besides, I did not think you would remember your offer to help me this morning.

ZEUS
Omén, you underestimate your friend Zeus. Zeus's word is as good as gold. Now hurry – the morning is wasting.

Omén hesitates a moment, then rises carefully, and unsteadily makes his way to the nearby streamlet, holds his head with his hands and moans as he goes. He drops to his knees, and as he cups some water in his hands and lets it run down over his head, there is another LAUGH from Zeus.

EXT – NEAR CITY GATES – FORENOON

Omén and Zeus drive five sheep, all older rams. Zeus does most of the work, willingly, and he smiles. A soldier leads to market a small group of slaves who are roped together. Zeus sees the slaves, stops abruptly, frowns, nervously fingers the golden collar around his neck. Omén watches.

ZEUS
Omén, I really have to go. There are a thousand things I just remembered I must do. You won't have any trouble with the sale. Just go where I told you last night.

Zeus walks quickly through the gates and disappears from view into the city. Omén stands and stares after Zeus, his mouth open in surprise and wonder.

EXT – NEAR OMÉN'S CAMP – LATE AFTERNOON

Omén returns toward camp with two young ewes. He has a sack over his shoulder.

SULTAN OMÉN VO.
Abdul said to always be on the lookout for a prize ewe or ram, if the price was right. I still had enough money left over for supplies, and to pay my boys. I wondered why

Zeus had disappeared so suddenly – I didn't see him all day. He had said something about being a slave once. Maybe the slaves brought back evil memories.

Omén shrugs his shoulders and continues driving the sheep. His camp is in the distance, his flock spread out into two groups, grazing contentedly. Omén spots THREE RIDERS on horseback crossing in the distance, and he stops and stares. After a few moments he turns back and urges the two ewes on.

The riders draw nearer and Omén stops and looks again. They have on splendid clothing, dyed in the richest colors. From the horses' bridles dangle brightly colored tassels. Tiny bells jingle on the horses' breast collars. The horses stride powerfully, their coats glisten in the sunlight.

The rider in the middle appears definitely smaller than the others. As they come nearer, it is obvious that this rider is not a man, but a woman. She has on clothes similar to the men's, and rides as well as the men, but her head is covered with a long veil that reaches her feet; only her eyes and hands are clearly exposed.

At a hundred paces, the Sultan's emblem shows clearly on their clothes. At thirty paces they pass in front of Omén. The woman looks at him boldly, then she bows her head and looks away. The group rides away and disappears in the heat waves of the hot earth.

SULTAN OMÉN V.O.
The woman was in my dreams every night, and in my thoughts every day. Those eyes... that noble bearing ... that grace ... Zeus said I was acting like a lovesick calf ... It was a week later that I saw her again in the flesh.

EXT – FIELD NEAR CAMP –AFTERNOON

Omén sits and combs the burrs from a sheep's legs. He combs almost lovingly and caressingly. He hears the thunder of hooves galloping across the earth, coming nearer and nearer and then the galloping stops. Omén is busy at his chore and chooses not to pay any attention. (There seem to be many riders around lately.) A few moments pass.

Close-up on Omén. He has the odd sensation that someone watches him. His heart BEATS evenly and steadily. He turns his head slowly to see if anyone is there. His heart stops a beat and then races. Before him is the woman on horseback, alone. Her name is SHAHRAZAD. She quickly jumps down from her mount and tethers the horse. Then she steps close to him.

SHAHRAZAD
Hello, shepherd boy.

Her smile is visible beneath her veil. His mouth opens, he bows his head as he gets up to greet her. When he lifts his head, he finds that she is tall, as tall as he is. He stares, then smiles, then looks apprehensive. She smiles again and removes the veil from her face – there is a sheer veil beneath.

SHAHRAZAD (Cont.)
Do not worry. Today I have managed to get away from the palace unnoticed.

OMÉN
I … I think I must be dreaming … I am Omén.

SHAHRAZAD
And I am Shahrazad.

She walks toward the nearby streamlet. Omén follows, as if in a daze. She sits down, gestures for him to sit near her He sits down and they gaze into the water for some fifteen seconds. Omén sneaks a peek at her a time or two.

OMÉN
I hope you do not think me too bold when I say that you have been in my thoughts ever since I first saw you.

SHAHRAZAD
No, Omén, you are not too bold ... you have been in my thoughts as well.

She smiles, then looks coyly away.

SHAHRAZAD (Cont.)
I have seen you many times when I ride out with the guards.

They sit for a few seconds in silence, watching each other. Omén moves closer to her. She looks away, then rises as if to leave. He rises also. Their eyes meet. They slowly touch fingertips with hands upraised in front of them; then they drop their hands.

OMÉN
Shahrazad …

SHAHRAZAD
You are not from around here, are you? Your speech is of the southern regions.

OMÉN
You are correct. I am from far to the south, from Oman, born in the village of Sur.

SHAHRAZAD
Did you then journey with a caravan this past year, or are you perhaps the young caravan leader?

OMÉN
My lady, I am but a humble shepherd, come with my flock these past six years.

SHAHRAZAD
Indeed! This is hard to believe. You are very young; you are hardly a man. You must have been but a youth when you began your journey. What possessed you to come to Kuwait?

OMÉN
My lady, I was but sixteen when I left my family and friends. Allah told me that I would find my destiny in Kuwait – and if it be his will, I have.

SHAHRAZAD
Is Allah then your father, and would he allow such a young man to leave him?

OMÉN
Allah is my God, and I speak to him often. He speaks to me in the sound of the wind-storm in the desert. My father would not let me leave, but I escaped and became a shepherd for livelihood on my journey.

SHAHRAZAD
Your God Allah is a new name to my ears. Your tribal god?

OMÉN
Yes, my lady.

SHAHRAZAD
I have a younger sister about your age, but no brothers ...

OMÉN
I am the oldest in the family. I have two brothers ... and a baby sister I was glad to be rid of.

SHAHRAZAD
I should not be speaking to you as an equal. I should not dishonor my father, the We-zir, the court advisor to the Sultan. Are you married, Omén?

OMÉN
No, my lady, but I have found the one I have been seeking.

SHAHRAZAD
That is good. You have been in town long enough now to know about the Sultan, and the dearth of available maidens. You should marry your love promptly, before the Sultan finds her and she dies.

OMÉN
I have heard nothing of this.

SHAHRAZAD
My father mentioned the problem directly to me not six weeks ago, and I have vowed to become the Sultan's bride and perhaps end the horror of this age.

OMÉN
Oh!

SHAHRAZAD
You look sad; why am I telling you all this? It is too depressing …

My father has raised us and has kept the two of us from the company of men since our youth, so that we would be an honor to him when we marry.

OMÉN
What do you do with your time? Do you work?

SHAHRAZAD
We read books and play together, and attend school – I am presently managing the kitchen help at the Palace.

OMÉN
Play together? What do grown-up sisters do together?

SHAHRAZAD
Whenever we can, we race each other around the Palace grounds to let off tensions. Also I love to ride horses, but my sister does not care for the sport.

I can run like the wind. My father says I am too old for that – I am twenty-four. Dunyzad, my sister, is twenty-two. How old are you, Omén?

OMÉN
Twenty-two years, my lady.

SHAHRAZAD
I like you. Will you be my brother? The marriage to the Sultan will be soon enough, and I feel my youth slipping away.

Do you run? Do you think you can keep up with me? Come, let us race to yonder hill and back.

She removes her sheer veil and head covering, exposing her long, flowing dark hair.

They race down and back, always keeping a few paces from each other. She laughs now and then, her hair flowing in the breeze.

When they get back, she sits down on the ground with her legs spread apart and her arms braced behind. Omén follows her example; they sit side by side. They both breathe heavily. Unexpectedly, Shahrazad leans over and puts her arms around Omén's neck and pushes him to the ground. She kisses him on the neck until their breath becomes more regular.

SHAHRAZAD
I have never been with a man before. Show me what I must do to keep the Sultan happy, Brother Omén.

They get up and sit close together, holding hands. They don't speak, but they are enamored of each other, and their thoughts turn to verses of love.

OMÉN V.O.
Shahrazad, I have never known woman like you. Shahrazad, your dear lips are like morning's sweet dew. Shahrazad, my whole head's filled with thoughts kind and true. Shahrazad, without you my whole being is blue.

SHAHRAZAD V.O.
Omén, your name brings a promise to be. Omén, I love you when first you I see; Omén, if only we both may be free, Omén, then I would take you, and you me.

INT – OMÉN'S HUT – MORNING

It is several weeks later. Omén now has a permanent hut. There was a windstorm last night and dust covers everything. The wind still blows and makes NOISES and the door covering flaps. Zeus appears in Omén's doorway with two loaves of bread and a comb of honey sandwiched between them.

ZEUS
Ho, young friend, how fare you from last night's storm? Is your new dwelling still sound?

Zeus takes the flask of wine Omén has on his table, pours the remains (about 1/3 flask) into a cup, squeezes some honey from the comb into the cup, washes his fingers in the cup to mix in the honey, and drinks some. This action takes place during the following exchange.

OMÉN
As well as can be expected. What brings you out so early in the day?

Zeus laughs his deep-throated laugh.

ZEUS
You wound me to think I cannot rise early to check on a friend! But you are right – I have another reason for coming.

Zeus puts the cup down, sighs contentedly, breaks off a hunk of bread and eats. The suspense builds in Omén's face as Zeus takes his sweet time.

OMÉN
Don't keep me in suspense, Zeus. Tell me.

Zeus smiles and continues eating.

OMÉN (Cont.)
Zeus!

ZEUS
Oh, very well. I have a message from Shahrazad. She will meet you at the usual place this afternoon. She seemed a bit troubled when I spoke with her, though she did not go into detail.
You be careful, my brother. The desert has a thousand eyes. I cannot be everywhere to see to your safety.

EXT – OMÉN'S HUT – MIDMORNING

Omén gets ready to leave to meet Shahrazad. He hears hoofbeats pound across the land. He sees THREE of the Sultan's GUARDS approaching. The hoofbeats merge into the sound of Omén's heartbeat as the riders slow to a canter.

OMÉN
(whispering to himself)
No one could know about my meetings with Shahrazad. We have been too careful … Zeus would not tell.

The heartbeats speed up somewhat. The riders come to a halt in front of him. The head guard calls out.

HEAD GUARD
Greetings, shepherd.

OMÉN
Good day to you.

HEAD GUARD
A fine day, is it not?

OMÉN
Yes, indeed. Indeed it is.

HEAD GUARD
The Sultan sends his regards and requests you bring three sheep to the Palace no later than tomorrow morning. A page will pay you as usual.

OMÉN
Oh ... yes ... yes, I will deliver them later this afternoon.

Omén is quite relieved that this is the extent of the call. He manages a smile. The Head Guard pivots his mount. Close-up. The horse rears and snorts not two feet from Omén's face and frightens him thoroughly. The heartbeat races. He hears the head guard ordering his men to their next assignment.

When the guards are off screen, Omén starts out for the rendezvous, the base of a grassy knoll seen in the distance.

ZEUS V.O.
The desert has a thousand eyes ...

EXT – GRASSY KNOLL – AFTERNOON

Shahrazad has not come. Omén is sitting down, and he looks dejected. He takes his walking stick, balances it vertically on the ground, and looks at the shadow's length. He gets up wearily and heads for the hut.

OMÉN
Shahrazad has never been this late. Something is wrong. I'll find out when I deliver the sheep. Zeus will know.

EXT – BACK OF PALACE – LATE AFTERNOON

Omén hurries the three sheep to a small paddock by the stable. A young boy returns with the payment. There is a noise inside the stable, the WHINNY and SNORT of a horse. Omén goes to investigate, to look at the Sultan's beautiful horses. He cautiously enters the dark stable.

INT – STABLE – DAY

The scene is through Omén's eyes. Almost nothing is visible except light from the entryway. Then some dark outlines of horses as his eyes adjust. The scene shakes slightly (a stone hits his shoulder), the stone falls to the ground with a muffled sound.

SHAHRAZAD O.S.
Do not turn around. Meet me in two days at the knoll.

A side door CREAKS and THUMPS shut, then silence in the darkness.

INT – OMÉN'S HUT – MORNING

Omén sits at the table and picks at his food. Zeus is there. Zeus does not smile. He tries to get Omén to eat.

ZEUS
Omén, Omén, you will see her this afternoon. Why so sad these past two days? Get your mind on other things … I say, have you not wondered about the golden collar about my neck?

OMÉN
What? What? I'm sorry, Zeus. You were saying something about a golden collar. Oh! Yes. I've wondered about that. What is the story behind it?

Omén speaks absentmindedly and continues to pick at his food. Zeus tells his story, plays out the action with theatrical gestures and expanded facial features.

ZEUS
Know, 0 Brother Omén, that I am an Indian of the Hindu religion. My mother was of the highest caste and betrothed to the King.

She was of an independent spirit and would on occasion walk the markets incognito, in disguise.

But my mother one day was accosted by a madman of the lowest caste. He pulled her into his stall where he was butchering a pig, and had his way with her.

At his trial, just before he was put to the sword, it came out that his wife had died not a week before, having been run over by the King's charioteers as they were returning to the city from one of their exercises.

As was the custom of his caste he could take no other to wife, but could become a eunuch for the palace, as they were always in short supply, the King not desiring slaves.

Naturally, my mother could no longer be the King's bride, and was ostracized. No man would have her, since she had been defiled. She became with child.

When I was born, her relatives begged that the infant Zeus be left in the fields to die or be devoured by wolves or jackals, as was the custom of the barbarian Romans.

But my mother could not do this – I was the only child she would ever have, and she found me comely, and she nursed me.

She took all her possessions and sold them and had a golden collar made, one that could expand to fit a growing boy, and placed it around my neck and declared to all that could hear:

"No harm shall come to my son. When he comes of age you will sell him to a caravan as a slave so that he may grow up in a distant land with the hope of manumission, unlike here where he would live and die, unwanted by high born and pariah alike."

When I became a man I was sold as a slave, still with my golden collar. I fetched a goodly price.

My mother desired to travel with me and so we departed India. After many adventures we arrived here in Kuwait.

The Sultan's Wezir, having lost his wife to a sickness, and having two small children, desired a cook and housekeeper and caretaker for his children.

He saw my mother was highborn and intelligent and handsome, and approached her concerning this matter with his two daughters.

She replied, "Yes, on condition you buy the slave with the golden collar and free him." The Wezir was taken aback by her reply and asked her if I was her slave and if she was dissatisfied with my performance of duties.

She replied, "The slave was sold to the caravan leader to pay for this trip. I was well satisfied with him and wish to see him free." And it was done.

I work for the Wezir and others for wages as I see fit, and am friend to high born and those of low estate alike. The collar I keep as a reminder of man's inhumanity to man.

Omén continues to pick at his food and to sigh forlornly. Zeus sighs, raises his eyes to heaven, and tries again. This time he does no acting out, but sits down close to Omén and watches for any signs of awareness. Omén pays no attention.

ZEUS (Cont.)
Know also, Omén: While my mother was betrothed to the King, she became privy to much knowledge and stories not known to others.

One of these stories concerned a certain water-clear sapphire chip, not a normal blue sapphire, nor yet one with a star blazing in its belly, but a chip as one of the points of a star – Sapphire Star was it called.

To the ordinary mortal it appeared nothing … But the sages polished the point and mounted the chip, and by looking through it up into the deep blue sky could discern worlds not visible to mortal, worlds even unto the foundations of the earth, and the substance from which all creation springs … Sapphire Star, my friend.

Omén raises his head and looks out into the distance, in thought, and the scene fades.

EXT – KNOLL – NOON

Omén approaches the knoll from the far side.

ZEUS V.O.
I'm sorry Omén, but rumor has it that Shahrazad's time with the Sultan is drawing near. Should she not please him, I'm afraid she may perish like the others before her.

Omén sees Shahrazad's back to him. She nervously watches for him and for the approach of riders. He pauses to watch her. She senses his presence and turns. Before he can move, she is in his arms. Hot tears flow down her face.

OMÉN
Shhhh, my love. Everything will be all right.

SHAHRAZAD
Oh, what am I to do? I fear so for the lives of us all.

OMÉN
Shahrazad, certainly the Sultan would not be so cruel …

SHAHRAZAD
Omén, Omén, you do not know … I must think of a way to give the Sultan peace of mind.

They both sit down. Omén holds her and stares out into the distance.

OMÉN
Shahrazad, come away with me. We'll go somewhere far away from here. Zeus can arrange passage …

SHAHRAZAD
No, my love, You know he would send his guards for us, and find us wherever we went … I made my vow in all innocence, in the idealistic passion of youth, and I will hold to it.

335

Perhaps my death will stay the Sultan's hand for the other maidens ... there must be some way to end his madness ... Oh, it hurts so to know my life is over and that I will never be with you again.

Omén holds her as she falls into a fitful sleep, watches her, memorizes every feature. This may be the last time he will ever see her. He traces her lips with his fingertips.

OMÉN
Shahrazad ...

EXT – KNOLL – AFTERNOON

Shahrazad stirs and wakes up. She looks about as if uncertain of her surroundings. She feels Omén's arms tighten about her shoulders and she relaxes. She lies there in silence for a spell, then turns to look at Omén. The faintest hint of a smile plays on her full lips.

SHAHRAZAD
My love, I think I have come upon the solution to the problem ... Mayhaps I can tell the Sultan a story that he likes, and so live another day.

Another silent spell. She is fully awake now. She frowns, becomes dejected.

SHAHRAZAD (Cont.)
I am well read, but my genius is small and the ideas few. I fear I die also like the others. How many stories ... how many days?

OMÉN
My love, I found this crystal on the shores of the Sea. It can excite the genius in one, if he but gaze into her eye.

SHAHRAZAD
Oh, Omén! I will give thee great treasure if thou wilt give me thy crystal.

OMÉN
Alas, ever since I was blinded by the lightning flash at her birth, and my sight fully restored by her at the first piercing ray of the morning sun, I have taken a vow upon my eyes never to part with my Crystal Ball.

SHAHRAZAD
Thou hast vowed a mighty vow, and strong it is indeed. Since thou canst not break thy vow, come, show me how it works.

Thou canst take the place of my sister to be at my side in the King's chambers, and when thou seest a convenient time, do thou say to me, "O my sister, relate to me some strange story to beguile our waking hour:" and I will, if it be the will of Allah, and with the help of thy magic crystal, relate to thee a story that shall be the means of deliverance.

Omén looks questioningly and moves his mouth as if to speak.

SHAHRAZAD (Cont.)
Yes, yes, Omén!

Shahrazad frowns and brings her hands up to his cheeks.

SHAHRAZAD (Cont.)
Oh, thou must pluck out thy beard.

Shahrazad moves her face to Omén's and kisses him on the lips. Then she drops her hands.

SHAHRAZAD (Cont.)
There! It is settled. Do not question. Now, show me how thy crystal works.

INT – SULTAN'S CHAMBERS – EVENING

The SULTAN is in his bed. Shahrazad is snuggled up to him. She gazes intently into the crystal in her hands. Omén is in woman's garb and sits at their feet.

OMÉN
(high pitch)
O my sister, relate to me some strange story to beguile our waking hour.

Shahrazad looks at him brightly, and smiles.

SHAHRAZAD
Most willingly, dear sister, if this virtuous King permit me.

The Sultan nods, and Shahrazad commences:

SHAHRAZAD (Cont.)
It has been related to me O happy King, that there was a certain merchant who had great wealth, and traded extensively with surrounding countries; and one day he mounted his horse, and journeyed to a neighboring country to collect what was due him ….

Shahrazad continues talking, the sound fades out.

INT – PALACE – SULTAN'S OFFICE – DAY

The Sultan sits at his desk and works on a stack of papers. He quickly reads each paper, signs his name, rolls it up. The AIDE heats up the end of a bar of red sealing wax in a candle flame and allows a puddle to drop onto the edge of the roll. The Sultan then impresses the warm wax with his signet ring and gives the roll to the aide to cool off while he starts on the next paper. There is a table nearby with many rolls.

The Sultan looks very tired. After the second roll is finished, he motions to the aide to draw near, and he whispers in the aide's ear. There are OTHERS in the vicinity who come and go on official business.

SULTAN
Go and seek Zeus and bring him here.

The aide bows and leaves. The Sultan sighs, and starts on the papers all by himself.

The papers are almost cleared from the desk, the candle is now very short. Zeus comes in with the aide and bows slightly to the Sultan. No one else is in the office. The Sultan motions for the aide to leave. The aide bows and leaves.

ZEUS
You wish to see me, my lord?

SULTAN
Yes. Please. Sit down … You seem to know much about the area and the people here, sometimes even more than the Wezir himself. Do you know somewhat about the Wezir's daughter Shahrazad?

ZEUS
Yes, my lord. She manages the Palace kitchen.

SULTAN
No, no, you know what I mean. I took her to bed last night and it is all over the Palace that she is still alive today. The Wezir took very ill last night, else I might ask him.

ZEUS
My lord, you know there are no other desirable maidens hereabouts, certainly none as virtuous as Shahrazad. You have seen to that. Why did you spare her?

SULTAN
I don't know. It was very strange. She told a strange tale 'til the light of morning, then left off in mid-sentence. I will not kill her until I hear the rest of the story.

ZEUS

Is Shahrazad not enticing to look at, pleasant to be with? Have your midwives not determined that she indeed was a virgin when you took her to bed?

SULTAN
Indeed … And a virgin she remains this morning. And what of her sister? Most pleasing, more handsome I would say than comely. Shahrazad seems to love her sister exceedingly.

ZEUS
My lord, have you not enjoyed your mutton these past weeks? Is the meat not sweeter to your palate lately?

SULTAN
Indeed. With the meat in my belly and the maiden by my side telling me strange tales, why, I feel like my old self. Tell me what you know of this matter.

ZEUS
The mutton is from the flock of a new shepherd in the area. He is the one who took the place of Dunyzad, sister of Shahrazad, last night.

Shahrazad loves him exceedingly – I have never seen man and woman so well matched – but as your midwives proved, she remains faithful to you.

The stone she held is the shepherd's and allows her to tell strange tales.

My lord, if you kill her, he will depart, and you will lose your fine meat and strange tales … and your lovely maiden.

SULTAN
I will kill her eventually. How many tales can she tell, and how long can she hold out from her lover?

ZEUS
My lord, I know Shahrazad from a little girl. When she vows something, she will not break that vow. She has vowed to be true to you.

Will you let off your killing? Because your Queen cuckolded you, you should not take it out on others.

SULTAN
No woman cuckolds the Sultan and lives.

ZEUS
So be it. I know Shahrazad. I will wager you one thousand dinars that she will be faithful to you for one thousand days more.

SULTAN
Ha! The easiest one thousand dinars I will ever acquire. I will let her lover be with her all the day, except Shahrazad must be in my chamber of an evening and checked first.

The first day she proves unfaithful, she dies. Do you still wager?

ZEUS
I do. I know Shahrazad. She will last the one thousand days.

SULTAN
Ha, ha. If she lasts the full time … she will be my Queen! But the lover must go after the feast.

ZEUS
Agreed!

The two rise and join hands to seal the agreement. Then the Sultan finally realizes what is necessary if Shahrazad is faithful – that he may not have her either. His exultation turns to somberness at the gravity of the situation. Then his face takes on a pained expression as Zeus leaves the room.

SULTAN
(to himself)
No mere shepherd is going to best me … Zeus, you drive a hard bargain.

INT – OMÉN'S HUT – DAY

Omén and Shahrazad are lying side by side on his bed. Shahrazad teaches him to write and to cipher. They giggle and caress each other.

EXT – PALACE GROUNDS – DAY

Shahrazad shows Omén how to mount and ride a horse.

INT – SULTAN'S CHAMBERS – NIGHT

Omén is in woman's garb. He writes down in a book the tales Shahrazad tells. Omén has Crystal, Shahrazad caresses the Sultan intimately, kisses him, tries to get him aroused. The Sultan appears disconcerted, flustered.

INT – PALACE DINING HALL – NIGHT

The wedding feast. The Sultan is with Shahrazad in royal robes. Many OTHERS are there, celebrating. Shahrazad looks neither sad nor happy, just resigned to her fate. Omén is not there.

EXT – HILLTOP – DAY

Omén is atop a chestnut-brown roan Mare. The horse has a blaze and a light brown mane and pasterns. Her coloring is as much like Zeus as is possible for a horse. There are considerable supplies packed behind Omén. He looks eastward toward Kuwait in the distance. His jaw is set.

SULTAN OMÉN V.O.
The Sultan was right to turn me out. I could not live in Kuwait now, knowing that I would never hold my Shahrazad again.

The flock was sold to the young men. They will continue the noble profession. I sent a letter to Halima stating as much, and wished her well with her recent marriage.

Zeus left early this morning back to India as a free man – may Allah keep him from harm.

Crystal says I must go now to Riyadh if I would fulfill my destiny. What do you suppose she meant by that?

The horse? No, I didn't buy it. Zeus gave her to me as a gift. Said he won her in a wager, but she was too small for him to ride. Said she was worth one thousand dinars. Zeus liked to joke.

Kiyah will keep me company. It should be easier without the sheep. I can work at odd jobs at any villages I meet. Maybe I'll stay out in the desert – with the three sisters – I am in no hurry this time.

Omén slowly breaks out into a smile. He wheels Kiyah around to the southwest and they move out at a walk. Then Omén gives a YELL and nudges Kiyah, and she breaks out into a full gallop. Omén YELLS again.

INT – PALACE – SHAHRAZAD'S BEDROOM – DAY

It rains steadily, a very dreary day. Close up. Shahrazad sits by the window, looks out toward the southwest – toward Mecca, perhaps? Silent tears glide down her sad face.

SHAHRAZAD V.O.
Omén, Omén, I miss you so!

Blue, blue your collar, Sad, sad my heart. Though I do not go to you, Why don't you

341

send word?

Blue, blue your beltstone, Sad, sad my thoughts. Though I do not go to you, Why don't you come?

Restless, heedless, I walk the gate tower. One day not seeing you Is three months long.

View source slowly moves back, and there is the Sultan her husband who stands behind her and massages her neck and shoulders. He, too, looks sad. She reaches up with one hand and puts it over his.

EXT – STABLE BY INN – EARLY EVENING

A windstorm. Omén rides up to the closed stable door, dismounts and hammers at it with his fist. The stable boy comes out, with a wet cloth over his nose and mouth. He sees Kiyah, goes back inside, then comes out again with a canvas-type bag and puts it over her mouth and face before taking her inside.

Omén walks the few steps to the inn. Through the dust and sand are hazy images of date palms and other evidence of an oasis.

INT – INN – EVENING

Evidence of fine sand dust covering the tables. The INNKEEPER is the only other person in the dining area besides Omén, who has just come in. The innkeeper is happy to have a customer. Omén goes to one of the few small tables.

OMÉN
Wine, please.

The innkeeper scurries around and then waits patiently while Omén drinks his wine. The innkeeper gets a cup and a jug of wine and joins Omén. After a lengthy silence, the innkeeper begins:

INNKEEPER
Nasty weather.

OMÉN
Yep.

INNKEEPER
Where you from?

OMÉN

(lengthy pause)
Kuwait.

The innkeeper raises his eyebrows.

INNKEEPER
Why'd you leave?

OMÉN
(lengthy pause)
Lost my girl.

INNKEEPER
Far from home, young man.

OMÉN
Oh, Kuwait's not my home. I'm from Sur, way down in Oman province.

The innkeeper raises his eyebrows again.

INNKEEPER
Where you headed?

OMÉN
Riyadh.

INNKEEPER
By the gods, you're not even thirty, and you've traveled the whole world! Well, I was born in this village and suppose I'll probably die here as well. I have little time to travel, taking care of the inn.

My eldest son lives in Riyadh and sends word as often as he can, raising a family and all being very hard, and letters written by the official scribes being very expensive, and Riyadh being so very far away, so that unless a caravan is going northward through Riyadh I very seldom hear anything and likewise I seldom send word unless a caravan is traveling south through Riyadh.

Would you care to take word to my son in Riyadh even though he will not get it for many months, Riyadh being so very far away and all, and I will be more than happy to give you my son's name and last address so you can look him up when you get to the city …

OMÉN
Well, I …

The innkeeper cuts him off. Omén's eyes get bigger and bigger and his mouth hangs more and more during the following:

INNKEEPER
We frequently get windstorms like this in the village which is why many of the villagers have left to seek a better life in Riyadh and the weather seems to have changed here noticeably these past ten years and when the storm comes you should cover your head and neck with a large heavy cloth well wet down with water even though water is precious and you are dying of thirst else you will breathe in much fine dust and your lungs will turn to stone and you will die then and there which is why there are no more sheep or goats hereabouts and what would you like for your dinner?

INT – RIYADH – TAVERN – DAY

Omén is thirty-five years of age, well dressed, chief scribe in the Palace. He sits and drinks his wine and mulls over his life in Riyadh. Crystal now is in a small pouch hung from a cord around his neck. He touches the pouch.

SULTAN OMÉN V.O.
Sultan's chief scribe and accountant for two years now and only thirty-five .... Life was hard when I first arrived here in Riyadh. No job satisfied me. I thought about leaving many times, but Crystal soothed me.

Just at my lowest, the innkeeper's son, whom I had met upon my arrival, put in the word that I could read and write, and cipher. I was made assistant clerk. My first day didn't go too well ...

INT – VISION – SCRIBES' CUBICLE – DAY

Omén is twenty-eight, in Riyadh about a year. SCRIBES interview him for the job. He nervously knocks over the India ink pot, then in his haste to right the pot, pushes a stack of ledgers to the floor and gets ink on his best white shirt, then they have him copy what he has messed up.

INT – TAVERN – DAY

Omén smiles, shakes his head, gets up and walks out of the tavern into the bright sun and busy streets of Riyadh.

EXT – STREET – DAY

Omén approaches the stable at the end of the street. The SOUND of hooves kicking angrily in a stall. Omén enters the barn as the young stable boys scatter. Omén comes out of the barn leading a fiery black STALLION with a bridle but no saddle. He swings easily onto the back of the horse and laughs as the stable boys hurry back into the stable, frightened out of their wits by the horse. Horse and rider walk out of town.

SULTAN OMÉN V.O.

Kiyah died giving birth to this beautiful animal. I call him "Zeus" … a fitting name, don't you think? He reminds me so much of the Black Stallion of the desert … and the three sisters …

I worked hard. The clerks did not like my quick ascent in their ranks. But I came in early, and often closed the door of an early afternoon to an empty office.

The Sultan Halidah took notice of me, and I was given special projects. One of these was the translation of many manuscripts into Arabic … Took two years …

I had the help of an old Greek scholar to translate while I wrote. He knew Greek, Hebrew, Latin, Arabic, Sanskrit, Babylonian, Egyptian … and was even learning some of the bastardized languages coming out of the Frankish territories!

One problem I had as a clerk was the cumbersome mathematics. There must be a better way. My head swam with all the different methods and symbols.

It had become an obsession – I thought about the problem constantly, even in my dreams. One night, about two years prior, I was in the office – I could not sleep …

INT – VISION – SCRIBES' OFFICE – NIGHT

Omén, age 33, is at his desk. Papers, books, manuscripts, scrolls are scattered about. It is very late at night and he is very tired. He puts symbols down on paper (hand made from rags, the newest method from China), symbols of numbers from all the various civilizations.

OMÉN V.O.

Let's try something new.

One, two, three, four Greek delta, five delta plus one, six delta plus one plus one

I don't like all these straight lines, and the six is a double delta and could be an eight. I'll make the six like a pig's tail.

The seven is a combination of the three and delta four – or maybe a two and a four. Let's make the seven look like the two, and add a stroke on the two and three.

Nine looks too cumbersome to write. What do you think, Crystal?

CRYSTAL V.O.
Turn the curlicue six upside down.

OMÉN VO.
The two, three, four, five and eight look Greek or Egyptian – I can round them off.

The six and nine can be confused.

That looks good.

For powers of ten, Egyptians have an arch, a coiled rope for hundred, a lotus plant for thousand. Greeks use "K" for ten, the tenth letter in their alphabet. And so forth. My head swims. Is there not a better way to represent large numbers?

CRYSTAL V.O.
Oh, Omén, look at me!

OMÉN VO.
Why, Crystal, you are so tiny, you are practically a dot. The space between powers of tens, if there be no number, can be indicated by a dot.

Scholars have taken to drawing a triangle or square around the dot so it will not be lost or thought an ink spatter or flyspeck.

CRYSTAL V.O.
Omén! Look closer. Look at me very, very close.

Omén brings Crystal closer and closer. The point of light from the distant candle refracting through her becomes larger and larger. When his eye almost touches her, the point of light is a large circle of light, and practically fills his eye.

CRYSTAL V.O. (Cont.)
What do you see, Omén?

OMÉN V.O.

I see a large circle of light. You are filling my whole head with light!

CRYSTAL V.O.
And can the masterful Omén make a quick sketch of what he sees?

OMÉN V.O.
Yes, yes!

Omén takes the pen and draws a large circle on the piece of paper.

CRYSTAL V.O.
Why do you make it so big?

OMÉN V.O.
Why, it fills my whole mind. It is very important.

CRYSTAL V.O.
Make it a little smaller, about the size of your other symbols. Omén puts on the paper:

$$0\ I\ 2\ 3\ 4\ 5\ 6\ 7\ 8\ 9\ \cap$$

OMÉN V.O.
Circle, one, two, three, four, five, six, seven, eight, nine, ten.

CRYSTAL V.O.
Why do you use the arch for ten? Why not "X" or "K"?

OMÉN V.O.
Well, what symbol would you use?

CRYSTAL VO.
(matter-of-factly)
Why don't you try the "one" with me after it?

OMÉNVO.
I don't understand you.

Omén puts down the "1" and struggles, but finally puts the "0" after it.

CRYSTAL V.O.
Now, was that so hard? What do you have?

OMÉN V.O.
(blank expression)

I have a one with a big sifr [cipher], a big nothing after it.

CRYSTAL V.O.
Why don't you call that "ten"?

Crystal says this as an older sister would talk down to her little brother.

OMÉN V.O.
(angrily)
Well, why not? And why don't I put another sifr after it and call that "one hundred" instead of the "C" of the Romans?

And why don't I put another sifr after that and call it "one thousand" instead of the "M"?

That is stupid, using two, three or more figures instead of one. Do you take me for a dolt? Crystal? Crystal, don't cry.

But it is Omén who cries.

SULTAN OMÉN V.O.
(quietly)
Crystal had just shown me how to number the universe with just ten symbols...Eureka! ...

INT – VISION – SULTAN HALIDAH'S OFFICE – DAY

SULTAN HALIDAH sits at his desk. Omén stands by his side and shows him his new system. Halidah puts the figures down on paper as he speaks them.

HALIDAH
So the sifrs can represent powers of ten. So say Jabal owes me three hundred sheep and four. In Roman it would be "CCCIV", but you have three sifr four [304]. Hmm. Suppose I owe King Saud six thousand and eight hundred and nine slaves. In Egyptian that is, uh, six lotus flowers and, uh, eight ropes and nine strokes. Oh, my! What do you have? Six eight sifr nine [6809]? A lot better. Can you add and subtract your numbers? You can? Hmm. I'll talk to my council about this. Looks good.

Omén, you are due for a raise. In fact, I think I will make you chief scribe and accountant. You seem to know what you are doing.

INT – VISION – HALIDAH'S OFFICE – EVENING

Sultan Halidah has convened his council of SIX OFFICIALS. They do not like

Omén. Halidah shows them how the zero can be used in calculations.

OFFICIAL #1
Sire, the alignment of the stars shows conclusively that this method bodes ill for your rule. Omén is a troublemaker and an upstart, and should be kept in line. Indeed, by the casting of the bones it is made plain that he should be removed from the Palace.

HALIDAH
But it looks like it would save time, and make it easier to understand your confounded calculations.

OFFICIAL #2
Sire, if you have your heart set on keeping this Omén, we will not dissuade you. However, he should be prepared to answer two questions: One, how large a number can he write with his system, and two, what are the names of all the numbers.

OFFICIAL #3
Sire, this sifr the man uses is not a number. Mixing numbers and that which is not a number is fraught with danger to your reign – you had best heed this advice. The astrologers have so told me, and you may certainly ask them yourself.

Halidah frowns, dismisses his council. They leave solemnly.

INT – VISION – OUTSIDE HALIDAH'S OFFICE – EVENING

Well outside the office, the officials huddle together.

OFFICIAL #4
Ha! The Sultan will certainly go to Omén and ask the questions. We have not long to wait for this interloper's downfall.

They all join hands and raise their arms in a victory celebration.

INT – VISION – OMÉN'S OFFICE – DAY

Sultan Halidah enters and goes to Omén. The other TWO SCRIBES talk and joke between themselves and pay no attention to Omén or to the Sultan. They do not like it that Omén has been put in charge, and are giving him his comeuppance. Halidah frowns at them, then looks at Omén questioningly.

HALIDAH
Omén, I have taken up the matter of your new system of calculations with the council. While they see promise in it, they feel it poses some danger. To clear the air, therefore, they wish you to answer two simple questions before they will examine it

further.

OMÉN

It seems a simple enough system. There should be no problems. What are the two questions?

HALIDAH

The first question: What is the largest number you can write with your system?

Omén takes a pen and a sheet of paper and puts down the figures:

OMÉN

One, and then a sifr makes ten, and then another sifr makes a hundred, and then another sifr makes … a thousand.

HALIDAH

But can't you keep adding sifrs? What is the largest number you can write with your system?

Halidah looks at Omén expectantly, with a half smile. He gestures with his hands and body to get the answer out of Omén. He hopes Omén will come up with a good answer he can take back to the council.

OMÉN

And then another sifr is … ten thousand … and another sifr is … another sifr is … a hundred thousand?

HALIDAH

Is that the largest number?

Omén becomes confused and adds sifr after sifr until he fills the line. Then after a moment he starts on the second line and puts down three sifrs. Then he stops and looks up at Halidah in embarrassment.

OMÉN

I don't know … I can't tell you the largest number I can write with my system.

HALIDAH

(crestfallen)

Is this the answer I must take back to the council?

CRYSTAL V.O.

Omén! Omén! Put me beside myself and call it "without end"…

Omén puts two circles side by side. Then he traces around the two joined circles –

around and around he traces. He smiles.

OMÉN
Here is the symbol of the number. You could call it "without end" … or "infinity" in Latin.

Halidah smiles.

HALIDAH
Aha!

Then Halidah frowns.

HALIDAH (Cont.)
The second question: What are the names of all the numbers?

Halidah sits down, his head bowed. The council has beat him and he knows it. Omén will have to go, and he was really getting to like the young man. He turns his head and looks at Omén sorrowfully. Omén sits and stares straight ahead. Seconds go by.

OMÉN
After the thousands, or the ten thousands, you really need no names. The symbols themselves show their values, depending on their location in the number.

HALIDAH
Is there a Latin name for the numbers smaller than the "infinity"?

OMÉN
(abjectly)
…No … there would be no name.

Both men sit in pure misery.

OMÉN (Cont.)
(to himself)
No name, nothing, nobody, no one. The sifr, a nothing. What is the Latin? Nemo!

OMÉN (Cont.)
But the sifr, being a number that is not a number, and doing the work that numbers cannot do, would be called in Latin, "NEMO".

Halidah looks up suddenly, breaks out into a beautific smile. He gets up quickly, walks, almost runs out of the room.

INT – VISION – SULTAN HALIDAH'S OFFICE – DAY

Halidah is at his desk. His six council members stand in a group before him.

HALIDAH
(frowning)
You wanted to know the largest number that can be written by Omén's system.

ALL SIX OFFICIALS
(smirking)
Yes, Sire.

Halidah takes a pen and a sheet of paper. He draws a large infinity symbol on the paper. Over and over he traces the symbol until he sees that they all are looking and are aware of what he is doing.

HALIDAH
Here is the symbol of the largest number that can be written by Omén's new system.

OFFICIAL #2
(weakly)
But what is its name?

HALIDAH
(smiling)
Omén calls it "without end". Or in Latin, "infinity".

Audible GASPS from some of the officials.

OFFICIAL #2
(obsequiously)
And, my Lord, what are the names of all the *other* numbers?

Official #2 smiles and waits patiently for Halidah's answer, his head up, eyes half closed. The other officials slowly break out into muted smiles. Halidah finally answers.

HALIDAH
After the thousands, or the ten thousands, you really need no names. The symbols themselves show their value, depending on their location in the number.

Official #2 lowers his head and looks hard at Halidah. He purses his lips.

OFFICIAL #2
We have *names* for all *our* numbers.

Halidah breaks the official's gaze and looks up at the ceiling, with his head cocked.

HALIDAH
But the sifr, being a number that is not a number, and doing the work that numbers cannot do, would be called in Latin, "NEMO"!

GASPS and CRIES of alarm from the officials. They stare at Halidah in terror and back away from him slowly, then run out when they reach the door, hitting into each other in their haste.

SULTAN OMÉN V.O.
The others seemed afraid of the sifr and would not use it. Oh, well, maybe some day...

INT – OMÉN'S OFFICE – D AY

Omén is in his early forties. He is the boss of a group of FOUR SCRIBES and ACCOUNTANTS. They are all working away. Sultan Halidah enters Omén's office and comes up to him.

HALIDAH
Omén, my brother is coming to visit next year and is bringing his family and entourage – four wives and sixteen children – or is it eighteen? (Who can keep track?) Would you please start the preparations for a proper greeting?

OMÉN
Yes, of course, Sir. Your brother, as yourself, must be of great importance and in high position to afford four wives.

I am sorry, but I have kept to my work and have not perhaps heeded the local gossip too well – I am not familiar with your brother.

HALIDAH
Oh, everyone in Riyadh knows about my brother, but no one discusses it, under my edict. You arrived here several years after the proclamation.

My brother suffered mightily in love, and it affected his mind. He had taken to bedding a virgin in his city every night and having her killed the next morning, because he believed no woman would be faithful to him...

Until his Wezir's daughter came and told him tales every evening and soothed his troubled mind, faithful to him for almost three years, until he finally married her.

My brother is the Sultan of Kuwait. Perhaps you have heard of him, or have even written to him in your official duties.

Omén appears thunderstruck. He nods his head, and Halidah leaves.

OMÉN V.O.
Kuwait! The Sultan! Shahrazad! Coming here to Riyadh! Will she still be alive and be one of his wives? Will she have children and be dumpy and fat?

OMÉN
(out loud)
Gentlemen, gentlemen, the Sultan has given me some unexpected news. I am not feeling well. I am sorry, but you will have to take the rest of the day off. I am sure I will be composed tomorrow.

INT – SULTAN'S OFFICE – DAY

Halidah has Omén on the carpet. Omén looks very depressed, fidgety, unsure of himself, at loose ends. He is somewhat unkempt, unshaven, needs a haircut, hollow-eyed.

HALIDAH
I have been working you too hard. Your office help have told me of your mood swings this past month. The preparations for my brother can wait, important as they are.

You need a change of scenery. Set everything aside and take a vacation. The Wezir will check on your men in your absence.

Pick out a pretty maid in this grand city and go sailing or something. Yes, you need a woman to take care of you. You really do. Pick someone you can live with. Be back in two months. 'Bye.

Halidah waves Omén off, and looks hard at him as Omén bows and leaves without saying a word, shoulders stooped, head down. When Omén's back is turned, Halidah shakes his head and clucks quietly to himself.

HALIDAH (Cont.)
Tch, tch, tch. Sad, sad.

Halidah gets back to the work on his desk. He motions for the aide to come over and assist him.

EXT – MESSAGE CENTER NEAR PALACE – DAY

A PAGE goes up to the billboard and tacks on a large note. The view source zeroes in on it:

All those young maidens of the City between the ages of fourteen and twenty four who would desire to take a pleasant two month trip by camel to the East Ocean and back, with some sailing if the winds be favorable,

Please meet with your chaperone at Market Square on the morning following the first sighting of the new crescent Moon. Only one will be chosen. Must be adventuresome.

By Order of SULTAN HALIDAH per Omén, chief scribe

When the page leaves, three older men mosey on up and read the message. One of them SHOUTS and beckons to his wife, who comes up, and they converse animatedly. Another hurries away; the third stands there in thought.

EXT – MARKET SQUARE – MORNING

A group of about thirty women, giggling young MAIDENS and older DOWAGERS, with heavy veils and robes – only their eyes show brightly, CHATTER away.

VARIOUS MAIDENS V.O.
Perhaps the Sultan will choose one of us for his new Queen.

Don't press your luck, dearie. I would be happy to be his concubine. Yes, the lap of luxury, bountiful plenty.

I am so pretty; that one is so ugly – why would she even think of showing up?

Will the Sultan like a young one, or perhaps an older one with more experience?

Well, you've sure had the experience.

His wives are a little thin, don't you think? Surely he would want one with a little more meat on her bones, like me.

Sure thing, honey. You're enough for a whole banquet.

The Sultan is so handsome; I am sure I could make him happy.

Am I not beautiful, do not all the men fall at my feet? How could the Sultan resist me?

DOWAGER #1
(to her charge)
Well, I got you up at the crack of dawn and prettied you up … For what? We've been

here half the morning and nothing … nothing.

Some of the others MUMBLE and GRUMBLE, and several pairs leave. The chatter dies down. It is not market day, and soon all is quiet. After an interminable silence, Omén walks into the Square with TWO BODYGUARDS. As the women see them, the chatter starts again, this time from the dowagers.

VARIOUS DOWAGERS V.O.
Oh, look, what a handsome man. Yes, but that's not the Sultan. Look how big the bodyguards are! Maybe we'll find out something now. I hope so. My feet are freezing.

Omén walks up to the group and waits for the chatter to die down. The guards remain at some distance. A dowager ogles Omén.

OMÉN
I am from the Palace, and I assume you, uh, are here in, uh, response to the notice I, uh, had posted. Uh, my name is Omén, scribe to the Sultan. I do not presently know, uh, all the details, and assume, uh, the Sultan may desire a, uh, con-concubine, or even a Queen. Are there any questions?

DOWAGER #2
What about our safety on the trip?

OMÉN
The two bodyguards will travel with us to ward off bandits.

DOWAGER #3
How many will be in the caravan, and will the Sultan be taking his wives?

OMÉN
There will be only six camels and six of us – the two bodyguards, you and your chaperone, the Sultan, and myself.

Omén reddens in embarrassment. Several more women leave. They mutter to themselves.

LEAVING WOMEN V.O.
What a tiny caravan! There is no planning at all to this. Six camels? He must be joking. The Sultan must be off his rocker, like his brother. Shhhhh!

MAIDEN #1
I like to rise early, before high noon, so I will have time for my servant to do my hair and makeup and nails. She will have to go along. She is small, so can she not sit with me on my camel?

OMÉN
The caravan will be traveling from the crack of dawn until it is dark, with only short rest stops. There will be no time or need for prettying up, unless you want to do it yourself after the evening meal around the campfire, when it gets dark and the stars come out.

MAIDEN #1
Oh, my!

Maiden # 1 and her chaperone turn away.

MAIDEN #2
Can we be sure of returning in exactly two months or less? My boyfriend will wait no longer than that.

OMÉN
If you are not a, uh, a virgin, the Sultan is, uh, is, uh, not interested.

MAIDEN #2
Oh.

Several more pairs of women leave at this astonishing announcement. There are now only four pairs left. In this remaining assemblage is still the ogling woman. She has been ogling Omén all this time. It has made Omén uncomfortable all this time. Also, every time he answers a question, her young charge turns away to leave, only to be pulled back by the ogler.

OMÉN
Please follow me to the Palace, and I will complete the inquiry in my office.

The eight women follow Omén, with the two guards at the rear.

INT – PALACE – DAY

As the women enter the Palace, they all OOH and AHH and crane their necks up and down and side to side; all except the ogler and her charge. The ogler continues to ogle Omén whenever possible; her young charge keeps her head down and her eyes on the floor. Omén takes them to a small anteroom adjoining the Sultan's office.

OMÉN
Please have a seat.

Omén takes up his notebook and begins checking off questions.

OMÉN (Cont.)
I will need your names and addresses, and you must swear that the young maiden is truly a virgin. Omén blushes violently.

DOWAGER #4
We really must go. I just remembered some pressing matters that must be attended to.

Dowager #4 leaves with her charge in tow. The Sultan pokes his head into the room.

HALIDAH
Ah, Omén, the business is about finished. Haven't you forgotten something?

OMÉN
Oh, yes. The trip by camel and on the ship can be very confining, and we may see each other naked at times. Is this a problem? No? Will you all please remove your veils so the Sultan can get a better look.

Omén turns beet red.

MAIDEN #3
I was trained to never remove my veil for a man until the wedding night.

Maiden #3 and her chaperone leave. There are only two girls and two chaperones now: eight eyes peering over black veils. Omén keeps his eyes on the ogler. Slowly she removes her veil. A shock of recognition as her veil drops.

OMÉN V.O.
Shahrazad? No, but very much like her. Where have I seen this face before?

Omén shakes his head as if to clear his thoughts. Then another shock when he looks at the ogler's companion as her veil drops, after a nudge from the ogler.

OMÉN V.O.
Oh, almost like Dunyzad, Shahrazad's sister! Are my eyes playing tricks on me? Am I that far gone?

Omén turns to the other pair, and they drop their veils. He looks at them for some time.

OMÉN
(out loud)
Yes, very pretty. Are they not, Sire?

Omén lowers his eyes to his notebook and begins writing furiously. The Sultan has been looking at the women all this time and he enjoys himself immensely. The Sultan addresses the ogler.

HALIDAH
Well, hello, love.

DOWAGER #5 [ogler]
Hello, yourself. Do you want the regular tonight or something special?

HALIDAH
Just a kiss will do.

Sultan Halidah comes through the doorway up to her, kisses her fully on the mouth, and pats her behind.

DOWAGER #5
No touching the merchandise until after the wedding.

The ogler smiles as she says this and breaks free. Then she pats Halidah on *his* behind. Halidah breaks out into a full, hearty laugh. He reaches out to take the hand of the other chaperone.

HALIDAH
And who do we have here?

DOWAGER #6
Hmpff! Well, I never! Come, child. You can do better than this. He is nothing but a dirty old man.

They leave, and everyone can hear the girl's wail.

MAIDEN #4 O.S.
But Auntie, he seems like a kindly old gentleman to me. He reminds me of my dear father.

DOWAGER #6 O.S.
Hmpff!

Two ladies are left. The chaperone is SARI and the maiden is DONA.

HALIDAH
What is it that allows you to take this trip with us? Will your family not miss you?

Sari looks pleadingly into Halidah's eyes.

SARI

My husband is gone these many years on a dangerous voyage, and I long to have him back in my arms.

HALIDAH
(softly)
May you find the one you are seeking.

HALIDAH
(to Omén)
By the way, Omén, I almost forgot to tell you. Sudden business has come up that I must attend to, and I am unable to take off for two months. Have a nice time. I will see if we can all have the evening meal together before you leave. Come along, guards.

Omén looks up from his notebook and bids the Sultan goodbye. Then he turns to Dona.

OMÉN
Young lady, you are very pretty, but you do not seem to fit our requirements. You must be at least fourteen.

DONA
(shyly)
I am fourteen, Sir.

SARI
She has just turned fourteen. Today is her birthday. And perhaps this trip will be her birthday present?

OMÉN
Can you two leave tomorrow morning?

SARI
Yes.

Sari ogles Omén shamelessly.

OMÉN
Very well, I will show you to your quarters. Make yourselves comfortable. Go home and get anything you may need, after you get settled.

Provisions should be plentiful – we will have a spare camel. And are you sure you like adventure?

DONA and SARI
Yes, yes.

OMÉN
And you two are mother and daughter?

SARI and DONA
Yes, yes.

OMÉN
And you both will have an enjoyable time?

DONA and SARI
Yes, yes.

Omén holds out his hands to Sari and she takes them immediately. He holds out his hands to Dona; she overcomes her shyness and takes them. Then he leads the way out of the room, still holding one of Dona's hands.

OMÉN
Come. It's just down the hall.

INT – PALACE DINING HALL – EVENING

At the table are Halidah, his THREE WIVES, Sari, Dona, and Omén. They finish the meal. SERVANTS hover in the background with dessert. No veils, nice eveningwear for the time, no ornate dress-up. The wives smile off and on at Sari and Dona, showing no jealousy whatsoever. Mainly they WHISPER among themselves.

SARI
So, Sultan, what have you done with that problem in the southeast section?

HALIDAH
That problem? … Oh, yes, I took your ideas under advisement. The Wezir is looking into it now. We should have an end to the robberies. Your descriptions were quite complete.

Omén looks at Sari with utter amazement. Then he looks at Halidah to see if the Sultan is joking. He is not.

SARI
And the entertainment … don't you think it is getting stale? Could you check around for me while we are gone and the place is closed?

Omén looks at Sari again with amazement. Who is this woman who talks business with a Sultan as an equal?!!

HALIDAH
We'll talk about it later, during dessert. Speaking of entertainment …

With this, the servants clear the dishes and bring on dessert. The Sultan's SIX ber-ibboned CHILDREN, all girls, come in and bow, and GIGGLE. Two of them are near Dona's age, and the three of them go off to play. The four youngest GIGGLE and hold hands and SING a song of welcome, then start to set up for a skit as the scene fades.

INT – PALACE – OMÉN'S QUARTERS – NIGHT

Omén sleeps. A CRY goes up off-stage (from Sari and Dona's quarters). There are commotion and running SOUNDS. Soon the MAID comes in to Omén and shakes him awake. He stirs groggily.

MAID
Blood … All over … Place a mess … Your guests …

OMÉN
Oh! Summon the court physician and the chief of police. Hurry!

The maid leaves in a hurry. She shakes her head no, no. Omén pulls on his robe and slippers and hurries out.

INT – PALACE – GUESTS' QUARTERS – NIGHT

Dona stands in the middle of the room. She SOBS uncontrollably. There is evidence of blood on the bedclothes and on Dona's face and hands.

OMÉN
(to Sari)
What happened? What happened?

SARI
Nothing, really. Please go back to bed.

OMÉN
(to Dona)
Did you see the intruder? Where are you hurt, child?

SARI
Please, it is nothing. My daughter is all right.

The PHYSICIAN and the CHIEF of police arrive with the maid. The maid cleans up, the Physician checks Dona behind a dressing screen, the Chief looks around windows and doors and the floor for clues. Everything is finally back in order. The Physician brings Dona from behind the screen and whispers in Sari's ear. She nods.

CHIEF
No intruder.

PHYSICIAN
No injuries.

SARI
(to Omén)
See, I told you it was nothing.

DONA
(cautiously)
It was nothing. I...I feel better now.

OMÉN
But what, then?

SARI
(smiling broadly)
Today, on the first day of our trip, my child is a woman!

EXT – DESERT – DAY

The ridge of a sand dune, in bold relief against the dark blue sky. From the left come the camels with their mounts. GUARD #1 in front, then Sari, then Dona, then Omén, then GUARD #2. The sixth camel carries much provisions and is led by a long rope attached to the fifth camel upon which the second guard sits. They pass out of view by the time Sultan Omén finishes his speech:

SULTAN OMÉN V.O.
It is amazing how quickly we travel. The trip was quite uneventful, except for two minor events that took place on shipboard after we reached the coast.

Upon our return from sailing we stopped a few days at the port city of Dhahran. Halima was fine, her children almost grown, her husband now had taken over the business after her father died.

We remain good friends … But I am getting ahead of my story.

EXT – DESERT – NIGHT

Tableau – the five around the campfire on their bedrolls. The tent is nearby, the camels are staked out some distance away. There is some sparse pasture here. Omén tells a story, Dona lies with her head in his lap and holds Crystal up to the glow from the campfire. The guards are asleep, Sari nods off.

SULTAN OMÉN V.O. (Cont.)
Every evening after the meal I would tell a little story. Dona was becoming quite proficient in using Crystal …

The travel must wear everyone out - I would start talking a little about astrology and constellations and star names as soon as it was dark enough, and everyone would soon be asleep.

When I fell asleep, I would dream about my childhood and my family, but especially about my baby sister, whom I could not abide. What ever became of her?

EXT – SHIPBOARD – DAY

It is perfectly calm. The sails do not move at all. The boat is large, two-masted with square sails, not the lateen sail of a dhow. In the far distance is land (Persia) and boats.

In the water some ten paces away are two inflated empty wineskins, each tied by a rope to sturdy fittings inboard. Both ropes are draped across the deck in front of Omén, who sleeps in his deck chair, an empty wine glass by his side.

SULTAN OMÉN V.O.
We sailed about a month in all. The ship mostly traded back and forth across the Sea. It had some rooms set aside for paying passengers.

We were out a week, in sight of Persia, before the winds died. It became very monotonous.

Things got so dull, I would take an empty wineskin, fill it from my lungs, and have Dona tie it to the ship with a length of rope and heave it into the water.

The wineskin would just sit out there. It was about the third day of the calm …

The floating wineskins move ever so slightly in relation to the boat. The ropes slowly move closer to Omén's feet and they tighten somewhat. Everyone else except the LOOKOUT sleeps, or works at some chore, or plays games of chance. The lookout points to the east and SHOUTS to the CAPTAIN. Smaller craft capsize in the distance, the dark cast of the water approaches along with a storm cloud.

LOOKOUT
Captain! The wind! The wind!

Everyone runs forward to see what the lookout has spotted – the first excitement in three days. Omén jumps up from his drunken stupor, he trips on the taut ropes at his feet. He falls and hits his head on the deck. He slips over the side, unconscious.

CAPTAIN
Down the sails! Down the sails!

All the CREWMEN furl the sails and tie down all loose items in preparation for the storm. Sari, Dona and the two guards come back and see Omén's chair empty. They look around and spot him in the water, floating face down.

SARI
Help! Help! Save him!

The guards find a grappling hook, but when they deploy it, they find it lacks a hand-span of reaching Omén.

DONA
(wide-eyed)
Do something!

GUARD #1
We cannot swim…

The guards turn away and discuss and gesture between themselves what to do. As they are engaged in this, Dona takes off her outer garments and jumps into the water. Sari and the guards watch in horror. Dog paddling, Dona reaches a rope, catches it in her mouth, then paddles to Omén. She wraps the rope around his limp body and pulls the wineskin through for the knot.

DONA
Pull him up!
No more than a minute elapses between the time Omén hits the water and when he is on deck. The guards turn him face down, his midsection over a coil of rope, and they work at clearing out his lungs.

About this time the storm hits. At hurricane force, the winds and rain pelt the ship and heel it over at an alarming angle. Fifteen seconds later the rain stops, the sun comes out, and a cool dry breeze blows.

Omén now BREATHES and COUGHS. All those on deck shiver uncontrollably, from the fright, from the cold rain, and from the cool dry breeze. They look for and put on garments or towels.

SARI
Dona! Dona! Get my Dona out of the water!

Crew, captain and all look over the side where Dona splashes happily around in the warm Persian Gulf. She uses the other wineskin for a float.

DONA
I am all right, Mother, really I am. Have them pull me up when you are all dried off … and they better not look!

EXT – SHIPBOARD – NIGHT

It is that same evening, after dinner. Dirty dishes are outside the closed door to Sari and Dona's cabin. Omén comes up and raps on the door.

OMÉN
May I come in? It is Omén. I must talk to the both of you.

SARI O.S.
Just one moment, while we get presentable.

The door opens after a few seconds and Omén goes inside.

INT – CABIN – NIGHT

SARI
How are you feeling? Were your clothes ruined?

OMÉN
I must get right to the point. You saved my life today, Dona. I must know all about you. I am forever in your debt.

DONA
There is nothing to tell, really. I have lived with my mother all my life in Riyadh and hope to marry some day.

OMÉN
But, yes, but … where did you learn to swim?

Dona casts her eyes down.

SARI
Is it really necessary to know? Girls do many things today.

OMÉN
Yes, I must know. I cannot swim, the guards cannot swim. Riyadh is nowhere near the Sea. How did you come to know how to swim?

Dona begins to cry softly. Then she speaks.

DONA
Your Crystal called to me to dive in and retrieve her.

OMÉN
But where did you learn how to swim?

The floodgates open, the tears flow freely, then the words pour forth.

DONA
My boyfriend pushed me into the fountain late one night and taught me. I am home-sick already. I miss him so. We were planning to be secretly married when he finds a good job.

He helps a local sheepherder, but wants to become a gardener – he likes to watch trees and flowering plants and grape vines spring out of the ground like magic wher-ever there is fresh water.

Sari does not like him – she wants me to marry up, out of my position in life.

Dona cries again.

OMÉN
And Sari, what is your story?

Tears form in Sari's eyes and course down her cheeks. She looks so sad and pitiful.

SARI
You have been so good to us. I must tell someone. I have been longing to tell some-one I can trust. Please do not tell anyone else, especially the Sultan. If he knew, my dream would be shattered, for he would laugh at the dreams of an old woman.

I was born in a small town on the East Shore far away. When I was five my oldest brother left to seek his fortune to the North. I worshipped my brother and was heart-broken to see him leave – I would never see him again.

When I became a woman, my parents tried to marry me to a local lad. I would have none of it. After two years of prodding my father was getting firm – I must be out, and I must be married.

A caravan came through town that year, heading north. I hopped on secretly after disguising myself and away we went. Perhaps I would see my brother yet.

(Silent scenes of bandits and caravan following along with the story.)

Several weeks later bandits held up the caravan and took all the gold and silver. Then they spotted me. They talked and argued among themselves until their leader said to the trail master,

"We have need of a young maid more than your piddling gold and silver." "Would that I could help you, but it is impossible – there are no young maidens in the caravan," said the trailmaster.

"That one there, sitting behind you." "I will go with them," I said. They will not harm me." "You do not know what you are saying," said the trailmaster.

I slid off the camel and approached the leader. "You will not harm me," I said, and I brushed his lips with mine.

"Take your gold and silver, and a good day to you," said the leader to the trailmaster, and he threw the money bags to the ground. The trailmaster looked quite upset, but I was off with my new companions.

I became with child at that time, but do not know the father, whether the trailmaster or one of the bandits. I like adventure, but that is the last time I was with a man.

I vowed to wait for a rich nobleman who loved me. The bandits took me to Riyadh, their home base, and there have I lived ever since.

My dream is to be truly loved by the Sultan and to have a boy child for him – he has no heirs to the throne, as you know.

In Riyadh I took work as a barmaid and presently own the tavern – I am training my daughter in my profession.

The Sultan comes in often, as does half the population of Riyadh, it seems. My tavern is on the south end, in a pretty rough district. I have never seen you there.

So now you know why the Sultan and I acted as old friends. We are – we have known each other for years.

He has told me much about you, Omén, and I decided that while I could never have the Sultan as a true love, perhaps my daughter could, or could have the shy clerk.

I am sorry, I want only the best for my daughter. Please forgive an old woman.

OMÉN
What town were you born in?

SARI
Uh … Sur, on the East Coast.

OMÉN
Where did your brother say he was going?

SARI
He said he was going north … to … to Kuwait.

The pulse beats more strongly in Omén's temples.

OMÉN
What was your brother's name?

SARI
That is the strange part. His name is, or was, Omén, the same as yours.

OMÉN
It is a common name. I had a baby sister and left her in similar circumstances. But her name was not Sari.

Sari looks at Omén wide-eyed, and her pulse quickens.

SARI
I hated my given name, and am Sari from my first day with the caravan.

Omén looks at her wide-eyed, intently.

OMÉN
I had a nickname for my baby sister, for she would bother me no end and was always jumping all over me and putting her arms around my neck and kissing me. I called her "Monkey".

SARI
Oh!

As soon as the cry is out, Sari puts her hands over her mouth. Then she composes herself.

SARI (Cont.)
Many older brothers no doubt call their bothersome baby sisters by that name.

Omén smiles; he is quite certain by now.

OMÉN
No doubt, but do baby sisters call their big brothers by this nickname?
Omén takes Sari to the corner of the small cabin and whispers … then he nibbles her ear.

SARI
Ouch! Ha, ha, Omén, hahahaha, oh, ohh, it IS you!

Sari LAUGHS and CRIES hysterically, flings her arms around Omén's neck, and pushes him onto the low bed. She kisses him all over his face, while he and Dona look at each other helplessly. When her hysteria dies down, she realizes where she is and she jumps up from the bed.

SARI (Cont.)
I'm sorry, I'm sorry. We really do not know each other. It has been many years. We are both adults. I'm sorry, please forgive me. It is out of my system. It will never happen again, Omén, I promise.

OMÉN
Come here, Monkey.
It is Omén's turn. He pulls her to him, picks her up in his arms, and sits down on a chair. He cradles her while he half-WHISPERS lullabies in her ear. Sari's eyes are closed, but tears of joy stream out and her mouth is open as if crying.

Her body shakes with SOBS, she puts her arms around his neck and hangs on for dear life. Then the sobs cease, the tears cease. Sari carefully gets up and kisses Omén on the forehead.

SARI
Thank you, big brother. I love you very much. Look, Dona, say hello to your Uncle Omén.

Omén and Dona smile at each other and nod.

OMÉN
(to Dona)
We have a lot of catching up to do, don't we?

DONA

(teasing)
Tomorrow, love. I must get my beauty sleep for the Sultan.

EXT – SHIPBOARD – LATE AFTERNOON

The two guards are side by side at the railing; They look out over the water toward the sun, low in the sky. Guard #1, out of the corner of his eye (he turns his head slightly), sees Omén, who goes into Sari and Dona's cabin.

GUARD #1
I win the bet today. The evening sun is higher when he goes in.

GUARD #2
Six days, and every day either they will visit him or he sees them in the cabin all night. If this keeps up, they will never come out at all.

GUARD #1
Ho, ho, the Sultan will be very pleased. Two at one crack!

GUARD #2
I should be so lucky.

INT – SULTAN HALIDAH'S OFFICE – DAY

Halidah works at his desk. He smiles profusely as Omén enters.

HALIDAH
Hello, hello, the guards tell me you have done famously. You look like a new man. Congratulations. When is the wedding? Where is the bride?

OMÉN
Sari and Dona are in their quarters here waiting for your word. But there will be no wedding.

Halidah looks at Omén quizzically.

OMÉN (Cont.)
Sari is my sister and Dona is my niece.

HALIDAH
What?!! Come, come, you are joking.

OMÉN
Indeed, it is true. Sari and I exchanged childhood secrets. She is indeed my sister.

HALIDAH
(frowning)
Then what do you plan to do? Your family, working in the seediest part of town?

OMÉN
I wish to take them in. It can be noised about that I have taken Sari as my concubine, and I will lawfully make Dona my adopted daughter.

Her boyfriend can also move in, as they wish to be married soon. He can start work as the gardener's assistant. Does any of this make any sense to you? Is it acceptable?

Halidah puts his fingers together and brings them under his chin. He purses his lips and remains in thought. His emotions come out plainly in his face and eyes as he considers.

HALIDAH V.O.
(thinking to himself)
Sari as Omén's concubine in the Palace complex would be very handy – perhaps I can at last get to bed her. She is very attractive and I have been after her for years, to no avail … as have all the others.

Omén would need larger quarters and an increase in salary … My wives like Sari very much: they have so commented often these past months.

The local gossips would be stilled, as there would be nothing to talk about. Men take concubines every day, and Omén would be supporting her child as well. The Palace gardener needs more help, especially with the preparations for my brother's visit.

Dona is turning into a very pretty woman, as I noted when I patted her backside the last time I was in the tavern. It could be like one happy family.

HALIDAH
(to Omén)
Sari could sell the tavern. That might provide sufficient funds to cover the increase in rent I would have to charge for your larger quarters ....

Oh, hang it all, Omén, you are due for a big increase in salary. Yes, I will approve of what you wish.

Call in the women and we will go over the details. Tell Sari to get a manager for her tavern. I still like to get out occasionally.

OMÉN
(worried look)
There is one other detail which I must mention, even though Sari begged me to tell no

one. Do not laugh at what I tell you.

Sari loves you very much. She knows she will never be your concubine, much less a Queen, but her dream is for you to truly love her, and she wants to give you a male child, seeing as how there are no heirs to the throne.

HALIDAH
She told you all that? Hmmm. Well, don't just stand there like a bump on a log. Go bring them in!

INT – OMÉN'S APARTMENT – EVENING

Sari is in bed. She calls out to Omén.

SARI
Big brother, come here to my room, please. I have a question.

Omén comes in, looking worn and haggard.

SARI (Cont.)
Why are you so sad, Omén? Is something wrong? You looked so happy when we returned and set up this apartment with Dona and her boyfriend.

And when cares wore you down again, the Sultan had you spend that week with his new dancing girl, Akasha. A whole week with a beautiful girl, and not a care in the world.

You were so happy again for a while. Come here and tell your sister while I rub your back.

OMÉN
You do not understand, Sari. I love a woman I cannot have, and she loves me.

Sari is silent for a time and rubs Omén's back.

SARI
What perfume dos she wear?

OMÉN
I don't know ... it is very haunting, very subtle ... exotic ...

Sari thinks for a while.

SARI
What does she look like?

OMÉN
She looks like … she looks a lot like you … But she has a hold on me I cannot shake. It is my destiny.

EXT – MARKET – DAY

Sari is at the PERFUMER's stall. He keeps her busy trying out various scents and combinations. PASSERSBY stare at her; the men smile knowing, secretive smiles – the concubine is fixing herself up.

INT – OMÉN'S APARTMENT – NIGHT

Omén is in bed, unable to sleep. He tosses and turns.

SARI O.S.
Big brother, come in and hold me. Monkey is 'fraid.

Omén comes in to her room and stumbles around. It is dark, but enough light to see Sari sitting up in bed. She has on a sheer nightgown.

SARI (Cont.)
Come here and lie down, love, and lay you head on my bosom and quiet my fears.

Sari quietly SINGS nursery rhymes from her childhood as she massages his body and kisses the back of his neck. His breathing becomes more peaceful.

SARI (Cont.)
(quietly)
I love you, and you love me, and we cannot have each other.

OMÉN
That is different, Monkey.

Omén's head moves somewhat. There is the slightest suggestion in the dark that he bites her tenderly on a nipple.

SARI
Ouch!

Sari's hand forms a fist and she hits him gently on the top of his head. Omén grunts and falls into a deep sleep. Sari gets up and carefully places him in her bed.

EXT – PALACE – NIGHT

Sari is dressed and is on the Palace grounds outside Halidah's window. She COOES twice like a turtle dove. Soon Halidah appears at the window. He signals "yes."

Close up of Sari and Halidah near the Palace.

SARI
Before we dance the night away, love, I must ask you not to pester Omén with available women any more.

HALIDAH
Why is that? I noticed his mood was down, and gave him Akasha, one of my new dancing girls, and the prettiest.

SARI
Because he is under the spell of a beautiful woman, and she is under his spell.

HALIDAH
Fine. What is the problem?

SARI
They cannot have each other ... I do not know why. I will comfort him as best I can. I am acquainted with his grief.

Sari kisses Halidah on the cheek.

HALIDAH & SARI
(together)
To the Tavern!

INT – PALACE – EARLY MORNING

Sari and Halidah are in his bedchamber ready for their embrace. The sky is just beginning to get light. A cock crows. Sari decides to tell her lover a story, and she speaks quietly in his ear.

SARI
(with trepidation)
Please do not think me forward, my sweet, but I had heard a story in my travels, and I must tell it now.

Once Abu Nuwas asked Harun Al Rasheed for permission to take one donkey from every husband in the kingdom who proved to be afraid of his wife.

Some time later the sultan was sitting in a palace window when he saw a cloud of dust on the horizon. Soon he made out Abu Nuwas driving a herd of donkeys toward the cattle market. "What is this?" asked the sultan.

"This is the sad state of your kingdom, sire," said Abu Nuwas. "Did you not give me leave to demand one donkey from every man who fears his wife?

"By the way, on my journey I saw a girl with cheeks like pomegranates and breasts like marble. I immediately thought of you ..."

"Shhh!" whispered the sultan. Queen Zubeida is sitting behind that screen – she will hear you!"

"Sire," said Abu Nuwas, "From the men of your land I have taken one donkey; for the king the fine is two donkeys – and make them white ones."

Sultan Halidah breaks out into a loud, long LAUGH. Sari then GIGGLES. They caress each other.

EXT – PALACE – MORNING

The sun is over the horizon. GIGGLES and LAUGHS for a while as the sun moves straight up, then SIGHS and GROANS, then silence for a while, then a cock CROWS.

EXT – PALACE – AFTERNOON

The caravan comes into the Palace area. First, the two Riyadh guards on horseback lead the procession; then one HUNDRED CAMELS: the Sultan of Kuwait, his FOUR WIVES, the EIGHTEEN CHILDREN, FOUR

GUARDS, sixty-nine camels with provisions, twenty of them carry men and women SERVANTS and ATTENDANTS, TWELVE Arabian racing HORSES with GROOMS walking them, then finally FOUR GUARDS on camels in the rear.

SULTAN OMÉN V.O.
(while the procession goes by)
The caravan arrived this afternoon, as I knew it would ...The Sultan of Kuwait...I had planned the whole week to perfection –

the welcome, the reception, the accommodations, the fetes, the music, the dancing, the banquets, the recreation, the flowers and decorations, the food and drink,

the nursery, the programs for the older children, the swimming, the archery, the falconry and horse racing, the games of skill and of chance, the relaxation periods, the quarters for the servants and attendants, the stables for the hordes of camels and horses … I had even stocked the livery with a complete replacement of bridles and tassels and bells and stirrups …

not to mention the gifts for presentations and awards … and Sari mentioned other needs of the attendants and servants that must be filled …

INT – OMÉN'S OFFICE – MORNING

Omén is at his desk and works away with his staff.

SULTAN OMÉN V.O.
I stayed away. I was sick of the whole thing. If it went well, fine; if not, I would not be there to be embarrassed. And the next morning, I am here at my desk as usual.

Suddenly the door bursts open and Halidah and his brother the Sultan of Kuwait come in – they leave the door open. As soon as it opens, there is a shrill, yet muffled NOISE in the distance.

Halidah shows his brother around, but with the noise only snatches of their conversation can be heard: "Ledgers … time saver … get another clerk … helps with taxes … really? … " They soon leave by the other door.

As soon as they enter and the noise starts, all clerks but Omén stop work and look up to see what is going on. Omén works away.

Now the GUIDE comes in, the noise increases to a shrill roar, and the six Halidah children and the eighteen brother's children pour in, followed closely by FOUR regal MATRONS in veils.

Some of the children play with the papers and inkwells. The noise gets so bad that Omén can stand it no longer, and he looks up. An ASSISTANT, whom one of the children harasses, comes up to Omén and shouts through the noise.

ASSISTANT
Omén, what are we to do with the children?

At that, a loud CRY comes from one of the veiled matrons, and she faints. The others slowly lower her to the floor, pat her hands and fan her face. The din from the children quickly stops. Soon the brothers come back into the room.

SULTAN OF KUWAIT
We heard a strange quiet. What happened?

A little GIRL cries out.

GIRL
Mommy died again!

MATRON
Hush, child, your mother just fainted.

Omén comes up to the woman on the floor, who now stirs, and helps her to her feet. His pockets are stocked with emergency supplies, and he feels around for the right item. He pulls it out and offers it to her.

OMÉN
Would Madame care for some smelling salts?

SHAHRAZAD
Yes, please.

SULTAN OF KUWAIT
Oh, it's Shahrazad. Is she with child?

The other women nod "yes".

SULTAN OF KUWAIT (Cont.)
That explains many things. She has not been herself this past year. I thought she had completed her change of life.

The brothers leave again. Queen Shahrazad turns and whispers in Omén's ear.

SHAHRAZAD
Meet me somewhere, anywhere. We must talk.

The crowd moves on and out of the office. Omén makes an announcement to his staff.

OMÉN
This office will be closed for the duration of the Sultan's visit. You will receive your regular pay.

Smiles from all his staff. Some MURMURS: "Boss is sure a great guy ... all right! ... great place to work ... how about that!" Omén leaves the office.

EXT – GARDENS – MORNING

Omén goes to the gardens where the tour was to end up. He sees Shahrazad with the other Queens. He walks up to her; his heart pounds.

OMÉN
Is Madame feeling better?

Shahrazad nods, then takes his hand and leads him out of earshot of the others.

SHAHRAZAD
How did you come to be in Riyadh, and in such a high position? Are you married? Oh, here comes my husband. I will find you later.

Shahrazad releases his hand and starts back to the other Queens. The Sultan of Kuwait sees her and Omén from a distance and waves for them to stay while he walks up, a smile on his face.

SULTAN OF KUWAIT
Ah, here is the young gentleman who planned this whole affair. Remarkable, wonderful, beautiful; I love it. Sorry that Sher caused such a commotion earlier.

SHAHRAZAD
I want the child, but really, darling, I am too old for this.

SULTAN OF KUWAIT
You look familiar, son. What name do you go by? Omén? I have seen you somewhere before.

SHAHRAZAD
Pshaw, love, he must be running all over the place to get things in order. You probably saw him a dozen times since we arrived.

SULTAN OF KUWAIT
(unconvinced)
Yes, of course.

EXT – GARDENS – DAY

Third day of visit; the falcon hunt. Halidah and his brother each have a hooded falcon on their arm; they stand about two hundred feet apart, with Omén between them. All the OTHERS stand in a large ring around the area. They place bets. Omén takes a dove from a cage, holds his arm up and lets the dove free.

When the dove flies approximately straight ahead of him he CALLS out.

The two falconers quickly remove the hoods. The falcons take off in pursuit. All eyes are on the birds. Omén moves back, Shahrazad moves up from the ring, takes his hand in hers and whispers.

SHAHRAZAD
Understand you have a wife and daughter. Congratulations. Please bring your wife when we have the opportunity to talk. She sounds like a gem. All the men I have met here praise her in the most glowing terms.

They return to their places. A SHOUT goes up from the crowd. One of the falcons returns with the dove.

INT – OMÉN'S APARTMENT – EVENING

Omén paces the floor. Sari comes in and Omén corners her.

SARI
Omén! I have to pick up some supplies. They are having a birthday party at the Tavern.

OMÉN
Sari, please tell me what to do. I am beside myself. This is already the third day and I have not had the chance to talk to Shahrazad in private.

She hopes the opportunity will arise, and she wants you to be there also. She has heard we are man and wife.

SARI
So your love is still alive. Is she still beautiful? As beautiful as your baby sister?

Sari bats her eyes at Omén.

SARI (Cont.)
Yes, Omén, love, I want to meet her. Are her feelings for you as strong?

OMÉN
I do not know. It doesn't seem so. She seems more mature.

Sari LAUGHS.

SARI
I would hope so.

EXT – GARDENS – DAY

Omén and Sari walk the grounds.

OMÉN

Sari, thank you for coming along. I can look on my side, you look on yours. Any damage or refuse should be noted for the groundskeepers.

SARI
You have nothing scheduled this afternoon; she very well could be out here resting. The grounds look quite clean – you should not have to spend much time with them.

Are you looking forward to the banquet tomorrow evening? They leave the morning after, don't they? Oh, isn't that her?

Shahrazad sits on a long bench, her veil and royal robes off. She wears a more revealing tea gown and soaks up the sun. Her legs are on the bench, her back against a large silk pillow held in by the armrest. Her eyes are closed, she faces the sun. Her young ATTENDANT stands behind her and shades Shahrazad's eyes with a fan.

SARI
Hello. I understand you know my husband.

OMÉN
Queen Shahrazad, please meet Sari, my love.

The two women bow to each other. Sari is by Shahrazad's side, Omén is at the end of the bench facing Shahrazad, who keeps her eyes half closed. She bows almost straight ahead, does not crane her neck to get a good look at Sari.

SARI
May we sit with you?

SHAHRAZAD
Yes, indeed.

Shahrazad turns her head slightly the other way, toward the attendant.

SHAHRAZAD (Cont.)
Shoo … go back to the Palace. We would talk in private. I will be fine.

Shahrazad moves her legs off the bench and adjusts the pillow as Sari speaks. The attendant walks away.

SARI
Your perfume is most pleasing. What is it, may I ask?

SHAHRAZAD
Why, thank you. It is only sandalwood … and patchouli … from India … I use very little … and only on special occasions.

The two women now turn and face each other directly for the first time. Shahrazad GASPS.

OMÉN
What is the matter, Sher?

SHAHRAZAD
Your wife, Omén, your wife! By the gods, hers is the face I see in my looking glass!

Omén looks at Shahrazad in amazement, then looks at Sari. The similarity of their features is frightening. Omén is at a loss for words. Finally he speaks.

OMÉN
Sher, you were told that Sari is my concubine, not my wife, were you not?

Shahrazad nods.

OMÉN (Cont.)
Sari is not my concubine. She is my baby sister.

SHAHRAZAD
Omén, I do not understand any of this … The new life inside me has stilled my passion. Lie down and put your head on my lap to quiet the pain in my belly.

Shahrazad looks closely at Sari to catch any sign of jealousy. There is none. Sari leans over and kisses Shahrazad on the cheek. Then Omén lies down, his head in Shahrazad's lap, his legs over Sari's.

SHAHRAZAD (Cont.)
Now tell me your story.

EXT – ROSE BUSHES – DAY

The attendant hides near the rose bushes, about thirty paces from the bench. She was returning to the Palace as directed, but when she heard Shahrazad cry out, she stopped and looked for a hiding place to keep an eye on her charge.

She has been here about an hour – the sun is definitely lower. The Sultan of Kuwait comes by with his Queen DUNYZAD and he sees the girl.

SULTAN OF KUWAIT
Child, what are you doing here? Dunyzad, your daughter does not follow orders.

ATTENDANT

Hush, Papa. Auntie Sher wishes to speak privately with the couple.

The attendant points toward the bench, then puts her finger to her mouth for the Sultan to be quiet. The father bends down and kisses his ten-year-old favorite on her forehead, tousles her hair, and slowly walks away down the path, his hands clasped behind his back, in reverie.

Dunyzad stays a while and stares steadily at the trio on the bench. The attendant had ducked her head and blushed when the Sultan of Kuwait tousled her hair, then she switched position, and now sits facing her father as he walks away, her arms clasped around her knees drawn up tightly to her chest. The attendant SIGHS.

ATTENDANT
I love him, Mama.

Dunyzad SIGHS.

DUNYZAD
Yes, dear.

Then Dunyzad turns to her daughter and utters a startled CRY: she realizes that her daughter does not talk about Omén, but about her husband, the Sultan of Kuwait, who walks away in the distance. Dunyzad runs down the path and quickly catches up to him before he is aware she was not with him the whole time.

EXT – GARDENS – AFTERNOON

Omén finishes up his story. The late afternoon air is a little cooler – Shahrazad has a covering over her shoulders.

OMÉN
…And so you see that Sari is indeed my sister, and that my passion for you will not go away. It is my destiny … Your husband the Sultan of Kuwait does not seem to desire you. Would he not be willing to allow you to leave?

SHAHRAZAD
Dearest Omén, if we became husband and wife, your passion would no doubt disappear in the humdrum of daily life. Then where would I be?

OMÉN
That would never happen.

SHAHRAZAD
Omén, do you still keep your Crystal with you, as you vowed those many years ago?

OMÉN
Yes, of course. I have her here with me now.

SHAHRAZAD
Well, as you have never broken your vow, so I have never broken mine. I am more a nurse to my husband than a wife and lover. If I left him, he would soon be back drinking wine and eating mutton, and the lives of the maidens in Kuwait would again be in danger.

The local mutton has something in it that affects him untowardly, which your mutton did not. I learned as much in the three years we were together evenings in his chamber. [To Sari] Did he tell you about our long tryst? Sari smiles.

OMÉN
What is Palace life like for you? Tell me about Dunyzad and your husband and his other wives and the children.

SHAHRAZAD
Oh, it is so boring. I will relate it to you in due course. Let not this sacred time vanish in the mist …

Omén, when the passion strikes and I long for your arms, I bother my husband no end until he submits; then while I am in his arms I think of you.

Do you not have someone you can hold thusly? What about Akasha, the dancing girl? Do you not find her attractive?

OMÉN
Yes, but …

SHAHRAZAD
Oh, you are making me very jealous.

Shahrazad tickles Omén until he holds her hands firmly.

SHAHRAZAD (Cont.)
We are both nearing fifty years. We are much too old for this. And yet we cannot help ourselves. Yes, it is Karma … You mentioned once long ago that your god Allah had told you that you would have me one day.

OMÉN
Yes, but when I ask when, I am told to go to his messenger, Crystal. And when I ask her, the stone dissolves.

I feel a shape, as a tunnel, and I see you at the end of the tunnel, but yet not as a tunnel, for your image fills my whole eye. And do not laugh: you are upside down!

Sher and Sari both start to laugh, but keep themselves in check.

SHAHRAZAD
And what am I doing while upside down?

A GIGGLE starts in Shahrazad's throat.

OMÉN
You are running to me, you are all bloody … I long to comfort you … The dream has come upon me many times and I do not understand it at all.

Omén closes his eyes and holds her hands even closer to his heart. His eyelids glisten at the corners.

SHAHRAZAD
Omén, promise me something.

Omén nods.

SHAHRAZAD (Cont.)
Promise me that you take Akasha as your concubine and do as I do. If it be the will of Allah, we will be together in our next life.

For the present we will be brother and sister when we are together, as you and Sari.

OMÉN
Sher … may I write to you in the Palace?

SHAHRAZAD
My husband reads all the mail, incoming and outgoing. You will have to get his acceptance if our letters are to be delivered.

OMÉN
Then I will ask him … and I promise to do as you wish.

INT – BANQUET HALL – EVENING

One large "U"-shaped table with Halidah, his three wives, his WEZIR and WIFE, his twelve ASSISTANTS, two main guards, maid, chief of police, physician, Omén, Sari, Dona and her BOYFRIEND, Omén's staff of four; Sultan of Kuwait, his four wives, his eight guards, his twenty attendants and servants, the twelve grooms for the racing horses; plus anyone else not listed. A separate table at the back for the twenty-four children. There are twenty WAITERS. In the center is a large stage.

The banqueters are seated on the outside only, so the stage is clear to view (except the small children are seated on the inside of their table). The meal has progressed to past the meat course; the waiters bring up the fowl.

A group of DANCERS (including AKASHA) just finishes up. There is the usual NOISE and COMMOTION and APPLAUSE. Akasha runs smiling up to Omén before she leaves the stage, and he gives her a flower; she holds it to her heart as she runs off. Halidah shouts over to Shahrazad as the applause dies down.

HALIDAH
Dear Sister Shahrazad, I have heard rumors that you can tell tales with the help of the magic stone which Omén carries with him. Is this true, and would you care to entertain us?

SHAHRAZAD
Dear Brother-in-Law, it has been many years since that was accomplished. If you will make ready on the stage with a bedchamber ... and if your brother is willing ...

and if my Brother Omén will allow me once more to hold his magic Crystal ...

and if my sister Dunyzad will accompany me in the tableau ... then I will attempt another story.

Those around the table have heard snatches of this conversation and the chatter gradually dies down during it, so that everyone hears Shahrazad's last words "will attempt another story."

BANQUETERS
Story! Yes, yes, story. Let us have a story!

Halidah tells his assistants to get the bedchamber ready, Shahrazad tells her sister Dunyzad what to say at the proper time. Then Shahrazad gets up and goes over to Omén, who gets up and gives the Crystal to her.

They stand together, shoulder to shoulder, as she peers into Crystal's eye. Omén watches her face intently all the while; he can feel her tremble. All is ready, a hush falls upon the whole room. Still, Shahrazad does not quit her gaze as she says out loud to Omén:

SHAHRAZAD
I do not understand what your Crystal is telling me. I feel anxious and afraid. Please, this must be the last time I tell a story by your Crystal.

She gives the Crystal back to Omén, the Sultan of Kuwait goes up and settles comfortably in the bed, Shahrazad goes up and snuggles in his bosom, Dunyzad goes up and sits at the foot of the bed. All seems in order. The attendants bow, leave the stage and return to their seats.

DUNYZAD
By Allah, Oh my sister, relate to us a story to beguile the waking hour of our night.

SHAHRAZAD
Most willingly, if this virtuous King permits me.

The Sultan of Kuwait nods his head, and Shahrazad begins, in a singsong voice, as if repeating a childhood tale everyone knew.

SHAHRAZAD (Cont.)
There once was a young boy who lived far to the South. One day his God Allah spoke to him and said, "My son, you must go North, and there you will find your destiny."

So the boy took leave of family and friends and became a shepherd to sustain himself while he traveled. Many years he went on, until finally he reached his goal and found that for which he was searching.

But this one, for it was a young maiden, had vowed to be true to another for good and sufficient reason. The shepherd, also, had taken a vow; neither vow could they break.

After three years he took leave and traveled far away to begin a new life. He became very rich and powerful and died in honor, never having broken his vow.

But it is the will of his God Allah that they be husband and wife in the next life.

Shahrazad stops speaking, and there is an uneasy silence in the room. Omén looks embarrassed; the Sultan of Kuwait looks embarrassed. There are WHISPERINGS: … not a story … know several friends in similar happenings … what is this "next life?" … dull … where is the drama? Some of the children TITTER. Then Shahrazad begins again, her face blank and her eyes closed, her voice now that of a gypsy fortuneteller.

SHAHRAZAD (Cont.)
I was born of a thunderbolt. I was plucked the next morning from the sandy beach by a young dreamer. I was buried alive with this dreamer when he died.

Soon after I was taken and sold to a passing caravan and traveled West and North, through Mecca and Deri-Seadet, to a city on the sea far away, and at last to a city on an island where tree worshippers dwelt.

I find my mate and await my dreamer so that we can lead him to his destiny far to the

South.

Again Shahrazad ceases. The room is quiet, but every eye is on her. She has their attention: buried alive, exotic lands, tree worshippers, mates and dreamers. Her trance deepens and her voice lowers and becomes staccato as an African medicine man. The faintest hint of jungle drums SOUNDS in the distance.

SHAHRAZAD (Cont.)
My lover comes to me in the mountains far to the North. We become husband and wife. Life stirs in my belly. Oh!

The cry comes from Shahrazad's lips in her own voice and her hands clasp her stomach.

SHAHRAZAD (Cont.)
The young wife, big with child, dies by the sword. The distraught husband has heard since childhood a tale of a stone whereby one can magnify his vision, and to keep his sanity, he begins his search.

Years pass … Many years … Many, many years. He finds the stone, now altered beyond recognition, and they direct him to me, born again in a far away land. We become one again, and live happily ever after … Together … Forever …

Shahrazad ceases and slowly wraps her arms around her husband's neck. The hint of a smile plays on her lips. In the hush, the audience hears her snore softly. The Sultan of Kuwait breaks the silence.

SULTAN OF KUWAIT
My Shahrazad is with child. This shall be the last. She is become too old to have more. Please excuse her ramblings. She has been like this now for almost a year. Excuse me …

The Sultan of Kuwait picks up his "bride" and carries her out of the room to her bedchamber.

An hour later. The candles burn lower. The banquet breaks up, some still drink, a juggling act finishes up, people leave and thank Halidah for the great week. Omén overhears one of the departing GUESTS.

GUEST
The Queen's story was very strange. I do not understand it – yet it haunts me.

Omén spies the Sultan of Kuwait, who returns for the festivities. Omén goes up to him.

388

OMÉN
Sir, it is unlikely that I will ever see your Shahrazad again. However, may I write to her as a brother?

SULTAN OF KUWAIT
Yes, yes, please do, Omén. She has been very moody of late, and letters from a brother and a friend will be most welcome. Yes, indeed.

The Sultan of Kuwait and Omén embrace, the Sultan whispers in Omén's ear.

SULTAN OF KUWAIT (Cont.)
I do not believe in an afterlife. She will be faithful to me in my lifetime, and this is enough.

INT – OMÉN'S APARTMENT – NIGHT

Omén tosses and turns in his bed. The lamps are still lit.

SULTAN OMÉN V.O.
In a gilded prison, she; Yearning always to be free. Kept in rein by high duty, Can she to her lover flee,

Lovely, lonely girl you see? Shahrazad, please come to me; We will be in ecstasy. Karma – 'tis our destiny.

Omén gets up, goes to his writing table and puts pen to paper.

SULTAN OMÉN V,O. (Cont.)
Sleep would not come that night. Her story was burned in my memory. I took pen and ink and fine parchment and wrote down her last words as told by Crystal.

INT – PALACE WORKSHOP – DAY

Omén shows the woodworker that he wants a thin ebony plate as a base for his "stone".

SULTAN OMÉN V,O. (Cont.)
The next day they left, but I busied myself preparing a safe hiding place for the parchment.

Omén goes to a small warming oven and puts the ebony base inside. He takes the parchment out of his robes and carefully folds it up and stuffs it into the cavity in the "shell" base of the stone. He takes a stick of sealing wax from his robes and melts the wax around the perimeter of the warm ebony plate in the oven. Then he puts the stone on the plate to form an assembly. He puts on workman's gloves and takes the assembly out of the oven and puts it to one side to cool off. He presses down carefully and centers stone and base.

SULTAN OMÉN V.O. (Cont.)
Now, in my next life, I will know I have been here before.

INT – SULTAN OMÉN'S CHAMBERS – EVENING

Sultan Omén continues his story from his bed.

SULTAN OMÉN
I wrote to Shahrazad faithfully every month, and soon began receiving her letters ... you had your wish, did you not, Sari? A boy child.

We took him in as our own for some years, until the Palace claimed him ... My staff would often tell me how lucky I was – two concubines ... But time passes ... One evening, late at night, I was called to the Sultan Halidah's chambers. Many were there. We knew he was ill for some time, but now he was on his deathbed. Why would he ask for me? ... He motioned me to his side, and began speaking, haltingly ...

INT – VISION – HALIDAH'S DEATHBED – NIGHT

HALIDAH
Omén, we have had many favorable encounters ... I have grown to like you as a person and as an employee ... I have come to depend on you and value your advice ... I think of your family as part of my family ... I think of you as a son ... My son, I wish to appoint you as the next Sultan. When your rule is ended ... my line shall resume.

INT – SULTAN OMÉN'S CHAMBERS – EVENING

SULTAN OMÉN
We clasped hands and this shepherd became Sultan ... I have tried to uphold the grandeur of the office ... I extended trade routes to China and Africa ... I set up a trade colony in Bombay ... the Hindus took to using the sifr ...

I became patron to many craftsmen – gold and silver, wood and metal ... I encouraged poets, writers, artists, musicians ...

The Sultan of Kuwait died ... the new regime put Shahrazad to drudge work in the nursery ... her letters slowed ...

Last year my letter to Shahrazad came back unopened ... on the top, there ...

Sultan Omén nods toward the open chest. The view source comes down and zeroes in on the top letter. The address says "Queen Shahrazad – Kuwait"; across the address is written, ugly and terse, "Unclaimed. Recipient deceased."

SULTAN OMÉN (Cont.)
The Seven Sisters have circled the skies over me now eighty seven times. It is enough … The line shall resume …

Sultan Omén gestures for the view source to come to his side. The view source moves up as people move out of the way. The view source "kneels", the right hand comes into view as Omén extends his right hand, and Omén and the new Sultan clasp hands for a time. Sultan Omén's hand gradually slips away.

SULTAN OMÉN (Cont.)
I will be with her … always …

The trilling WAIL of the mourners.

FADE OUT

Credits roll.

EXT – OMÉN'S TOMB – EARLY MORNING

Two GRAVE ROBBERS approach the small tomb. It is very dark – the sky is just brightening in the east. The robbers have cloths over their nose and mouth to protect themselves from the odor.

ROBBER #1
Ha! Didn't I tell you the guards would leave after ten days? The tomb is free for pickings.

ROBBER #2
I don't feel right doing this. What if someone finds out? I would have my hand cut off at least, maybe lose my job in the kitchen. I would become a beggar.

ROBBER #1
Who would find out? If we don't take it, someone else would tomorrow. It would be the guards' fault. Let them have their heads chopped off. Ha!

ROBBER #2
I don't know. I don't like it. I liked the Sultan – he was good to me. He even asked me to be present with the others at his deathbed. Me!

ROBBER #1
Don't quit on me now, Faris. Didn't you tell me he was buried with great treasure?

ROBBER #2
Yes. So I heard in the kitchen gossip. But maybe that's all it is – gossip.

ROBBER #1
But maybe not, eh? Would a Sultan be buried with nothing of value? Even you and I will be buried with something of value. Ha, ha. Something of value.

Enough. It's getting light. Open the gate and let's get inside. We can't find any treasure standing out here.

They duck down and squeeze into the small tomb.

INT – TOMB

The ceiling is low; they can barely stand up. The casket is ordinary wood. The lid is not locked.

Credits end.

ROBBER #1
Whew! What a stench. They must have saved a little on the embalming, no? Look, the lid is not fastened.

Robber # 1 takes off the lid and places it on the floor.

ROBBER #1 (Cont.)
There's the treasure box. Ha.

Robber #1 takes out the box. It, too, is not locked. He opens it and takes it to the doorway to get more light. He MUTTERS to himself.

ROBBER #1 (Cont.)
Not very heavy. Maybe you were right.

Robber #1 feels around, takes out some letters.

ROBBER #1 (Cont.)
By the Gods! Letters! They have no value. Son of a bitch! Omén, you son of a bitch! Take the body out.

ROBBER #2
I … I can't.

ROBBER #1

There must be treasure under the body. Here, I'll help you. You, who carry sheep around the Palace kitchen for butchering, afraid of a dead old man.

They lift the body out and drop it on the lid lying on the floor of the tomb. They feel all around.

ROBBER #1
Nothing!

ROBBER #2
We've got to get out of here. The sky is brightening. Help me get him back in.

ROBBER #1
Yes, I'll get you back in, Omén, you miserable miser, you. Away from Mecca I'll face you. How do you like that?

Robber #1 picks up the body and unceremoniously drops it into the casket and goes outside. He MUTTERS to himself. Robber #2 puts the lid back on and goes to the treasure box. He looks in and feels around.

ROBBER #2
Here is a pouch! It feels like a large stone inside. It must be the stone that can talk, the stone that can tell stories, the stone that can tell the future. It must be the stone of great value!

ROBBER #1
Take it and let's get out of here.

The two robbers leave, close the gate, and depart in a hurry.

EXT – SECLUDED EDGE OF RIYADH – MORNING

ROBBER #1
Let's see what you have in the pouch. If it's a gemstone, maybe we can sell it to the caravan. I hear it's coming soon. We will have the money, and the stolen goods will soon be far away. No one can connect us to this deed, and we will be rich, my friend. Rich!

Robber #2 takes the stone out of the pouch and they look at it. Behind them the sun peeks over the horizon and the rays strike Crystal. The HEAVENLY SOUND and the RAINBOW FLASH of colors. The flash gets brighter going from the blue to the red, and it dims the rest of the scene, until the screen is almost filled with bright white light.

FADE OUT –

172 minutes as written

MS. BALL II
The movie begins at the point where Sultan Omén says:
"The Seven Sisters ..." through the point where the robbers hear the heavenly sound and see Crystal's rainbow.

INT – RIYADH PALACE – DAY

The NEW SULTAN is in his office with his WEZIR.

SULTAN
Well, what word do you have?

WEZIR
Omén's tomb has been robbed this morning.

SULTAN
They didn't waste any time, did they? What was taken?

WEZIR
Only the pouch. But Sire, they desecrated the place. Sultan Omén was almost doubled up, like they pulled him out and threw him back in. We repositioned him and put everything back in place and locked it all up, as you commanded.

SULTAN
Well done. All has been completed as Omén wished. He can rest in peace. His treasure is now free to seek her destiny. Do you know who did this?

WEZIR
Yes, of course. Do you wish me to bring them to trial?

SULTAN
No, of course not. They had a job to do and they did it well. Just keep an eye on them to see if they come into some money soon. Maybe the stone *does* have some value. If they get more than you think their services were worth, find some excuse to fine them. The tomb *was* expensive to build.

WEZIR
As you wish, My Lord.

etc.

www.ingramcontent.com/pod-product-compliance
Lightning Source LLC
Chambersburg PA
CBHW060810030726
47503CB00002B/422